A.C. DONAUBAUER

Schemes – Book 3

Schemes -
The Order: Book 3

A.C. Donaubauer

First published in as ebook in August 2016
Paperback
2nd edition

Astrid Donaubauer-Grobner
Waltenhofengasse 3/3/3302
1100 Vienna, Austria

The author online:
www.ac-donaubauer.com
www.facebook.com/acdonaubauer

Cover: Biserka Design

Editing: Jürgen Donaubauer
Proofreading: Philip Scott

Print: CreateSpace, an Amazon.com enterprise
February 2019

ISBN 978-3-904142-07-6

To Jasmin and Jennifer, my little sisters.
I'm proud of you.

CHAPTER 1

Returning Home

Enric looked grim as he stared out over the sea. There was nothing in sight, the horizon was no more than an endless straight line that separated the brighter blue above from the darker colour below. No interruption in the form of land promised relief anytime soon.

The last time he crossed the sea he had not felt any of the effects most others in his party, Eryn included, had been suffering. Seasickness, they called it, he remembered. But this time it seemed his stomach was not as resistant to the constant pitching of the ship as before. He was told that the body got used to it after a few days, so suffering from it now when it had not affected him before seemed strange.

His troubles were not as grave as Eryn's, though. She lay immobile on the plank bed in their cabin downstairs, her stomach empty of everything that had been in there. It was unfortunate that healing away the symptoms did not work in this case as long as the cause was present every single moment and caused them to return immediately.

But at least they had half of the journey on the ship behind them already, only one more day left until they would reach the small village of Bonhet where they had boarded the ship that had brought them to the Western Territories. Right now that seemed like an eternity ago. He had quite grand plans for the village and wondered how people would react to them. Eryn was right in that one regard: the willingness to adapt to new developments was not exactly considered a virtue, not in the city of Anyueel, and even less in remote places like that fishing village.

He felt the tension in his stomach relaxing and decided to look after Eryn. Maybe he could persuade her to let him put her to sleep for a few hours now that Kilan and Grend were not there to tease her about choosing the easy way out. It was reluctance to be forced to listen to any jibes from their travel companions that had made her reject his offer the previous time, when they were bound for Takhan.

But when he opened the door to their small cabin, he saw that she had fallen asleep already, one arm hanging down to the floor limply. She couldn't have been asleep for very long, the tea he had made for her was still warm. Probably no more than a minute or two, pretty much when his stomach had given up complaining.

His head jerked up and he frowned down at her. No, surely not. That would be highly unlikely, wouldn't it? And this was surely no more than a coincidence, nothing that justified jumping to any premature conclusions, he warned himself. He would keep his eyes open, though, he decided. His suspicion was maybe no more than that, but it certainly paid to be on the safe side.

He turned and left the cabin, closing the door behind him carefully. They would soon reach the barrier and he had been told that the captain would show him how to overcome it, once and for all putting an end to the limitation of going to sea for the Kingdom.

* * *

Eryn woke when a warm hand kept shaking her shoulder.

"Are we still on that bloody ship?" she murmured without opening her eyes. "If yes, you have quite some explaining to do for waking me."

Enric smiled down at her. "The village is in sight already, so you have another hour of suffering ahead of you." An hour that would surely provide some interesting insights for himself.

"That is one hour you might have spared me!" she moaned. "You are doing this on purpose! Is there anything I have done to you recently that justifies tormenting me like that?"

He pretended to think for a moment. "No, nothing that I can think of. But then it is well known that I have a penchant for heaping agony onto helpless women. And now get up and come on deck for a bit of fresh air. It will do you good."

"You are joking, aren't you? You know very well what being on deck does to me! Why are you inflicting it on me?" she wailed and felt herself being pulled up to her feet and more or less hauled up the stairs and outside. The sudden brightness of the sunlight blinded her and she quickly lifted a hand to shade her eyes. There was a stiff breeze that made her shiver and she felt Enric's arm around her shoulders pull her against his warm body.

"We need to change out of these clothes. They are not exactly suited for the climate back home," he murmured and watched her stare at the waves around them that made the ship pitch up and down.

Then she closed her eyes, her face growing pale again. He also felt the feeling from before returning, causing in him the urge to hold on to something firm to convince his stomach that this sense of being tossed up and down was no more than an unjustified overreaction.

He smiled despite the unpleasant sensation. It seemed as if Eryn might be up for a little surprise, though none that would make her very happy. He would see how long it would take her to figure it out on her own.

* * *

"There it is! I can see it!" she exclaimed delightedly. "Never would I have thought that there will be the day that I am overjoyed to lay my eyes upon it!"

Enric looked up as well at the hazy outline of the city of Anyueel at the horizon. "It warms my heart to see you so happy to return to it, my love," he smiled and took her hand to kiss it. And it truly did. She had, as far as he could remember, never once mentioned missing her little cottage in the town where she had spent most of her life. That had to mean that she now considered their house in the city her home, he hoped.

Urban trotted beside the horses and had turned her head to look at Eryn when she had called out her delight at spotting Anyueel in the distance.

"The yard should be finished for her by now," Enric remarked with a glance at the cat. "Trees, rocks, everything. With a little luck the passage between the buildings is ready as well. The servants will otherwise very probably turn out to be just a little... jumpy."

Eryn shrugged. "Why would they? She has never hurt anyone so far."

"Still. We are talking about a fierce animal here. After all, not everybody has known her since she was small enough to fit into your palm. And though she is still not fully grown, she has definitely lost the advantage of being considered cute rather than frightening."

"One would think that if a four-year-old girl is not afraid, adults should be able to handle Urban as well," she pointed out.

"Children at that age do not yet have a proper understanding of danger, Eryn. Obal would just as likely have tried to cuddle a completely wild animal if there was one around. Vran'el's reaction was the more natural one. And consider that part of my reputation in Takhan was based on the fact that I was wandering the streets of the city with what was perceived as a very impressive wild animal," he explained.

She sighed. "Alright, I bow to your superior wisdom. Once again. Then let's hope that passage is ready or we will have to do our own cooking and cleaning for a while. Not that I would mind that too much - I had to do it for quite a while when I was living alone. But I fear that there will not be very much time left to devote to it. I wonder what the healers' place looks like. Utter chaos? Or will nobody even have noticed that I was gone? I don't know which would be worse."

"For you? The latter, very likely," he smiled. "I am getting hungry. We should be in the city in about an hour and a half. It will be early evening by then. We will have time to get home, have a bite to eat then wash and change into clean clothes, but that is practically it."

She furrowed her brow. "So there is no chance whatsoever to ask the King to see us tomorrow instead of tonight?"

"None. He already waited for us rather longer than he had planned - about two weeks longer. He wants to make sure we really are back. And to learn about the latest developments as soon as possible. The last message he received from me is several days old already. After that we will have to see Tyront. He will want to learn about everything the King did not tell him. Kilan was only instructed to inform the King, after all. Whatever has been passed on to Tyront was thus filtered."

"So this is going to be a very long day yet," she groaned. "And I just wanted to fall into my own bed and catch up on the sleep I missed these last few nights."

"Sorry, my love. Not much chance for that in the next few hours."

* * *

The four guards at the western gates bowed as the two high-ranking magicians passed them. Odd, Eryn thought, how strange this formal behaviour seemed after only a few weeks in Takhan.

They rode through the city to their house and Enric whistled through his teeth when he saw the people assembled in front of it.

"Look at that. It seems somebody has spread the news of our impending arrival when we were first spotted," he murmured.

Eryn urged her horse on until she was close enough to dismount and as soon as her feet had touched the ground, she found herself in a tight embrace with a certain sixteen-year-old boy.

"Finally!" he whispered. "I was so afraid they would not let you leave again!"

She squeezed him back, noting how his cheeks were not any longer level with hers. Was it possible that he had grown so much since she had left here?

"So was I," she replied, "I can't tell you how glad I am to be back."

"Let go of her, Vern," Orrin scolded him mildly when he made no move to release her again. "There are a few others who would like to greet her as well."

Vern removed his arms from around Eryn with obvious reluctance, and moments later Orrin's much firmer embrace squeezed the air out of her lungs. She smiled at the unusual physical display of affection from his side.

"Look at you, you old softy! You have gone all mellow in my absence without anybody to torment and goad! Or is that Junar's influence?" she laughed and hugged him back.

"Shut up," he growled. "We were worried sick about you after we learned that they had accused you of some crime over there. It seems even with your companion at your side there is no keeping you out of trouble. Next time you go there, I will be sure to accompany you myself. One of us is clearly not enough to keep an eye on you."

"That's enough, now it's my turn," Junar complained from behind them and Orrin stepped aside so the two women could hug next.

Enric watched the scene, wondering about the feeling of regret and loss inside him. Nobody dared embracing him here, unlike in Takhan, where he had been hugged and kissed by a number of people, both male and female. For the first time in more than ten years he wondered if the reputation he had been so careful to build was worth the solitude that was its consequence. His stay in the Western Territories had introduced him to quite a different way of social interaction. There were those in awe of him who were mostly people he had met when negotiating, and others who were sufficiently impressed by him, but met him in a more private setting that allowed them to look behind that official mask. Here in Anyueel there was hardly anybody who dared look behind it. Apart from Tyront and the King, that is. Although they did not do so for mere social reasons but because he was, just like them, a player in the political game, and knowing one's fellow players was essential to ensure both survival and success.

He looked up in surprise, when he felt a hearty slap on his shoulder. Orrin gave him a nod.

"Good to have the two of you back," he said simply, yet it sounded like he truly meant it.

"Good to be back. Finally," Enric replied and smiled at the warrior. Who would have thought that Orrin would be the only one to give him at least some feeling of being welcome?

At the back of his mind, he wondered if he wanted to change that somehow, if he wanted to work on establishing friendships here in Anyueel. Would such a thing even work? People here were less open, less casual, more easily intimidated by rank and power. He imagined that Eryn would feel the contrast of being addressed with Lady again even more noticeably. But then she had quite a few people around her who would refrain from doing so anyway, as she had let them come close enough for them to forego the title.

In the entire city there were no more than four people who addressed him without *Lord*. Tyront, his companion Vyril, Kilan and Eryn. Before Eryn, there had been only two, since he had not had any contact with Kilan in these last ten years.

He saw Eryn frown in confusion while talking to Plia and wondered if she had caught on to his feelings, wondering where that melancholy came from when she felt herself happy and relieved at being back.

"Is everything alright, my love?" he enquired and put an arm around her shoulders.

She nodded and plastered on a smile to conceal her puzzlement. "Yes, I am just a little exhausted, that's all."

Enric noted how Junar, Vern and Plia around them had taken a small step back at his approach.

Junar widened her eyes as Urban squeezed her way between them to rub her head against Enric's legs. "Look at that cat! She has grown quite a lot in these last weeks. If she grows any larger, you can use her instead of a horse next time."

"She may still grow a little more over the next two or three months, but that should be it," Enric explained and bent down to rub the cat's cheeks.

"Look at that! So you managed to escape the claws of the foreign senate!" an amused voice from behind them called out.

They saw Kilan approaching them. The few people around them collectively turned their heads around, and jaws dropped in surprise as the two men hugged affectionately. Lord Enric hugging people was not exactly a common sight.

Kilan then turned to Eryn. "They said you were trouble. But I didn't want to believe it. I stand corrected."

She rolled her eyes at him. "Says the man who jumped aboard the ship and sailed off in my hour of distress."

His expression became serious. "Believe me, in all my life that was one of the most difficult things I have ever had to do. I hope I will not be in such a situation again anytime soon. But I had my orders."

"I was not serious, Kilan," she sighed. "Your returning was the only sensible thing to do. Especially as the King would of course need first-hand information about the whole mix-up."

He smiled in relief and squeezed her hand. "True enough. But next time we will just try not to have you accused of anything, shall we?"

"I'll do my best, just to keep you happy," she grinned. "But I suppose there will not be another opportunity for us to go to Takhan together again anytime soon, so no worries about that."

"I would not count on that too much, Eryn," he shook his head.

"Why not?" she frowned, then her brow furrowed. "You are not trying to tell me that they are sending you back there, are you?"

"Well, there is an opening for someone as permanent ambassador to Takhan, since the man who initially applied for the job decided not to remain after his companion was released from custody," he smiled.

That caused a few frowns around them and Eryn remembered that they were very likely not informed of the important things that had happened. There would be some explaining to do, she thought, and sighed inwardly. And that meant once again telling the story of her father's death. Though not today.

"What are the plans for the next few days?" Vern cut in. "Unpacking? Distributing gifts among your most valued friends?" he added, with a gleam of hope.

That made her laugh. "Well, that last one *obviously*." Then she turned serious. "Tonight we will have to do some reporting to the upper ranks, and tomorrow I want to have a look how things are going at the healers' place."

"The Magic Council might want to see you tomorrow," Enric reminded her.

"I was counting on *you* to give them all the juicy details. I really, *really* want to get back to my work," she said, hoping he would see things her way, and smiled when he assented by nodding.

"I will try to convince them that they don't need to see you tomorrow. But you will have to show up there sooner or later."

She nodded. "Very well, as long as it is not in the next one or two days, when I have more important things to take care of."

Orrin sniffed. "The Magic Council will be so pleased to hear that you do not consider them important enough to be worthy an hour or two of your precious time."

"Well, they won't be hearing it from me," she shrugged.

"You are aware that myself and Lord Orrin are members of the Council, aren't you?" Enric said. "So strictly speaking the Council *has* heard about it already."

She chuckled. "But I trust that my two favourite members will not get me into any trouble because of it."

Orrin grinned broadly and put an arm around her shoulders. "Trust, my girl, is something of a luxury. It makes you vulnerable."

Eryn's face fell. "Yes, that lesson I learned well enough in those foreign parts," she said quietly.

Orrin frowned. "Hmm, it seems that was exactly the wrong thing to say. I am sorry. You will have to tell me about it. Soon." It was not an order as such, but definitely more than a polite request. She smiled at him and nodded. It was good to see that some things would probably never change. No matter how high up she was, this was one man she could always depend on still to tell her what to do.

"So, everyone, let's give the two of them a little space to return to their home after their journey. They have some work ahead of them yet," Orrin called out, following which the two of them were finally able to take the last few steps towards their home.

* * *

Eryn frowned in confusion when one of the Palace guards in front of the doors to the throne room indicated for them to follow him instead of admitting them.

"Judging from the direction, the King will be seeing us in his study instead," Enric murmured. "Probably a concession to our having travelled all day long. Provided he lets us sit down," he added dryly.

She nodded slowly. Sitting down in a study was definitely a more appealing thought than standing before him on weary legs. She had never been to his study before and wondered if it would look any different from others due to the importance of the man occupying it.

The guard bowed to them and left when they had reached an unassuming looking door.

"That's the right door? Are you sure? It looks unexpectedly modest," she commented.

"This is the right place, really," Enric nodded and knocked at the door.

"Come," a muffled voice from inside called and they entered and faced Marrin, who rose from behind his desk and seemed, to Eryn's surprise, genuinely pleased at seeing them.

"Lady Eryn, Lord Enric. What a relief to have you back safely. His Majesty is expecting you," he smiled and indicated a door to his right.

"Thank you, Marrin," Enric replied. "We are happy to be back." Then he opened the door and let Eryn enter first. Marrin followed them into the room, closing the door behind him, stepping aside as usual to more or less merge with the surroundings like an unobtrusive piece of furniture.

Eryn looked around, almost a little disappointed at how undistinguished the room looked with its books, papers and writing utensils. Elegant, but not much more elaborate than her own study. A room for working, not for fancy displays of power the way the throne room was.

The King was standing behind his desk, facing the window behind it, and turned when they entered and bowed.

He looked at them for a while before nodding, obviously satisfied with what he saw. "Finally the delegation has returned in full. You had us all worried a little there."

Eryn suppressed a snort. *He* had been worried? Not half as much as she herself had when facing the threat of being detained in that place across the sea for two years, she thought.

"I am sorry to hear that my troubles caused you distress, Your Majesty," she replied with a thin smile, "I assure you it was not done deliberately."

The monarch raised an eyebrow at her. "I see that your stay in Takhan has not changed your attitude towards authority one bit, Lady Eryn. I think we may consider ourselves lucky you had your companion with you, or the outcome of the trial might have been less favourable."

The warning undertone in his voice let her reconsider the wisdom of speaking without being explicitly asked. Right, back to where they had been before their departure: Enric would do the talking.

She wondered at the mild sensation of disapproval she felt and looked at Enric. Was she imagining that? She searched his face, but it did not reveal anything - just the usual composure when he was in public. And in control of himself. So what had caused that impression had probably been her imagination. She had come to know him quite well, after all. Of course he would not approve of the way she had just spoken to the King. Interesting, though, that she seemed to have switched from not only anticipating his feelings, but also imagining an echo thereof.

"Is everything alright, Lady Eryn? You seem a tiny bit distracted," the King observed.

"Sorry, I am just a little tired. It was a long voyage."

"Then I would ask the two of you to take a seat and rest your weary limbs," he smiled. "I must say that like Kilan after his return, your appearance strikes the eyes as slightly exotic with your tanned skin and Lord Enric's bleached hair. How did you cope with the climate?"

Eryn smiled politely and waited for Enric to reply. He wanted to talk about the weather there? Really?

"It was unusually warm by our standards, but after adapting our wardrobe to the local conditions it became fairly pleasant. The locals have adapted their schedules to the climate and avoid being outside when the day is at its hottest, which means they generally stay up longer in the evening before retiring," Enric explained.

Oh, she thought. So the weather question had obviously been an invitation to elaborate on the local customs instead of just meaningless chatter. Implications, she thought tiredly. Why could people not just say what they wanted and thus avoid depending on others to guess correctly?

She felt Enric's hand take and squeeze hers. She couldn't help the impression that it was meant as a warning. But why? She was not displaying any outward sign of the impatience she felt, she was absolutely sure of it.

"I am of course aware of the general developments due to Kilan's report upon his return and the message you sent me after the senate's decision, but there is surely a lot more. Your message informing us that the proceedings had gone in your favour and that you were about to return in a few more days was rather terse," she heard him say, a slight hint of reproach discernible in his tone.

Enric nodded. "You assume correctly, Your Majesty. Allow me to expand on what occurred. You are aware of the situation with Ram'an and Lady Eryn, I assume?"

The King nodded. "If you mean his claim to her due to an arrangement between their families when they were still infants, then yes. From what I understand, Lady Eryn was placed under his care for the duration of the proceedings."

Good, Eryn thought glumly, at least they did not have to go into more detail than necessary. Kilan had obviously provided a thorough report.

"Yes," Enric confirmed. "Though the senate was considerate enough to have the arrangement carried out at the residence of Lady Eryn's father's family instead of Ram'an's."

"Due to a rather impressive display of your disapproval, if my information was correct?" the King prompted with a raised eyebrow.

"That might have been part of the consideration, yes," Enric admitted unabashedly. "I myself was made to stay with the strongest of the three triarchs. It seems that in comparison my strength also ranks somewhat above average in the Western Territories. Thus it was considered wise to have me under observation as well for the duration of my extended voluntary stay."

"They would have let you leave any time had you expressed a wish to do so?" the King enquired.

"I trust that they would have, yes," the magician nodded. "Although they might actually have preferred it if I had left. They were not entirely sure what to expect of me."

"I understand it was Lady Eryn's own mother who made the accusations. I assume this influenced the nature of the political landscape quite a bit. From what I heard Lady Eryn has turned out to be the sole heir in a powerful family. An inconvenient development, if you will allow me to say that much."

Eryn smiled grimly. "None that will serve to cause you any further concern, Your Majesty. I corrected that inconvenient circumstance after the trial by renouncing House Aren and thereby severing all bonds with it." She shot an annoyed look at her companion. "Or at least that's what I thought at that time."

She admired the King's command over his facial features. All that spoke of his surprise were pursed lips.

"Renounced a powerful House, did you? I would imagine that you gave up quite a considerable personal advantage by doing so, unless I am mistaken. The status of belonging to a House, as I am given to understand, also reflects the social standing of a person, especially of a magician in the Western Territories."

"It does indeed. However, I have not given up that advantage as such as I was subsequently adopted into another House," she explained. So much for letting Enric do the talking.

The King remained silent for a few moments before he smiled faintly. "House... Vel'kim, I assume? You father's family?"

"Yes," she confirmed, slightly annoyed at his quick thinking. Why was it so hard to catch him off-guard? Well, it remained to be seen how much he liked Enric's own small gambit.

"I would have thought you to be more reluctant to bind yourself to another family after what happened with your mother. Am I right in assuming that there was a reason behind this very quick connection to another House?" he asked.

Damn him, she thought. How did he do it? Was there not a single detail she could keep to herself? This was too closely connected to her own personal story with Ram'an. Too private for him to know. Though by refusing to tell him when he asked her directly was equal to disobeying an order.

She breathed out steadily. "There was, yes. My cousin is a lawyer and suspected that Ram'an had been planning to claim me as a member of his House under an ancient but still active piece of legislation. The still valid companionship agreement our mothers had entered into would have made that possible."

"But only if you had not been a member of another House already?" the King asked.

"That is correct," she nodded.

"You mentioned that you thought your bond with your mother's House would be severed. This conveys the impression to me that it is not?"

"I would rather let my dear companion elaborate on that, with your permission. He may be able to outline the motives behind his actions more... convincingly than me, I believe."

The King's questioning gaze moved to Enric.

"Lady Eryn refers to my compliance with Malriel's request to adopt me into House Aren as her son," he said slowly.

Eryn felt a surge of triumph when the King's eyes bulged. "Pardon me?"

Finally! So it *was* possible to surprise even that seemingly cold-blooded fellow.

The monarch covered his eyes with a hand for a moment before he had regained his control. "So what you are telling me, Lord Enric, is that you let yourself be adopted into a powerful House to take Lady Eryn's place as heir to the title of Head? This means of course you have subjected yourself voluntarily to the local jurisdiction as a consequence."

"Indeed," Enric confirmed. Eryn cast a quick look at him. He seemed completely at ease, no sign of tension at all discernible in his features or posture. Why then did she have the impression that he was taut with unpleasant expectation, dread even?

"Lord Enric," the King said slowly and carefully, linking his fingers. "This means that you have made yourself answerable to two masters, as it were. From what I understand, the Houses in Takhan are also an important part of the local political system. You are already politically involved here and, sooner or later, will be also in the Western Territories. This puts us in a very difficult position here as we shall at some point have to consider where your true loyalties lie."

Oh dear, Eryn mused, that did sound as if Enric was in trouble. It wasn't a good portent.

"How about your intention of assuming the position of Head of House Aren, Lord Enric? Do you have any ambitions in that regard? I assume this must have been a major consideration in adopting you in the first place. I can see why you would be a desirable choice for Malriel, being both an experienced leader with considerable influence and the companion to her renegade daughter. I can see why you were the obvious choice for the position. Yet I can't help being curious as to your own motivation for that step."

Enric took a deep breath before replying. "Let me assure you, Your Majesty, that my loyalties lie with the Kingdom and the Order, just like before. My primary reason for accepting Malriel's adoption proposal was to keep harm away from Lady Eryn's new House. As you may imagine, owing to the history of both Houses, Malriel was quite unhappy over the impending adoption of her daughter into the House of the man who had stolen her so many years ago. Malriel's condition for not causing them considerable hardship was my consent to serve as a kind of... compensation for her loss."

The King considered him carefully for a few moments before smiling. "That seems like a noble, selfless gesture resulting from a very strong attachment to your companion. And yet I can't help but think that you yourself will profit from it as well."

"Not only myself, Your Majesty," he replied mildly, "all of us stand to profit. Being in constant contact with a high-ranking member of not only the society in Takhan, but its senate as well will strengthen our political connections considerably."

King Folrin nodded. "True. And yet a decision I would have preferred you not to have made without my assent."

"I understand, Your Majesty," Enric nodded.

The monarch raised an eyebrow. "No excuse that time was of the essence, Lord Enric?"

Enric smiled faintly. "I was under the impression that you would not have appreciated such a thing, Your Majesty."

The King leaned back in his chair and sighed heavily. "I would not have, no. Though in general this does not stop people from tiring me with them. Is there anything else you wish to inform me of? Maybe why your departure was delayed for several days after the trial had ended in your favour?"

"The reason for this, Your Majesty, was that Lady Eryn and I entered into what is in the Western Territories known as a *third level commitment bond*," Enric explained.

"You are full of astonishing news today," the King commented tartly. "I was informed of their nature. A magical binding only recommended to those truly connected to each other in great devotion." His gaze rested on Eryn. "A bond, I am given to understand, that needs to be entered into voluntarily."

She smiled. "I assure you, Your Majesty, that Lord Enric's decision to accept my request to enter into the bond with me was entirely voluntary. I did not apply any means of duress whatsoever."

The King's look at her was intense as he nodded slowly. "*You* were the one who expressed the wish to be joined magically, were you?" He noted the quick flicker in her eyes and smiled. "Yet there is a little more to it, would I be correct to assume? You were the one who asked finally, but not the one to ask initially, I cannot help but think?"

His smile grew wider as she pressed her lips together in annoyance. "You do not have to answer that, Lady Eryn. Your reaction is quite revealing in itself. I admit I am pleased to see that the commitment I made you enter into so hurriedly has grown into something more substantial in a matter of mere months. On both sides." He rose from his chair, causing them to follow his example. "I will expect a detailed report from you, Lord Enric. I have little hope of receiving one from Lady Eryn, having heard of her dislike for written reports when it comes to her superiors," he added pointedly. "Do include some information about the legal situation of both your new family situations and the magical commitment. I assume you familiarised yourself with each of those instead of entering into them blindly. And now you may leave. Lord Tyront is doubtlessly eager to hear about these most interesting developments."

Eryn bowed, grateful to have the first of the two meetings behind her. Though she did not have great hopes that the one with Lord Tyront would turn out to be any more pleasant.

* * *

King Folrin pressed the thumb and index finger of one hand into his eyes.

"I am at a loss whether to admire or curse Lord Enric. Publicly I need to commend him for his merits, of course. It would not do to make our new friends across the sea think I disapprove of his connection to their society, would it?" he sighed tiredly. "I need information, Marrin. We have received the formal invitation to establish a permanent ambassador in Takhan, and I am recommending your son leave here and take up his new position as soon as possible. Though I fear the kind of information I need from him will put his own loyalties to a test."

Marrin lifted a questioning eyebrow.

"The commitment bonds. You are aware, of course, that the bond we place our own magicians under when they have finished the training is what is considered a so-called second level commitment bond. I imagine they have worked out a way to counteract the binding effect. This will sooner or later become common knowledge here as well and change the nature of the bond between the Crown and the Order. As yet we have more or less forced magicians to bind themselves to us. If the bond can be easily reversed, this would change into a voluntary bond," the King explained with a dark expression.

"So you assume that the Order itself is not aware how to dissolve the binding to the Crown?" Marrin enquired.

The King smiled at his adviser. "You know me too well, Marrin. You are right of course. I am sure enough that at least Lord Tyront could reverse the effect of the binding any time he chose. Probably even Lord Enric, especially after his journey to Takhan."

"So if your assumptions are correct, Your Majesty, the Order would anyway have kept the binding intact in the past voluntarily," the older man pointed out.

"True. But only the Order's leader or leaders would be aware of it. Other magicians would not be. It seems like a detailed conversation with Lord Tyront is overdue. Before that I will allow him a day or two to recover from the news he is about to obtain from our two voyagers," the King smiled without humour.

* * *

Eryn flopped onto the bed, face first, intoning something muffled that was swallowed up by the mattress.

"This was not exactly a clear statement, my love. Try again without your mouth buried in fabric," Enric advised her.

She lifted her head, "I said that those two summonses have managed to reduce my happiness about returning home considerably. I feel spent and weary. Exhausted. We should have pretended to be returning tomorrow and instead have spent the evening in secret with Orrin, Junar, Vern and Plia."

The unexpected amusement she felt made her frown and she lifted her eyes up to his lopsided grin.

"You know," she said deliberately, "somehow I have the feeling that something is wrong here."

She saw the expression in his eyes become more intense.

"Indeed?"

Her eyes narrowed. "Yes, indeed. And I can't help thinking that you are very well aware of it. What is this? A little game to see how much time I would need to work it out?"

"What is it you think is wrong, dearest?" he enquired gently and leaned against the chest of drawers behind him with folded arms. "What *have* you divined?"

"That I seem to be a little more perceptive than before when it comes to judging your moods, I think," she said carefully. "I wonder if this is because I have finally admitted to myself the true scope of my attachment to you or if this is one of the side effects of our bond."

"Then let me add my own impressions to yours," Enric offered. That would probably make the evening even less enjoyable for her, he thought. "I do not believe your first assumption is the true reason. I have been aware of my own feelings for you for quite a while, though for the first time - and only recently - have I experienced the effect you are describing."

She nodded. "So it is the bond, then. A closer connection than before, the need to share more. This may include an enhanced sensitivity to the other person's moods, I assume."

He sighed. "Eryn, I think it is a bit more than that. I suffered from seasickness this time."

"Did you?" she asked.

"Only while you were awake. It was gone when you were asleep," he added quietly.

"Well, that is unfortunate for you, but I don't..." Her voice tapered off when the full implication of what he had just said hit her. She jumped off the bed and shook her head frantically. "No! Tell me that this is not true!"

He exhaled slowly. "Judging from the level of panic that I feel inside me that is clearly not my own, I would say that denying it does not make much sense."

She buried her face in both hands. "But Vran'el said this hardly ever happens! That I don't need to worry about it!" she wailed. "Why? Why is there always something that hits me on the head when I decide to open myself to somebody?" She gasped at the surge of anger that shot through her like a hot spear and stared at Enric, who did not show any sign of agitation apart from narrowed eyes while still leaning against the chest, apparently calm.

"How can you keep that inside you without any outward sign?" she groaned and returned to what had in the past worked reasonably well when dealing with strong emotions: breathing.

A thin smile spread across his lips. "Good. A very effective and direct way of communicating my sentiments. You just received a little impression of what goes on inside me when you talk of binding yourself to me and *regretting* it."

"I didn't mean to say *that*! I don't regret it, I promise!" she called out, relieved once the anger he projected had noticeably subsided.

"We need help with that," he told her. "If we fight, neither of us has a chance to stay calm and reasonable if we keep experiencing each other's feelings in addition to our own. I will despatch a message to Valrad tomorrow and ask him to send us whatever information he has on mind bonds. Do not count on it being too much, though. You heard Vran'el; not a lot of research has been done on the topic as it does not occur very often."

He sighed at her desperate expression and pushed away from the chest to sit on the bed with her. "This is not necessarily a burden, my love. It is a way of sharing something most people never would have a chance to experience like this. The trouble is just that we have yet to learn how to deal with what it brings. The upside, though, is that only strong emotions seem to be reflected in the other, which is quite a relief. We will need to see if distance has any effect on the potency of the sensations. Maybe there is even a way to reduce their influence."

She lifted her face to him and nodded unhappily. "That would be good, yes. Just now your anger almost brought me to my knees. Oh dear, I hope this is also something we experience with positive emotions in the other."

"It is," he nodded. "I felt your glee at the King's surprise when I told him of my adoption into House Aren."

She gave him a shaky laugh. "If you could call that a positive emotion..."

He smiled. "I also felt your joy at finding your friends waiting for you when we returned here earlier."

Her eyes widened when she thought back. "That feeling of regret I couldn't quite place - that was you, wasn't it? Why?"

So it seemed the bond was already causing him, too, to share more than he would have otherwise, he mused. "Seeing you being received like that, and coming back from a place where I had for the first time in many years formed friendly attachments with other people, made me understand how I have not exactly been the social type here."

She blinked and thought for a few moments. "People here are mostly either awed by or afraid of you. Just like myself not too long ago. I suppose that socialising is not exactly easy for you here," she conceded. "Funny, I wouldn't have thought that something like that mattered to you very much."

He shook his head. "Interestingly enough, me neither." He took her hand and squeezed it. "You see? The intimacy aspect of the bond has been working already."

"Yes," she smiled, "and I am pleased to see that for once not only on me. Our usual discussions about personal matters tend to be rather one-sided and result in your analysing me. Maybe it will be liberating to have that work both ways now." Then she said, more hesitantly, "So keeping secrets from you from now on will really be impossible, won't it? If I feel guilty about keeping something from you, you will sense it immediately."

"That I am counting on," he said with a raised brow. "It is a habit I have been trying to break you loose of for quite some time now. Though you did show some first signs of improvement in Takhan, I have to admit."

"High praise indeed," she murmured. Then a thought occurred to her and she narrowed her eyes. "You woke me one hour too early on the ship to experiment with this, didn't you? You made me suffer intentionally to verify your suspicions! You were aware of it back then already!"

He smiled apologetically. "Will it console you if I tell you that I had to suffer with you?"

"No," she growled, then shrugged. "Well, a little. How much did you suffer?"

"Terribly," he replied earnestly. "Like my empty stomach was on the verge of upending constantly without anything in there to bring up other than the bitter fluids that left a burning sensation in my throat."

She considered him thoughtfully, then nodded. "Alright, that is adequate. How do we deal with this mind bond for now? Avoiding strong emotions seems somewhat difficult."

"I am used to dealing with them, but from what I have seen, you have yet to get used to mine. You have a hard time keeping your own emotions under control, so sensing mine in addition to that might turn out to be quite a burden for some time."

She swallowed. "What if there is no helpful literature on how to deal with this?"

"Then, my love," he kissed her hand, "your enormous aptitude in the category of explorer will doubtless turn out to be very useful. You will have the unique chance to experiment and thus contribute to a field of expertise that will bring you fame and glory in both countries."

He smiled at the spark of interest which ignited in her eyes.

CHAPTER 2

Back to Work

Enric held her hand in his while they were strolling through the streets of Anyueel on their way to the healers' place. He was relieved that yesterday evening she had taken what must have been to her distressing news reasonably well. He had pondered his own point of view on that unexpected development and found that he was slightly worried about how to deal with it in a way that did not cause them any undue disadvantage. But all in all he did not consider it the curse Eryn seemed to regard it as.

"Do we need to tell Lord Tyront about this?" she said, interrupting his thoughts. So her mind was occupied with this matter as well. "He was not any happier about your adoption than the King. And unlike the King, he was not too thrilled about our commitment bond either. What did he call it? *Playing around with magic we had no understanding of*?" She grimaced at the memory of their superior's foul mood. She did not envy Enric the task of seeing him again at the Council meeting today.

"We might want to wait a while with that," he sighed. "He needs to come to terms with the news we have given him so far. Let's not overstrain his frayed nerves for the moment."

"Good. I don't think I want to deal with him again anytime soon."

"Give him some time to deal with the new situation. He is not a great friend of surprises but does not need long to adapt to them. His bad moods tend not to linger for long." He stopped when they had reached the healers' building. "Here we are. Eager to get back and show your colleagues what astounding new things you have learned?" he smiled and kissed her on the forehead.

"That would be fabulous," she nodded. "But I dare say there will be quite a lot of work to take care of first. Good thing today is not a treatment day. Not that I expect too much peace and quiet, though. I am a bit worried after the hints Plia dropped yesterday before we left for the meeting with the King."

"How bad can it be? The building is still standing, after all. No angry mob has ransacked it or burned it down."

"Very funny," she growled and started to open one of the large double doors, but felt herself gently pulled back into a warm embrace.

"Don't work too long today. I need you fit to participate in an experiment."

She raised both eyebrows. "What experiment?"

"With the mind bond. It concerns how the more intense positive emotions are conveyed."

Her eyes narrowed. "Are you using fancy words to mask the fact that this is about sex?"

He chuckled and shook his head. "I wonder why you even have to ask. Of course it is." He bent down to press a quick kiss on her mouth and turned to continue his way to the Palace. After a few steps he half turned and lifted a finger. "Return home timely, do you hear?"

She rolled her eyes and then looked down at the symbols on her wrist that were growing fainter with every few steps he took away from her. When he turned the next corner, they disappeared completely.

As she lifted her hand to push against the door, it was opened from the inside and she saw before her a familiar face. Rolan.

"Lady Eryn," he sighed and she blinked at the relief in his voice. "I am so glad you are back. Really glad."

"Rolan," she smiled uncertainly. "It's good to be back." Rolan happy to see her? That was probably not a good sign. "Would you like to tell me what's wrong now or do I need to sit down for it?" she said with a slightly ironic smile at him.

He blushed slightly. "Sit down, probably. With a nice warm drink."

"That bad?" she sighed.

He seemed to think about that for a few moments, then shrugged. "You know, now that you are back I am not so sure about that any longer." His voice sounded surprised. "Interesting."

Indeed, she thought but didn't say it out loud. It seemed as if his confidence in her having the solution to whatever catastrophes had occurred was as unexpected for himself as it was for her. That had to be a sign of trust, didn't it? Or perhaps just plain desperation. Well, she would know soon enough.

She looked around surreptitiously while walking after Rolan to the small kitchen to get her drink. Everything seemed clean, undamaged and the way it was supposed to be. Her assistant waited for her to fill a cup with water, stir in a spoonful of finely ground herbs and heat the mixture with a touch of her finger and a little magic, then he preceded her up the stairs and held the door to her study open for her.

Happiness about seeing her as well as almost overbearing courtesy? Now matters were shaping up to be scary indeed, she thought.

Her study did not look too messy, she decided. After an absence of more than six weeks it was a bit more untidy - with papers strewn about - than she had left it, but nothing to shock her or make her recoil.

She went to her desk, placing the cup on it before letting herself sink onto the chair, exhaling and smiling contentedly.

"Now I am back. Truly back." She motioned for Rolan to sit as well. "Alright - shock me. What has gone wrong?"

"Vern," her assistant said carefully.

"*Vern* has gone wrong?" she enquired gently.

Rolan thought for a moment, then obviously reached the conclusion that the term was suitable. "Yes, I think we could phrase it like that."

"Very well," she said slowly, "could you elaborate some more? A few more details would be good."

"He was not getting along very well with the other healers," her assistant supplied.

"What do you mean by that? Rolan, fill in the blanks for me! This is very tedious!" she exclaimed impatiently.

He grimaced unhappily. "Vern seems to have developed certain qualities of a tyrant. The healers were on the verge of revolting against him openly. I was afraid I would soon be standing here alone with a house full of patients and the healers refusing to work."

A tyrant? Vern? Well, she mused, judging from how she had seen him act when he was negotiating, that was probably not so very unlikely. There was definitely a propensity for that in his character.

"I see. What was the reason for his behaviour in your opinion?"

"Youth. Inexperience. Idiocy," Rolan threw up his hands. "I don't know!"

"Think again," she said gently. "I need a neutral point of view from you. Give me your thoughts."

"A voice of reason," he murmured and shook his head. "That seems luxury in the mayhem we had here in these last weeks." He cleared his throat and looked up again with less desperation and more focus in his eyes, she noted, relieved.

"He was overwhelmed with the double burden of heading a group of people much older than himself where he had to struggle to be taken seriously, and healing and teaching in his other role. He spent long nights here, doing the paperwork, despairing over it at times," he explained, some sympathy clear in his voice.

"How did *you* get along with him?"

"Well enough. I tried to take as much off his shoulders as I could, but my own experience with leading people and healing or teaching is not exactly noteworthy. All I could help him with was the paperwork." He sighed. "As well as with getting him out of the safe room once when they had blocked the door while he was in."

"They?" she asked. "The healers?"

Rolan nodded.

"What else have they done?" She felt anger rising at the stupidity of adults teasing a young man several years their junior who instead would be best shown their support.

"Wilfully misunderstood orders, from what I have gathered. Hidden his clothes. Locked the study door. Twice."

Eryn closed her eyes, calming her wish to hit out at someone. There was steel in them when she opened them again. "Alright. Tell me what he did to provoke those things. They are not normally that stupid."

"He resorted to shouting at them quite a lot. Made them stay longer, gave them more to learn than they could cope with. It seems he is used to a rather more rapid rate of progress when it comes to learning things."

Yes, she thought, and she had always taken advantage of the fact that he was smart, interested and a very speedy learner. Had she inadvertently encouraged him to think that this was the way everybody should be tutored? Obviously she had.

"They tried to talk to him first," Rolan continued. "But they made demands, which he did not take very well, either."

She thought back to the hug Vern had given her. The panic in his voice when he had told her that he had been afraid they wouldn't let her leave any more from Takhan. There had obviously been a little more behind that than merely missing her as a friend.

"Oh dear," she sighed. "So it seems I will have to start mending that breach again. They need to be able to work together again as professionals. And Vern is still far enough ahead to train them occasionally or at least supervise their work. I need to get them to respect each other again. Any suggestions?"

Rolan straightened. She couldn't help but notice that he very much appreciated being asked for his thoughts. She tried to think back. Had she never bothered to ask him before? It seemed as if Vern's approach to leading people was not the only one that needed mid-course corrections, she thought.

"I think what both sides have been missing over these last weeks is appreciation," he ventured and waited for her reaction to that.

"Appreciation? As in telling them that they have performed good work?"

He nodded. "Something like that, yes."

"Alright, I can do that." She emptied her cup. "Do you have any information for me about training progress, stock, treatments?"

She saw him smile for the first time since her arrival and couldn't help but relish the sight. He had never once failed to produce a piece of paper with lists, numbers or whatever else on it since they had started working together. It was what he was good at. So now they were about to enter *his* realm of expertise.

* * *

Eryn had just finished reading the reports about the nature and quantities of medicines that had been administered to patients in her absence, when there was a knock at the door and upon her invitation a liveried Palace messenger entered.

Oh no, she thought. Not a summons from the King or the Council. Not now when there was so much to be taken care of. However, he did not seem to have a written message on him, so he was surely here to tell her to come with him.

She sighed before he could speak. "King or Council?"

The messenger blinked. "Magic Council, Lady Eryn."

"Right now or do I have time to finish a few things first?"

He grimaced sympathetically. "Right now, I am afraid."

She pushed back her chair. "Of course. What else? Lead on, then. I suppose you were told not to leave without me."

He nodded and waited for her to slip into her robes and adjust them before preceding her down the stairs.

Enric had warned her that they might want to see her soon enough, but she had hoped that whatever they needed or wanted to know could for now be dealt with by him alone. Whatever concerned trade or politics he would surely be the one to satisfy their curiosity more effectively. She stopped and slowed her breathing. But there was one area in which *she* herself would be the one to ask. Healing and everything concerned with it. Of course. They wanted to talk about the barrier inside their heads. That was the most likely explanation.

The messenger turned to her and waited patiently until she resumed walking. When they had reached the doors to the great Council hall, he bowed to her and took his leave. She knocked three times and the door opened immediately. She entered and found herself the centre of attention from not only the twelve Council members but also an exalted visitor to these halls: the King.

The Council sat around a large round table with one chair for the Order's leader slightly more elaborate than the others. The King's throne was off to one side as if he had the role of a mere observer in these halls.

Twelve members, she mused. Exactly like the number of Houses in Takhan. It was the first time she had noticed this coincidence. Funny, the things the mind came up with when it wanted to escape the immediate reality. She knew she was not in any trouble, and yet standing before the Council and the King was not particularly pleasant.

"Gentlemen," she spoke before any of them had a chance to address her, "Here I am. Let's keep this brief, shall we? As you may imagine, there is quite a lot of work I need to take care of after my return."

She saw a few of them exchange amused or annoyed glances with each other. Orrin lifted an eyebrow at her, perhaps in warning, while Enric seemed slightly amused and Lord Tyront gave her a stare which - while not exactly hostile - did definitely lack warmth. The King's expression was as unreadable as it tended to be most of the time.

Maybe it had not been the most advisable of greetings, she considered. Though summoning her at such short notice had not been the most considerate thing to do, either. From where she stood, they were even.

"Lady Eryn," Tyront said pointedly, "allow me to welcome you back amongst us in the name of the Council, however inconvenient our request for your presence seems to be for you right now."

She shrugged. "Thank you. As long as this does not require too long, I would say the inconvenience is not going to be too great." Stupid, she scolded herself. What was it about this man which made her want to provoke him? She considered the King's words only the evening before about how her stay abroad had not done anything for her attitude towards authority.

Tyront took a deep breath and smiled at her coldly. "Then the Council will do its best not to unduly waste your very precious time, Lady Eryn."

She didn't reply to that and just waited for him to go on. The statement might have seemed harmless enough, but his tone implied he was clearly far from happy, so it was probably wiser to keep her tongue in check for now and limit herself to answering when she was spoken to. A strategy which Enric had been trying to impress its merits on her for quite some time now.

"You might have guessed why we have called for you," he went on. She noted that he didn't offer her a seat. Small revenges won. So she had to stand there like she was accused of a wrongdoing. It reminded her of the day when she and Vern had been brought to his study after being discovered during their unapproved magical fighting lessons. And the senate in Takhan, where she had stood before the representatives of the Houses during the trial. She pushed the images aside and focused on the here and now.

"I assume you wish to talk to me about the barrier existing inside your heads," she ventured. She saw Tyront nod in mild surprise. So he had not counted on her really supposing the reason and had tried to make her appear bad as punishment for her behaviour. Charming. Enric's approving grin was hardly discernible, but clearly visible to the knowing eye.

"Indeed. From what I understand you were granted the knowledge of how to detect and remove the barrier and were even shown how to do it by your..." He paused, clearly not certain how to term the family situation she was now in after the adoption.

"By Valrad," she completed his sentence. "Yes. He was kind enough to show me how it is done by instructing me in the removal of Enric's barrier."

She saw a broad smile spread on Lord Woldarn's face. "Then we have now two magicians who are in a position to bear magically-gifted daughters. And most convenient that they happen to be joined as companions."

Eryn gave him a cool stare. "Your eagerness to embrace that new development is understandable, My Lord, but I assure you that I have no intention of starting a large family to accommodate other people's wishes for such things."

"I do beg your pardon," he said in a placating voice and lifted both hands, "that was not what I meant to imply, My Lady, I assure you. I just meant to say that however many children yourself and Lord Enric intend to have, we all look forward to seeing them develop, *particularly* if girls number among them."

Enric closed his eyes for a moment. That would not receive a favourable reply either, and he doubted that Tyront was in any mood to deal with more of her insolence for now. Which was why he spoke up before Eryn had a chance to reply.

"Lord Woldarn, I appreciate your interest in our procreation plans, but suggest this is hardly the right setting for such discussion," he commented dryly, not leaving any doubt whatsoever that he did not at all appreciate it.

That earned him a few chuckles and Lord Woldarn leaned back with folded arms and a sour expression.

"Lady Eryn," Lord Tyront resumed his initial topic, "we have summoned you to inform you of our decision to allow removal of the barrier inside the heads of both magicians and non-magicians at your earliest convenience."

She gulped. "All of them?"

"Preferably, yes. I imagine that this might take up some of the time that you would rather wish to dedicate to other matters for now, but you will surely understand that this needs to be taken care of soon," he pointed out.

Eryn exhaled and nodded. "I do, yes. Though I don't even know how long it will take me to remove every barrier. I have performed it only once so far, and I had help with that. How is this supposed to work? Do I go knocking from door to door, and have people let me look inside their heads? What if somebody objects? Not everybody is comfortable with a stranger doing things they don't understand inside their own heads," she pointed out.

"There will be a Royal order that will make people comply," another Council member supplied.

She shook her head in disbelief. "Really? We are forcing them? Or rather you are making *me* force them? What am I to do if they refuse point blank? Bash them on the head with a stick and go ahead without their consent?" She folded her arms. "This contradicts the principles of the healing profession. I do not intend to subject anybody to this order who is not willing to allow it. Additionally, I will not show my healers how it is done if you intend to put them under pressure instead." Her chin was lifted defiantly and she glared at the Council members.

Enric saw Tyront go pale at the blatant refusal to carry out a Royal order, especially as the one who had issued it was present. They had returned less than one day ago and she was already getting herself into trouble again. This woman really had a knack for it. Unfortunately for the Order and the King, though, she had a very powerful advantage on her side. If she refused to remove the barrier, they had nobody else who would or could do it. And asking for a healer from the Western Territories to take care of it because Eryn refused would look very bad. Then there was the question of whether they themselves would refuse as well under such conditions. It was likely enough that they considered the same principles applied to healing as she.

All of them looked up when they heard the King's calm voice.

"Lady Eryn. I can assure you that none of us intends to violate the strict ethical principles you consider necessary for your work. I am sure we all feel safer when offering ourselves into your capable hands because of those. What approach would *you* say was appropriate in this matter, my Lady?"

Good, Enric mused, it seemed the King had reached the same conclusion. But then that was no great surprise. He did have a certain aptitude for thinking on his feet.

Enric watched Eryn thinking over the options for a moment before she turned to the King. "I propose making the removal of the barrier voluntary, Your Majesty. If we communicate that there is no danger whatsoever involved and point out the likely benefit of being able to conceive female magicians, this might convince the majority of people to do it. Citizens could come to the clinic to have it removed. It might be that granting them a waiver on taxes for this year would help persuade them..."

The King raised his brow at her. "A most intriguing proposal. I will certainly consider it. You have resorted to calling the place a *clinic*?"

Had she? She thought back and then realised that she had indeed. "Yes, it would seem I have," she said slowly.

"Not entirely consciously, though," the King remarked. "A term adopted from our new friends in the west, no doubt." He looked at the Council members. "I assume that the Magic Council has no objections to having their barriers removed as soon as practicable?"

Heads shook.

"As you see, Lady Eryn, those magicians present do not have to be compelled. May I therefore impose on you to do it right here and now? Let me be the first one you work on to set a good example."

She swallowed and nodded, not sure how to proceed. Was she to walk to the throne? Did she need an invitation for that? Had that just been one?

King Folrin rose and indicated for her to step closer. "Where do you need to touch me, Lady Eryn?"

"Somewhere on your head would be right. The forehead, for example," she replied and walked the few steps until she stood directly in front of him.

"Do you prefer sitting or standing for this?" he enquired further.

"As I am not sure how long it will take, I would prefer to sit if this is in order."

"Naturally," the King nodded politely and took her hand to lead her to a small bench in front of one of the many windows. It was hardly wide enough to accommodate two people, she noted with slight unease. Back to playing games, it seemed. Though she doubted the wisdom of making her uncomfortable while she was meant to work inside his head without causing any damage.

He waited for her to take a seat and then sat down a little closer than would have been necessary, before taking her hand and laying it on his forehead.

"I am ready if you are, my Lady."

She nodded and closed her eyes, conscious of his eyes on her. Fighting down her nervousness, she found that place of peace and quiet inside her, and only then let the magic follow the outline of her arm and enter the skull under her palm. She found the spot reasonably quickly as it was now the third time she had looked for it. It seemed to become easier the more often she did it. As she had been instructed by Valrad, she slowly and carefully increased the barrier in size by feeding it with magic until it was large enough to be dissolved without causing any shock to the sensitive tissue surrounding it.

When she opened her eyes, the King was still regarding her with this unnerving gaze of his. She nodded and removed her hand from his forehead. "It is done. The barrier inside you has been removed."

King Folrin smiled approvingly. "Well done." Then he rose and turned to the Council.

Tyront had risen from his chair already, knowing what was expected of him. "I shall be the next one." He walked over to her briskly and took the seat the King had relinquished only moments ago. His posture was as calm and confident as ever, but she saw the warning in his eyes. So it seemed he was not entirely comfortable with the thought of granting her access to his head.

"Don't concern yourself, Lord Tyront," she said quietly enough for only him to hear. "I promise it won't cause you any pain. I will behave; no nightmares or images of giant cats chasing you through the streets."

He didn't comment at that but merely raised an eyebrow at her as she lifted her hand to place on his forehead.

* * *

Tyront joined his second-in-command, who was leaning against a column while observing his companion on the small bench as she was working with her brow furrowed in concentration.

"Kilan told us that in the Western Territories her family is notorious for their short temper," he remarked. "Pity we couldn't have had a more docile one of them find her way here."

Enric just smiled. It seemed that Tyront had overcome his anger at the news of his adoption from the evening before, just as Enric had expected him to.

"I must say that I am happy enough with the way things have turned out so far. What's more, you have to admit that we have benefited from her knowledge. We have reintroduced female magicians after more than three-hundred years. I would say coping with her temper and insolence is a small price to pay for that," he pointed out.

Tyront sighed. "You are right, and we both know it. Though I don't appreciate it when you come across as the voice of reason instead of the sympathetic listener I need when airing my frustration, my dear boy."

"*My dear boy*," Enric repeated with a slight shake of his head. "I am thirty-five years old. When are you going to stop calling me that?"

"When our age difference starts shrinking or you take over my position," Tyront replied with calculated smugness.

"When I take over your position? That means after you would be dead," Enric pointed out.

"That would certainly stop me from addressing you with *my dear boy* any longer, wouldn't it?"

"It would stop you from doing a lot of things, I would say," the younger man remarked dryly.

"True enough. But then there is the question of whether you would even be available for my succession with your new status as heir of a House in Takhan, isn't there?"

Ah yes, Enric thought grimly - so they were back onto that topic. Of course there was no avoiding it in the long run; he was second in line for two positions which more or less excluded each other, if simply for reasons of geography.

"I have great expectation of not finding myself in that situation in the foreseeable future," he said, trying to placate his superior. "I trust that there will be other opportunities to find a capable Head for House Aren in time. Malriel is not yet fifty, so I doubt that she will want to relinquish her position anytime soon. Or you yours, for that matter."

That seemed to reassure Tyront to a certain degree. "That may be true. Although it is not a matter that needs to concern us right now, it does not mean that we are absolved from finding a way of dealing with it, however. Right now it looks as if the Order's succession is under threat." His gaze wandered over to Eryn, who was working on Lord Poron's barrier at the moment. "Number three," he murmured. "Apart from the fact that she would probably dissolve the Order or lead it into utter chaos, that is not even the main problem, as you would take her with you to Takhan anyway. That leaves Lord Poron, who I would wish to live forever, but who is still twenty years older than I and will very probably not outlive me to take over my position."

"Orrin then," Enric smiled. "Now, that would be a good choice. Apart from the fact that he would refuse outright. Too honest, too straightforward for the political dance."

Tyront released his breath audibly. "I hope you see in what situation I find myself due to your chivalrous gesture to take your companion's place in her old family so as to protect her new one."

Enric nodded sympathetically. "Let me assure you of my compassion."

"I would rather hear you assure me that you will find a solution to this dilemma. Don't think this is only my problem, Enric."

"I wouldn't dream of doing so. But then there is always the chance of another unexpected addition to our high ranks," the younger man said cheerfully.

"Stop trying to comfort me," Tyront growled. "I will surely not have to deal with this a third time if there is any justice in this world." He turned his head to Eryn once more. "Is she still as opposed to having children as she used to be? She has entered into this magical bond with you, after all."

"Yes, she is. Moreover, if I had not intervened at Lord Woldarn's question previously, I am in no doubt that she would have told you about it herself in very colourful words. Are you wondering about sending my offspring to Takhan to take over House Aren?" He shook his head. "That would not work quite so easily. According to their laws, our children would be members of House Vel'kim. Children we are very likely never to have, though," he added in a tone that made Tyront narrow his eyes at him.

"Not too happy about that, are you?" he enquired carefully.

Enric sighed. "I respect that decision. And it was something I was aware of before I entered into the third level bond with her. So no complaints. It was not as if I were so very likely to start a family without her any time soon, in any case. If there is the question either of having children or of keeping *her*, I don't even have to think about the answer."

The older man nodded slowly. "I see. A pity that those are the choices, though."

Lord Poron joined their circle and smiled. "Over and done with. It seems I have now the ability to father magical daughters," he laughed. "My Aurna will be very tickled to hear that."

"It is more the gesture that counts," Tyront told him. "We should be able to say that the entire Magic Council has had the barrier removed - otherwise how can we justify asking others to have it done if there is a single one of us who hasn't?"

Lord Poron waved a dismissive hand. "You won't hear me complain, Lord Tyront. I found it interesting to watch, though Lady Eryn kept telling me to stop following her every move and asking inconvenient questions that broke her concentration."

"Well, I would say diverting a healer who is working inside your head might not be the wisest course of action," Enric pointed out. "Anyway, I am sure there will be ample opportunity to observe how it is done when she removes the barriers at the healers' place."

"Yes, or the *clinic*, as it seems we will be calling it from now on," Lord Poron said. "Though people will probably keep referring to it as *Lady Eryn's* anyway."

They straightened when King Folrin stepped towards them.

"Lord Enric, I am sure you are aware that there is a custom of the Crown's granting a favour to those who earn the Kingdom's gratitude by accomplishing something that benefits it?"

Enric smiled faintly. "I admit I am, Your Majesty."

"Then I am surely right in further assuming that you have something in mind that you would wish to propose to me for that purpose?"

"There is indeed an idea that I would very much like to discuss with you, Your Majesty."

"Very good," the King smiled. "Then I suggest we meet to take care of this soon. Do you need time to prepare a detailed proposal, Lord Enric?"

"No, I happen to have one ready."

"Excellent. And not entirely unexpected, I have to say." The King nodded to the three magicians. "Excuse me now. I need to leave." He waited for the magicians to bow to him before he walked away.

"So, what is it going to be?" Lord Poron asked curiously.

"Nothing I wish to disclose before it is granted," Enric chuckled. "That is said to attract bad luck." He looked over at Eryn. "It looks like she will be kept here for quite some time yet. That means her work remains unfinished and she will not be in a very relaxed mood tonight. I assume I will have to drag her home before she falls asleep across her desk again."

"That's the downside of being joined to such an important woman, Lord Enric," Lord Poron chuckled. "The most important one we have right now."

* * *

Eryn returned to her study and flopped down on her chair. Two hours gone. Two hours she could have employed much better than in removing the barriers of the King and the Council members. But then at least she had improved her skills somewhat by practising. Towards the end she had been a lot quicker than with the first few. As soon as she was done with the last of them, she had all but fled the Council hall when she detected first attempts at getting her to join conversations.

She had seen Enric standing on one side and talking first to Lord Tyront and later to Lord Peron. At one time Orrin joined them as well. Soon after the removal of Lord Tyront's barrier she had felt a surprising pang of sadness that had not been her own. She wondered what the two men had been talking about that triggered such a feeling in her companion.

A knock came from the door that joined her study with Rolan's and she called out for him to enter. He stuck his head in.

"Vern has been looking for you. I told him I would let him know as soon as you are back. He is in Plia's laboratory now," her assistant reported.

Sighing, she stood up. "Alright, then I'd better fetch him. It looks like there is not going to be much chance for me to get any work done today. I wonder why I ever thought there was."

She walked out onto the corridor and knocked at Plia's half-open door.

"Plia?" she called out. "I was told Vern was here." When she entered, she saw Plia examining a bunch of dried herbs that had very likely been delivered by the herb gatherers and Vern leafing through one of the books on the table next to her.

"I told you," he then announced triumphantly, "the blossoms are to be plucked before drying!"

They both looked up when Eryn entered.

"There you are!" Vern complained, "I have been waiting here for more than half an hour! Where have you been? I would have thought that you have enough to do after your trip not to run off just like that in the middle of the day!"

She snorted. "Don't tell me, tell the Magic Council! They thought this was just the right day to make me take care of a little task for them. Plia, I hope he is not keeping you from your work? Just kick him out if he is a nuisance."

"No," the girl smiled, "he has been very helpful, in fact. It helps that he has aided you in putting the books together, he is a lot faster at finding things in them than me."

Vern put aside the book and waved goodbye to Plia before following Eryn into her study. As soon as the door was closed, his stance changed completely. His shoulders drooped and his expression became unhappy and worried.

"What's the matter?" she enquired immediately. "That's not a good reaction when you enter my study."

"I have come to apologise. I suppose you have heard about a thing or two already. My taking care of this place here was not exactly a grand success," he murmured. "I failed you."

Eryn looked at him and considered how to handle things. Sympathy was not a path that would lead anywhere with him right now. His self-esteem was low at the moment, and treating him with gentleness would just confirm this to him. What he needed now was not a friend. He needed a superior.

She picked up a few sheets of paper and pretended to look through them, then she looked up in confusion.

"I have looked through the reports Rolan is so eager to throw at me on every possible occasion, and it seems there was an increasing number of patients who were treated with mostly good results in these last weeks." She pulled out one list. "It says here the quality of the herbs and medicines was adequate, so no complaints here. The complaints that were made - all four of them - were taken care of quickly. The money kept flowing in and was stored properly, the patient reports were completed and I have not returned to utter chaos and mayhem." She put aside the papers. "I heard that you met some trouble with the healers, but as the healing services seem to have been provided continuously at the standard that I demand, I do not consider the term *failed* appropriate here."

He blinked a few times and frowned. When he was about to speak, she lifted her finger to stop him.

"I am sure that your time in charge of this place was not exactly a very relaxing and uncomplicated one, but full of challenges, especially personal ones. Yet this did not stop you from keeping it going, nor did you fling everything aside and make a bolt for it when most people would surely have understood if you had. So, however you yourself assess your performance, from a rational point of view *failed* is certainly not accurate. Also, if we are to work together, I need to be able to rely on your assessment of situations." She leaned back and steepled her fingers the way she had seen Lord Tyront do. Oh dear. Was she really imitating him now? "I would invite you to think again and then give me a more realistic evaluation of what has happened here in my absence." She was proud of how cool her voice sounded, making her statement just sound like the order it actually was.

Vern straightened and his face drained of all but an insecure expression, as if not entirely sure how to deal with authoritative Eryn when he was so much more used to either explosive, annoyed or funny Eryn.

His eyes scanned the floor for several moments, then he started speaking. "The treatment of the patients worked well; I established a rota where each of the trainees worked with me before being paired up again with another trainee. I took care of the more complex treatments myself while the others healed minor things and were instructed to fetch me if they had any questions." Then he paused, thinking again for a few seconds before continuing, "The supply of herbs was a little erratic at the beginning, but Plia devised a way to plan in advance for the medication she needs and instructed the gatherers accordingly. In some cases the quality was a bit of a problem, especially when it came to the gatherers who were not on the excursion with us. But Plia was very strict in accepting the material, so they mended their ways, as it were." A small smile appeared on his face.

"What else?" Eryn prompted.

"The administrative matters were taken care of by Rolan, and while I sometimes found it hard to get on with him at the beginning, it turned out that this place was more or less destined for rack and ruin without him. At least when you are not here."

She suppressed a smile and refrained from telling him for now that such a fate was not much changed now she *was* here.

"I would have been totally and completely lost without him. Really. I think I owe him my sanity. Or what is left of it," Vern sighed.

Good. At least he had seen that there was something positive as well, she thought. Time to move on to what had not worked out that well.

"What was the trouble with you and the other healers?" she enquired mildly.

"I don't know, it was just..." he started and stilled immediately, when she shook her head.

"No, Vern. Switch off the self-pity for now and think. I need proper answers, not complaints," she insisted.

He seemed slightly taken aback, but then nodded and started anew. "I had the impression that they found it hard to take me seriously."

"What do you think was the reason for that?"

He looked at her as if this was obvious. "My youth, I would think."

"Alright. I heard there was a certain... discord when it came to the training?"

"You could say that, yes," he replied darkly. "They either didn't attempt the assignments I gave them at all or did only half of them."

"Did they give you a reason for that?"

"They kept saying it was too much, that they didn't have the energy after work."

Eryn nodded. "I see. How did you react to that argument?"

"I told them to put more effort into their training and had better take it seriously instead of trying to take advantage of the fact that you were away," he informed her.

Oh dear. "So there was no doubt whatsoever in your mind that they might *not* have been trying to shirk the assignments out of laziness but because they really found it too much?"

He concentrated his stare. "I did much more than that when I started my healing training with you! I stayed up until midnight reading books, practising the things I had learned and drawing pictures. I set them a lot less to do than that, so I really don't see what there was to complain about!"

Eryn leaned forward. "Vern, you know very well that your aptitude in everything remotely connected with books and understanding things is above average. This is not something only I kept on telling you, but also what you no doubt experienced with the rest of your classmates and teachers. Applying your own standards, based on your personal abilities to other people with strengths either not as developed or in different areas, can be a dangerous thing to do."

"So you, as well, think I expected too much from them?"

She breathed out slowly. "Vern, I am not in a position to judge anything here. I have no idea what or exactly how much you gave them to do, whether it was too much or not. I am just trying to encourage you to see their point and be slightly more conscious of not everybody's being like *you*. It does not mean that they are any less important as healers, mind you. They probably have other strengths, which you may not," she added in a warning tone.

That seemed to make him reconsider the issue.

"They locked me in several times," was all he finally said, rather quietly.

"That was wrong of them," she nodded. "Quite childish. But people tend to react unreasonably when they feel misunderstood and frustrated. That's the trick, you see? Listening to them." She smiled. "Do you remember all those troubles we had with the changing room?" How far away that seemed now. "I insisted on keeping the arrangement in place, no matter what Enric caused me to suffer. Then the healers themselves came to me to tell me that they wanted it changed. I was not too happy about that, believe me. Even though if felt like losing this battle to Enric, I still gave up my fight and did what they asked me to. Doing so didn't make them respect me any less. Insisting on keeping everything the way it was despite their request would surely have cost me their goodwill. And despite all the trouble you had with them, from what I have seen they have never let this influence the quality of their work. You know, that is something you need to credit them with."

Vern rubbed his face, feeling suddenly weary. "That shows me that I am clearly not cut out for leading people."

"Utter rubbish. It just shows that you are sixteen. Leading people is a matter of experience and a willingness to learn. Willingness to learn has never been a problem in your case. I'm sure the experience will come with age. I have no intention of letting you off the hook when it comes to filling in for me."

He eyed her doubtfully. "After all this you still think that is a wise idea?"

"I do, yes. I have no intention of wasting that potential and talent of yours because you have not yet learned to control your tendencies to lead from the front like a dictator. You will sooner or later assume a position of responsibility of some kind, there is no avoiding that. So you'd better start learning how to work with people. Though we will make sure you are better prepared for facing that the next time."

"You hear people talk of *born leaders* all the time! So it is not necessarily something that can be learned but is a gift," he pointed out.

"Born leaders, Vern, are people who can indulge in the luxury of not having to learn all this because most likely they were born with considerable strengths in that area. They might, however, be neither good as healers, nor as artists nor as negotiators. If you ask me, I would rather be born with a gift that cannot be learned and take the trouble of acquiring the skill of leadership. You have heard what people say about Enric, haven't you? A lazy, useless scallywag when he was young - certainly *not* a born leader. But just look at him now."

She decided that this was a good time to return to her role as a friend. "Vern, you have not failed me. Apart from with your totally inaccurate assessment of the situation, that is," she smiled. "I am proud of you, very much. Always have been. And I am confident that you will give me more than enough reason to be so in the future."

He relaxed and returned the smile. "It's good to have you back. Really good."

She grinned. "Good. So don't you forget it."

"What am I to do with the other healers?"

"I will talk to them, listen to their side of the story. Tell them that they have done some good work, show them appreciation. As for the rest - well, it is up to you to make them respect you again. There are two significant advantages you have: greater knowledge and experience in healing than they have. Use that to help them, but don't let them treat you with disrespect. That is pretty much it for now." She cast a quick glance at the door to her assistant's room. "So he did a good job in my absence?"

Vern shook his head. "Not merely a good job, but he saved my life day after day. He did so much paperwork, I don't even know what all of it is. He only came in here when there was no way of avoiding it, when he needed a signature or something to keep the place running. He stayed late almost every day, was here early in the morning. I don't know when he had time to sleep. And he tried to stop us from bickering."

Eryn nodded. That was high praise indeed and she decided to be nicer to Rolan from now on. He had really earned it.

She smiled and leant forward. "I learned some very helpful things in Takhan. Things I can imagine you will be very eager to learn "

A glint had entered Vern's eyes. "Such as what?"

"I learned how to make people appear younger. Ten years, twenty, however much you desire. And I met a very talented and smart non-magician healer who taught me about non-magical methods of diagnosis."

A broad grin split his face. "Seriously? That is awesome!"

"There is more. I learned how to enable people here to give birth to magically-gifted daughters."

Vern stared at her. "You are joking!"

"I am not," she smiled, satisfied at his reaction. "And I have just been commissioned by the Magic Council to work on that. I could use another healer to help me with it. You don't happen to know anyone who would be interested in that task, do you?"

CHAPTER 3

Side Effect

Junar laughed delightedly as she opened the door and found herself facing Eryn.

"Hey, what an unexpected honour! I didn't think we would be seeing you here for a while yet! You must be swamped with work, I imagine. Orrin - look who is here," she called out. Then she noticed her visitor's slightly pained expression and stopped herself. "Something is not right. Come in."

"I need to talk to you," Eryn sighed and stepped inside the parlour that had noticeably acquired a few more female touches in the course of these last few weeks. Flowers in vases, colourful throw cushions, little items that served no other purpose than decoration.

Orrin stepped out of his study and lifted his brow at her. "Trouble, dear girl?"

She nodded. "One could say that, yes."

"Did you cause it or are you suffering from its effects?" he enquired further.

"Tough question. I suppose one could say both, in a way," she replied after thinking for moment.

"Well, if that isn't being cryptic..." Junar lifted her eyes to the ceiling and led Eryn to a settee. "Sit. I'll get you something to drink."

"So, what is the matter?" Orrin asked and strolled closer.

Eryn regarded him for a few moments, then said, "I am not really sure if *you* should hear this. It is tenuously connected to sex."

He fought down a slightly uncomfortable expression, but not before she had spotted it. She smiled faintly. "Last chance to run, warrior. What is it to be? Will you brave the news now or will you make Junar tell you after I have gone?"

He huffed indignantly. "What makes you think I would do a thing like that? I don't remember ever expressing an unhealthy interest in that element of your life. Or having one, for that matter," he amended.

"I think you would be terribly curious as I don't normally run around talking about my intimate partner problems to people," she remarked with a raised eyebrow.

"I will stay," Orrin announced. "But only because you phrased it as a challenge."

"Brave Orrin," she murmured and accepted the warm drink Junar brought her.

"Out with it, then!" the seamstress urged her, before taking a seat between them.

Eryn took a sip and felt the comforting warmth in her throat and stomach. How best to start, she wondered. There was quite a lot connected to this they were not aware of yet.

"Enric and I entered into something called a third level commitment bond before we left Takhan," she started. "It is a magical commitment only two magicians can have. It binds them very tightly."

Junar's eyes bulged and Orrin frowned. "A magical binding? Like the oath to the King?"

"Yes, similar to that. Somewhat stronger, though. They have three commitment bonds, and the one between companions is the strongest one. It induces more intimacy, more awareness for the other's feelings and pulls companions back together if they become separated."

"And *you* entered into this?" Junar asked incredulously. "*You* bound yourself to a man magically?"

"Voluntarily?" Orrin added in that same tone of disbelief.

"Come on!" Eryn exclaimed and threw up her hands in frustration. "I was joined with Enric for several months before that, why would it surprise you that we took what could be considered the next step?"

"Because you were forced into the commitment with him and did not at all take it well at that time," Orrin replied.

"As well as because you have serious commitment issues," Junar said.

"Well, consider them overcome! Can I now go on or do you wish to discuss what you think of as my bonding issues?"

"Fair enough... so you entered into this strong magical commitment." Orrin motioned for her to go on.

"It has side effects," Eryn murmured.

"Apart from the things you mentioned before?" Junar asked.

"Yes. At least in our case it has. I am told it hardly ever happens, so not to worry about it. *Of course* it has to happen to us, Enric and I, of all people," she sighed and pressed her fingers to her temples. "Far away from the people who know at least a little about it."

"And that side effect concerns your sex life?" the seamstress asked carefully.

"Among other things, it does. We have what is referred to as a mind bond. That means we have somehow developed a connection that makes it possible for each of us to experience the other person's feelings in our own consciousness if they are strong enough,' Eryn explained.

Both of them stared at her in surprise. Junar was the first to recover. "Really? Such as what?"

"Just about everything - good and bad emotions. When I learned about this I said something that angered Enric very much, and the force of his reaction almost doubled me over."

Orrin looked surprised. "Amazing. And in bed this is a problem why exactly?"

Eryn gave him a pained look. "Because having his emotions in addition to my own is so intense that my brain doesn't seem to be able to cope with it. I fainted." She snipped her fingers. "Just like that. Out like a light."

Junar replied helpfully, "Oh my. That is inconvenient."

"Inconvenient?" Eryn called out. "That is putting it very mildly! It is a catastrophe!"

"Why?" her friend asked in puzzlement. "I assume the emotions you felt were positive ones?"

"Yes. So what?"

"I would guess that quite a large number of women would be more than thrilled at the prospect of losing consciousness after sex due to a wave of overwhelming positive emotion," she shrugged. "Not me, though," she added with a sly glimpse at Orrin. "I am perfectly happy."

Eryn frowned at her. "Enric was in a panic! He thought for a moment that he had killed me! Can you imagine that? I wonder if he will ever dare touch me again. Or whether he even should."

"Can't you ask somebody in the Western Territories about what to do? Or if this is a risk to your life?" Orrin prompted.

"Enric sent a message to my uncle, who is a healer. But as we have not yet managed to encourage those bloody birds to breed, the answer might involve a long wait."

"Then what will you do now? Sleep in separate rooms?" Junar enquired.

She shook her head. "No. He is adamant about avoiding that. It seems after our initial difficulties, where I refused to sleep in his bedroom but instead stayed in his guestroom, he rejects the idea of sleeping apart. We were separated in Takhan for the duration of the trial, and he did not take that very well."

"The trial, yes," Orrin said slowly. "That is something I would very much like to hear more about. We were only told that your return would be delayed due to accusations you had to face."

Junar opened her mouth to say something but then closed it again.

"What?" Eryn asked.

"I was about to invite you to dinner, but I am not really sure how to go about it. Can I even do that? I mean, your companion is Orrin's superior. Is that appropriate? Would he even accept? What if he does? I admit I am a bit out of my depth here," she sighed.

"Then let me help you out here, will you? I would very much like to invite the two of you, plus Vern, to have dinner at our place in three days."

Junar smiled in relief. "Thank you. That does make everything a lot easier."

"Glad to have eased your mind. So, any advice for my fainting problem?" Eryn enquired.

Junar shrugged. "I admit I don't really see the problem. So you faint when the pleasure is too much for you to bear. That does not sound like that much of a test of endurance to me. Why not just revel in it? Or are there any objections from the healer's point of view? Might it cause any brain damage? I assume you have checked that?"

Eryn shook her head. "I did, yes. And no, none that I am aware of. But fainting makes me feel so helpless! It's weak, pathetic!"

"Ah yes," Orrin smiled. "And there we have the root of the problem, don't we? It is certainly not a matter of what Lord Enric thinks of you. He wouldn't think less of you for it. But you have issues with seeming weak, probably as a consequence of how you came to stay in the city. Not to mention joining your companion in the first place. By being *made* to do so. Control. You feel you are losing control of your life again, and this does not sit well with you."

Eryn blinked a few times in astonishment. "That was surprisingly insightful."

"Unlike my usual, uneducated approach to things, you mean?" he asked with a raised brow.

"No!" she protested. "It's just that you tend to be a little more blunt from what I have experienced."

"You are aware that there are books in my study, right?"

"I am, yes," she confirmed tactfully.

"They are not for decoration. I have read almost all of them," he said dryly.

"I'm sorry if I insulted you, Orrin," she sighed. "So you think I don't trust Enric enough to be able to tolerate my own loss of control?"

He shook his head. "That's not what I said. Control is an innate human need. If we have the impression that we cannot influence things around us no matter what we do, we feel helpless, frustrated. You fought for control when you were kept prisoner. At first by defying me whenever you could, and when that didn't work, you started healing people on the street."

Eryn stared at him. It seemed Vern was not the only smart one in this family. However could she have underestimated him that much?

"So in letting me roam the streets with Vern...," she began.

"I returned some control over your life to you, yes. And you became more cooperative after that. Though you kept pushing your limits and I had to set you boundaries, like that one night when you healed Junar's sister and didn't return to your quarters. There is only so much control that one *should* restore to a prisoner, after all."

"Orrin, Orrin," she murmured and nodded her head, "you sly old dog. You are more dangerous than I would have thought."

"How do you cope with that emotion sharing in general? What is it like? Do you suddenly feel things and you have no idea why?' Junar wanted to know.

"Well, it's different from my own feelings, I know instantly when I am perceiving something from him. Mostly it's confusing, especially when I am somewhere else and have just the emotion but no context for it. Like yesterday, when he was talking to Lord Tyront. There was a short moment of sadness or regret and I had no idea what was causing it."

"And asking him about it is not something you feel comfortable with?" Junar prompted.

Eryn grimaced. "I don't know. I'd imagine if he wants me to know about it he will tell me. This whole matter is exhausting. It is like we are melding somehow and I am starting to wonder where exactly he ends and I begin. I want to preserve a certain amount of privacy. It is intimate enough to share the emotions first hand without knowing each tiny detail around them as well."

Junar nodded slowly. "I guess I can understand that. But then who would have thought that there are so many emotions within him anyway? He always seems so calm and collected."

"He has strong emotions alright; he just doesn't let people see them. He has no trouble whatsoever controlling how much he lets out. And now I think this is already a lot more than he would want you knowing about him." She rose. "Thank you for your time." She smiled at Orrin. "You are more useful than I give you credit for."

"Obviously," he remarked. "So you are leaving us again already? That was a very brief visit."

"I need to get back to the clinic. Vern is meeting me there so I can show him how to remove the head barrier from the other healers."

He cleared his throat. "I do not have the impression that Vern and the healers are getting along terribly well at the moment."

"I am sure they will behave themselves, especially when I am there to back him up. I am confident that they can manage to work together. I had a little chat with Vern yesterday."

Orrin nodded. "I know. He told me about it. He was rather surprised at some of the things you said to him. And so was I, to be honest. Growing up, aren't you?"

She sighed and chuckled. "It seems we are both bubbling with surprises these days, eh?"

"I wish you were. I am still waiting for my presents from far across the seas," Junar pouted.

"In three days, I promise," Eryn smiled and closed the door behind her.

* * *

She entered the parlour and whistled through her teeth when she saw the preparations that had been made for their guests. They would be arriving in about two hours and she was immensely pleased with the efforts. It had a touch of the Western Territories, she noted. Throw cushions in colourful fabric, a table cloth in the same style. When had they bought all those?

Enric had told her that he intended to introduce their guests to a little of the new culture they were both now more or less a part of now. So he had been on a hunting trip the day before with Orrin and of course Urban to follow the Western tradition of serving to guests only what the host had hunted himself. The warrior trainer had been surprised at his superior's invitation to join him, and so had Eryn.

It seemed that the scene on their return really had made Enric think over his lack of attachment to other people here in his home country, and he was working on changing that. Orrin was a more or less obvious - if not completely uncomplicated - choice, considering their not exactly harmonious history together.

The trip seemed to have gone well enough, they returned with several kills and parted amicably.

"Enric?" she called out and went to his study when no reply came. The room was empty, and so were the others. Was it possible that he was not at home? She looked out of her study window into the yard and saw Urban sleeping on an elevated place on a rock, paws and head hanging down limply. So Enric could not be very far away. He only left the cat at home when he attended Council meetings, and as far as she was aware there was none scheduled for today.

Shrugging, she went upstairs to consult her wardrobe and found a note pinned to the door. It told her to wear something appealing in her home country's colours. Smiling, she pulled out a colourful tunic and dark trousers to slip into after washing. Enric really seemed to be enjoying playing the host tonight judging from the details he paid attention to.

She stilled when a thought occurred to her. Her gaze wandered to the window that overlooked the yard and the opposite building that housed the working rooms. Such as the kitchen. He would not really be taking over preparation of the meal himself as well, would he? No, she thought, amused at herself - that was probably too much to assume. Or was it?

She decided that there was still enough time left for a quick bath. The last three days had been exhausting, so she surely deserved a little relaxation before receiving her guests.

Nonetheless, her thoughts did not exactly care about resting when she was leaning back in the refreshing, warm water a little later. They seemed to have been waiting for a small break to spring out and announce themselves from all sides.

Vern and the healers. The first encounter following her return had been noticeably tense and overly polite, but after a few hours all of them seemed to have found a way back into their roles which were there before her departure, as colleagues with no hierarchy between them, only a gap in knowledge. Vern seemed most relieved afterwards, glad that they had started talking to him again.

He had been busy these last two days, removing barriers whenever he had seen a chance. First Junar and Plia, then Rolan and his classmates. He was eager to continue with the patients, but Eryn had to hold him back. He was still recovering from six very stressful weeks and needed to focus on the things he had missed in class instead of continuing to do *her* work.

The mind bond had been surprisingly unproblematic these last three days. She had once caught a flare up of anger from Enric and asked him about it in the evening. He told her that one of his fellow Council members had expressed his opinion of Enric's adoption rather too freely and had been rebuked accordingly. Very likely with an icy smile and a warning stare that had not revealed the extent of anger inside him. She wondered if this was something that could be learned. Keeping her feelings inside like this, only letting them out when she wished to use them as a weapon.

Plia seemed to have been the only one working at the healers' place who had not been affected by the tension between Vern and the other healers. She had been working steadily in her secluded safe haven with the door closed, receiving herb gatherers and apothecaries to accept or refuse their goods and preparing her own stock of medicines. Eryn had tried to encourage her to join them tonight, but Plia refused politely by pretending to have a prior engagement. Enric and Orrin together in one place was probably too much for her - she still bowed to Enric whenever she met him in the house, even though he kept pointing out to her that this was rather excessive formality when both lived under the same roof.

The yard came as a pleasant surprise once they had returned. The grass, planted shortly after their departure, had covered the ground nicely with the large rocks, trees and tree trunks very much to Urban's liking - probably because she finally had a place where she was allowed to wreak havoc to her heart's content. Enric had told Eryn that people kept pointing out to him how much the cat had grown since they had last seen her a month and a half ago and also asked expressly how much she was likely to grow yet further. Eryn didn't really see the change, but then she wouldn't have noticed it, having seen Urban every day. The crate they had used to transport her in had seemed a little more cramped on their journey back, though.

She felt heaviness tugging at her eyelids and promised herself that she would close them for no more than a minute.

* * *

Enric was surprised when he found the bedroom empty. She was clearly already at home - he had seen her robes on the hook downstairs. On the bed lay the clothes she was intending to wear for the evening. Just as he requested, she had selected something she ordered in Takhan. Their guests were due in less than half an hour and now there was no trace of her.

When he entered the wet room, he saw a limp arm hanging out of the tub and his tensions relaxed in a long sigh. She looked so much at peace, snoring quietly in the water. Nonetheless, taking a warm bath after a strenuous few days was never a good way to stay awake, he thought, and crouched down next to her.

"Eryn," he nudged her slightly and once again with more force when she didn't react.

She opened her eyes halfway and gave him a drowsy smile. "Hello you."

Then she sat up abruptly, causing the water to splash onto his shirt with some swilling on the floor. "Did I fall asleep? Oh no! How much time do I have left?"

Enric merely smiled and dried his clothes with a little magic, watching tiny curls of steam rising from them. "Half an hour."

She exhaled in relief. "Good. I can manage that."

He watched intently as she stood up from the tub, with the water running down her body in tiny streams, finding natural lines in skin folds, while Enric smiled appreciatively.

"Stop that," she scolded. "I know exactly how it ends when you look at me like that usually. We really have no time for that now."

His smile didn't waver. "I am looking at you in a particular way? I was not aware of that."

Rolling her eyes, she stepped out of the tub and wrapped a large towel around herself. "Of course you are. That ravenous look, when your eyelids are half closed, but your eyes following my every move. Like an animal of prey ready to pounce on its next meal."

"Interesting assessment," he mused. "And not entirely unwarranted, I admit. Unfortunately you are right, there is no time." Especially as she had taken to fainting in bed lately and always needed a while to recover afterwards. He watched her dry her hair with a touch of her fingers and brush it until it hung down her back in gentle, dark brown waves.

"I have been wondering whether to cut it off," she said conversationally when she saw him observing her even strokes of the hairbrush. "Rather impractical. And I tend to wear it either braided or pinned up anyway."

"Don't you dare cut it," he growled. She wore it down in bed. From his point of view, nobody else needed to see her with her hair down like that.

"You don't ask for my permission when you cut *your* hair," she pointed out with an annoyed look. "You more or less pick my clothes and now you want to tell me how to cut my hair?"

He shook his head. "No. I wanted to tell you how *not* to cut your hair: at all. But we can discuss it all some other time. Now get yourself ready. If we are to grant our guests a glimpse of Western culture, we might start by being authentic when it comes to punctuality."

"How very conscious of authenticity you are. This has, of course, nothing to do with your own notorious approach to punctuality," she joked and went ahead of him back to the bedroom in order to dress.

"Eager to offer the best to every single guest," he murmured and made her stop and turn to him.

"You have taken to speaking in rhymes lately, haven't you? First the commitment vow and now spontaneous little verses for humdrum purposes. It's really charming."

He shrugged and handed her the tunic on the bed. "I used to write a lot of poetry when I was much younger. Mostly to abuse my teachers and my father in colourful language. But just like drawing, writing poetry is not exactly a skill that is encouraged in a magician."

She stared at him in surprise. "You did?"

Chuckling, he pulled down the tunic when she seemed frozen in astonishment. "Yes, indeed. Though nothing inspiring or heart-warming. It was more or less a science for me to find words that rhymed and put them together in the most insulting combinations possible. Not exactly what most people would consider an artistic approach, I am afraid."

"That would probably depend on which people you asked. I imagine most people here would not consider Vern's work exactly artistic, while they were absolutely stunned in Takhan when they saw his book."

Enric grinned. "Some people would probably show a similar reaction to *my* early works, though not in appreciation but in shock."

"You don't happen to have a few of them lying around somewhere still, do you?" she enquired with curiosity.

He shook his head. "No, my teachers kept confiscating them from me and probably burned them soon after. I once wrote a particularly unflattering one about Orrin. He made me do ten hours of kitchen duty as punishment."

She laughed out loud at the thought of inviting that very man here tonight to have dinner with them.

"It seems you were not very good at hiding them, then," she smiled.

"I didn't want to. That was the point, after all - having an audience."

Funny, she thought, how very different their priorities had been in their youth. He had been seeking attention while she had been eager to avoid it at all costs.

* * *

Eryn hurried to the door when she heard the firm knock. "That is Orrin's knock; I would recognise it anywhere. It's the one I dreaded when I was still in my cell in the warriors' quarters. It was usually what preceded his kicking the door open or scolding me. Or both."

Enric smiled. "It seems we neither have too fond memories of him from those early days. Remind me why you have invited him here?"

"So we can prove to ourselves that we are now stronger and higher in rank than he and do not need to fear him any longer," she laughed and opened the door.

She gasped in feigned astonishment and laid a hand on her chest. "Orrin, no matter how often I see you in smart clothes, it is a shock each time!"

"Is that the kind of greeting a guest has to endure here? Your manners have not improved since being sent to foreign parts," he retorted and let a happy looking Junar enter first.

She immediately took Eryn's hands and held them off to both sides before taking a step back to let her professional eye assess the garments she was wearing. "Very interesting! Turn," she instructed.

"The woman you brought with you is not too good with manners, either," Eryn tossed back at him, but turned obediently when Junar twirled her index finger for emphasis.

"Bad influence, I am afraid. She has a very poor choice in friends actually," Orrin replied evenly. "Same as my son. You have been a corrupting influence on the whole family."

Eryn noted how Junar blinked and suppressed a smile of what could only have been delight at being included in the term *family*.

"Lucky you, then, that you seem to be the only one with enough strength of character to weather it." She turned to her friend. "So, Seamstress - am I done posing for now? Not that this cosy place in front of the door is not immensely comfortable or anything, but I would like to move into the parlour, if you don't mind."

"Well, *Healer*," Junar replied with a raised brow, "then you had better let us enter instead of standing in our way."

When they had hung their cloaks and moved out of the way, Vern came in and rolled his eyes when he closed the door behind him. "Finally! I was about to start a fire and catch myself a rat to roast out there!"

"You could have brought one of those your feline monster likes to catch and deposit on the carpet," Orrin huffed.

Enric smiled at their guests who all bowed to him. "None of that tonight, this is a casual social get-together. Welcome. What may I offer you to drink? I can offer you wine and different types of juice from the West."

Junar let her gaze wander over the decoration and nodded appreciatively. "A glass of wine would be lovely, thank you."

"Same for me," Orrin chimed in.

"Me, too," Vern nodded.

Eryn raised her brow at Orrin. "Is that alright for you?"

He shrugged. "He has proven that he can work like a man, so who am I to deny him a drink if he wants one?" He narrowed his eyes. "Hey, don't you pretend that you never let him drink alcohol before. Or need I remind you of that one evening at the ambassador's quarters?"

She bit her lip and looked at Vern, who smiled apologetically. "You stabbed me in the back with that, Vern!"

"He noticed the smell in the morning! What should I have done?"

"Leave my name out of it, for one," she sighed.

"Why take the blame myself if I can pass it on?" he shrugged.

"Valid point," Enric agreed and presented his guests and Eryn each with a brimming glass before raising his own. "To pleasant evenings in good company," he said solemnly and they took a sip.

"Would you mind terribly if I took a closer look at your shirt and trousers, Lord Enric?" Junar asked hesitantly.

Eryn smiled. So her shyness around Enric wasn't going to remain still with her professional curiosity pushing forward.

"By all means," he replied softly and put his glass aside to raise his arms on both sides and afford her a better look.

"Very nice," she said softly as she walked around him. "The cut is more along the natural outline of your body. Very advantageous for a slim proportioned man such as yourself, definitely less so for a stockier gent." Then she looked up in shock, realising too late that she had just commented on his physical form rather more freely than circumstances warranted.

Enric raised a brow and smirked. "I know. That's why I had them made. I was hoping for you to be able to duplicate the pattern and make me a few more of them."

Junar nodded in relief. "That I can do, surely. I would just need one shirt for the pattern. You prefer dark colours to the more vibrant ones that are obviously favoured in Takhan," she added with a sideways glance at the cushions and Eryn's own tunic.

"Yes," he replied. "I am told that I can afford to do that because of my *exotic* hair colour."

She turned to look at Eryn again. "And you chose the other combination of *our* cuts with *their* fabrics, I can see. Not bad at all. It is quite a picture the two of you make together."

"Hey, what is this?" they heard Vern asking. Eryn turned her head and saw him standing in front of a small picture frame on the wall next to a tall cupboard. She had not noticed that little addition yet.

Stepping closer, she saw that it was a slip of paper with tiny handwriting on it. She drew in a surprised breath when she realised what it was: the King's message in which he informed Enric that his request to remain in Takhan as ambassador for two years in case of her conviction was granted.

She swallowed hard, feeling a lump in her throat. "My uncle gave that to me. It was what made me tell Enric that I love him and ask him to join me in the third level bond." And he had framed it. Like something precious that needed to be preserved.

She felt an intense wave of genuine affection growing inside her that made her blink rapidly for a few times to hold back the moisture that threatened to overwhelm her eyes. She saw a slow smile spreading on Enric's face when he felt the echo of what was going on inside her.

"Are we watching that mind bond doing its thing just now?" Junar whispered.

Orrin nodded, staring at them alternatingly in fascination. "I dare say we are, yes."

"What mind bond? And what's a third level bond supposed to be?" Vern enquired, watching all four of them in puzzlement.

Eryn fought to return to the present. "A little something we caught when entering into a magical commitment in Takhan," she explained.

"Something you *caught*?" he asked, taken aback. "Like an illness? And you did *what*? Voluntarily?!"

She covered her eyes with her hand. "Why do people keep asking me that question? Seriously! Do I look as if I was forced, taken advantage of or compelled into submission lately?"

"Alright, alright," Vern mumbled, "Back to this mind bond, then. What is it and why do you have it?"

"A direct line that conveys strong emotions between us, more or less. All I know is we ended up with it, but I have no idea why. No clue whatsoever. It hardly ever happens, so it seems there is also not a great deal of literature on the topic available in the Western Territories."

Vern looked at her in bewilderment. "What were you doing there, Eryn? First they refuse to let you leave the country because of some kind of crime you committed, and then you just enter into a magical bond without considering the consequences?" He looked at Enric with an accusatory intensity. "I thought you had been sent along to keep her safe and stop her from doing anything stupid?"

Orrin grabbed his son's shoulder and turned him towards him abruptly. "You may be invited as Eryn's friend here tonight, son, but let's not forget who you are talking to. You'd better consider your words before you talk from now on and make sure they are appropriate before you let them leave your mouth. Or bear the consequences."

The boy closed his eyes for a moment, clearly fighting down an urge to dig even deeper. Then he turned back to Enric and bowed his head. "I apologise, Lord Enric. I spoke out of turn. Let me assure you that it was concern for Eryn's wellbeing that led me to speak without thinking. Which is of course no justification."

"Apology accepted," Enric replied mildly. "And let me assure you that at times even my considerable skills find themselves rather outdone by Eryn's dark gift of getting herself into trouble," he added dryly.

"I resent that statement," Eryn growled.

"Of course you do," he smiled and kissed her forehead. "The truth is hardly ever pleasant. Shall we have a seat and serve our guests, my love?"

"*We* will do the serving?" she asked with a raised brow and smiled. So he really had been in the other building, actually cooking the meal himself, when she arrived here earlier.

"That's how it's done, I am told." He then took Junar's hand and put it on his arm to guide her to the table, Vern and Orrin behind them.

When they were all seated, he motioned for Eryn to follow him into his study where he had placed two colourful bowls in larger pots with hot water to keep the contents warm.

She raised both brows when he pushed six bowls into her hands. "When did you buy all that?"

"Let's say I had a lot of time to kill when I was stuck with Golir," he replied with a chuckle.

"And you did that by buying up household items? Is that where the cushions and table cloth came from? So he simply let you wander the streets alone instead of guarding you like a proper overseer?"

"Of course not. He accompanied me. I think he imagined it wiser to occupy me somehow instead of having me locked in and getting restless."

She smiled at the image of the two powerful, high-ranking magicians making purchases such as these, discussing colours, quality, patterns and so on.

"Don't just stand there grinning," he reprimanded her. "Get the bowls out for our guests so we can feed them." He then lifted one of the large bowls out of its water bath, blotted off the dripping underside with a towel and walked ahead of her back into the parlour where he placed the bowl in the centre of the table before going back to collect the other one.

He smiled at their guests' badly-concealed astonishment at seeing him serve food. "In the Western Territories it is customary to cook for one's guests as a host. And if meat is served, it is expected to be an animal hunted by the host as well. Anything else would be an insult and would expose him to ridicule. I have prepared two different dishes as Eryn has decided to renounce eating meat. You are of course welcome to try them both."

Junar said, "I admit I am quite overwhelmed at how well you seem to have adapted to the local customs there." Then she stared at Eryn in disbelief while Enric filled their bowls after asking each of them which dish they preferred. "Now you don't eat meat anymore? What happened?"

Eryn accepted her bowl from her companion and turned to her friend. "We were invited to accompany my cousin and his... friends on a hunting trip, and that turned out to be quite a rude awakening for me. Later I learned that it is considered an acceptable lifestyle choice not to eat meat there if one is not prepared to kill it oneself." She shrugged. "That sounded fine to me. It still does."

"So you don't miss it? This does not smell at all tempting to you?" Vern asked incredulously and pushed his bowl under her nose.

"No to both. I will thank you kindly for not making me breathe that in." She set her face in a rigid expression and turned away until he had placed his bowl before himself again.

They then looked at Enric expectantly, waiting for him to start eating.

"A host is supposed to wait until all his guests have taken the first bite before he starts eating," he explained. "Because only then he can be sure that everybody has been provided with something to his or her liking. I would thus invite you to do just that."

"It seems like you had to learn a lot there after your arrival," Orrin remarked.

Eryn nodded. "True enough. Though be glad that we are sparing you the rest of it for now. Next time you come here we will make you sit on the cushions they use there instead of chairs and wash your hands in bowls they use for that purpose," she added with a smirk. "As Enric was occupying his time there with shopping, he probably bought all of those as well." Her eyes widened when he shrugged. "You really did? Oh my!" Shaking her head, she turned back to Orrin. "It seems my empty threat was not quite as empty as I thought."

Junar swallowed her first bite and looked up at Enric. "That is really good. Where did you learn cookery? It is not a skill I would associate with magicians."

"Eryn's cousin Vran'el taught me. Over there, it seems that providing for oneself is considered a basic skill just as healing is," he explained.

"Cousin?" Vern asked curiously and turned to Eryn. "You mentioned an uncle before. So you have met family there? What are they like?"

She began explaining slowly. "Let me start at the beginning, shall I? When we got off the ship in Takhan, we were greeted by three people plus Ram'an. One important politician and two more people. One of them turned out to be my uncle from my father's side who has given me the message you saw on the wall. The other one introduced herself as... my mother."

Three pairs of eyes stared at her. "As in your *dead* mother?" Junar asked confusedly.

"Yes, that turned out to be a bit of a misinformation," Eryn remarked wryly.

"So your mother is really *alive*?" Vern looked astounded. "Unbelievable! Why don't you look happy when you are talking about this, then?"

"Because it turned out that I was the only daughter of a very powerful family who was expected to one day take over the role of the leader, or Head of House, as they call it."

"Then you really are a kind of lost princess!" Vern laughed and clapped his hands. "I was right!"

"Yes, congratulations there," she snorted. "But that entailed a little more. I was also expected to enter into a commitment with Ram'an."

"What?" This time it was Orrin's astonished voice who had called out. "So that's why..." His gaze fell on Enric and he fell silent at once.

"It's alright, Orrin - he has learned about Ram'an's little interrogation attempt in the meantime," she sighed.

"Why?" Junar enquired.

"My cousin told him about it. Ram'an made his manoeuvre public knowledge in Takhan."

"What? No! I meant why you were supposed to join Ram'an!"

Eryn grimaced, then answered her question. "Because the Houses have a custom of promising their offspring to other Houses as spouses to reaffirm their political alliances. As the only daughter of a powerful House, I was intended for the son of another one."

"But you already had a companion when you went there!" the seamstress exclaimed.

"They didn't really acknowledge Enric as my companion since we had no third level bond in place. So Ram'an tried extremely hard to prise me away from him." She shook her head and sighed, glad that all that was over.

"Unsuccessfully, obviously," Orrin smiled thinly.

"Obviously," Enric confirmed grimly, his smile equally weak.

"Had it not been for my cousin Vran'el, Ram'an would have managed to make me stay in Takhan for quite a while," Eryn told them. "If Vran'el had not arranged for me to be adopted by my uncle, I would have been claimed as a member of Ram'an's House by him."

"You have been adopted by your *uncle*?" Junar cried out in complete desperation. "Can you please tell things in the correct order? My head is spinning! How can all that have happened in such a short time?"

Enric sighed. "Why don't I go on? Eryn hasn't exactly made it easy by jumping back and forth all the time. We had managed to negotiate trade agreements and Eryn had until then managed to keep Ram'an at a distance. After three weeks we were supposed to return home. As we were about to board the ship, we were apprehended by guards who brought us to the senate, which is like our Council here. It turned out that Malriel, Eryn's mother, had accused her own daughter of causing her father's death thirteen years ago. I shall leave it to Eryn if she wants to recount this story one day herself. But rest assured, it was clear from a legal point of view that Eryn was not to blame for it and would never have been made to endure the trial if it had not been for her mother's considerable political influence." He stopped to take a sip of wine before continuing. "For the duration of the trial we were separated, and each of us was put under the constant watch of a guardian who was stronger in magical powers than us. Ram'an volunteered to guard Eryn and was granted the task, though he had to do it at the residence of her uncle's family instead of his own." He stopped when he saw Orrin looking puzzled.

"Wait," the warrior frowned. "But Ram'an was not stronger than Eryn. That day in his quarters she managed to break his shield."

Eryn closed her eyes and stifled a groan. Oh no. That was the only little detail Enric had not been aware of, that she had managed to keep from him. Until now.

It fell quiet at the table. Nobody so much as dared make a noise. Enric's deep breath escaping his tightened lips was the only sound.

"Eryn?" he asked in a calm yet threatening voice. She could feel his rage fiery in the pit of her stomach. "Would you care to elaborate? How come I was not aware of any fighting on that occasion?"

"I thought you said he was aware of it, Eryn!" Orrin reprimanded her sharply. "When will you finally stop keeping secrets, you bloody idiot!"

"I would be very interested in that answer myself," Enric added with narrowed eyes. "Out with it!" he demanded with more force.

She picked her words carefully. "It was just a minor thing. He tried to keep me from leaving that day with a shield across the door after I had freed myself from his grip. I hit it twice and barely managed to break it. So I assumed that I was a bit stronger than him. Which was obviously not correct. He told me later that he had not used all of his strength to create the shield, meaning his shield was weak enough for me to break. I really am sorry."

He shook his head. "No, you are not. I feel a mix of annoyance and unease, but no regret." His blue eyes had narrowed. "And another stab of annoyance at me looking right through you. Let this be a lesson to you. No lying to me. Ever again. I am really starting to appreciate this mind bond."

"Even though it causes me to faint in bed?" she parried at him angrily, hoping to embarrass him in front of their guests to exact a little revenge.

He just smiled at her attempt, not in the least thrown off balance. "I find I do not care about that little side effect very much right now. Consider it a gentler way of knocking you out. Remember, we have tried it only twice so far. You might well develop a certain immunity to the effect after a while. We will just have to keep practising, won't we?"

Her face had flushed scarlet and she hastily grabbed a glass of water and gulped it down.

Enric gave her a last disapproving look, then returned his attention to their guests. "So much for that. As I said, Ram'an was made Eryn's guardian and took full advantage of his position as much as this was possible while her uncle and cousin were close by. Ram'an was one of the senators to vote on the outcome of the trial and was initially determined to vote against Eryn as a two-year house arrest in Takhan as punishment was what her mother intended. But then Eryn decided to renounce her mother's family after the end of the trial in the event the decision was in her favour. As Ram'an was caught between accepting the leading role for his own House and getting Eryn as heiress of another House as his companion, he saw his chance of getting both Eryn *and* this position. Thus he managed to obtain his own plus three more votes in her favour that tipped the verdict of the senate."

"What?" Vern asked, "Why did he have to choose between Eryn and leading his House?"

"Because Eryn was the sole heiress to her House, but he still had a younger brother who could take over the position. Two heirs of Houses cannot be joined as companions in the Western Territories," Enric explained patiently. "That's why Eryn renouncing her House and thus giving up her position as heiress to it was an attractive option for Ram'an."

"But why did he imagine she would stay in Takhan after winning the trial? She was free to leave then, wasn't she?" the boy then asked, wondering why each answer just led to new questions.

"Because he was very well versed in historical law and its application. There was one law that would have aided him considerably. It was an old rule about an intended companion having the right to claim the partner into his own house in the event she renounces hers in order still to fulfil the companionship agreement. This law was made before the fulfilment of the agreement became voluntary and was meant to keep children from freeing themselves from it by simply renouncing their Houses."

"But her cousin put a stop to this because her uncle then adopted her?" Junar now asked, working hard to keep up with all the details.

"Indeed," Enric nodded. "Thus Eryn is no longer the heiress of her mother's House, but an official and legally confirmed member of her father's family, namely House Vel'kim."

"So there is now no heir for her mother's House?" Vern asked.

"Oh yes, there is," Eryn cut in. "It turned out that Enric let himself be blackmailed into being adopted by my mother. *He* is now the new heir of House Aren, the one I renounced." She watched their stunned expressions with evident satisfaction. It was good to see that she was not the only one who found that utterly and completely ludicrous.

"Am I understanding this correctly," Orrin said very slowly, "that you, Lord Enric, are now the son and heir of your companion's mother?"

"Yes," Enric nodded, "that is correct."

"Does this mean that you could be made to succeed her at any time? What consequences are there for your position in the Order? You are meant to be following in another's footsteps here yourself one day," Orrin asked worriedly.

"Theoretically, yes," Enric admitted, "though practically this is not very likely for now. I am confident that in time another solution will be found for that obligation."

"And that's all now? Apart from you joining into that bond before you left?" Junar wanted to know, brow furrowed.

"Well, almost. Enric took revenge on Ram'an for not keeping his hands to himself by compelling him into hosting our ceremony and celebrations at his residence and forcing him to participate in the ceremony itself," Eryn added. "But that is it now. Really."

"Incredible," Orrin sighed and opened his eyes wide in wonder. "Eryn, it seems there really is no way of keeping you out of trouble for long."

"How about the ceremony itself?" Junar asked. "You said it was a magical bond? How did that work? Like the oath to the Kingdom here made with joined hands?"

"Pretty much so, yes," Eryn nodded. "Only that there are five hands involved instead of two and you are required to write your own vow for it. Enric's vow even rhymed." She turned to Orrin. "There is a little something I wanted to ask you. Enric told me that he once wrote a poem about you when he was a boy. An insulting one."

Orrin smiled. "I remember that, yes. I was not the only teacher whom he bestowed that honour on. We compared them and tried to figure out who it was he hated most. Let me think..." He leaned back and looked at the ceiling for a short while before he started reciting, "Wherever Orrin often lingers / You will find toes or ears or fingers, / That were part of a student's body / That walks the land now maimed and bloody."

Vern stared first at his father, then at Enric. "You wrote that? Seriously?"

"I admit I did. I recognise it," Enric smirked. "Though it is only an extract from it. I am surprised you still remember the words, Lord Orrin. It seems to have made a permanent impression on you."

Orrin chuckled. "It has indeed, yes. I was one of the first teachers to be so honoured. Disrespectful and insulting, but hilarious to read. It got so bad that the teachers who didn't find themselves targeted by that insolence felt left out."

Eryn laughed. "And there you were, thinking artistic talent was not appreciated in these parts at all!"

"It wasn't," Enric remarked, "I was made to work in the kitchen for that particular poem. I don't even remember the punishment from the other teachers."

"Then it seems that my response impressed you in turn," Orrin smirked.

"So it seems, yes," Enric nodded thoughtfully.

"And today, about twenty years later the foul-mouthed poet and the merciless teacher are sitting together at the same table, eating dinner the foul-mouthed poet cooked because your female partners happen to be friends," Vern said, sounding impressed as well. "I bet if anybody had told you that back then, you would have either panicked or denied it would ever come to pass."

"True enough," Orrin nodded. "Though telling me back then that I would find myself one day be subordinate to Lord Enric would have been bad enough anyway."

Enric leaned back and regarded his old teacher with a thoughtful expression. "It did not turn out as bad as that for you, I hope."

The older man smiled. "There were a few times when insubordination did seem quite attractive. Especially over this last year." His gaze darted to Eryn.

Both men shared a lopsided grin at memories of challenges well mastered.

Eryn exchanged a look with Junar, who cast her eyes to the ceiling. The two men seemed far too blasé for her taste. She leaned forward.

"There is something I haven't told you about yet. It's something I tried in Takhan that I think you might find very interesting. The magicians use golden belts for hunting to block their magic."

Both Enric and Orrin exchanged a slightly panicked look. One at the prospect of having yet another intimate detail revealed, the other at being coaxed into following the younger man's example.

Vern smiled indulgently and got up to step towards the drinking cabinet to return with the half full bottle a moment later.

"I trust I am not the only one who needs a refill, am I?" he sighed and then refilled the two glasses which had been hastily pushed towards him.

CHAPTER 4

New Developments

Eryn looked up at the messenger who was standing in her study doorway. Palace, she noted to herself with an element of weariness.

"Lord Tyront requests your presence," he announced after he had bowed.

"This is not something I can do right now. I am on my way to return to treating a patient. I can hardly let the poor woman wait until I have come back from the Palace, can I?" she snapped at the man, completely unwarranted as he was hardly likely to be the one to have summoned her, merely in the unhappy position to be carrying out the order. She took care to sound less aggressive when she went on, "Please inform Lord Tyront that I am not available right now and will visit him at my earliest convenience."

The messenger looked ill at ease.

"Listen," she went on, "I know that you have been instructed to take me there, but it simply can't be done right now. You are hardly in a position to *make* me come if I refuse, are you?"

He bowed stiffly and left quickly.

Shaking her head, she turned to collect the patient report on her desk she had come for and went back to the treatment room. Yes, she *was* late with the report Lord Tyront had wanted. Though she had hardly been back more than two weeks and there was still enough work she had to catch up with, in addition to going through new books from Takhan and integrating all the knowledge into her teaching plan. Surely a status report was the least important of her worries right now, and even mighty Lord Tyront should be able to understand that.

It was about half an hour later when there was a knock at the door to the treatment room she was working in. Lebern rose from his chair to open it a crack and see what was important enough to interrupt a healer's work. She heard a few murmured words, then the trainee turned to her.

"Lord Orrin is here to see you."

"Tell him to wait outside or in my study. I am in the middle of a treatment here," she said testily. "I will come to him when I am finished."

Lebern was about to inform her visitor of this, when the door was pushed open impatiently and Orrin stepped in with a dark glare.

"Don't you dare make me wait! You will come with me right now or there will be trouble," he growled.

She stared at him, taken aback. "What? I am in the middle of healing an irritated stomach here, I can't just get up and walk away! Out with you! Now!"

The warrior narrowed his eyes and looked at the other healer. "Can you heal an irritated stomach?"

Lebern swallowed. "I have done so before, yes," he said slowly.

"Good. Then get on with it." Orrin stepped towards her chair, completely ignoring the wide-eyed patient and pulled Eryn up into a standing position none too gently by seizing her upper arm.

She ground her teeth and decided not to shout at him in front of her patient but in somewhere less public. Letting him all but drag her out of the room, she nodded to Lebern to indicate for him to comply with the order he had been given.

"I will be back in a short while," she muttered.

"No, she will not!" Orrin grunted and shut the door behind them noisily once they were out in the corridor.

She jerked her arm free of his grip and pointed to the small kitchen a few steps to their left. "In there," she hissed and entered without checking if he followed her.

She decisively pushed the door shut, then whirled to face him. "What do you think you are doing here? Storming into my treatment room and dragging me out while I am in the middle of healing a patient? Have you lost command of your senses?" she snarled. "This is not acceptable to me! Next time you try a thing like that I will be less lenient and just push you out and raise a shield to block you from coming in!"

"*You* will be less lenient with *me*? You had better shut up right now before I forget myself," he snapped at her. He grabbed her arm once more and stepped close enough for their noses to almost touch. "I was sent to escort you to Lord Tyront's study because you ignored the messenger he sent to get you! Do you think I have nothing better to do than drag your insubordinate butt to the Palace?"

"You couldn't even drag me there if I don't cooperate! You are not strong enough," she hissed back.

He pulled out a pair of golden shackles with a humourless smile. "Don't provoke me. I am authorised to instruct whatever magician I want to assist me in *convincing* you to accompany me. Lord Poron should be here today, shouldn't he? You may be strong, my girl, but not more powerful than the two of us together." His eyes narrowed. "Are you coming of your own accord or will I have to shackle you before throwing you over my shoulder, you accursed nuisance?"

Breathe, she commanded herself. There was no winning this. Apparently he was not doing this for entertainment, she reminded herself, so it was not his fault. Quite the contrary - he was obviously no happier about this than she herself and was just communicating this in his usual, assertive way.

She nodded slowly. "You can put those damned things away, I will come," she said calmly.

He let the tension go in his face and let the manacles slide back into his pockets. "Good. Though I will admit that right now I really would have enjoyed doing something unpleasant to you. Come on. We shouldn't keep him waiting any longer than you have already." He grabbed her by the wrist and pulled her after him.

* * *

Enric blinked at the surge of wrath that rolled over him and took a sip from his cup to steady himself. He was used to masking his emotions, but doing so when they jumped him unexpectedly was a different challenge. So it seemed Tyront had made good on his threat to have her dragged to his study if she didn't start reporting to him regularly. Judging from her current mood she was likely to get herself into trouble with her superior again. He considered going to the Palace as well, seemingly dropping by for a random visit at Tyront's study and see if there was any damage control possible, but then decided against it. She really needed to learn. And judging from the past, there were certain things she would not internalise without pain.

He smiled slightly when his thoughts returned to the day Orrin had trained her for the very first time. He had been standing at the window in his old study at the Palace with Tyront and watched the warrior carrying her to the arena over his shoulder. Then she had refused to pick up the practice sword and Orrin had had to strike her hard with his own sword several times until she had finally taken it to avoid any more bruising. He had lost a gold piece to Tyront that day, he remembered. They had bet on how many hits she would take before giving in. It seemed as if Tyront had assessed her fairly accurately already back then. Her pride and reluctance were at times stronger than her ability to learn fast. It seemed nothing much had changed there, he thought, and wondered how many hits it would take this time.

He smiled to himself. Maybe it was time for another bet with Tyront.

* * *

Eryn carefully closed the door behind her as she left Lord Tyront's quarters. She would have preferred slamming it shut, but that was of course not something that would get her in any good books. Slamming his door would land her in even worse books than she was in already.

She raised an eyebrow in surprise at seeing Orrin leaning against the wall in the corridor, his arms folded.

"He is now free for you," she said without a trace of irony or anger.

The warrior looked at her directly. "I have been waiting for you, not for him."

She noted that his mood had changed. He seemed to have calmed down considerably since he had more or less dumped her here no more than twenty minutes ago.

"Have you now."

"Yes. There is the little matter of your combat lessons we need to address. I gave you two weeks to settle back in here again. Now it's time to resume our work."

"Orrin, no!" she protested with a wail. "I have so much to do right now! Spare me for another two weeks, I beg of you!"

"No," he replied and shook his head, unimpressed. "This is still a prerequisite of the Order and I see that my leniency in granting you those two weeks led to nothing more than your trying to procrastinate further. How often have you picked up a sword in these last eight weeks, if I may ask?"

She flashed him an annoyed look. "I was rather occupied, if I might just remind you," she huffed.

"So - not at all. Just as I thought. One more area where you have some catching up to do, then," he nodded.

"That's not true!" she protested. "Enric made me fight." Well, twice he did. Once before they had left for Takhan and another time at the ambassadorial residence when he had needed to get rid of his tensions after learning that she had more or less been promised to Ram'an. But that was not of the essence right now, was it?

"Did he? I somehow doubt that teaching you fighting has been among his priorities when he had to trouble over trade negotiations or not losing you to another man," Orrin said mildly. "But I will see about that tomorrow morning. Tomorrow is no treatment day, so you will be able to make the time."

He only smiled when she cursed colourfully. "Now, now - that is surely not appropriate for such a high-born lady as yourself."

"What in the world made you think that addressing this matter after dragging me to Lord Tyront was a smart idea?" she glowered at him.

"I thought he probably would have dampened your rebellious spirits enough for me to profit from it. Any new horse manure assignments we need to consider in our training schedule?" he asked with a broad grin.

"No, *deliveryman*, I behaved myself. Though I can see that you would have enjoyed it if I hadn't." She had been dangerously close to getting punished a couple of times for what might probably, with deeper inspection, be considered remarks slightly less respectful than appropriate, but she would surely not be telling Orrin about that. He was far too smug already. Waiting for her seemed to have improved his mood considerably while hers had slipped even more after her little chat with the high lord.

"Deliveryman," Orrin pondered thoughtfully, then shrugged. "Let me tell you this much: That term will become even more appropriate if you fail to turn up tomorrow after sunrise, as I shall again deliver you, this time to myself. Also I trust that your companion will aid rather than impede me." He gave a small wave and sauntered off, whistling happily.

The trouble was, she fumed, that he was absolutely right. Enric would not lift a finger to stop it but just watch her being dragged off by Orrin while bearing this placid expression he liked to show the world.

* * *

Enric smiled when she walked into his study and let herself collapse onto the sofa to one side of his desk.

"Hard day, my love?"

She sighed. "Did you talk to Lord Tyront or was I angry enough for you to experience it first hand?"

"The latter. Twice, in fact. Once it was anger, the second time was more annoyance mixed with a pinch of desperation."

"A pinch?" she smiled despite herself. "You really have taken to cooking, haven't you?"

He leaned back and waited for her to tell him of what had aggravated her so much today.

"First Lord Tyront summoned me to his office and then sent Orrin to drag me there when I didn't jump immediately to attention. Seriously - was that just because of a report? I offered to send Rolan to provide him with whatever information he needs, but he insists on talking to *me*. As if I had nothing else to do!" She threw up her hands in frustration.

"Eryn, making time for your superior when he asks you repeatedly is a sign of respect and obedience. You are still not very promising in those qualities, I must say," he admonished her mildly.

"But making me abandon a patient in the middle of their treatment? That is little short of outrageous!" she complained.

"It was a drastic step to teach you that you had better report regularly if you want to avoid scenes like that in the future. You know, it really *is* in your power to avoid them. There are two people whose summons you must never ignore: The King's and Tyront's. Well, and there is me, technically anyway."

"Technically?" she enquired with a raised brow.

"Yes. Technically I am your superior as well, but practically I am at liberty to punish you for ignoring *my* summons in ways that would not be considered appropriate for a mere superior, but are deemed acceptable while unusual for a companion," he smiled.

"Lucky you to have such ample resources at your disposal, then," she said sourly.

"Indeed," he nodded. Then he pointed to two books on his desk. "These were delivered today. With best regards from Takhan."

She jumped up immediately. "The books on mind bonds?"

"Yes. Though after leafing through them I am afraid that they will probably not turn out to be all that helpful. Most of what's in there are suppositions, theories and observations without giving reason or advice on how to deal with a mind bond," he told her, careful not to raise her hopes too high only to have them dashed afterwards.

Eryn's previous delight fell flat. "So no advice about how to avoid regular fainting when making love with one's companion?"

"Nothing whatsoever, no."

"Why don't you ever fall unconscious?" she frowned. "Why is it always only me?"

"Well, either you are not experiencing it strongly enough to overwhelm me, or I am just better at taking in a lot more than you," he shrugged.

"Charming. Any other theories that do *not* make me seem either lacking in emotional depth or weak?"

He thought for a moment, then shook his head. "No, not at this moment."

"How about this one: that I am opening up a lot more for you than you for myself?"

Enric rolled his eyes. "Really now, how likely is that? Do I really have to remind you which one was the person who continuously shrank back from anything remotely emotional?"

"I *did* ask you to join me, didn't I?" she remarked testily.

"You did. After refusing me twice," he pointed out.

"I don't count the second time - it was only meant to bind me to you so they couldn't keep me in Takhan that easily."

"I would never have suggested it *just* for that reason, and you are well aware of that. Why exactly are we discussing this right now?

"Because you said that the reason for my fainting is that I am either weak or emotionally shallow! And I resent that very much!" She grabbed both books and pressed them to her chest. "I shall retire to my study and do some reading, if you will excuse me." She went a few steps and then stopped and turned. "One of the Council members, don't ask me what his name was, congratulated me today on the very advantageous favour the King granted you. I somehow think I should know about things like that, it makes me feel awkward when I pretend to be perfectly aware what he is talking about when I am not. Simply asking him what favour it was exactly seemed rather out of place as well. It would appear as if we're not talking to each other. So? Would you care to enlighten me?"

"With pleasure. I do think you should take a little more interest in what keeps us rich and powerful. The King has granted me permission to begin a shipping business. This requires quite extensive construction work as we are not exactly equipped to deal with large shipments of assorted goods from across the sea - namely to store, register and distribute them properly. Thus I have commissioned a few builders for building docks, a tally house and warehouses, as well as houses for people to live in, in addition to another pub in Bonhet." He smiled. "I think we will be hard pressed to recognise it when we next pass through the place."

She blinked in surprise. "Another business in addition to the ones you already have?"

"More like a whole range of them, but yes. As I am for now the only one to have been granted the permission, I imagine we will make quite a lot of money from the enterprise in the years to come."

"More money? I thought you have more than we could ever spend already?" she frowned.

"Let's say there is no danger of descending into poverty anytime soon, anyway."

"So you want more still?" That seemed wrong somehow, she felt, as if he was using his considerable wealth to remove the chances for others to earn honest money.

He saw her irritation and rose to step away from behind his desk and sit on the sofa instead, patting the space next to him. "Sit with me, will you? I don't think this is a matter to be discussed when you are about to leave the room. Put aside the books for a few minutes longer, they will not run away."

She nodded reluctantly and went to take a seat next to him.

He took her hands in his. "Eryn, I couldn't help but notice that you seem to have a rather negative attitude when it comes to wealth. I understand that you were raised in modest - but by no means poor - circumstances by your father, and that a man who willingly gave up his own prosperity to follow his principles might not have had the most positive attitude when it came to money."

"I don't mind that you are rich," she protested.

"Really? Then how come that you still speak of it as *my* money when I keep impressing on you that I consider it *ours*? And why is it such a great fight every time I wish to spend money on you? Why don't you draw wages for your work?"

She lowered her voice to what sounded like a whimper. "This feels like I am on trial again."

He sighed. "That is not what I'd intended. I see why your father was frustrated by what he considered a society of rich and powerful people violating what he saw as the vital rules of life. I also see that you find it so much more difficult to deal with rich people here in Anyueel than with those of more modest origins."

"Are you trying to tell me that not all rich people are bad? I know that, thank you so much. I happen to be friends with Orrin, and he is not exactly a pauper."

"You may know it in your head, but I don't think this is how you feel."

"My family in Takhan is rich," she pointed out. "I don't despise them for it."

"No, because they are subject to mitigating circumstances, are they not? They are healers. What about House Aren?"

She gave him a cool stare. "You know exactly what my problem with House Aren is, *Enric of just-that-House*."

"Do I? I can't help wondering whether your troubles with Malriel would be quite so severe if she wasn't rich and influential - if just her attitude would be the problem even without the means behind it to cause you trouble," he mused.

Eryn sighed exhaustedly. "Where exactly is this going?"

"I am trying to point out that *having* money is probably not the most important thing, but how you got it and what you are doing with it."

"I see. And using your... *our* money to earn even more is the right thing to do. Is this what you are telling me?"

"No," he shook his head, reminding himself to be patient, "but I think providing a chance for other people to make a living without exploiting them does count for something, wouldn't you say? The construction of the buildings in Bonhet will help a lot of families to get through the winter without freezing or starving. In early spring I will commence building the shipyards, which will provide even more work - and not only for a limited time period, but permanently. This does not only concern construction in the long term, but also operating the buildings, whether it is the tally house, the warehouses, the pub or the shops that will open soon enough once the village has started to grow."

"So you are saying you are basically providing a public service that just happens to enrich your own wealth?" she asked, with a deliberate tone of irony in her voice.

"That would probably be going too far," he said. "But you are more than welcome to use some of that money I keep making so self-servingly to provide public services, if you wish."

She stared at him. "Such as what?"

He shrugged. "Such as whatever else you feel is in dire need of improvement, I would say. You already have established an affordable place for healing services in the city, so what else is a thorn in your flesh?"

"The orphanage," she murmured, thinking back to the day when she first visited Plia there. "A breeding place for the criminal elements of tomorrow due to lack of food, clothing, education and affection."

Enric nodded slowly. "I see. Then I suppose you have just found the favour you will permit the King to grant *you*."

"Me? Permit *him*? But I thought *you*..."

"That I was the only one worthy of being rewarded for my magnificent accomplishments?" he chuckled. "No, my love, everyone who was part of the delegation except you has informed the King of what they wish."

"I wasn't even aware that I could do that! Why did nobody inform me?" she called out in astonishment.

"The King approached me, so I assumed he had done so with you as well. And he probably assumed that I had talked to you about it." He chuckled. "He is probably wondering at your uncharacteristic reserve."

"So I can ask him for permission to take over the orphanage? Or rather level it to the ground and rebuild it, for that matter?"

"And administer it, I would say. Adding a school, maybe. Having a caterer provide regular food. What is more, in time maybe even training those who are so inclined in a medical profession." He smiled at the amazement he felt rising in her, closely followed by excitement and impatience.

She stared at the floor unseeingly for a while. He observed her quietly, wondering what was going on inside her head right now.

"I will need even more time to take care of this as well," she murmured, tension forming creases on her forehead.

He lifted her chin and smiled at her when he indicated she was wrong. "No, you don't. And that's the beauty of it, my love: You have the money to pay someone else for it. You see? Having money is not such a bad thing after all."

* * *

Enric cringed slightly as another one of Orrin's blows must have hit her. This was a definite downside to the mind bond – having to suffer through her trainings with her. Orrin didn't act at all gingerly with her, not hesitating to use his advantage in strength - especially as she was wearing shackles during their trainings that reduced her own power level down to his.

Tyront watched Enric and spoke in a concerned voice. "That mind bond of yours again? Is she having another training session with Orrin? Seriously, Enric - we need to take care of this somehow. I can't have you suffering second-hand physical pain all the time when we are supposed to be working. What about these books you were sent a few days ago? Nothing useful in there at all?"

"No," his second-in-command shook his head wearily. "Not really. The only thing we did learn is that usually after dissolving the third level bond the mind connection slowly decreases in intensity until it is completely gone after a few days."

"Which is not something you'd want, I assume," Tyront stated with eyebrows raised in question.

"Not at all," Enric confirmed determinedly. "I have no intention whatsoever of doing that. The benefits outweigh the disadvantages by far in my opinion."

"Eryn agrees with this assessment of the situation?"

"She does now," Enric nodded. They had of course discussed that option, though not for very long. A wave of his iron resolution, annoyance and dread had silenced her quickly and she had dropped the idea again.

"Her uncle has promised to look whatever else he can find and to consult his colleagues about the mind bond effect. I have great hopes in one healer who specialises in everything inside the head." Ikan, he remembered - the man who had removed Eryn's memory block. Or rather instructed Enric to do so, as the magician who had placed it there was too strong for the healer to overturn the block otherwise.

"So for now there is nothing else for you to do than endure her training sessions? We could suspend them for now, or at least have them practice sword fighting instead of unarmed combat," Tyront offered.

The younger man raised his brow. "Surely not. I would never hear the end of it. If I stop them because I find the pain bothersome, she will ask me why she is being made to suffer it if I myself - the mighty warrior - am not willing to. And she would be right," he sighed and then closed his eyes for a moment. Another punch connecting, no doubt. He did not feel exactly where the pain occurred, only that it was there. "But I am starting to consider training her myself to encourage her to faster progress. The more punches she avoids, the sooner I will be able to relax again. Though she keeps pointing out how pressed for time she is presently, so she will not exactly rejoice at the prospect of additional combat training."

"Her lessons have started again," Tyront nodded. "So now she is back to teaching her healers, being taught herself, healing and keeping the clinic running. Though I am informed that young Rolan has virtually taken over the administrative duties as much as he can. It seems he has finally found something he is good at. I am glad about that; I was starting to run out of ideas." He chuckled. "Who would have thought that those two would be a match, professionally speaking?"

"Not me," Enric grinned, "Not after watching where she kicked him during their training together. Repeatedly."

"I heard she has finally asked the King for that favour she was entitled to. An unusual one, but not exactly surprising, considering her disposition. So she will be taking over the orphanage. No doubt the inspiration stems from her friendship with the orphan girl. Plia, I think it was? Interestingly enough, she has not requested any funding, from what I understand. Am I to assume that *you* will take care of that minor detail?" Tyront enquired with a knowing smile.

"That is a valid assumption, yes," he agreed. "I have finally managed to get her to spend some money. Imagine that."

"Not the usual challenge men find themselves facing in a companionship," Tyront remarked airily. "But then you have not exactly chosen the usual kind of companion." He spoke more seriously, "I hope she finally starts delivering her reports on time. I think she has already told you that I sent Orrin after her?"

"She has. I'll admit I was rather surprised that she made it out of your office without any punishment. Is she finally learning to control her temper, or are you getting soft with old age and decided to allow her some latitude?"

"Neither. She came fairly close to getting herself into trouble twice. I swear, if she had added another word, it would have been off to the stables for her," he growled. "But at least everything at the Lady Eryn's seems to be going well enough. The trouble between Vern and the healers is also taken care of, from what I hear. They are all more than happy to have her back, even Rolan, and that is saying something."

"Yes, it seems she makes a better leader than a subordinate." The amusement was plain on Enric's face. "They like her. Or at least appreciate her, in Rolan's case." And another stab of pain, this one less intense, however. "I heard that the messenger birds which are being bred on the Palace roof will soon have grown enough to make the journey to Takhan. That is handy. Kilan took care to have a bird pen erected on our own roof after his return more than a month ago, but our young have only just hatched. It will take another two months before they are something we could use for messenger services. For now we have to be content with sending messages speedily by bird and then waiting for quite some time for the reply."

"How many different Houses have given you birds up to now? Your roof must be quite a sight."

"Houses Aren and Vel'kim, obviously. And then Arbil, Ram'an's House. So three in total," Enric listed.

"Ram'an has given you birds for easier communication with him? But I suppose he gave them to Eryn rather than yourself. So he wants to stay in contact with her. Is that wise?" Tyront sounded doubtful.

Enric shrugged. "She has taken a shine to him again after the trial. And she feels sorry for him. Now that he has no more chance of claiming her I don't see much danger in indulging her in that - quite the opposite, in fact. She would not take well to my forbidding her to write him. And would ignore it anyway. After that whole jumble of woe involving her mother I am glad she has people she actually wants to stay in contact with on the other side of the sea. Which is time consuming enough right now, especially as the ships are not yet crossing the sea at regular intervals."

"That will change soon enough as soon as you have finished your buildings in Bonhet. Then we can finally manage the merchandise properly. Up to now there have been two smaller shiploads - a dummy run, as it were. Any time estimate when the construction works will be finished?"

"The initial estimate was three months for tally house, warehouses and dock," Enric replied.

"That does sound a trifle optimistic."

"Not with the manpower I have set to work there, it isn't." He smiled as a surge of triumph went through him. "I think Eryn just managed to deal Orrin her first blow. Good girl."

* * *

She sighed with relief and put aside the pen she had been using to copy the letter painstakingly to Ram'an from the draft sheet to the small slip of paper that would be rolled up and tucked into the tiny tube, which would in turn be fastened to the bird's leg.

"You look tired," Enric commented from the door frame against which he was leaning and regarding her.

"It's just my eyes. Writing in such small letters to fit as much as possible on the slip is quite a feat. How many of those tubes can one bird carry?"

"Two at the most, one for each leg. They have to spend quite a time in the air carrying them, after all. We wouldn't want them to tire themselves and fall spent into the sea instead of reaching their destination. Who are you writing to? Vran'el? Valrad?" he enquired.

She shook her head. "Ram'an. I wonder how he is adapting to his new position as Head of House."

Enric strolled closer and looked down on her drafting sheet. A few words had been crossed out, others inserted in several places.

"Do you mind if I take a look at it?"

She smiled. "No, go ahead. No secrets in there."

He let his gaze wander along the lines. She had written about all the work that had expected her upon her return, resuming her training with Orrin, staying true to her resolve not to eat meat anymore and adapting little things from Takhan into their lifestyle, such as still wearing the clothes they had had made there and occasionally cooking their own meals, which puzzled the servants a lot. She also enquired as to how things at House Arbil were going, whether he had found adapting to his new role very hard.

He nodded approvingly and let the page sink onto her desk again. "And you managed to fit all that on one paper slip? I am impressed. I hope it is still decipherable."

"Had I known that I can use two of them, I wouldn't have squeezed it all onto one," she sighed. "But at least I know now that I can send both Vel'kim men a message with the same bird."

"Is there anything you would like to send to Takhan? Kilan will be leaving here tomorrow and has asked me to remind you."

"Is that day tomorrow already? How time flies. Yes, I wanted to send along a few bottles of wine for Neval and one copy of each of the books Vern has illustrated for Valrad. I think he will be interested in the local herbs we have here. I also want to send him a few seeds, maybe he would like to try and grow them in that garden of his." She got to her feet. "How about yourself? Any tokens of appreciation to be delivered for you?"

"Well, in two out of three cases you could say that, yes. I will send along some wine as well. For Golir, Uvel and Malriel."

She nodded curtly. Of course he had to send *her* something as well, she reminded herself. She was his Head of House, after all. It would not look good for either of them if he sent along presents for two other people, but not for her. Especially as Eryn herself also sent along something for her own Head.

"So we are both sending wine to House Tokmar? At least Neval and his father won't have to fight over it. Let's just make sure to send them the same number of bottles."

Enric nodded. "A box each, I would say. That should keep them going until the ships are crossing the sea regularly and they can order some more."

"So Kilan will really go back there." She thought for some time. "The notion itself makes me shiver - even though our time there was not unpleasant, if we don't count the ten days of the trial. But I really need some distance from that place. Spatial distance, that is," she amended. "I am happy enough that I can communicate with them. From a distance."

"Don't worry," he smiled, "I do not intend to take you back there for a while yet. But we are expected to show ourselves there occasionally. I would say we should go back there for two or three weeks in about a year's time. Which I hope will be enough time for you to get over the less savoury aspects of our first stay."

"Yes, I think I can work with that. At least this time I will be able to plan ahead much better. A few weeks are definitely not enough, especially as we stayed longer than intended. I was no more than lucky that everything went that well in my absence." She stretched and yawned. "There have been a few requests for cosmetic corrections over these last weeks. They will ensure the clinic's financial independence from the King for another few months. I think I will get them over and done within the next few days."

Enric sighed resignedly. "That means I will experience quite a few hours of irritation and anger. And that's just before you get home."

Laughing, she wrapped her arms around his waist. "Regretting the bond, dearest?"

"No," he grinned. "I was just preparing you for the fact that I will be demanding adequate compensation for my suffering."

CHAPTER 5

Progress

Eryn leaned against a desk and watched the girl's delicate fingers pushing seeds into small pots and then covering them with a thin layer of earth. There had to be at least twenty vessels in different sizes and shapes she had somehow managed to accumulate. Mugs with chunks chipped off their rims or with broken handles, old cooking pots, old bowls and in one case even a vase.

"Where did you get all this junk from? If I had known that you needed pots for planting, we could have ordered some."

Plia shrugged. "But why? These work fine and didn't cost anything. And if this doesn't work out, at least I won't have wasted any money. I got them from the Palace. Cook collected them for me, otherwise they would have been thrown away."

Eryn smiled. Pragmatic and frugal, but no less effective. And it wasn't as if the shape or general appearance mattered so much for growing plants. As far as she knew the only characteristic to limit a plant's growth was the vessel's size. Well, provided it was not crafted containing material such as copper which would slow growth in higher concentrations.

"What are you planting?"

"Mostly the herbs we gathered during the expedition. These are the ones I know most about. This is just an experiment for now. I don't even know if they will grow at all. Most of them need little light as they grow between trees, that will not be a problem." She pointed to a group of pots she had placed on another table. "Those over there, though, might be a bit of challenge. They grow higher up where they enjoy more sun than a place at the window here will afford them."

Eryn nodded slowly. "Say, have you ever been up on the roof here?"

Plia halted in mid-action, soil-covered hands hovering over a pot and frowned in confusion at the seemingly abrupt change of topic. "On the roof? No, why would I have?"

"Then finish your plants. We will take a look afterwards."

"A look on the *roof*?" the girl enquired slowly, as if she started doubting Eryn's sanity.

"Yes, the roof. Go on, I will tell you my reasons later. Why are you using soil from different bags instead of using up one bag after the other?" the healer frowned.

"I asked some of the herb gatherers to get me some earth from different places. It very likely contains the different nutrients the plants prefer, I suppose," the girl explained, unsure. "I mean, we saw the same plants in different places; sometimes they looked lusher, at other times stringy with hardly any blossoms. I told them to bring me some soil from places where they looked healthier."

Eryn stared at her. "You paid attention to things like that? And then you came up with the idea of using the same soil as in their natural habitats?" Was that really the girl she had saved from a back alley a year ago who had worried about things like where to get her next meal from? Now she was analysing planting requirements for herbs!

Plia gave her an apprehensive look. "Does that sound too peculiar?"

The woman sighed. But they still had to work on her self-confidence. "Peculiar? That sounds brilliant to me, Plia. And even if I didn't think so, why would I be right? Never in my life have I wondered about planting anything. I have always left that to nature which means my expertise in that area is strictly limited." An idea hit her. "But my uncle is a very dedicated collector and grower of plants. His garden really is a sight to be seen. I can ask him about books on planting and nurturing plants, if you are interested."

The girl's eyes brightened, but the light dimmed almost immediately. "But that would surely cost a lot, first to have them copied and then sent here..."

"Let's make that my problem," she smiled and then blinked. That situation suddenly seemed absurdly familiar, only with reversed roles. She was the one who had to persuade another person to let her do something pleasant for her by spending money.

"Why are you looking shocked?" Plia enquired cautiously.

Eryn rubbed her face. "I think I have just learned another lesson for my life with Enric," she sighed.

"I am not sure I follow you."

"I just realised that money really is not *such* a bad thing to have. That you can do things with it. Good things."

A bemused smile spread across Plia's face. "That's what you realised? Just now? I could have told you that. When did you last eat something or have some sleep?"

The magician rolled her eyes. "Shut up, smarty-pants, and get those plants ready."

* * *

Rolan seemed doubtful as he regarded the crude drawing Eryn had placed on his desk. "What exactly am I looking at here? A dolls' house? Another one of those breeding cages on the roof for messenger birds?"

She rolled her eyes at him. "Dolls' house? Seriously? And the cages have *bars*. Do you see any bars on *my* drawing?"

"I am not sure what I am seeing on your... yes, why not call it a *drawing*?" he pointed out. "Would you care to elaborate?"

"It is a small house for growing plants in."

He stared at her as if she had lost her mind. "A house. For plants. Why? Don't they like it outside anymore?"

She took a deep breath and let it out slowly. Keep being nice to him, she reminded herself. He had more or less kept this place from collapsing while you were away.

"It's for Plia to grow herbs in. She came up with a few interesting ideas, and I think having our own supply of herbs would be advantageous, especially for those varieties hard to come by," she explained patiently.

"And her laboratory doesn't give enough protection against the weather?"

"This is not just to protect them against the weather, but to provide more light for them as well. Her room is too dark to grow some of them. And if this works out, there will not be enough space in it anyway."

"And putting that thing," he pointed at her picture, "in there will increase the available space?" he asked in confusion.

"Rolan," she sighed, suddenly becoming jaded with the whole *being nice* routine, "please tell me that you are doing this on purpose! At least that would give me a reason to just whack you instead of wondering where you left your brain today. You make it really hard for me to be civil to you right now."

He stared at her with a raised brow. "That's what you are like when you are being civil to me? Sorry, I hadn't noticed. It felt like it always is. No difference from your *not* trying to be civil discernible for me." Then he frowned. "Why would you try to be civil to me anyway?"

"To demonstrate my appreciation for your keeping the place here running and Vern out of mischief."

Rolan blinked, then smiled faintly. "Then show me your appreciation by *not* trying to be civil to me. It kind of frightens me."

"I will try harder."

He was quick to reply. "That is not necessary, but thank you for the offer."

She frowned at him. "Why? I would have thought that you would surely prefer a more... placid style of communication."

A shake of his head. "No, I think we are fine."

"We are?" Her eyes bulged incredulously.

"Absolutely."

"But... I am not exactly always polite," she pointed out.

"True. But as you have come to accept that I pretty much reply in kind, that sits well with me. It is dynamic, at the very least," he smiled.

"Really?"

"Really," he shrugged.

"So I don't need to tell you how very satisfied I am with your work and praise your efforts?"

"Not for my sake. Only when the mood strikes you and you can't hold it inside any longer."

She leaned back and looked at him in amazement. "You know, I think it does strike me right now. Thank you for all your outstanding work. I wouldn't know what to do without your being here."

Rolan nodded sheepishly, clearly unused to compliments, especially from this direction.

"Well, let's have a look at your dolls' house, then."

"Plant house," she corrected him sternly.

"Yes. Right. That."

"You didn't really think I wanted to put it inside Plia's laboratory, did you? It will be too large for that. And what sense would that make, anyway?"

He cast another sceptical look over the sheet in front of him. "How am I to know how large you want it? I don't see any numbers to indicate size or anything else here. It might well be the size of my chair."

"Rolan, don't make me kick you! It is obviously more like the size of this room here than your *chair*," she growled. "It is meant to be on the roof. Good place for taking advantage of the full light, you know."

"I assume I am to take care of its construction?" he enquired.

"That would be good, yes," she nodded.

"So be it," he said and nodded slowly, carefully picking up the sketch and turning it upside down as if to see if it made more sense that way round. "May I ask Vern to draw another one for me or am I supposed to work from this here?"

Now he was doing it on purpose - she was absolutely sure of it. "Why are you even asking me that? You don't normally bother me with any details when I tell you what I want, but just provide results and ask me to sign the payment drafts."

"To contribute something to that new cooperative spirit you seem eager to establish between us," he said with a slightly malicious glint in his eyes.

She got to her feet with a sigh. "Why exactly do I put up with you?"

"Because you wouldn't know what to do anymore without me. Your very words."

"I am starting to regret them."

"No," he said and looked at her with conviction. "You are not. Aren't we supposed to hug now or something? Cuddle?" He opened his arms wide and grinned, comfortable in the knowledge that she wouldn't take him up on that offer.

"Oh, shut up," she murmured and fled through the connecting door to her own study. She preferred it infinitely when she was the one doing the teasing.

* * *

Eryn smiled when she found the letter on her desk in her study, which must have been delivered while she was at the clinic. Ram'an had written back.

She unrolled the tiny slip of paper and took a seat in her comfortable chair behind the desk to read it. It was rather shorter than she had been hoping, but then he had probably not a lot of time left at the moment to indulge in lengthy replies.

He thanked her for her letter and told her that he had been pleased to hear from her. The members of his House had finally all taken the second level commitment bond with him, which was proof of loyalty whenever a new Head took over the family. Eryn frowned at that and wondered why she had not been asked to take that bond with Valrad when she was adopted into his House. Not that she minded, though. *Not* being bound by another magical oath - the third one in her case - was surely nothing she could complain about.

His father's health seemed to be declining even more rapidly now, as if his body was indulging in the luxury of finally giving in to the illness after being released from the burden of taking care of the family.

He wrote of the many trading and other contracts with other Houses that he had needed to look through, either to renew or to terminate them in the near future. It seemed that some of the contracts were not exactly to his House's advantage. She noted a hint of bitterness here. Though he did not go as far as openly accusing his father of carelessly having entered into imprudent arrangements, she couldn't help feeling that it was somehow implied.

Good that he was a lawyer, she thought. If there was anybody qualified to deal with things like that, it was very probably him.

She placed the letter on the desk. He seemed to have quite a lot on his plate right now. It was not exactly an upbeat letter, but then that was hardly to be expected. She would write back to him tomorrow and try to cheer him up a little by telling him the story of how her assistant had refused to be treated in a more civil manner in exchange for being allowed the freedom to be ironic and annoying.

She stood and stretched. The days had started becoming noticeably shorter again. And slightly cooler, too. Enric had been pleasantly surprised when she had voluntarily and without pressure ordered some new clothes for herself from Junar. The seamstress herself had dramatically impersonated someone suffering heart failure upon hearing this unexpected request. Vern had been watching her, a critical expression on his face, subsequently pointing out to her that she had got most of the symptoms wrong. Eryn had sipped her drink with an amused look as Junar was treated to a lecture on what she was supposed to consider next time she intended to fake that particular affliction in order to appear more credible.

Her friend had not exactly been idle in these last few weeks since their return from Takhan, either. She had happily taken away different items of clothing from their wardrobe to use them as patterns, unpicking all the seams, critically appraising the single pieces, marvelling at tiny details. In Takhan Enric had purchased a selection of several bales of cloth in assorted colours, among them a few that Vran'el had personally approved as suitable for Eryn, and gave them to Junar. She was absolutely thrilled and Eryn herself was pleased with this small thoughtful act which made her friend happy. Orrin was as well, for that matter. Not that he had found it worth his while to let her benefit from his appreciation by being a bit more lenient during their training sessions or anything of that sort, though.

Plia had also used part of her income to buy herself new clothes for the winter. Eryn had tried to make Junar charge a good part of it to her instead of the girl, but the seamstress just winked at her and told her that this was not necessary as she had given Plia quite a generous discount on prices already.

Junar also hinted that Eryn was to show herself in public more often without her robes in order to show off her new clothes in the foreign style and perhaps even drop a hint every now and then about who had made them for her. When Eryn rolled her eyes and refused to be used as some kind of walking display for another's merchandise, Junar pointed out that Enric was the more suitable object for this anyway, as he was the one wearing the items with foreign tailoring instead of simply the fabrics. Though she had not dared proposing to him that leaving his robes at home from now on would be helpful to her.

Tomorrow Eryn would need to start looking for somebody to handle everything in connection with the orphanage, from working with builders to planning and carrying out the renovation, to implementing a proper plan for feeding, clothing and educating the children regularly and handling the administration connected with it all. She was unsure exactly what to do with Mistress Walchan, the current matron of the orphanage, though. She had not been a shining beacon when it came to caring and providing for her young charges. She would talk with Plia about this, she decided.

The girl was currently spending as much time as possible up on the clinic's rooftop, observing every single step of the construction of what would afterwards become her domain. She had worked with Rolan on the drawings, daring for the first time ever to actively contradict him and improve his plans and construction proposals. More glass, fewer walls, more solid surfaces that could bear weight, shutters that could be lifted or closed individually over each glass pane according to the plants' requirements, containers to collect rainwater, an extra shed for storing the tools she would need and so on. Vern had sat between them sketching plans as he followed their instructions and had told Eryn afterwards that this was the first time ever he had seen Plia stand up to Rolan, not giving in when she was convinced that her ideas were better than what he was proposing.

She looked down at the note on her desk, large and conspicuous: a reminder to see Lord Tyront tomorrow and report to him. And before that she had a training session scheduled with Orrin. Which was probably not the best order of events, considering that being in a foul mood when dealing with her superior hardly ever ended well.

"Eryn?" she heard Enric's voice from the parlour after the entrance door had closed. Moments later Urban strolled into her study and brushed her cheek firmly against Eryn's thigh in her usual affectionate greeting.

"Eryn? Are you there?"

"Yes," she called back. 'In here." He sounded as if he had news, she immediately decided. Good news probably, as there was no hint of irritation in his voice.

He entered the room and pulled her into his arms, kissing her firmly on the lips.

"There was a message from Takhan today to the King, the very first one to be delivered to us by bird, mind you. Basically, a historic occasion," he smiled. "And it is something that should be of great interest to you."

"Out with it, then," she urged him. "I can hardly bear the suspense."

"Valrad has been busy, it seems. We were asked for permission to have a healer sent over here for three months to work at the clinic with you."

He smiled at how her brow rose and her mouth lolled open in surprise. "No! Seriously? When? Who?"

"In two months' time. So we have a while to take care of a few things in advance, such as preparing adequate quarters, your furnishing another study at the clinic and so on. As to the *who* - they are still in the process of selecting somebody. Either they have nobody willing to come to what they doubtless consider a rather backward place or too many applicants with a pioneering spirit," he grinned.

Her thoughts raced. "I can't believe it! This is really going to happen!"

"There is even more. The healer who comes will be authorised to test you on most of the disciplines that are required for official recognition of being a certified healer in the Western Territories. The only exam you would have to take at a later point would be the one in non-magical applications, as it seems that Sarol is the only healer qualified or willing to undertake that. Valrad writes that he will be sending you a couple of extra books to prepare from, in addition to those you brought with you already."

Eryn let lose a squeal of delight that made him flinch. "That is the kind of noise that makes animals run off to hide in caves," he chuckled.

"A healer! That will be fantastic – not having to be the expert for this time, but being able to consult somebody else! I can't wait!" She grabbed his collar and pulled him down, her eyes glistening, her voice breathless when she murmured, "Are you in the mood for making me faint?"

* * *

"Your companion has been quite busy since your return from foreign parts," Tyront mused and poured himself another cup, raising a questioning eyebrow at his colleague's empty one.

With a nod, Enric accepted the refill. "That she has, yes. I sometimes fear she takes on a little too much, never wanting to wait until one area is sorted out before starting on another one. As soon as she has an idea, she wants it to be taken care of. No patience, that woman. But at least she doesn't insist on doing everything herself any longer. Rolan took care of overseeing the plant house on the clinic roof being erected, and now she is looking for somebody to take over the orphanage."

"There may be hope yet, then," Tyront smiled. "Yesterday she came here to deliver a progress report. Imagine that. It would have been even more impressive if she had made an appointment with me first, but then I suppose that would be hoping for too much."

"Definitely," Enric agreed. "Right now she is busy preparing for the healer from Takhan. She keeps wondering who they will send. She is hoping for someone she worked with during her stay, but I am afraid that is not very realistic. As Valrad's niece she was treated as an important person, a lot of people indulged her by letting her work with them, but they will hardly wish to leave their city to come here for three months."

"How well will she respond to another healer's coming here, probably telling her what should be done better?"

"That very much depends on the personality of the healer, I would say. Somebody who can deal with her temper would be an asset. Seniority alone does not carry much weight with her," Enric said.

"Yes, tell *me* more about that," Tyront quipped. "But learning about what people there call the *Aren temper* at least makes me feel better about not always keeping my cool with her. Though learning that they seem to have a tendency for powerful magical potency when arranging their commitments in addition to confirming political alliances makes me wonder why they haven't taken care of that anger trait yet. A few generations of having children with milder mannered partners should have done the trick, I can't help thinking."

Enric shrugged. "From what I have seen, Aren temper is not necessarily considered a weakness. Rather the opposite. It makes people stand back in fear - or awe. They generally try not to provoke an Aren woman if they can avoid it. Eryn's mother is very good at using this to her advantage. She controls her temper very well, but when on occasion she gives people a sneak preview of it, they tend to talk about it for a while. I was considered some kind of local hero there for stepping between Eryn, Malriel and Malriel's mother one time. The family is known to have collapsed entire buildings when they have their little quarrels."

Tyront chuckled. "So you stepped between three of them? Were you feeling particularly bold that day or was your protective instinct stronger than your need for self-preservation?"

"A combination probably," the younger man admitted. "Though it did not exactly earn me bonuses with any of the Aren women involved, mind you. Eryn stopped talking to me after she woke again, her grandmother stormed off indignantly, and Malriel played the gracious loser only later to prove to the world that she had the upper hand in the end through adopting me. The audience was impressed, though," he added dryly.

"You need to introduce me to that woman one day. The more I hear about her, the more curious I become."

Enric grimaced. "I hope to keep Eryn and Malriel apart for a while. After the trial and the renunciation they did not exactly part amiably, as you might imagine. At least not on Eryn's side. I can't help the impression that Malriel somehow seems to enjoy the challenge her daughter presents."

Tyront smiled. "A sentiment you share, unless I am mistaken."

"True. I was told that the danger of ever becoming bored with an Aren woman as companion is basically negligible."

"Do they now consider you an Aren man over there?"

"Even better," he smirked. "They consider me a man who not only managed to tame the legendary Aren temper, but also be accepted into their sacred inner circle."

"So you have assembled quite a reputation for yourself over there in a short time," the older magician noted.

"So it appears, yes. That I had a thigh-height predator accompanying me wherever I went helped as well. Especially since it is public knowledge that Eryn more or less presented me with Urban."

He bent down and scratched the cat's brown cheeks, earning himself a lazy flicker of feline whiskers.

"I assume you will be going there regularly from now on to visit your families, as it were?"

"Yes, her uncle made me promise him to take her back to them regularly. They have grown very fond of her and want to see her occasionally. Well, the *men* in the family, that is. It seems she does not have such a fortunate hand with her female relatives. Her mother on the one side, and then there is a cousin a few years younger who rejected her at first sight, or probably even before that," he sighed.

Tyront smiled. "As she is the only female member in the Order for now, it is an advantage that she does seem to get on well with men in general."

"That's *your* point of view," Enric replied darkly.

"Still jealous, my friend?"

"I can't help it. With each bit she opens up more, there is more I could lose, so to speak." Then he smiled. "But the third level bond helps. If she felt any undue attachment to another man, at least I would know right away that there is somebody in need of a lesson."

"You may not be subject to the Aren temper, my dear boy, but I wonder if your cold relentlessness is not even more dangerous than that."

Enric smiled thinly. "According to you, this is just what they need as a counterbalance."

"Maybe. But it provides food for thought how dangerous the two of you together could be if you put your minds to it," Tyront stated calmly.

"Lucky for you then that we each took an oath binding us in loyalty here."

"Ah yes, the oath. The King recently invited me to have a very interesting chat about that topic. Smart lad, I grant him that. It seems he never really took it for granted that the oath is something which binds us reliably. Our new friends in the west very likely know how to dissolve what they call the second level commitment bond, so the King is eager to find a way to keep the partnership between Crown and Order intact without turning it into something more or less voluntary for every individual magician."

Enric sat up attentively. "For the individual? So he acknowledges that it might at least be a matter of voluntary cooperation for the Order's *leader*, as it were, to bind his magicians to the Kingdom?"

"It seems he is aware that this virtually has been the case already. Amazing, the things that remain unspoken," the older man opened his eyes wide in wonder. "I admit that I underestimated him in this regard."

"Have you reached a conclusion on the matter?"

"We discussed a few options. He advised me to talk to you and then reach a consensus with the Magic Council."

"Any suggestions so far?"

"There has been one, yes," Tyront said slowly. "We have discussed the possibility of one magician not being a member of the Order but instead directly subordinate to the King. The chosen magician would then be able to bind whoever leads the Order to the King with an oath. That magician could not be instructed by the Order to dissolve the oath again, only by the King himself. It would have to be somebody rather strong, of course."

Enric frowned. "You are not thinking of me for this, are you?"

Tyront looked at him appalled. "Surely not! If there is one thing I am quite determined to avoid, it is having you on a different side than mine in that game. No," he smiled without humour, "I won't be giving you up to the King anytime soon. In any case, I am sure that he would prefer a magician less tightly bound to the Order. Somebody young and mouldable, I would imagine. However, we can consider that when we have a final decision on the change."

"So you approve of the idea in general? This would cost you the advantage the Order's leader has had these last hundred years - freeing yourself and any Order magician from the oath, if necessary."

Tyront nodded. "I know. But there is one further thing to consider. Dissolving an oath is a matter of magical strength, just like forging it. And this, my friend, is where our new associates across the sea may turn out to be useful contacts. Conveniently, I happen to be fairly well acquainted with two members of powerful magical families in Takhan. Both of them very strong magicians."

Enric laughed appreciatively. And there was Eryn thinking that adapting to new situations was something people here were averse to or unable to manage. That obviously did not apply for the man in front of him.

* * *

Eryn stood in front of the door to Lord Tyront's quarters, slightly tense. That was not exactly one of her favourite places. Not much good had taken place when she had been ordered here in the past. Though this time it was different - as it was not Lord Tyront but his companion who had asked her to come and have a drink with her. So it was basically not a summons, but an invitation. She was here voluntarily this time. Or as voluntarily as possible when it came to an invitation sent by her superior's companion.

She got along well enough with Vyril in the past on the few occasions when they had met. A strangely vital and apparently happy woman, considering who her companion was, Eryn thought. One would expect that being joined with a man like him would after a while all but drain the will to live from a woman. Though he would of course treat the woman he loved a lot better than the one he had an edgy professional relationship with, she conceded, and finally lifted her hand to rap at the door.

Vyril opened only moments later, smiling and taking Eryn's hands, squeezing them affectionately.

"Lady Eryn, how very nice of you to make time for me at such short notice. I heard about all the projects you are trying to keep moving. I keep wondering how one person alone can handle all that. But do come in and take a seat, won't you? I simply love that dress you are wearing! Did you bring it with you from Takhan?"

Eryn shook her head. "No, not directly. Enric purchased the fabric and my friend Junar used the articles we had made there as a pattern for new clothes. The ones from the Western Territories are not really up to the climate here, I am sorry to say. It really is a lot warmer there than we are used to in our region."

Vyril regarded her thoughtfully. "So your seamstress friend has managed to copy the style of Takhan clothing? That is very interesting to know. I wonder if you would find it at all objectionable if other people adopted elements of it in their own style of dressing for certain occasions?" she asked, being careful to choose her words.

"No, certainly not. Quite the opposite, in fact. What's more, I know that Junar would be happy to oblige in advising you on cuts and colours. And then making up whatever you choose, obviously," she added as an afterthought.

Vyril smiled in relief. "Oh, excellent! Then I can imagine my probably being the centre of attention at the next dinner we are invited to. Provided *you* have managed to find a reason to shirk it again, naturally," she grinned. "No, don't look panicked. You are known for doing so, but people have accepted you as a touch different from most of us, so it has become more or less tolerated. The surprise is all the greater when you really do turn up once in a while. It is something the hostess will of course use to brag about in the weeks to come."

Eryn blinked. "I was not aware that my not going to these occasions regularly has quite such an effect on the social dynamics of our city. I thought that trying to keep out of all this as best I can makes me less noticed."

"My dear Lady Eryn, ask your trade-savvy companion whether, in his experience, reducing available quantities of a commodity tends to lower or increase the demand and thereby its price. You will find that the rarer something is, the more it is sought after. And you tend to make yourself *very* rare." Her gaze darted to the door Eryn knew to lead through to Lord Tyront's study. Ah yes, so he had probably complained about the stubbornness with which she often avoided reporting to him. "So you see I appreciate it all the more that you agreed to visit me tonight. What may I offer you to drink? I would normally suggest wine from the Western Territories, but you more than likely have plenty of that on hand yourselves. But I have something very nice that you will not come across that often. My father makes liqueur, and I find he has improved his recipe considerably these last years."

"Then I would be happy to try a glass," Eryn smiled politely.

She seemed somewhat less relaxed than usual, Eryn observed. Her movements were a tiny bit jittery. Although the two women had always been on friendly terms, it was somehow amusing to see her superior's companion like that. It had probably something to do with the reason why she had asked for the meeting. The purpose had surely not been pointing out that she was known to duck out of social events or asking for permission to adapt to Western fashion styles.

"You are wondering why I have asked you to come here tonight, I am sure," Vyril started when she had placed two tall, slim glasses filled with a somewhat syrupy, dark reddish-purple liquid on the small table between them.

"Yes, I admit that question did cross my mind," the younger woman nodded.

"Judging from what I have heard about you and also experienced first-hand, I think you are not a friend of lengthy talks, thus I will get to the point quickly. Tyront told me that you have asked the King for permission to take over the responsibility for the orphanage in the city. That you will even be paying for everything yourself. And that you are looking for somebody to handle all the matters connected with the place."

Eryn raised an eyebrow, wondering where this could be leading. "That is correct, yes. Do you know somebody who would be interested in doing that?" Probably a maid's aunt, daughter or someone who was looking for employment, she mused.

Vyril straightened and drew in a breath as if collecting all her courage for her next words. "I do indeed. Myself. I would very much like to take it on."

The younger woman stared at her incredulously. "You? Seriously? Why?"

That had obviously not been the reaction Vyril had been hoping for. Her face fell slightly. "So you don't consider this a good idea. You do not approve."

"What?" Eryn blinked. "No! I am just wondering why somebody in your position would want to, er, even..." Her voice trailed off, at a loss how to phrase this without insulting Vyril even more than she might have done already.

"...get my delicate, sensitive hands soiled? Make myself useful for a change?" She gripped her glass and emptied it in a single, unladylike gulp before rising. "You think you are the only rich woman in the city who wants to fill her days with something more than sipping tea and planning the redecoration of her home? Or is even *able* to do something more than that?!" she said in a voice slightly more raised than the setting might have merited.

Oh dear, Eryn thought horrified. What exactly was happening here? How had she managed to turn this amiable, charming woman into a fury within a few seconds? That was quite an accomplishment, even for somebody with her unparalleled skills for provocation.

"Vyril," she said slowly and soothingly in her best, dealing-with-snapped-patients' voice, her hands raised as if to defend herself with palms facing outwards, "I assure you I did not wish to imply that you are useless or unskilled. Not for one moment - you are educated and doubtlessly used to organising things. I was just wondering why you would even be interested in doing this. You have to admit that this is not necessarily the kind of work a woman in your position is expected to do."

Vyril closed her eyes for a moment to collect herself, then linked her fingers and lifted them to her chin.

"You must think I am terribly foolish, Lady Eryn. I apologise for losing my cool like that. You are right, of course. Forgive me. I admit I was a little nervous to talk to you about that."

A little? Eryn scoffed in the privacy of her head. More like a jumble of nerves.

"Don't worry about that. Tell me why you wanted to do this in the first place."

Vyril sighed. "You made me wonder about a few things a while ago when you began by healing people on the street. And particularly when you did not stop, but increased your efforts after being joined to Lord Enric. The former is what generally happens when a woman lives with a rich man, you see. If they did some work before, they usually don't do so afterwards but dedicate their days to maintaining their contacts to others in the same social niche. But not you." She shook her head. "You stay away from us as well as you manage, fill your days with hard work and do something to make a difference. All this is even more amazing now that I have learned how you are not the humble country healer's daughter we thought, but born as high as any other self-proclaimed important woman in this city - even more so, probably! But this did not induce you to reduce your efforts, since you took on even more responsibility!" Opening her clenched fingers again, she gestured helplessly. "I started feeling useless beside you. Something like that does not feel good. I hinted at this when talking to friends of mine, but they don't share this sentiment but thought I needed to take over a more active role in commanding the servants about. The servants!" she exclaimed in frustration. "They don't need anybody to command them, they know better than I what I eat, drink, wear and buy!"

The study door opened with care and Tyront stepped through, looking with interest at the two women. "Is everything in order out here? I heard... something," he finished tamely with a glance at his companion.

"No, not everything is in order here! Do you also consider me useless, Tyront? That I am wasting my days with pointless tasks that may as well remain not done because nobody would even see the difference?"

Tyront's gaze snapped to Eryn. "Did *you* say that?" he demanded sharply.

"No, she did not say that!" Vyril called out, agitated. "I am saying that! My friends had their children to take care of, and many didn't even do that but employed a nurse to do so. And even those who made an effort and raised their children themselves don't do anything else now that they have grown up and gone from their homes."

He stared at her and looked visibly uneasy. "Are you telling me that you want children? Now of all times? Is this why you invited Lady Eryn here? To heal whatever reason there was that didn't work for us in the past?"

"What? No! I am forty-eight years old; I no longer have any intention of having children! People would think I was the child's grandmother if they saw me with a baby!" Then she seemed to deflate, as if all anger and frustration had torn away from her completely leaving no more than an exhausted shell. "I just want to do something useful for once," she murmured sadly. "I was hoping to take care of the orphanage, but I do not seem to be exactly what is needed for that job."

Eryn closed her eyes for a moment and slowly breathed out. There was obviously a lot that had been in need of getting aired. So Vyril's motivation was partly the wish to feel useful and needed - to contribute something that mattered - and partly to compensate for never having had the chance to raise her own children. That was not a bad combination as far as motivation was concerned, Eryn pondered.

"I never said anything like that and I'd thank you for not putting words in my mouth, especially such absurd ones," Eryn replied coolly. "I don't think you are in any condition to discuss this reasonably at the moment, so I shall invite you to come and see me tomorrow at the clinic after lunch. We can then talk over what exactly needs to be done, the matter of your remuneration and how we will coordinate this. Preferably in a way that will not involve me too much as this is the reason why I am looking for some capable person to take this off my shoulders."

Vyril stared at her in confusion when she rose. "What? I don't understand."

Tyront sighed resignedly. Why him? Why? "It seems, my dear, that you have just been accepted for the position. Lady Eryn is from now on your superior."

Eryn smirked at the picture they made. Vyril's face slowly lit up in incredulous delight while her companion's expression by contrast seemed to darken with each moment.

"Yes," she nodded and turned to leave, "Funny, the way things work out, isn't it?"

CHAPTER 6

The Challenge

"Your training today was a bit more... dolorous than the last few times, I couldn't help but notice," Enric commented when she put a bowl of the dish she had cooked for dinner before him.

"Believe me, you were not the only one to have noticed that," she snorted. "I was the one with the bruises, after all."

"Which you have undoubtedly healed away, so no sympathy there."

"He cracked my rib. Again!" she complained. "I think I deserve a *little* sympathy at least."

"Why were you slow enough for him to hit you so often today?"

"I was bit preoccupied after my talk with Vyril yesterday evening. She seemed so agitated. Yet at the same time vulnerable."

Enric nodded. "Tyront mentioned that he is a little concerned about Vyril's working for you right now. Having your companion subordinated to your own subordinate is a touch complicated and might provide cause for trouble in time."

"As would have rejecting her," Eryn countered.

He thought for a moment, then nodded. "Yes, I see the quandary. So you agreed to work with her to make Tyront happy? Why does this sound wrong to me?"

She shrugged. "Because you underestimate my willingness in making an effort to improve the relationship with my leader?"

That made him chuckle. "Try again. This is so outrageously absurd I wonder that you can keep a straight face."

"I didn't do it to please Lord Tyront," she admitted. "Her outpouring in the evening impressed me. I have trouble with suave, elegant women whose dresses always match their jewellery."

"Which is the case with Vyril," Enric smiled.

"Yes, but after watching her snap at her companion yesterday, I am inclined to forgive her that."

"You told her to meet you at the clinic today, didn't you? How did it go?" he enquired curiously.

"Very well, I must say. She has not been idle since yesterday." She leaned forward, her expression serious and anything but pleased. "Did you know that there is an increase in new born orphans every year about nine months after Freedom Night? And that there are a lot more children without parents than deaths of people in the city would suggest?"

He shook his head. "No, I didn't know that. Vyril told you that?"

She nodded. "Yes. She obtained the lists from the Palace and showed me the development over the last ten years. I find this really shocking! And the next Freedom Night is no more than two weeks away. I shudder at the risk people take so thoughtlessly in just copulating with a stranger without considering the possible results. Then they refuse to accept what happens by simply depositing their children at the orphanage where they will grow up like... well, you know the conditions there."

"I see. So, what's your plan, then?" he enquired.

"What makes you think I have a plan?" she asked in return.

"That feeling of grim determination inside me that is not my own, I would say," he commented dryly.

Smiling, she leaned back again. "Alright, I do have a plan. I have sent the King a message to propose linking the participation in the Freedom Night to a condition. People need to do no more than agree to let the healers protect them against unplanned pregnancies."

Enric frowned. "How do you plan to carry that out?"

"By using a bit of magic to render them infertile for a short while. That effect will wear off after no more than two or three days. With men it's fairly easy - just blocking a certain duct. And as for women, I have ample practice there as I have been performing that regularly for the last ten years on myself," she explained. "Then only those who have agreed should be permitted to enter the area and enjoy the night, as it were."

"An interesting suggestion," he nodded appreciatively. "I would be surprised if the King doesn't agree with it."

"I hope he doesn't tell me to first obtain Lord Tyront's permission, or the Magic Council's," she sighed. "They are both tiresome to deal with."

"You either keep forgetting that *I* am a member of the Council or maybe you say things like that to vex me," he noted.

"The latter," she grinned and winked at him.

"But as for your concerns, I don't think he will delegate this to the Order. We are neither in charge of the orphanage, nor of the Freedom Night, and only to a certain degree of healing as long as the Crown is officially funding the clinic. So he is the right person to have approached, I would think."

"I hope you are right. I will wait for a week, and if I hear nothing from him by then, I will request an audience to petition him about it directly. Or fail when trying to sneak past Marrin and ambush him in his study, now that I know where to find it."

"He doesn't usually just ignore messages, so I wouldn't worry about that. Especially not yours. He will tell you soon enough whether he approves or not."

"What do you mean, especially not *mine*? I wasn't aware that I have any special privileges here," she frowned.

Enric smiled lopsidedly. "You are known to make yourself as rare as you can, so when you do want attention, you are sure to get it. You are still an important person, my love. People are bound to listen when you speak up."

She thought about Vyril's words about her being a very welcome guest at every possible social gathering due to hardly ever turning up. The rarer something was, the higher the demand.

"Vyril said something about me keeping my distance from her and the other women to fill my days with work instead of decorating," she murmured.

Enric pursed his lips. "You can't deny that there is a grain of truth in that, dearest," he said carefully.

"So you are saying that I avoid them because I think I am cut above them?" she exclaimed.

"I have never said a thing like that!" he protested. And he wouldn't as long as he did not feel particularly suicidal for any reason. "Why? Do you think that you are superior to them?"

"Of course not!" She paused. "Well, not as a human being. Or as a magician."

"But maybe as somebody who is engaged in doing something useful compared to them?" he suggested with a smile.

She gave him an intense look. "Then I would also have to consider myself above any other magician in that Kingdom. Apart from my healers."

"Because warriors are the least useful items in the world, I know," he sighed.

"You won't hear me deny that," she retorted airily, then frowned. "But you don't exactly run from one dinner invitation to the next, either."

"I know. Though I have been trying to mend my ways at least a bit in that respect since we were joined. The trouble is that you keep sabotaging my plans. I have to more or less drag you everywhere I think we should go."

"So now this is my fault because I am as reluctant to do this as you are, but am more honest in admitting it? You want to comply with the social convention of suddenly being expected to join these occasions, just because you have a companion now?"

He thought for a moment, then nodded. "That is a pretty accurate assessment of the situation, yes."

"So you admit that you don't want to do this either and are just pretending to be social?" she enquired once more to be on the safe side.

"Absolutely. Most of these people are immensely tiresome. But then this is about maintaining contacts, as you are well aware. I dimly remember having a similar conversation with you months ago."

"I did attend all three balls with you," she pointed out, trying to collects points in her favour.

He lifted a brow at her. "Yes, because you were *ordered* to go there by the King. Next time you should look at the invitations other people receive – they are phrased a little less... emphatically."

"They are?"

"Yes. The King more or less grants people the privilege to attend, while in your case he has to threaten you between the lines because he knows that you will try to stay away if he doesn't."

"Isn't it nice to be special," she said quietly and pushed aside her empty bowl. "Well, I hope there will not be another ball anytime soon."

Enric shook his head at her. "You know that the Western Territories will be sending a permanent ambassador to Anyueel soon? We have established one there already, after all."

She bit her lip. Of course, this was only logical. "Any idea who they will send? And when?"

"Yes to both. Sanaf of House Finran. He will arrive in no more than three weeks."

"House Finran?" she frowned. "That's Legara's House, isn't it? Malriel's friend." She recalled the woman well from the trial.

"Yes. I think they sent somebody from a House allied to my own to make the start up as smooth as possible."

To *his own* House, Eryn thought. He had adapted well enough to his new family situation, so to say. All that was missing now was that he started calling Malriel *mother*.

Enric watched her expression darkening, then she shivered. "Are you thinking of the ball that is likely to be given to welcome the ambassador or of a certain member of my House you are not too fond of?"

"I was thinking of Malriel. And mentioning the ball just now does nothing to improve my mood, thank you very much," she growled.

"What *would* improve your mood?"

She thought for a moment. "A hot bath, a good book that has nothing to do with healing and an obscenely large glass of that sweet wine House Arbil is famed for."

He nodded. "That can be arranged. And to improve my own mood, I will be waiting for you when you are finished. I find it very entertaining when you've had some alcohol. Especially in obscene quantities," he grinned broadly.

* * *

Vern opened the door at the knock and made a sympathetic face when he saw Eryn's expression.

"Cosmetic correction again?"

Eryn nodded. "Yes. Inad once more. This was the third time she has had something done now. First her feet were shortened, then she wanted smaller ears and now she had me remove some of the flab from her hips and upper arms. This is, of course, so much easier than just cutting back on the sweets she keeps stuffing herself with," she grunted.

"Well, as you ask outrageous prices for your services, I dare say it was worth the ordeal," the boy pointed out. "Come in, I need to feed Ram'an, then we can move on to unravelling the secrets of nerve fibres."

She entered the parlour and walked towards an untouched lunch tray. "Don't tell me you didn't eat your meal? I would have to do a complete check on you right here and now to sort out that unheard phenomenon," she grinned and snatched a piece of vegetable that had not been in contact with the meat.

"Very funny. No, it was Junar's. She wasn't hungry. Upset stomach or something. She didn't want to let me check. She says she does not want to give up her ability to somehow survive without magic now that she lives with two magicians."

Eryn raised both brows. "So she has finally given in and officially moved in here?"

"Yes, that she has. Father has been moving her things here bit by bit and when she realised that her own place was more or less empty apart from a few plates and chipped cups, she told him that she gave in."

"Sneaky. She didn't say anything to me about that."

"Don't worry, its being official is still new. It was only two days ago, and she is very busy right now. It seems the women here have gone crazy about clothes from the Western Territories, or rather the styles. And, thanks to you, Junar is the only one in possession of patterns and fabrics to make them, so people keep going to her instead of their usual tailors."

"I hope they don't cause her any trouble because of it?" she frowned, thinking back to how the apothecaries had taken to having competition months ago. They had even tried to murder her.

"What? No, why would they? They want to buy from her," Vern asked and seemed confused.

"No, not her customers, the other tailors! How have they reacted?"

"Oh, them," he waved them off dismissively. "They are not happy, of course. Two of them have tried to buy the patterns from her, but of course she declined to sell them. One even broke into her shop and tried to take the patterns, but she always locks them up tightly, so nothing was taken."

"They broke into her shop?" Eryn exclaimed shocked.

"Yes, but they caught the burglar and he will be spending a few months in the dungeon cooling his heels. Father was not too happy and has made it known that he will make sure the next person who attempts anything like that will not get off so lightly."

Eryn nodded. When a threat like that came from a man of Orrin's status, people usually tended to be very careful. Good thing for Junar that she had not only a magician, but a renowned fighter by her side. Otherwise she might have had to face difficult times. She remembered when Enric had insisted on making their romance public so that she would be protected by his status even without an official arrangement. It pretty much worked like that now for Junar.

"She had to hire two more girls - now she has five," Vern said into her thoughts. "Amazing, when you think that only a few months ago she was able to do all the work herself. Having you as a friend did turn out to be advantageous."

"As well as the considerable benefit of my charming company, I hope," she remarked with a raised eyebrow.

"Yes, sure. There's always that, obviously," he sneered. He put down a ceramic bowl filled with small chunks of meat for the cat who dashed out of his room at the sound of the vessel touching the floor, as if he had not been fed in weeks.

"How is that creature getting on with Orrin now? Have they befriended each other yet?"

"I wouldn't go that far. I would call it more of a truce. Father doesn't throw things after him anymore, and in turn Ram'an has stopped peeing over his shoes. But they still maintain a minimum distance of several steps. It's funny to watch," the boy sniggered. "How about your plans for the Freedom Night? Have you heard anything from the King yet?"

"Yes, he has granted it graciously, thanking me for my effort in serving the common good and all that."

Vern nodded thoughtfully. "I see why this is a good thing to be done, yet I can't help thinking that seventeen years ago, such a measure would have prevented my ever being born."

She blinked and then sighed. Putting an arm around his shoulders, she briefly touched her head against his. "And that, my friend, would have been a great loss, not only for me personally, but for the healing profession in this country. I don't know how I would have stayed in my right mind during captivity without you. But your situation is not what usually happens to children who are conceived in the course of that night. Only very few of them have the chance of staying with a parent. The rest are either abandoned or left on the doorstep of the orphanage."

"I know," he nodded. "Father thinks this prevention is a good thing. He said that as long as this anonymity is not lifted and there is no way of sharing the responsibilities between both parents afterwards, the current way of doing it is just not right. He says that most of the women have very likely no other option than to give up their children, as raising them alone is not something they can afford when they have to work to survive and no family to support them."

"*Orrin* said that?" she marvelled. That was a statement that showed true greatness coming from a man who had been left without warning with a baby boy by the woman he had romped with on that one fateful Freedom Night. It had not made him bitter but instead he had enough sympathy in him really to see the situation many of them were in.

"He did, yes. And he told me that he considers me a gift and has never once regretted ending up with me as a son."

Eryn shook her head in mock amazement. "An uncharacteristic show of affection and emotional attachment. I hope he at least used an inappropriately stern tone of voice for this declaration of fondness for his only son?"

Vern grinned. "He did. And a frown that gave him the troubled look of a man who had to face an unpleasant but necessary duty. And being who is he, he never shies away from things he considers necessary. Assuring me of his paternal affection despite our bumpy start seems to fall into that category. He wanted to make sure I don't feel unwelcome after his approval of your new scheme to make this city an even better place. If you carry on like that, this city will soon be some kind of tedious paradise with nothing but healthy, well-fed and happy people. Oh - I forgot *beautiful*, as you are also doing the cosmetic stuff regularly now."

"Yes, that makes a good picture. I am sure there is a great danger of it happening quite soon," she snorted. "Now get your book and tell me about repairs to nerves. I have asked one of my patients to drop by in about one hour. He has a numb foot and I asked him to come here so you can practise on him."

"Experiments on patients? Is that alright?"

"Sure, or I wouldn't be doing it," she pointed out. "I told him that it is for training purposes and that I would repair any untoward damage you cause. And let's not forget that he will walk out here in a better condition than he comes in. Of course the treatment is free as he will be assisting the healing profession with his readiness to let us work on his condition."

The boy frowned. "So you just sent away a patient who came to you to return later?"

"Not quite like that. He did not come because of his foot, but because of a skin rash. I asked him if I could use the old injury on his foot for teaching purposes, and he was thrilled about it. He became so used to not having any feeling in it that he hadn't even considered having it healed."

Satisfied that the healing principles had not been violated, Vern then walked into his room and returned with the book she had sent him for a moment later.

"How is the plant house doing?" he enquired.

"Well enough, it was finished yesterday afternoon. Plia spends every free minute up there, filling pots with soil, planting out I have no idea what, playing around with her tools."

"I suppose I will take a look at it tomorrow, then," he said a little too casually.

She narrowed her eyes. "Could it be that you fancy Plia?"

He looked at her with a start. She watched a blush start at his throat, progressing to his ears and finally taking over his face. "What? No! What an absurd thing to say!"

Eryn sighed. "Yes, right. Complete nonsense, I can see that. You are aware that you need to keep your hands off her for a while yet? She is thirteen years old now. If I catch you doing anything I don't approve of before she is at least fifteen, I am going to hurt you.'

"I... you... that..." he stammered, his eyes wide.

"I take this as agreement," she nodded. "And now let's move on with your studies. We don't have all day."

* * *

Eryn regarded the letter in her hands with a bewildered look. It was Ram'an's second message to her, and while the first one had maybe seemed a little cooler than she would have expected, this one was almost impersonal, like something he would write to a stranger. Formal, inexpressive, without any trace of the friendship he had assured her he still felt for her before her departure. She looked down at the bracelet he had given her as a farewell present. The simple though elegant string encircling her wrist with the crest of House Arbil fixed upon it.

Right now it felt strange to glance at it after reading that letter. She wondered if he regretted giving the bracelet to her and hoped that he didn't. Unfortunately that was not what the paper in front of her suggested.

She let her eyes wander along the few lines once again, trying to convince herself that it was not as bad as she thought. He had written next to nothing about himself, just that he was at the best of health as was his family. The rest contained bits and pieces about trade and politics, things Enric would know in more detail anyway due to the messages he was exchanging with Kilan on a regular basis.

She decided to have a second pair of eyes look at it and put it aside to show it to Junar when they next met.

Vern had told her about receiving a message from Ram'an in which he asked if he was interested in working together with a cousin of his who was in the middle of writing a book on the development of children in the womb. He had seen Vern's drawings in the book

Ram'an had brought back with him and was very eager to have him provide the illustrations for his own work.

The boy had been thrilled not only at having his work appreciated in another part of the world, but also at being invited to participate in something that would then bear his name beside the author's and be there for everyone to see.

He had written back and then come to Eryn to ask if he could use one of her birds to deliver the message more speedily than sending it by ship would be. She looked down at the little tube containing his reply. He wanted it sent as soon as possible, so she would not have the luxury to ponder Ram'an's message for a while longer before writing back if she didn't want to use more birds than necessary.

She would adapt her own reply to his letter, she decided. Maybe not quite that cool, but she wanted him to see that she was not exactly content with his style of communication presently. Could it be that he was not aware of how his letter must seem to her? She sighed and scolded herself for her attempts at deceiving herself. Ram'an was a lawyer, and a good one at that. He knew perfectly well how nuances in phrasing could change the whole message. If he sent her a detached and nondescript letter, then it was exactly what he had intended to do.

Well, if this was how he wanted to do this, she would oblige him with an equally charmless one.

She pulled a blank sheet out from her drawer and started writing about the weather in Anyueel, how the preparations for the impending visit of the healer from Takhan were going and that they were now trying to grow their own medical herbs on the clinic's roof.

"You look grim," a voice said from the door. Enric was leaning against the door frame, just how he preferred, with his arms folded. He had his sleeves pushed up so that the dark symbols on his wrist were visible against his skin.

"Just taking care of my correspondence," she shrugged.

He entered her study and walked to her desk to take a seat at the corner closest to her. "Tomorrow is Freedom Night," he said.

Lifting one eyebrow at him, she nodded. "I know, thank you. I will be there aiming to prevent unplanned pregnancies, remember? It's basically work time for me."

"But only for one or two hours, I would think. How about the rest of the evening? Would you like to stay there?" he enquired.

She put aside her pen and leaned back, considering him curiously. "Stay there as in dancing and having a wild, untamed night of passion with a random stranger? Sure, why not?" she said lightly. "Don't ever let it be said that I don't embrace variety."

His expression became dark and menacing, just as she had known it would. "Very funny. You know very well who you will spend the night with."

"How can you be so sure of that? It won't be quite that easy for you this time. I would change my hair colour, of course. I would really be anonymous. You wouldn't even recognise me."

"I would be able to recognise you if you wore a bag over your head. A mask is nothing much of a challenge," he professed.

"Would you really?" she smiled. "Well, then I challenge you to prove it. I will be there. What if you don't recognise me?"

"This sounds suspiciously like a bet," he grinned back.

"Does it now?"

"Yes. And I accept. If I do not manage to identify and whisk you away to one of the huts before midnight, I shall consider myself the loser of this bet. What is it you want in that very unlikely case?"

She let her eyes wander over the ceiling while she thought about it. "Nothing you could buy, money is not an item for you, you simply have too much of it," she mused. "Time. Yes, I want some of your time. Ten days' work at the clinic. You'll assist me in writing my patient reports, help Rolan with his administration, that kind of thing."

He nodded. "Alright, ten days it is. And if I win, you will take up combat training with me again in addition to the lessons you have with Orrin. I am tired of feeling the numerous punches he lands while I am supposed to be working."

"How often?" she grimaced.

"As often as I see fit until your progress is to my satisfaction."

She snorted. "Hardly. I gave you a specific time frame, now you do the same, please. I don't trust your estimate of my progress. You might prolong this unduly because you enjoy it so much."

"Alright, ten evenings, two hours each. They don't need to be in one go, but within the next month."

"Agreed." She held out her hand for him to shake. He did and then held on to it to pull her closer.

"You have no chance whatsoever. I know your face very well, having the upper half covered will not be a problem at all." He traced a finger along her mouth. "Your upper lip is slightly fuller than the lower. And there is this slight dimple in your chin. And these three tiny moles to one side of your throat are a dead giveaway as well."

"Really?" she purred and closed her eyes for a moment.

He watched the small brown dots become paler and disappear within seconds. Then the dimple in her chin evened out.

She opened her eyes again, her mouth in a smirk. "You know, it is interesting to see that while the only visible sign on your face are slightly narrowed eyes, there is a real storm of annoyance at work inside you. And if I have interpreted this correctly, you are a lot less sure of winning now."

"We did not agree on that," he pointed out.

"Neither did we exclude it," she grinned. "Which was rather incautious of you, as you know that I improved my skills in cosmetic alterations considerably in Takhan. Sarol was very insistent on that. And now I find he was right. Useful skill, after all. Who would have thought that it could be used for more than serving personal vanity and earning money for the clinic?"

He nodded slowly. "You are right, that was careless of me. But this does not mean that I won't find you amongst them." He rose and pointed at her chin. "And I want that dimple back."

* * *

Eryn rose from the bench that had been placed there for herself and the other two healers who had volunteered to take care of the pregnancy prevention with her.

"Gentlemen, I think this was it for tonight. There hasn't been another newcomer for the last half hour, so we can raise the shield in case somebody tries to sneak in without complying with the new rule. Vern, off you go."

The boy complained, "I am old enough to keep others from getting into trouble but am not allowed to join the fun? Really? This is not fair!"

"You are sixteen, that is too young, as you are aware. And you volunteered for this; I wouldn't have ordered you to do it," she pointed out. "So now go home, or I will get Orrin to drag you off. That would not exactly benefit your reputation, I dare say."

Lord Poron rose as well. "Then I will now be taking my leave as well. It was nice to see the setting again after such a long time. It must have been ten years since I last attended one of these. The huts were not as nice back then." Then he grinned, the wrinkles around his eyes deepening. "And you are joining the dancers now to see if Lord Enric can find you among the masked ladies?"

She nodded. "That's the plan, yes. With a bit of luck we will have a helper for a couple of days to do menial tasks for us." Not that anybody but herself would dare give him any, she thought. But still.

"Confident," Vern stated. "You really think you can win this? The idea of him losing feels somehow wrong."

Lord Poron nodded in agreement. "Yes, he is not normally known to lose. But then maybe there is always a first time. The best of luck to you, Eryn." He nodded to both of them and then left.

Vern frowned and waited until the old man was out of earshot before he asked, "Eryn? When did that happen? No more title?"

She shook her head. "I asked the healers to stop using it. I find the whole concept absurd, to be honest. That's one of the things I liked very much in the Western Territories – they have their titles, but they are more of a job description than something they use to address each other with on a daily basis."

"So no difference if you are a humble healer or a mighty Head of House?"

"Not even if you are a triarch," she nodded. "Though they address the Heads of Houses as such when there is an official occasion or they want to express their disapproval by being extra formal. Ram'an kept calling Enric *Lord* for quite a while, even though Enric asked to be addressed without the title."

"You can hardly blame him for it, can you? Lord Enric was his competition for getting you," Vern pointed out. "Speaking of Ram'an, you have sent him my message, haven't you?"

"Sure, it went out yesterday evening together with my own. Unless that bird took a detour, he should have received them by now." But she didn't want to talk about Ram'an any longer. "Now go home. I need to do a few minor things."

"Things like what?" he enquired curiously. "You are not going to cheat somehow, are you?"

"I don't think you can call it that when you have warned your opponent in advance that you intended to do it," she shrugged.

"You haven't answered my first question," he insisted. "What things?"

"Minor changes to my appearance. Hair colour, lips, shape of the ears, minor things."

"Really? Cosmetic alterations? I hope you remember what exactly you have to change back afterwards. Doesn't sound like responsible use of healing resources, I must say," he scolded her with a lifted brow.

She rolled her eyes. "Are you going to leave now or what? I remember sending you home twice already. If you don't go right now, I really will send for Orrin!"

He mumbled something that did not sound particularly friendly and sauntered off with a final disapproving look over his shoulder.

She scanned the area quickly to see if anybody was paying her any undue attention and then ducked behind one of the huts that were meant for intimate togetherness. She quickly slipped out of the tunic she was wearing and into the same off-white dress every other woman was wearing. Closing her eyes, she changed the nature of her hair structure so that it started curling in playful, blond ringlets and thereby seemed a lot shorter than before. Then she changed the colour of her eyes from brown to the same green as Orrin's. A pot of face paint took care of disguising the symbols on her wrist so they wouldn't give her away should he come too close and manage to push back the long sleeves of her dress to check.

Next came the lips. She reduced the volume of her upper lip slightly and made the dimple in her chin a little deeper.

Then she opened her eyes again and lifted up the little hand mirror she had brought, smiling broadly when she did not find much that was familiar in the reflection anymore.

"Eryn?" she heard a whisper behind her. Junar's eyes widened behind her mask. "Is that you?"

"Yes, it's me," she whispered back. "Did you bring the wristband? Good. Now put it on and make sure to keep it exactly in that position at all times. It is meant to look like you are trying to cover your wrist. And now to the other things." She took the seamstress' hand and closed her eyes, letting magic flow into her friend's body. When she opened them again she nodded in satisfaction. "Good. That should do it."

Junar's hair was longer than before and fell down her back in gentle waves. Her eyes were now brown instead of grey and her breasts noticeably fuller.

"Look at that!" the older woman marvelled. "The eyes and the hair I would change back, but can I keep *these*?"

Eryn shrugged. "Whatever you want. Consider them a little token of appreciation for aiding me in that scheme here."

The other women snorted. "Little token? I have heard about the prices you ask for cosmetic alterations. This is more in the scope of what I earn in three years."

"I can slim them down a bit if you think I am being too generous," the magician grinned.

Junar grabbed them possessively, "No, you can't! You have given them to me, they are mine now!" Then she looked questioningly at Eryn. "I really wonder, though, if winning a bet is worth all this effort."

"Kilan once told me that there is no way to permanently defeat Enric, the only thing that may be achieved - with luck - is delaying his victory. I want to prove to him and myself that this is not true. He *can* be defeated. And he will be. By me. Tonight."

"Then let's hope that your plan doesn't work too well, or I will find myself in a really awkward situation with him when he takes me to one of the huts."

"He won't. He will spend some time trying to work out if you really are me, but it will not convince him in the long run. And isn't meant to. It will just make him waste time he would otherwise have spent looking for me."

"You are lucky Orrin avoids the Freedom Nights," Junar sighed, "or you would have had to do this alone. You still may have some explaining to do after he learns about this."

Eryn shrugged. "Once I win this bet, I will explain to him whatever he likes. Are you ready?"

"I am, yes. But you are not. You are still wearing the bracelet Ram'an gave you. It's kind of a giveaway, you know," the seamstress pointed out crisply. "Come, let me take it off."

* * *

Enric leaned against a tree and watched the couples on the dance floor moving. He had noticed that the bench the three healers had been sitting on was now empty. So the game had begun. She had to be there somewhere, hiding not only behind her mask, but also her healing skills that she had no doubt used to change herself enough not to be that easily recognisable any longer.

Maybe it had not been too smart to provoke her into that, he mused. But there were still two things in his favour: the symbols on her wrist and the mind bond.

Like last year he had opted for a sleeveless open vest instead of going bare-chested like many other men around him. A woman with curly hair and green eyes passed him and gave him a curious and appreciative look before moving on to the table with the drinks.

There had to be about three-hundred women, he estimated. The question was how much she would have changed her appearance. Not too much, he hoped. He started dismissing the options. She had very likely refrained from making herself appear shorter or taller, something that would have involved working with bone growth and was much too involved for a bet and would also have left her exhausted and unsteady on her feet. So her height would be the same. That left soft tissue such as muscles and skin. And eyes and hair, obviously. That was still a lot to work with, he pondered.

Two hours until midnight. Time to get started.

* * *

Eryn sipped her wine. It was not particularly good, especially not compared to what she was used to. But then this occasion was not meant to provide gustatory pleasures but catered to a different kind.

She had spotted Enric quickly enough, but then that was fairly easy if one knew what to look for. Tall, muscled without seeming bulgy but rather sinewy with broad shoulders, confident – and on the prowl.

When she had passed him, his gaze had brushed her without lingering. That had been a good sign.

She saw him pushing away from the tree and step towards a woman about her height with her hair pinned up in a sturdy knot. Moments later they moved into the circle that was reserved for dancers and she watched them move together.

Turning away, she put her empty glass back on the table. She needed to avoid watching him too openly, that would make him suspicious. Better to behave as naturally as possible, just as a woman looking for a little adventure would. Time to find a dancing partner.

* * *

One more hour until midnight and he had three women left on his shortlist so far after discarding the two he had already danced with.

One of them was currently dancing, the second was in deep conversation with two other women and the third was about to take a seat. He would start with her.

Stepping towards her, he smiled and lifted his hand. "May I request this dance, if you are not too exhausted?"

The woman's eyes wandered up and down his tall, well-built form and then beamed. "I would be absolutely delighted."

* * *

Eryn smiled to herself when he led the woman he had just danced with back to where he had picked her up. The set of his mouth told her that he had dismissed her too.

She wondered whether he would recognise her despite her changes if she danced with him. Or was that just a little too chancy? It would surely mean testing her luck. But then if she remained undiscovered, she would enjoy telling him about it afterwards immensely. Was that worth the risk? Definitely.

The musicians started playing a non-magical song, so that was perfect. She made her hips swing when she walked over to him and wordlessly stretched out her hand for him to take. He blinked, seemingly slightly taken aback by such a demanding approach. His eyes darted to her curls and green eyes with their smouldering expression, then he smiled politely.

"Forgive me, but I am afraid I need a break." He nodded his head and then walked off.

She stifled a laugh and saw a blond woman with a piece of fabric around her wrist step next to her.

"That was daring," Junar murmured. "What if he had danced with you?"

"It's not a magical song, he wouldn't have noticed anything. And he didn't even accept my invitation!" she sniggered. "So much for recognising me even if I had a bag over my head. There is now less than half an hour left. I need you to get yourself noticed by him."

"Why do I feel like bait?"

"Because that's exactly what you are, my dear. Now off you go to flirt with my companion, but subtly. Pretend you are reluctant," Eryn smiled.

"That really must be one of those things one is never really prepared for hearing," Junar murmured and sighed before strolling towards where Enric was leaning against another tree.

* * *

He watched the woman walking towards the wine table. He had dismissed her as a possible candidate already, but started wondering if this had been wise. It was not that she did not fit the picture, but rather that she seemed to measure up to it a bit too much. But there were currently no other options he was following, so why not take a closer look. Maybe Eryn had counted on him dismissing everything that appeared too obvious.

He took the glass the woman had picked up out of her hand and smiled down at her. "Would you mind dancing with me first, if your thirst permits it?"

She swallowed, then smiled nervously before taking his hand. That was new, he pondered. None of the others he had asked to dance had reacted with so little enthusiasm. Maybe he was on the right track here, after all.

A pity that this was another completely non-magical dance, he mused when he heard the first notes of the song the musicians started playing. He observed her closely while moving with her in his arms. Brown eyes, he noted. But that was not exactly a reliable cue here. The general proportions were right, though the dress did not cling enough to judge reliably.

"A very nice evening," he said conversationally. His dancing partner just smiled faintly and nodded.

When she didn't comment, he continued, "Very warm for this time of year, don't you think?"

She shrugged.

Reluctant to talk so he wouldn't recognise her voice? That was promising. He smiled at her and made no more attempts at conversing with her, instead making sure to brush against her seemingly accidentally, now and again, satisfied with the nervous flicker he saw in her eyes. Very promising indeed.

After the music ended, he accompanied her back to the wine table and handed her a fresh glass. "Thank you very much. Here is your wine. I would be delighted if you would grant me another dance when you have finished it."

A hesitant nod.

He watched her lift her glass to her lips and his smile grew when her sleeve slid back slightly to reveal her wrist – and something that looked like the edges of a piece of fabric fastened around it as if to cover something.

She took her time with sipping her wine, he noted grimly. There were only a few minutes left to midnight, and he wouldn't want to let her win like that. Determinedly he plucked the half-empty glass from her hand.

"That is a little more time-consuming than I had anticipated. Come on," he said dryly and led her back to the dance floor when the next song started.

He held her pressed towards him more closely than before, feeling how she stiffened. Not too pleased about knowing that she had very likely been found out, he deduced. He grinned at her and lifted her slightly off the ground at the next twirl.

"Do you remember the first time we danced together a year ago?" he asked. "You kept fighting the magical music. And me when I held on to you while ordering another magical song. The one that made you more or less melt in my arms, so to say. A pity they don't play seduction songs here, but with your being the only one who can dance them with a magician, that would be rather cruel." He stopped moving and pulled her even closer. "Let's stop this now, shall we? You have lost our little bet. I have identified you. I will of course comply with the other requirement and take you to a hut." He smirked. "A bet is a bet, after all." Then he bent down and held her when she made to step away, his lips slowly nearing hers until they were only a hair's breadth apart.

"No!" she exclaimed and squirmed in his arms. "Please don't!"

He stopped and looked confused. There was a feeling of annoyance that did not come from him. The women in his arms didn't look annoyed, but panicked. Something was not right here.

He straightened and lifted her left wrist, unclasping the wristband and cursing when there was nothing but pale skin. This was surely no coincidence. He wanted to take off the woman's mask, but held back as this was against the rules. Public unmasking was not something that would be taken lightly. But he didn't really have to, did he?

"Junar," he said evenly.

She sighed, half apologetic, half relieved. "Yes."

"You just won that bet for her. Well done. I hope she has compensated you accordingly, because Orrin will not be pleased about that little scene here when I inform him about it."

Her eyes widened. "It was not my idea!" she protested. "There is no need to worry Orrin unduly! Really not!"

He held on to her when she wanted to leave the dance floor and pulled her back to the dance. "Now you wait just a moment. The dance is not over yet. I don't want to be seen being left here like that. It would make me seem like bad dancer, wouldn't it?"

She hesitated, but fell back into the rhythm with him obediently.

"The thing is this - I know very well that this was not your idea, none of it was. But the fact remains that you willingly participated in making me lose that bet. As the consequence of this, namely my helping out at the clinic, will be quite public, I feel I am justified in exacting some kind of revenge on you. We wouldn't want to encourage those around us into erroneously thinking that this is something I accept without struggle, would we? It would set a bad precedent."

"So your revenge is telling Orrin about it?" she sighed resignedly. "Alright, I suppose I had that one coming."

"That will be one part of it," he smiled thinly. "The second part is that you will not only be accompanying Orrin to the next ball - probably taking place after the ambassador's arrival sometime - but also to the next three dinner invitations he receives where we will also be present."

Junar closed her eyes for a moment. "Yes, Lord Enric."

"You don't need to sound so downcast, Junar. Comfort yourself with the prospect that I will also make Eryn go there. You know well enough how much she hates these occasions."

"So you are punishing us both for her winning that bet?"

There was a ripple of discontent audible in her tone, Enric noted.

"I would not put it like that, no. It would make me seem like a bad loser, wouldn't it? Let's say I wish to encourage you both to stick to more acceptable means next time, methods that do not border upon trickery that closely. And when I say *border on* I am being very generous."

The music stopped and he released the seamstress before etting his gaze wander over the people surrounding them. One woman seemed to be particularly interested in the two of them.

"Curly hair, green eyes, exaggerated hip swing?" he asked.

"Yep, that's her," Junar confirmed.

He sighed at his own ignorance. "And she even asked me for a dance."

CHAPTER 7

A New Ambassador

Eryn slipped out of the tunic after Junar had stuck a few needles in it to mark where minor changes were necessary.

"That's the last one. I should have them finished in two days and will send them over. The fabric is a little different to work with, more stretchy than what I am used to, so I can't use our usual patterns with it," the seamstress explained and rolled up the garments into a bundle. "So, that was business. I haven't really had a chance to talk to you since the Freedom Night two days back, so I am a little curious. Lord Enric didn't seem overly pleased when he whisked you off."

Eryn shrugged. "That was to be expected. He is not exactly familiar with losing and so doesn't have too much experience of handling it, it seems."

"I had the impression he thought we'd tricked him?" Junar prompted.

"Well, we did, didn't we?" she giggled. "But then he is a strategist, so he admitted that I did well enough."

"He said I have to go the next ball with Orrin *and* three dinner invitations following that."

"You know that you don't have to do this, don't you? He is big and powerful in the Order, but you are not a member, so he can't really bring anything against it if you don't comply. He has no *real* authority over you," Eryn pointed out.

"Are you insane?" the seamstress snapped. "He is Orrin's superior, and I am buying my fabrics from him at very favourable prices! I can't afford to anger him. If he says I have to go to these important occasions, then that is bloody well what I am going to do. Next time you go and find somebody else to help you outwit him; from now on I will try to stay on his good side."

"You are not on his bad side now, believe me."

"Maybe not, but Orrin was not particularly thrilled when he learned that Lord Enric had confused you and I and was about to take me to one of the huts," Junar scowled. "He is very happy with the punishment Lord Enric handed me and of course insists that I bow to it."

"Which you intend to do anyway, so don't pretend to be annoyed at him for agreeing with it," Eryn pointed out.

"Still. What about that wager? Has he started his clinic duty yet?"

"Yes, today was his first day. I just let him stay until noon since I don't want him to fall too far behind with his own work. He is quite busy with his tax negotiations with the King right now. It seems a whole new abyss of taxation has opened up with the import of goods from another country. The King wants to adopt the model they use in Takhan, but Enric says that he is the one providing the infrastructure, not the Kingdom, so there should be a considerable discount, plus whatever else they are quarrelling about right now."

"So not a good time for him to lose ten precious mornings of work," Junar said with a sympathetic sigh.

Eryn shrugged. "He should have considered that before betting against me. And I am not making him come for ten subsequent days but only every second day when we treat our patients."

"And how did it go? What did you make him do?"

"Letting him take minutes of patients' treatments and file them afterwards. He did well enough, I have to admit. Though the patients were a bit unsettled at having him there, as you may imagine. Afterwards he started reorganising the filing system, telling me how much more efficient his ideas were. I didn't understand all of it, but Rolan was thrilled and started carrying boxes and files from one room to the other, muttering something about a referencing system."

"So he is kind of taking over the place?" Junar chuckled.

"I wouldn't go that far - *I* am still in charge. Well, for now. Ask me again when his ten days are over and I am not able to recognise the place," Eryn sighed.

"At least he is eager to help you improve things. That's nice, isn't it?" Then she cleared her throat. "About improving things, there is a small matter I need you to fix for me."

"What little matter?"

"My breasts."

"What about them? They look fine to me. Don't tell me you want them bigger?" Eryn frowned disapprovingly. "I would advise against that, it would not look very natural anymore and you would probably get back problems after a while."

"No, not bigger. Smaller. Orrin doesn't approve. Not at all."

"What?" The healer shook her head incredulously. "You are joking, aren't you? Why wouldn't he? I did some very good work there!"

"He says this is not *me* any longer and he liked them the way they were before. He...," she hesitated and started to blush.

"What?"

"Well... he likes it that each fits inside one cupped hand," Junar finished.

"That is... quite charming," Eryn smirked. "So back to their former size it is. Give me your hand, so I can restore you. It's a matter of a few minutes."

"Well," the seamstress smiled, "maybe we can just reduce them a tiny bit instead of all the way back to their original size. Just enough to still make a nice cleavage."

"What is a *nice* cleavage for you? Give me something work with here," Eryn sighed.

"Well, now I am about your size. Can you reduce it halfway to what they were before?"

"Alright, I can do that. Why didn't you ask Vern? He could have done it as well. He knows how to manipulate that kind of tissue."

"Vern? Are you joking? You are suggesting I let a sixteen-year-old boy reduce the size of my breasts? A young man who is effectively my stepson?" Junar covered her face at the mere thought. "Surely you can't be serious!"

"He is a healer," Eryn pointed out. "And very professional about his work. I am sure he would not have done anything inappropriate."

"Well, *he* may be a professional, *I* am not! It would have been awkward for *me*."

"That's saying something after him learning about the two of you through finding you about to have fun in the parlour," Eryn sniggered.

Junar rolled her eyes. "Are you going to shrink them now or not?"

"Sure. You'll need to start working on a ball gown for yourself soon, after all, won't you?"

"Oh, just shut up and do your thing, will you?"

"I find that sort of funny, you know. This is probably the only occasion ever where I have to do the procedure the other way around," she grinned and closed her eyes to oblige her friend.

* * *

"Did he say what he wants? I hate these short-notice summons," she growled and felt how Enric pulled at her hand when her pace was about to slow.

"When does he ever?" he remarked dryly. "But I assume it has something to do with the arrival of the new ambassador in a few days."

"Why does he need *me* for that? That is time I could have better employed by going through the books Valrad has sent me. Or checking the progress of the reconstruction works at the orphanage. Or preparing figures for the bloody meetings Lord Tyront is so fond of," she whined.

"Complaining doesn't help you one bit. As you have hired Vyril to take care of everything around the orphanage there is no need for you to interfere with anything there. Concerning the books for your exam - well, the healer will be here for three months, so there will be plenty of time to fill in your gaps of knowledge. Your next meeting with Tyront is not due for several days and Rolan is the one preparing the figures, anyway. So I think sparing the King a few minutes of your precious time is surely not too much of a drain on your resources," he explained matter-of-factly.

"I hate it when you are all reasonable when I just want to air my frustrations," she moaned.

"There is a lot of hating going on with you today," he said. "Better get a grip on your mood before you meet the King."

They passed the guards at the Palace entrance and moved on towards the throne room.

"Did he summon Lord Tyront as well?" she whispered.

"No. Just the two of us."

Another pair of guards bade them to wait in front of the large double doors to the throne room and admitted them a few moments later after announcing them.

The King was sitting on his throne and watched them approach with that little smile of his. Marrin stood to his left, solemn as ever, Loft to his right, with his usual expression of having just bitten into something sour.

When they stopped before the dais and bowed, King Folrin rose and descended to take Eryn's hands into his and lift them to his lips. "Lady Eryn." Then he turned to nod at her companion. "Lord Enric."

"Your Majesty," both replied and waited for him to go on.

"As you know," he began and climbed the few steps again to take a seat on the throne, "we will soon be in the very happy position of welcoming Sanaf of House Finran as new permanent ambassador to Anyueel. In three days, to be precise." He waited for them to nod in confirmation before he went on, "You are surely aware that the selection of a suitable candidate was no doubt quite a delicate matter for the triarchy."

Eryn frowned, thinking of what Enric had told her about them selecting somebody from House Finran, because they were allied with House Aren.

"At the final voting at your trial, Lady Eryn, the Houses were made to choose their side of being for or against Malriel of House Aren. Being against her meant being *for* you. But now that your companion has joined her House, things have changed in a manner that has set the political wheels spinning, as it were. For the selection of an ambassador, the triarchy had the choice between either a House that was on your side before, but is now no longer, or one that had voted against you, but in favour of House Aren. So whoever was on your side before, was against House Aren and vice-versa. House Finran is the only House allied with both House Aren and Vel'kim, and this makes it a most suitable choice when it comes to supplying a representative."

"I was not aware they were allied with House Vel'kim," Eryn murmured.

The King raised his brow. "That, my dear Lady, is immensely negligent of you. You should at all times be aware of your allies. And of those who are not, obviously."

"I find it hard to consider somebody an ally who voted in favour of convicting me," she pointed out.

"And yet you are expected to bow to the arrangements made by your Head of House, I understand. I wonder, Lady Eryn, if another personal lesson in political strategy is not overdue for you." He smiled at her when she looked down uncomfortably.

"Lord Enric, I know I do not need to impress on you the importance of a good relationship with our new friends, especially as your own business interests depend on this so very much. They sent us a man whose family is allied with both your Houses, so they are making an effort we need to acknowledge by making their ambassador feel welcome and at home in our city. I am depending on *you* for that, Lord Enric, and henceforth am putting you in charge of dealing with him and making sure everything is to his liking."

"Yes, Your Majesty," he replied calmly.

Eryn felt a stab of annoyance and irritation from her companion. She stared straight ahead, gulped and looked unsettled. Of course he would not be thrilled about this assignment as not only did it relegate him to a chaperone, but introducing the newcomer to whomever he needed to know in Anyueel would also cost him precious time.

The King nodded. "Good. Lady Eryn, I should congratulate you on acquiring Vyril as administrator for your orphanage. And your companion as a helper at your clinic," he added with an amused expression.

"Thank you," she replied dryly, "They are both performing well, I am happy to say."

"As for your companion's assignment, I am sure I may depend on you to support him in his task to the best of your abilities. Lord Enric will of course be required to attend a number of social occasions in order to carry it out." He looked at her pointedly.

"Which I will be delighted to accompany him to?" she asked with a slightly pained expression.

"Very good. Just what I was hoping to hear," the King smiled. "Now that we have this taken care of, I will not take up more of your precious time. You are dismissed."

Both of them bowed, then turned to leave the throne room.

"That was strange," Eryn muttered when they had left the Palace gates and were walking along Kingsway back towards their house. "He just summoned me there to tell me I was to be a good girl and accompany you on your dinner invitations?"

Enric sighed. "No, he summoned you to get a first-hand impression."

"Of what?" she asked.

"Of the mind bond. He was informed of it and just tested its effect. And we complied beautifully. He annoyed me on purpose and observed your reaction. I dare say he will find some reason or other from now on to summon us both together as frequently as possible.'

She stared at him in horror. "Then I am more or less being used as a mirror for your emotions because you are so damn hard to see through? That means I am a liability to you! A weakness!"

He stopped and turned to her, taking her face in both hands. "No, my love, whatever you are, a liability or weakness you are not. Never. But this is something we need to work on. The sooner the better."

* * *

Eryn impatiently unfolded the letter, almost ripping it in the process. It was from Iklan. If there was somebody who might be able to help her, it was him. She had been waiting for him to write after Valrad had promised Eryn he would talk to him about the mind bond and hoped his letter would be worth the waiting.

Her eyes darted from left to right in quick succession, then she looked thoughtful and leaned back in her chair, considering his idea. That was certainly an interesting approach. It sounded unreal, mad, impossible. But it was still the best shot yet at learning somehow to control this - in most cases inconvenient and troublesome - flow of emotions between them. If that idea of his really worked, though...

She got up abruptly, causing her chair to tilt backwards and hit the floor. A few moments later the adjoining door to Rolan's study opened and he stuck his head in.

"What was that? Anything broken?" he asked and then looked at the tipped chair and her tense posture. "Obviously not," he concluded. "Just a very energetic way of standing. Going somewhere?"

She all but ran to the door, grabbing her robes from the hook next to it, struggling into them. "Yes. I need to see Vern."

Rolan rolled his eyes and stepped closer to help her when she desperately clawed the fabric to find the exit hole for her head.

"Bloody robes," she growled. "Awkward, useless, stupid, damn..."

"There you go," he said soothingly and pulled down the fabric to guide her into the light.

"Don't talk to me like I am a child!" she grumbled.

"Right, because that would be in crass contrast to your very grown up style of behaviour," he said aptly. "And you should take a cloak with you! It is raining out!" he then called after her when she ran down the stairs.

"I am a bloody magician, Rolan! There is a popular technique called *shielding*. Very useful against attackers. And *raindrops*," she called back sarcastically and then marched out into the rain towards the warriors' quarters, Iklan's letter still clutched in her hand.

"Wide-eyed, impatient and slightly scary," Junar commented after opening the door at her, not bothering with a greeting. "Orrin or Vern?"

"Vern," Eryn just said and pushed past her to knock at the door to the boy's room.

"Go away, Eryn," she heard his muffled voice through the door. Without hesitation she pushed it open to enter despite the less than welcoming words.

"How did you know it was me?" she asked and let herself fall on his bed.

"You think you are the only one able to recognise knocks. You are not," he glowered at her. "I am trying to learn Political Strategy here, so what do you want? Our next lesson is not scheduled until two days from now, I am absolutely sure of it."

"I need your help. It's important."

He indulged her and closed his book with a small, resigned sigh. "When is it ever not?"

She pushed Iklan's letter into his hand. "Read this."

He took the paper that was now slightly creased from her grip and smoothed it before going over the lines. He whistled through his teeth.

"That works?"

"I don't know, that's why I need you."

"You haven't tried it yet? Wouldn't Lord Enric be a bit more helpful in finding out whether this works?" he frowned.

"Ultimately, yes. But there is a little something I need to work out first. For that I need a healer. And apart from me, you are the most skilled one around."

"True," he nodded honestly. "So what have you come to seek my advice about? How may my wisdom be of aid to you today?"

"Oh my," she said quietly and shook her head. "You are so full of yourself. Now listen. I need you to help me find out where in the brain emotions take place, where they originate. Iklan seems to think I know that, but emotions have not been a focus in my healing efforts so far. That's not exactly the kind of stuff that helps mend damaged tissue. I have never done anything that required knowledge of the finer brain functions so far, apart from repairing torn nerve fibres."

"So you really want to try shielding parts of your brain? I mean, he says in his letter that this risks being dangerous if you perform it wrongly. Like making the shield too dense for any impulses to pass through or having it in place for too long," he pointed out. "Maybe you shouldn't play around with this on your own without even knowing where to place it. You should have another trained healer supervising this. There happens to be one due in a few weeks, so why not wait at least that long?"

She groaned. "Because I am tired of fainting all the time! And being taken advantage of because people think it is a great idea to use me to gauge Enric's feelings since he keeps them hidden too well!"

"I don't approve of what you want to do at all," Vern said darkly. "What if you end up damaged, unable to feel any emotion at all any longer, or even worse?"

"Come on!" she cried out impatiently, "If nobody dared to take risks, we would never have found out anything new. And if I happen to incur damage, there will be a healer here soon enough to repair it again."

"I don't know. I still don't like it," he protested and folded his arms. "What is my part in this, anyway? To hit you and see where the resulting emotion regarding the pain takes place? To anger you and then keep you from hitting me long enough to look inside your head?"

She raised her brow. "It sounds strange when you put it like that, but in essence that is pretty much what I had in mind, I'll admit."

Vern looked at her in exasperation. "Great. And I know exactly who your tall, bulky companion is going to come looking for when I send you back home with whatever deficiency you might end up with - little me!"

"Don't be ridiculous! As if Enric wasn't already eager enough to blame *me* for whatever he disapproves of."

"Sure, and people who are dumb enough to help you don't have to bear any of the consequences, do they? Look at Junar!"

"Being made to go to social events is hardly a despicable, inhuman torture! Well, not unless Inad is there," she corrected herself, "Her voice alone makes me shiver, not to mention the things that come out of her mouth."

"We are talking about words here, aren't we?" the boy asked with a slightly disgusted expression.

"Hey! Yes - words! So, are you helping me now or not?"

"What if I refuse?"

"Then I will order you to and have you punished if you disobey," she glared at him.

He threw up his hands in frustration. "Why did you even ask me, then?"

"To give you the illusion of choice. I am told that making people think they have a certain degree of control over their life makes them more likely to cooperate."

"Super. Then let's get this over with. I will only monitor and report, just to make that very clear. I am not going to place a shield inside your head, no matter how much you think you can force me to. I would argue before the Council that you were trying to make me violate the healing principle of not using my skills to harm people."

"Smart lad," she smirked. "I am fine with that, though."

"Why can't you do that alone, anyway? Just wait until something makes you angry again and then look inside to see where it is coming from. Should only be a matter of time in your case," he added tartly.

"Because when I am a slave to my emotions I am not nearly focused enough to do any internal exploration as delicate as that," she explained. "And I am not particularly happy with that last comment of yours. There are people across the sea who are very careful not to arouse what is commonly known as the *Aren temper*."

He shrugged. "Can't be worse than what I have come to know as the *Eryn temper*."

"If you are trying to make me angry, you are off to a superb start," she growled.

He put a hand on her forehead and closed his eyes. "Good. Then shut up and let me do my thing."

She felt a mild surge of warmth enter her head and extend small, carefully probing tendrils into her brain.

"Increased activity located," he murmured, then opened his eyes and picked up a pen and started drawing on a blank sheet of paper which was, after a few strokes, recognisable as a rough sketch of the human brain. He took another colour and made a dot about the size of a fingernail close to the underside at the centre.

He then pointed his pen at the dot. "That's where anger or rather annoyance seems to be at home. Let's try something different. How about something nice for a change, like joy or pride?"

"You just annoyed me. Do you think I am that prone to mood swings?"

"For my own sake I am not answering that question," he chuckled. "What if I tell you that the Magic Council has decided to let you stop your combat training because they assessed your skills as adequate for a healer? Father told Junar only half an hour ago."

She perked up, her expression incredulous, before a slow smile started spreading across her face. "What? Really?"

He quickly put his hand back on her forehead and followed the emotions back to their source, then opened his eyes again and grinned. "No, not really. But look at all that joy everywhere!"

She pressed her lips together and narrowed her eyes. "Brute!"

He yowled when she punched his shoulder hard. "Ow! Stop that! I was only doing this to help you! We are back to anger again. Great."

They tried another few emotions such as glee, sadness, curiosity, disappointment, anticipation, disgust and relief before Eryn lifted both hands.

"Stop, I think that is enough. That was quite a journey through a jungle of emotions. Thank you for that story with the hairy spiders," she remarked. "That will probably keep me awake for a few nights to come."

"Well, it disgusted you, didn't it? So it did its job well enough."

"A bit too well, if you ask me. But from what I can see you made all your dots in pretty much the same general area, so I think we are safe to assume that these three points here are almost certainly where emotions come from. They are close enough together that a small shield should cover them all, even if I should happen to jump from one extreme to the other within a short time."

Vern nodded. "I agree. So now you will start playing around with shielding yourself in there? I can't stop you from doing that until the healer from Takhan has arrived here, can I?"

Eryn was insistent. "No chance. But don't worry, we have a little experience with shields inside heads, don't we? We have removed quite a few of the barriers up there, after all. If I keep the density below one of a complete barrier, there should not be a problem. I am not going to ask you to place a shield, but I would really appreciate if you could have a look at what I am doing and intervene in case I am starting to feel woozy or anything like that."

He sighed in resignation and nodded. "Go on, then. If I don't have an eye on you, you will just do it alone anyway - which would be more dangerous."

She grinned broadly. "You are a good lackey, I am going to keep you on."

"Oh, just shut up and get on with it, or I will never manage to return to my book. I did mention at any time that I am supposed to be learning?"

She waved him off dismissively. "You are learning something already. So stop complaining."

"I would rather learn how I could quickly limit your vocal cords' or tongue's function enough to keep you from talking," he said under his breath.

"I heard that!"

"Excellent. I wouldn't have wanted to waste a good insult."

* * *

Eryn raced home through streets all but empty due to the heavy rain which still was falling in fat drops. It was rather early for her, but she was too excited to return to the clinic for paperwork.

She lifted her arm to edge open the entrance door to their house and smiled at the glowing dark symbols that had emerged on her wrist. So he was at home. Perfect.

Closing the door behind her with her foot, she wrestled the robes to free herself from their relentless grip and once again swore to have Junar redesign them as soon as possible. Why did she only ever think of it while struggling in and out of them and almost immediately forget about it again afterwards?

"Enric?" she called out.

"Yes?" his voice answered from his study.

She walked to his door and saw him sitting on the settee, a cup before him, and smiled. The lord of the house, taking a break from his tedious paperwork. She would give him a break from it alright.

Her hands grabbed the collar of her working shirt and ripped it apart, not enough to expose her chest completely, but still sufficiently to grant a very generous view at the top of her bosom.

"Come to bed with me," she purred and watched his eyes widening in surprise and something else she couldn't quite identify. "There is a little something I would like to try with you. If it works the way I hope, we can resume our little... wake-up activities without my taking another hour to regain consciousness." She had come closer and leaned forward, bracing her hands on his knees to grant him an even better view.

"Um, Eryn?" he said quietly.

"Shhh," she whispered and laid a finger upon his lips. "Whatever is awaiting on your desk will surely still be there in an hour."

"Do you want me to come back later? Like in, let's say, one hour?" a deep voice offered dryly from behind her.

She almost fell forward in an attempt to turn and close her halfway-ripped shirt in one movement. Enric caught and steadied her on his knees. She stared at Lord Tyront next to the drinks cabinet behind the door open-mouthed, feeling heat and doubtlessly colour rise to her face.

The words she wanted to say got stuck in her throat and she just opened and closed her mouth helplessly. So much for the unidentifiable look on Enric's face when she had come in. She gulped hard and got off Enric's lap, holding the tear at her chest together with one hand.

"Lord Tyront. How unexpected. I didn't see you," she said stiffly.

"Yes," he nodded slowly. "I had gathered that much."

Enric cleared his throat to keep the grin that wanted to grow at bay. He wasn't sure which one of them looked more abashed, though he could of course sense Eryn's considerable embarrassment through the mind bond.

"If you would excuse me now," she murmured and averted her eyes from her superior's, "I should change into something less... shredded."

Tyront looked at the door she had closed behind her very carefully.

"I am learning far too much about the two of you," he sighed. "She tries to avoid me as best she can even without being unable to look me in the eyes. I think we ought to continue this tomorrow."

Enric nodded. "That will probably be best, yes. I dare say she will not come down again as long as you are here." Pity though, that she would hardly be in the mood for experimenting anymore now that Tyront was leaving...

* * *

Eryn looked up at the grey sky, wondering if it would start raining before the ambassador passed the city gates and if they were expected to raise a shield to keep the onlookers dry.

She was shivering in her robes, cursing herself for forgetting her cloak. Once again. She smiled at Enric gratefully when he lifted his arm around her shoulders to press her close and at the same time envelop her in his own cloak.

Why was this taking so long? Hadn't they been told that the ambassador was due in only a few minutes?

"You radiate impatience and grumpiness," Enric murmured low enough for only her to hear. "You are not still disgruntled because the shielding thing didn't work, are you? We will try again. Figuring out a thing like that is not something that can be done in a hurry but requires time and patience."

"Yes, how right you are," she snorted. "And I am well known for that quality, am I not?"

She caught a glimpse of Lord Tyront approaching from the Palace speedily, and kept looking straight ahead, still feeling awkward after the little scene in Enric's study yesterday.

"Lady Eryn," he greeted her and she could see that he was not completely comfortable in her presence, either. Well, that was something at least. The only one who was not only completely unperturbed by this but also seemed to find it amusing was of course the calm and unflappable Enric.

They looked ahead once the ambassador and another rider had finally passed the city gate and neared the group of people who were standing awaiting them in front of the Palace. Eryn couldn't help but thinking back to the day when Ram'an had arrived here. The weather had been fine that day - the air clear, the sun shining. And she had been so excited at meeting somebody from her home country. And angry at the Order's and the King's trickery at making her bind herself to Enric and the Kingdom only days before his arrival. All that seemed to have been in another life, and yet it was barely nine months before today.

She considered the two men on their horses. The older one was very likely Sanaf, the ambassador. He was stocky and his long hair was bound to a tight, greying ponytail at the back of his head. His face and hands showed the tan that was usual for people from the Western Territories. It would probably pale soon enough, especially as the winter was approaching slowly but steadily. The trees had started shedding their leaves only days ago. He didn't look particularly comfortable and seemed to shiver every now and then, even though his clothes seemed warmer than what was generally worn in the Western Territories. He had not come entirely unprepared, but still not quite well enough.

The second man who had to be either an assistant or servant seemed to be about half his age with a short, artfully trimmed beard and a posture that suggested that he was either too relieved at arriving to feel the cold or was just dressed in clothes that suited the local climate better.

When both horses had stopped in front of the Palace gates, the older man dismounted first, his legs obviously stiff from time in the saddle and the cold.

"Welcome to Anyueel, Ambassador Sanaf of House Finran," Tyront said and stepped forward to greet the ambassador by grabbing his forearm in the way of the Western greeting Enric had shown him.

Sanaf smiled and then bowed the way he had obviously been told to when encountering a high-ranking magician.

"Thank you very much, Lord Tyront, if I am assuming correctly?"

Tyront nodded. "You are, yes." Then he indicated Enric and Eryn. "I don't think you met Lord Enric, my second-in-command or Lady Eryn in Takhan."

"I did not," he confirmed, "at least not officially. I was present at the final hearing of the trial and saw them, of course." He bowed to both of them. "It is my pleasure finally to meet you officially. You know Legara, of course, my Head of House and cousin."

Eryn smiled thinly. "We met her, yes."

Enric sent her a warning look. There was no sense in acting offended because Legara had voted against her in accordance with her loyalty to House Aren, even though it had not exactly aided her alliance with House Vel'kim. But then Malriel was the more powerful – and surely the more unforgiving of the two Heads of Houses.

Sanaf seemed to have detected the slightly cool undertone in her voice and turned to Enric.

"Lord Enric, allow me to convey Malriel's warmest regards and her hopes for your wellbeing. And for your companion's, of course."

"Of course," Eryn said dryly, ignoring the warning elbow nudge Enric somehow managed to make look accidental to the unsuspecting observer.

"Allow me to introduce to you my assistant, Erbál."

The young man bowed with a smile. "I am honoured."

"You must be exhausted, Ambassador," Enric then said. "Allow me to show you to your quarters, where you can have a quiet meal and warm yourself up. His Majesty will receive you in the evening, so you have a few hours to start making yourself at home. The things that were delivered in advance have already been brought to your quarters, but of course you will have to arrange them to your liking."

The ambassador smiled with obvious relief. "I admit that a warm drink and a soft cushion are welcome prospects indeed right at this moment." He nodded to Tyront and Eryn and followed his guide inside the Palace, his assistant trailing behind.

"We need to work on that attitude of yours, Lady Eryn," she heard Tyront say when they were out of earshot. "He will be staying here for quite some time, and the King has ordered the two of you to take care of him until he has settled in. You better get that misguided grudge under control."

She flashed him a dark look and folded her arms. "I don't like him. We sent them Kilan – smart, charming, pleasant, humorous – and this is who we get in return? He looks shifty and untrustworthy. I think we were short-changed," she grumbled.

"Your assessment of his character is no doubt not at all related to his cousin's voting against you at the trial, I assume?" Tyront asked pointedly.

She raised an eyebrow at him. "I am not going to dignify that question with an answer."

"Good," he smiled grimly, "I am not in the mood for being lied to in any case."

CHAPTER 8

Considerations

Eryn yawned and stretched in her chair in her study at the clinic. Yesterday had been a long and less than stimulating evening. Banquets - whoever invented them? She had been placed close enough to the ambassador to listen to his endless chatter when answering inane questions with extensive monologues. And the King had commissioned them to go to the same gatherings as himself for the next few weeks. Brilliant.

Erbál, his assistant, had not appeared too thrilled with the ambassador, either. That alone earned him a few credits in Eryn's book even though they had not talked much with each other so far.

And now, after only five hours of sleep, she was supposed to be staying awake while checking her healers' patient reports. Just splendid.

At least Orrin's training in the morning had served to awaken her if not to teach her anything aside from the reminder that strikes from that man were something best avoided. She rubbed her shoulder without thinking, even though she had already healed away the pain and bruises.

A sharp knock at their connecting door told her that her assistant most likely needed something from her. That would be a welcome distraction from the letters that kept dancing up and down in front of her eyes, even though the quality of the knock did not suggest that he was in a particularly good mood.

"Come," she called out and watched Rolan enter with an unhappy look and a sheet of paper in one hand.

"I have turned up something on the expenses list that is not right." He took a seat on the other side of her desk. "The list for personnel expenses is either not correct or there is a little matter you failed to inform me about," he snapped and put the sheet in question before her and turned it so she could inspect the line his accusing index finger pointed out.

It said *Head of Administration*. She raised both eyebrows. So the Palace had granted her request finally, she mused. It had taken them long enough. They could at least have informed her of it instead of just doing it behind the scenes.

She sighed. "Alright, you found out about it, then. I wanted to tell you myself, but I wasn't aware that the Palace has already agreed to it."

Rolan stared at her and she wondered at his injured expression. "Yes, I think it would have been a little more appropriate to hear it from you instead of finding out like this."

Eryn narrowed her eyes at him. "I think we are not talking about the same thing here - is that possible?"

"How would I know? You don't tell me so much, do you?" he exclaimed in frustration, his eyes widened and his face pale, as he jumped up.

"Rolan," she said in her most reasoning and calm voice, "do sit down again. Tell me what exactly you see when you look at this list.'

"I see that you have hired somebody you put in charge of administration of the clinic. I first thought that you had hired a new superior for me, but my position does not appear on the list anymore!"

"True, because your position as such is no longer required." Well, she admitted to herself; now she *was* doing this on purpose. A little fun at somebody else's expense was just what she needed right now to lift her spirits.

"You are kicking me out, just like that? After everything I have..." His voice trailed off and his head sunk in disbelief. "I have watched this place grow, helped make it what it is! Without me there wouldn't even be tables in the teaching rooms or paper on your table! Nobody would get paid or supplies get reordered!" When he became quiet and seemed to be holding back tears, she decided that she had maybe let this go on too long.

"Rolan, come on. I am not kicking you out. I am promoting you."

He stared at her, his eyes even wider if such a thing were possible. "Me? *I* am the Head of Administration?" he whispered.

"Yes, you are." She looked directly at him. "And I am a little insulted that you think me capable of just dismissing you like that without even telling you myself."

"Head of Administration," he repeated. Then he snatched the paper back from her desk and his eyes followed the line to its end where the figure for his new salary was given.

"That's a lot," he frowned, his voice unsure.

She shrugged. "A bit more than you had before, yes. Let's look at the last few months as your probationary period, shall we? You have performed well enough to be in charge of all that tedious stuff you seem to enjoy playing around with. That means you now need fewer signatures from me to buy, pay, order and grant things. That not only increases your standing, but also frees me of some of the paperwork and leaves me with more time for all the other stuff the Order thinks I should be doing. Isn't that nice?" she concluded with a smile.

"Then you no longer have an assistant?" he asked.

"What would I need one for, anyway? I am not sure if an assistant is expected to know so much more about what needs to be done than me, anyway. But I have seen the hours you have been working, so we might in time have to think of securing *you* one, though."

"Why did I have to learn about this from a list?" he suddenly exclaimed. "Why didn't you tell me? My heart almost stopped!"

"I told you, I wasn't aware that the Palace had already granted it. I didn't want to get your hopes up in case they refused." She lifted a brow at him. "I am still waiting for some kind of expression of pleasure or satisfaction here. Or is the shock of finding an unexplainable item on your list greater than your joy at being promoted and having the gap between us diminished quite a lot?"

He blinked, then straightened. "Of course not." He obviously remembered what social conventions required of him in a situation like that. Obviously *not* complaining. "I am very grateful for your trust and will prove myself worthy of it. Thank you."

"How cheery and emotional," she sniffed and opened her arms wide with an impish grin. "How about that hug you offered me after my return? Want it now?" She sniggered when he all but fled to his room and called after him, "Come on! Don't be shy! You know that you want it! It's waiting for you right here - just pick it up any time you want!"

* * *

Vern closed the book and pushed it to one side. "Another one finished. I like being able to close a book and have the feeling that I have wrestled all the knowledge from it, claimed all its secrets."

Eryn chuckled. "A very energetic approach to reading, I am sure. I like to think of books as friends. I give them a home, treat them well, we share our knowledge and at times I will revisit them."

"You share your knowledge? Like scribbling your thoughts in there and stuff like that?" he enquired, looking critical.

"I'll thank you for not calling adding my own notes to my father's books *scribbling*, but basically yes - I add my own knowledge to what's in the book and in doing so enrich it for myself and future generations. Though I can see you are not a great fan of that."

"No, I think books are one-way. You read them without debasing them by using them as note pads. The only person privileged to write in them is the author," he stated plainly. "Or should be, at least. Who knows what people write in there afterwards? If it's even correct? Or is done properly?"

She regarded him thoughtfully. "I wonder if this attitude has something to do with your starting to work on creating books yourself. I think you just don't want others to annotate and expand your work. Is that it?"

He thought for a few moments. "Probably," he then admitted. "I mean, I spend really a lot of time working on them, and then somebody simply writes in them? Just doesn't feel right."

"I am not a great writer of books, too much effort. I like to improve the ones that have been written already without having to bother with organising the content," she shrugged. "And from what I saw in the libraries in Takhan, books exist on pretty much every healing topic already, so there is not a lot I could contribute to the field, anyway."

"Apart from a certain area where hardly any research has been done because the condition has hardly ever been observed," he pointed out. "Speaking of which, how are your experiments coming along? Any progress so far? I haven't noticed any obvious major brain damage from your behaviour, well, none that wasn't there already... Ow!" He rubbed his upper arm. "Why always on that same spot? It will get deformed one day!"

"Better your arm than your head, I'd say," she growled. "And no, nothing worth mentioning. I have tried changing the nature of the shield, making it denser and less dense, stronger, weaker, smaller, larger, placing it earlier, but nothing has helped. Same effect as before. I have written to Iklan about it, but he as clueless as I am. I am getting sick of trying again and again and failing."

"I thought you were tested for being crazy about discovering new things? What did they term it? Explorer? Shouldn't this include a certain tolerance for failure?"

"Well, obviously not. It seems to focus on the strengths you were born with or developed in your early childhood, not so much on the character traits that would be helpful in using them."

Vern thought for a moment. "Maybe shielding is just not the way to do it. I mean, shielding against emotions sounds rather strange, doesn't it? Emotions are nothing tangible, so how can they be stopped by a barrier anyway?"

She stared at him open-mouthed, then leaned back and slapped a palm against her head. "I am so stupid. So incredibly stupid! How could I not have thought of that? It's so obvious! Of course it can't work! Stupid, stupid, stupid! So much for experimenting first instead of thinking!"

He held on to her wrist when she was about to jump up from the chair. "Oh no! Don't you dash off without sharing your epiphany with me! Sit and talk!"

She gave him a pained look, but sat back again. It was not as if she didn't understand his need to learn about new things, especially revolutionary new things he had basically just witnessed her come up with and aided to a certain degree. But then she wanted to test her idea right now without delay, and having to explain it to him would be just that.

"Alright, I'll make it brief: The concept I used before so stupidly was indeed blocking the physical transfer of emotions through the substances in the blood, but that is the wrong path. This is why Iklan warned me of the dangers. This could lead to malnourishment of the brain and thereby severe consequences after no more than two minutes. The shield is not supposed to deal with the physical aspect of emotions, but instead the *magical* ones!"

"But emotions are not magical," Vern threw in, clearly confused. "If they were, non-magicians wouldn't have them."

"Absolutely. But there is magic involved in the *transfer* from my head to Enric's – that is not a physical thing, but a gap that is bridged by magic somehow. And that magic is what needs to be stopped. But that requires a different kind of shield. It's like blocking a magical bolt with a barrier that is merely meant to protect you from rain. It would go through without even slowing down."

The boy straightened. "So you need to increase the strength of the shield without making it impenetrable for your body fluids. You can do that! We have worked with these kinds of shields before!"

She nodded, thrilled at having him understand the principle so quickly. "Exactly! All I need to do is change the nature of the shield and stop the magic from passing. That should keep me conscious when we... you know," she added sheepishly with a vague wave of her hand.

"Yes, I know," he said, looking away. "Well, then, off you go. Tell me tomorrow if it worked."

"I will," she promised and left his room to return home, forgetting her robes hanging on the hook in her haste.

* * *

Rolan knocked at her door and entered without waiting to be admitted.

"Lady Eryn? Erbál is here to see you. He says he needs your help."

She sighed and beckoned for him to step inside for a moment. "You are aware of course that you are the only person who works in this building still addressing me with the title *Lady*?"

He blinked. "No, I am not."

"Really? If there is one digit out of place on one of your lists, you yell murder and mayhem, but things like that slip your attention? We need to work on getting you in contact with people more," she said. "But be that as it may, I would like it more if you could leave off my title."

He gulped. "Do I have to?"

She gave him a dark lock. "That is one of those things that make me want to sock you. May I enquire why you feel you cannot accept this gesture of appreciation I just offered you?"

"Professional distancing," he murmured. "Next we will be sitting in your parlour and chatting about our feelings."

She closed her eyes for a moment. "You keep provoking and insulting me and now you want to maintain *professional distance*? Really? And believe me, there is no danger whatsoever of the two of our ending up in my parlour sharing private thoughts."

Rolan nodded slowly. "Alright, from now on just *Eryn*, then."

"Thank you so much," she nodded, letting the *just* Eryn slip for now. "Then send the man in - let's see what he needs."

Erbál walked in after the Head of Administration had left, smiling apologetically and looking rather more pale than when she had seen him before. "Lady Eryn, I thank you so much for seeing me. I was told that today is not one of your treatment days, but I would very much appreciate if you could still help me with a little matter." He lifted his arm around which he had slung a colourful towel that showed only after careful inspection traces of blood interrupting the pattern. "I have somehow managed to hurt myself when I put away my things. I smashed a bottle on the floor and then slipped on the wine and fell onto the shards. Can you believe such clumsiness?"

Eryn looked concerned at the injuries. "That is bad luck. Let me have a look, will you?" She carefully peeled away the fabric and kept her expression unchanged when looking at the small, glistening fragments that were still half-buried in numerous bleeding wounds. "I think we had better go downstairs to a treatment room. There I have all the tools I need for removing those shards of glass. Come."

She took his uninjured arm and guided him down the stairs and into the room she needed, making him lie down on the bed. "I will first numb the pain with a little magic, then I will remove the glass pieces and finally close the wounds."

He nodded gratefully, a relieved smile spreading across his lips when the ache vanished.

Eryn then grabbed a pair of tweezers and a bowl and started removing the tiny fragments of glass.

"I assume you are not a magician, are you? Otherwise you would probably not have come here but healed yourself. Unless you were desperate to meet me, that is," she said conversationally.

"I am not, no," he confirmed, keeping his eyes shut.

"Good. I was wondering if your entire city only consisted of magicians. Somehow I was never really introduced to anybody without magical capabilities. Apart from Sarol, that is. And that almost got me into trouble because he happened to be from the wrong House," she grinned lopsidedly, remembering the walk Malriel had taken her on to point out to her what an impression it made if her daughter was seen to be consorting with the enemy, as it were.

"Well, it seems you were too important to waste your time with introducing yourself to mere mortals such as me," he smiled, but there was a tense undertone in his voice.

A different kind of two class society, she remembered. One that was not only determined by wealth, but also magical ability. Of two children in the same family, the one born with magic would always be the more valuable. And if there were a boy and a girl with magic, the girl would be the favoured child as her children would ensure succession in the House.

In the Kingdom it was sufficient to be either rich *or* a magician, she thought. Though being a magician ensured at least a certain degree of wealth sooner or later. Or at least a comfortable lifestyle. The Order provided well for its own.

"Pity," she said lightly, "I could have gone without meeting some of the magicians in exchange for a few nice level-headed people no matter whether magician or not."

He opened his eyes to regard her curiously. "Not a statement one expects to hear from a magician, especially one as powerful as yourself."

She smiled wanly. "You have met Malriel of House Aren, I assume? I would exchange her for a non-magician anytime. And I bet my strained relationship with my cousin - or I should probably now say *sister* - Pe'tala, is surely also no secret."

"No, not exactly," he admitted.

"So, the glass is completely removed now. At least the pieces I can see with my eyes. I will now check for any smaller or deeper embedded ones with magic and remove them before I start healing the wound."

She waited for him to nod before she closed her eyes and took his hand into hers to do her work.

When she opened them again several minutes later, his skin was unscathed and he touched it gingerly.

"No matter how often I see it done, it is still an amazing sight every time," he marvelled. "Hard to believe that half an hour ago I managed to bury half a bottle in my arm, and now there is nothing left to see."

Eryn shrugged. "It was not nearly as bad as it looked; you managed to damage the superficial tissue, but the muscles were mostly unharmed. That made it easy to repair. Be sure to eat enough today and tomorrow and drink water instead of wine."

He nodded. "I will. I am very grateful to you, Lady Eryn. Will I settle the payment with your administrator?"

"No, that will not be necessary. Consider it welcome gift, if that is the right term."

"That is very generous of you. Thank you," Erbál beamed and bowed his head to her. His white teeth gleamed in stark contrast to his dark beard.

"Just a minor thing, really," she shrugged. "Would you care for a cup of something warm to drink before you brave the walk back to the Palace?"

"Would I be taking that drink with you?"

"That was my intention, yes," she smiled and got up from her chair.

"Then I accept with the greatest of pleasure," he replied and swung his legs off the treatment bed to follow her as she walked out into the corridor and to the small kitchen to prepare two generous mugs. She reached for two glass jars each of which contained a different one of Plia's herbal brews she stocked after having tested them to her own satisfaction first.

"I will give you something that increases the production of fresh blood, as you have lost quite a bit," she explained when taking a few spoons of green-grey powder from one of the glass jars. For herself she then selected the other one.

"And which one is it you have chosen for yourself, if I may be so curious?" he enquired.

"This one helps the muscles to relax. I have to do regular combat training, so I am a bit tense in the back and shoulders at times," she explained.

She added cold water to both mugs and heated it with a little magic. In a short while both mugs were steaming and she handed one to Erbál. Then they went up into her study and sat down.

"Tell me about yourself," she invited him. "What brings you to Anyueel? I am afraid if you are looking for fame and adventure, you will find us rather disappointing here," she smiled.

"Well, I am the youngest of four children, so it is not as if I cannot be spared at home due to there being some family business I am supposed to take over."

"Are you telling me they sent you here because they had no use for you at home?" she frowned.

He stared at her, then chuckled. "I was told that your style is rather direct, and yet it took me completely unprepared nevertheless."

Eryn sighed. "I apologise. In my head I associate certain places with expected behaviours I need to adapt to. In the throne room with the King I need to be careful and talk as little as possible; in the treatment rooms it is sympathy, calmness and professionalism; and up here in my study it is the luxury of being myself. Which happens to be a blunt, at times rash and not always as polite a person as the title *Lady* would suggest."

"Then, my dear Lady Eryn," he stated with an earnest nod, "I feel exceedingly privileged at the happy chance of spending time with you here, where I can experience the true you."

"Gallant," she smiled. "But I suppose with three older siblings you might have learned to be very careful in how to express yourself."

"It was not that bad, I assure you. You have met my sister, have you not? Her name is Intrea."

She stared at him, then grinned broadly. "Not Intrea of House Feral?"

"The very same, yes. I am glad you still smile when you speak of our House," he then said carefully.

Eryn nodded. "Ah yes: there was the minor matter of voting in favour of Malriel and against me at the trial. But so did the Ambassador's House, after all."

Erbál's mouth tightened. "With the small difference that his House acted in accordance with their alliance with House Aren, but we did not do so when it came to supporting House Vel'kim in the way that would have been expected of us."

"Why didn't you, if I may be so bold as to ask?"

"Bribery, of course," he smiled unabashedly. "But in hindsight that was not such a smart route to take as your companion turned out to be the new heir of House Aren and so it might have been wiser to support our old allies." He shrugged. "But it is always easier to be wiser when looking back, is it not?"

"I suppose, yes," she said slowly, surprised at his openness. "Then why have you been sent here? Your House is probably not the most unproblematic choice, I assume. I am sure you were not the only available person in the whole city," she added.

"That may be the case, but then there is the trouble of my still being one of only a few suitable candidates," he replied with a confident smile. At her raised brow he elaborated, "I was trained as a diplomat, you see."

"Were you, then?" She wasn't even aware that there was any training for that. What did they learn? Political strategy to excess?

"Yes. Unfortunately my exact House was an obstacle in sending me here to this place as an ambassador, and so was the fact that I am not a magician."

Eryn looked at him sceptically. "The argument with your House I can understand, but not the one about not being a magician. Society here does appreciate the usefulness of magicians, but we do not look unkindly on non-magicians. The fact that all the important women in the city are non-magicians would alone make that very unlikely." Then her eyes narrowed. "Why did they send you anyway? *One* trained diplomat is not enough for this assignment?"

"One is considered sufficient, which is why I am here. Sanaf is not trained in the art. He received what I would term accelerated preparation over the course of three weeks. Which, while being a handy thing, is hardly comparable to the six years of schooling in skills I received." There was a crumb of resentment there, she noted.

"So you are the one who is supposed to be doing the real work here while Sanaf will grace us with his presence due to having been born into the only House they deem a safe choice to pick a delegate from? That probably limited the number of available applicants, I dare say. Judging from what you said before, he was currently conveniently available and unencumbered by any duties that would have kept him in Takhan?" Basically useless, she added silently.

"That is quite an apt summary, yes. Which of course I will deny fervently of ever having admitted to you," he smiled sweetly, winking at her.

She pursed her lips. That felt a lot like political strategy. But at least she was now aware that she needed to be careful with that man.

"Why did you divulge this to me, then? Even if unofficially?" she enquired.

"Because, Lady Eryn, I am very confident that Lord Enric is either aware of all this already or soon will be. He does have very good contacts to Takhan, after all."

She sighed and nodded wearily. "And you came here to show me your goodwill and encourage me to like you. Was that arm of yours even a real accident?"

He laughed. "It was indeed, dear Lady. My commitment to my task goes only so far. Though it happened to be a very convenient excuse to come here and see you. I could have asked the ambassador to heal me, after all."

"You know," she frowned in puzzlement, "I really wonder at that diplomatic training you received. I thought that diplomacy was a bit less about complete openness but more about the arts of obfuscation and illusion."

He emptied the last drops from his mug and placed it on her table while he got to his feet. "A part of my training, Lady Eryn, was assessing people quickly and making use of information received. Your personality type does not take well to obfuscation and illusion, as you call it, but is frustrated and annoyed by it. You appreciate directness, so that is what you will get from me."

She stared at him in dismay. And with a certain admiration.

"And I am glad to see that it has worked superbly. You are already starting to like me." He bent over her table to take her hand and kiss it the way that was custom in the Western Territories before he bowed. "I thank you very much for the drink. And the treatment of my injuries. I look forward to seeing you at the next tedious social occasion."

She watched him walk out and close the door behind him, then leaned back and stared at the ceiling. Damn him if he wasn't right. She had indeed started to like him.

* * *

"Yes, and...?" Vern prompted when the other healers had left the teaching room and she was the only one left. "Did it work?"

She motioned for him to close the door, then sighed. "No, it didn't. It seems my new revolutionary approach was not as game-changing as I had thought."

The boy squeezed her shoulder affectionately. "It sounded good, though. I really wonder why it didn't work. You shielded in time? Not too late?"

"No, I was careful to be on the safe side, believe me." She rubbed her chin. "Back to the start, then. But let's leave that aside for now. There is something else I have been thinking about. The healer from Takhan will be arriving here in one month."

"Yes?"

"That will be the first free magician who will use magic regularly here without being a member of the Order and thus answerable to it," she pointed out.

Vern seemed puzzled. "But that's not true, is it? What about Ambassador Sanaf? He is surely a magician as well?"

"Yes, but putting his powers to daily use is not a part of his function here. His duties are non-magical. However, the healer will be using magic for his or her work on a daily basis. This is why they wanted me in the Order, don't you see? There shouldn't be magicians around who can't be held accountable for their actions."

"But wouldn't that healer be under your command anyway as you are pretty much the leader in that field?"

"Theoretically, yes. But practically I am a member of the Order, and that would also subject that healer to the Order's rules, which can't be right as it is an institution concerned with the defence of the Kingdom. You can't make a citizen of another country answerable to a bunch of warriors who are defending a country that's not their own," she pointed out.

"I see what you mean," he said slowly, "but I don't see much of an alternative here."

"I thought that maybe we should have a healers' association. Something like the Order, but for all professions associated with healing, not just for healers. It could include the herb gatherers and the apothecaries as well."

"So you want magicians and non-magicians in the same union, as it were?" he asked doubtfully. "But the Order is not responsible for non-magicians."

"Exactly!" she beamed. "That's why an organisation outside the Order is the only logical solution!"

Vern swallowed. "Have you talked about this to anybody else yet? Such as Lord Enric, for example?"

"No, I want to prepare a detailed plan before I propose this to the Magic Council. And I suppose Enric would not be too happy about not having me subordinated to him any longer."

His brow rose in alarm. "Are you telling me you intend to leave the Order? You can't be telling me this!"

She nodded grimly. "Why not? What sense does it make for the Order to be responsible for healers if their focus is clearly on another discipline? It's just an encumbrance for them, anyway. I am practically doing them a favour."

"Well, ye-es," he said carefully. "Practically."

"You don't agree."

"Well, I think it would be brilliant for you, and probably all of us, if they agreed to this, but I strongly suspect that they will not just let you leave the Order after taking all that trouble to make you join."

She waved him off. "That was just to keep me from leaving here. That shouldn't be a problem now that I am bound to the Kingdom *and* to Enric by magic."

Vern nodded, determined not to fan the flames of her anger by opposing her. It was not as if he was the one denying her the idea she seemed so fond of that she refused to see the obvious obstacles that would very likely doom it to failure. So why offer himself up as a target?

CHAPTER 9

Junar's Surprise

Eryn leaned back after emptying her bowl. Vran'el had sent her a few more spices and she had been a little overzealous in adding them to the dish.

"Very spicy," Enric commented and popped a piece of bread into his mouth to soothe the sensation aflame on his tongue.

"That was on purpose. Spices keep us warm and as it keeps getting colder outside..." she improvised, rather desperately.

He pondered her excuse for a moment, then shook his head. "No, that doesn't convince me. As we have no more plans for going out today, this doesn't seem a valid excuse."

"Then I will from now on have the servants add spices to your breakfast instead," she grinned.

He grimaced at the thought of sweet bread with hot spices. "Thank you, but no. That will not be necessary."

She shrugged. "Then there is no helping you, I am afraid. Speaking of helping, I had a very interesting encounter today."

"In the morning after your training session with Orrin, I suppose? I remember feeling surprise that had surely nothing to do with my Council meeting, so it and must have been yours."

Nodding, she took a sip of wine before she continued. "Yes, surprise was definitely a key element in that conversation. Did you know that Erbál is the real diplomat of the two of them and Sanaf no more than a figurehead?"

Enric smiled. "Yes, I received a few interesting bits of information about the two of them. Sanaf was a convenient choice because they didn't want to risk unsettling the two of us and thought that sending a member from the right House would help. But House Feral is not exactly rich in expertise when it comes to ambassadors, so they sent Erbál as his assistant despite the fact that he is much better qualified."

"Why does this kind of information never find its way to *me*?" she complained. "Why do I have to depend on strangers to fill me in on such things even though you know about it already?"

"Because it is a political matter and I did not have the impression that this is a topic you are too eager to deal with," he pointed out. "Though I am more than happy to share this kind of information with you from now on."

"I would value that very much, thank you."

"So he came to you to tell you that he is the more important one of them? Blunt," he said.

"He came to me to have his arm healed after falling onto a broken wine bottle. We had a drink together afterwards and that's when he told me. And it seems he has taken the trouble to analyse my character in order to determine the most suitable approach to make me like him. How delightful. I do so like to feel important," she snorted.

"Well, that would be openness in your case. If he told you that, too, he really follows the concept through."

She thought back to the day before she left for her expedition, when the King had tested her knowledge of political strategy. "I was once told that the master level of the game is playing with open cards and still winning."

Enric raised both eyebrows at her. "There are not many men I would expect such a statement from. Tyront is not exactly the open type, so that rules him out. The King?"

"Yes. But Erbál informed me of this because he was convinced that you would learn about it sooner or later anyway. So he was no more open than he had to be, revealing nothing I wouldn't have learned from you anyway. He just used it to endear himself to me."

Enric nodded appreciatively. "You are getting into the line of political thinking. Knowing that we are being manipulated does not always protect us from the effects, though. Did it work? Has he managed to endear himself to you?"

"He is off to a good start there, yes," she chuckled. "How did you learn about Erbál? Through Kilan?"

"No, Vran'el. They are family, after all. And that is another point in his favour he might be using to win you over. You share one niece now, after all."

"A niece who isn't particularly, or rather, *not at all* fond of me," she pointed out. "And why would he be so eager to make *me* like him, anyway? Wouldn't it have been smarter to suck up to *you* instead?"

"That would have been risky. He doesn't really have any official reason to get in contact with me yet. But his injury allowed him to do just that with *you*. And judging from what people know about us, he can be sure that any man who is in regular contact with you will sooner or later also be sure of my attentions. Particularly considering what the last ambassador tried," he explained. "And there is also the matter of mending fences with House Vel'kim again after voting against you. You are of House Vel'kim, so you will probably put in a good word for them. And if you, the one who was accused, have forgiven them, who are the others to not follow your noble example?"

"I dare say having Intrea and Obal in House Feral would not keep Valrad angry for long, anyway."

Enric smiled weakly. "I think you underestimate your uncle, my love. He may be a grandfather, but he is also a Head of House. If he had shown any weakness in that position over these last years, his House would surely not be so very influential and wealthy anymore, I can promise you that."

Eryn blinked, trying to imagine kind, calm, benign Valrad breathing fire and bringing doom to another House. That seemed strange. But then it was usually not wise to dismiss Enric's words just like that.

They looked towards the door at the knock.

"That must be Junar. She is a bit early. She told me she would bring over the winter clothes today," Eryn told him and stood up to let her in.

The seamstress walked in, a bundle of clothes heaved over her shoulder.

"Let me relieve you of that," Eryn offered and took the pile of garments from Junar to put them on a table while the seamstress hung her cloak on a hook.

"Thank you, I had started feeling like a packing horse... Oh, Lord Enric," she swallowed. Enric nodded at her and suppressed a smile at her obvious discomfort. This was the first time they met after the Freedom Night, where she had avoided his kiss only at the last moment.

"Good evening, Junar. I hope you are well?"

"I am, thank you," she replied awkwardly. "I have not come at a bad time, I hope? I am a little early."

He rose. "No, not at all. Let me get you something to drink before I retreat to my study and leave the two of you alone. Wine?"

She shook her head. "No, not when I have work to do. Some juice would be nice. I could eat and drink sweet things all the time at the moment. If I don't take care and go on like this I will gain weight."

Enric stepped towards the drink cabinet and filled a glass with berry juice before putting it on a table for her. "Have fun, ladies." Having bidden them leave, he walked the few steps to his study and closed the door behind him.

"You act strangely around him," Eryn pointed out. "Don't worry about him, he has forgiven you already, or he wouldn't be offering you a drink but staring you into submission."

"Oh, please!" Junar rolled her eyes. "As if you were not all stiff and awkward every time you have a row with Orrin. The only difference is that you are less careful than me because you happen to outrank him."

"Nonsense," Eryn objected. "I am not stiff and awkward, but angry and resentful. That's a huge difference."

"Yes, Lady Eryn. Whatever you say, Lady Eryn," Junar sighed resignedly. "Let's get this over with, shall we? I want to get back home, my stomach is a bit sensitive at the moment."

"Still?"

"What do you mean, *still*?" the seamstress frowned.

"When I was with Vern the other day, he told me that something was wrong with your stomach but you didn't want him to have a look at it."

"Why were the two of you discussing my body functions uninvited? That is really creepy. Stop it! Bizarre healer bunch," she added with a mutter and shook her head. Then she looked up, checking if Enric's door had really been closed, before saying, "By the way, there is a little something I wanted to tell you. My breasts have grown again. Is that some side-effect from the change of size? Are they supposed to do that?"

Eryn frowned. "What do you mean, they have grown? Just like that? Maybe you haven't got used to their new size yet."

"No! I swear to you, they have grown! This is not normal, is it?" She swallowed and her hand went up to her throat. "Don't tell me – this is some fatal illness, isn't it?"

The healer exhaled. "What can I say? You guessed correctly. You are about to die a horrible death: choked by breasts that will never stop swelling out until their weight stops you from breathing altogether."

"Stop that, you! How can you make fun of something like this? Is this how you treat your patients? Then I wonder that you still have any!" Junar hissed.

"Junar," Eryn said calmly, "if there is a fatal illness, it is very likely that I would be able to do something against it, don't you think? Now give me your hand and let me have a look, will you?" She pushed her friend down on a settee and took a seat next to her, taking her hand and sending in a weak exploratory pulse of magic.

"Nothing amiss from what I can see," she murmured. "No unnatural growth, no lumps that shouldn't be there." Her pulse went further south to examine the organs that generally triggered mammal growth and sucked in a surprised breath.

"What?" Junar exclaimed panicky. "You have found something, haven't you? Can you fix it?"

Eryn opened her eyes again. "Well, not exactly, no."

"*No* what? No, you haven't found anything or No, you can't fix it?"

"I did find something," the healer said slowly.

"Out with it!" the seamstress demanded. "I am sweating blood here!"

"Junar," Eryn said calmly, "you are pregnant."

The older woman stared at her for a moment, then started laughing. "That is very funny! But if you want to shock me you need to resort to something a bit less unlikely. I am infertile, remember? Does it mean this was a crude joke? Everything is alright?"

The magician swallowed. "Junar. You are pregnant. There is a child growing inside you. This is why your stomach troubles you. And why your breasts have grown," she insisted.

Junar had gone pale. "Stop that, Eryn. It's not funny anymore."

Eryn just stared at her, wondering how she could phrase it to make it clear to the woman in front of her that this was no clumsy attempt at being humorous, but the real deal. But looking at her serious face, Junar seemed to be reaching the very same conclusion on her own.

A shrill shriek escaped Junar's mouth before she covered it with both hands and started breathing heavily.

The door to Enric's study banged open and he dashed outside, looking around for what might have alarmed them. When he found nothing, he took in the seamstress' pale face and obvious state of shock. "What happened?"

"I just told her that she is expecting a baby," Eryn said slowly and watched an expression of disbelief form on his face that matched the feeling she felt him projecting. But it took him only moments to recover from it. He straightened, swallowed and came closer, crouching in front of the two women.

"She is not taking the news very well, it seems," he frowned and gently took her hand that felt too cold. "Junar?"

She started wobbling her head slowly from side to side, then with more and more vigour. "No. This is a mistake. Healers are people. People make mistakes." She gripped Eryn's hand with her free one. "Check again."

The healer looked at her for a moment, then decided to indulge her if it made it any easier for Junar to believe it finally. She let her magic enter the woman's body once more, moving down to her abdomen and to the area where a little blob of life was forming and dividing. There was no doubt about it.

"It was no mistake, Junar," she then sighed. "But we can send for Vern, if you would like to have a second opinion."

"This is impossible," the seamstress whispered, then looked up at the two sympathetic faces in front of her. "How is this possible? I was trying to have a baby for more than ten years, and it didn't work! I know that *I* was the problem, *he* had three children with another woman after he left me! How? What have you done to me?"

Eryn swallowed. Her? "I have not done anything as far as I know," she then said, determined not to let anything Junar said insult or annoy her. She was not exactly in a shape to carefully consider what came out of her mouth right now.

"You must have! I was infertile! You must have healed *something* somewhere, restored whatever was behind my infertility!"

The healer thought back to the occasions when she had healed her friend. There was the cut from a broken plate about a year ago Then the sore feet at the ball. And finally the cosmetic things, like the breast sizes and colour of her eyes. Wasn't there something else? A gland in the throat that had not been performing the way it was supposed to. Could that have been the reason for her infertility? She had never read anything about that, but then her resources were still limited. So she would have to write Valrad and ask him; he would surely know.

She forced herself to smile. "Junar, whatever the reason may have been, there is an embryo inside you, growing into a child. This is nothing bad - it is a gift from Nature to you and Orrin."

"Orrin!" Junar exclaimed and covered her face with both hands. Moments later first tears formed at the corners of her eyes. "How am I to tell him this? He will think I have tricked him!" She then stared angrily at Eryn. "A gift? Really? How would *you* react to news of a gift like that inside you?"

"Humbled and grateful," she lied without hesitation. Enric flashed her a glance at once sympathetic and penetrating, but didn't comment on the outrageous statement. But Junar's next words made that abundant anyway, as she seemed to have reached the same conclusion.

"That is complete nonsense! How can you lie to me in a situation like this now?" After that outburst she sank back as if all energy had left her. "What am I to do now? Orrin will hate me! And how can he not? This is the second child he had no say in conceiving!"

Enric rose from his crouch. "Come on. Let's get you home."

"Home," Junar murmured. "I shouldn't have given up my own place."

"What nonsense!" Eryn called out. "He will not kick you out." She hoped. Really, really hoped.

They hauled her up from her seat, wrapped her in her cloak and Enric hailed a coach, paying the coachman before sending both women off to the warriors' quarters. He then returned to the parlour, stepped to the drink cabinet and selected a bottle of strong liquor that would very probably come in handy later. Pulling his own cloak around him, he stepped outside and created a weak shield against the drizzle that had just started. Then he started walking, remembering with a sigh his words to her earlier about not having any plans for going out tonight. So much for plans.

* * *

Vern raised both eyebrows when he opened the door. "You are early. Normally you don't get back so quickly when you visit Eryn." Then he frowned. "Where is your sewing bag? And why are you so pale? Have you been crying?" He looked at Eryn. "And what are you doing here? Is everything alright?" He pulled them both inside. "Father!" he then called.

They heard Orrin's chair being raked back across the floor in his study then moments later he emerged, watching his son take the cloak from Junar's shoulders.

"You are early," he repeated Vern's comment, then he, too, frowned when he took in the women's faces, one pale, wide-eyed and tear-streaked, the other tense and concerned.

"What happened?" he just asked urgently in his brisk way and took Junar's face in both hands, searching her eyes worriedly.

The tears began to flow again, and Junar held on to his forearms. "I am so sorry, I have no idea how this could have happened! I never would have done something like that to you on purpose, I swear it!"

Now the warrior's expression became really troubled. "What are you talking about?"

"I just want you to know that I will take care of this," she sobbed, "and that I won't... won't... won't... force you to bear the consequences."

"Junar!" he growled. "Tell me what this is about!"

He stared at her for a few more moments, and when she just shook her head, he turned to Eryn.

"Explain yourself! Now!" he commanded.

Oh dear. *She* had to be the one telling him? Just dandy.

"Eryn!" he barked when she hesitated.

"She is pregnant," she said with a calm she didn't feel, observing him closely.

Orrin just stared at her, then blinked. Vern's stood agape and he stared at Junar, who had commenced sobbing again.

"The stomach...," the boy then whispered. Eryn had to stifle a wry smile. Analysing symptoms, now of all times.

Orrin seemed to recover his ability to move and did so stiffly, turning and walking the few steps to the drinks cabinet where he took out a small glass and filled it to the brim with a clear, golden liquid. Then he lifted the glass and tilted his head back, draining it in one go. He exhaled when the alcohol hit his stomach and closed his eyes for a moment.

Then he walked towards the door, opened it and stepped outside into the cool corridor. He descended the stairs as though in a trance, his feet leading him towards the exit of the building on their own accord without any involvement from his brain. He pulled open the heavy door aside and stepped outside into the dusk, lifting his face towards the rain. After a few seconds he started walking without a destination in mind, just following the urge to move. He didn't see the shadow that detached itself from the house wall it had been leaning against. Only when the man had drawn level with him, did he turn his head to take a look at Enric.

Enric, he thought; him of all people. He was about to say something to send him away, perhaps tell him that he was in no mood to talk, but then felt something cool and heavy being pushed into his hand, and gripped it automatically. A glass bottle. A full one. The strong stuff. He uncorked the bottle with his teeth and took a long pull, feeling the warmth radiating pleasantly in his stomach.

He resumed his walk, not minding any more when Enric fell into step with him. They hadn't spoken a single word and just walked along the emptying streets in companionable silence.

* * *

Vern and Eryn exchanged a look, then each took one of Junar's arms in unspoken agreement and led her to a sofa.

"A hot drink, something herbal, if you have it," Eryn instructed and the boy took out a cup and stirred a few spoonsful of powder into hot water before returning to them.

"He just left," Junar said stunned. "Just like that - without saying a word. Just gone." Her head shook slightly, her eyes fixed on a spot on the carpet. "I made him flee his own home. He didn't even shout. Nothing. Just left." More tears rolled down her cheeks.

"Well, it came as a bit of a surprise for him, too," Eryn conceded.

"He will be back," Vern nodded confidently, then took both of Junar's hands in his. "Would you mind if I had a look at it?"

The seamstress' eyes lifted to him uncomprehendingly. "What?" she sobbed.

"The baby," he explained with a smile. "I would very much like to have a look at it. May I?"

She looked at him, searching his face. "You would?"

He looked surprised. "Sure! Why would I not? It's my brother or sister, after all, isn't it?"

"But... you don't mind?" She stared at him through teary eyes.

"Well, that will depend on how often you make me babysit. I am a busy man, after all. With healing, classes and all that. But a few hours every now and then won't be a problem, I think."

Eryn smiled at him warmly. He had a way of astonishing people sometimes. In a good way. Junar's tears had stopped flowing for the moment, her eyes wide.

"Babysit?" she asked weakly, sniffing.

"Yes, unless you manage to give birth to a self-sufficient child, that will be an issue, I would say. Have you thought about taking on a nurse? I suppose you will want to continue your work, so having somebody for a few hours a day would probably be good. Though you have hired quite a few people lately, so most of the work you should be able to delegate for a while. And I suppose you can do some supervising carrying a baby on your arm," he shrugged.

Eryn shook her head. He was doing it on purpose. He was overwhelming her with things that stopped her from crying and at the same time demonstrating his support and affection. What a boy.

"Work?" she breathed.

"Of course. It would be a shame to stop working, now that your business is going so well. I dare say the demand for clothes in Western styles will increase, especially now that the ambassador is here. There surely are a few desperate women who want to capture his eye – not that he is that much of a looker, mind you. Can I have a peek now?"

"What?" she asked, completely flustered by the changes of subject.

"The baby," he nodded to her abdomen. "I won't harm it, I promise. Just a peek."

She blinked, then nodded. Eryn watched him close his eyes and moments later a smile spread on his face when he found the tiny creature.

"Small, about the size of my thumbnail," he murmured. "So many things visible already," he continued, marvelling quietly at what he was seeing. "The head, beginnings of the spine, hands and legs, even a tiny nose..." Then he opened his eyes, staring at Junar for a moment before jumping up. "You are *pregnant*!" he exclaimed and clapped his hands.

Junar seemed completely overwhelmed with the situation and now Vern's odd reaction, and Eryn, too, frowned at him in confusion.

"What? Have you gone completely off your rocker? Of course she is pregnant! We established that fact only a few minutes ago!"

"No, I mean, that's just what I need! I am expected to illustrate this book on the development of children in the mother's womb, and now I have a mother here! I can draw every minor change, can check the development on a daily basis!" he exclaimed delightedly. "This is fabulous!"

Junar rose slowly, a strange calm seemed to have come over her. "You are welcome to draw whatever you see, Vern. You will always be welcome." A single tear ran down her cheek and she wiped it away with her hand. "I will stay with my sister until I have converted my storage above the shop back into a place where I can live."

Vern blinked at her, then rolled his eyes. "No, Junar, you are not going to staying with Gara," he explained matter-of-factly. "I don't wish to explain to my father why I let you leave here. Do you want him to kill me? I am very attached to this life, thank you so much! And I am too brilliant to die young. Even more, I have only just started shaving! My life is just about to become interesting. Take your drink to the bedroom with you."

She started to object, but he cast his eyes sternly down at her. "Don't think I am beneath wrestling a pregnant woman into submission. Go and get some sleep - you look exhausted." He pushed the cup into her hands and opened the bedroom door. "In you go!"

Junar was perplexed enough to obey, letting herself be shoved towards the bed. He lit a lamp for her on the bedside table and kissed her on the forehead before turning to leave again. "Don't worry, Junar. Everything will be fine." Then he stepped outside into the parlour, closing the door behind him.

Eryn shook her head at him and sighed. "You are a piece of work, my boy."

"Either you appreciate the way I handled Junar or you take issue with my benefiting from her condition for my project. I can't tell right now," he said and let himself slump into a chair.

She smiled faintly. "Both, I think. But the way you treated Junar just now impressed me more than your shameless exploitation of your own on-demand live study model. I can't help but marvel at that warm, affectionate manner of yours in combination with that cold-blooded opportunism."

"Doesn't hurt anyone, does it?" he grinned.

"No, or I would have taken your hide, my friend," she told him with a warning barely concealed in her voice.

"I know. So, where do we go from here?"

"We wait, I would say. I suppose Orrin needs some time to think, so going after him right now might not be so wise. If he hasn't returned before tomorrow morning, we will go looking for him." She stretched. "I'll send Enric a message that I will be staying here for the night. Can you get me one of Junar's nightshirts? Or one of yours? I'll also have a glass of whatever Orrin gulped down before he left. I hope it is wickedly expensive."

Vern smirked. "It is. And tastes fairly awful."

"Does it?" she grimaced. "Doesn't matter - the main point is that it cost a lot. Bring the bottle." She watched him go to the drinks cabinet.

"Splendid," he sighed. "Then this is my first night of babysitting. In one room there is a desolate pregnant woman, and here there is you, soon to be drunk. And I am the remaining responsible adult here."

"Good way of getting used to the role," she smirked. "Have I ever showed you how to heal away the aftereffects of overindulgence?"

* * *

Enric had walked through the now darkened streets, trailing Orrin, for more than one hour, watching him take a generous swig from the bottle every now and then without flinching at the strong liquor at all. One third was gone by now, and he didn't show any sign of its having any effect on him: his steps still energetic, tense and determined, even if directionless. He was soaked, not bothering with a shield to keep off the rain and neither had he brought a cloak.

They had not exchanged a single word, just walked. Then Orrin suddenly stopped and turned, looking at Enric as if truly seeing him for the first time only now.

"Junar is pregnant," he stated.

Enric nodded. "I know."

The warrior nodded slowly. "You would, of course." Then he let his gaze wander along the rows of houses. "It's no coincidence, I assume, that we are close to your house." It was not a question.

"No," the younger man confirmed calmly. "It's not. Are you done walking and ready to get inside where it's warm?"

Orrin sighed, rivulets of water running down his face, his hair plastered to his head. "Smart lad. You always were. Lead on, then."

They reached the house only a few moments later, the cat greeting them and complaining loudly at having been left alone while her master had obviously been out on a walk without her. Enric ruffled the fur on Urban's head in passing then hung up his cloak, while Orrin concentrated and moments later his clothes started steaming as he dried them with magic. The cat circled him curiously, sniffing the warm, humid air around him and then followed the men when they walked into the parlour to take a seat on a settee each.

Orrin stared at the cat. "I wonder how your beast will react to having a toddler nearby."

"Flee. We tested it in Takhan on Eryn's niece. It's quite a sight to see her running away from a four-year-old girl while grown man hold back in fear," he smiled at the memory of Obal and Vran'el.

"Cold-blooded," he remarked, still not taking his eyes of the animal.

Enric shrugged. "Maybe. But Urban didn't suffer any permanent damage."

The older man looked up in confusion, then smiled faintly when the joke sank in. "Do you have a glass for me? I am not normally the kind that drinks expensive liquor from the bottle. Makes me feel like a street drunkard. One wants to retain at least the pretence of decorum, after all. Doesn't do to show weakness in the upper ranks of the Order, eh?"

The host rose to fetch two glasses and placed them on the small table in front of them. "Depends on who is watching, I would say."

Orrin filled the glasses halfway and placed the bottle on the table without putting the cork back in. He regarded his opposite number thoughtfully.

"*You* are watching. But not as closely as Lord Tyront. Very fond of his spies, he is," he murmured. "Probably knows already that we were roaming the streets."

That was likely, Enric agreed, but didn't say anything out loud.

"I don't approve of what he has done. To you and Eryn. Just watching when you were being made to join like that." He shook his head vigorously, as if freeing his ear of an insect. "And not telling you about the visit of the ambassador back then."

Enric remained silent.

"Joining somebody shouldn't be something you are made to do," he continued and stared up at the ceiling. "I have been thinking about asking Junar. But somehow I have never got around to it, worrying about her bad experience with her first companion. Might be she has no intention of taking a risk like that ever again." He took a generous sip from his glass and swirled the remaining liquor around, watching oily streaks clinging to the glass. His superior had been generous with his selection, but then he had probably nothing cheap in his cabinet anyway.

"*Wherever Orrin often lingers You will find toes or ears or fingers, That were part of a student's body That walks the land now maimed and bloody,*" he quoted the lines from the poem Enric had written about him about twenty years ago and chuckled. "What a bother you were. Your laziness wouldn't have been so annoying if you hadn't been so clever. But not clever enough to stop rebelling against that father of yours by fighting every attempt at teaching you. Not back then."

Enric smiled in reminiscence. "You were about my age then."

"Yes. And you are Junar's age." He sighed. "Junar. I am old enough to be her father. Old enough to be the grandfather of that baby."

Good, Enric thought, they had arrived at that topic finally.

"True," he said lightly, "but then you are a magician. From what we learned in Takhan you are in the lucky position to prolong your life for several decades and make yourself look younger while doing so. So it's not as if you won't see that child grow up. Or be likely to die before you have grandchildren."

Orrin stared at him. "I have heard about that. It hasn't seemed like a particularly attractive option but rather strange and unnatural. Until now."

They each stared at different spots on the wall without saying anything for many seconds.

"You did a good job with Vern," Enric then ventured. "Amazing boy. In so many ways."

The older warrior closed his eyes. "Luck, nothing more than luck. If it hadn't been for the recent developments, he would be forced to choose between an administrative position and being a reluctant warrior. Neither working in healing nor drawing would have been on the table."

"Probably," the younger man shrugged. "But seeing a chance and seizing it are still two different things. Not every warrior would have seen any value in his son's turning his back on fighting and following his true talents the way he has. A lesser man might have seen it as disregard for his own profession."

Orrin smiled. "A lesser man. What distinguishes a better man from a lesser one, then, Enric?"

Enric, the younger man thought. It had been thirteen years since he had last been addressed without his title by Orrin. It felt right, though. Like something long overdue. Should he have offered it before, he wondered? Would Orrin have accepted it? Probably not. The last year had not been free of tension. The more amazing it was that they were now sitting together like that, discussing where fate had led them.

"The way he treats others, I would like to think," Enric mused.

"Then we both proved to be lesser men indeed in our dealings with Eryn after she was brought here, didn't we?"

"Not you," Enric shook his head. "That's why Tyront picked you. He knew you wouldn't break her. Like you haven't tried to break me. Neither when I was a boy, nor when I was made second-in-command."

"Starting it all again," Orrin muttered. "A child. I am too old for it. People will laugh at me."

"As long as you are strong enough not to take cheek from my companion, I'd say you are not too old to raise a child. And people don't laugh at you. They don't dare," he added dryly. "Which is probably another indicator that you are hardly too old. For anything. Probably never will be until you fall down dead clutching a sword in your hand while training a bunch of stubborn youngsters."

"A warrior's favoured death," the combat trainer sighed. "Raising Vern was not easy. I am not exactly the warm and nurturing kind. That's why he clung to Eryn so closely after she arrived here. An older woman who gave him the attention he needed so desperately. Who appreciated and at the same time mentored him."

Enric looked unconvinced. "Warm maybe not, but the supportive kind you are and always have been. And will again be with your second child. This time it will be easier. You have Junar." Eryn, he thought. Yes, she had been good with Vern, very much so. A shame that she was so dead set against having children herself. He would have loved to see her in the role as mother.

Orrin watched the expression on Enric's face growing thoughtful and a bit regretful. That was not a usual sight. One that made him seem more human, less cold and invincible, though never weak. He looked at the empty glass in front of the younger man and smiled to himself. Maybe it was time for a refill. He leaned forward to grab the bottle and do just that. It was easier to talk to a man of flesh and blood instead of that marble statue the city knew him as. Though that perception had changed since Eryn had arrived and caused a few visible ruptures in the stonework.

"Junar said she wouldn't make me bear the consequences," he sighed. "That means she thinks she has to leave me. To not inflict on me what Vern's mother did so many years ago." He rubbed his face. "I can't let her do that. I am terrified of raising another child at my age. And I am even more terrified of *not* having the chance to do it."

Enric took his glass and stared at the golden liquid. "I understand that very well," he said quietly. "So you had better hold on to both of them."

Orrin regarded him closely. There was some regret there. And, he realised, envy.

* * *

Eryn slowly opened her eyes and turned her head immediately to escape the searching rays of sunlight. Her back was stiff and one of her legs hung down from the over-short sofa she had fallen asleep on. She was relieved at not feeling any after effects of the few glasses she had indulged in yesterday evening. Vern was very likely on his way to fetch Orrin from their house, as Enric had sent a note that this was where he had spent the night.

She rose stiffly from her resting place and walked the few steps to the bedroom door, still closed. The aroma of freshly-baked bread buns reached her nostrils as she passed the table. Vern had obviously ordered breakfast before he had left.

Holding her ear against the door, she tried to discern any noises that would point to Junar's being awake. She looked slightly alarmed when she heard something scratching quietly. A moment later the door burst open and Eryn cried out, tumbling forward, finding herself on all fours on the carpet.

"Really now," she complained, "is that a way to treat an eavesdropper?"

"What are you doing?" Junar asked confusedly.

"I was trying to figure out if you were already awake. I didn't want to wake you." She climbed back to her feet. "But now that you are, we can have breakfast." She scanned inside the bedroom. "In here. The bed looks cosy. Get back in it - I'll fetch the tray."

Junar looked exhausted, as if she had not had a particularly restful night. Which was no wonder, of course.

"I am not hungry."

Eryn shrugged, determined not to let herself be brushed off like that. "Then you will keep me company while I fill Orrin's bed with breadcrumbs. It's one of those things a lady can do only when the bed owner's girlfriend keeps her company. It would look strange if he returned here and found me in his bed alone, seemingly waiting for him. He would drag me to Enric and I would have to try and explain everything to both of them." She turned to pick up the tray. "And you should eat a bite or at least drink something. That's free advice from your personal healer. Well, one of them."

Junar stood in the doorway, obviously unsure of what to do. Returning to Orrin's bed had clearly not been her intention.

"Go on, back into bed with you. I am not going to let you leave the room until I have made that bed of his a lot scruffier," Eryn insisted and carefully balanced the heavy tray on one arm to grab Junar and pull her along with the other hand.

Her friend was sparing with words, so she continued with her chatter. "I love those bread buns of yours. You get your food from the Palace kitchen, don't you? That's the only thing I miss since we have moved out of the Palace," she sighed. "The breakfasts. So I am not too displeased that I won't have to share this with you. It will have to keep me happy until I find another excuse to have breakfast here. Why do adults never have sleepovers? Not that I had many as a child, mind you. Too dangerous, I might have given away my secret. But I knew other children who had. Next time we do this, you come to my place and we make Enric sleep in the guest room and spend the night gossiping and eating sweets."

"Eryn," Junar said quietly, "I am afraid. Of being alone. And unable to cope with all this."

Eryn let out the breath that would otherwise have been converted into more meaningless jabber. "Don't. Even if things do not work out the way they should, there is always a place for you at my home." She smiled and pulled Junar into an embrace. "Enric would hardly mind having our own live-in seamstress to boast of. It's the kind of decadence he appreciates."

Junar gave her a teary smile when she released her again.

They heard the entrance door opening and two pairs of feet moved towards the open bedroom door. Orrin walked in determinedly, looking unshaven and wild, his hair standing on end, his clothes crumpled. He lifted his index finger to point at a wide-eyed Junar.

"You will join me as my companion!" he all but barked. "I will not tolerate any resistance in that matter. If it turns out to be a girl, don't even think of calling it *Eryn*. I am not a great friend of challenging fate like that." He stared at Eryn with narrowed eyes and his finger swerved to point at her, this time in warning. "And when I get back from the washroom, I don't want to find a single crumb in my bed!" With that he turned and stomped away, leaving both women staring after him in shock.

Eryn turned to Junar, who had begun sobbing softly. "What does he think?" she cried out. "No need to be upset! Don't worry, I will..." She stopped when her friend said something. "What was that?"

"I am not upset," Junar sobbed and smiled, "I am happy."

"You are *what*?" the healer called out incredulously. "How can you be happy after a proposal like that? It was a command, no less! I wouldn't let him go through with that!"

Junar took her hand, squeezing it affectionately. "Eryn, that's the way he needs to do things. And I don't mind letting him. He is kind and generous, and I really, *really* want to keep him. And he wants to keep me. To keep *us*. I don't mind how he phrases it. I find it even flattering that he thought I might consider resisting him. The seamstress rejecting the noble warrior!" She laughed while another tear ran over her cheek. "How absurd! I am ashamed that I was ready to give him up that easily."

Vern coughed from his place at the door. "I don't want to disturb this very female and emotional moment, but I have to, as I see the breakfast on a tray that was originally intended to be my second breakfast disappearing in Eryn's greedy fangs. Come on - at least share with the pregnant lady!" He walked the few steps to the bed and climbed on it, snatching away a bread bun before Eryn could react.

"Second breakfast!" she exclaimed. "You greedy glutton! We haven't even had our first! And I can't get these buns for breakfast anymore, so let *me* have them for once!"

"Get your own! And you should return to Lord Enric at once; he is surely worried about your being out of his sight for several hours at one go. There is no saying what trouble you might have got yourself into, after all," he sneered.

"You do know that I am still your superior, don't you? Both as a magician and as a healer! I order you to give those two bread buns back!"

"Superior? Really? You throw that at me while you are lying with me in my father's bed? Let's talk about appropriate leadership, shall we?" he shot back, grinning broadly.

"Brute," she murmured.

"Termagant," he retorted.

"Glutton," she replied.

Junar shook her head at them. "That child will really not be allowed to play with the two of you. You are terrible role models!" Then she snatched a bread bun from Vern's hand. "And that is *mine*. Now get out of my bed and get yourselves ready for whatever you are supposed to be doing today. Vern, I am sure you are supposed to be in class right now. Eryn, you are almost certainly due at the clinic, whether it is a treatment day or not. Be off with you!" Then she leaned back contentedly, smiling at herself as they stared at her. "Dear me, I am already quite good at this child-rearing thing! A natural, it would seem."

Vern snorted and looked at Eryn. "I pity the kid. Being raised by a warrior and our born-of-Nature mother here will hardly be a walk along Kingsway for the poor brat."

She shrugged. "Not my problem. Give me that bun." She snatched it from his hand and grinned when he cursed.

CHAPTER 10

Orrin's Troubles

Tyront sighed and held up a sheet of paper that bore Eryn's seal.

"Your companion keeps pestering me about making basic healing skills a compulsory part of the teaching schedule," he sighed. "This is the second letter in as many weeks. And that from a woman who does not normally send anything to me if she can help it. I think she only does it because she knows that it will unnerve me."

Enric smiled. "This does not surprise me in the least. I rather wonder what stopped her from demanding it earlier. I take it you are not in favour of the idea?"

"There is a trouble from making things compulsory, you see. People tend to resist. Especially as there does not yet seem to be a general agreement for considering healing a positive development. There are still quite a few magicians who are not too thrilled with the way things have been turning out. Healing is to them still something outlandish that needs to be avoided as much as possible. I have heard discussions, well, I had them reported by somebody who has heard them," he amended, "where magicians said that healing the human body robs it of the natural ability to repair itself."

The younger man raised a brow. "I wonder how they would react if they had to suffer a serious injury that would cause them to lose a limb. I doubt they would still insist on letting the body do its own mending the way Nature intended."

"That is likely, yes. Yet however absurd their reasons for rejecting it are, many of them have children or grandchildren and would not react well to having them more or less forced to learn it," Tyront pointed out. "I don't have to tell you that I cannot afford to alienate the Council members through something like this. Though I don't have much hope of getting Eryn to understand that," he sighed. "I tried to discuss it with her two days ago when she delivered her status update, but she got angry, telling me to not let the considerations of stupid people hold me back from doing what is good for all of us, the stupid ones included. What am I supposed to say to that? Defend the rights of the stupid? Tell her that there is no law against being stupid?"

"Better not," Enric laughed. "Her next letter might otherwise be a demand for just such a law."

"I wonder where she gets the energy from. One would think she is busy enough with her orphanage project and Junar's pregnancy in addition to her usual duties."

"She doesn't really do a lot herself when it comes to the orphanage. But I would have thought you knew about that, you live with the woman who *does* take care of everything in connection with it."

The older man rolled his eyes. "That's what one would think, yes. But Vyril has decided that as I am not at liberty to talk about most aspects of my work with her, she will adapt to this same policy and also not tell me about hers. I think she is enjoying that new-found importance very much," he remarked dryly. "It seems being a magician's companion is not the right occupation for every woman. But then who am I telling this to? Are you aware that you and I are the only magicians with working companions? Well, Orrin will soon join that elevated circle. When did he schedule the commitment?"

"In three days. They want to keep it very small and simple, as Junar had a large ceremony the first time and doesn't feel the need for another one. She says that from her experience a grand celebration is hardly a guarantee for a happy companionship but often enough only a waste of money. And she tires more easily these days, so organising a large festivity is not in her interest, especially as she does not exactly enjoy social gatherings as such. Just like Eryn. Those two have found each other alright," he commented.

Tyront smiled. "Orrin finally taking a companion. Who would have thought it? And having another child, as well; I was surprised enough when he ended up with the first one. He is only a little younger than I. I wonder how this happened." He took a sheet of paper out of one of his drawers. "I was told that her former companion left her because she couldn't have children. Eryn doesn't happen to have anything to do with that, does she?"

Enric wasn't surprised that there was a report about Junar in that monstrosity of a desk with its many drawers. He wondered how many hidden compartments there were and what kind of dark secrets they held.

"According to the letter her uncle sent her, that seems indeed to be the case. Eryn healed a gland in Junar's throat at the ball before we left for Takhan because it was not working properly. That gland, it seems, was the sole reason for Junar's infertility, and after it was given attention it was restored to normal function. With all that entailed. Eryn is somewhat angry at herself for that. She said that she needs to learn more, so things like that just don't happen again."

"Well, the healer from Takhan should be arriving in only a few weeks. That should give her ample opportunity to extend her knowledge."

"Yes, she is very much looking forward to that. She had Rolan prepare a study at the clinic and has started going through the books for the exams her uncle sent her. That woman never really manages to lean back and do nothing for even a short while."

The older man smiled. "I don't recall seeing you idle in these last years, either. How are you dealing with that mind bond of yours? Have you got used to it by now?"

Enric shrugged. "Fairly much, yes. Though every time I sense a strong emotion from her I wonder what she has been up to. That is quite a distraction at times. She is doing some experimentation on it, but so far there have been no ground-breaking discoveries." He didn't let the chummy atmosphere entice him into thinking that this conversation was anything other than a report to his superior.

"How is the ambassador settling in? I hope Eryn refrains from displaying her dislike for him too openly."

"She is trying to avoid him as best she can. After exchanging a polite greeting with him she usually turns to his assistant. She gets along much better with *him*."

Tyront smiled. "Which is handy, isn't it? As he happens to be one who really matters. I wonder a bit about Sanaf's lack of decorum when it comes to conversations, though. One would think he would be a little more sensitive to what is accepted in our society. Do you remember the welcoming banquet, when he complimented Inad on the work she had done on her upper arms? She almost passed out from embarrassment. Though I distinctly recall your companion's badly concealed amusement. A hastily lifted napkin may cover the smile on her mouth, but not the malevolent glint in her eyes."

Enric nodded. "I was glad enough she didn't laugh out loud. I think it was one of the few occasions when she has actually enjoyed herself at one of these gatherings."

"I hear the dinner invitation at Lord Seagon's two days ago was very entertaining as well. Orrin inadvertently made the forthcoming addition to his family public knowledge."

"It's the way he is treating Junar," the younger man chuckled. "Like something very breakable and delicate that must be protected from every sharp point or whatever other dangers are lurking around every possible corner. People noticed that quite soon and started whispering amongst themselves. When Junar then took him aside and told him that she was pregnant, not fatally ill, well of course there was somebody close enough to hear and spread the news. By now it is common knowledge."

"Well, it's not like they could have hidden it forever. It is bound to show in a few months. Come in!" he then called out when there was an urgent knock at his study door.

A servant opened the door, permitting a breathless messenger. Both men arose. This did not have the hallmark of good news.

"Lord Enric," the messenger panted, "Lady Eryn sends for you. She says to come immediately. Lord Orrin has attacked a man and is now being accused by him of having used magic against a non-magician."

Tyront turned to his second-in-command. "You go. Have the man who was attacked brought to me here. As Eryn is there, I imagine he shouldn't be suffering from any injuries now and so should be able to walk. You need to talk to Orrin and find out what is going on here. Maybe we can avoid a Council hearing."

Enric nodded once for confirmation and indicated for the messenger to lead the way.

Orrin had attacked a man? That was unusual. There must have been some very strong provocation indeed.

He motioned to one of the Palace guards to follow them as well so he could send the man back to Tyront later.

The messenger led him towards the city centre along Kingsway and then turned right. Enric soon recognised the street where Junar's shop was located, and only a short while later he indeed beheld a crowd of onlookers, indicating that something must have happened there.

He saw Orrin standing to one side, holding a very distressed looking Junar in his arms. Eryn stood with her arms folded, in front of a lean, angry-looking man in his late thirties who was shouting something at Orrin. The words he couldn't make out, but the tone sounded accusatory. Enric wondered at the wisdom of provoking a man such as Orrin like that.

Vern stood on the other side of Junar, watching the shouting man with narrowed eyes.

"What happened here?" Enric enquired once he had got close enough. Eryn turned and immediately looked relieved to see him.

"It seems this person here," she pointed to the man in front of her, "is Junar's former companion. He came to talk to her while Orrin was out buying something. However," she flashed the man an angry look, "his temper seems to have got the better of him and he started bawling at Junar and even grabbed her by the shoulders and shook her."

Ah yes, Enric thought grimly - a man shaking his pregnant companion, whom he was immensely protective of, was of course something to make Orrin react with physical force.

"That is an outright lie!" the man protested. "I never even laid a finger on her!"

"Didn't you?" Eryn snapped at him. "Then you surely will have no objection to repeating that while I use a truth block on you, right?"

That made him hesitate for a moment before he admitted, "Well - not shaking as such, I mean. Not really. A tiny bit."

Enric motioned to the guard he had brought with him and instructed him to escort the man to Lord Tyront, then turned back to Eryn. "Why are *you* here?"

"They sent for me because the man was injured and Vern had refused to heal him." She turned her head to look at the boy, rage blazing on her face. "Come here, you."

Vern's jaw was set stubbornly when he came closer, obviously preparing himself for the storm that was about to hit him.

Eryn lifted her index finger and stabbed him in the chest with it. "If I ever hear about your not healing an injured person who is before you, I am going to tan your hide, you can rely on that! Everybody has the right to medical help and we do not - and let me be quite clear about that - absolutely not discriminate between people we like and those we don't. We can't have people worrying about who is on duty when they attend the clinic! Imagine Junar needed something and was refused treatment because she happened to get into an argument with a healer... You must never decide who gets help; none of us must! You see an injury, you do something about it!"

"He touched Junar!" Vern protested angrily.

"Then your father has put a stop to it! Aren't you listening? You are not the one to choose whether somebody gets to be healed! Nobody here is! And we certainly cannot deal out punishment to people by not healing them! Have I made myself clear?"

Vern pressed his lips together and nodded briskly.

"Good. Now go home. I expect Enric will want a word with Junar and Orrin now."

"I will stay with them," he protested.

"No, you won't," she objected, then took him by the shoulders and twisted him around in the direction he was supposed to walk. "I will stay with them myself. You go home and keep out of the way."

The boy turned and gave his father and Junar a pained look before reluctantly walking off.

Enric walked over to the two of them. "Come on, we need to talk. Our house is closer than the Palace." Without waiting for an answer, he turned and heard three pairs of feet fall into step behind him. Of course Eryn would not be returning to the clinic right now.

A few minutes later he opened the entrance door for them and walked ahead into his study where he took a seat behind his desk. He was now acting as Orrin's superior, and that had to be clear to all present.

"Lord Orrin," he said when all of them had taken a seat. "Tell me what happened."

"Vern and I were accompanying Junar to her shop and left her there. She needed to pick up fabric samples or something similar. Vern and I decided to get some bread while we were waiting for her to finish. When we came back, the door to the shop was ajar and I heard loud voices from inside, one of them Junar's. When I walked into the shop, I saw that man with his hands on her shoulders, shaking her, while she kept yelling at him to take his hands off." His stare was furious and fixed to the desk in front of him, as if he was reliving the scene once more. "He didn't see me coming in. When he didn't remove his hands, I bodily dragged him away from Junar and punched him. Twice. Once in the face, once in the abdomen. He collapsed. Vern knelt down in front of him and did his diagnosis thing. It seems I had broken the man's cheekbone and two ribs. Vern said something about a ruptured spleen, whatever that is. He refused to heal the man and sent somebody to fetch Eryn instead. She came here and healed the man, then sent somebody to bring you."

Enric let his breath out slowly. "Where was that control you have kept lecturing me about over more than ten years?"

Orrin smiled weakly. "Where was it the day Eryn was attacked by the apothecaries and you almost laid into *them* after finding her lying on the floor?"

Eryn's head snapped towards her companion. What?

Enric's eyes narrowed. How on earth did he know about that?

"I like to maintain good contacts with the Palace guards," the combat trainer explained, as if reading Enric's thoughts. "Every now and then one learns interesting things. Such as the air crackling with magic and Lord Tyront threatening to take you down a peg if you didn't behave yourself."

Enric felt Eryn's surprise at the revelation. He turned to Junar. "Eryn said that the man is your former companion. What did he want from you?"

Junar sighed, and Orrin put his arm around her shoulders to pull her against him. "He heard about my being pregnant. The news seems to have spread through the city like a wildfire. He was so angry, accusing me of deliberately avoiding having children with him during the time we were joined. I told him that this wasn't true, but he didn't believe me and just became angrier and angrier. Then he grabbed me and started shaking me - I was so afraid he would hurt me. Or the baby." Her hand went down to her flat abdomen.

"Lord Orrin, the messenger told me that the man is accusing you of using magic against him. Did you?"

"No, I did not," he said simply.

"Not even to enhance your muscle strength and be able to hit harder?"

"No."

Enric regarded him thoughtfully, then nodded. "Very well. Tyront is talking to... what is his name again?" He looked at Junar questioningly.

"Orlek," she supplied.

"Tyront is talking to Orlek right now. We will see what the next steps in this matter should be." He arose and stepped away from his desk. The official part was over. "How are you doing, Junar?" he asked gently.

The seamstress smiled weakly. "A bit shaken, but otherwise everything is fine. Vern checked me. And Eryn, too."

"Then I would suggest returning home now."

Orrin nodded and turned to Eryn. "Is Vern in trouble for not healing that man?"

She nodded. "He is, yes. But only with me. Nothing you need to worry about."

He closed his eyes for a moment, then picked up Junar's cloak to spread it across her shoulders before they left.

Eryn leaned against a bookshelf. "Is he in trouble?"

"Probably. If Orlek persists in his accusation of Orrin's having used magic against a non-magician, then there will be a hearing before the Magic Council."

"Do you believe he used magic? He denies it."

Enric shook his head. "No, I don't think so. His punches are forceful enough without magic. Believe me, I experienced them often enough when he was training me in unarmed combat. When he hits you during your training, he holds himself back. Rather a lot, I might add."

"He broke two ribs and ruptured a spleen! And that without magic?" she frowned. But then she remembered Enric hitting Ram'an back then when he had tried to make her dance to the seductive music. Ram'an had been thrown back and over an entire seating arrangement before hitting a wall or column. That had been done without magic as well.

"So it should be fairly easy, shouldn't it? You could make Orrin repeat his statement that he didn't use magic, under the influence of a truth block. That would surely convince the Council, wouldn't it?"

"I am afraid it is not quite that simple. Magicians often use their magic without realising it when it comes to things we do automatically. Orrin is a trained fighter, he might have enhanced his muscles without even realising it. That makes the statement using a truth block useless."

Eryn frowned in dismay. "And there is no other way to prove that he is strong enough to do this without magic?"

"There is one, but that is not something we want to try," Enric said grimly.

"Which one?"

"Shackling him in gold, letting him punch somebody and then comparing the injuries."

She swallowed. "Dear me. There won't be many volunteers for that, I imagine."

"I would volunteer. But not with the mind bond in place. You would feel the pain."

"You would do this?" she asked gently. "To get him out of trouble?" She thought back to the tension between them only months ago. It truly was amazing how much had changed between them.

"I would have, yes. But my priorities have changed now. He has Junar to protect, I have you," he said.

She shook her head sadly. "Then I truly have become a liability."

He stepped towards her and leaned his forehead against hers. "I know what you are trying to do here. It will not work. I will not cause you pain to help him, no matter how willing you are to endure it."

She let herself be pulled into an embrace, wondering how to make him change his mind.

* * *

Eryn made herself lean back and relax as much as was possible in this situation. Lord Tyront had acted fast. As Orlek had persisted in accusing Orrin of using magic in hurting a non-magician, a Council meeting had been scheduled only one day later. A high-ranking Order member being accused of a thing like that needed to be dealt with as quickly as possible.

She was staring at the double doors to the Council hall. They had summoned her here to testify as a witness to report the injuries that Orrin had inflicted on Orlek. They were not particularly happy about having to ask her to do it, Enric told her, but the alternative would have been Vern, and that was even worse. How could they ask a sixteen-year-old boy to give evidence which would disadvantage his own father? But of course they would ask it of *her*. She was known to be Orrin's friend, but then she was number three in the Order and expected not to let that influence the execution of her duty.

The double doors opened and a Palace guard motioned for her to enter.

"Lady Eryn," he announced before she walked in and took in the round table with eleven of the twelve Council members. Orrin would of course not sit with them this time. He was made to stand in front of them, the accused, made to justify himself before his colleagues. He looked tense, but it was the tension of a man who seemed determined to face whatever he needed to, not one caused by fear or dread. He was willing to brave whatever was thrown at him. Courageous Orrin, she thought, and stepped beside him, resisting the urge to squeeze his arm or otherwise touch him in reassurance.

Everything would turn out well. She was determined to make sure of that.

On one side of the room was the throne, and just like the last time she had been summoned here to remove the barrier inside their heads, it was occupied. So the King wanted to witness this in person, not relying on his informants in this event. But then why would he want to miss the show?

"Lady Eryn," Lord Tyront spoke. "You have been summoned to bear witness to the injuries you found when you were sent for yesterday and examined Orlek before healing him. Should the Council have reason to doubt the veracity of your words, we will be forced to employ a truth block to verify what you say."

She understood this was a warning for her not to lie about the injuries, diminish the extent of harm she had seen. She gave him a forced smile. "I assure you that will not be necessary. I would not lie to the Council."

His considered look and raised eyebrow gave her a good idea of how credible he considered *those* words.

"That is a relief to hear, My Lady," he smiled coldly. "Be so kind as to let us hear what you found upon your arrival at the scene."

"I found a man lying on the floor of Junar's shop, clutching his upper abdomen and breathing rapidly. In addition he was bleeding from his left nostril and his cheek was visibly swollen. When I examined him, I found his spleen ruptured and two ribs and his cheekbone fractured."

"How severe would you say these injuries were?" Lord Tyront enquired.

"The ruptured spleen might have turned out to be a problem in time. The blood loss could have led to unconsciousness in a while and at some point he might even have died. But we are talking about days here, as the rupture was not that extensive. I expect he would have found his own way to the clinic before then or somebody would have summoned a healer to help him. This is only one possible scenario, mind you. I don't have too much experience in watching an injury like that run its course, I usually tend to heal it once I see such a thing," she explained calmly. "The two or rather three fractured bones would have healed in time, though not without causing pain for some weeks."

Enric gave her a short nod of approval. So she had obviously appeared worthy of trust. Very satisfying. She doubted that her next words would earn her any additional applause from his side.

"Is there any additional information you require concerning Orlek's physical status yesterday?"

Lord Tyront shook his head. "No, that will be all, thank you very much. You may leave now. Thank you for your cooperation."

She remained standing where she was, raising her head. "If I may be so bold as to speak out of turn, gentlemen? I wish to make a proposal that might shed light upon the question that brought us all here - namely whether Lord Orrin used magic in hitting that man or not."

She saw Enric frowning for a short moment before realisation dawned on him. She could feel the rage inside him boiling up. He jumped to his feet. "No! I cannot permit that!"

Lord Tyront looked at both of them in turn, then motioned for Enric to be seated again. "What proposal would that be?"

"I can prove to you that Lord Orrin had no need to make use of magic to cause those injuries. He is a trained warrior with considerable physical strength," she explained. "I would like to ask for the Council's permission for a little demonstration."

Lord Tyront regarded her for a moment, then turned to the other magicians. "Show of hands. Are there any objections against the demonstration Lady Eryn is offering us?"

Heads shook, only one hand was raised. Enric's.

"Go on, then," he told her and watched her take out a pair of golden manacles before she turned to Orrin.

"Orrin?" she said softly. "Your hands, please."

He looked into her eyes, clearly confused, but did as she told him. "What are you up to?" he asked quietly.

She didn't answer, but fastened the shackles around his wrists and closed the seams with magic, robbing him of his command over his magical powers.

Enric rose from his seat and turned to the Council members. "I must ask you to put a stop to this. Now. Or *I* will."

"You will do no such thing," his superior warned him. "Sit."

But Enric ignored him and pushed back his chair to march the few paces to his companion and grab her upper arm to turn her to him.

"What do you think you are doing here?" he hissed. "I forbid it. Do you hear me? This is an order!"

Eryn freed herself from his grip. Her voice was calm and apologetic. "I am sorry, Enric. But you can't order me not to do it when Lord Tyront has approved. Take a seat, will you?"

Orrin watched the two of them suspiciously. "What is going on here?"

Enric closed his eyes for a moment, then opened them again and looked at the warrior. "Eryn wants you to hit her to show the Council that you don't need magic to hurt somebody."

"What?" Orrin boomed and turned to her angrily. "You take those manacles off me right now! Have you gone completely crazy? I am not going to hit you!"

She placed herself right in front of him, folding her arms, taking a few calming breaths. "You will. This is an order."

The world seemed to stop when for several seconds nobody moved, as if time itself had frozen.

"No." His voice was not loud, but carried well enough in the silence to reverberate in the high-ceilinged hall.

"You will either follow my order, Lord Orrin, or you will face a charge of insubordination in addition to the one you have to face already," she threatened him. "And no holding back. This is supposed to be a demonstration of what you can do without physical restraint, after all."

Orrin started at her, not even seeing the furious gaze in Enric's face that warned him not to dare and raise a hand against her. Then he slowly turned to the Council.

"I admit to having used magic to increase my strength and hit Orlek harder," he stated with grim determination.

Eryn grabbed his arm and held on to it with the aid of a little magic when he wanted to free himself and then bound him with a truth block.

"Repeat that," she barked at him. "Now."

He opened his mouth, then closed it again when the words refused to come out. His glare was deadly. "Stop that right now," he growled. "I am not going to hit you, whatever you do. I appreciate what you are trying to do, but no. That is not worth it."

Enric drew in a deep breath, then grabbed Eryn's shoulders and steered her away from Orrin. He just lifted a finger and gave her a warning stare when she attempted to object. Then he turned back to the accused, stepping before him.

"Lord Orrin, you were completely correct in choosing not to hit Lady Eryn, and I commend you on your chivalry. There will be no consequences for not obeying that particular order," he said loud enough for all present to hear him. "The Council, however, has expressed a wish to see the demonstration Lady Eryn has promised them. You will thus oblige them by hitting *me* instead."

Orrin shook his head at him. "What difference is it supposed to make for her which of you I hit with your bloody bond?" he yelled.

"The difference," Enric said fiercely, "is that *I* will take the blows, not her. She will heal me immediately afterwards, so this is a matter of no more than two or three minutes if you cooperate. Hit me. And make it count."

The older man didn't move, his eyes flickered to Eryn for a moment, then he shook his head. "No. I cannot."

"Don't be a fool, Orrin," Enric murmured. "She wants to do this for you. As I would have, with no hesitation, without the mind bond. She will suffer a lot more and for longer if you are made to pay unjustly for protecting Junar."

Orrin closed his eyes for several seconds, then nodded resignedly before he opened them again.

"Lady Eryn," the King's voice rang out, "You may want to sit down for this."

She looked at him, missing the usual smile when he demonstrated knowledge people didn't expect him to have. Enric had been right. He knew well enough about the mind bond. And he did not look forward to seeing it in effect in this case. She went to sit down in Enric's chair and grabbed the armrests tightly, bracing herself for the pain that would soon come.

She watched Orrin pull back his arm and a moment later she heard first the sound of his fist hitting something solid, then only a moment later felt agonising pain in her abdomen, taking her breath away and making even screaming impossible. She dimly felt a warm hand on her shoulder before a second punch made her head explode into shards of glowing hot sparks of agony that took away every other sensation.

Tyront pointed at Lord Poron and barked, "Go and dull his pain, somehow, but hurry!"

Moments later Eryn exhaled in relief when the fist of ache that had held her head and abdomen in a tight grip loosened. Only then did she realise that she was on the floor, curled up in a foetal position with her knees pulled towards her chest and her head in her hands. She hadn't even noticed falling down.

Lord Tyront and the King each held out a hand to her and helped her back to her feet. She saw Enric lying on the floor on his back, staring at the ceiling. She could feel that he was no longer in pain, but the sight of him lying there was like a spear through her innards. Lord Poron was kneeling next to him.

"Lord Poron, can you assess the damage?" Lord Tyront asked.

The healer closed his eyes and put his hand on the recumbent man's arm. "Multiple jaw fractures, three broken ribs on the left side. And..." His eyes flew open in distress, "his lung is damaged, if only slightly."

Eryn all but ran towards Enric and ripped his robes apart so her hand could touch him where the damage was instead of having to send the magic on a detour through his arm. Her eyes closed and she needed several long moments before she could control the agitation inside her that would make healing him more difficult and thus dangerous. When she felt her breathing calm, she sent in a first searching impulse to locate the small rip in his lung. She could see the pressure in his lung decreasing slowly and started mending the rip immediately, careful not to work too fast in her eagerness to restore him. When the damage to his lung was mended, she moved her attention to the three ribs that were fractured, healing them one after the other. Then she put her other hand on his cheek without opening her eyes and started at the shape his jaw was in. It was broken in three places. She worked on each fracture. When she had at last repaired the final area of damage, she opened her eyes to look down upon him again and into blue eyes that were fixed on her face.

Enric sat up slowly, took a tentative breath and then felt around his jaw, satisfied when nothing hurt or felt different to the touch.

He then got to his feet and pulled Eryn up as well. The Council members and the King were no longer seated on their chairs or throne, but were standing around them in a circle and had been the last twenty minutes Eryn had been working on him.

"I don't know about you, but from what I have just experienced I would assume that Lord Orrin does not need to harness magic to hurt a man if he so desires. And let me point out that he hit me reluctantly, while yesterday he had been provoked and was therefore angry when he punched Orlek. I marvel at his not suffering greater injury than he did," he added pointedly.

The Council members exchanged looks and Tyront sighed. "You heard about the injuries Lord Orrin caused a trained fighter like Lord Enric is with a mere two punches. Which of you doubts that Lord Orrin was able to inflict the injuries on the man who was manhandling Junar without the use of magic?" Not a single hand was raised. He nodded, then asked, "Which of you thinks that Lord Orrin is strong enough to have caused the injuries without magic and should thereby be cleared of the accusations of having used magic to hurt a non-magician?"

Eleven hands went up without hesitation.

Tyront nodded and stepped towards Orrin to remove the golden shackles. "Congratulations, Lord Orrin. You have been cleared."

The warrior nodded once and shot Eryn an evil look before he turned and left the Council hall with large, angry strides.

Eryn sighed and turned to Lord Tyront. "You couldn't order him not to be mad at me, could you?"

Tyront raised his brow at her. "It would be like ordering you to show more respect," he replied.

She grimaced. "That unlikely, eh?"

Lord Woldarn, one of the senior Council members, cleared his throat. "I would say some explanation of that very interesting phenomenon we just witnessed is in order. How come Lady Eryn collapsed to the floor herself when Lord Enric was being hit? This was a rather more... vivid reaction than mere compassion would warrant."

So the great moment had come to make it known to the world, Eryn sighed quietly and looked up at Enric. He put an arm around her shoulders and started to address his colleagues.

"What you have just witnessed is referred to as a mind bond and is a rather rare and unexpected consequence of the third level commitment bond we entered into in the Western Territories. It couples strong emotions between us, of which pain is one, unfortunately."

For a few moments nobody said anything, then Lord Seagon nodded. "Then your willingness to demonstrate Lord Orrin's ability to cause physical damage was an even greater sacrifice than it might have appeared at first glance."

"Which also explains Lord Orrin's foul mood just now. For him it was essentially like hitting a woman," another Council member pointed out.

Eryn noted her companion's clenched jaw. For him it had not only been the same as letting another man hit her, but even encouraging him to. She sighed. Somehow she had the feeling that she was about to get an earful once they were alone.

* * *

Eryn felt his fingers digging into her arm when he all but dragged her with him back to their house. She knew he wouldn't start on his tirade as long as they were out on the street. He would wait until they were alone. She thought frantically about choices she had to avoid just that for just a bit longer.

"I need to make a quick stop at the clinic, because there is..."

"No."

She sucked in a sharp breath when they turned the last corner that brought them into view of their house. Orrin was leaning against the wall next to the entrance door, waiting for them. For her.

"No, no, no, no," she protested and tried to free herself from Enric's grip, but he just smiled wickedly and held on to her.

"Well, look who we have here! So nice of him to drop by for a little chat, isn't it?"

"Come on!" she wailed, "Not both of you at once! This is not fair!'

They reached the house and Orrin waited for Enric to open the door and pull a struggling Eryn inside after him before he himself followed.

Eryn blinked in surprise when she found her wrist locked in Orrin's tight grip a moment later. He really was fast. Too fast for her liking.

His green eyes were bright with anger. "Right now I would really, really like to give you a good thrashing, you bloody fool," he hissed.

"Just missed your chance for that, I'm afraid," she shot back and clenched her teeth as he strengthened his grip.

"Do you have any idea what punching a woman is like for me? Hitting somebody weaker? And in your case without the chance of defending yourself?" His voice had become louder with each sentence.

"Come on, Orrin!" she protested. "It was just a few moments of pain, then Lord Poron did something to help me manage it. No harm was done! And your unblemished record of never having hit a woman remains intact as I was not the one who needed physical healing afterwards."

His grin was more a baring of teeth than anything else. "Really? Though that was not your initial plan, was it? I distinctly remember your standing before me and *ordering* me to hit you!"

"An order you chose to ignore!" she growled back, deciding that meeting anger with anger was probably the best strategy. "I am your superior - don't you see how that makes me look in front of others?"

"I don't care in the least what you looked like after ordering me to *hit* you!"

She raised her free hand to pry loose his fingers around her wrist. "I don't see why I am the one having to justify myself when I was just trying to help! And I was the one you disobeyed, so you should be *apologising* to me instead of yelling at me!"

"Apologising?" he roared. "I watched you collapse under my blows, and you think I should *apologise* to you for making me do this? And let me thank you so much for then being placed in the hapless position of being made to strike my *superior*!"

"So you would have preferred being found guilty? They might have booted you out of the Council, taken away your position! How was this not worth a few seconds of pain? I don't see why *I* am the one who is a fool here!" she threw back at him.

"I don't need your protection!"

She blinked. Was that the trouble? Big, strong Orrin couldn't stand being helped out by a woman?

"You would do the same thing for me, wouldn't you? You would hurt any man who laid hand on me," she asked quietly.

He didn't answer, but he didn't have to.

"I can't do that for you. Not really, as nobody would dare attack you. But that doesn't mean that I don't feel the need to protect you as well when you are in trouble. I just do it my way. And what I have learned from training with you is that a good fighter needs to take the blows as well as deal them out. So I chose a warrior's path, didn't I?" She squeezed his hand. "Even though you didn't let me walk it after more than a year of preparing me for it."

Orrin sighed. He seemed to have calmed down now. "Because taking the blows might have been the warrior's path for you, but *dealing them out* wasn't for me."

She grinned at him. "Next time we will make you hit something else. Like a sack of bricks or a stone column."

"Next time." He shook his head in an almost hopeless way. "I have been in more trouble since your arrival here in the city than I was the twenty years before."

Enric gave a disappointed sigh. "I can see you have forgiven her already. Pity. I had hoped for some kind of retribution, to be honest. Would have saved *me* the trouble."

Orrin smiled. "Oh, there will be that. I have just started combat training with the first years. And I hereby wish to request a teaching assistant. I think they would profit a lot from the female approach."

"Granted," Enric said immediately and went to the drinking cabinet to pour himself a glass of wine despite the hour's earliness.

"I don't have time for this!" Eryn wailed. "And I don't see why he is able to punish me for *helping* him! Or why *he* can punish me, anyway!"

"Well, he didn't do it alone. I helped," her companion pointed out. "Let's call it a joint effort, shall we? Does that make you feel any better?"

She just beamed a devastating look at him and turned towards the stairs to get as much distance between herself and the two of them.

CHAPTER 11

Intimate Details

Junar and Eryn stood in front of the tall mirror in Eryn's bedroom regarding their reflections with less than happy expressions.

"Where again is this thing taking place today?" the magician asked wearily. It had been a long day at the clinic, and she would have preferred a hot bath and an early night. But no. The ambassador had been invited to another dinner and this meant she and Enric had been forced to accept as well.

"Lord Seagon's I think," Junar said with equally flat enthusiasm. "Orrin has been unusually eager to go to these occasions lately," she sighed.

"He wants to show you off. That is kind of sweet," Eryn shrugged.

"Why do you fail to find that sweet in Lord Enric's case? Why is it not sweet that he maybe wants to show you off as well?" the seamstress protested.

"Because I am not the kind suitable for being shown off."

"But *I* am?"

"Of course you are. Considerably younger companion to a middle-aged man, an apparently infertile woman impregnated by the mighty warrior. If you are not the kind who should be shown off, I don't know who is," Eryn snorted.

Junar touched her flat belly and smiled. "I suppose I am." Then she turned to her friend to lay a hand on her shoulder, her tone serious. "I never really got to thank you for what you did for Orrin. And I am sorry that he is making you pay for it. And that Lord Enric helped him with it. Idiots, both of them."

The magician rolled her eyes. "Tell me something new. They are just angry because their manly pride was hurt by my proactive approach."

"Well, Orrin's manly pride was hurt by watching you collapse under his punches, more or less. Which I find reassuring. I wouldn't want to be bound to a man who didn't mind about anything like that," she pointed out.

That was a good point, Eryn had to admit. Though being punished for this noble disposition of his was not exactly the best way of making *her* appreciate it.

"Isn't there supposed to be a ball sometime soon?" Junar asked. "I thought the King would give one to welcome the new ambassador. However unjustified that turned out to be."

"You don't like him, either? Good. I was beginning to think I was the only one who didn't."

The seamstress shrugged. "Not particularly. He is awkward. Always making strange remarks that make you wonder whether he is simply socially inept or insulting people on purpose. I can't help but wonder how they could send a man like that here. You said something about his being born into the right family, didn't you? That basically means we can thank *you* for his gracing us with his presence."

Eryn grimaced. "Don't say that! I would have preferred somebody else from the wrong house with better manners. I would rather feel guilty about liking somebody I shouldn't than not liking somebody I am supposed to."

"Really?" Junar looked at her doubtfully. "That is not at all the impression I have from you. Since when have you cared what others expect of you or who you are supposed to like?"

"Since I was adopted into a family that actually likes me and kept me from becoming stuck in Takhan. I owe them loyalty, and not getting along with one of their, or rather *our*, allies is not so great."

"Well, it's not like you are enemies. Though I admit that after Ram'an that new ambassador does seem rather awkward and unappealing. Not that Ram'an's motives were that pure, mind you," Junar sighed. "Are you ready? I would really like to pin up your hair."

Eryn shook her head. "Not tonight. I want to be able to untangle my hairstyle speedily after getting back here, no plucking pins out of my hair for half an hour before I am able to fall into bed. The braiding will have to do. See? I did a more complicated one than usual. With four strands."

"Very sophisticated, yes," the seamstress snorted. "Come on, then - let's get moving. If it is too tedious I will pretend I am unwell and you as my personal healer need to tend to me." She smiled conspiratorially. "We could leave the men there, alone."

"You wouldn't," Eryn sighed. "You have only just been joined, it will probably take you years to reach that level of selfishness."

Junar lifted an eyebrow at her. "*You* would do it without hesitation. And you have only been joined for, what, nine months?"

"*I* am a natural. I was practically born into it."

They descended the stairs and Eryn was surprised that the parlour seemed empty. Then she heard voices coming from Enric's study; the men were standing in front of the window, looking out at the dark street. Only the light of occasional lanterns lent the scene outside some faint glow. They both turned when the women entered.

Enric smiled at the picture they made. Junar elegant in a pastel shades sort of way and with glowing skin, very probably due to her new life circumstances. Next to her Eryn, who was trying to avoid any effort at decoration that exceeded the absolute required minimum and yet could not avoid the classy effect Junar's clothes lent her.

"Good. You are both ready. Orrin and I were discussing your new assignment. We consider that once a week for two hours for the next two months should be sufficient."

She sighed and looked at the warrior intently. "Orrin, don't you remember the effect I had on those kids you dragged to the training sessions with me?"

He smiled. "I do. And be sure that I will warn them not to run when they see you appearing with foam dripping from your mouth again or some similar ruse."

"Spoilsport," she muttered.

"The coach arrived a few minutes ago and is waiting outside, when you are ready," Enric urged them on, aware that his companion would take every chance she would get to defer their departure.

Both men laid cloaks around the women's shoulders, then donned their own before ushering their companions out the door and into the waiting coach.

"Vern asked me to enquire how your experiments with the mind bond are going. Though I just realised that this is a rather intimate question, considering," Junar conceded and steadied herself when the coach started moving with a sudden lurch.

Eryn grinned at Orrin's obvious discomfort. "It is. But I will oblige you as I see that listening to this is much harder for your companion than talking about it is for me. I do like to see him squirming. Happens rarely enough. Since the little incident at Orrin's hearing there has not really been any progress. I still receive his emotions unfiltered. My efforts to shield myself against him haven't really helped at all."

Both men stared at her, then looked at each other as if to see if they had really heard what they thought they had heard.

Enric frowned at her. "This is what you have been experimenting on? Shielding yourself from my emotions?"

She nodded. "Yes. Didn't I tell you?"

"No, you didn't give me any details, just that you were trying something with shields."

"It was Iklan's idea. I have been experimenting on the consistency and nature of the shield, but somehow it doesn't make a difference. None whatever." She frowned in annoyance when Orrin chuckled at something he seemed to see as a private joke. And was even less amused when Enric smiled quietly, as if the two men were sharing the same joke. "May I ask what's so funny about my fruitless efforts?"

"That after all that training you received it seems you have not managed to internalise the one very basic principle of shielding that determines success or failure," the combat trainer explained.

When she just looked puzzled, Enric added, "That a weaker magician cannot shield successfully against a stronger one. Really now. How could that not have occurred to you? You can't shield against *me*, I am much too strong for you."

Eryn rolled her eyes. "This is medical shielding we are talking about here, not a fight where we attack each other with bolts. I can place shields inside your body for medical purposes without any problem. I did so a few days ago when I healed your lung, which was to stop the pressure from falling. And it worked fine, no matter how superior your strength."

"Because I didn't resist it," he pointed out. He reached out for her to take his hand. "Try again."

She clasped his hand and closed her eyes, trying to place a shield inside his chest. He pushed against her with his own powers and she gave up after several attempts.

"Well, you are right," she shrugged and let go of him again, "it doesn't work if you resist. But I am not sure what exactly we have just proven with that."

"That medical shielding follows the same rules as combat shielding," Orrin explained patiently.

"But emotions are hardly subject to combat shielding, are they?" she smiled indulgently.

"Emotions penetrating your internal defences and even robbing you of your consciousness are an attack alright, my love," Enric clarified. "An attack you can't brave. *I* need to be the one doing the shielding, not *you*."

She considered his words, feeling how her heart started beating faster. They did have a point, she thought, excitement suddenly coursing through her veins. Her eyes had started sparkling and she reached out to take his hand again.

"I will place a shield inside my head. Watch and remember where it is located. Look at the consistency of the shield, its density and size," she instructed.

Enric thought about telling her that this here was probably not the most suitable place to do this, in a rocking coach with the clapping of horse shoes on cobblestones and the rattle of wheels, but decided against it. She would not be able to contain her impatience all evening long if he didn't oblige her here and now. Thus he just nodded and took her warm hand in his before closing his eyes and following her lead.

"Alright," she said after no more than two minutes, "now you place a shield just like that inside your head in the exact location I showed you. Be careful not to make it impenetrable, or you will cause severe damage. It needs to let fluids pass, but not the magic that will transfer the feelings to me." She watched him create and adapt the shield until it was to her satisfaction. "Good. That should do the trick." Now for the test. She turned to Junar. "Have I ever told you about the romantic dinner Ram'an made me agree to in Takhan when he was my guardian? It was a payment for his and three more votes at the end of the trial. It was actually quite a nice evening, we cooked together, had wine, went for a walk in his garden with all the lanterns he had hung there and he even hired musicians so we could dance. The only trouble was that he had his hands all over me all evening. And his mouth." She looked at Enric, whose eyes had narrowed and whose expression had become fierce and dangerous. His hands had balled into fists and she saw that his jaw muscles had become clenched.

"You look furious, and not just a bit!" she called out in delight. "Yet I can only feel a mild echo of it! It is not completely gone, but considerably dampened!" Clapping her hands, she leaned back against the bench and laughed. "We did it! I can't believe it! I won't have to faint again! Yes!"

Enric closed his eyes for a moment, reminding himself that she had just said these things to provoke him enough to be able to test the shield. But knowing that this was very likely exactly what had happened that evening, made relaxing particularly hard right now. He felt a certain very familiar urge, to reacquaint Ram'an's face with his fist, rising inside him and fought against it with sheer willpower. He couldn't go to a dinner invitation with a storm like that brewing inside him.

Eryn followed his inner fight with an apologetic grimace. "Sorry. Not a good time for this, was it?" Then she beamed at him. "But think about what we have just accomplished! This is revolutionary progress! I can't wait to write to Iklan about this! And I need Vern to do some illustrations about where to place the shield. After that I need to write a report about it, with instructions on how to carry it out and send it to Iklan," she murmured. "I'd better get started with this right away..."

"No, you will not," Enric said calmly. "No worming out of this dinner invitation. If you can't wait until tomorrow, you can sit down and get it out of your system *after* we return home."

She looked at him, disconsolate. "You really are insisting on my going there? Now? After what we just worked out? That is incredibly heartless!" she protested.

"No more for you than for me, my love, I assure you," he sighed with a lopsided grin.

"What? Why?" she frowned.

Junar grinned broadly. "Because I think he would very much prefer putting that shield to the proper test with you himself instead of going to that dinner right now. Not one to recognise subtleties, are you?"

Eryn frowned. "What proper...? Oh." Then she gave him a lascivious smile. "That is definitely still open for us to choose, you know!"

He let his breath out slowly and gave her a stern look. "No attempts at bribery, Eryn. We are expected at that dinner, I have confirmed the invitation." He winked at her. "But we do not need to stay too long."

Orrin rubbed his face with both hands, then asked, "And the two of you couldn't have worked this out a *little* earlier? Before a certain Council hearing, for example?"

"Well, yes," Eryn admitted sheepishly, "I suppose we could have. There is definitely some need for improvement in our communication, I would say."

"You don't say," the warrior commented sarcastically.

* * *

Eryn slapped on a smile when a servant opened the door to Lord Seagon's House. She felt a gentle urging pressure against her back as if Enric wanted to make sure that she didn't try to run. That made her smile.

"Pity I showed you how those bolts for penetrating the special barrier work. Otherwise I could have escaped now," she said, quietly enough for only him to hear.

"Yes. Pity."

After handing their cloaks to the servant, they were shown into a spacious parlour with numerous people all wearing elegant clothes and carrying wine glasses in their hands. Eryn's smile became less forced as soon as she spotted Vyril, who excused herself from her current conversation partner and walked over to them.

"I am so delighted to see you! Tyront told me that you would probably be coming, but then with you it is always a matter of luck to see you at one of these occasions," she smiled at Eryn. "Junar, how are you doing, my dear? You look fabulous, and I don't just mean your dress! Either your companion or your pregnancy seem to be doing you a lot of good. How is that baby of yours coming along? Any troubles so far?"

"My stomach can be a little rebellious at times, but that is pretty much it," she shrugged. "If Vern didn't keep drawing these pictures I wouldn't even realise that something is growing in there."

Vyril nodded. "I have heard that he works on a book with a healer from Takhan, who specifically requested *his* pictures. That is so exciting! Lord Orrin, you must be so proud!"

He nodded. "I certainly am."

Then a number of people greeted them, including the obnoxious Inad, Lord Seagon - who was still not too pleased whenever he saw Eryn - Lord Tyront and of course the ambassador and his assistant. When they were lead to the dinner table, she noted with relief that they had seated her far enough away from Ambassador Sanaf not to be forced to converse with him. The hostess had furthermore taken care not to sit Inad too close to him, either, due to his last remark over her cosmetic changes.

But it seemed there were still a number of people anxious to converse with such an important man. They had obviously not been exposed to him or had any insults from him, Eryn thought. Yet. Occasional shrill eruptions of female laughter around him marked either genuine amusement or the wish to indulge him. She exchanged a look with Erbál who was sitting opposite her. He also appeared a fraction unnerved by his, for want of a better expression, *superior*. Lord Poron sat next to him, focused on his food and unperturbed by everything going on around him. His companion Aurna sat to Eryn's left and kept her gaze fixed on the plate in front of her.

"I heard that you have stopped eating meat. Is that true? I fear that there is not a lot to sate you tonight, then," she said with an expression of sympathy.

Eryn shrugged. "I am used to it. I usually make sure there is enough to eat at home when we return. I am not exactly good company when I am hungry."

"What news is there from Takhan, Ambassador? Anything spicy to keep us entertained as well?" a nasal female voice was asking. The companion of one of the Council members, Eryn thought, but could of course remember neither her name nor her companion's. She wondered briefly if she wanted to do something to remedy these gaps in her knowledge, then decided that it was probably not worth such effort. Why waste time on minor things like that? Junar would probably know and could supply that information if it were ever needed.

Sanaf smiled and looked at Eryn. "Well, Lady Eryn and Lord Enric have launched quite a few discussions in different expert circles and meanwhile also everywhere else with their mind bond. The matter of her fainting problem has really kept people wondering. And envious, of course," he chuckled. "Men wish they could accomplish the same feat, and the ladies long to experience such a thing."

Eryn's heart threatened to stop beating from the shock of what she had just heard. No. He had surely *not* just told them this, had he? Orrin, Junar and Enric stared at each other in horror, the rest of the people at the long table looked about in confusion.

"Oh dear! Lady Eryn, I didn't know you had a propensity for fainting?" Inad cried out, forgetting that she was mad at the ambassador. "I hope it is nothing serious?"

Yes, Eryn thought angrily, we wouldn't want to lose our source of unnecessary cosmetic alterations, would we?

But before she had a chance to answer, Sanaf waved off Inad's concerns. "Let me assure you that it is nothing to worry about. It is a consequence of intense intimate ecstasy, as it were." He laughed. "There are much worse causes of fainting than that, I am sure."

Eryn closed her eyes, feeling the heat rush into her face. And there she was, thinking it couldn't become much worse. This halfwit had just shared her intimate problems with people she was subordinated to, barely acquainted or on bad terms with or newly befriended, or - in Lord Poron's case - superior to.

Aurna next to her took a sip of water and then pronounced, "Oh dear, that was quite rude. That dreadful man really does not have any sense of propriety."

The conversations around them had virtually all fallen silent and the guests were showing different expressions ranging from delight through glee, sympathy, shock, disbelief, to disapproval.

Erbál's face showed some anger, but only briefly before he had himself under control again. He showed Eryn an apologetic expression in his glance. A situation such as that was of course a nightmare to any trained diplomat.

Lord Tyront stared at Sanaf grimly, clearly not thrilled of having his two most high-ranking magicians derided like that.

How was she to look these people in the eyes ever again, she wondered, and fought the urge to hide her face behind her hands. Striking him here and now was not something any present would countenance, in any case. Fantasies of knocking him out with a single strong bolt emerged in her imaginings.

"Lady Eryn," Aurna's quiet voice whispered next to her, "you can only be embarrassed by others if you allow it. Dignity should be your weapon of choice right now."

Dignity, she thought, and clung to the word. How was she supposed to react now? Pretend nothing had happened? That was not anything she could do. Take the chance and flee from this house never to return? That would look like running away. Which it practically would be. Saying something to deny it? Hardly credible. Scolding him publicly for his lack of tact? That might lead to diplomatic tensions if she wasn't very careful. What was the dignified way around this?

All eyes turned when Enric put his cutlery on his plate and cleared his throat.

"Ambassador Sanaf, I appreciate that you are still in the process of adapting to our local customs and societal rules. Let me take this opportunity to acquaint you with one of them. While I have experienced people in your country as being very open and uncomplicated when it comes to more personal topics, this is not the case in our country. Matters that pertain to what happens intimately between companions behind closed doors are generally considered private and are not discussed in public." His voice was not unkind, yet there was hardness behind the velvet.

Eryn exhaled. Of course she could depend on Enric when it came to communicating resentment without invoking any unwelcome consequences.

"The Ambassador did surely not intend to cause yourself or Lady Eryn any distress, I can assure you," the same nasal voice from before cut in and the plump woman who owned it put a protective hand on Sanaf's arm.

"I certainly did not!" Sanaf called out with a grand gesture, "It would horrify me to have you think that! Let me apologise for my words and assure you that I will from now on be more careful in adhering to the accepted rules of conversation. As they differ quite considerably from those in my own country, I beg your oversight for this until I have managed to internalise them completely."

Ram'an never had this kind of trouble, Eryn thought sternly and refused to return the modest smile Sanaf flashed her.

"Let us not talk about it anymore," she replied stiffly and resumed eating, signalling to the ambassador and the other guests that for her this matter was thereby concluded. She wondered if this incident had earned her the right from now on to show her disregard for him rather more openly than before. She was sick of pretence. Friendliness was too good for him. What he would face when dealing with her henceforth was no more than functional politeness.

The rest of the dinner was characterised by sporadic attempts at starting conversation by the hostess and significant glances being exchanged between certain people that promised that this would be talked about on the first undisturbed occasion.

When the guests then rose to return to the parlour, Eryn tried to stand off to one side and avoid having to talk to anybody if at all possible. She soon found herself in the company of Lord Tyront, who pressed a small glass of something sweet-smelling into her hand. He was closely followed by Vyril.

"*Now* I give you leave not to like him," he sighed and looked critically at the ambassador who was standing in the centre of the room with a crowd of women around him. Even Inad - who'd borne the brunt of his remarks before - had decided to join her friends now that somebody else was being talked about.

Eryn smiled weakly. "With all due respect, Lord Tyront, I would have taken *that* liberty even without your permission." She watched Junar and Orrin come closer and join them. "And I have decided to leave such things as dislike behind me for the moment."

"In favour of forgiving him for putting his foot in it?" Vyril asked, clearly impressed by such generosity.

"No, I am afraid my disposition is not as noble as that," Eryn said and sipped her liqueur. "I have moved over to hating him."

Both Vyril and Junar sniggered while the men exchanged indulgent looks.

"How likely is it that Enric will not drag me to another one of these dinners anytime soon?" she asked wearily.

"Not very, my dear," Vyril replied with a sympathetic tone. "Especially now you need to be seen not to care enough about his remarks to hide."

"I would have hidden anyway, whether that man keeps making a fool of himself and others or not!" she whispered.

Aurna approached them with a dark look on her wrinkled face. "What an unappealing man!" she hissed and put hand on Eryn's arm to squeeze it reassuringly. "I am considering having a dinner party just so I can deliberately *not* invite him."

Eryn smiled at the demonstration of solidarity, especially Lord Tyront's.

"Lady Eryn," she heard a young male voice behind her and turned to look at Erbál. "Would you allow me to join you for a moment?"

She nodded and stood aside so he could stand among them. "I must apologise most sincerely for the Ambassador's remarks. I assure you he had no intention of embarrassing you like that and was completely unaware of the effect his words would have," he then spoke.

"I know," Eryn growled. "That makes it even worse. I can appreciate a well-aimed attack, but not outright blind ignorance." She noted a few worried expressions around her and sighed. "It's alright, Erbál knows how I meant that."

Erbál smiled. "I do, yes. Just the way you said it."

She couldn't help but grin. "Exactly. You don't happen to have any scheming plans for getting him removed from his position and ordered back to Takhan, do you? If I can somehow assist you in taking over his place, then..."

The ambassador's assistant laughed quietly. "No plans at the moment, but I surely know now where to go if I decide to pursue that angle."

"Count me in," Orrin added dryly.

"Now, now," Lord Tyront said with a warning undertone, "let's not start any conspiracies here."

"Why not?" Eryn retorted. "Because it is not in line with good taste and appropriate behaviour?"

"No," he replied with a chuckle, "because it's too public."

She stared at him for a moment, then grinned. His brand of humour was so much more appealing when she wasn't its target for once.

* * *

Eryn stood in front of a group of ten boys ranging in age between ten and twelve years, her arms folded, and stared at them without expression. They stared back, clearly at a loss what to do with that sinister looking woman who did not look like she was enjoying being here very much.

Orrin cleared his throat. "Good day to you. I assume you all know who Lady Eryn is?"

Several of the boys slowly moved their heads in hesitant and obviously uncomfortable nods, their eyes still glued to the woman in front of them.

Smart kids, Orrin thought with dark amusement. They recognised trouble when it was standing in front of them.

"She will be helping me with your training over the next two months," he went on and nodded to a skinny boy who had raised a finger. "Yes?"

"Why?"

Eryn pursed her lips and waited for Orrin's reply. He would, she hoped, not tell them about this stint being her punishment. It might cause their respect for her to diminish to nothing if they learned that she, too, had been subjected to corrective measures like a child. But then their expression so far pointed not so much towards respect but rather fear. Funny - most people around her took to admiring her due to her valiant efforts at healing. But these boys hadn't had any contact with her in that capacity. They probably only knew what their parents had told them and of course the other boys who had been unfortunate enough to be selected for Orrin's training with her when she was a prisoner. Their tales were without doubt not of the most flattering kind.

She allowed herself a small smile. She could work with that.

"Lord Orrin is considered too lenient and clement," she replied. "That's why they sent me. To show you that swordplay is not always fun and games."

Eyes widened in distress when their gazes flickered to Orrin with the thought that anybody might consider *him* too lenient.

"My grandfather says this is a discipline for you," a boy with a defiant glint in his grey eyes offered. "Because you angered Lord Enric."

"Your grandfather?" Eryn said slowly and focussed her attention on him. "And who might that be if I may ask?"

He drew in a breath and puffed himself up to his full unimpressive height that hardly reached Eryn's collarbone. "My grandfather is Lord Remdel, member of the Magic Council."

She blinked in surprise. Lord Remdel? That meant she had Inad's grandson before her. That woman had genuinely had offspring? And right before her stood the defiant and much too cheeky result.

Eryn leaned forward, careful to maintain eye contact with him as she smiled, showing too many teeth. "Indeed? What an interesting little theory. I suppose I will have a chat with your grandfather. I really do not appreciate my subordinates gossiping about me."

The boy looked pale and pulled his head between his shoulders, clearly not happy with the thought of having caused trouble for his grandfather. Eryn had no intention of following through with that threat, but the boy wasn't to know that. And it had been a happy reminder that however important he thought his grandfather was, she was still higher positioned.

She looked at Orrin and his studiously blank expression. Was he unnerved or amused? It was hard to tell.

The combat trainer cleared his throat. "We are not here to talk but to fight. Lady Eryn will now instruct you on how to adopt a steady stance and why this is essential in any fight." He nodded to Eryn. "Whenever you are ready, My Lady."

She forced herself to smile and began to impart to her still uneasy audience the first thing that Orrin had taught her back then when she had been compelled to start her training with him.

Orrin leaned with the low stone wall against his back, arms folded, and watched contentedly. He could see that she was used to teaching, it showed in her posture, her gestures, the confidence even though she was talking about a subject that was not at all to her liking. She slipped into her role as teacher, wearing it like a robe and even forgetting to maintain the fearful façade she had doubtlessly intended to show them in order to make this an unpleasant experience for her class.

He smiled. She would deny it fervently later, but it was obvious that she was enjoying herself. Well, at least a little. His gaze drifted across to Lord Remdel's grandson. It would be interesting to see if he behaved himself. And how Eryn would react if he didn't.

* * *

"I assume you are aware of the current situation between the Western Territories and their northern neighbour, Pirinkar?" Tyront asked without transition after they had concluded the matters of funding and reporting for that month.

Enric nodded. "I am, yes. The situation is tense. From what I know it is about the claim to a small strip of land along their border that seems to contain mineral deposits, deposits which both countries would be interesting in tapping. The matter of where exactly the border lies has in the past never been much of an issue, as the mountains themselves formed a natural one. But now that exploiting the area is a topic, they need to decide who is entitled to dig where, and formalise ownership. They have not yet been able to agree on a clear, official border and each keeps rejecting the other's proposals."

Tyront nodded. "Indeed. They are on the verge of halting all trade. So this is not going well." He regarded the younger man thoughtfully. "Have you ever wondered if this was one reason why Malriel of House Aren was so eager to adopt you?"

"No, not exactly wondered. I am convinced that it was a reason. The Western Territories have next to no practical experience remaining when it comes to fighting techniques, strategy or defence. Having an expert on that in one of the Houses is not only a practical asset for the country, but also one for House Aren. I would say Malriel will manage to profit from that somehow in the future," he explained. "Why do you ask? Are you aware of any Royal plans to interfere in the dispute? I would think that our relationship with the Western Territories is a little too new and frail to offer them assistance that might lead to our being involved in a war that is not of our own making."

Tyront shook his head. "No, I doubt that the King intends to offer anything like that for now. Though he is without a doubt interested in keeping trade with the West going as the taxes he earns on goods traded are surely not to be sniffed at. But you would know more about that than me, being the one who pays them to him. This is why I am wondering if the King will be sending you there. Not as his delegate or an official advisor pertaining to matters of war, but to encourage you to spend an extended holiday with your new family there."

"I do hope this is not going to happen especially soon; Eryn would throw a pink fit at the prospect of not only encountering her mother again, but spending a longer time in the same city with her. And she can hardly just leave Vern in charge of the clinic again so early on – especially as he can only train the others to a certain degree and is supposed to be attending his classes as well. Let's not forget that he is only sixteen years old."

"I am not saying that this is what will happen, just that we had better be prepared for it," the older man warned. "I am not particularly eager to send the two of you off to another country for who knows how long. Enough trouble came out of it when you stayed there for only a few *weeks*."

"Hardly our fault," Enric shrugged. "But then we arrived there completely unprepared for what was awaiting us. This will not happen a second time. We now have an ambassador and family there to keep us informed."

"So you are in contact with Kilan?"

"Certainly. It is nice to compare his and Vran'el's messages and see how much they each know or have chosen to tell me, for that matter. Kilan is of course restricted to what he thinks the King will approve of me learning about."

"Which is completely irrelevant as you have more than one information source there," Tyront chuckled.

"Yes. But Kilan needs to maintain appearances. If we seem too close, the King might doubt his trustworthiness."

"Speaking of ambassadors, how is Eryn dealing with your mind bond and its effects having been made public?" the older man enquired.

"There are not a lot people who have dared ask her about it and the few who have been brave or rather stupid enough to do so have usually been silenced with a cold stare," Enric smiled. "And as it is by now common knowledge in Takhan and now here as well that we have the fainting under control, there is not so much talk going about anymore. At least not here. It seems the healing community in Takhan is thrilled by our discovery. They keep sending Eryn messages with questions and asking her to write a book about it. Which she resists because she thinks writing a book about something that can be explained as well in a few minutes does not make sense."

"So she is not exactly after fame and glory," Tyront smiled.

"I would think that she has had enough of that since she was brought to Anyueel," her companion pointed out. "The main purpose in her life was remaining unnoticed, so being the centre of attention wherever she goes unnerves her."

"The healer from Takhan is due in less than a week. I suppose Eryn is busy preparing herself for the exams now?"

"Yes. She has finished most of the books and wants to be through with them when he arrives. Her extra morning every six days teaching Orrin's first-years takes away additional time she could use now."

Tyront grinned. "I heard about that. I wonder who the punishment was intended for, because from what I was told she seems to be enjoying herself considerably more than her students are. One of them kept complaining and she just locked him behind a soundproof barrier and only removed it shortly before he would have fainted. I read the letter of complaint his parents sent to Orrin. He gave it to Eryn and she answered it. Then the parents complained to me about Orrin *and* her. But it seems to have done the trick, at least as far as the boy is concerned. I hear he keeps his mouth shut whenever she is close."

Enric sighed. "Please tell me we are not talking of Lord Remdel's grandson here. I will never hear the end of it."

Tyront shook his head. "No. His boy is a troublemaker, but he has stayed away from making himself her target so far. Which shows impressive restraint considering his behaviour towards most of his other teachers. Eryn's victim is of less exalted origins. His father works at the treasury under Lord Seagon. So there shouldn't be any unpleasant consequences. But there are still several weeks of teaching left for Eryn. I dare say it is not the last we will be hearing about it."

"I am inclined to agree with you on that. She certainly has a way with children," Enric grimaced.

"She is still determined not to have any? No change of mind now that her friend is expecting one?"

"No, nothing. But she is still young - she might change her mind," he said, obviously without much hope.

They heard a loud yawn from under the table and Urban then stretched and got to her feet to sit in front of Enric and stare at him pointedly.

"Feeding time already?" Tyront shook his head. "I would get really nervous if that animal stared at me like that all the time."

"She is restless. It has been a while since we were on a hunting trip. But I have been thinking about taking a trip to Bonhet soon to see how things are progressing there. They should soon be finished with the building work. That would give her enough opportunity to run and hunt. Though she has discovered that hunting messenger birds is another way of keeping fit,' he sighed. "The birds that hatched on our roof are old enough to carry messages, so we sent them to Takhan for Malriel, Kilan and Valrad. The first one made it back to the roof, the second one was eaten and only this morning another one arrived and she snacked on that one as well. These birds were clearly bred for endurance, not for intelligence. They think the yard is a good place to land before returning to their cages on the roof."

Tyront laughed. "Well, at least she keeps herself fit if you don't have time to go hunting."

"The birds keep breeding, so that is not the problem. We will just send them others. The messages are a different matter. We managed to retrieve the first one as it had fallen off during the bird's fight for its life, but the one today she devoured whole - nothing left, not even the metal tube. I have no idea who sent the bird. I hope it was nothing urgent. I don't even know if looking for it coming out the other end makes any sense as I have no idea how durable those tubes are or if they seal tightly enough for keeping the paper slip in there legible."

"Any ideas how to increase the birds' or rather the messages' chances for survival for the future?"

Enric nodded. "I have been thinking about putting a few trees on top of the roof, so they land there instead of the yard. Though getting fully grown trees on top of the roof is going to be a challenge. I'll have to ask a few magicians for help here." He smirked. "Time to show Orrin and Vern what they have got themselves into by befriending Eryn."

"Well, that sounds like an interesting idea. And as long as it keeps the air mail flying. I heard young Vern is corresponding with Ram'an regularly for that book he is working on with that healer friend of his," Tyront remarked.

"Yes, he uses the Arbil birds on our roof for that. Eryn is a little annoyed at it, as her own correspondence with Ram'an has more or less come to a standstill. It seems his last few messages were not exactly very friendly."

"They weren't? That is interesting. Any idea why? Any trouble between their Houses?"

"Not according to Vran'el. It just seems that Ram'an's resolve to remain friends with her changed once she left Takhan."

Tyront pursed his lips. "Some delayed resentment due to having repeatedly been rejected by her?"

Enric shrugged. "Probably. But that is his problem."

"I imagine you are not particularly disappointed about that?"

"I didn't mind that they wanted to stay in contact, but if his letters keep upsetting her it is better to stop them."

"Well, the arrival of the healer from Takhan will keep her busy enough not to dwell on this too much, I would imagine," Tyront pointed out.

"True enough. But luckily her healers have progressed far enough to take care of the greater part of the treatments without her, only calling her to aid them in more complicated cases. Promoting Rolan has taken a part of her administrative duties off her shoulders. So she has more time for fighting lessons and following up her own teaching schedules. There should be five or six more exams until she is done, not counting the ones for her healing certificate, of course."

"That certificate, it would enable her to work as a healer in the Western Territories, if I understand it correctly?" Tyront enquired.

"It would, yes. Not that this is her plan, though. It is more about catching up with what the required level there is in order to be able to provide the same standard here," Enric assured him. "She is thinking about establishing something similar here. And is toying with the idea of some sort of governing body for healers, but I suppose she will be approaching you with that soon enough."

"In her usual demure way, no doubt," Tyront sighed. "And now get out of here and feed that cat. These staring hungry eyes are making me nervous."

* * *

Orrin ducked hastily when a fist came flying towards his chin and nodded appreciatively. That had been a splendid feint.

"So that healer is due to arrive tomorrow, isn't he?" he asked conversationally.

Eryn nodded. She knew better than to be negligent of her cover just because he was talking to her of something completely different. Like Enric, he was a great advocate of learning not to be distracted, never to feel too safe, to be prepared for an attack at all times - no matter what tactics one's opponent employed for luring one into a false sense of safety.

"Who is he, then?"

She jumped aside when he was about to sweep her off her feet with a well-aimed move. "A colleague of my uncle's. He specialises in illnesses, which will be useful since I am pretty good with handling injuries already. I am confident that he will be able to teach me a few useful things from his discipline."

"Good for you, then," he remarked and tried to grab her when she aimed a fist at his stomach, but she slipped away under his arm and a moment later her arm was around his neck in a headlock.

He tensed his neck and reached behind, gripping her upper arm and throwing her forwards over his shoulder.

Eryn landed on her back with a heavy thud that pressed the air from her lungs; she closed her eyes for a moment until her organs remembered how to apply the simple technique of breathing again.

"That was not very clever. You were within reach of my arms. And even if you had not been, this is a grip you might not want to use on a much stronger opponent. Even if I had not been able to grab you, I would have been able to walk away with you clinging to my neck to dash you against the next available wall until you had let go of me."

She climbed back to her feet and gave him a pleading look. "Are we done for today? I need to check a few things before my guest arrives tomorrow. Preferably without first healing any major injuries."

Orrin sighed, then nodded. "Very well. I will graciously allow you this half hour. You almost landed one or two good punches today, after all. I am not an unreasonable man."

"Thank you," she smiled, the relief clear in her voice and lifted her shackled wrists for him to free them. "If you would be so kind?"

"Funny, taking them off is never as much fun as putting them on you," he smiled.

"How lovely. But as you have just spared me the last half hour, I will graciously forgive you for that remark."

"Lucky for me. Off with you, then. Same time in four days."

"Ah, yes, about that. You see, as the healer is arriving tomorrow and there is a lot...," she began.

"No chance. Here in four days. No excuses." Thus he turned and walked off, carrying her shackles in one hand.

Well, she had not really expected him to accommodate her, but it definitely had been worth a try. She brushed the worst of the dirt off her trousers and started walking home to wash and get changed before going to the clinic.

When she opened the door and entered the house, a servant greeted her and handed her a paper slip. Well, at least some of the birds seemed to have been able to make it to the roof alive, she thought, and unrolled the message. It was from Vran'el, informing her that Ram'an's father had died.

Oh dear. She sat down on a sofa and stared at the message. It had been more than a month since she had last had contact with Ram'an. She had even considered sending his birds back empty, as a gesture that was meant to show him how unhappy she was with his letters. But she had not really been able to bring herself to do it. And Vern needed the birds to write to Ram'an about his drawings for the book, after all.

But now there had been a death in his family, and not just anybody, but his father, who he had lived under the same roof with and who he had probably been close to. The thought of him suffering right now was not a pleasant one, no matter how impersonal his messages had been before. Sighing, she got up and walked into her study to write to him.

CHAPTER 12

Foreign Guests

Rolan rolled his eyes and cleared his throat. "Are you even listening to me?"

Eryn looked apologetic. "I am sorry. I am finding it a little hard to concentrate on anything today."

He nodded. "I understand that you are excited and that you are expecting a messenger every minute to tell you that they are in sight, but we need to take care of a few things first, especially as you have now decided to dedicate some of your time to teaching fighting to children," he ended a touch reproachfully.

"That last one was not my idea!" she protested. "They made me do it!"

"Who made you do it? Lord Enric?" He shook his head. "That is a really complicated relationship you are in." He gave a leery grin. "Even without the fainting."

"Oh, come on! Aren't you following the gossip, Rolan? That is no longer an issue."

"What can I say? People are, unfortunately, very careful about what they share when I am around. At times it really is a disadvantage to be working so closely with you. They think I am either not interested in any gossip about you or disapprove of it."

"Which is, of course, complete nonsense," she retorted.

He looked at her as if this was self-evident. "Well, yes. I do feel left out, I'll admit. If I want to learn about things I need to come to you directly and hope you are in the mood to share, after all. Anyway, you managed to counter the effects of the mind bond? How?"

"Shielding," she sighed. "But this is not really what you came to talk about, is it? I thought we had things you want taken care of before I rush off to receive the healer."

"Not if you are willing to answer my questions at the moment. I feel I should have a certain advantage here. People ask me things, after all. That is the trouble, you see? On the one hand they are so very careful what they say in my presence and on the other they expect me to know more than anybody else! Which is a tiny contradiction."

Eryn shook her head at him. She remembered that Vern had said something similar several months ago when she had knocked out Lord Tyront in the Palace square when he wanted to show her that he had mastered her double barrier. Vern had admonished her for not being more considerate and making sure he was in a position to watch such things as people expected him to be well-informed about everything concerning her.

"I wasn't aware that you are such a gossip yourself," she replied. "I thought your life is too unsocial and solitary for frivolities like that."

He shrugged, unperturbed by this less than flattering evaluation of his character. "My market value has risen since I was promoted, as it were. I get invited a lot more frequently and I feel I owe it to society to participate more actively in social life."

She sniffed. "How very self-sacrificing of you. All for the common good, eh?"

He didn't reply to that but instead returned to consulting his sheets. "There have been a few requests for a night service," he said, returning to the reason why he had come to her in the first place. "Most of the healers, apart from Lord Poron and yourself, have been summoned by messenger time and again to attend to perceived or real emergencies."

She frowned. "Apart from Lord Poron and myself?"

"Of course. The two of you are too important to be shaken awake in the middle of the night. And Lord Poron is not exactly a young man. Though he does appear a little less wrinkled these days," he added thoughtfully. "One of your cosmetic tricks?"

"Are you telling me that my healers are being repeatedly woken at night to rush off healing people and then have to get up in the morning to work? What happens to the money they collect at these occasions?"

Rolan exhaled. "Generally there is none. They have no idea what to ask without my being there, so they don't. I would therefore recommend establishing some kind of night roster whereby one healer is here at the clinic and makes it possible for all the others to have a good night's sleep. And I have taken the liberty of preparing a tariff list for the most common ailments that seem to occur at night." He handed her a sheet of paper.

"But these are higher than our usual rates!" she protested.

"Yes, but additional working hours are required to provide this service, so it is more pricey," he explained. "If they want to save money, they'd better attend during our regular treatment hours. Did I mention that the patients' waiting times have increased? Now that the initial distrust and scepticism is over, more people are making use of our services, even those from outside the city. More patients, the same number of healers. Do the arithmetic."

Eryn rubbed her face. "I know. But the trouble is that the Order is not willing to increase the quota for healers presently and even if they did, I couldn't provide training for them anyway. I first need a few fully-trained healers who are able to teach others. And I don't have enough knowledge to train non-magician healers for now, so that is not a way of circumventing the quota, either."

"We do get applications every now and then," Rolan told her.

"That is good to hear, but firstly, we are not the right place for people to send them to - that should be Lord Tyront - and secondly, I am not in a position to take on anyone else due to the quota."

He shrugged. "I was just telling you about it because I thought you would appreciate the interest in the profession."

She sighed and made herself smile. "You are right. I do." Then she straightened when she heard footsteps approaching her door.

Rolan smiled. "Mighty Lady Eryn getting nervous?"

Flashing him a dark look, she awaited the knock, then called out to permit the messenger who had indeed come to inform her that the visitor from Takhan had been sighted and should arrive at the western gate in no more than half an hour.

"Finally!" she exclaimed and raised a triumphant fist into the air once the man had left. "I can't wait to meet him!" She fished a hand mirror out of a drawer and held it in front of her, regarding the reflection critically, smoothing a strand of hair that had managed to free itself from her braid and putting it away again.

Rolan stared at her. "Oh my. I didn't even know you possessed a thing like that, or cared enough to."

She ignored that remark and got up to take her cloak from the hook. "Make sure everything is ready for the healer. That his study is clean, there is enough paper and pens, whatever else is needed. He will very likely want to see his quarters first, but maybe we will drop by later. If not, I will bring him over tomorrow. And now you will have to excuse me. I have a guest to pick up."

* * *

Eryn reminded herself to be calm and collected, not to appear overexcited like a girl. She was a grown woman, a professional, and that was what she wanted the newcomer to see when he looked at her.

This time the traveller from Takhan would arrive not on horseback, but in a coach. The season was too cold to ride such long distances comfortably, especially for a man used to a much warmer climate.

She smiled broadly when the carriage came into sight and waited for it to stop in front of the Palace gates. She watched impatiently as the coach driver jumped down from his seat and opened the door, refraining with an effort from hurrying towards the coach.

"Welc..." The word became lodged in her throat and her smile froze and then turned into a scowl of shock and dismay. "What? No! Where is the healer?"

Pe'tala sneered and descended the few steps to the ground, stretching her arms to remove the stiffness and then raising both eyebrows. "You are standing in front of her. *I* am the healer."

"Oh no, you are not!" Eryn all but shouted. "They sent a man! I read the message, I am absolutely sure! What is this? A cruel joke?"

Pe'tala laughed. "No, *sister*, there was a last-minute substitution. The healer who was supposed to be coming had to deal with a family problem. Pregnant daughter or something. So they sent the next candidate on the list: me."

Eryn balled her hands into fists, breathing heavily. No. This could not be true. She would wake from this nightmare any moment now. She squeezed her eyes closed, then opened them again.

Her cousin looked amused. "Trying to wake up, are you?"

"Why? Why would you decide to come here? I don't understand this! This is a dreadful mistake!" Eryn wailed. "You go back to Takhan at once and get them to send me somebody else! Anybody!"

Pe'tala's expression became tense. "You listen to me, Eryn. You can consider yourself lucky to have me here, or do you imagine the list of applicants for coming to this backwards place was so very long? There is a reason why I was number two: Despite my young age I am one of the best. So quit whining and show me to my quarters. It has been a long journey and I really need to warm myself. And, well - it could be worse. Malriel could be here."

Eryn stared at her, unable to come up with a reply. Then a movement at the coach door caught her eye and she watched in horror as another woman alighted from the coach. Malriel of House Aren.

"Oh my," Pe'tala laughed, "I suppose it *is* worse!"

* * *

Enric's head jerked up at the wave of shock and annoyance he felt. It was then followed by another stab of anguish, anger and helplessness. What was happening? This should have been a joyous day for her with the healer from Takhan arriving. Or was that what had triggered those emotions in her?

He got to his feet, looking at the Council members. "My Lords, I am afraid I need to leave you. There is something I need to take care of."

Tyront gave him a questioning look, but assented. "Of course, Lord Enric. Inform me of the outcome later in my study."

Enric nodded and left the Council hall, running along the corridors towards the Palace gates. The shock he had felt before had turned into desperation and he fuelled his muscles with magic to run faster. Several pairs of surprised eyes turned towards him. Seeing the man in the blue robes run was not an everyday occurrence.

He spotted the coach and knew that it must indeed have been the newcomer that had made her so unhappy. He skidded to an abrupt halt at the scene in front of him and blinked, unable to believe what his eyes were showing him.

Pe'tala stood to one side, arms folded, sneering. She seemed positively gleeful. To her left stood Malriel, regarding her daughter in front of her with half-closed eyes and a faint, indulgent smile. She had obviously not expected any sort of warm welcome but counted on the outburst that her arrival had obviously caused in Eryn.

"You can't come here! Neither of you!" he heard her yelling. "This is my home, my own safe haven, where I don't have to deal with either of you! Shouldn't have to! Go away!"

Malriel spotted Enric and raised her hand to wave at him elegantly. "Enric, my dear boy, it seems Theá is a little out of sorts. The surprise of our arrival was obviously too much for her. I am sure you will manage to calm her down somehow."

He quickly wrapped his arms around Eryn as she attempted to attack her mother, lunging for her throat, and pressed her against him, keeping her immobile for as long as her violent outburst needed to be kept under control.

"Malriel. Pe'tala. That really is a surprise," he said calmly. "It seems we have been misinformed about the healer. Nor were we told about your plans to come here, Malriel." But of course the King would have known about this, he realised. A high-ranking politician from one country didn't simply travel to another without sending word before, or rather without obtaining permission to do so. He held on to Eryn, who was flailing about in an attempt to free herself with the aid of magic from his restraining embrace.

"At home we tranquilise mares when they become rebellious. Allow me to assist you," Pe'tala grinned broadly and made to step towards Eryn.

"Pe'tala," Enric warned her. "This is not amusing."

She shrugged, but stayed where she was. "That is your opinion."

He regarded both women, who seemed to find Eryn's reaction tickling, and wondered what in the world he was supposed to do right now. If he let go of Eryn, there was no telling what she would do. Knocking her out was not a good idea - she would run amok with him as soon as she woke again. Showing Pe'tala to her quarters while dragging a kicking Eryn with him was also not the easy choice here. And he didn't even know where Malriel was supposed to be staying.

He turned when he heard footsteps behind him and Marrin, the King's advisor, approached them. His eyes took in the scene with little surprise, but widened when he beheld Malriel. His gaze darted from mother to daughter several times, clearly thrown off track by the resemblance he had surely heard about but still not expected to be so close.

He bowed to both women. "My ladies, I am very happy to welcome you to the city of Anyueel. My name is Marrin, I am His Majesty's advisor and will be at your disposal should there arise any questions or concerns during your stay." He stepped towards Malriel and lifted her hand to kiss it in the Western way of greeting. "Malriel of House Aren, we are honoured to have you here." Then he turned to Pe'tala to kiss her hand as well. "Pe'tala of House Vel'kim, we hope that your stay here will be a pleasant one and we are grateful that you have allowed us to benefit from your expertise. I am sure you are eager to rest and get warm again, so please allow me to show you to your quarters."

Both women nodded graciously and followed him after a last glance at Eryn, who was staring at Marrin as though she wanted to do painful things to him.

Once the three of them had disappeared into the Palace, the tension vanished from her muscles and all that kept her upright were Enric's arms.

"He knew," she whispered. "He knew exactly that it was them coming. He was not in the least surprised to see them. He knew their names. And he had already got quarters for Malriel prepared!' New anger was sparked. "And he was obviously waiting to greet them until I'd had a good look at each of them, knowing you were there to keep me in check, before venturing out!"

"Very likely in accordance with the King's orders," Enric suggested gently and released her carefully from the grip to take her hand and pull her along with him. There was no sense in letting her return to the clinic right now. Or for him to go back to the Council meeting. "Come on, let's go home."

She didn't object and let herself be pulled along, shaking her head in disbelief. "Why Pe'tala? I can understand that Malriel would enjoy doing this to me, she even threatened us with it when we left Takhan. But Pe'tala? She detests me! Why would she come here of her own choice? And why did nobody tell me! Valrad must have known!"

Enric frowned. "I suspect they might have been trying to warn us. You remember the bird which Urban caught? The one which she didn't bother spitting out the message tube it was carrying?"

Eryn looked at him in dismay. "We have to work on keeping the birds safe from her."

He smiled. "I am far ahead of you, dearest." Then he turned serious again. "We will pay Pe'tala a little visit tonight. Then you can put all these questions to her."

"I am definitely not going to visit her!" Eryn exclaimed.

"Of course you are. You need to clear the air between the two of you or you will hardly be able to work together at all. She is not the healer you had expected or wanted, but that doesn't mean that you can't learn something from her expertise," he pointed out.

Eryn sighed in defeat, then released a sudden stream of curses.

"What?" he asked.

"I am supposed to take the healing exams with her!" she wailed. "She will never assess me fairly! I might as well accept failure now!"

Enric tried to placate her. "No, you will not. You will not allow her any chance to let you fail the exams, because you will be prepared well enough." And he intended to have a word with Pe'tala about that, anyway.

* * *

Eryn looked up from her letter when Enric stood in the doorway to her study. "Are you done? I have sent word to Pe'tala to expect us after dinner. Which would be now."

She nodded. "I am, yes. Just let me despatch the bird to Valrad."

"I hope you have been careful not to take your anger out on him? This is about his daughter, after all. He would almost certainly not appreciate your abusing her or rejecting her outright. If he hadn't thought that she was suitable for this assignment, he wouldn't have agreed to sending her here."

She looked down at the paper slip in her hands, then sighed and screwed it up into a tiny ball. So much for that. "I suppose I'll write another one later. And address it to Vran'el."

They walked along the streets silently. Enric held her cool hand in his and studied her contemplative expression. He hoped she was pondering how to keep the conversation with her cousin from escalating. But it was far more likely that she was indulging in fantasies of how to maim her.

She hesitated only for a moment once they reached the Palace, took a deep breath and followed him up the stairway. He stopped in front of a door not far from where his former quarters had been and knocked three times.

Pe'tala opened up only a moment later, looking calm and determined. She stepped aside to permit her visitors to enter. Eryn felt the gentle push in her back that made her take a step inside. She then turned and waited for Enric to follow, but he remained standing in the doorway.

He took Pe'tala's hands in his and pulled her close to kiss her on both cheeks the way family were supposed to greet in the Western Territories. She accepted this with a smile at Eryn's displeased frown.

"Would you, too, like to greet me properly, *sister*?" she then said.

"Consider yourself properly greeted by not being booted out of that window," Eryn growled and folded her arms.

"I trust the two of you will manage not to strike each other for the next half hour until I pick you up again," Enric said, his voice carrying a mild rebuke.

"What do you mean, until you pick me up again?" Eryn frowned, sudden panic widening her eyes. "Where are you going? You just stay here!" How dare he drag her here without the intention of standing by her? She had counted on the advantage of their facing Pe'tala in greater numbers!

"I am going to pay Malriel a short visit. Unless you wish to accompany me there, then of course I will stay here and we can go there afterwards. Together."

She shivered. "No, thank you very much. That is rather more than I can manage in one evening."

He nodded curtly. "Good. Then I hope you will behave and be halfway civil to each other. Goodbye for now." Thus he turned around and was gone a moment later.

Pe'tala slowly closed the door. The two women faced each other for several long, silent seconds.

"I suppose I should offer you a drink," the hostess said.

"Don't bother with insincere politeness," Eryn barked and walked over to a sofa to take a seat. "Talk to me! What are you doing here? A sudden yearning to deepen our family bonds when before you were so eager to avoid me at all costs? So disgusted that you wouldn't even remain in your own house as long as I was stuck there with my guard? Don't tell me you suddenly realised that I was not to blame for Ram'an's behaviour?"

Pe'tala remained standing in a broad-legged stance and folded her arms. It was almost as if she too were prepared for combat. "I am well aware that the latter was not your fault. But then I got to know you in the meantime and decided not to like you for completely different reasons, if I could put it so."

"Super," Eryn muttered. "Which brings me back to my first question. If you don't like me, why are you here at my place? They did tell you that you are supposed to be working with me every single day for the next three months, didn't they?"

"Yes. A downside, I admit. But then you did come to my city to spoil a few weeks of my life and I thought, well, why not return the favour?"

"This is a joke, isn't it? You are willing to suffer through something just to make me suffer more? What are we, arch enemies? I thought we just didn't like each other! I wasn't aware that we had entered into a pitched battle!"

Pe'tala closed her eyes for a moment. "It was not just that. I could not stand the pity any longer. Poor Pe'tala, discarded like an old pair of shoes by the man who was supposed to be her companion in favour of her very own cousin. And when you slipped through his fingers, people expected him to turn back to me. But he did not." Her expression became angry for a short moment. "And I would have hurt him badly if he had dared to. Though I admit it would have done me some good to crush him. But people thought I was waiting desperately for him to recall that I was still there as somebody to fall back on for him and was devastated when he failed to. I could not stand their stupidity any longer, their looks of faux commiseration, their attempts to match me up with somebody else." She looked up, her eyes free of the usual mockery. "So when the healer they had intended to send here was not available any longer, I took the chance without hesitation. Since whatever you are going to throw in my face here, pity will surely not be part of it."

Eryn sighed. "Yes, you may safely rely on that. You are aware that you are subordinate to me as long as you are here, of course? I am the Head of Healing here, after all."

Her cousin chuckled. "Subordinate to *you*? My knowledge outstrips yours by far, so what sense would that make?"

Ah yes, who would have thought that this would be the first item to quibble over? "If you cannot live with things as they are, you are welcome to return to your city. I am responsible for whatever you do here, so you had better make sure not to do anything that will get me into trouble. Have I made myself clear?"

Pe'tala narrowed her eyes and nodded reluctantly after a few seconds. "So be it. You are aware that I will be the one who is testing you for the qualification, are you not?" she went on to ask with a venomous smile. "I am sure we are going to have so much fun together."

Eryn ground her teeth. "If you fail me without justification, I swear to you that I will make sure people in Takhan don't only consider you as pathetic, but also vindictive and a disgrace to your profession."

"I would not sink as low as that. I am confident enough that you will not meet with my high standards anyway," the younger woman sneered.

"We will see about that," Eryn hissed. "In the meantime I expect you to adhere to the working times at the clinic, treat my healers with the respect they deserve and do what you have been sent to do here: help me in improving my knowledge and the medical services we provide here."

"That will by my pleasure, dear *colleague*." Pe'tala leaned against a chest, still not willing to sit. "Then I suppose we will be spending a lot of time together tomorrow. First the working day, then the welcoming banquet your King has planned for us. When am I supposed to be at your clinic?"

Damn it, Eryn thought. The banquet. Her dismay at finding the two women here in her city had led her to forget about that. An entire evening in Malriel's company.

"I will pick you up after breakfast and show you the way there." She stood. "You might want to see a tailor and have yourself outfitted with warmer clothes soon. It is going to get colder and you will not be too happy with the clothes you are wearing now."

She walked to the door placing a hand on the knob, then stopped and asked without turning. "What exactly does Malriel want here? Why has she come?"

"I do not know. Believe me when I tell you that I am not particularly thrilled at having *her* here, either. One of you is enough - I could do without the mother-daughter Aren package for an entire month."

Eryn looked over her shoulder to give her a cold look. "I do not consider her my mother any longer, as you should by now be aware of. I'll thank you for considering that little fact as long as you stay here. And that I am not a member of House Aren, however much my belonging to your House displeases you."

Pe'tala shrugged. "Duly noted. Am I to address you with *Lady* here? Or am I among a privileged few who may forego the title?"

"The people I work with do not use the title. And neither does family. Good bye, Pe'tala. Tomorrow after breakfast; don't expect me to wait." With that she opened the door and slipped outside, closing it carefully behind her.

* * *

Malriel smiled broadly when she opened the door and took both of Enric's hands to pull him closer and slightly down towards her so she could kiss his cheeks. He noted how her eyes quickly checked if he was alone and saw the very short and hardly discernible flicker of disappointment which she then masked immediately. So she had obviously been hoping to see her daughter here as well.

"Enric, what a pleasure to set eyes on you again. I see you have had new clothes made for yourself in our style here." She felt the fabric between her fingers. "Warmer, of course, to get you through that nasty cold season you have here."

"Malriel," he nodded and let himself be led to a sofa. She held on to one hand of his and pulled him down with her.

"I was told upon my arrival in Bonhet that you had pretty much taken over the village - though I doubt that it will now remain a village for much longer. It is remarkable what they have built in such a short time; I assume that you started only after your return here," she said conversationally. "From what I hear all the trade with the Old Kingdom is currently being handled by you. Which means that you are earning quite a lot from that side in addition to the businesses you already had before."

Small talk about money, he smiled. She really came from a completely different world than him.

"Yes, the King has granted me permission to establish a shipping business."

She nodded. "A smart thing for you to request. But then this comes as hardly a surprise for me. Have you been thinking of establishing a shipping route between the city and the sea? I would have preferred to have got here by ship instead of having to travel by road, to be honest. And I believe that it would also make it easier to get the goods from Bonhet to here. I am assuming the river the city is sited on and the one flowing into the sea at Bonhet is the same?"

"It is, yes," Enric confirmed. "And yes, I have been considering that already. I am currently negotiating with the Palace. There is quite a lot of construction work necessary so shipments can be unloaded here properly, and now we are discussing whether I would get tax relief and pay for the construction myself or if it will have to be the other way around."

He lifted his hand when she was about to say something else. Now there was the foremost question he wanted answered. "Malriel, why are you here? Don't tell me you had been missing Eryn that much. We have been gone from Takhan for no more than three months now, and you two were not exactly close."

She sighed. "Straight to the point, as always. I was wondering how long you would let me deflect you from asking about that." Then she stood up. "Would you like a drink first, my friend?"

"No," he answered, "I would like to have the answer first."

"But you would not mind, I hope, if I poured myself a glass," she smiled and opened a small box to take out two glasses and a rounded bottle.

"Not at all."

When she returned to the table with the glasses and the bottle, he waited for her to take the first sip and lean back.

"I have come here, Enric, to establish a good relationship with your King and have a look at the place where my heir calls his home."

A reminder of his status in her House. He wondered why she thought it necessary at this point.

"Why would you have a particular interest in befriending the King, if I may ask? We have your ambassador here for that, after all."

"Sanaf?" She laughed and shook her head at him. "Oh dear - do not tell me you have not determined by now that he is a complete buffoon?"

Enric blinked. That was blunt. "Well, he has not exactly endeared himself to some people, but ladies of a certain age and standing seem especially taken with him," he replied carefully. It was one thing for *her* to insult the ambassador, but he couldn't afford to do so or even to agree.

She rolled her eyes and he couldn't help but smile at how much she resembled Eryn at that moment. "That is because the title Ambassador carries enough weight for them to overlook the fact that there is nothing more to him than that title. But you wait, it is only a matter of time until Erbál takes over the position. How is Theá getting along with him?"

"Very well from what I have seen," Enric said. "Why?"

"Because the fact that his House voted against her despite their alliance with House Vel'kim is one of the reasons he was not eligible for the position of ambassador here. But the triarchy is aware that he is a much better fit for the assignment, so they simply sent him along under the guise of Sanaf's assistant. My guess is that they wanted to see how well he gets along with Theá. If he manages to earn himself respect here, I expect them to recall Sanaf to Takhan soon enough and instead send an assistant for Erbál over here."

"Many of us would not regret that, to be perfectly honest. The ambassador has a talent for making inappropriate remarks, at least when judging by our standards here."

Malriel chuckled. "I know. Erbál has written to me about his informing society of how the mind bond caused her to faint during bedtime, shall we call it... activity? Has he also told them that you managed to solve that little problem already, if that is how you would like to term it?"

"I have no idea," he admitted. "I haven't had the heart to drag her to another one of these occasions since then, especially as there will be the banquet tomorrow, plus a ball she is expected to attend in about one week." Then he raised an eyebrow. "You are in correspondence with Erbál? I thought Aren and Feral were not allied?"

She smiled mischievously. "Well, let us say that the alliance we had was not exactly of a political, but more of a private nature. We became lovers for a short while and kept in touch. I advocated the idea of sending him here."

Enric remembered her reputation for preferring younger men, but was still surprised at her taking a lover a few years younger than her own daughter. But then what did age really matter for a magician who had the ability to make herself appear older or younger according to mood or occasion? He regarded her thoughtfully.

"Is it just my impression or are you looking rather younger than the last time I saw you?" he then asked.

"No, you are right. I decided to slough off a few more years for now. As I will be being introduced here as your mother, I may as well do something to make their eyes pop," she said, with a smirk.

"That is very likely what will happen," he nodded, "as you look as old as I do myself now. And of course it was no consideration at all that any similarity between yourself and Eryn will now be even more obvious to whoever looks at you, was it?"

"An added effect I am willing to accept, yes," she smiled in a calculating way. "If I cannot call myself her mother any longer, I may at least have others do it for me."

He rubbed his face and took a sip from the bitter liquor. "I don't think having the two of you here will become humdrum any time soon, then. How long did you plan to grace us with your presence here, can I ask?"

"Asking me when you will be seeing the back of me on my first evening here, are we, Enric? How very ungallant of you." She wagged her finger at him in mock reprimand. "A month. I cannot afford to stay any longer, unfortunately, as a House cannot remain that long without its Head. This is a law, but it also makes sense, practically speaking."

Yes, unfortunate indeed, he thought wearily. One month with herself and Eryn in the same city, where they would without any doubt be invited to the same occasions, would be enough of a challenge.

"How is Theá managing with the surprise of having Pe'tala here instead of the healer who was supposed to be sent?"

He sighed. "Not particularly well, as you can probably imagine. They are talking at the moment and I hope they will manage to set a few rules that make working together feasible. Three months is a very long time if they keep on resenting each other the way they did. I wish Ram'an had saved us all a lot of trouble and just gone through with getting committed to her."

Malriel looked at him indulgently. "He fell in love with Theá when he came here. How could he have joined another woman? Would you have done that in his place? Imagine how Pe'tala would have felt. I am convinced that dissolving the agreement was the right thing to do, even though pursuing Theá the way he did was clearly not. He has always been the dogged but patient type. And considerate, whatever else you may think of him."

"Judging from the letters he has been sending to Eryn these last months, I find that hard to believe," he objected. "They were dispassionate, distant and bordering on unfriendliness. It was he who insisted on keeping in contact with her, after all."

"I would imagine that writing to her has proven to be a little more of a challenge than he is able to handle right now. House Arbil is currently facing financial troubles, so he is not as level-headed and balanced as he used to be. His father died the day before we left Takhan as well, and from what my sources tell me, the real impact of years of imprudent business decisions he took is only apparent now that all the papers are accessible to Ram'an." She sighed. "It is a shame when a House with a talented lawyer such as Ram'an enters into so many disadvantageous agreements because the Head of the House is too proud to consult his own son."

Enric leaned back and stared at the ceiling for a few moments. "Then I suppose I will contact him to ask if he is interested in undertaking some serious trading with that wine of his instead of the small quantities we now manage to purchase through a third party."

Malriel's smile widened. "I admire the fact that you are such a gracious winner, Enric."

He lifted his brow at her. "Which is no less than you expected, otherwise you would not have mentioned this. I expect you wish to restore House Arbil to its former glory, as a powerful ally is more useful than a weak one. And another House might profit from this weakness, one that is less well disposed towards our own."

"I see I selected my heir well," she beamed and emptied her glass.

"Did you now," he said flatly. "I wonder how honestly you would answer me if I asked you if your visit has anything to do with troubles in the north that the Western Territories are currently facing."

She just looked intently at him, a faint smile around her lips. "Whatever gave you that idea, Enric? I certainly did not come to drag your Kingdom into a war, in case you were wondering."

Enric smiled and got to his feet. "Of course not. Whatever was I thinking? I thank you for your hospitality, Malriel. We will meet again tomorrow evening at the banquet." He bent down to kiss her on each cheek and left. It was probably better to check on the Vel'kim sisters a bit earlier than he had announced.

CHAPTER 13

Introductions

Eryn breathed out in a resigned manner before knocking at Pe'tala's door. When a servant opened it, she went in and looked around for any sign of the healer she had come to collect.

"Where is she?" she addressed the middle-aged woman.

"In the bathroom, Lady Eryn," she answered obediently and pointed to a door to her right.

"Pe'tala?" she called, then knocked.

"What?" a muffled voice came from within. "You are early! Do not rush me without good reason!" she protested.

"I have something for you to change into. Working clothes. I'll set them in front of your door," Eryn called back and placed the bundle on the floor before she went over to a chair next to a window and looked outside. It afforded a view of the western gates, the ones she had tried to escape through the first time, a few days after having been brought here, only to be stopped by Enric. Last year. An eternity ago.

She didn't turn when the door opened.

"You could have given me these a bit earlier, could you not? I am already fully dressed," Pe'tala complained.

Eryn now turned and shrugged. "Suit yourself. You can change with the men at the clinic, if you prefer that. Who am I to force unwarranted privacy onto you?"

The younger woman huffed impatiently, picked up the clothes and put them on a chair before undressing again right there in the parlour. Eryn resumed her observation of the city gates and watched a cart being checked over by the gate guards and then waved through.

"Done. We can leave now."

Eryn eyed her sceptically. "Don't you have a cloak or something? You are going to freeze wearing that."

"Cannot be helped right now. I need to see a tailor first," Pe'tala shrugged. "And you can surely lend me one of yours until then."

"Sure, especially when I am asked as nicely as that," Eryn replied with mock cheerfulness and unfastened the cloak from around her shoulders to throw it at her cousin. Well, at least her healer's robes would keep her reasonably warm until they reached the clinic. "I want that back when you have your own."

Pe'tala snorted. "Like I would need a reminder for such a thing. It is not as if I were so very eager to hold on to your worn items of clothing."

"Then you can give it back right now if you prefer freezing." Eryn smiled sweetly.

"Hardly," came the dry reply.

They then turned to leave the quarters and follow the corridor to the staircase that would lead them to the Palace gates and out into the cool and grey morning.

Pe'tala tugged the cloak closed and shivered. "This really is a cold place. Why would anybody choose to live here?"

"Because not everybody is in favour of perspiring all the time," Eryn retorted.

They walked on, drawing a number of curious glances. People were fairly used to seeing one dark head in the city, and nowadays also to the two men from the West, but two dark haired women were something new.

"Incredible," Pe'tala murmured. "They really are yellow-haired, all of them. I feel like some kind of exotic animal among them."

They reached the clinic after a few minutes and Eryn pushed the front doors open to enter first. They had not yet opened up for patients and she heard voices from the little kitchen.

"Come on," she said and motioned forwards. "Let's get ourselves something warm to drink. It's how we start our treatment days here."

"Treatment days? You do not treat patients every day? Why ever not?"

"Because presently there's only me with five healer trainees, so I alternate treating patients with them for practical experience and learning on the job, and every second day I teach them theory."

They had reached the kitchen and six pairs of curious eyes swivelled towards them.

"Good morning, everyone!" Eryn called out. "I would like to introduce you to Pe'tala of House Vel'kim, the healer who will be spending the next three months with us. Pe'tala, these are the healers Lord Poron, Onil, Felden, Lebern, Vern and our medical herbalist, Plia."

Various greetings were uttered.

"I thought they wanted to send a *man*?" Felden asked in confusion, then added hurriedly, "Not that I would have preferred that!"

Vern's eyes narrowed. "Pe'tala of House Vel'kim? As in *Maltheá* of House Vel'kim? That same House?"

Eryn pressed her lips together. Why did that kid always have to be so quick-thinking?

"Yes," Pe'tala smiled broadly. "I am Eryn's *sister*. Her much *younger* sister."

"You have a sister? I didn't know that!" Plia exclaimed excitedly.

"Yes," Eryn said lamely, "it is a rather recent development."

"She is a grown woman, how recent can that development be?" Onil frowned.

"She is adopted," Eryn explained.

"No, *dearest* sister, let me assist you in getting our facts right," Pe'tala objected with a sneer, "*Eryn* is the one who was adopted."

"You were adopted?" Lord Poron asked, perplexed. "By whom?"

"By my uncle," she replied tiredly. Why could Vern not just have kept his mouth shut for once?

"So your sister was your cousin before?" Onil chuckled. "That's novel. Why did they adopt you, anyway?"

"Yes, that is a question we have not stopped asking ourselves since then," Pe'tala smiled. Several pairs of astonished eyes rested on her.

"We are still working on getting into that sisterly spirit," Eryn growled and shot the younger woman a sour glance before turning back to Onil. "My uncle adopted me because otherwise the man I was promised to would have claimed me for his House."

"Promised? To another man? You?" Lord Poron exclaimed.

"Can we talk about that some other time? Please? And get out of my way, I need something to drink. It is really cold outside today."

"No wonder you are freezing, you don't even have a cloak on!" Vern admonished her.

"I have given it to Pe'tala for now. She needs to have some clothes made for herself. So you should rather be complementing me on my generous heart than chiding me for not wearing any cloak today."

The boy nodded. "Alright. Then I suppose you come home with me today, Pe'tala. Junar can take your measurements after we are done here. She is currently *the* seamstress in Anyueel thanks to Eryn here. And she can make you things in the Western style, she has the patterns at home."

"I don't know if this is such a good idea," Eryn narrowed her eyes at him. "Junar should not work so much, she needs to take it easy now. We don't even know if she is willing to accept any new customers. As you said, she is in great demand at present."

Vern dismissed that statement with a hand gesture. "Oh, don't worry about it. She will surely make time for your family."

She wasn't sure if Vern had done this on purpose just to tease her or if he really wasn't aware that she was trying to keep Pe'tala away from her friend.

"Eryn's seamstress?" Pe'tala smiled. "Well, then of course I will take you up on your offer, young man."

Eryn gave the boy an angry look, then turned back to her healers.

"As Vern is here to assist us today, I will be able to show Pe'tala around. Plia, maybe you can accompany us to the roof later and present your realm yourself? I don't really know half of what you are doing up there."

"Sure," the girl beamed. "Just collect me when you are ready."

Eryn remembered that she had wanted to get hot drinks and mixed them for herself and Pe'tala before handing one cup to her.

Both women wrapped their cold hands around the steaming mug appreciatively.

"Where is Rolan?" Eryn then asked.

"Here," his voice came from the door. "Just finished the..." He stopped and frowned, examining Pe'tala critically. "This is *not* a man," he then stated after careful consideration.

Pe'tala narrowed her eyes at him. "You are a particularly smart one, are you not? I suppose knowing the difference between men and women is the first useful skill when working at a place of healing."

He blinked, taken aback.

"She is Eryn's sister," Vern explained with a grin.

Rolan nodded slowly. "Yes, I can believe that alright."

"Did he just insult me?" Pe'tala frowned.

Eryn glared at her. "Did *you* just insult *me*?"

"Oh my," Lord Poron chuckled, "these will be three very interesting months, you mark my words."

* * *

Enric sighed and poured himself and the two men waiting with him another drink.

Orrin frowned. "So, why exactly did they send a different healer now? And why did nobody tell you that it would be her cousin or sister - or whatever you are calling her now - whom she can't stand? Does seem a little twisted, if you ask me."

"I think somebody tried to warn us, but Urban caught and ate the messenger bird before we were able to save the message. We have sent word to her family and Kilan, asking them if they knew about that. I suppose I will receive their reply tomorrow," Enric explained, then turned to Vern. "How did you get along with Pe'tala? Eryn hasn't told me anything about her day; she just rushed home at the last possible minute and up into the bedroom, from where she has not emerged since."

The boy shrugged. "She is a bit rough at times, but after working with Eryn for a time that is nothing to throw me off balance. Most of us are still getting used to her rather direct way of pointing out mistakes, though. But listening to Eryn and her is entertaining, at least. They really can't bear each other, can they?"

"Not at all, no," Enric sighed. "I am hoping that they may in the course of time come at least to respect each other as professionals when they have been working together for a while."

"Junar got along fairly well with Pe'tala today," Orrin told them. "But then it normally doesn't pay to rub one's seamstress up the wrong way. Next time you go to a ball, and people ask you why you are looking so pale and ill, just try to remember if there was something insulting you said to the person who picked your colours and cuts."

"That is frighteningly insightful for a man who has until recently avoided dressing up," Vern remarked. "But then I suppose being joined to a seamstress can do that to any man."

All three of them turned their heads to the stairs when they heard two female voices discussing something.

"You can't ask me to reject her on principle just because *you* don't like her!" Junar complained. "We are grown women, after all! Well, *I* am," she amended. "You seem to have fallen back into infantilism, as it seems."

"Come on!" Eryn's voice moaned. "Liking her is basically a violation of our friendship! It betrays a certain loyalty, don't you think?"

"Why don't you travel in the coach with them and I'll walk there?" Vern said softly and emptied his glass in one go before rising and taking his cloak from the hook.

"Coward," Enric murmured.

The boy shrugged and grinned. "Well, you chose them, I more or less got stuck with them. So it is only right and proper that you should be the ones who suffer." And he was gone before the women had entered the parlour.

Junar frowned. "Where is Vern?"

"Took flight from all your bickering," Orrin said.

"That was no bickering, it was a discussion," Eryn said haughtily and grabbed her own cloak to fasten it around her neck before Enric had a chance to.

"And? Will you give Junar leave to like Pe'tala or will she from now on have to consult you first whenever she meets somebody?" Enric asked cheerily and grinned when his companion gave him an angry look. "Well, Junar, I would say she will forgive you in time as long as you don't make the mistake of finding Malriel remotely pleasant."

The seamstress smiled. "I admit I have become rather curious about her. From what Eryn tells me she must be some kind of monster escaped from the depths of the darkest seas or something equally unpleasant."

"She tried to get me convicted! Her own daughter! What more do you need to assess her?" Eryn exclaimed.

"Well, I do try to meet people first before damning them," her friend replied.

"Doesn't sound a very good use of time to me," Eryn said and opened the door. "Are you ready? Can we leave?"

Both men looked at each other and quickly emptied their glasses before following her on to the coach.

"You seem unusually eager," Orrin remarked. "Not impatient to get there all of a sudden, are you?"

"The earlier we get there, the sooner I can excuse myself, I hope," she explained.

"You know, I don't think that's how this works," Junar pointed out. "Especially in your case. They are both related to you, after all. You are not supposed to run away even earlier than you usually do in order to escape their company."

"Oh dear! You really are determined get on my bad side today, aren't you?" Eryn growled. "And don't think I haven't noticed that you have put me in that pale-yellow dress that you put aside for taking revenge on me because it makes me look like a corpse!"

Orrin lifted his brow at Enric. "See? What did I tell you?"

* * *

Eryn stepped out of the coach and turned to her companion. "I am not going to introduce her. She is now *your* mother. You chose her voluntarily, you bear the consequences."

Enric looked directly at her. "You are aware that people will realise that the two of you are related, aren't you? There is a striking family resemblance."

"Then it will be an even clearer signal that I don't want to have anything to do with her." She lifted her chin and strolled on into the Palace.

The double doors to the ball room where the banquet would take place were wide open allowing her to see that most of the guests seemed to be there already. Of course. They would be curious about the newcomers. They had met several men from the Western Territories already, but this was the first time there would be any women from somewhere they must consider an exotic, distant land.

Eryn turned when she heard hasty footsteps behind them. Vern looked slightly out of breath when he drew level with them.

"Where have you been? Why didn't you ride in the coach with us?" she asked with a frown.

"Self-preservation, I suppose," he shrugged. "Are we ready to go in? I am curious about your mother."

"Don't call her that," Eryn hissed at him. "She is *Enric's* mother now."

He rolled his eyes. "Sure. And nobody will wonder about her having dark hair and sounding foreign, I'm sure."

"You shut up or this will be your first and last banquet because you won't survive it. Next time the King sees fit to invite the healers as well I will discourage him," she grumbled and felt Enric take her arm.

"Come. Time to brave them. And keep that temper of yours on a leash. Control always starts with oneself," he warned her quietly. "Don't let people see that she gets to you. Don't let *her* see it."

She nodded. That she wanted to avoid alright.

When they entered, they saw the guests that had arrived already divided into two groups, each surrounding a dark-haired woman.

"I suppose there will not be any introductions necessary now," Enric said quietly.

A moment later Malriel's eyes locked with Eryn's and she freed herself from her many admirers with an exclamation of delight.

"There they are!" She approached them with wide open arms as if she had taken over the role of hostess and was welcoming her guests. "Enric, my son, and his lovely companion Maltheá," she chirped breezily with a lively sparkle in her eyes. Eryn saw Pe'tala smirking from several paces away and merely glanced icily in her direction.

A moment later she found herself being kissed by Malriel and clenched her teeth. "People call me *Eryn* here, as you are well aware," she growled.

"*This* is your mother?" Vern breathed incredulously. "She looks hardly any older than you! You could almost be twins! How astonishing!"

Malriel turned to him. "Ah, you must be young Vern, the outstandingly talented young man who illustrated that book Ram'an brought back from here. It is a pleasure to meet you. I am Malriel of House Aren."

Vern just nodded, speechless. This glorious, powerful, confident woman knew his name and was delighted to meet *him*!

Enric introduced her to Junar and Orrin, as Eryn made no move whatsoever to take this upon herself, just as she had informed him before.

Malriel's eyes rested on Orrin thoughtfully. "The man who somehow managed to teach an Aren woman combat skills against her will. That is quite a feat. You are to be complimented. I assume this was a hard and challenging task for you, Lord Orrin?"

He gave her a thin smile. "Indeed it was. An unbroken trial for my nerves."

Malriel gave him throaty laugh. "Good. I would not want to think that we are tamed so easily."

"That is something we have given up trying to do now," a deep voice from behind them spoke. Tyront smiled and lifted Malriel's hand to kiss it. "Judging from the similarity in your facial features and build, I assume you are Malriel of House Aren. I am Lord Tyront and this is my companion Vyril."

Eryn exhaled slowly. Why did people find it necessary to keep pointing out how much alike they looked?

"Lady Eryn," her superior then addressed her and looked in Pe'tala's direction, "Why don't you introduce us to your..."

"Sister," she supplied with a tense smile and nodded. "Of course." She went over to Pe'tala and smiled at the people standing around her. "If you would excuse us for a moment? I need to borrow her for a short while."

"Am I to be introduced to the mighty leader of the Order?" the younger woman sneered. "What an honour."

Eryn didn't reply to this and put on a polite smile. "Pe'tala, I would like to introduce you to Lord Tyront, the Order's leader and his companion Vyril. You have met Junar, Orrin and Vern. Lord Tyront, this is Pe'tala of House Vel'kim, my *little* sister."

She watched with satisfaction the annoyed glint at the diminutive in Pe'tala's eyes.

They turned to the entrance when Sanaf and Erbál entered.

"Malriel!" the ambassador boomed jovially, causing her to gulp visibly as he approached her with arms widely spread.

Eryn gleefully watched the plump man envelop her in a clearly unwelcome embrace which Malriel was in no position quickly to free herself from without seeming impolite.

Erbál smiled at Pe'tala and kissed her hand. "Tala. It has been a while. I admit I am surprised you decided to come here."

She grinned broadly. "Erbál, I in turn am not at all surprised that you ended up here. Still the big adventurer. And how could I not avail myself of the opportunity of visiting my *much older* sister, who is so very dear to my heart, and spending some time with her?"

Vern covered his snigger with a hasty cough.

"You don't laugh at *her* insults," Eryn hissed at him quietly. "You laugh at *mine*! Where is the loyalty in your family, I ask?" She then watched in surprise when Malriel and Erbál greeted each other with kisses on both cheeks and then exchanged what could only be called a very private smile. Not another one of her lovers? She really *did* like them young!

She looked up in relief when the signal was given for the servants to lead the guests to the large table. She didn't really care who they would sit her next to, as long as it was not Malriel. She would gladly endure Sanaf, Lord Seagon or even Inad instead.

And this time she really was lucky. Malriel was seated close to the King, as was Pe'tala, as they were the guests of honour. Enric was placed next to Malriel, and Ambassador Sanaf and his assistant next to Pe'tala, who seemed anything but thrilled about her neighbour. Erbál smiled in delight when Eryn took her seat next to him. His smile froze, however, when she whispered to him, "Did you have sex with Malriel?"

"Pardon me?" he asked with a slightly panicked expression.

"You heard me," she growled. "And don't pretend to be offended. This is a question nobody would raise their brow at where you come from. And you have classified me as blunt already. So out with it."

He sighed in defeat. "Yes."

"Brilliant," she muttered, the annoyance clear on her face. "So you are going to pass on to her everything I ever said or will say to you?"

"No, Lady Eryn, I will not. I am a diplomat, after all. And Malriel's knowing too much is not necessarily an advantage for myself," he pointed out. "She is a politician, when all is said and done."

"Good, at least you do not harbour any illusions about her being too refined to use you for her purposes."

He chuckled. "Not at all, no. This is one of the things that attracted me about her. I find a woman who causes me to be on my guard at all times very stimulating. You resemble her a lot in that regard, though your methods differ."

She looked at him with a sudden angry stare. "You are not trying to flirt with me, are you? Because let me tell you that comparing me with *her* is not a promising approach here."

Erbál grinned at her lopsidedly. "I would not dare to. Your companion is a lot taller and stronger than me. And he already has his eye on us for whispering."

Eryn looked up and indeed saw Enric observing them with a concerned face. She smiled at him reassuringly and shrugged.

A moment later the doors at the other side of the room opened and the guests rose as King Folrin entered, waiting for him to reach his ornate chair and bowing when he finally did.

He first nodded to Malriel, who bowed low.

"Malriel of House Aren, welcome to my Kingdom. It is a great pleasure and a privilege to welcome you here."

"Your Majesty," she replied graciously, "the pleasure is entirely mine."

Then he turned to Pe'tala. "Pe'tala of House Vel'kim, your stay here is proof of our countries' willingness to share more than goods in trade. We thank you very much for your willingness to spend time with us here to allow us to benefit from your knowledge."

"I thank you, Your Majesty," she replied and bowed as well.

The guests let themselves sink back onto their chairs as soon as the King had taken his seat.

Eryn saw how his eyes darted between Malriel and herself a few times and prepared herself mentally for another remark about that astonishing similarity, but nothing came. But of course he would be aware of the tensions between them and how little she would appreciate remarks of that kind, she realised. Not that he normally minded what she did or did not want to hear, however.

She spotted Onil and Lebern at the other end of the table and nodded to them. They seemed rather ill at ease, not usually being invited to occasions such as these. Felden looked more relaxed, having been seated next to Lord Poron, who was always eager to talk about healing. How she wished she could sit next to them instead of being so close to the King.

"How are you adapting to the local clime, Malriel?" she heard the King enquire.

"I admit I have my difficulties getting used to these temperatures," she smiled. "I intend to see a tailor tomorrow to order a few garments for my stay here."

"I can recommend somebody," Pe'tala spoke up with a malicious smile at Eryn. "Junar, Lord Orrin's companion, is a very able seamstress and a very close friend of Eryn's. I went to have my measurements taken only this afternoon."

"Indeed?" Malriel smiled. "Then I will see her as soon as possible. Thank you *so* much." The women exchanged a frosty glance that conveyed openly that they were not at all fond of each other, but both delighted in causing Eryn distress.

Eryn caught Enric's warning gaze.

"Let me first talk to Junar about a special price for you," she smiled sweetly. More like three times her usual rate.

Malriel seemed to rumble the lines her thoughts were going along. "Oh, please do not bother. I would not want to trespass on her generosity."

"Honestly," Eryn assured her dryly, "I wouldn't let you."

Inad's voice rose over all others. "Malriel, if you allow me one question - you and Lady Eryn are...?"

"Completely unconnected by any family bonds whatsoever, members of completely different Houses," Eryn supplied happily and took a hearty bite from the vegetable dish that had been especially prepared for her.

She narrowed her eyes in suspicion as she watched Malriel's face fall. It was not like Malriel to show a weakness like being hurt by a remark so publicly unless she was up to something.

"This is only true up to a certain point, dear Maltheá," she then said with a strained smile. "I am your companion's mother, am I not? That *is* a connection, after all."

The puzzlement among the guests was almost tangible.

"You are *Lord Enric's* mother?" Lord Seagon, the Order's treasurer asked confusedly. "Or have I fallen victim to some misunderstanding here?"

"No, My Lord," Malriel replied, "You have not. Lord Enric is a member of my House and heir to my position of Head of the same as well as my seat in our senate. In Takhan he is known as Enric of House Aren."

Eryn saw a number of unbelieving eyes darting between Malriel's and her own face.

"This is all... rather unexpected," Inad said carefully. "I would have expected there to be some family connection between you and Lady Eryn, to be honest."

Eryn nodded earnestly. "A common misconception. The only family connection at this table I can currently offer you is the one to my dear *little* sister Pe'tala."

Pe'tala blushed a shade when she suddenly found herself the centre of attention.

"I have heard about men who prefer women similar to their mother, but this..." Lord Woldarn said in what had very likely been intended as a whisper but was audible for all guests thanks to his booming voice.

Eryn saw Junar hastily covering her mouth with a napkin to hide the grin which wrinkles around her eyes nevertheless betrayed.

Enric closed his eyes for a moment, a whistle of a sigh escaping his lips, before he cleared his throat and thereby managed to still all talk at the entire table immediately. Neat trick, Eryn thought, impressed. Was that something *she* could learn?

"Allow me to satisfy your curiosity in this. I understand that this must seem rather baffling to you. Malriel of House Aren is indeed my mother, legally speaking. I was adopted into her House - which is, as most of you surely have guessed already, similar to an extended and powerful family in the Western Territories. Eryn, or Maltheá, as she is known as in Takhan, was born as daughter of Malriel, but decided to terminate the connection to her family for personal reasons. She was then adopted into her father's House, namely House Vel'kim, of which also Pe'tala here is a member."

A muttering went around the group, which was after several moments interrupted by a female voice.

"So Lady Eryn's mother is now *your* mother as well, Lord Enric?" Inad asked in confusion. "Wouldn't this make you her brother, legally speaking?"

"No, dear," Lord Remdel, her companion, corrected her patiently. "Lady Eryn has left the family and joined another, so they are not related."

"Oh, good," she nodded, apparently relieved. "It would have appeared a bit off kilter otherwise, I would say, no matter how open and tolerant our new friends in the Western Territories are in this regard."

"Not *that* tolerant, let me assure you," Pe'tala said dismissively, earning herself a few appreciative glances.

Eryn leaned back and took a sip of the very fine wine the King always served at events. There were quite a few things that could be said about Pe'tala, but surely not that she had a habit of sucking up to the rich and powerful. One had to give her that.

"Malriel," Inad's voice sounded out again, "let me congratulate you on you most youthful appearance, considering that you are mother to a child... well, an adult. You must let me in on your secret!"

Malriel smiled. "Of course, Inad, is it not? Healthy food in moderation, regular exercise and of course regular magical corrections."

"Magical?" Inad called out in delight. "Indeed?"

Eryn felt a sense of despair as Inad's gaze darted towards her greedily. Great move there. Now Malriel also served as walking proof of what magic could do when it came to combatting the outward effects of aging. Eryn saw herself removing wrinkles, smoothing skin and rehydrating tissue for weeks to come. As if she had time for such frivolous things without being granted more healers and the time to train them in!

"A messenger for Lady Eryn," a servant said quietly next to the King's ear. King Folrin nodded to permit the interruption and Eryn accepted the folded piece of paper with a blank expression.

All eyes rested on her as she read the short message, then quickly got to her feet. "Your Majesty, there is an urgent case at the clinic that requires my presence. I thus beg your permission to leave. I do not know how long this will take, so please do not trouble to wait for me."

"A moment, Lady Eryn, if you will," the King stopped her when she was about to step away from the table. "I was not aware that you have already established the night duty you informed Marrin you were planning. How can it be that there is somebody at the clinic right now when all your healers are present?"

"The message is from Rolan, Your Majesty. He tends to work late and was present when the patient in question was seeking help," she replied with barely contained impatience.

"Of what nature is this urgent case, Lady Eryn?"

"I beg your pardon?"

"The gravity of the injury or illness."

She blinked. "The message does not give any particulars about that, Your Majesty. I should really be going..."

He just smiled and motioned for her to sit again. "Then I assume that it is a matter that might as well be handled by one of your healers, My Lady."

Onil rose at once. "I would take care of this for Lady Eryn, if you will permit it, Your Majesty," he offered hastily, obviously having beaten Lebern to it just in time, judging from the other healer's hands, placed on the armrests to lift himself up.

"Commendable. I am convinced that your abilities will be up to the task." He dismissed the healer with a nod, and Eryn watched Onil leaving the hall with a relieved smile. So much for her escape plan. At least *somebody* had profited from it.

When she looked back at the King, he just nodded his head slightly at her, his brow raised in faint diversion. Enric's face was a serene mask, but he very pointedly was avoiding shielding his disapproval.

* * *

"What in the world made you think that that ruse would work?" Enric asked as soon as he had closed the door behind them, his tone anything but gentle. He lifted a warning finger at her when she opened her mouth. "And don't you dare go denying it!"

"If that man wasn't so damn suspicious, it would have worked well enough!"

"A messenger who brings a note that happens to require your immediate departure from the kind of occasion you are known to avoid? And especially today when two women are present you are known not to get along with?" He covered his eyes for a moment. "This could hardly have been more obvious. You are lucky that the King seems to find your little antics amusing, or you would have been in real trouble. He might have insisted on meeting the patient or have somebody sent along to watch the healing done."

She hung her cloak on the allotted peg and then let herself collapse onto a sofa. "Don't scold me! I behaved very well, considering the circumstances, didn't I? What is a harmless, little escape excuse? And it's not even like I profited from it anyway! Onil was the one to be released instead of me! How unfair is that?"

"Are you really complaining to me?" he asked incredulously. "You would have left me there with them, so don't expect any sympathy from *me*."

"Why would *you* have minded staying there, anyway? Malriel and you seem to be such great friends, after all. Inad doesn't pester you about cosmetic corrections, and Pe'tala doesn't keep regarding you as something distasteful that got stuck to the sole of her shoe."

"Don't try to justify that ill-fated scheme of yours," he sighed, suddenly tired. "Just don't ever try such a thing again. Especially as it has now lost all believability. Should you ever again receive an urgent message that requires your presence during one of these occasions, you had better be prepared to prove it. The King's soft spot for you doesn't stop him from setting you boundaries if you keep treating him like an idiot." He held out a hand to her. "And now come to bed. It's late."

She took his hand reluctantly and let him pull her to her feet. "Can we skip the ball at least?"

"I am not even bothering to answer that," he growled.

CHAPTER 14

Learning the Ropes

Eryn opened the classroom door onto the corridor when she heard loud voices discussing outside. Pe'tala and Rolan were facing each other, both with their arms akimbo and wearing angry expressions.

"What is going on here? I am supposed to be teaching in here!" Eryn glowered at them.

"Your errand boy here tells me my ideas for improving your work here are neither practicable, nor financially viable," Pe'tala complained. "This is why I am here, after all! To tell you what you can do better! Why does he not listen to me?"

"I don't know what you are used to working with, but we have no more than six healers here, only one of them being fully trained! Your proposals require a minor army of them! As well as the administrative effort!" Rolan cried out in despair. "Who is supposed to do all that? We can't just hire three more people on the spot! They need to be paid now and then, after all!"

Eryn closed her eyes for a moment, then stepped towards them and grabbed one arm each. "You bloody children could at least take your argument to one of your studies! This does not create a very professional impression. Neither of you comes off looking very good at the moment." She pushed open Rolan's door with her foot and guided them both inside. "In here you may yell at each other – as long as I am not in the adjoining room, mind you. Once you are done abusing each other, you can sit down and compile two lists." She placed two empty sheets of paper in front of Rolan. "Don't look at me like that - I know you like lists. And you are good at them. One list is for everything Pe'tala proposes that should be changed, improved, established or whatever. And on this list you will write down *everything* she says."

"Even the...," he began.

"Even that!" she interrupted him sternly.

"You don't even know what I was going to say!" he protested.

"I don't have to. I said *everything*, and you started a discussion! What is so hard to understand about the word *everything*? She says it, you write it down, no matter how stupid, irrelevant, expensive or impractical you find it. No evaluation, just writing it down." She pointed at the second sheet. "And then afterwards - preferably when she is no longer in the room - you make another list where you write down those points from the first list that you see as useful, affordable, sensible and practical."

"And then?" he asked in a resigned way.

"Then you will come to me and discuss both lists with me. We will see what we really can do and want to do," she explained patiently. "And after that you will get back together with Pe'tala and ask about details for the points we decided to implement in the interim."

"Nothing I tell him is stupid or impractical! If you do not want my help, I may as well return to Takhan!" Pe'tala blurted out, folding her arms defiantly.

Eryn stepped closer and glared at her. "You will stay where you are and do what you have come here to do. Which of your changes is suitable for us is definitely not for you to decide, but for us, as we are the ones who will be paying for them. Accepting your help does not mean that we have to do everything the way *you* see fit. Have I made myself clear?"

They stared at each other for several moments, then Pe'tala nodded reluctantly. "Of course, *Lady* Eryn. Anything you command, Lady Eryn."

Eryn smiled thinly. "If you use that tone with me in front of my healers or my patients, I am going to make you suffer. Badly. If you feel the urge to insult me, do it when we are alone."

Pe'tala lifted a brow. "So errand boy here is allowed to witness my disrespectful behaviour?"

"He obviously has to suffer your arrogance himself. It will comfort him that he is not the only one you are treating like that," she replied. "Any more questions or can I return to my teaching without the two of you interrupting me again with your shouting match?"

When each of them had nodded without looking either at her or the other, she left Rolan's study and made sure to close the door firmly. Before pressing her ear to it.

"Mean temper," she heard Pe'tala murmur. "Typically Aren, no matter what she calls herself now."

"You should hear her when Lord Tyront has her dragged to his study because she has failed to report to him on time," Rolan snorted. "That just now was nothing. That's what she is like when she is in a *good* mood."

Eryn rolled her eyes and walked away from the door to return to her healers. Well, at least they had managed to exchange a few civil words, even if they were not exactly flattering for her.

* * *

Tyront held up a message with a familiar seal. "She has asked me for permission to speak at the next Council meeting. Is this about the healers' association you mentioned?"

Enric shrugged. "I don't know for certain, but this is a valid assumption. Especially now that we have a foreign healer in our midst, who theoretically is not subject to any authority other than Eryn herself. And in Pe'tala's case that is probably not the best solution, considering their background. Maybe something official would be better with the two of them."

"How are the two of them getting along so far? I haven't received any reports of explosions, shouting matches or other indicators of escalation. To be honest, I am almost disappointed, especially after the banquet. I suppose working at the clinic has become a lot more interesting recently," Tyront teased.

"From what she tells me Pe'tala has turned out to be useful. They agreed only to throw abuse at each other in private, which should make working together easier for them. Pe'tala has taken over a few hours of training the new healers and Eryn even joins them every now and then if she thinks the topic is useful for her. I admire her readiness to admit to gaps in her knowledge; I would think that her cousin doesn't always make that easy," Enric sighed.

"Eryn will stand her ground with Pe'tala, I have no doubt about that. I am more concerned about Malriel. She is no doubt a formidable opponent. I find being in the same room with mother and daughter rather unsettling. The tension is almost tangible. Speaking of having them in the same room - we missed you and Eryn at the dinner at Lord Seagon's yesterday evening. Vyril has been increasingly disappointed after not seeing you at these occasions these days. Since she has started working with the orphanage, her friends have been treating her differently. It seems using your *labour* is considered something reserved for women of the *labouring class*, as far as they are concerned," he snorted. "What does that say about our society, I ask you? So being among the only two like-minded women is more pleasant for her." He leaned back and took a sip from his cup. "Malriel was there as well. She gets invited a lot. But then of course people are doubly curious about her, which is understandable considering her relationship with the two of you. I was surprised about her acting as grieving mother, though. From what I have heard about her she doesn't seem like the type who makes her grievances public."

Enric nodded. "She isn't normally. But I think she is playing a game here. Eryn told me that the situation between Malriel and her has been noted by several people who have tried to get her to make up with the desolate, suffering mother who desires nothing more than to hold Eryn in her arms again. The day before yesterday Eryn almost kicked out a patient who was imploring her to go to Malriel and forgive her, as the bond between mother and daughter is such a precious one."

Tyront grimaced. "Yes, I can imagine that she didn't take too well to that. So even patients are trying to appeal to her conscience?"

"Yes. Especially the kind who call her to perform cosmetic corrections on them and then feel the need to help her get her life back on track," Enric shook his head. "The smarter ones wait until *after* she has done her work."

"And the less smart ones?"

"I am glad to say that she merely gets up and leaves, instead of adding another ten years to their faces," he grinned.

"So Malriel's arrival here has increased the flow of money into the clinic's vault. That should count for something," Tyront shrugged. "Even though she doesn't enjoy the work as such, it keeps her financially independent from the King." Then he cleared his throat. "Rumour has it that Eryn is in truth in her mid-forties and is just hiding her age very well with the help of the same cosmetic alterations she now performs so regularly on others."

Enric exhaled and rubbed his eyes with a thumb and forefinger. "Pe'tala has become tired of being referred to as her *little* or *baby* sister and kindled that rumour as revenge. But Eryn doesn't mind. She just shrugged and said that this at least makes people think that her services are superior."

Tyront laughed at that. "Not prone to vanity, that one. I know Vyril would have a fit if somebody made her fifteen years older than she really is."

"Vanity has never been much of a thing with Eryn, but pride is. As soon as she learned about what Pe'tala was spreading about her, she started telling people that the reason why her cousin was sent here was to avoid her from bedding all the senators back in Takhan as their companions had objected strongly. Especially the male ones." Enric shook his head wearily. "I am telling you, it is like living with a teenage girl. A second one, I mean. Though Plia does not indulge in such idiocies, or I would go crazy with the two of them. There is Malriel on one side who she tries to avoid as best she can, and on the other side Pe'tala, who cannot be avoided and thus fights battles with in her private time. I marvel that they manage to leave it outside the clinic and work together every day."

"I heard that Pe'tala has at times a less... sympathetic approach to advising patients than has become customary?" Tyront enquired.

"That is one way of putting it, yes. Though the patients are obviously willing enough to put up with it, they seem a little afraid of her. And fascinated as well. Some of them even ask specifically if they can be treated by her and then delight in sharing their stories with their friends. The more unfriendly she is, the better the story, or so I am told. Eryn is not very thrilled with that development, but she knows that she can hardly get Pe'tala to change a habit she has been stuck in for years now. And Pe'tala's work is outstanding apparently, which makes dressing her down a lot harder."

"Well, as long as patients are asking for her it is probably no real problem," the older man shrugged. "I expect I will be seeing you at the ball tomorrow? Or does Eryn have any other bright plans for making the King excuse her? If she has, I hope they turn out to be less clumsy ones. I am seriously considering adding another few lessons in Political strategy to her schedule."

"Don't do it for now. I think dealing with her mother for another three weeks will probably turn out to be enough education there."

"Possibly," Tyront conceded. "Malriel has started observing Eryn's combat training. Any thoughts on that?"

Enric smiled. "Oh yes. I think she wants to see what we are capable of here. She casually enquired whether I also keep fixed training hours myself, so it may be she wants to see what exactly she has in her own stable. And it's another occasion for watching her daughter and at the same time showing people how desperate she is to spend time with her."

"And will you let Malriel watch some training lesson of yours?"

"I might do, yes. Preferably one with Eryn, although she is unlikely to agree to perform for her mother."

"But you would?" Tyront raised a brow.

"Why not? Whatever keeps me in favour with her. *I* am pretty much what keeps her from turning on House Vel'kim, if you look at how Eryn and Pe'tala treat her. My adoption is just about all that keeps her friendly with them, and that I keep up a good relationship with her."

"Is that a purely political consideration? I have the impression that the two of you get along pretty well personally."

Enric nodded slowly. "We do, actually. Though Eryn is anything but thrilled about that. They are similar enough deep down, but Malriel had her skills of manipulation honed by decades of being politically active while Eryn has been taught to be considerate of other people's needs, and abhors playing power games. But both are in their own way determined when they want to reach something, which is something I respect very much. In each of them."

"Then I suppose I will send Eryn her permission to speak before the Council in six days. Though somehow I have a feeling that I am not going to like what she will propose."

Enric smiled thinly. That was a sentiment he couldn't help but share.

* * *

Junar sipped a glass of water while Vern held her hand and used his other one to draw on a sheet of paper with closed eyes.

Eryn sat beside them, watching him in fascination. The pen strokes looked connected, as if his hand did not at all depend on his eyes to aid it in its efforts.

He opened his eyes for a moment. "You can talk to each other, it doesn't disturb me, you know. Quite the opposite, in fact. Your just sitting there and staring at me is what really spoils my concentration."

"Alright then," Junar shrugged. "Then let's not hamper the artist by being too quiet. Did you get the invitation to Inad's dinner?"

Eryn grimaced. "Don't remind me! If there is one place I definitely don't want to go, it's there. Well, and Lord Seagon's. He is still angry at me because Enric punched his nephew in the face when he got too physical in his admiration of me at that one ball. Why do you ask or does the question mean you are going?"

"I will be going, yes. It is good for business, after all, to stay in contact with the customers. Especially the Council members' companions. That is where it money is at home." She chuckled. "But from what I was told I should be staying in close contact with *you* when it comes to rich Council members now that trading with the Western Territories seems to have got off to such a healthy start."

"I knew you just wanted me for my companion's money," Eryn ribbed.

"Don't forget that you are now somebody of distinction also through your own noble birth lineage instead of only through your advantageous relationship," Junar pointed out. "That also counts for something in my book."

Eryn rolled her eyes. "Speaking of noble birth, Malriel has started observing my training lessons. Can you talk to Orrin about chasing her away? He doesn't listen to me. He says that as the training grounds are publicly visible, he can't actually forbid people watching. What kind of attitude is that? Is he a big, bad, scary warrior or not?"

"I don't see that I can do much with that. I know he isn't too thrilled about her watching you himself. He says it distracts you. But since she is the King's guest, shooing her away is not really something he has free reign to do, if you think about it."

"Yes, I know that," Eryn sighed resignedly. "If it were, I would drive her away and back all the way to Takhan. Can you believe what she is telling people?"

"About her desperately trying to mend her relationship with you?" Vern put his pen aside and straightened. The drawing looked finished from what Eryn could see.

"Yes! She told Lord Woldarn's companion that she was only trying to maroon me in Takhan for two years so as to get to know me better, after my having been snatched away from her so many years ago. That woman has been spreading the tearful tale among her new friends, and those fools believe her, of course! And now I so am cruelly refusing to acknowledge her pain and am keeping my heart closed to the needs of a mother who just wants to give me her love." She screwed her face up in disgust. "Did you see her at the ball yesterday? How did she even learn to dance so quickly? And the King of course opened the ball with her, falling prey to her well-applied charms just like everybody else."

"I think maybe you should go to Inad's dinner, Eryn. If only to make it harder for her to further pass around her sad tale. Isn't there something you can do here? I thought they had taught you malicious deceit, concealed manipulation or something?" Junar frowned.

"Political strategy," Vern smiled and refilled her water glass.

"Yes, that then," she nodded. "Shouldn't you be able to trip her with this somehow? In a diplomatic way, of course."

"Of course," Eryn couldn't help but smile.

"And there is one other thing that you might want to consider. It seems there is a story about your having clandestine relationships with several members of the senate in Takhan so they would vote for you to be cleared of the charges," Junar said carefully.

"What?" Eryn cursed and almost spilled her drink. "That bloody bitch!"

"You know," Vern shook his head, "I think that rumour game you are playing with your cousin is a bit immature, don't you think? You are supposed to be professionals, after all! People come to you to entrust you with their health. Seeing you behave like two silly teenagers is hardly bound to make confiding in you seem like an attractive proposition."

She flashed him a hurt look. "But she started it!"

He sighed and rolled his eyes. "Thank you, that is exactly the kind of grown-up remark I was hoping for."

* * *

Enric leaned against the wall of a building opposite the clinic and waited. The temperatures had dropped even further and he could see his breath condensing in front of his face. It was colder than was usual for the time of year, and he wondered if his vineyards would be affected by the weather.

His cloak disguised the blue robes underneath well enough for him not to draw curious glances, so he was at liberty to observe the street. He had left Urban at home, so people wouldn't just identify him at first glance due to his feline follower.

Today was no treatment day, no patients anywhere. So she would very probably not stay too long today.

And indeed, only several minutes later one half of the double doors opened and she stepped outside, wrapping her cloak tightly around her before starting to walk briskly towards the Palace.

He pushed himself away from the wall to catch up with her with a few quick strides. "Pe'tala?"

She turned with a frown at hearing her name and relaxed when she recognised him. "Enric. To what do I owe this unexpected pleasure? You are not normally lurking in the shadows waiting until I pass."

He smiled faintly. "Too little sun today for any decent shadows. Very bad weather for lurking in them. May I accompany you to the Palace? There is a little matter I would like to talk about."

"By all means. Who am I to deny the mighty Lord Enric something he wishes?" she shrugged.

"Good. Hold on to that thought," he remarked dryly. "I have been told of rumours pertaining to how a certain companion of mine managed to be found not guilty at the trial back in Takhan. Namely by having sex with both male and female senators and persuading them to vote for her."

"Oh no!" Pe'tala cried out in mock astonishment. "Whoever would dare to commit such slander?"

"Who indeed," Enric smiled without humour.

"She has hardly been any more considerate herself! She told people that I was being banished here for my promiscuity!"

He stopped and held on to her arm. "Your childish little games are your own business, however idiotic damaging each other's reputation is, as you are both supposed to be trustworthy adults who provide a highly dependable service. But let me warn you that if you invent stories that compromise my own standing, I will have no other choice than to intervene." His voice was stern and he noted with satisfaction that a certain unease and maybe even a tiny glimmer of fear were visible in her wide eyes. "And having people think that my companion might make a habit of sleeping around to gain favours with her body definitely has a negative impact on my reputation. You will thus oblige me in being more careful with any future slander of your cousin, and in addition circulate that this was misinformation. Have I made myself clear?"

Pe'tala swallowed and nodded silently.

"Excellent." He let go of her arm. "And now kiss me."

"What?" she stared at him, completely taken off guard by his demand.

"We have observers and I don't want to give rise to any rumours of you and me being at war. So we should be seen to be parting as friends. A kiss should convey that impression easily enough, though I would suggest a less... enthusiastic and more brotherly one than last time." He grinned when her face flushed red. "On the cheek, perhaps."

He bent down slightly and she obediently gave him a quick peck with cool lips.

"Well done, my dear. And now off with you to a warm place. You are still not sufficiently well dressed for our climate." He watched her turn and all but run the last few steps to the Palace gate before she disappeared without looking back.

Then he smiled and turned back to where he had come from.

CHAPTER 15

The Proposal

Eryn drew in a deep breath and shook her shoulders and arms to loosen them. She would have to be careful, stay in control, argument logically, respectful and point out the benefits for the Order instead of for herself. That did not sound that difficult, she told herself, trying to calm herself. She could do that. They would surely see reason if she presented it to them properly, wouldn't they? It was not as if she was dealing with unreasonable people here. Absolutely, she thought; an institution that had focused on nothing but fighting for centuries would of course be eager to listen to her rather revolutionary ideas. It was not like they were traditionalists or anything...

She looked down at the sheet of paper in her hands on which her notes were scribbled in various degrees of neatness. It was a list that had grown over the course of several days. She would first explain to them what the current situation was, why this was not ideal, what she proposed to do to reform it and what benefit they would ultimately derive. Logical, clear, comprehensible.

She straightened, let the paper disappear into her pocket and squared her shoulders when the large double doors opened and she was announced to the Council members. She felt thirteen pairs of eyes on her. So the King had sent an observer, curious to learn why she had decided to address the Council.

"Welcome, Lady Eryn," Tyront nodded to her. "You have asked to speak before the Council today. We are eager to hear what you have to tell us. It is the first time you have chosen to address the Council of your own accord, so you will find us curious to learn more."

"Lord Tyront, thank you for giving me the opportunity to speak before you today. I will not take up too much of your valuable time and try to make it short." She noted Enric's amused smile and forced herself to look away from him to avoid being distracted. It was a strange feeling to stand before him, reminding her of what she tended to forget when having nothing to do with him in his official capacity for a while: that he was one of the most powerful men in this country. And her superior.

"Gentlemen, I wish to propose to you the establishment of an association for healers." She let her words sink in for a moment, then continued. "The current situation is not exactly one conductive to providing high quality medical services in the city. We have all seen how the League of Apothecaries carried on, and the remnants that remained after the... the..."

"Execution," Enric supplied softly when the word seemed to refuse to come out of her mouth.

"Yes, that," she nodded, uneasy for a moment before she collected herself again. "Well, the organisation itself has not exactly thrived, to put it mildly. There is no coordination about which apothecary provides what products. In fact, they seem to have started competing with each other to a degree that is neither desirable nor necessary. The herb gatherers have so far refrained from forming any governing body for their services at all, as the apothecaries' example deters them. And then there is the matter of the healers, of course."

"They are subject to a governing body already, are they not, Lady Eryn?" an amused elderly voice asked. Lord Seagon. "It is called the *Order*, if I remember correctly." That earned him a few throaty chuckles.

Eryn smiled politely. She needed to retain her cool. This was important. No reaction to provocations or jokes at her expense.

"Indeed, My Lord. But as I intend to open the training scheme for the profession to non-magicians as well, I would prefer a governing body that includes *them* as well."

"The Order is not responsible for non-magicians," another Lord said and frowned.

"Exactly," Eryn agreed tensely. She could see from the narrowing of Lord Tyront's eyes at what exact moment he was realising what she was leading up to.

"You are surely not proposing to form a governing body for healing services which exists *outside* the Order, are you?" The warning in his voice was clear as fresh spring water.

She clasped her hands together. That was not how she had wanted this to play out. She had wanted to tell them more about the current situation, painting them a picture of darkness and doom before presenting her simple but practicable solution. No such luck. Damned interruptions! Next time she would just ignore them. If Lord Tyront ever permitted her to speak in front of the Council again, that is. Right now her chances of getting that didn't look too good.

"I am indeed, Lord Tyront. But I would kindly ask you to hear my proposal in full first," she pleaded quickly before the Council members started their typical chattering at any unforeseen comment. "The Order, you see, has for many hundred years been commissioned with keeping the Kingdom safe and defending its people. A task which has been performed admirably so far and will, I have no doubt whatsoever, be fulfilled as admirably in the future. The Order's focus has, for obvious reasons, been on warrior skills and fighting, while my efforts have gone in a completely different direction. As the services I provide with my healers are not being subject to the funding of the Order, I thus do not see why being subject to its rules is justified."

She risked a quick glance at Enric and felt immediately deflated. He did not look happy, not at all.

"What *exactly* is it you are proposing?" Lord Tyront asked with narrowed eyes.

Lifting her chin, she looked him in the eyes. "I am asking for all magicians who choose the profession of healing over a path in warrior skills to be released from the Order and be subject to an independent institution."

The smile on his face was somehow dangerous, though she couldn't exactly place why. "And tell me, my dear Lady Eryn, am I right in assuming that this independent institution would then be headed by yourself?"

"Not necessarily, though it is one of several options, of course," she replied and felt how her palms had started sweating. Why was it suddenly so damn warm in here?

"So you wish to start your own Order, as it were, only with the focus on healing instead of fighting, if I understand you correctly so far," he said, with an audible sigh, as if he couldn't quite believe what was going on.

"Not at all!" she protested, "Nothing like the Order! This institution would primarily not govern magicians, but instead focus on different professions and promote and coordinate their services. Magic and its application for healing would only be one of several areas it would monitor." She took a deep breath. "Could I just say, well... I know that some of you have always been sceptical about the idea of healing, and if you granted my proposal, you would not have to concern yourselves with that any longer. I am almost doing you a favour in taking this issue, of which you have no understanding anyway, out of your hands!" She regretted the words even before her mouth had completely finished articulating them. That might have sounded a little too direct and even offensive.

She saw Lord Tyront's gaze darken and took an involuntary step back when he slowly got to his feet. Had he always been that imposing?

"Let me make one thing very clear to you, Lady Eryn: Not a single one of the magicians in this city will be leaving the Order. And least of all *yourself*. You will continue to justify your actions to the Order and act in accordance with its rules." He smiled grimly. "You have been in the Order for less than a year, and I am not going to let you slip out of it again like that. You stay where you are: under *my* command."

Her first impulse was to nod obediently and look to the floor, but she fought it down determinedly.

"Healing will always come long, long after fighting! You make it compulsory for healers to practice combat training, but not a single non-healer has ever to learn basic healing principles!" she exclaimed, her fists balled at her sides. "Apart from Lord Orrin and Enric, not a single one of you here could heal a broken bone, even if someone's life depended on it! The profession of healing needs to be independent from the Order, or it will never be valued the way it should be!"

She saw Orrin covering his eyes with one hand and shaking his head slightly. When had this started going so very wrong? And why couldn't she manage to keep her mouth shut for once?

"Not valued the way it should be," Lord Tyront mulled her words, with a thoughtfulness that had an edge to it. The other Council members all but held their breaths. "Would you care to elaborate what we have done to give you this impression?"

Eryn gulped. Now was a bit late for silence. But maybe she could placate him with a calmer, more controlled tone. "The healers' quota is one issue which we are finding very difficult to deal with. The demand for our services has increased, while the number of healers has not." She barely managed to stop talking before Rolan's words slipped out - do the arithmetic. "And the Order's understanding of hierarchy is based on no more than chance, namely the strength with which a magician is born. This might be a serviceable approach to fighting, but for healing it is not. I require people who don't primarily have a lot of magic at their disposal, but know how to use it properly. We could complement each other - you keep the stronger ones, I get the smarter ones."

It was then she saw Enric closing his eyes. Damn it! Why did that mouth of hers never give her brain a chance to contribute something? Most of the other Council members were now regarding her with a slightly hostile expression, and they all had folded arms, narrowed eyes, furrowed brows, pursed lips, the whole range of disapproving body language, she saw.

"So we are to divide magicians into smart healers and dumb warriors?" Lord Tyront said with a voice that hinted that he found keeping his cool quite a challenge right now. "What a very, *very* novel idea. If I wasn't aware of your own companion and your good friend Lord Orrin being warriors and that you know very well that they are anything but slow-witted, I would start being massively offended right now, Lady Eryn," he growled. The room seemed to reverberate with the deep rumbling in his throat. "Also, if we were indeed to follow your suggestion, you yourself would have to give up healing and join the warriors, as you clearly belong in the class of *strong* ones. What's more, your current behaviour genuinely makes me doubt whether you would qualify for the *smart* class, anyway."

"I am not your enemy!" she protested. "I am just trying to provide a setting which might enable people to use those talents that have nothing to do with warrior skills but are valuable nevertheless!"

"Unlike wasting them like we are doing now?"

"Yes!" She hesitated for a moment and frowned. "What? I mean, no!"

"This is quite enough, Lady Eryn!" Tyront was now all but shouting, his hands braced on the large stone table. "Three days of stable duty! Lord Orrin, please get her out of my sight! Now!"

Eryn stared at him, taken aback, until she felt Orrin's hand taking her arm and lead her towards the double doors that were hastily opened for them.

She half turned and gave Tyront an angry look. "I take it this means that you are thinking about it?" she called over her shoulder, forcing a cold smile onto her lips.

"Five days!" he thundered behind her, and Orrin hastily dragged her out of the chamber and along the long corridor.

"Damn," he murmured. "You just lost me three gold pieces."

"What?" What in the world was he talking about?

"Vern and I had a little bet going. I thought you would walk out of here with three days, but he said that with your proposal and that nasty temper you would end up with between five and ten days."

"I can't believe the two of you were gambling on a thing like that!" she growled at him and jerked her arm loose from his grip.

"Oh, shut up, you," he sighed and shook his head. "Watching you in there and losing that bet were bad enough."

* * *

"What is that woman doing to me?" Tyront muttered and raked his fingers through his hair in agitation. "I ask myself why? Every time I think we have reached some comparatively peaceful form of coexistence, she does something like that! What am I to do with her?" He let himself fall into his chair. "I can't believe I lost my countenance, and in front of the Council, too." He shook his head at himself.

Enric took a seat at the sofa next to the window in Tyront's study and smiled consolingly. "Don't worry about that, I think it doesn't hurt to remind them every now and then why they should avoid making you angry. I liked the vibration effect. I did something similar in Takhan at the senate building. Never fails to impress."

"Enric, how can you joke at a time like this?" the mighty leader sighed. "I am starting to understand why that temper is feared in her home country. Did you observe her? I think she was at times angrier at herself than me for simply being unable to keep that mouth of hers shut despite knowing that she was making it worse with every word." He shook his head wearily. "And that parting remark of hers? I swear to you, it has been quite a while since I had to exert that kind of willpower to avoid myself lashing out with magic. I have always considered myself a balanced, even-tempered sort of man. I would very likely go out of my skull living with a woman like that. I wonder how you manage it."

"It has its merits. I never get bored. This last year must have been the most eventful in my life, and I have great hopes for the future."

Tyront rubbed his face. "That I believe. And now the King has even let her mother come over here. Two of them. In the same city. They don't even like each other. I shiver at what might happen if we can't keep them far enough apart."

"Well, back in Takhan they are known for causing buildings to collapse when they have their little family feuds," Enric told him. "The Aren residence is pretty much the most modern-looking grand family home there as they needed so much reconstruction work done at regular intervals. Her grandmother is said to have blown up a wine cellar once when she found her companion cheating on her."

Tyront stared at him in horror. "What misguided man dares to cheat on a woman like that? It would hardly surprise me if you told me next that the poor fool was still in there when it happened."

Enric looked thoughtful. "You know, people did become a wee bit nervous and taciturn when I asked them that, so that probably *is* a realistic scenario."

"I wonder how you can even go to sleep without worry of what might befall you."

"She has come to like me and pretty much given up battling against me, save for special occasions," the younger man grinned.

"It seems she has taken up battling with everyone around her instead," his superior added dryly. "Myself, her own mother, her cousin... is that woman ever happy without making somebody's life a trial?"

Vyril knocked at the open study door and entered when Tyront motioned her inside.

"I heard you come in, dear," she ventured with a tense glance at her companion. "Judging from the energy with which the door was shut I assume that your Council meeting did not go particularly well?"

"No, not particularly. Your most charitable superior Lady Eryn outdid herself today. I don't even remember the last time when I was that angry. No wait - I do remember. It was when she tried to get herself killed by lowering that shield when I had fifteen magicians shooting bolts at her."

Vyril shook her head as if showing her displeasure with a child. "You were not unpleasant to her, were you?" she asked with a slightly accusatory undertone in her voice. "None of this is easy for her, you know. Being forced to endure the mother of hers whom she can't stand - and rightly so! Added to which working with a cousin she is not exactly on good terms with. Then she has so much work on her plate with the healing, the training you are making her do and also now the orphanage. I have never had a single unfriendly word from her whenever I come to see her, no matter how trivial my concerns are and how busy she is. And look what she is doing, so unselfishly, for the city!"

Tyront looked at her in dismay. "You are on her side? You should have seen her today! Have you never wondered why there doesn't seem to be a single woman in her family who gets along with her? Or hardly any woman in our city?"

"No, Tyront, I have not! I decide on her character from how well I myself get along with her, which is exceedingly well! And I see how she has managed to make Enric here befriend other people for the first time in a decade and turn Vern into a confident young man with pride in his abilities! So don't you start talking like that about her in my presence!" Thus she turned on her heel and marched out again, her chin indignantly held high.

Enric whistled through his teeth. "Look at that."

"I think I must be dreaming," Tyront murmured with a disbelieving stare at the door through which Vyril had just stormed. "How is it possible that this day is becoming even stranger? My companion is obviously a great admirer of the woman who will drive me to an early grave! Now that is simply marvellous."

"You are aware that you need to admit Eryn to the next Council meeting, aren't you?" Enric asked casually.

Tyront closed his eyes and leaned back in his comfortable chair. "Don't remind me. I will give her another two weeks to get that tongue of hers under control and present me with an idea that I do not have to toss out before she even finishes speaking the introductory words."

"I will pass that on to her. I am sure she will appreciate your cooperation."

"Yes," Tyront growled. "As if I have much of a choice. The trouble is that we *need* an arrangement of some sort for the healers. But nothing like what she suggested. We can't have people thinking that warriors and healers are about to repeat history and divide into factions only to attack each other at some point in the future. The Order needs to remain a unified body, and I would value it if you could impress this on her. Add a small history lesson, if you must. And convey my warning that if I have the impression that my little stable assignments are not helping her to remember the respect she needs to show me, I will devise something else. Such as combat training with *me*, for a change. And if she thinks being punched by Orrin is unpleasant, make her consider how superior magical strength and unresolved issues can merge into something she surely does *not* want to experience."

Enric lifted his eyebrows. "I will pass all that on. And I would like it if we could change the subject away from your hurting my companion, if you don't mind." His tone was detached.

Tyront breathed out heavily. "Forgive me. I am not normally the kind to threaten women with violence."

Enric nodded once and then got up. "If you would excuse me now, I need to leave. There is a little matter I need to take care of."

"Trouble?"

"Nothing major. Urban killed a bolting horse today. One of Lord Woldarn's, unfortunately. Somebody dropped a shovel next to it, it became scared and ran. That awakened the cat's hunting instincts and she ran after it. Let me tell you that a few children out there will not be having pleasant dreams for the next few nights after that sight. So I have to buy him another horse. Now the horse breeder is in the city and I need to see him about a replacement."

"Funny how your females keep getting into trouble with the Council." Tyront finally managed a weak smile.

* * *

Eryn carefully put aside the book when the door opened and Enric entered the house. He smiled when he saw her cautious expression. So it seemed she had come to realise what exactly she had done now that she had calmed down again.

"Good evening, my love," he greeted her and lifted her chin to kiss her before sitting down on the sofa and pulling her onto his lap. "You made quite an impression today, I should say."

She looked chastened. "I must admit I expected you to be a little less... unperturbed when I imagined your coming home."

"I am not the one you should worry about. Tyront was a little out of sorts today, I have to tell you. But he is not one to bear a grudge for too long, or otherwise you wouldn't be doing anything but shoving horse manure all day long for the foreseeable future. He seems to have his doubts that this punishment serves its purpose, though. He is considering new, less agreeable options for future offences, so you might want to tread carefully," he warned her. He leaned closer to sniff her neck. "You smell good. What is that?"

She giggled when his nose tickled her throat. "Medical herbs. If you like the bouquet, I can put them into my bath water from now on."

He nodded. "Do that." Then he returned to the matter at hand. "Tyront has given you another chance to present something less outrageous in two weeks' time at the next Council meeting. You had better make sure this works out, or he will not give you another opportunity very soon. He told me to remind you of a few historic facts that are relevant to warriors and healers here a few hundred years ago. He reminded me that your attempts at leaving the Order would make a few of us rather nervous about that piece of history."

Eryn frowned. "You think I am about to stoke another war between the professions? That was not my intention at all!"

"I know that. Still, be careful of the latent fears you might awaken with these revolutionary proposals of yours. And, to be blunt, I am completely opposed to your idea of leaving the Order. I am with Tyront on this one. You stay where I can keep an eye on you."

She looked sceptical at this last remark and was about to get up from his lap, but felt his arms tightening around her to keep her in place. "I am serious, now, Eryn."

"I resent the implication that I need a caretaker," she replied stiffly. "And it's not as if there was any chance for me get out of it anyway."

"No, there isn't. I am glad we have established that," he confirmed sternly. "I wasn't even aware that this is an issue. I thought your days of running off were behind us."

Eryn leaned back against him. "I am not trying to run. I just thought that freeing myself from the restrictions of the Order will help me with my healing services. And I am not exactly getting along too well with Lord Tyront as my superior."

He shook his head. "No, this is not the way to do it. We will never permit you to leave the Order, under any circumstances. Not after what it took us to get you into it in the first place. You will have to thrash something out that does not exclude the Order." He smiled and chuckled. "And you started so well by telling us what a fabulous job we were doing in defending the Kingdom and how understandable it is that we are focusing our efforts on that purpose."

She sighed. "I had it all planned out so well. I had made notes."

"But the proposal would have been the same, and we would have rejected it in the end, my love. The only difference would have been that you wouldn't need to be getting up a lot earlier for the next few days."

"Don't remind me," she groaned with an unhappy expression. "Why now? I bet Malriel and Pe'tala will have a lot of fun when they hear about it."

"That is something you should have considered a little earlier, I would suggest."

"Yes, of course," she murmured. "Side with your superior, why don't you?"

"I try to avoid siding with anyone when it comes to the two of you. I would always come out the loser, after all," he pointed out. "Vyril subjected Tyront to quite a speech in your defence when we were back at his quarters today. He was aghast at first, then rather miffed. So maybe you find comfort in the knowledge that even though I am not on your side, Tyront's companion clearly is."

Eryn grinned widely. "That's good to hear. I should ask her to have a cup of tea with me some time. We only ever meet at these ghastly dinners you drag me to or when we meet up to talk about the orphanage."

Enric nodded. "You should, yes. She is having a rather difficult time at the moment and would surely appreciate that."

She frowned. "Vyril? A difficult time? Why?"

"Because she has started working. That seems to make her a bit of an outsider among her friends and acquaintances. It is not customary here for a rich woman to work, after all. Just be attentive and listen to some of their remarks next time I drag you to another ghastly dinner instead of visualising yourself doing horrid things to Inad."

"I won't deny that Inad provides material for a few immensely satisfying daydreams, which help me get through these evenings, so I won't allow you to make me feel guilty about that. As for the other, I don't think it is as bad as that. Junar and I are also joined to rich men, and we don't get treated worse because of working."

"That is because Junar was part of the working class before she joined Orrin, so she will probably never really be accepted into the elaborate circle of the high-born ladies, anyway. They more or less accept and some even like her because her companion is highly respected and outranks theirs. But you may depend on it that after a while they will very likely start dropping little hints that she doesn't need to work any longer. They probably think she hasn't realised this yet."

She wanted to object, but thought about it for a moment. It did have a plausible ring to it, she admitted. Especially considering some of the women's attitude. She was getting to know them much better than she cared to thanks to her new social life and the cosmetic corrections that were escalating in frequency.

"And what about me?"

He laughed. "You, my love, are a different book entirely, with pages they can't decipher because they don't understand the language."

She lifted her brow at him. "I like the book analogy, especially in connection with me. As I can't quite see what you mean, though, you will have to elaborate."

"Most magicians are known to work, no matter how rich we are. And magicians have until now always been men. So they are not really sure how to categorise you: as a magician who is supposed to be working or a rich woman who is not. But as you have decided that yourself, they are happy enough to go along with it and convince themselves that this is just the way it should be. They want to like you because you are important. As well as that, you come from another country, so they do allow you more latitude as a result."

"From another country? I have lived here since I was five years old! The fact that I work has nothing to do with my origins, I was raised *here*!"

"By a man who applied the standards of his home country when raising you," Enric pointed out. "But this doesn't really matter as not *your* perception but *theirs* accounts for how they treat you. And they have decided that your being from the Western Territories earns you their indulgence."

She grimaced. "I don't need their indulgence!"

"Yet you have it. Now in Vyril's case there are none of these factors to account for her sudden interest in getting involved with actual work. She is high-born, joined with a very powerful man, never before worked and was not subjected to any foreign influences in her childhood. She is just plainly and inexplicably different to them all of a sudden. And the only way they seem to be able to handle it is by making her feel bad about it."

Eryn looked at him disconcertedly. "And it works? Should I ask her to stop working with me?"

"Don't do that, no!" he protested quickly. "It would give her the feeling that not only are her friends turning away from her, but you are as well."

"I wouldn't! I just want to help her! If working for me results in her friends treating her badly, how can I let her continue?"

Enric raised both eyebrows at her. "That coming from you really surprises me. How would you react if somebody treated *you* like that? Making a decision for you because somebody thinks he or she knows what's best for you?"

"Vyril is not like me, I have been used to being without close friends all my life. I wouldn't waste a thought on them. But she depends on them a lot more and probably has done for decades."

"And for that reason you would deny her the chance to reconsider her priorities and make her own choices?" he enquired. "Stop arguing with me, Eryn. We both know that you are just doing it because you don't want to admit that I am right. Which I am, by the way."

"That must really be a burden," she sighed and rolled her eyes. "However do you bear it?"

"With dignity, as you can see," he stated.

"Funny, *I* only see smugness," she countered.

"That's how perceptions can differ," he smiled, then his face became serious. "Eryn, I would like to hear you say it again."

She blinked. "You would?" She shrugged. "Alright. Whatever makes you happy. I only see smugness," she repeated her words.

He exhaled slowly and closed his eyes for a moment. "Not *that*."

"Then be more specific! What do you want to hear?" she exclaimed baffled.

"I want you to tell me again that you love me."

"Why?" she asked, obviously completely at a loss.

He stared at her. "What do you mean, why?"

"But I have already told you! You know that I do. I asked you to join me in a third level bond, after all."

"You *already* told me?" he repeated and shook his head. "So you had no intention of ever telling me again? Because you established that fact once and for all time?"

"Pretty much so, yes," she nodded, but couldn't help feeling that he didn't really embrace the logic of his own words.

"This is not like a piece of information that you pass on and then it is taken care of. Being in a relationship means that there is a certain need to reaffirm our feelings every now and then," he said.

"There is? So you want to make sure that nothing has changed? That I haven't stopped loving you? Let me put your mind at ease then: I haven't. Nothing has changed."

"Eryn," he sighed resignedly, "*I haven't stopped loving you, nothing has changed* is not what I was expecting."

"Look," she swallowed, "I am trying to indulge you here, but you don't make it easy for me. And it's not as if *you* had told me that, not even once since our commitment."

"That's because I wanted to give you time and avoid scaring you away. And I was hoping you would say it voluntarily again, but now after more than three months I have given up waiting and decided to simply tell you that I need to hear it every now and then and also that I would like you to let me say it to you."

She sighed and nodded. "Alright, give me a moment."

He raised a brow at her. "You need some preparation time? Really?"

"Shut up," she muttered. "Or what I am going to say will hardly match up to your requirements." After a few moments of silence she turned to him on his lap and lifted her arms to put them around his neck. "Enric, I would like you to know that I love you. Still." She watched an amused smile spread on his face and then he shook his head slightly. "What now?" she asked in annoyance.

"You just couldn't stop yourself from saying that last bit, could you? But it was not bad for a first try. And that was not so hard, was it?"

"It felt a bit strange," she shrugged. "Like stating something obvious. But if you want to hear it, I suppose I can work on that."

"It's good to see that you are willing to make an effort and brave that inhumanly difficult task I had the audacity to impose on you," he nodded solemnly. "And now let me show you how this is done in accordance with the rules."

"There are rules? Really?" she quipped.

"There are, yes. No snide remarks. That one you broke by adding *still*. Phrasing it in a positive way. Which you broke as well by telling me that you have *not stopped* loving me. Saying it voluntarily and at regular intervals..."

"...which of course I broke by making it necessary for you to ask me to tell you because I neglected doing it for three months. Yes, I get it," she grumbled.

"Good. Then let's move on to the actual statement, shall we?" He smiled at her. "Eryn, I love you. You are the first thing on my mind when I wake and the last before I drift off to sleep each night. You warm my heart and stir my blood. I will never let go of you again." He leaned forward and pressed a gentle kiss onto her lips.

She gulped, feeling oddly touched. "I admit that was... a little different. Pleasantly so," she admitted after a few moments of reflection.

Enric smiled. "I am glad you liked it. Did you notice the little flourish at the end? It is not a rule as such, but a kiss is just that extra touch that makes it perfect."

She laughed and rose. "I will bear that in mind. Thank you for the helpful guidelines. And now I really should be going to bed; I'll need to rise early tomorrow due to a certain unpleasant assignment. Feel like joining me? I could make sure that I really am the last thing on your mind before you fall asleep tonight."

He nodded and rose quickly. "Maybe we could turn this into a rule? Every time I tell you that I love you, you invite me to follow you to bed."

"Hardly," she snorted. "I would have to impair your vocal cords to keep you from saying it several times a day."

He grinned. "That's probably true, yes."

CHAPTER 16

Society Games

Eryn pulled her cloak tighter around her shoulders and yawned widely and noisily, marvelling at how the dark, overly empty streets threw the sound back at her. There were the first signs of dawn visible, but it would take some time yet until the city woke completely. The few people out on the streets threw her curious glances. Seeing a magician up and about at this time of day was unusual; they normally didn't have to rise that early. And so they didn't.

She saw the outline of the stables at the end of the street and, as she got closer, that a pitchfork and cart had been prepared for her, exactly like last time. Well, she thought, at least the poor sod who usually did that work had a chance to lie in for a few days thanks to Lord Tyront's punishment. Why did it always have to be in the morning? Why couldn't she muck out those damn stables in the afternoon? Because the mucking out was not the issue, she realised. It was the getting up that got to her. Unfortunately he was well aware that her pride would not really suffer from being seen by the public doing such menial work, but instead knew that getting up early was the real problem here. Almost three hours too early. And this for five days in a row. Once again anger niggling at herself for not shutting up in time awoke briefly.

She had been doing fairly well before her trip to Takhan. But somehow after returning here it seemed that whatever she had learned was gone again. Six weeks away from Lord Tyront had obviously let her forget that she needed to be more careful around him. He was one of the very few people in this city she needed to avoid provoking, and yet that was apparently an impossible task.

She thought about his threat of making her undergo combat training with him. That was definitely something she wanted to avoid. She knew that he was not as able a swordsman as Orrin or Enric, but nonetheless superior strength was always enough to defeat a considerably weaker opponent. Even she, with her barely more than rudimentary skills, was able to defeat Orrin, the blade master, with not much more than sheer brute strength.

The night guards patrolling the streets around the stables bowed to her when they spotted her and wished her a good morning. They had obviously been informed of her assignment as they did not appear at all ruffled by her presence. She nodded briefly in acknowledgement and pushed open the stable doors, finding the lantern just where it had been last time.

Ah yes, she thought sarcastically, wasn't coming home a comfort? The ten horses in their boxes were in various states of sleep, some dozing while standing with their heads and necks drooping, others lying down with their legs folded beneath their bodies or on one side with all four legs stretched out.

The dozers' ears twitched when she came in and she could almost feel the level of skittishness rising at her entry. They could smell the scent of mountain cat on her.

She opened the stable doors wide and irritated the horses even further by letting in cooler morning air.

"Can't be helped, girls and boys," she murmured. "I can't sleep, so why should you?"

She hung her cloak on a hook outside, pulled the cart closer, grabbed the pitchfork and commenced her noisome work.

About one hour later she had cleaned out about two thirds of the stable when she heard a sigh of satisfaction behind her. She turned towards the stable doors, where a very smug looking Pe'tala was standing, arms folded and grinning broadly.

"I do love that sight very much. One does not see a mighty Aren shovelling horse muck all too often," she sneered.

"Then I would advise you to enjoy the sight while you can, as it will not become a regular one," another exotic female voice replied softly.

Eryn glared at the second woman who stepped into view behind her cousin. Malriel. Seriously? They had both risen early to come here and watch her do this?

"Malriel," Pe'tala said, obviously equally unenthusiastic about the other woman's presence. Eryn turned away from them, her lips pressed together in determination, and resumed her work. She would not let them provoke her. At least they didn't enjoy each other's company so very much either, so watching her was not an undiminished pleasure for them.

"Pe'tala," Malriel replied with a nod. "What a perfect morning for studying stable cleaning."

Pe'tala focused her attention back on Eryn. "I must say you clearly are very capable when it comes to this kind of work. You are being sent here regularly for practice either because you cannot keep that Aren temper at bay or working as a healer is the wrong calling for your abilities."

Clenching her teeth, Eryn didn't reply but kept up her rhythm of bending down, driving her fork into the soiled straw, lifting it, carrying it the few steps to the cart before depositing it and walking back to start anew.

"Not very talkative today, are you, *sister*?"

Eryn hid a smile. That last one was clearly not only aimed at her but also at annoying Malriel. Maybe having them watch her could turn out to be entertaining for her as well if they kept provoking each other.

"How very inconsiderate of her when such a charming conversation partner is at hand," Malriel smiled thinly.

Pe'tala gave her a disgruntled look. "Do you even recognise your own reflection any more, Malriel? Ageing with dignity was obviously never something you considered trying, was it?"

"We will talk about that when you are my age, little Tala," Malriel replied calmly. "We will see how much *you* enjoy the visible signs of ageing when you are quite grown up."

"Visible signs of ageing," Pe'tala mused. "Yes, I gathered that you are not a great friend of those, and not only when it comes to yourself. You are known to avoid them in the men you take as lovers, too. Have you ever had a suitor who is not young enough to be your own son over these last ten years?"

"Not envious, are you?" Malriel raised her brow. "You do not have to be, I can assure you. You are a pretty girl. Do not let the fact that Ram'an cast you aside for a woman he cannot have drag you down. Put a smile on your face, keep that spiked tongue of yours under control, and in time you might even find a willing young man who is not terrified of spending some time with you."

Eryn could hear her cousin hissing in annoyance. That was funny, she had to admit. Their four-day journey here must have been a real trial for both of them. A cheerful thought it was, as she lifted another pitchfork of manure. It seemed they had even forgotten that they had come to tease *her* instead of each other.

"I do not require a pool of lovers to make me feel appreciated, but thank you so much for your advice. I was told always to listen to *much older* people. Though one cannot always trust their words as there are certain illnesses that befall a very... mature brain and suddenly their words cease to make sense if untreated. Would you like me to have a peek at yours, Malriel?"

"No, thank you, girl. I remember well enough what happens to people whose head you play around with," Malriel said, obviously hinting at the incident about ten years ago when Pe'tala had been forced to justify herself after letting an admirer think he was continuously being chased by huge birds. How handy that Ram'an had told her that story back in Takhan, or that stab would have been lost to her.

"Do not worry, Malriel," Pe'tala said. "It would not be birds for you. I would choose for you to think that only men of your own generation found you appealing. That would surely come as a nasty shock for you - probably bad enough to make you swim all the way back to Takhan in one day. Or I could make your face reflect your true age. Around sixty, was it not?"

"How very witty, Tala. I only hope for your own sake that your clumsy jibes do not reflect your level of intelligence. Or one would have to wonder if you are truly a Vel'kim. They are said to be rather bright, after all. Or was that only in the male line?" Malriel retorted.

"Probably. Ved'al was obviously smart enough to rectify his mistake of joining you by taking flight at the first opportunity," Pe'tala lobbed back nastily. "Though a really smart man might have managed to avoid getting stuck with you in the first place. Is it not alluring what Aren money can buy?"

Eryn swallowed. That had been a low blow, but then they had not exactly been gentle with each other so far. She put aside the pitchfork, glad that she was finished. Being spared nasty remarks on her own account was a relief, but listening to them for an extended period of time was scary. She hadn't been aware that they detested each other so much. What a trio they were, she thought wearily as she grabbed her cloak from the hook. Each one of them despised the other two. Whatever they said about one's enemy's enemy being your friend clearly did not apply when it came to her own relatives.

She passed them without having spoken a word to either and quickly left the stable area to get out of earshot and back to her house where she had still time for a quick bath before she was due at the training grounds to play Orrin's assistant.

* * *

Junar entered the parlour as Vern completed packing together the books and papers he had needed for the lesson with Eryn and was about to disappear into his room.

"Are you done for today?" she asked.

Eryn nodded. "We are, yes. And I am glad we are. My concentration is not too special right now. I'm really missing my sleep in the morning. I go to bed earlier, but it's just not the same." She stretched her arms wide and yawned.

"No pity for the cheeky girl," the seamstress said. "I hope you didn't put Orrin's poor class through undue exertions? It's not their fault that you are not getting enough rest."

"No, I didn't. It was a rather peaceful session. Since I locked that one boy inside a shield his peers are very careful around me."

Junar shook her head. "I am still amazed that they let you get away with that. That is not considered use of excessive force or something?"

Eryn shrugged. "Obviously not. But I dare say the consequences would have been different ones if I had done it with Lord Remdel's grandson. Or if I wasn't that high up in rank. Which does still not protect me from certain punishments it would seem. Imagine - today I had to carry out two different ones in succession. That is a new record."

"Next time you might want to employ that well-worn method of thinking before talking."

"I will give it some thought," the magician nodded tiredly. "But today was the third out of five days at the stables, so that's more than half of my sentence. I wish Pe'tala and Malriel wouldn't keep showing up. The first day it was quite funny - at least at first. They were really catty to each other, no pretence at politeness there at all. But yesterday and today they obviously remembered that they didn't get up that early to torment each other, but *me*. I swear to you, if they don't leave me in peace, there will be trouble."

"Were they mean to you, darling?" Junar cooed. "Do you want me to kick them for you?"

"I wish you could," Eryn snorted. "But they are bloody magicians. I am beginning to think that it might not be such a bad thing to live in a place where women don't have magic."

"Yourself excluded, of course."

"Of course. *I* use it responsibly," she replied haughtily, then took a sip from her water glass and considered her friend thoughtfully. "Can I ask you something personal?"

Junar nodded, curious. "You know you can."

Eryn leaned forward, casting a quick look at the half-open door to Orrin's study and lowered her voice. "Do you tell Orrin that you love him?"

Her friend raised both eyebrows in surprise. "Of course I do. Don't you?"

The magician grinned. "No, I hardly ever tell Orrin that I love him. I think his companion wouldn't appreciate it. She is even moodier now that she is carrying his child."

"You idiot," Junar sighed and popped a piece of fruit into her mouth. "Is there any deeper significance to this question or are you just nosey?"

"Enric told me he wants to hear it from me occasionally."

"So? Why should that be a problem? Are you not the sharing kind?"

"Well, let's say I feel awkward telling him the same thing time and again. It's not that he is likely to forget it, is he?"

Junar shook her head. "You are not being serious, are you? Telling your companion that you love him should not be a bothersome duty, but a privilege. So you yourself don't feel the need to hear it?" Then she sighed. "But then I am forgetting who I am talking to."

"What is that supposed to mean? That I am cool and distanced?"

"No, just that you have been raised to keep people at arm's length and are only starting to get over that. One only has to look at your family to see that."

Eryn groaned. "Really? You use *those two* to measure my character by? The woman who dragged me before the senate in an attempt to have me sentenced after I had made a little slip of confiding in her. Not to mention the other woman who hates me because the man who was supposed to join her dropped her, owing to his wish to be joined with me... You should rather be giving me credit for not hitting each of them on the head with something blunt and heavy every time I see them. I feel I show great restraint in that."

"Don't change the topic. So, are you complying with his simple wish to make your companion feel loved every now and then or not?"

"I am working on it. I told him a few days ago when he asked me to. I am not sure how often I am supposed to say it. Is once a week a good interval? Would once a month suffice?"

Junar covered her eyes for a moment, a habit she seemed to have adopted from watching Orrin. He somehow seemed to do that a lot in her presence, she thought.

"This is not something you write on a list and make a check mark next to it! It springs from the occasion. That may at one time be on two subsequent days or even hours, and at other times a week may pass until you will want to say it again. I can't believe we are having this conversation," she sighed.

"Don't be like that! I was raised by a single parent who fled his companion and even went to another, forbidden country to escape her. Where exactly am I supposed to have learned this? The fleeing thing I have come to understand completely in the meantime, mind you," she added darkly.

"I wonder if you and your mother will manage to exchange a few civilised words before she leaves here again. It really is a pity with the two of you," Junar stated.

"Oh, come on!" Eryn exclaimed. "Not you, too? People keep telling me what a shame it is that we are on such bad terms. The braver ones even tell me that I should be ashamed of myself for treating the poor woman like that."

The seamstress grimaced. "Brave? That is loopy! Have those people ever been heard from again or did you dispose of them discreetly?"

"Very funny, Junar," Eryn growled. "I usually rise with a polite smile and leave the room. Instead of following my first impulse of hitting them with a nearby heavy object. Interesting. That urge has become more frequent since Malriel's arrival. Maybe I should start carrying such an object around with me."

"Oh, quite - because being the third strongest magician in that country doesn't make you dangerous enough," Junar sniffed.

"Not for non-magicians, there is this little law about not hurting them with magic if you care to remember? The one that got Orrin in trouble?"

"Did I just hear my name?" a voice came from the study door. "I felt a cold shiver running down along my spine, so I thought that probably has something to do with the two women in my parlour," he smiled and came closer, kissing Junar on the forehead.

Eryn nodded. "Yes, these are my misguided powers of stirring up unease." She touched the back of his hand and sent a small pulse of magic into his body to his spine, whispering, "Orrin!"

He grimaced at the unpleasant sensation of a cold shiver running down his back and pulled his hand away quickly. "You stop that! Misguided powers indeed. Everything in your hands would probably turn the wrong way sooner or later."

Junar sniggered, then linked her fingers with his. "Orrin, did I recently tell you that I love you?"

He smiled at Eryn's grimace. "Not recently enough. I love you, too." He bent down to place a small kiss on her lips.

"Really? That *had* to be just now?" the healer moaned. "If you want me to leave, just tell me!"

"Don't behave like a teenager! Not even Vern reacts that childishly. This, my dear, was a little demonstration of how painless it is to say it when the mood strikes you," Junar lectured. "Now you go home and try it out yourself."

"You are kicking me out?"

"I am, yes. I have agreed to go to Inad's dinner and need to get ready for it. Remember? It's the one you refuse to attend because it's one of the two places in this city you don't want to be."

"Make that three," Eryn muttered and stood.

Junar gave her a warning glare. "Don't provoke the pregnant woman, kid. I may not be able to throw a bolt at you, but I swear to you that a carafe of water is just as painful when it hits your head."

Eryn cleared her throat. "Oh my, so late already? I am afraid I really must leave now." She turned towards Vern's door and called out, "Vern? I am leaving now. Stay out of Junar's reach, she's just threatened to throw heavy breakable objects at people!"

"You are not supposed to provoke the mother-to-be!" he called back, his voice slightly accusatory.

Junar grinned broadly. "What did I tell you? You have to like that boy."

* * *

Eryn ground her teeth and kept on shovelling, indulging in fantasies of burying her two observers up to their necks in a heap of strong-smelling, steaming dung. They had turned up every single day of her punishment to mock her. Today's the last day, she reminded herself. After four days she would surely get this final one behind her as well. She was proud of herself. Not once had she acknowledged their presence in any way. Not by talking to them, shooing them away or attacking them with whatever stable tools were so easily accessible. It just wouldn't look good to have them walk away with a pitchfork stuck into each of their chests. It might make people wonder if she was the kind of healer they wanted to entrust their health to.

"What a pity this is your last day," Pe'tala remarked. "But from what I have heard this will surely not be the last time they send you here. That Lord Tyront definitely does not like you, does he? I cannot imagine why somebody would choose not to like *you*, of course," she added with a sneer.

Eryn dumped another fork load of manure into her cart and returned to the box. It was the last one. When that one was clean in no more than a few minutes, she would just leave here not to return anytime soon.

"I heard about the nice dinner the day before yesterday hosted by that impossible woman who does not seem ever to have enough cosmetic restructuring done," Pe'tala continued, unperturbed by the lack of response. "It seems Malriel keeps spreading that very sad mother-daughter story and impresses on people how very unfairly you treat her. Poor, suffering mother, being cursed by such a heartless, unforgiving daughter. Though I am not supposed to term you *mother and daughter* anymore, am I?"

There are a lot of things you are not supposed to do, Eryn thought angrily. Like slowly wearing away at my nerves. One had to give it to the two of them, though – they were persistent. Four days of being ignored had not stopped them from returning a fifth time. That was high tolerance for frustration. Though Malriel mostly settled for just leaning against a convenient wall and watching her. Which was unnerving enough. Pe'tala, however, preferred the more active approach of constant teasing and baiting.

"You will not believe who visited me yesterday at the clinic while you were upstairs training the healers. Vern and Junar."

Eryn froze for a moment, then carried on with her work. That was surely just another try to make her react somehow.

"I see that got your attention, *sister*."

She could hear the glee in Pe'tala's voice. "Vern brought her to me to have a real healer have a look at her. Somebody with real experience, training and healing awareness. Did you know that it is going to be a girl? This will be interesting, her being the first girl to be fathered by a magician after you removed the barriers. I wonder if she will have any magical abilities. That would be quite a sensation here, I imagine," she rambled on.

A stab of anger, a sensation of betrayal made Eryn slowly release her breath. So Vern really had taken Junar to see her cousin. Without telling her about it. She would have to have a word with him about that.

"I find Junar a very pleasant woman, I really must say. Not one of these tiresome society persons with more money than sense. I am thinking about inviting her to have dinner with me one evening. And I will ask her to bring Vern along. An amazing young man. I admit I had my doubts about him at first, but he is a smart and very talented boy. And a very good healer. I wonder why he puts up with you. But then this is the only way you are allowed to work as a healer around here, is it not?"

Enough was enough. Eryn lifted her last fork load, heavy with watery manure, from the ground. They wanted a reaction? Well, they would get one. She fuelled the muscles in her arms with extra strength, hurling the load of manure into the air, and used two bolts of magic to split it into two and give each part direction. A moment later the dripping clumps landed on each woman's face and neck. She saw them frantically wiping the remnants of the missiles from their faces and spitting out the taste from their mouths. Pe'tala cursed loudly between noises of coughing and retching, but Malriel simply laughed.

"Good, my girl. You had me worrying for a while whether my looks were the only thing I had passed on to you."

"You just watch it," Eryn spat at her, an index finger lifted in front of her face, "or the next thing that gets thrown in your face won't be soft but instead a lot more solid and spiky."

Then she turned and leaned the pitchfork against the wall for the last time before she walked back home with the feeling of a job done properly.

* * *

"Is it true that you stabbed your mother with a pitchfork and then covered her in horse manure?"

Eryn looked up from her desk and saw that Vern had stuck his head into her study.

"What? No! And since when haven't we knocked before annoying people?"

The boy shrugged and entered. "I did, but you didn't answer."

"Perhaps because I didn't hear you due to being so busy? Which could possibly indicate that this is not a good time to disturb me, couldn't it?"

"Don't tell me that your paperwork is more important than your good friend who really wants to hear about your latest nasty trick?"

She glowered at him. "My good friend? The same one who brought Junar to my beasty cousin to have her checked over without informing me? Imagine how pleasant it was to learn about this from her while shovelling horse manure."

He grimaced. "I didn't intend to keep it a secret, I just haven't seen you since then. You are not angry about it, are you?"

Eryn rubbed her face. "No, not about your seeing her. She knows things I don't, I freely admit. But *telling* me would have been a courtesy. And how is it she thinks that you are about to become best chums?"

"Well, I do get along with her quite nicely," he said after an uneasy pause. "She came by a few times to have her measurements taken, try on the clothes, pick them up when they were ready, order new ones... So we just sat down with her, had a drink or two..."

"You really are being good to her?" Eryn hissed. "How can you? You are my friends! She can't have you! What's next? Inviting Malriel for dinner over at your place?"

"Don't be so petty! That is not very grown up behaviour! Why can't we like your cousin or sister or whatever just because the two of you are too stubborn to get along with each other?"

"I am not the one justifying myself here! You are!" she protested.

"Can we just leave that topic alone? I don't need your approval to make friends with other people," Vern said in a matter-of-fact way. "Now, did you just stab Malriel with a pitchfork or not?"

"Of course I didn't! What kind of a question is that? I just hit her in the face with a bit of horse dung. Seriously, who comes up with a story like that?"

He shrugged. "You know how stories change with the telling. I have no idea how many mouths passed it on before it reached my ears. But it's good to hear that you kept your violent urges under control. Well, almost."

Eryn sighed. "Can we change that topic, as well? What did Pe'tala say about the baby? Everything alright?"

Vern beamed. "Yes, everything is just fine. A healthy girl, right on schedule with size and whatever is supposed to be going on in there. She showed me a few things that she says should be looked at when examining a mother-to-be. I can show you later, if you like."

She nodded. "Very well. I will come by later. How was that dinner at Inad's two days ago? Did your father or Junar say anything?'

"They did," he said hesitantly.

"Spill it out, then," she sighed. "It was about Malriel and her rejected mother routine, wasn't it?"

"Yes," he admitted. "She really seems to be determined to get people on her side for this one. Junar told me that she was once again telling the sad story that her only reason for accusing you back in Takhan was to make you stay longer after finding you again after decades instead of losing you again after a few weeks."

"Great," Eryn rolled her eyes. "At least people will get sick of that story soon enough judging from how often she is telling it."

"Not from what Junar says. No matter how often they hear it, they seem to hang on to her words every time. And when one of them hints that your behaviour might have been rather heartless, Malriel defends you."

"Which of course makes people sympathise with her and despise me the more. This is just brilliant," she muttered, beginning to see the calculation at work in Malriel. She needed to stop her somehow. She had written to Vran'el about what Malriel was doing and he had urged her to stop moaning and instead start doing something about it. But he had not told her *what* to do about it. He either had no idea but didn't want to admit it, or thought that the answer was so obvious that he clearly didn't have to point it out. What was she to do? Challenge Malriel to a duel?

"And Junar told me about Vyril," the boy continued. "She says her friends are not being very civil to her, making snide remarks about her work all the time."

Eryn frowned. So Enric really had been right - again. Damn him.

"How did she react?"

"By giving them polite and offhand smiles and conversing with other people at the table who were less rude. The dignified, passive-aggressive routine with the cold shoulder. What are you going to do about Vyril?" he then asked.

"What am *I* going to do about her?" she exclaimed. "I can't even do anything about Malriel making me seem like a daughter out of a nightmare, how am I supposed to help Vyril?"

"So you will ignore what she is going through? It is a pity; Vyril is so pleasant and so decent. If she had a bit more of Pe'tala or you in her, she would only need to shut them up with a few very harsh words and be done with it."

"I can't do that! Enric and Lord Tyront would drag me out of the room each by one ear and give me a right Royal dressing down! They keep impressing on me that I am a public figure and need to start behaving like a responsible adult. Lord Tyront even threatened to relieve me of my role as head of the clinic if I don't!" A sudden thought hit her. *She* had to comply with that requirement, but Pe'tala didn't, did she?

"You know what, I might have an idea. Go. I need to talk to somebody."

The boy got up. "That's my girl," he grinned.

"You can't say that to me, Vern," she sighed. "I am twelve years older than you."

"Not in spirit you're not, Eryn, not in spirit," he winked and left her study.

She shook her head and stood as well to walk over to Pe'tala's study a few doors down the corridor. An impatient "What?" came from inside after she had knocked.

She decided to consider this an invitation and entered.

"What do you want?" her cousin called out unhappily.

"Don't play that insulted routine with me just because teasing me for several days rewarded you with a clump of horse dung in the face.

You provoked me for that and you know it. So shut up. I need something."

Pe'tala raised an eyebrow and leaned back in her chair, clearly intrigued. "Do you now? Mighty Lady Eryn comes to a mere underling to ask for help?"

"I need to you to go to a dinner with me and do something for me there."

"Why would I?"

"Because I am going to pay you for it. And it is something that you will very likely enjoy anyway as you are such a natural at these things."

"I am not normally for rent, whatever you may have heard about me," Pe'tala said with narrowed eyes. "And I am a natural at which sort of thing?"

"At being a real bitch. See, I happen to need one for an evening. I'll pay ten gold pieces. Take it or leave it."

Pe'tala pursed her lips. 'Ten gold pieces? That equals about twenty gold slips. Handsome pay for what exactly?"

"For being the bitch I would like to be but am not allowed to be anymore."

"Keep talking."

* * *

Enric smiled to himself as he was reading the progress reports from the Bonhet construction sites. Things were progressing fast indeed. There were two factors that helped a lot when it came to ensuring that structures were completed on time: being a magician, which made people generally eager to comply with whatever he asked, and promising the workers a generous bonus for finishing within the agreed time. The bonus he paid them would be well spent, as being able to handle the goods shipped from the Western Territories properly would earn him quite a lot more than his outlay on incentives.

He looked up when he heard a sound and saw Eryn and Urban standing in his door. They were each of them on their own an impressive sight - both lithe, elegant, beautiful with this underlying tension and power that made each of them dangerous in their own way.

"Why do you look so amused?" Eryn enquired.

"I am just so happy to behold my two ladies. You are home early. Today was the last day of your stable duty. I heard that you hurled manure at your two observers."

She folded her arms, clearly expecting to be told off for it. "So?"

He shrugged. "Nothing. You won't hear me blame you for doing it. They had it coming, in my opinion. I think they can consider themselves lucky that they had no implements stuck in any part of their body when they left. There are rumours about that, by the way.

I had heard that you severed Malriel's toes with a shovel, but that is clearly not your style. If you resorted to measures like that, I doubt that you would stop at her toes," he added serenely.

"Charming," she snorted. But then he had a point there.

"I don't harbour illusions about you, my love. I know that you have a propensity for expressing your temper rather fiercely if provoked enough. Though from my past experience I know that you would avoid inflicting physical harm, being a healer and all that. You didn't even truly try to hurt *me* when you were still our prisoner. And after learning more about your healing skills and what happened when you were a girl I know very well that you could have." He saw the look on her face. This area was not a pleasant topic for her. "And she is still your mother, no matter what she has done to you or what the official legal status is."

"You just had to say that, didn't you?" she said sullenly.

"It's not as if never hearing it will let you forget it, I imagine," he chuckled. "But at least Malriel is going to leave again in two weeks. Your dear cousin will be spending a lot more time here before she returns."

Eryn's expression darkened. "Yes, and there is a tiny matter I have to discuss with her, anyway. She is getting a bit too close to Vern and Junar. It is one thing to continue our private feud, but pulling my friends into this is not something I will accept."

"You think she is befriending them just to vex or even hurt you?" he enquired carefully.

"Of course she is! She sees that whatever else she does doesn't bother me enough."

"Right. And a good example for her complete inability to get to you is the load of manure you threw in her face this morning," he pointed out.

"That was just because she told me about her evil intentions to invite the two of them to dinner at her place."

"Doubtlessly not because she likes them, but to annoy you."

"Exactly!"

He sighed. "That is not a very flattering opinion of your own friends you have here. You think nobody but yourself might like them for their own sake, but just pretend to do so in order to hurt you?"

"Of course not! They are both great, and you know that!"

"I do, yes. But it seems like you have forgotten it for a moment. Why don't you give Pe'tala the benefit of the doubt? Even she might be able to recognise great people when she meets them," he added. "And from what I remember she might accuse you of the same. I dimly remember your befriending a certain non-magician healer she is close to."

"That was hardly my fault! Valrad introduced me to him, and I didn't even know that they were friends at that time!" she protested.

"Indeed? I wonder what Pe'tala's point of view on that little matter would be."

"Stop making me feel small and petty!"

"I am not. I can't make you feel anything. I can just fan the blaze that is already burning there."

"Very poetic," she said. "Alright, I won't accuse her of anything the like for now." She narrowed her eyes. "But I will be watching her. Carefully."

Enric nodded. "Which you should as a good friend. That I tell you not to judge her prematurely does not mean you should discard your doubts about her intentions just like that. There is still the chance that you are right and she really is using them."

"You are doing that on purpose! Just when I reluctantly agree with you, you change course back to what I was saying at the beginning of this discussion!" she exclaimed.

"I didn't say that you were wrong, just that you are not necessarily right. Which means that you need to be prepared for both cases. But you didn't come in here to talk about this. Is there anything I can do for you? You don't normally come to my study for a casual chat."

She straightened. "There is indeed." After hesitating for a short moment, she said, "I need money."

He furrowed his brow in surprise. That was new. "You do? How much?"

"Ten gold pieces."

He opened one of the desk drawers and took out a leather pouch, which made a jingling noise as he put in on the desk surface. He silently counted out the amount she had asked for, got to his feet and pressed the coins into her hand.

"There you are, my love."

She stared at the shiny heap of gold on her palm. "You didn't ask me what I need it for."

He nodded. "Very true. I didn't. And I have no intention of doing so. Do you need a pouch for it?"

"That would be good, yes," she answered slowly, clearly surprised by his readiness to part with a sum like that without even wanting to know what she intended to use it for.

He opened another drawer, took out a small leather bag and motioned for her to drop the coins into it. Then he pulled the strings close and handed it to her.

"Next time you need money you can also go to the money lenders. There is a box in your name containing five hundred gold pieces. If it is empty, the lender is instructed to inform me so I can replenish it."

She stared at him. What? Five hundred gold pieces? How was one person ever to spend a sum like that? That was simply frivolous! And he would just replenish it if it were empty?

"Why?" she just asked, caught between surprise and dismay. Why was he so careless with his money? What if she just went on a spending spree and spent it all on jewellery and clothes or, well - more realistically - books?

He sighed and looked directly at her. "Don't look so alarmed. You will need it, believe me. You have to pay Vyril every now and then, I would imagine. And give her money for the expenses of the orphanage, construction work, food, clothes and so on. Or you just give her the authority to withdraw what she needs, however you wish to handle this." He kissed her forehead. "But you are, of course, always welcome to come to me directly. Though I don't have larger sums here in the house, so for that I would ask you to go to the money lender's or give me notice of an hour or two."

She looked up at him miserably. "What are you doing here? I just wanted ten gold pieces, and you push five hundred at me! I am not used to handling that kind of money! What if I bankrupt us?"

He laughed. "Honestly, it would take a lot more than spending a few hundred gold pieces to empty us out. And you may depend on me to keep an eye on our expenses, so don't worry about that. I wouldn't give you more than we can afford to lose."

"I find that unnecessarily trusting of you. I thought you were that calculating, hardened businessman! At least that's what people keep telling me," she complained.

He stared at her, utterly amazed. "I share my *emotions* with you, and you think giving you a few hundred gold pieces is too trusting?"

"You are not sharing your emotions voluntarily!" she protested. "It's nothing you chose, it just happens, so it is not an argument that stands up."

"I would have chosen to share if there had been a choice."

"You would have? Really? Just like that?" This time she was the astonished one.

"Yes. Just like that. So in comparison with the mind bond giving you a few hundred gold pieces is a minor thing."

She considered him for some moments, lips pursed. He really meant it, but when did he ever not do? She supposed that always having had more money than he needed at his disposal must have made him see it as a minor thing. One probably had to experience poverty first really to appreciate the value of money.

"Alright, then let me thank you for this," she jingled the pouch, "and the wealth you have deposited for my use. I will try to make it last."

"I have no doubt that you will," he smiled. Not with that strong aversion against spending, he thought.

She turned to leave and stopped at the door frame. "Ah yes, about that dinner invitation we got for tomorrow."

"Yes?"

"I accepted it."

His eyes bulged. "You did *what*?"

She rolled her eyes. "Don't act so surprised. It's just a dinner invitation. I thought you wanted me to be more sociable, make useful contacts and all that?"

"I did," he nodded slowly. "And I still do. Though until now you have kept fighting against it instead of voluntarily accepting invitations I would have let you skip."

She smiled broadly. "Isn't it nice that even mighty Lord Enric, who always prides himself on being prepared for whatever may happen, can occasionally be surprised?"

"I have never really managed to prepare myself for the things you keep throwing at me, my love. There is no preparation for it, apart from expecting the worst."

"Let me remind you of that when you are angry at me next time."

He smiled weakly. "Don't. I wouldn't take it well."

* * *

"I hear Vyril and I are going to see you at Lord Aldon's tonight. That surprises me a bit. I thought you had no intention of going?" Tyront enquired.

"I didn't. Eryn wants to. Don't ask me why. It was an evening of surprises yesterday. In addition to volunteering for the first time to attend a social gathering of any kind, she also asked me for money."

"Did she now? I assume you didn't enquire what she wanted it for?"

"No, I didn't. I don't want to make her feel like she has to account for anything she spends," Enric said with a shake of his head. Nonetheless, he would love to know what was important enough to her to come and ask him for money for the very first time.

"Provided she doesn't spend it in large quantities, I assume," Tyront chortled.

"Yes, always provided that," Enric grinned. "But for now I don't see much danger for that. She accused me of being too trusting in her when I told her about the money lenders' box I have filled for her."

"It seems as if she didn't really trust herself with money, then," the older man pointed out.

"That thought occurred to me, too."

"Does Eryn know that her mother will be at the dinner as well?"

Enric shrugged. "I assume she knows that this is very likely. Malriel has been getting herself invited to every occasion of late. And the number of occasions has also increased since she has arrived here. People are eager to spend time with her, to include her into their elite circles."

Tyront smiled. "Not entirely unselfishly, I would say. Malriel is a powerful woman, after all. And she is connected to a very powerful couple here. From what I hear she is also getting along very well with the King."

"Yes, she certainly does know how to win friends. Yet getting her own daughter to like her is a challenge she has not yet overcome. What's more, I doubt that her little games will aid her in that respect," her adopted son sighed.

"Well, it's not as if things could become any worse between them than they are now, is it? So what does she have to lose?"

"Nothing much probably. But I would think that she is rather aiming at winning something, and making people put pressure on Eryn to forgive her mother will not win her anything."

Tyront nodded. "I have heard that people still keep on suggesting that Eryn make up with Malriel. I wonder why they don't learn. It is no secret how Eryn treated those who did so in the past. I hope they will stop before she resorts to less pleasant measures than showing patients the door or just rising and walking out herself. She will be meeting a few of those people at the dinner tonight. I hope she will behave herself." That last remark did contain a warning.

"I am sure she intends to. She has *chosen* to go there, after all. For whatever reason."

Tyront looked disgruntled. "You think she is up to something?"

"Don't you?" Enric asked.

"Probably. I just hope it is nothing that will make the Order come out looking bad. I do have the impression that she tends to forget or rather block out that she is a high-ranking representative of it. But judging from the fact that she tried to get out of it only recently, she is obviously not too concerned about how her actions reflect on us," he said sourly.

There was no use in denying that, Enric knew. She didn't make any effort to keep her low opinion of the Order secret.

"At least she chooses to communicate it to the Order itself, not to outsiders. That must count for something," he said.

"The trouble is not that she communicates it, the problem is that she thinks of us in that way in the first place. I seriously hope that she will present us with a halfway sensible concept in a few days. One that will enable us to show her that we are willing to cooperate with her and I hope improve her opinion of us. Which should in turn make her more ready to work with us instead of just obeying reluctantly."

"That is going to be difficult as long as she still feels unfairly treated due to warriors' privileges in comparison to healers."

"I am aware of that, Enric. The problem is that I am not the only one making decisions in the Order. She needs to convince the Council of a need for major change, not just myself. And if she doesn't modify her attitude when she addresses the Council the next time, she will not manage to convince anybody in it, no matter how reasonable her ideas are."

Enric nodded. Yes, that was the real nub of it. He had no doubt that Eryn would be able to come up with a concept that was more appealing to the Council members. Presenting it to them without making them feel that agreeing to it would be nothing more than what she was due anyway would be the real challenge.

"Anyway, there will be a few Council members at the dinner tonight, so Eryn can start trying to improve their opinion of her. Maybe it will help her."

Enric snorted. "Can you imagine *her* trying to endear herself to people?"

Tyront laughed. "No, not by any stretch of the imagination. But then one should always be prepared for the unexpected."

The younger man smiled, thinking of how he had expressed a similar sentiment with regard to her only the evening before.

* * *

"Are you ready?" she asked, and caused Enric to shake his head at her reflection in the mirror.

"Now you are really starting to scare me. Out with it. What are you up to?" he demanded while buttoning up his sleeves.

"Me?" she called out, all hurt innocence. "What would make you think a thing like that?"

He rolled his eyes. "Alright, don't tell me, then. Just hint if I need to be prepared for a speedy retreat."

She smiled. "That will not be necessary. I am sure of it. Or let's say optimistic about it. Well, fairly positive. Full of hope."

"That rapid decrease of your confidence is not exactly reassuring," he sighed. "Come on, then. Let's go to that dinner. Do you even know the host's name?"

Eryn thought for a moment. "It's another Council member, isn't it?"

"Yes. Lord Aldon. So I assume whatever you are planning has nothing to do with him or his companion as such, as you can't even remember their names," he concluded.

She frowned impatiently. "Are you coming now or not? The coach is waiting outside already."

He sighed and checked his reflection in the mirror one last time before he followed her out the door. He knew from other men that this was how it was supposed to work: the women all eager to leave, the men being more or less dragged along to another tedious evening they would rather have spent alone with a good glass of something and a good book or at one of the upscale pubs. But experiencing it himself for the first time was... just unnerving. Under normal circumstances it would have amused him to find himself in that situation when only a year ago he had pretty much reconciled himself with the fact that he would probably remain a bachelor for the rest of his life. But this was so unlike her and he wondered if he should insist on determining what was going on here or just hope for the best. She would not react well if he used a truth block on her. That would very likely spoil the evening for her. And for him as a result.

Which meant that he had already decided in favour of the second option. He grabbed her cloak from the hook next to the door and fastened it around her shoulders before draping his own over one arm and opening the door.

She pulled her cloak around her tightly, grateful that Enric had insisted on having another one made for her with a warm fur lining. It was much too cold for the one she had used until only few days ago, especially when wearing one of those elegant dresses that were made for looking elegant in but hardly for keeping a woman warm.

"The next Council meeting is in only a few days. How is that proposal of yours coming along?" he spoke into her thoughts.

She looked grim. "Not too well, I must be honest. I am trying to find valid reasons that won't sound offensive, but they sound confrontational even to my ears."

"You know that an important characteristic of a leader is to know one's own weaknesses. And that there are two ways of dealing with them."

"Which two? I suppose one of them would be getting rid of the weaknesses by developing one's character, skills or whatever," she ventured.

"True," he confirmed. "But that is not always possible or even preferable. What might be a weakness in one situation might turn out to be a strength in another, so getting rid of it is not always the best solution. The second way of dealing with it is delegating it to somebody who is better at accomplishing the task than you. Which is another thing a good leader should be able to do: surround yourself with people who are able to do the things you can't or have no time for."

"Delegating? I can hardly delegate a matter like that..." Her voice trailed off. Maybe she couldn't delegate it entirely, but instead make another person work on it with her. Somebody good with structures. Who delighted in playing around with details. Rolan. Unfortunately he was not the most diplomatic person to present this to the Council in her stead or assist her in discussing and even negotiating. But then she had somebody else who was really good at that. Vern.

Enric watched a thoughtful expression spread across her face, followed by a smile.

"You know," she nodded slowly, "I think I will heed that advice. You sometimes really are useful to have around. At least when we don't get mixed up in our different roles. Although it probably doesn't really matter if you tell me off in your capacity as my companion or as my superior."

"Glad to be of service, dearest. I will graciously ignore the rest of what you said for now."

"How very gracious of you indeed," she grinned. "How much longer until we arrive? Does it make sense to sit next to you and have you warm me?"

"A few more minutes. And it always makes sense for you to snuggle up to me, no matter for how little time." He lifted his arm to let her slip under his cloak with him.

"As long as you keep your hands to yourself," she murmured and all but fell against him when the coach turned a corner.

"I don't think I have to, unless I am very much mistaken. You are mine. I can do with you as I please. Didn't anybody tell you?" he quipped and pulled her close.

"Just you, and you are not trustworthy," she shot back and pushed his hand away from her bosom. "Behave, Lordling."

"That one I haven't heard in a while. Lucky for you that was not a public insult this time, so the retribution will be private as well."

She laughed when he lifted her chin despite her attempts to turn her face away. "Stop that! You really are a bother when we are alone in a coach! Next time I'll make sure to have Junar and Orrin with us again."

"It's not my fault she wasn't feeling well today. I am just using an opportunity that presents itself," he remarked and kissed her, careful not to mess up her hairstyle while cradling her head.

Next time she looked up again was when she felt a cool draught across her face. The coach driver had opened the door for them to exit, first staring at them in surprise, then quickly averting his eyes. She couldn't be sure in the dark, but she had the impression that his face was about as red as her own felt. Without looking at him, she let Enric help her out and guide her to the entrance door.

"What was his name again?" she whispered when he knocked loudly.

"Lord Aldon. His companion's name is Eliar," he replied quietly a moment before a servant opened the door.

After their cloaks were taken away, the host and hostess, who did look familiar to Eryn, greeted them warmly, clearly delighted at being graced with their presence. They were led into a parlour, where a few guests were already assembled and were standing together in small groups, each person talking over a glass of wine. Around fifteen heads turned towards them as they entered, two of them dark haired. Pe'tala was here. Good. Malriel as well - which was hardly unexpected and couldn't be helped.

Malriel approached them with a smile and greeted first Enric with kisses on both cheeks, then turned to Eryn, who had quickly wandered away to join the group Vyril and Lord Tyront were talking to. Lord Tyront was surely not her favourite person to spend time with presently, but still preferable to Malriel.

"Lady Eryn," Vyril beamed, sounding relieved at seeing her. "I am so delighted that you could make it tonight. I hear Junar had to decline the invitation due to feeling unwell?"

"Yes, the baby does not seem to approve of her meals and is regularly making her bring them back up lately," she explained.

"Isn't this something a healer could take care of?" Lord Tyront enquired.

"No, because the cause for the sickness is still there, and the symptoms would return soon enough after healing them away. It is something which would have to be repeated every few minutes. It is the same with sea-sickness. Only after the ship has stopped pitching on the sea does it make any sense to heal the stomach," she illustrated.

"Eliar!" They heard a booming, nasal voice that made Eryn close her eyes for a moment. "Your dress is simply ravishing! I wish I could wear that colour!"

Vyril smiled sympathetically. "It seems Inad has arrived. No dinner is complete without her. There is always the danger of missing something otherwise," she murmured in a low voice.

That was not so bad, was it? Inad was one of those to spread news quickly, after all. Which did not exactly make enduring her presence any more bearable. But then it probably paid to be acquainted with somebody who was in close contact with Inad – that was a sure way of always getting the latest gossip.

When the last guests had arrived, Enric stepped next to her and took her arm to lead her to the dinner table. Eryn sighed under her breath. That was always the least pleasant part of these evenings. Before and after the meal she could stand together with the people she preferred being with, but while eating there was the seating order the hostess had laid out and she was more or less forced to talk to the people next to and opposite her. Her spirits sank when she saw that Malriel had been placed directly in front of her. So the hostess was one of these well-meaning sorts who was trying to make everything between them come good again. How very considerate of her.

Vyril and Enric had been placed as far away from Eryn as possible as if to make sure nobody she delighted in talking to was close by and might make ignoring Malriel easier for her. One had to admire such deviousness.

"Malriel," Inad's voice not far away to her right sang out, "you must be so very proud of what Lady Eryn has accomplished here in our city. She is our entire pride and joy here!"

Eryn forced a polite smile. What a clumsy, transparent attempt to make her feel guilty after hearing Malriel say something positive about her.

Malriel smiled. "Of course I am. It does not exactly diminish the pain of being separated from her, but at least I know that people here are benefiting from her commitment and her wish to make this world a better place."

"Really?" Eryn replied with a smile that turned out more a baring of teeth, "That makes me wonder why you attempted to get me held in Takhan without any chance of returning here. I would say your concern for the people here was not so high just a few months ago."

Malriel's bearing became stiff when she shook her head sadly. "It was a plan any desperate mother on the verge of losing her only child again would make. It pains me that you do not feel you can forgive me for it."

Eryn clenched her jaws. She knew it wouldn't make a difference if she pointed out to their audience that they were witnessing nothing more than a carefully studied act on her mother's side. That would just make herself seem more heartless and unforgiving than she did already.

"Whatever you say, Malriel," she uttered dismissively, then shrugged and resumed eating without sparing the woman another glance.

There were a few moments of silence until a few of the chattier guests resumed their chatter to cover the awkward gap in the conversation.

Eryn's ears perked up when she caught a snippet of the topic she had been hoping for at the other end of the table. Around Vyril. She saw Pe'tala straightening slightly. Good. She had been seated pretty much at the centre of the table, which was useful. Lord Tyront's face seemed neutral at first glance, but Eryn had learned to recognise the tension in his expression. It was a survival skill in her case, after all. Not that she had figured out how to react to it appropriately, of course. Playing dead, maybe? She had heard about certain animal species coping fairly well with that trick.

"...at the orphanage, my dearest? I heard you are in discussion with the *builders* now. How very novel!" a nasal voice said with barely contained amusement.

"I am, yes," Vyril replied calmly, without the usual warmth Eryn was accustomed to when hearing her talk.

"For the life of me, I wouldn't know how to talk to people like that! I am sure you are learning a lot of things in your *work*."

Before Vyril could answer, Pe'tala's voice spoke above everyone. "I can tell you a little something about talking to builders, though I have to say that this is a task I am happy to leave to other people who are more proficient in that area. It requires a lot of different skills, such as the ability to decipher construction plans, determination, a certain direct insistence when it comes to negotiating schedules and costs, and last but not least quite a lot of insight into human nature to see when they are trying to get the better of you. I respect anybody who can handle such people properly. It is a talent, I think."

The woman who had spoken to Vyril blinked, clearly taken aback by having her words of hidden disdain turned into a compliment.

"But hardly a task for a lady of such high standing," the woman remarked loftily, being more pointed in her insult to make sure it was perceived as such this time.

"Where I come from," Pe'tala said, smiling mischievously, "determination, intelligence and diligence are also occasionally to be found among the high-born and rich women." Then she leaned forward slightly. "May I enquire what *your* profession is?"

Several polite and indulgent smiles appeared on various faces.

"Our ladies do not have to bear the burden of everyday labour in the *classic* sense," Lord Whateverhisnamewas replied. "In our society we take pride in showing our regard for our companions by not subjecting them to pursuing a *profession*. It would just not look good."

"Indeed? Wouldn't it?" a gentle male voice asked. Enric. "My, oh my. Then I dare say Lord Tyront, Lord Orrin and myself really should be ashamed of ourselves."

Eryn hid a smile.

"I assure you, Lord Enric, this was not the way I meant it! Of course everybody knows that your companion's humble origins..."

Eryn cleared her throat. "I assure you that my origins never were humble, neither before I left the House I was born to originally, nor after joining my father's. For this discussion that is hardly an appropriate argument."

She almost pitied the poor man. First he had insulted three of his superiors by making them seem like unloving and inconsiderate companions and then he had tried to make amends and in the course of this managed to slight her, another superior, strictly speaking. He seemed very much aware of this himself, judging from the sallow appearance that had befallen his face.

Pe'tala cut in before he could make any more ill-judged attempts at defending himself. "So the ones with access to resources such as time and money for proper education do not contribute to society as such?" There was an incredulous undertone in her voice, nicely accompanied by a scrunched-up nose as if she found the thought somehow repellent.

"We do not consider contribution to society limited to engaging in work in the *classical* sense," Inad pronounced in an imperious tone. "We do not think that our kind of efforts are worthy of any less value, though. Maintaining contacts, keeping the social life running and providing a comfortable home for our companions is surely worth something, even in your country, I would think?"

Pe'tala nodded. "Absolutely. Making a comfortable and safe home for your family is a task that indeed deserves recognition! I have seen that people here do rely on servants a lot for this - having them cook all the meals, do all the cleaning, raise the children... But it is good to see that some of you still make an effort to stay in contact with the challenge of providing for themselves."

Inad stared at her, eyes wide, her mouth snarled in contempt. "Cooking and cleaning? But of course we employ servants for this! The work of a lady of the house is hardly up to doing these tasks herself, more to instructing the servants accordingly and keeping note of the effectiveness and standard of their work!"

"Instructing people? So you tell them how to do the things they do every day anyway? Things they have done for years and that you are not experienced in undertaking yourself? And then you *check* on them? Like walking after them and letting your finger glide over surfaces to see that they are adequately dusted?" Pe'tala asked with a chuckle. "Yes, I can see how that might keep you busy all day long. It seems my dear sister Eryn and Vyril have a better quality of servants, as following them around all the time does not seem to be necessary in their cases. They even have time to make themselves useful outside their homes," she added pointedly, before turning to Vyril. "I have to commend you on your commitment to such a noble cause. Helping those who cannot help themselves is a show of true magnanimity where I come from. And especially in your case, where you have to take on so many responsibilities that often require several people to handle them. Let me assist your cause not with my physical effort, but with something that will I hope be equally welcome."

Pe'tala rose and Eryn gaped when she pulled out a familiar small brown pouch from between the folds of her dress to put it next to an equally surprised Vyril with a distinct jingling noise. "It is all I have on me right now, but I hope it will aid your efforts. This is another little thing we like to do back home: Those who can afford to, like to support the less well-off members of our society if their line of work does not go in that direction anyway."

"Why, I have to thank you very much Pe'tala," Vyril said with a smile which disclosed her perplexity at both the words of praise and the generous gesture. All eyes on the table were on her when she carefully lifted the pouch to remove it from the table, with people were trying to gauge the amount to which it was filled by how much it bulged.

Eryn shook her head slightly and leaned back. That had been unexpected. She had a pretty good idea about how much was in that pouch. Very probably exactly ten gold pieces.

Enric caught her eye and raised his brow. He, too, had of course recognised the pouch. Judging from his slightly amused look he had a pretty good idea why it had been in Pe'tala's possession before she gifted it.

Vyril took her time putting away the pouch, completely unperturbed by the silence around her. When she was done, she returned her attention to the generous donor.

"So this is a custom that is acknowledged and practised in your home country? How very interesting. I admit that giving something back to society, and not just the wealthy part of it, was my main motivation for taking over this task which Lady Eryn was kind enough to entrust me with. I find the idea of this being part of the regular way of caring for others a very appealing one, I must say," she smiled.

"It is," Pe'tala nodded. "I was rather surprised at finding that this is not the case here. Well, not generally, to be precise. It seems only yourself and my dearest *sister* have it in yourselves to care for people who are less privileged."

"We do pay our taxes, which fund both the clinic and the orphanage," Lord Aldon, the host, said stiffly, very probably regretting inviting this impertinent foreigner to his little gathering.

"From what I know the clinic is self-funding, so there is hardly any need for your tax money there," Pe'tala returned. "And I had a look at your orphanage while taking a walk; from what I saw there, the amount spent on keeping your parentless children fed, warm, clothed and educated must be rather small. But I am sure that Vyril here could tell you a lot more about this. Though I doubt that you want to hear it."

"This is hardly the right setting for a discussion of this nature," Lord Seagon remarked with a critical look at Pe'tala, who merely looked at him with the innocence of one wrongly accused of a crime.

"See? Just what I thought," she shrugged.

Eryn marvelled at her. Pe'tala had made use of her position to her best abilities. She was a guest, so there was a certain restriction on what people would say to her, due also to the fact that she was related to two of the three most powerful magicians in the country. Nobody would hold her accountable for being impolite as she was not subject to any authority but the one back in Takhan. And to her cousin - but that was more or less a voluntary arrangement.

To be allowed to voice opinions freely to all these stiff, conceited, self-important people like that again! Eryn remembered the days wistfully when she had been a prisoner and when nobody had really expected her to be very civil to her captors. Somehow this had changed as soon as her captors had become her superiors.

"Well, the clinic is funded principally by fees Lady Eryn asks for some of her... custom services," Lord Woldarn interjected. "Quite handsome prices, if I may say so. Which means that *we* basically are the ones paying for the medical services in the city," he pointed out.

"But you get the service in return for it, do you not?" Pe'tala countered. "You do not do it from the goodness of your heart, but because you want to keep your companions, or some other female company you keep, happy and beautiful. That counts as no more than trade, nothing you can claim as an accomplishment."

Eryn smiled at the lord. "Dear Lord Woldarn, I am not forcing anybody to engage my services if he or she cannot *afford* to. They are entirely voluntary. I do not impose them on anybody, people come to *me*."

"I did not intend to imply that I was in a position not to afford them," he huffed. "I just..."

"I am glad to hear it," Eryn interrupted him with a nod and then looked away from him to show clearly that she considered this conversation with him over.

Malriel cleared her throat and many expectant and hopeful faces turned towards her, as if whatever her next words would be, they would surely salvage the evening. Eryn herself was curious about how the experienced politician would handle the situation. Pe'tala's behaviour did not reflect on herself too favourably, after all.

"I think, my dear Pe'tala, that we do not have the right to pronounce on customs that differ from our own. I am sure there are matters people here would not approve of in our own home - ones which we consider normal." She then smiled at the other guests. "Do not let my fellow countrywoman make you think that this spirit charity is something we pursue only to satisfy our own need to serve people less fortunate than ourselves. We do enjoy social gatherings as much as you do here, which means we like to combine these two things and use enjoyable festive occasions with good food, wine and music to make helping others as pleasant for ourselves as we can."

That seemed to mollify the others. Not bad, Eryn thought with reluctant respect. Telling them that her own people were not necessarily better people as such, but just enjoyed social gatherings under the pretence of doing good seemed to have won her many points with her audience. And it also made Vyril's efforts more acceptable, as caring for the poor was something that the high and mighty in Takhan considered a matter important enough to be taken care of by themselves.

"How very fascinating! Malriel, you must tell me more about these occasions!" Inad called out, sensing an opportunity of being seen to do something nobody else had done here before.

Malriel's smile became a fraction strained, though only to the keenest eye, as she answered, "Of course. It would be my pleasure."

When the host then rose to accompany his guests into the spacious parlour in order to serve them drinks, Eryn casually strolled over to where Pe'tala was leaning against a windowsill with a quiet smile.

"Satisfied?" the younger woman murmured.

"Completely. I really did hire myself the right bitchy woman for the job. Though it seems I owe you another ten gold pieces as you employed the ones I gave you for a very impressive gesture," Eryn replied in the same low voice.

"No, you do not. I got my pay, and I decided to spend it the way I saw fit. And I do like the thought of your owing me a favour. And of you not being too happy about it," she grinned while sipping at her wine.

"Terrific," Eryn growled, but there was no real gripe in it.

* * *

Tyront and Enric watched the two dark-haired women standing together in front of the window.

"I assume we have just found out what she wanted the money for," Tyront said after making sure that nobody was close enough to overhear them.

"We have, yes. It was one of my pouches."

"Damn it," Tyront murmured. "Now I shall have to like her again after sending her off to the stables."

"Don't bother," Enric smirked. "I promise you she did it for Vyril, not for you."

"I know that, but she refrained from behaving badly herself, delegating it to somebody whose conduct would not make the Order appear in a bad light. So I need to value her consideration at least. And I definitely don't have to explain to you why doing a good deed for my suffering companion lets Eryn rise in my esteem nevertheless."

"No, not really," the younger man admitted.

"All the same, I am surprised at her resorting to measures such as that, though," Tyront mused. "She is not really on good terms with her cousin, so it was probably not pleasant for her to ask. But then I suppose it would have been easier for her to ask a favour for somebody other than herself."

"Do you think it will have the desired effect? Will that end the sniping remarks Vyril has had to suffer?"

"I believe it is very likely, yes. Now, someone who says something even remotely derogatory about her work aiding orphaned children will make themselves seem petty and miserly after this evening. An effective way of ending things as it appeals to people's vanity. And if you look at the women here today, most of them are your companion's customers for these so-called *custom services*. So vanity is definitely the topic here."

Vyril joined them, sipping at a small glass of something dark and sweet-smelling.

"What did I tell you, Tyront? That woman is a gem. In fact, both of them are. That is the real tragedy - that the two of them are not able to find some way to get along well - not that this devious mother of hers plays the injured victim."

Enric hid his smile behind his wine glass when as he took a sip. Unusually harsh words from gentle Vyril.

She then turned away from them to cross the room and stand beside Pe'tala and Eryn.

"The two of you really are a pair, you know," she sighed.

"Pardon?" Eryn enquired politely.

"Don't play any games with me, my dear. You did know that Enric's pouches have a very small, hardly discernible, seal affixed on the bottom-left corner, didn't you?"

Damn. "No, I wasn't aware of that." How was she to disburse money anonymously for the dirty deeds she bought when he used marked pouches? Really now!

Vyril smiled smugly. "I liked the part about praising Inad for keeping her house clean and cooking meals. I swear to you that woman has never in her life touched an uncooked vegetable."

Pe'tala grinned widely. "I thought she was about to pass out from the shock of the insinuation that she would get her soft hands dirty with such menial work."

"But luckily serene, sovereign Malriel was here to conciliate people with her remarks," Eryn said somewhat darkly.

Vyril considered her for several moments, then shook her head. "You need to do something about her, Lady Eryn. You are fighting the game she plays because you are open and direct. But this is not the way to set her boundaries."

Eryn looked at her thoughtfully. Maybe this was what Vran'el had meant in his message. "And what might be the way to accomplish this?"

"Play the game. She has selected the role of the victim for herself. That leaves only the role of the offender for you."

"You are not suggesting that I battle her for the role of victim, are you?" Eryn grimaced. "Nobody would believe me, anyway!"

"No, not with your attitude, they would not," Pe'tala stated dryly. "From what I heard they did not even see you as a victim when you essentially were one during your captivity here."

"I don't see why I should have to be ashamed of that!' Eryn protested.

"You haven't," Vyril soothed her, casting a surreptitious look around to make sure they had no unintended listeners. "But appearing as the victim is not automatically a position of weakness - quite the opposite. People are sympathetic and want to support the victim, if they like her. You would have to be a reluctant victim, just the way Malriel plays it. If you handle this deftly, the shock at seeing you show an apparent weakness will convince people that you really are the one to be supported." Then she smiled impishly. "I have the feeling that Inad is on the verge of planning a dinner intended to coax people into giving away money for good causes. Very soon, I imagine. I suggest you think of something you would like to show people." At Eryn's uneasy expression, she added, "I know you are a proud person, so showing weakness is probably not something that comes easily to you. But consider that blatantly demonstrating a false weakness may spoil Malriel's plans and cause her immense annoyance."

Eryn nodded slowly. "Alright, I can work with that."

CHAPTER 17

Malriel's Affair

Enric looked up at the knock at his study door. His companion held up a piece of paper that looked suspiciously like a Royal summons.

"Have you also been instructed to meet the King tomorrow afternoon?"

He shook his head. "I haven't, no. This means it is probably about either the orphanage or the clinic. These are virtually the only two concerns of yours that have nothing to do with the Order, but with you and the Crown."

She nodded slowly. That did not sound too demanding or alarming. She would surely be able to deal with either of these matters without a problem as they were running smoothly enough now.

"I wish he would deign to write in his messages what he wants. A hint would suffice! That would at least make it possible to prepare myself adequately," she sighed.

Enric smiled. "I think that is exactly what he wants to avoid. He wants authentic reactions, not practised behaviour. Not that he isn't very good at seeing right through the latter, mind you."

Eryn walked over to the sofa to one side of his desk and sat down with a tense look on her face. "I don't want to see him alone. I find being alone with him disconcerting when he tries his little games with me. If it is about the clinic, I could send him Rolan, and Vyril would be the better concerned party for anything connected with the orphanage, anyway."

"He wouldn't react well to that, my love. He sent for you because *you* are the person he wants to see. And you have not been called to him for quite a while now, so it was to be expected sooner or later. As you said, he likes to toy with you a little every now and then."

She looked concerned. "You don't think he will subject me to another test in political strategy, do you? I'm afraid I wouldn't perform very well in such a thing right now. I am struggling with games of my own which I am buried up to my neck in at the moment."

"You mean Malriel?"

"Yes. And Vyril, though I hope that this one has pretty much been resolved now. We will see about that at Inad's dinner."

He nodded. "We should, yes. Though Tyront thinks nobody will dare make another snide remark about Vyril's work after your little trick at Lord Aldon's."

Good, she thought, that would enable her to concentrate energies on Malriel instead.

"Will you be paying Pe'tala another ten gold pieces now, since she used her payment for this interesting gesture?" he then asked.

"I offered to, but she declined. It seems she delights in knowing that I owe her a favour. And it's not exactly as if she needs the money, anyway. I bet she was granted a nice allowance, and Valrad wouldn't have let her come here without sufficient funds to live on comfortably, either."

"True enough," Enric acknowledged. "Have you seen Junar today? I remember you said something about wanting to check on her."

"I have, yes. We had lunch together. Or I had lunch while she was watching me with a slightly nauseated expression."

"So she is still having trouble with keeping her food down?"

Eryn nodded. "Yes. But that's nothing to worry about, I have read that this is completely normal and should pass in a few weeks at the latest. Pe'tala agrees. Though Junar was not exactly happy about probably needing to endure this for another few weeks."

"Neither would you be," he pointed out.

She grinned broadly. "I wouldn't, no. But then this is not exactly going to be a thing for me, is it? That's one of the few experiences I can very well live without." Then her expression changed when she saw a paper slip with familiar handwriting lying on the edge of the desk. "You are corresponding with Ram'an? Seriously?" How was it possible that that man seemed to be on speaking terms with everybody else here but her? First with Vern, and now even with Enric, who he had more than enough reason not to like!

Enric nodded slowly. "I am, yes," he said carefully. "Business matters."

"I wasn't aware that you are engaged in business with him. I thought his House refused to enter into any trade agreements with the Kingdom when we were there," she pointed out.

"That was when his father was still in charge of House Arbil," he explained. "Now the situation has changed."

Eryn's eyes narrowed. "And why would he be corresponding with *you* about that, now that we have a permanent ambassador in

Takhan? I would have thought that this would be one of Kilan's areas of responsibility now."

"That is, of course, quite true," Enric conceded, "But the business matters are not between House Arbil and the Kingdom as such. The official trade agreements with the Kingdom are signed, so for the time being there is not much Ram'an can do to rectify his father's short-sighted course of action."

"You are doing business with him *directly*?" She narrowed her eyes. "Why? Why would you care about Ram'an's House so much? It's not like the two of you parted as chums."

"House Arbil is in serious financial difficulty," he told her. "Malriel told me about that. The Houses not allied with Arbil are trying to help matters go their way by not granting the family any credit until they get back on their feet. They see a chance to get rid of one House and strengthen their own standing. House Aren - and also Vel'kim, by the way - would not benefit from that. We need to get House Arbil back on its feet. A strong ally is better than an ailing one."

She nodded slowly. That did sound reasonable enough. "So there is nobody but you to help them recover? I would think the other Houses allied with House Arbil would share in that aim."

"They do. Your uncle has renewed some of the agreements with House Arbil despite the risk that they might not be able to pay in time. Luckily, Ram'an's brother took over the management of their crops quite a while ago, so at least they have something to sell, even though the agreements their father entered into were anything but advantageous to them. Then House Partém granted them a loan."

"And now House Aren has started buying goods from him, it would seem," she sighed. Why did that annoy her so? Probably because she was still angry at Ram'an for treating her in such an offhand way in his letters. She looked down at the bracelet he had given her on her commitment day to wear as a token of House Arbil's friendship. His friendship. That friendship had not lasted very long, yet she was reluctant to take the bracelet off, as if this gesture would mean that she truly and finally was convinced that he was no longer a friend.

Enric watched her pondering expression. "Don't worry about him, my love. He has a lot of problems on his plate right now, so I dare say he is not exactly the most pleasant person for a conversation at the moment."

She made herself smile. "I know. I will give him time. Let's see what will become of him in a few months." Then she got to her feet. "I am hungry. You know, I feel like cooking. Do you have any plans for tonight or is it going to be a quiet evening at home with the two of us and Plia?"

"No plans that I have. I don't know about Plia - has she even returned from the clinic yet?"

Eryn shook her head. "No. She said she wanted to test planting seeds out during different phases of the lunar cycle. I really wonder where she gets these ideas from. Probably from the herb gatherers when they bring her their plants."

"Don't tell me this bothers you? I can't imagine your being against experimentation and working out new things?" he raised a questioning eyebrow.

"Not really, but she is still a young girl and her walking home from the clinic around midnight is probably not the best way to ensure her safety."

"No," Enric agreed with a mild smile. "That is why I asked Grend to take care of her whenever she works late. He has been accompanying her back here for the last two weeks."

Eryn stared at him open-mouthed. "Really? That was... thoughtful of you," she concluded lamely. "Why don't you let me in on such things? It would save me from worrying."

"Why would this surprise you, my love?" he countered. "I would have thought that by now you must be aware that I like to take care of things. And as long as Plia is living under my roof I feel responsible for her. This includes making sure that she does not fall prey to whatever dregs of society are roaming the streets at night."

Great, now he had made her feel small-minded. "Very well," she muttered. "How could I have had any doubts about your protective instincts?"

"Because maybe you thought that you are the only person to trigger them?" he guessed. "But you know that there is no need to be jealous, don't you?" he smirked. "There is enough primal drive to protect in me for both of you to share."

That made her chuckle. "No, I am not jealous, I promise. Quite the opposite, I am touched. And maybe a little angry for not having thought of that myself."

"Don't worry. Just consider yourself lucky that in me you have a companion who takes care of the practical matters of life so you can keep playing around with discovering revolutionary new things in whatever disciplines you like dabbling in."

"Playing around? Dabbling? Thank you so much," she growled. "I'll have you know that I am considered somewhat of a rarity in Takhan due to my very high score in the category of exploration. I am sure nobody there would dare accuse me either of playing around or dabbling. And it's not like I have a lot of time for that, anyway. Which some people would definitely consider a shame as it more or less stops me from living up to my full potential."

"Let me guess," he sighed. "A few more hours a week to yourself would change that completely. Hours that could easily be won by not having to go to any combat training."

Her face fell. Why had he seen through that one so swiftly? It had been weeks since she had last bothered him with an attempt at being exempted from her training.

"Well, it was worth a try, wasn't it?" she mumbled and walked out to prepare some food for them.

Enric shook his head and smiled while he watched her leave. It had been a while since her last try. He had already started worrying that she might have given up. That would have been a pity.

* * *

Eryn breathed deeply in and out once to calm herself, then knocked at the door she knew Marrin would be sitting behind. When he called out his permission for her to enter, she turned the door handle and stepped inside the room. Marrin smiled at her.

"Lady Eryn. What a pleasure to see you. His Majesty is expecting you."

"Marrin," she nodded back and squared her shoulders before opening the door next to his desk that led to the King's study.

King Folrin didn't look up from the paper he was studying but instead pointed his index finger to the chair opposite him at the other side of his desk.

Eryn wondered briefly if she was still supposed to bow to him if he wasn't even looking, but decided against it. He would of course notice that she didn't, but if he wanted her to follow protocol, he could at least do her the courtesy of looking her in the eye.

She sank onto the hard chair and leaned back, stifling a yawn. It had been an exhausting day. Treatment days usually were, but today it had been worse than usual as there had been an accident at a construction site and more than twenty workers had needed rapid help. So four of the healers had followed the messenger to the location of the accident while the remaining two, Lebern and Lord Poron, had remained at the clinic to take care of the remaining patients. Unfortunately Vern had not been free to work with them today, being caught up in his classes.

The King was still reading, so she closed her burning eyes for just a short moment to rest them. She had washed out the dust from the construction site as well she could, but every now and then she felt a slight prickling sensation that told her that she had not been thorough enough. Her eyes were not the only part of her body affected by the dust. It clung to her hair and between her teeth and was lightly ingrained in her robe. She did not make the neatest impression right now for sure, she mused, but then he should have summoned her in the morning before her work if he placed a value on things like that. Or given her time to go home and take a proper bath instead of making do with a bowl of water, a stiff brush and a bar of soap.

"Lady Eryn? Are you asleep?" the King's dry and slightly amused voice addressed her.

She immediately opened her eyes and saw him regarding her with this thin smile of his.

"No. Forgive me, Your Majesty," she said quickly and straightened in her chair. Meeting him in the throne room would have been a lot better. The windows were a lot taller there and made the room more brightly lit. Which would have made staying awake and alert a lot easier.

"From what I have heard you must have had a long day, what with the accident today," he nodded. "I will not detain you for too long, then. I can see that you are in need of a bath and some rest. What I want to talk to you about is the forthcoming Council meeting in only a few days. The one where you are expected to present another idea of how to handle the matter of magical healing in the Order."

Her brow furrowed in concern. Why would he care about that? It was a matter for the Order, not the Crown.

"You are probably asking yourself why this is of interest to me," he went on, smiling in delight at her annoyed look of having been found out. Again. "I need the Order to be stable, a beacon of solidity, trustworthiness and superiority. You, my dear Lady Eryn, are at times perceived as a slightly... disruptive element to those values. Lord Tyront's usual stoic calm does not seem to be a match for your ability to make him lose it. And having people see you doing stable duty is not exactly a picture that conveys confidence in the institution that is supposed to prevent magicians from misbehaving in any way."

She suppressed another yawn and frowned. "Forgive me for the blunt question, Your Majesty, but are you telling me to *behave* next time I meet the Council?"

"Lady Eryn," he replied patiently, "I am telling you rather more than that. I am trying to impress on you the importance of presenting to them an acceptable proposal that will help to set up clear structures around magical healing in this Kingdom. The walls have ears, dear Lady, so your bickerings with the Order have not remained exactly a secret. Since you have managed to gain people's trust here in quite a short while, they tend to side *with* you which means *against* the Order. I would instruct you to put an end to this. Lord Tyront will not give you another chance if you fail to present your new proposal in a more respectful manner. He can't be seen to be letting you treat him in that way again. So I shall also warn you to be prepared for a more... severe punishment if you once more forego the rules of politeness and respect towards your superior."

She gave him a worried look. "By you?"

He raised both brows. "By me? But of course not, Lady Eryn. Lord Tyront would hardly thank me for taking away his right to discipline you when you have violated his rules. It would seem as if he couldn't deal with you himself. I did not mean to extend any threat to you, merely advise you to be careful. In your own interest."

Nodding, she sighed. "I have taken measures to increase the likelihood of success for my next attempt."

The King smiled. "Such as including Rolan and young Vern in your preparations?"

Confound him and his spies! How did they manage to find out what she talked to those two about behind closed doors? Especially in Vern's case, when she sat with him in Orrin's quarters in his room!

Both of them looked up when a door opposite the one leading to Marrin's room opened and Malriel ambled into the study, wearing nothing more than a flowing, silvery shimmering nightgown, her long dark hair failing down her back in gentle waves, her feet bare.

"Folrin," she purred, "I thought you wanted to return in only a few minutes."

Eryn's mouth dropped open at the sight. Malriel's face looked younger than she had ever seen it before, now she looked as old as Eryn herself, all lines gone, her skin fresh and glowing.

She smiled at her daughter. "I thought it was your voice I was hearing."

The King smiled and lifted a hand which Malriel took and let herself be pulled onto his lap.

"I had to answer a few letters. I would have returned to you as soon as I was finished with Lady Eryn."

Eryn exhaled and closed her eyes. "This is not happening. I am having a nervous breakdown and this is no more than an illusion. A nasty, impossible, ridiculous illusion," she intoned quietly, breathing heavily.

When she opened her eyes again, both of them were regarding her with indulgent expressions.

"Theá, do not be absurd. Or course this is not an illusion. And why would two healthy, attractive, interesting, powerful people not feel a certain attraction towards each other?" Malriel smiled.

"Because he is the King, damn you! You are not supposed to work your little games on *him*! Have you ever considered the consequences of your actions? Or are you too busy with stumbling from one barely grown-up lover's love nest to the next?"

Malriel's eyes narrowed. "You be careful what you say, my dear. Or you will be the one facing consequences."

Eryn ignored her and looked at the King instead, hissing, "And you! I wonder if you knew that she is old enough to be your mother? Literally? As well as being a manipulative politician who tried to get her own daughter convicted just because she felt that being held in her city would be a good opportunity for some mother-daughter bonding time?" She leapt up from her chair, causing it to tip over backwards. "I would have expected more of *you*, at least! She is well known for toying with young lovers and casting them aside when she no longer needs them or when she has found a fresher, more intriguing one. But you are smart! Yet obviously not quite the master of your impulses! Such a pity!"

The King's expression had turned stony and he motioned for Malriel to get off his lap before he rose.

Eryn whirled angrily and grabbed the door handle to leave, when his cold voice rang out. "You stop right there, Lady Eryn!"

She cursed under her breath and removed her hand from the door without turning back to him.

"Turn around," he commanded.

With her hands balled to fists, she slowly turned and saw him step towards her with a dangerous look on his face. Without thinking she raised a shield before her, now caught between it and the door one step behind her.

He stopped, lifting a careful finger to touch its tip to the barrier and pulling it back when he felt the crackle of magic.

"You will remove this *at once*." The threat in his voice was clear, even without putting words to whatever he would have Lord Tyront do to her in case she failed to comply.

She closed her eyes, cursing herself for this unthinking reaction. He had never before become physical with her, so why did she think that he would now, especially with his lover watching? She lowered the shield and sucked in a shocked breath when she felt a moment later both his hands on her upper arms, grabbing her tightly and pushing her back against the door behind her.

His face was close enough for her to see the specks of dark grey in his blue eyes. "You do *not* turn your back to me. And you do *not* leave before I have dismissed you. I distinctly remember impressing this on you before. And you *never* raise a barrier against me," he said with narrowed eyes, looking down at her.

She felt helpless, resisting the urge to push him aside with magic. If raising a shield to keep him away from her made him react like this, using magic actively, even if only to increase her own strength, would get her into serious trouble. Though that was a state she had probably reached already.

"Have I made myself clear?" he asked, staring into her eyes unblinkingly.

Not sure if her voice would obey, she just nodded.

"Excellent. I am glad we have re-established the rules of behaviour towards me. Then we can move on to another matter." His grip on her arms became firmer. "I do not require your permission or even acceptance for my choice of lovers, no matter what your relationship with those lovers is. I would not even have required it had I taken *you* to my bed on the evening of your commitment so many months ago."

She clenched her teeth and turned her head to one side. That had been a low blow. A moment later the pressure at one arm was gone when the King moved his hand to grip her chin and turn her head back so she faced him again, his fierce stare locking onto hers.

"Do not ever again assume that you are in a position to question or criticise my actions in such a manner. The consequences would not make you happy." He raised his brow questioningly, clearly expecting some kind of affirmative.

"Yes, Your Majesty," she pressed out from between clenched teeth. She couldn't see Malriel as the King was blocking the view, but she was probably enjoying herself well enough, Eryn thought grimly.

"Good. You may leave now before Lord Enric comes storming in here as your bond surely conveyed to him your current distress," the

King spoke more calmly and released her, stepping back enough for her to open the door and retreat after a stiff bow.

When he turned back to his desk, Malriel was sitting on a corner, watching him with a slightly amused expression.

"Dear me, that was interesting," she smiled. "I was not aware that you are attracted to her."

The King stepped towards her and took her hand to lift it to his lips. "What can I say, Malriel? I seem to have developed a preference for a certain type of woman lately."

She laughed and glided off the table with an elegant move. "Come with me, Folrin. There is a little thing I would like to ask of you."

He shook his head and smiled thinly. "I never grant favours in bed, Malriel."

She lifted a brow. "Where do you usually grant them, then?"

"Here in my study. Or in the throne room," he replied.

A glint had entered her eyes when she took his hand and pulled him to his chair to push him into it. "Alright, I can work with that."

* * *

Enric turned the corner and skidded to an abrupt halt, looking worried when he saw Eryn in the corridor in front of the King's study, slowly and repeatedly bumping her forehead against the stone column in front of her.

He was relieved at seeing her. On his way here he had worried about her getting into serious trouble, that the emotions he received might have induced her to act unwisely towards the King. But he seemed to have let her leave again without calling for guards, magicians, shackles or whatever else he might have deemed fit for dealing with an impertinent magician of such considerable strength.

"Eryn?" he asked carefully. "What happened?"

She closed her eyes and leaned her forehead against the cool stone. "I insulted the King. And not just a bit. Really. Unmistakably. And then I used magic against him."

Enric's heart stopped for a moment. He grabbed her upper arm and pulled her next to him, making her accompany him. That was not good news. But when had being summoned to the King been lately?

When they had left the Palace, he walked on with her until they turned a corner and were out of sight of the Palace guards. Gently, he moved her against a wall.

"Tell me again. More details this time," he insisted.

She nodded, her expression troubled. "He called for me to tell me that I am to make a good impression with the Magic Council when I present my new proposal to them. He wants a solution for organising magical healing."

Enric nodded. That alone could hardly have triggered such a reaction in her. "Go on."

"Then Malriel suddenly came in. Just like that, without a warning - no knock, nothing." She gave him a pained look. "In her nightgown and with no shoes! She is having an affair with the King! Can you believe that?"

Enric began to understand. That bit of news was surely enough to kindle such a fiery reaction in her.

"I can, yes. It is not exactly untypical for her, if you think of it. What happened then?" He kept his voice calm.

She closed her eyes. "I first insulted her, then told the King that I am disappointed and would have expected more of him. And that it seems that his intelligence had no chance against his male urges."

Enric grimaced. The King would hardly have appreciated that. "What else? We haven't reached the part with your using magic against him yet."

Opening her eyes again, she raked a shaking hand through her hair. "I tried to leave, but he stopped me. He looked so angry, so boiling, that I automatically raised a shield. I didn't plan to, it just happened!"

Alright, he thought, that was not as bad as he had feared. She had used no more than a defence. They had trained her to do just that instead of attacking. Magicians were allowed to use shields against non-magicians, straight shields that didn't lock anybody in couldn't do any harm. It was the kind of reaction he would have wished she had shown when she had been attacked at the inn during her expedition. They had chided her for not using a shield back then. It seemed his and Orrin's words had worked through. Just on the wrong occasion.

The King would not have been very happy about that, either.

"What happened after that?"

She rubbed her arms unconsciously. "He grabbed my arms and told me very plainly that he does not appreciate my behaviour towards him, and that he does not need me to agree to his choice of lovers."

Which was true enough, Enric thought but remained silent.

The memory of the King's words chafed at her. Her expression turned angry. "And do you know what he said then? That he wouldn't even have needed me to agree to his taking *me* to bed back then! The audacity!"

He swallowed hard. It was a miracle that she had not given him quite bit more than harsh words after that. He fought down his fury at the King's words. They had either been a sign that the usual admirable command over his emotions had failed him for once, or that he had wanted to provoke her. Either way, the remark itself had been a highly offensive one, both considering the implication that he wouldn't have shied away from taking her to bed without her consent, but also that it had been his way of blackmailing her to enter into a commitment she would otherwise never have agreed to.

"You did not use any magic against him after raising the shield?" he asked, just to be on the safe side.

She shook her head. "No, I didn't. And really, holding myself back from doing that was an act of violence." Her eyes narrowed. "I hope he falls in love with her and she crushes him like a mite crawling on a leaf," she growled.

"Careful," he warned her and threw glances around them. "We are not exactly in a private place here and we have no soundproof barrier in place." Which, in hindsight, was not too smart - careless even. But he had been too concerned about hearing what had happened after her less than calming words at the Palace to think of a practical thing like a protection against being overheard.

"Let's go home," he suggested. "You need a bath, and I need to think."

* * *

Enric paced the yard, the mountain cat's eyes trained on him as he walked the same line repeatedly. His study and the parlour had become too small for him tonight. He needed space to move, get rid of the nervous energy in his muscles, the inflamed thoughts in his head.

Apart from the fact that the King had in his opinion overstepped a narrow line by not only making that remark but also laying hands on Eryn, it was clear he was playing one of his games again. It was no coincidence that Eryn had learned about the King's affair with Malriel today, he was absolutely sure of it. He did not normally allow his lovers to interrupt an audience, so this had to have been planned.

But to what purpose? Provoking her? To do what? Defy him? What would that gain him? And he would have needed witnesses other than Malriel for using it against her later.

Widening the gap between the two women? Was that even attainable? And if it were, to what end? He discarded the idea again. Malriel would hardly have participated in that case as her own little society games were aimed at *bridging* that gap.

Gaming with Eryn, making her uneasy by showing her that he might not be in a position to enjoy *her* company, but had managed to take her mother, who resembled her so very much, to bed instead?

He balled his fists. That last one would imply an attachment to Eryn that exceeded casual attraction. For the first time since he had been joined with Eryn he wondered if the King had ever regretted that she had not refused to be blackmailed but had given in.

He rubbed his face. That was the trouble with a woman like Eryn in a place like this. Securing her for himself did not mean that no other man was interested in her. She was still special, different from the other women here for so many reasons, her personality traits not even considered.

Could he have done something to protect her more sufficiently? By keeping her away from the King, however he might have achieved this without disobeying direct Royal orders? Or by keeping a closer watch on Malriel, especially as he himself had pointed out that her behaviour was hardly that much of a surprise given her penchant for much younger men?

But pondering what he could have done in the past to avoid this was of no use now, he reminded himself. This was nothing more than self-pity and would not help him find a way to handle this situation properly in the future.

He paused his running over the arguments and turned towards the house. Had he just heard the sound of somebody knocking at the entrance door? When he listened a few more moments and heard nothing, he was about to resume his restless pacing but stopped when he looked at Urban, who sat straight with twitching ears and bristling whiskers. That was not her reaction to the usual night sounds of the city beyond the walls. So there probably really was a late-night visitor.

He raised his view up to the first floor and saw the faint shimmering of light from the bathroom through the bedroom window. So Eryn was very likely still soaking in her hot bath, which left answering the door to him.

As he walked back to enter the house, Urban followed him in, always curious about visitors. He needed to take her hunting again soon, he thought. She had appeared a little restless these last few days.

He opened the entrance door and blinked a few times at the sight. His brain refused to acknowledge the information the eyes kept sending.

The man in front of the door looked up at him with a determined expression, then his gaze sank and his eyes widened at the large cat that stared at him unblinkingly.

"What is that?" the man whispered hoarsely, his expression slightly panicked.

Hearing the voice finally convinced Enric's brain that denying the facts was no use. He really was here. In person. And there he had thought that this evening could hardly become any worse.

"A mountain cat. What are you doing here," he sighed, "father?"

* * *

Eryn frowned at the top of the stairs and stopped to listen. She heard two male voices talking, one of them Enric's, the other one she didn't know. It was a little late for visitors, she thought. Hopefully there was no emergency; but the voices did not seem urgent as such, just a little strained from what she could make out. She turned back into the bedroom to slip out of her nightgown - which would hardly be appropriate for receiving visitors - and into clean trousers and a tunic. She had received a stab of dismay before she had climbed out of the tub, but he had used a shield quickly to mask his emotions as well as he could. He was demonstrating quite some skill at it, much to her annoyance.

She descended the stairs and entered the parlour, smiling at both men when they stood to receive her. The visitor had to be in his early sixties, his hair was more grey than blond and he was quite a lot shorter than Enric. His upper lip sported a thin beard as if to accentuate the curve of the mouth. It was probably meant to look genteel and noble, but seemed in her opinion rather incomplete, not really suitable for the rather rugged face.

Enric's expression was blank. It was the cool mask he used to hide tension and dismay. Her interest in the other man increased immediately.

"Eryn," her companion said calmly. "Allow me to introduce to you Anwin. My father."

Eryn's jaw dropped in surprise. His father? Here? Just like that? Well, that surely was an explanation for Enric's tenseness.

"Father, this is Eryn. My companion."

Anwin's eyes were glued to her unusually coloured hair and Eryn gave him a few more moments to take it in before she stepped towards him.

"It is a pleasure to meet you, Anwin," she smiled politely.

He nodded slowly, looking her up and down as soon as he had managed to tear his eyes away from her hair. "Eryn. The spy from the Western Territories."

Oh dear, she thought. What a charming greeting.

"I changed professions," she replied lightly, "I am a healer now."

Anwin stared at her, clearly not comprehending her attempt at humour.

"I heard that you had taken a companion," he said to his son without taking his eyes off her for a moment. "As you are noble and important now, inviting your family to the ceremony was clearly out of the question. Proud Lord Enric cannot be shamed by allowing people to see how humble his origins were, can he?"

Enric didn't reply to this, instead folding his arms.

"Why are you here?" he asked instead.

"I heard about your companion and wanted to take a look at her for myself. I did not expect you to bring her to us at all soon," Anwin replied sourly. "Your mother is very disappointed in you. She surely would have appreciated meeting your companion. She had already given up seeing you joined to a woman."

"Indeed, had she?" Enric retorted, "I wonder why you didn't bring her with you when you came here. But then you never took mother along on any of your journeys, did you?"

"I am not here to justify myself to you, my boy," the older man grunted.

"No," his son remarked mildly, "you came here to make *me* justify myself to *you*."

Anwin stared at Enric for a long moment, then obviously decided that talking to his son was no use. He turned to Eryn and walked towards her before circling her like she had seen prospective buyers do at horse markets with an animal they were interested in. She flashed Enric an amused look.

"Trousers. I hope you just wear them at home?" the man asked disapprovingly.

She shook her head slowly. "No, not really. I find them more practical and wear them wherever I go."

"Then it seems my son has not learned how to keep a woman under control," Anwin mused. "That is the trouble when a boy is taken from his family at too early an age, I always said. It doesn't leave him enough time to learn how things need to be done properly."

"Like forcing women into wearing dresses if they don't want to?" Enric threw at him. "This is not the kind of companionship that would make *me* happy."

Eryn looked at Enric curiously. So it seemed she was not the only person who managed to really get to him. There were probably quite a lot of unresolved issues between the two men.

His father just shot him a withering look and returned his attention to Eryn.

"I hear you are a magician. I didn't know women could be. But then I suppose in that place you are from a lot of strange things go on." His eyes narrowed suspiciously.

She nodded seriously. "Oh yes, strange things indeed. That's why I came here. Too strange there for me."

His brow furrowed, clearly not sure if she was teasing him. "Are you making fun of me?"

"No, I would never dare to," she replied, wide-eyed with innocence, and saw Enric smiling from the corner of her eye.

Anwin turned back to his son. "Why did you move out of the Palace? I thought the important magicians had to stay there? Lost some of your standing, did you? The King is probably not happy about you joining the spy," he pondered.

"If you say so," Enric shrugged.

"You have always been careless, as everything you have has been more or less been forced on you. Your power of magic is wasted on you," Anwin spat. "Your brother, he would have appreciated the gift for the chance it really is. He wouldn't have lazed about all day long, leaving his teachers no choice but to send me notes again and again saying they were dissatisfied with his grades and general attitude. You were just ungrateful then, and you still are."

"Probably," his son smiled. "But then you would have been stuck with me and my attitude instead of being able to send me away from home at the age of twelve years to bring fame and glory to the family. You know as well as I do that we would not have got on well together. So spare me your lamentations. We both came away with something useful, and you know it. You can brag with a magician in the family, and there is still another son to take over your business. I don't really see any gratitude there for how well things turned out for you."

Eryn quickly cut in when Anwin took a deep breath to reply.

"How long will you be staying in the city, Anwin?"

He seemed to think about expressing his opinion about Enric's words first, but then reconsidered.

"For three days." Then he added with a sideways glance, "Some of us have real work to do, after all. Not just sitting in a nice study all day long and getting paid for having a title."

"Well, it seems you have figured out life in the Order pretty accurately," Enric nodded solemnly.

"Being paid for playing a bit with swords in case of a war that will probably never come is hardly a worthwhile occupation for a real man," Anwin sniffed.

Eryn grinned widely. "He has a point there, you know."

"And yet you were eager enough to spread the news that your son was a member of the Order twenty years ago," Enric countered, while giving his companion a dark look for her remark. "Why, if we are little more than a waste of money? Shouldn't you rather have been ashamed instead and kept it a secret?"

"You still are as disrespectful and impertinent as you always were!" Anwin said pointedly. "I can see that nothing has changed in you."

"That is because you have still not managed to earn my respect, father. Nothing much changed there, either," Enric lobbed back.

"I don't have to listen to this!" the older man thundered.

His son nodded emphatically. "Indeed, you don't." He stepped towards the door and opened it wide. "Here is the door. If you don't want to hear what I have to say, you had better leave, because as long as you are in *my* house, there will be no avoiding it."

"You are throwing your own father out?" his father called out incredulously. "After not seeing me for more than seven years?"

"I am, yes. I can see now that I haven't missed much. Since I didn't invite you to come here, I have no qualms about getting rid of you now. I much prefer spending a quiet evening with my companion to a battle of wills with you. Good night, father. I trust we can meet again before you leave the city and return to working hard for your money. Unlike myself." Enric folded both arms, adopting a broad stance and glaring at Anwin.

His father narrowed his eyes and grabbed his cloak from the hook next to the door. "If that's how it is to be, then. If you have no misgivings about treating your poor, old father like that, I will be gone."

The younger man rolled his eyes. "Oh, spare me that *worn-down, resigned and rejected father* routine. It failed to impress me back then; it will not work now either." He swung the door shut as soon as Anwin had crossed the threshold. When he turned to Eryn, he looked questioningly at her smug expression.

"What?"

"I thank my lucky stars for allowing me to witness that scene! It is balm for my soul! Just what I needed after dealing with Malriel today." She laughed and went to the drinks cabinet to pour herself a glass of sweet wine.

"I am glad I could assist in cheering you up," he remarked dryly.

"You did, there is no denying it," she smiled. "I have discovered a side to you that I wouldn't dream was buried there under all your dignity, superiority, strictness, eagerness to adhere to rules and all that. You were cheeky, snotty, uppity, ironic, disrespectful..."

"So basically, like *you*?"

"Exactly!" she beamed, not feeling the least bit insulted. "I am not the only one here being cursed with a parent who rather resembles some frightening monster in a story for children instead of a real person. But I want to say that you are still the one who is the better off of us," she said.

"Am I?" he sighed. "I wasn't aware that we had entered into competing for whose parent is more obnoxious. But do enlighten me."

"Compared to you, I did at least show you the courtesy of not liking your father. You, however, get along much too well with Malriel. I feel I should mention this for proper balance. And unlike me you are not an only child. You have siblings who can absorb some of his attention. Malriel's ill-conceived plans all focus on *me*. There is nobody else to distract her or keep her busy."

"I feel we should take into consideration that my father lives a lot closer to Anyueel than your mother. Proximity must count as increasing the annoyance factor," he countered.

"He said that he last saw you seven years ago! So it's not as if this spatial proximity brings you into closer contact with him. Malriel lives on the other side of the bloody sea, and yet I am having to endure her for the second time within a few months – and not only for three days, but over many weeks!"

Enric sighed. "Alright, I see your point. How about the fact that I had to spend the first twelve years with him while you were growing up with a caring and dedicated father?"

She snorted. "Please! He took me away from her to spare me the torture of growing up with her. That does not make her less, but more appalling."

He took in her sparkling eyes and relaxed manner. Before she had walked upstairs to take her bath, she had been downcast and worried. So that unexpected and unpleasant visit had at least had one positive side effect.

"Alright, dearest. I have to declare you the victor: You definitely are the one of us with the more terrible, awful, nasty parent. I hope such a sad triumph makes you happy."

She shrugged. "I know it shouldn't, but I take what I can get. Is there a prize?"

"Oh, yes, there is actually. I graciously bequeath Anwin to you. He is all yours," he smiled wickedly. "Compared to your apparently unbearable mother he should be an improvement. And it is only fair – I have taken your mother off you, so you might want to return the favour for my parent."

Eryn drained her glass and looked straight at him. "You know what? I think I will forego the prize. You can keep them both. Isn't that great?" she beamed. "Now your father *and* mother are in the city! This must be wonderful for you! I wonder how he will react if he learns that you have let yourself be adopted by another Western spy!" She smiled when he closed his eyes for a moment and exhaled, his face just a little paler than before.

Enric took a seat. "There is the chance that he will never learn about this."

She looked at him indulgently. "He learned about your being joined with a Western spy in that village of his. What makes you think that he won't hear of that other detail - especially now that he is in the city the same time as she is?"

"Because a man can still dream?" he ventured.

She thought for a moment, then nodded. "I'll grant you that. Dreams don't have to be realistic or likely, after all. They can be as imaginative, absurd or creative as you please."

"Yes," he groaned, "thank you so much. Just to remind you: My father will be gone in only three days. Malriel will be here for another week. And then there is still your delightful darling cousin. Or sister, as she now is. She will be here for another two months."

Now it was his turn to smile as her expression turned sour.

CHAPTER 18

Striking Back

Junar's eyes bulged. "What? No! I don't believe it! With the King? Really? And she just walked into the room?"

Eryn nodded wearily. "Yes. Then just sat on his lap. Can you imagine that?"

"But she is old enough to be his mother!"

"You are not being serious, are you? You are aware that *your* companion is twenty years older than yourself, aren't you? Or did that somehow slip your mind? And actually, Malriel did not look at all like anybody's mother yesterday – she had managed to heal away another five years at least, and looked *my* age!"

"Well, Orrin is only eighteen years older than me," Junar retorted sulkily.

"Sure, let's focus on that right now, shall we?" Eryn complained. "It's not like I just told you that this malicious creature is having an affair with the King!"

"What's so bad about it, really?" the seamstress shrugged, then grinned. "Or are you afraid of having to call him *father*?"

"You are not being at all funny," the younger woman growled. "Who knows what she is up to? She is a magician, and as you know we can do... things," she finished, a little lamely.

"In bed, you mean?" Junar smiled sweetly. "I am aware of that, yes. You think she will seduce him into submission with her magical erotic skills and then entice him to grant her whatever she asks?"

Eryn flashed her an annoyed look. "You can make that sound as ludicrous as you please, but that is actually the concern I have, yes."

"I suppose warning him about it is really not something you can do easily, is it?"

Just then, Orrin's study door opened wide. "Warning who about what?"

"The King about Eryn's mother and her sinister plans of dominating the Kingdom," Junar grinned.

Orrin frowned. "What?"

"Malriel is having a little fling with King Folrin," his companion explained with a gleeful smile.

"Junar, you are an idiot," Eryn groaned. "Why can't you just be sympathetic when I tell you something like that? Isn't that what friends were for originally?"

She shrugged. "I like to think that I am a modern woman who does not like to follow traditional definitions."

"Wait, wait, wait," Orrin lifted both hands as if to slow them. "Your mother is having an affair with the King? *Our* King?"

"Of course *our* King! *They* don't have any kings over there," Eryn called out impatiently.

"And you are planning to *warn* him about her now?" He grimaced. "A grown man in his position will not take well to that."

She snorted. "You bet he wouldn't. Especially not after what happened yesterday."

He looked resigned and took a seat next to Junar. "What have you done now?"

"Why would you automatically assume that it was my fault? I utterly resent that!" she complained, folding her arms stoically.

Orrin just lifted a brow. "Was it?"

Her chest fell as she exhaled. "Well, kind of," she admitted. "Though I still resent your attitude!"

"Duly noted," he replied dryly. "Are you going to tell me what you did or are we to discuss your aversion to people accurately assessing your character?"

She gave him another annoyed look, then straightened. "I used magic against him."

Orrin blinked, then stared at her. So did Junar.

"You did *what*?" His voice had become raised. "You are aware that not only is he a non-magician and so protected by the law against magicians using their powers against him, but also happens to be the sovereign of our country, aren't you? What were you thinking, you imbecile?" He forced himself to breathe steadily while closing his eyes for a moment to calm down. "Alright, let's think it through. You are here instead of in a cell and I don't see any shackles binding you. That means that you escaped relatively unscathed from what I can tell."

"Orrin," she moaned, "I am not completely stupid! I didn't attack him or anything! I just raised a shield."

His expression became first relieved, then thoughtful. "I am not sure if there is a *just* in the King's case. It is a token of your disobedience, after all. Did he threaten you in any way?"

She gestured helplessly. "Well, not as such. He just looked massively angry when he walked towards me. I raised the shield automatically without thinking. It was a reflexive action - nothing more."

Orrin sighed. "At least your training finally showed the first signs of success. Unfortunately, however, not at a very suitable time. We need to work on your perception of danger. When a stranger tries to rape you at a country inn, you don't think of raising a shield, but when the King looks angry it seems like a good idea?" He shook his head in exasperation, then raised his brow. "Why was the King mad at you? You didn't say anything that might have inflamed him after finding out about his affair, did you?"

Eryn looked guilty. "You could say that maybe, yes. I did sort of insult him. A tiny bit."

Now Junar looked incredulous. "You first insulted him and then raised a shield against him? Why do people even allow you to leave your house unsupervised, seriously?"

"What happened after you raised the shield?" Orrin asked tensely. "How did he react?"

"He ordered me to remove it. Which I did. Immediately," she emphasised. "Then he gripped my arms none too gently and warned me. Thoroughly."

"He grabbed you? King Folrin? Really?" Junar exclaimed with wide eyes. That was unheard of.

Orrin nodded slowly. "He had to."

Both women now looked at him in puzzlement.

"He had to demonstrate that he was still in charge, and after you protected yourself from him with magic, he needed to show you that whatever he wanted to do, you had to endure. He needed to show you that he was still in control, no matter if you are a magician or not. You wanted to protect yourself against his physical contact with you? So *that* was exactly what he *had* to do."

"But he provoked me! On purpose! Why else would he have wanted me to find out about his affair with *her*?" Eryn objected.

He pursed his lips. "That is the interesting question here, isn't it? Why indeed did he want you to know about this?" He leaned back and studied her for a few moments. "He would have taken you to bed that one night if Enric had not managed to persuade you to join him."

She rolled her eyes. "Why does everybody assume that the King would have managed such a thing? I had the shield inside me."

"He would very probably have found a way around it or he wouldn't have used it as leverage. Otherwise it wouldn't have worked on Enric the way it did," he pointed out. "But let's leave this aside for now. Your mother looks very much like you. The similarity is astonishing, especially with her ability to make herself appear a lot younger than she actually is."

Junar gasped and a protective hand came to lie on her belly in an automatic gesture. "You think the King is in love with Eryn?"

Orrin waggled his head. "I don't know about being in love, but definitely more attracted than a man of his position should be to a magician in the first instance, and secondly to a woman whom he personally joined with another man."

"So Malriel is the closest thing to taking Eryn to bed he can accomplish without making waves?" the seamstress frowned. "This is really awkward."

Eryn stroked a hand along her forearms to smoothen the hairs that were standing on end. "That is absolute nonsense!" she stated with more confidence than she felt.

Orrin looked at her indulgently. "No, it is not. And you know it. He has physical contact with you more than any other woman. Kissing your hands occasionally, and once he even kissed your cheeks. That is quite unusual for him." Then he smiled thinly. "Ask your companion. I am positive that he agrees with my assessment of the situation."

She looked at him in dismay. "I never encouraged anything of that kind, I swear!"

"I am sure that you have not," he nodded. "But consider that it is not only women who feel drawn towards power. Men often do, too. And being the only woman here with the use of magic makes you powerful enough."

"I was once not too long ago told that I needed a man with more magical power than myself or he would never manage to get close to me," she murmured. "It seems power attracts even more power."

"Who told you that? Enric?" Orrin enquired.

She shook her head. "No. Ram'an."

Orrin studied her. "He managed to get to know you within very short time, then. That must have been a very turbulent time you had in Takhan."

"It was, yes. I can't tell you how relieved I was when we finally boarded that ship back home," she sighed. Then she straightened. "Dear me, I almost forgot! Imagine who came to our house last night! Enric's father!"

Orrin's expression became wary. "He is here? Anwin is in the city? Why?"

Eryn looked at him in surprise. "Then you don't like him very much, do you? I wasn't aware that you even knew him."

"I met him several times when Enric was still a boy and he was visiting him or doing business in the city. I was trying to impress on him that telling Enric off was not the right way to motivate him into making more of an effort but rather increased his stubbornness, but he didn't listen and was convinced that more pressure would bring better results in the end. He even encouraged me to give the boy a good beating if he deserved one. He himself was clearly not willing to lay a hand on him, magical powers can cause quite some harm, after all," he concluded carefully.

"He told you to strike his own son?" Junar called out disgustedly.

"More than once, yes. I am glad the Order does not hold with this kind of education measures." He turned back to Eryn. "What does he want here?"

"He said he wanted to look at me as he had been told that Enric had taken the Western spy as his companion. Without inviting his own family to the ceremony," she told them.

"Western spy? That's what he said to you? Still his tactful, charming old self, then," the warrior said wearily.

"Tactful, very much so. Then he reprimanded me for wearing trousers and Enric for not controlling me properly," she grinned.

"You seem to think that is funny," Junar asked confusedly. "I would not stay as unperturbed if Orrin's parents turned up here and voiced their dislike of me so plainly."

She shrugged. "I am just relieved that I seem to be not the only one with an incorrigible parent. Now I can appreciate Enric more as I know where he comes from. Good thing he was the rebellious and not the compliant type in his youth, I would say. If he had turned out like his father, things would not have turned out so conveniently for the Order."

"Or for you," Junar added.

"For me?" Eryn snorted. "I would never have let him touch me with an attitude like that. The King would have needed a very different scheme than making me join Enric to keep me here." She shook her head in wonder. "Isn't this crazy? His father and Malriel here in Anyueel at the same time. I hope they will both be gone a week from now so our life can go back to normal. Or as normal as life has ever been for us. How come the two of you don't seem to stumble from one catastrophe into the next the same as us?"

Junar raised an eyebrow at her. "Because we are mature adults who have adopted the common practice of thinking before talking and acting."

"Unlike Enric and I?"

"Unlike *you*. Lord Enric, fortunately, is mature enough."

"Oh, thank you so much. So everything that has gone wrong or awry was *my* fault," Eryn complained.

"You got me pregnant," Junar pointed out.

"Can we rephrase that?" Orrin rolled his eyes. "I do so like the illusion of having been involved in conceiving that child to at least a minor degree."

"You know what I mean," Junar shrugged. "It seems like minor things she does more often than not turn out to have some unwanted impact nobody, least of all herself, counted on. Don't tell me it is a coincidence that this always happens to *her*?"

Eryn folded her arms defiantly. "That is a massive exaggeration."

Junar mirrored the gesture. "Is it? What about your little assignments to shovel horse manure? Do you even consider that there might be unpleasant consequences for you when you provoke your superior? What about that one ball where you changed your hair colour and ended up with a man's nose broken? His uncle is *still* angry at you for that. Or the little matter of your trying to go to Takhan without Lord Enric? Without him you would probably still be marooned out there!"

"Or when you kept your weapons out of reach during your expedition," Orrin joined his companion. "Not to mention the time you tried to blackmail me. And most recently, insulting the King and raising a shield..."

Eryn growled, "Just stop that, the two of you! Alright, I am a walking catastrophe and will one day single-handedly bring on the end of the world. I got it. Just hand me that bloody dress I came for and then I will leave. I have no more nerve to endure your endless list of my wrongdoings."

Junar pointed to chest of drawers on which a puffy-looking parcel lay. "Right behind you. And don't call my dresses *bloody*. I'll have you know that my services are in immensely high demand right now, especially since it became known that Malriel and Pe'tala have their clothes made by me. I have to turn orders down because I can't find enough women to hire for the work."

"So it seems I directly and indirectly promote your business. That should entitle me to call your dresses whatever I will. It's not as if I don't keep ordering quite a number of them for myself."

"Please!" Junar rolled her eyes. "Lord Enric more or less orders them. He told me to have one ready for you for whatever occasion you are expected to attend."

Orrin rubbed his face. "Is this apparel discussion ever going to come to an end?"

"No," both women replied in unison with a stern look at him.

Eryn got up from her seat and went to pick up the parcel. "I suppose I will see you in the evening at Inad's unless you fall victim to another qualm."

"Shouldn't be a problem; today has been a good day so far," Junar shrugged. "I am confident that I will be able to attend. You promised me a show, after all," she added with an impish smile. "I wouldn't want to miss that."

* * *

Eryn held on to his hand before he could raise it to knock at the door of Lord Remdel's house. Enric raised a questioning eyebrow at her.

"Don't tell me you have changed your mind about attending?"

She shook her head. "No, that's not it. I just wanted to warn you that you might find some aspects of my behaviour tonight a little... unusual."

"Unusual? Would you care to elaborate?" he frowned. "What are you up to this time?"

"Let's say I have been advised to counter Malriel's efforts."

He sighed. "Please tell me that you have not planned anything that will end up with our two Houses being enemies? You do remember that I let myself be adopted by Malriel to avoid just that, don't you?"

She squeezed his hand reassuringly. "Sure. Don't worry. Just don't be shocked. Well, you may be a bit shocked. Just react the way people would expect you to."

"Could you be more specific?" he urged her. "I don't appreciate it if I have no idea what to expect. This feeling of impending cataclysm makes me nervous."

She just winked at him and raised her hand to knock at the door.

Inad opened the door herself and exclaimed their names in delight. "Lady Eryn! Lord Enric! I am so delighted you could come!"

"We wouldn't have missed this for anything in the world," Eryn replied with a smile. "The idea of hosting a social gathering for the benefit of the underprivileged is completely new here, after all. You are pioneer, as it were."

Inad beamed at her. "I am, kind of, if you say it like that, am I not?" she replied immodestly.

Eryn nodded seriously. "Quite. A shining beacon of charitableness and philanthropy - a role model for us all."

"Certainly not for you, my dear," their hostess waved her off. "You were my inspiration, after all!" Then she turned to answer another knock.

Enric took her cloak to hand it to a servant and whispered to her, "I don't know what you are up to, but that just was plain scary."

"Why?" she murmured back, "She collects money for my orphanage, so I think she is due some flattery. If she feels that it is appreciated, maybe her snooty friends will follow her example and for once use their riches for something useful instead of more jewellery and scent."

"You are aware that Vyril and Aurna are two of what you term her *snooty friends*, aren't you?" he remarked.

She shrugged. "So what? Vyril has braved her friends' disdain by starting to work, and Aurna is joined with a healer. That clears them."

"Aurna is cleared from being snooty because her companion is a healer? How convenient. Then this would also apply for me, I would say?" he smirked.

"Absolutely. But then you were never really in danger of being categorised as *snooty* as you don't spend a lot of money on frivolous things. And you are funding the orphanage, after all," she pointed out.

"Eryn! There you are," Junar beamed at her and approached her as they entered the parlour. "Lord Enric." She bowed to him and nodded to a man at the other side of the room. "Look who else has graced us with his presence tonight."

Enric sighed when he spotted his father in conversation with Orrin, who looked anything but happy about the dubious honour.

Eryn grinned broadly and turned to Inad when she presented her with a glass of wine.

"Thank you so much, Inad! And I have seen you invited Anwin. How very considerate of you!"

"I thought it would be a nice surprise for you," the hostess beamed and then excused herself to answer the door once more.

"Did you drug her or anything?" Junar whispered to Enric. "Must be very potent stuff."

He looked unsure. "I am as surprised as you."

They turned when Tyront and Vyril entered the parlour and without hesitation walked towards them.

"Look at that," Tyront shook his head. "If somebody had told me only a few months ago that I would keep running into you and your companion at evenings like this I would have broken out laughing." He nodded at Junar. "And I had given up on Orrin ever taking a companion a long time ago. Amazing how some things develop." Then his gaze wandered over to where Orrin and his conversation partner were standing. "Oh my. She invited Anwin as well?"

"Yes," Enric said under his breath. "It doesn't seem to be common knowledge that we don't get along very well."

"I do have a feeling that this is going to change soon enough," Tyront remarked dryly.

"Enric, my dear," they heard a throaty voice behind them and turned. Malriel smiled at him and kissed him on the cheeks. "And Vyril and Junar, how lovely to see you here. Lord Tyront," she bowed to him and then turned to Eryn. "Theá, my dear, I am glad for another chance to spend at least *some* time with you, however many people I have to share you with."

Eryn saw from the corner of her eye how several heads turned towards them at Malriel's words. She saw sympathetic smiles and heard a *hmm* or two that expressed commiseration with the suffering mother.

"That was your own doing, Malriel," Eryn replied coolly. "Do not blame me for your own heartless choices in how you acted with me." She swallowed audibly and turned her head away. "If you'll excuse me now, I don't think I can even..." It was as if she couldn't bear to continue talking Malriel, and walked over to Orrin, who looked at her with immense gratitude at her freeing him of the chore of having to keep a conversation going with Anwin alone.

"Eryn," Orrin smiled with relief, "good to see you here tonight."

She smiled at him knowingly and then turned to Enric's father. "Anwin, I am very pleased to see you here. We did not really have a lot of opportunity to talk yesterday."

He shook his head. "No, Enric was never much of a gracious host."

Orrin raised his brow at that statement as he himself had never experienced Enric as anything else but a considerate and generous host when he had been invited to social occasions. Not counting being summoned to his home for other reasons, of course.

Eryn nodded earnestly. "I see what you mean. But then it is always a burden for a man to be in the shadow of a successful father, don't you think?"

Anwin blinked, then a slow smile spread across his face. "I would think that coming to terms with this is what growing up means," he replied good-naturedly, clearly pleased with what he considered an accurate observation by that woman who looked a little too foreign for his taste, but clearly had a sharp mind.

"Oh, quite," she agreed immediately, ignoring Orrin's incredulous expression. "But then I feel that being grown up is always a bit more of a challenge when our parents are present."

He nodded generously. "Probably." Then he looked over to where his son stood and frowned at the other dark-haired woman. "That woman over there, is she your twin sister?"

Eryn looked at Orrin. "Junar has been asking for you. Maybe you should go over to her and see if everything is alright."

The warrior gave her a conspiratorial smile and folded his arms. "She looks fine from here, I am sure it is nothing urgent."

That implied he was curious to see what she would answer. And people thought womenfolk were the nosey ones, she thought wryly. Only two minutes ago he had looked as though he would welcome any opportunity to flee Anwin's presence, and now there was no getting rid of him.

Turning back to Enric's father, she replied. "No, my sister is here in Anyueel at the moment, but it's not this one. She is Enric's mother."

Anwin looked at her as if she had lost her mind. "Enric's mother?" he repeated slowly. His gaze darted from one dark-haired woman to the other a few times before he carefully said, "She really does look a lot like *you*." He cleared his throat and then continued in a voice that suggested that he didn't want to provoke the crazed person, "I am his father, so I am absolutely sure that this person," he nodded towards Malriel, "is *not* his mother. I should know."

Orrin rolled his eyes when Eryn's mouth formed an almost perfect circle when expressing her astonishment. "I am so sorry - nobody told you?"

Anwin frowned. "Nobody told me *what*?"

Eryn grimaced. "Oh dear, this has become really unpleasant now. This is Malriel of House Aren, one of several influential families in the Western Territories. She adopted Enric as her son a few months ago. He is the sole heir to her position as leader of her House and whatever wealth it has accumulated over the centuries."

The man stared at her with his jaw dropped for several moments, before his gaze slowly pivoted to his son, who seemed to smile at something the older man at his side was saying to him. His eyes narrowed.

"*Adopted* him? How can she adopt a grown man? What's more he has a family, anyway," he grumbled.

She nodded sympathetically. "I know! Ridiculous, isn't it? Unfortunately the laws in the Western Territories are not as reasonable as ours. And Malriel is not exactly the type to care about other people's feelings, I am afraid. Enric had not much of a choice back then, she all but coerced him into it. She would otherwise have harmed my own family had he not agreed to it."

Anwin's stare had become hostile, she noted with satisfaction, and saw Orrin slowly nodding in recognition at the seeds she had sown.

"If you will excuse me," Anwin said, then walked towards the group around Enric without waiting for her reply.

When Anwin was out of earshot, Orrin said, "I don't like where this is going. You are using that poor fool. I would be interested in what exactly you are using him for. It doesn't have anything to do with the show you promised Junar, does it?"

Eryn shrugged. "Let's say I saw him and took the chance to let him aid me in my endeavours."

"And your endeavours aim at making Enric pay for something he did to you? Because Anwin really looks like he is in a mood to say a few very brisk things in public," he warned her.

She nodded. "That he does. But I am counting on his addressing them to Malriel, not to Enric. I just pointed out that Enric only let himself be adopted to protect my family, after all. A sure proof of the manly protective instincts that must appeal to a traditionalist such as Anwin."

Orrin lifted an eyebrow at her. "You are rather worrying when you take time to think before acting, you know. Let's see how accurately you have managed to judge his character, shall we?"

Both turned and took a few surreptitious steps closer to be able to hear Anwin when he addressed Malriel.

"Good evening. My name is Anwin," he started without waiting to be introduced. "It appears that you recently adopted my son. I do not recall agreeing to anything like that. And one would imagine that someone adopting somebody else's son at least would have the decency to ask for the parents' consent if they are still alive."

Eryn noted gleefully that his voice was loud enough for all other guests in the extensive parlour to overhear him without difficulty. It would not even have been necessary for Orrin and herself to step closer.

Malriel's smile looked slightly strained, but never faltered. "Anwin, what a pleasure to meet you," she purred, all charming and flirty, "I can see where Enric got his fabulous looks and his determination from."

"Smooth," Orrin remarked under his breath with an appreciative undertone.

Eryn rolled her eyes at the comment. "Oh, please! Flattery is so easy to see through."

"Eryn, Eryn, Eryn," he sighed disappointedly. "You started this off so well. Anwin is not a complicated man, which means elaborate approaches do not work on him. Flattery is simple - he can understand it."

And indeed, his ire seemed to melt away immediately.

"Gullible fool," she murmured. "One would think that the man who fathered Enric would be a bit fitter in the head."

They heard Malriel continue, "I can understand that this arrangement is not pleasant for you as his father, but let me reassure you that I have no intention at all of taking him away from you. His status as my son is only a legal one, while you will always remain his father. Blood binds stronger than the law, after all." Her focus darted across to Eryn at the last sentence. "And I want to let you know that I only did it to protect my own family, which would otherwise have been without a successor for the position of leader. Enric was kind enough to help me out in my hour of desperation."

Nicely played, even Eryn had to admit.

"This is not what I had heard," Anwin said with considerably less force than only a few moments ago.

Malriel looked back to her daughter. "Really? What is it you heard, if I may ask?"

"I heard that you coerced him into it," he accused her.

About twenty pairs of eyes were glued in fascination to the group at one end of the room. While Anwin clearly didn't care about the spectacle he was making, Malriel was very obviously more than aware of her audience.

"Yes, certain... less enthusiastic parties may choose to see it that way," she nodded slowly with another sideways glance at Eryn, who gave her a thin smile, curious about how she would continue. This was tricky ground, after everything that had happened. Claiming Enric had done it voluntarily would not improve his standing with his father. But admitting that she had coerced him would make *her* look like the unscrupulous person she really was, but didn't want to show here, and Enric would seem weak and vulnerable by letting himself *be* forced into it.

"I was in a very dire situation, you see," she went on after a moment's consideration. "I had just lost my own daughter and heiress to... unpleasant circumstances, and Enric, paying no heed to any disadvantage for himself, agreed to help me and my family in our time of need. A brave and noble gesture that reflects the values he was undoubtedly taught as a boy. It seems I have finally met the man I need to thank for this," she added with a beatific smile.

"Should you ever again need to adopt somebody to inherit your wealth, Malriel, let me know and I will send you my son as well," Lord Seagon called out, and caused a collective chortling. This meant Anwin had no other choice than to let his anger drain away and instead accept the compliment.

"Yes, he was taught to be obliging, especially when it came to the weaker sex," he nodded.

Malriel's stare wobbled for a moment at the wording, but her smiled remained in place. "Oh, how true."

The guests looked towards the door to the dining room as Inad cleared her throat and announced that dinner was ready to be served.

"That did not go quite the way you planned, did it?" Orrin asked.

Eryn shrugged. "I must say she handled that better than I had hoped. Well, at least a few people will start wondering if she is maybe not as harmless as she wants to make them think."

"So you are after destroying Malriel's reputation as the wronged mother she has been building these last few weeks?"

She nodded grimly. "I am. This should stop people pestering me about making amends with her. Every time somebody tells me to give my heart a push I feel an urge to punch him or her. And as you keep showing me how to do just that effectively without even having to resort to magic, I am sure that restraining myself is getting more difficult with every remark I have to listen to."

They watched as Anwin offered Malriel his arm and she accepted graciously. Enric gave Orrin a questioning look and when the warrior gave him a nod, offered Junar his own arm.

"That leaves you with me, girl," he said and waited until the other couples had left the room before he offered her his arm. "Am I to assume that act two is about to follow soon?"

She smiled tellingly. "Oh yes. You may depend on that."

* * *

Eryn leaned back contentedly after finishing her dessert. The food had been very good, and Inad had even instructed her cook to prepare something without meat for Eryn. Inad was not such a bad sort, she mused. Just not that well-endowed with intellectual capacities and with a tendency towards vanity that at least kept the clinic's vault from emptying too quickly. And even though she was not exactly hosting this evening for purely or even mainly charitable motives but to establish herself as benefactress and earn praise and respect, this hardly mattered to the orphans benefiting from the money.

"Where is your sister this evening, Lady Eryn? Such a pity she couldn't join us!" Aurna asked her.

"She is on night duty," Eryn told her.

"Night duty?" Lord Remdel, the host, enquired curiously. "I thought you did your healing only in the mornings?"

"That was the plan, yes," she smiled. "Unfortunately medical emergencies are not always very considerate of our treatment schedules when they occur. Every now and again healers have been woken by messengers to take care of problems during the night and are not very fit the following morning as a result. So my sister established a rota where each of us needs to be available one out of every few nights for emergencies and make sure the other healers can get some sleep," she explained.

"But surely, *you* do not participate in this rota, do you? Considering all your other important responsibilities," one of Inad's less appealing friends enquired. Eryn really needed to start remembering those names, especially as she always seemed to meet virtually the same people at these occasions each time.

"I do, yes. I am a healer as well, after all. And as their superior I need to set a good example. How can I ask of them what I myself am not ready to do?"

"A very important principle of good leadership, dearest Lady Eryn, is the ability to delegate," Lord Woldarn said, smiling at her condescendingly. "Let Lord Tyront be an example to you. If he took over all the tasks he is ultimately responsible for, there wouldn't be any time left in his day for taking care of the really important business his office entails."

Eryn returned the supercilious smile and adapted her tone accordingly. "Thank you so very much for that insight, My Lord. I may be superior to the other healers when it comes to knowledge and making decisions, but since about one third of my work consists not of leading or teaching, but of healing patients, we are equals at least in that area. Leaving the less pleasant tasks to people that are equal to you will not endear you to them in the long run. And then there is the matter of my still being the most skilled healer we have here, not counting our guest, of course. So being the only one not participating in the night duty rotation would mean wasting my abilities, don't you think? My understanding of delegation is handing on tasks to people if I have either no resources to take care of them myself, or if the others are more suited to handling them. Neither case applies here."

"Or course," he said coldly, "it is your decision to lower yourself to the standards that apply to your underlings."

"I do not appreciate that term very much, Lord Woldarn, considering that I am one of them," Lord Poron spoke softly. Eryn saw several mouths around her being covered by casual movements of hand or napkin to hide smiles.

"And technically speaking, My Lord," the septuagenarian magician continued, "*you* would also be termed an *underling*, as you chose to phrase it, as Lady Eryn outranks *you*, too."

"My Lords," Inad cut in, her face a mask of forced cheerfulness, bravely facing the danger of having her evening ruined by unkind words. "Let us not talk about business matters, I beg you!"

"Inad is absolutely right," Eryn nodded. "This is not a topic to be discussed at an occasion like this when our hostess has made such an effort to provide an exceedingly charming setting for our enjoyment."

She saw Junar shaking her head slightly and exchanging an exasperated glance with her companion. Enric, too, looked at her dubiously. Promoting the idea of a peaceful meal instead of enjoying the chance to watch two magicians having a go at each other to provide entertainment was clearly not the kind of behaviour they expected from her. But she had an agenda and their discussion didn't fit her plans right now.

Vyril was the first to speak after the table had fallen silent.

"Malriel, your stay will soon be coming to an end, won't it? How have you enjoyed your time here?"

"I have to admit I am rather reluctant to leave here again so soon. I did not quite accomplish what I came here to achieve. But unfortunately duties call me back to Takhan," Malriel explained with a sad smile.

Some of the guests exchanged knowing looks, then looked in whatever direction was not Eryn's.

Only Vyril seemed to be at a loss as to the nature of that unaccomplished task. "Really? I am sorry to hear that. Would it be too bold of me to ask what business it is you will leave here unfinished?"

Malriel's face disclosed some inner struggle as she looked down at the hands she had laid in her lap. "I had hoped to improve my relationship with my daughter. But it seems I was a little too optimistic on that score."

"Then there remains no unfinished business for you here, Malriel," Eryn replied pointedly. "As far as I know you have no daughter here, but a son. And from what I have seen your relationship with him is quite in order. Nothing to prolong your stay here unnecessarily, even if you weren't due to return soon."

"Lady Eryn," Lord Seagon's companion called out, taken aback, "don't you think it is a catastrophe when mother and daughter can't seem to find a way to work around their difficulties? Especially when one of them is trying so very hard?"

Eryn shook her head and replied stiffly, "I think that valid reasons may make a situation more desirable where no connection is maintained due to impossible differences, than attempts to fix what is beyond repair."

"My dear lady," another well-meaning voice cut in, Lord Aldon this time, "sometimes our perception as to what is beyond repair may change in time if we opened our minds."

"A mother is such a precious person to have," Inad cut in with a pleading look at Eryn. "Not a person to be cast aside carelessly due to an argument!"

Just a bit further, Eryn thought. Vyril gently dabbed the corners of her mouth with her napkin after finishing her dessert, then folded the fabric in an orderly fashion in front of her before she spoke.

"I agree with Inad. Lady Eryn, won't you try to use what energy you have and at least sit down with your mother to have a good, honest talk? Share all that misery and find a way out of this situation, one that cannot be pleasant for either of you?"

Eryn stared at her, then at the other faces, most of nodding in agreement and imploring her to give in. A few faces, though, did not at all appear convinced. Junar had raised a brow at Vyril, Lord Tyront seemed puzzled, Orrin was looking tickled, clearly expecting something entertaining.

Enric narrowed his eyes to warn her not to do anything stupid that would require his intervention, probably by knocking her out before she could cause any major damage. Or injury.

He watched her averting her face and covering her mouth as if to stifle a sob. A lump in her throat, she closed her eyes before two large tears, one at the corner of each eye, formed and ran down her cheeks.

The entire table had fallen silent and just stared at her. The next sob was clear and audible.

"I can't," she whispered. "Every time I see her I have to think back to when she betrayed me." Now she covered her face with both hands, her shoulders shaking.

Impressive, Enric mused. But then for a healer weeping on command couldn't be much of a challenge, considering that they knew very well how to control every organ and fluid of their bodies to a certain degree. He watched the other guests exchange looks that ranged between surprise and sheer panic, sympathy and incomprehension, fascination and disbelief.

"I trusted her when I told her of my father's death," she sobbed and made another tear run down her face. "And she used it to have me accused of killing him! To stop me from leaving her city again! To hold me there in captivity like an animal!"

She removed her hands again, allowing her audience to see the reddened eyes. The pale complexion was a nice touch, Enric mused. Red eyes were so much more effective when there was a good contrast to an almost white skin.

"I still wake up at night, looking around to see if I really am home again or if escaping her intrigues was just a beautiful dream I somehow made up to stay sane."

Time to be seen to comfort her, Enric thought with a certain resignation, just like a considerate and compassionate companion was supposed to. He got to his feet and walked over to her, crouching down next to her chair when Aurna quickly move hers aside for him.

"Eryn?" he asked gently, "Would you like me to take you home now?" Of course she wouldn't, he knew. She was not yet finished with them.

She indicated the negative with her head, but held on to his hands to press them against her wet cheeks. "No, I need to make them understand," she said in a soft yet desperate voice, loud enough to be heard by those around her.

She then straightened in her chair, bravely wiping away the tears that kept trickling down her cheeks. "I was raised by my father, as all of you know," she started, valiantly trying to keep the sobs under control that threatened to keep her from speaking. "I was raised in the belief that my mother was dead. So when I went to Takhar only a few months ago and discovered that she was not dead, it was an incredible feeling." She saw understanding nods and continued. "But I soon found out that she had been hardened by what had happened so many years ago, by my being taken away. Hardened not only against my father, but also against *me*..." She broke off, obviously not able to go on due to the anguish the thought caused her.

Enric had to work hard at keeping his face serious and worried. He could feel through the mind bond that she was truly enjoying herself by playing to her audience. Malriel seemed to be as aware of the manoeuvre as he was, but couldn't afford to put words to it without seeming even more unfeeling than her daughter's words had already painted her.

"She tried to have me convicted for causing my father's death. He was killed because he had protected me, and it took me so many years to deal with this." She let her sobs die down, but the tears kept running down her cheeks for good measure. "Being dragged before the senate and then having to relate the story to all of them... being accused of this terrible thing... by my own mother!" Once more her hands covered her face and Enric nodded gratefully to Aurna when she relinquished her chair for him so he could sit and pull her against his chest. She let herself be held by him for a few moments, before she sat up again, collecting herself before going on.

"I was found not guilty and permitted to leave Takhan. But these ten days of suspense, of fear at not being allowed to return with my companion..." She put one hand on Enric's cheek and leaned her forehead against his for a moment, closing her eyes to demonstrate their affection for each other.

"That was the worst period of my life so far. After being kept a prisoner here for so many months, I was so terrified of losing my freedom yet again over there, being once more forced to leave behind everything I had built." She finally wiped away her tears with a napkin. "And worst of all was one certainty: I no longer had a mother. I came to Takhan as an orphan, and I am grateful and humbled that my uncle gave me the family I had always dreamed of. He was the one to help me through that ordeal that Malriel made me endure. He is my family to me. She is not." She straightened and looked each of the other guests in the eye for a moment before saying, "I never had the luxury of trusting people when I grew up, always having to hide who I was. Then I came to meet family, believing that I had to hide no longer and was then taught otherwise by Malriel. Even now I find trusting my closest friends hard, thanks to her. As a result I would ask you not to try and make me do something I do not have in me any longer: being able to forgive her. Because there is so much fear, anger, helplessness and coldness in me when I think of her - not to mention when looking at her, like now - that I know I will not be able to overcome this in the foreseeable future. I need time to heal first."

Her wide, doe-like eyes rested on Malriel, whose expression was hard to determine, but seemed to contain elements of amusement, dismay, respect and mild surprise. She looked as if she might even start applauding any moment.

If only, Eryn thought. But that would be foolish, as all of the people around her, save a selected few who were on Eryn's side anyway, believed her and would not take well to a sarcastic gesture from the woman who had been shown to have caused so much suffering.

Some of the looks moved from Eryn to look at Malriel instead, clearly expecting some kind of reaction to such an incriminating outburst.

The silence stretched and Malriel finally drew in a deep breath. "Theá, my child," she said, careful to maintain a soft and gentle tone in her voice, "it pains me so very much that this is how you experienced all of this. I had no idea that this had been so immensely hard on you. I may have hardened my heart against your father for taking you away from me, but it was never against you. I will do whatever you require of me to make things between us whole again.'

Eryn shook her head resignedly. "There is nothing you can..." Her voice trailed off as if inspiration had just struck her.

"Yes?" Malriel asked calmly.

"Your presence here in the city is a great burden to me, has been for the last three weeks," she said quietly.

"Then I will lift this burden from your shoulders, my child," the older woman replied, "and leave tomorrow."

Eryn stared at her in surprise. That was unexpected. Pleasantly so.

"If," Malriel smiled sadly, "you will share a glass of wine with me tonight, here in Inad's beautiful parlour, and promise me that you will come to me when you feel that you have healed enough to have it in your heart to talk to me again."

Eryn saw people around her looking sad, but with understanding, at this. If she refused this seemingly very reasonable offer now, she would again be the one to have pushed her mother away by not accepting such a small, desperate request to share a glass of wine. Doing it would ensure Malriel's departure an entire week earlier than expected. One week fewer in which she could inflict suffering of whatever sort. Eryn nodded slowly.

"Very well, Malriel. One glass of wine and that promise." A worthless promise given from one player to another.

Inad rose quickly. "I will prepare some wine for the two of you in the parlour."

"Thank you so very much, that is considerate of you," Malriel smiled at her with a resigned expression.

Enric leaned closer and pretended to kiss Eryn's cheek while he whispered, "Nicely played, my love. Very accomplished."

She smiled with a sad irony, nodding as if he had just told her to face up to the enemy, then said, "I would appreciate your taking me home after..." She looked at Malriel. "This."

He nodded solemnly. "Of course, my dearest. Whatever you wish."

Malriel got up from her chair, waiting for Eryn to do the same before she stepped away from the table to walk into the parlour. Inad had placed two glasses and a bottle of red wine on a tablet on a chest of drawers and retreated hurriedly to give the two women privacy.

When the doors were closed and the two of them were alone, Malriel sneered at her.

"Well done, daughter. I was wondering when you would finally give up sulking and strike back. But your countermove was worth the waiting. Those were some very nice theatrics." She strolled over to the two glasses and the bottle. "I admit I would not have thought that your pride could bear your bursting into tears in front of these people." She motioned towards the dining room. "But then I might imagine the little incident with the King yesterday helped you to reassess your priorities, did it not?"

She turned her back to Eryn to open the bottle and pour them out a glass each.

Eryn turned to look out the window into the night beyond. It had been raining during the day and there was fog as the damp air rose from the streets up into the uncommonly warm night air. The lanterns outside made the scene seem eerie and unreal.

She accepted the glass Malriel pressed into her hand as she stepped next to her.

"You have no intention of keeping that promise, do you?"

Eryn shook her head. "No, I don't. But if it is any consolation to you, I don't think that I will ever recover from your deeds enough to feel the need to talk to you."

"It is not," Malriel replied dryly and took a sip of her wine. "Quite the opposite." She sighed heavily. "We cannot continue like this forever, Theá. You are bound to me by blood, and your companion is bound to me by law. There will always be contact between us due to the latter, as Enric is my heir now. Added to which you will frequently be visiting House Vel'kim, I am sure. You will not be able to avoid me completely on these occasions. I will not allow you to."

Eryn sighed and swirled the wine around her glass. "Stop this, Malriel. The most intimate relationship you may expect between the two of us is that of indifferent strangers. That would actually be a great improvement compared to what is going on inside me right now."

"No, Theá. Indifference can never be better than reluctance. Indifference is when all feelings are lost, when we have reached a point where we cannot even manage or bother to hurt one another anymore because there is nothing left. I would prefer you to *hate* me instead of that."

"Hatred is always more painful for the one doing the hating than for its target," Eryn said. "I will leave this behind me one day in favour of that indifference you reject so much. Be assured of that."

Malriel looked at her angrily. "Pain, Theá, is exactly what you *should* be feeling if you hate your own mother!"

Eryn downed her wine in a few gulps. "You brought this upon yourself, *mother*," she spat. "Now live with the consequences " She put her empty glass aside. "And now you must excuse me. I have fulfilled your condition of sharing a glass of wine with you. Now I will have Enric take me home. Do not bother to say goodbye to me before you leave tomorrow. I wouldn't thank you for it." With this she turned and walked briskly out of the room towards the entrance hall.

Malriel watched her and then looked down at the empty wine glass on the windowsill. And smiled faintly.

CHAPTER 19

A Second Chance

Eryn opened the door for Junar to enter and took her cloak.

"Good morning, you," the magician smiled. "Come in and tell me what happened yesterday after we had left."

Junar went to a settee. "First you will be hospitable and offer me something to drink, as is due and proper for a lady in my circumstances."

"Your circumstances? You mean being pregnant? I wasn't aware that you are due any special treatment due to that," Eryn said but obediently went to the drinking cabinet to take out a bottle of juice.

"Not only the pregnancy. I am the companion of an important man, after all," the seamstress grinned, then frowned. "But then it just occurred to me that you are the companion of an even more important man and also outrank Orrin yourself, so I should probably keep quiet before you make *me* serve *you* something to drink."

The younger woman shrugged and placed a glass in front of her guest. "Not today. I am in a forgiving mood."

"Alright, mighty enchantress, then I shall in turn comply with your request to relay the later happenings of yesterday evening to you." She took a generous gulp from her glass. "First of all let me tell you that your performance yesterday was extremely convincing. Not for those who know you reasonably well, mind you. Too melodramatic. When you burst into tears, I would be expecting things to crack or explode instead of a show of misery and pain, but fortunately most people there were not close enough to you to figure that out. Next time you pull of a stunt like that, *I* want to be the one to assist you."

Eryn frowned at her. "What?"

"Last time at Lord Aldon's you had Pe'tala to play her part, yesterday it was Vyril. Next time I want to help you with whatever sinister plot you might plan."

"I do not intend to make manipulating people at social dinner gatherings a habit."

Junar rolled her eyes. "Oh, please! Yesterday was the first time I didn't fear for you falling asleep at any moment. I take that as a sign that you had a lot of fun there. A pity that I wasn't there to witness Pe'tala's performance. I will make sure not to miss another evening when you are attending. Even if I have to bring my own bowl to vomit into."

"That is most considerate of you, really," Eryn retorted. "The guests will definitely appreciate seeing you retching over your very own bowl while they are trying to enjoy their meal."

"Tough luck for them," the seamstress shrugged, then returned to the topic of the evening before. "When you and Malriel had gone into the parlour, people started expressing their concern about that unusual outburst of yours and that they had no idea that this situation bothered and burdened you so much. Then they started talking about having noticed signs in the past of some inexplicable sadness they had glimpsed when you considered yourself unobserved. I had to work really hard to stop myself from bursting into laughter at that. It seems that now, in hindsight, most of them had some indefinable feeling about it all the time. Every rude word you ever uttered was quickly overlooked, as they attributed your unfriendliness to that terrible strain of being in conflict with your mother." She shook her head. "Lord Enric, Lord Tyront and Orrin kept avoiding looking at each other, probably for fear of otherwise not being able to maintain straight faces. Vyril valiantly joined the conversations, expressing her own sympathy with your situation and telling people how brave she thought you are, having been tested by fate like that."

Eryn snorted. "I am glad I put Pe'tala on night duty yesterday. She would probably have spoiled the whole thing."

"You kept her away on purpose?"

"You bet I did! If I had not, she might either have ruined everything with her sarcasm or it would have been necessary to ask her not to, and I would have ended up owing her another favour."

"Oh, you and your families," Junar mused. "Is there even one single woman you are related to that you get along with?"

Eryn thought back to her grandmother Malhora and their all but harmonic encounter at the Aren estate. "No, I don't think so. I don't know all female members of both Houses, but the ones I do are clearly not my kind of people. It seems I get along a lot better with the men for some reason. Anyway," she grinned broadly, "Not only did I manage to stop people from pushing me toward mending fences with Malriel, I also shoved her off home a week early. A successful evening indeed!"

"The King will probably not be too pleased about it," the seamstress pointed out. "You shooed away his lover one week earlier than he'd expected. I suppose it will be a while until he has another chance to enjoy a magician as a lover again."

"There is still Pe'tala," Eryn shrugged. "I dare say she would benefit from a little... work out. That would certainly loosen her up a bit."

"Eryn!" Junar exclaimed. "What a wicked thing to say!"

"Why? From a healer's point of view, sex is a very healthy thing. It improves circulation, tones the muscles, strengthens the body's defences against illnesses, releases substances that help brighten someone's mood..." she explained, then grinned. "I might even offer her to the King in compensation for prematurely depriving him of Malriel's company."

The older woman snorted. "I am sure your cousin would really appreciate that."

"Well, it would be for her own benefit, wouldn't it? You know, she could do worse than having sex with a young, fit King."

"And all but dreadful, as well," Junar agreed. "And yet she would not be at all thrilled about being offered by you like that."

"Then in the interest of good sisterhood I will refrain from doing so for now," Eryn gasped in mock surrender.

"Speaking of family, Anwin ended up completely confused yesterday. We had to explain to him why Malriel was suddenly supposed to be your mother while she appeared no more than Lord Enric's age. He was very generous about your outburst, conceding that women were generally given to dramatic emotional displays." Junar sniggered. "I can tell you that this earned him a few concerned looks. He didn't hang around very long after that for some reason."

"How did the rest of the evening go? Did people even remember that they were being invited to part with their money instead of just enjoying the show?"

She nodded. "Yes, Inad steered them back onto the path of virtue, as it were. She started auctioning off a few things like her aunt's earrings, a small box of gems and other things like that. People tried to outbid each other good-naturedly though without much enthusiasm, not really feeling motivated to part with their money for the items she offered. That changed when the last item on the list was presented."

Eryn raised her brow curiously. "What was it?"

Junar sneered wickedly. "A cosmetic correction carried out by *yourself*."

She stared at her friend. "What? I don't remember having offered that!"

"No, you forgot. Luckily *I* remembered in time and told Inad that you had wanted to surprise her with it," the seamstress replied gleefully. "Count that as my little revenge for always being left out of your schemes. Let it be a lesson to you."

"Marvellous," Eryn muttered. "And did they bid for it?"

"Not at the beginning. I think people were loath to be seen to show interest in it. But then Vyril said that this would be a fabulous gift to a friend, and that seemed to have been all the pretence the ladies needed. Suddenly they started trying to outbid each other for it.' She shook her head in amusement. "You should have seen them The greedy look in their eyes in contrast to the all too casual hand gestures to indicate their bids. Pretenders, all of them!"

"And who won in the end?"

"Lord Woldarn's companion, Elset. And good thing, too. She looks like she could use a bit of help in the facial department. Crimping her lips together in dismay over decades has left them with more than a few wrinkles," Junar jibed.

"You are not turning into one of these hateful society gossips, are you?"

Junar sighed. "Sorry. Being in their company for too long or too often within a short time does not agree with me, it would seem. They are a bad influence."

"Obviously," the magician observed dryly.

At that moment the door opened and Enric and Urban entered.

"Hello Junar," he smiled, then went over to Eryn and kissed her on the mouth before sitting down next to her. "There is something I need to tell you. I will leave for Bonhet tonight."

Eryn stared at him in surprise. "With *her*? Why?"

"I had planned to go there sometime next week or the week after, but now that Malriel is leaving earlier, I may as well keep her company. I should be back in no more than five days. I just talked to Tyront, and he agreed to it. The only thing we needed to reschedule was the Council meeting in two days where you were supposed to present your new proposal."

She nodded. "Well, we can hold it when you are back, I would think."

"No, he wants to take care of this rather sooner than later. It is rescheduled for the afternoon today."

Eryn jumped up. "What? Today? No! Come on! I thought I still had two more days of preparation left! I need to talk to Vern immediately!" She raked her fingers through her hair. "Enric, I need you to write me a note exempting him from his lessons today."

He raised an eyebrow at her. "You are number three in the Order, my love. You don't need me to write it for you, your seal and signature are quite sufficient, believe me."

She thought for a moment, then nodded and dashed off to her study. "Yes, of course!"

When she returned two minutes later she was waving a letter in her hand to dry the ink and sealing wax and opened the door to wave to the next person she saw, a young girl, pressed a coin into her hand and told her to get the message delivered. The girl stared at the money for a moment before her face split into a broad grin and she nodded and ran off.

Eryn closed the door, then started pacing the room. "I don't like it. I don't like having to do this today. And I don't like your being on the road with Malriel for two entire days. More or less alone!"

"You know you can trust me, I would hope," he responded.

"Of course I know that! I just don't trust *her*, that's all," she responded.

"I will protect my virtue, purse and life at all times," he promised solemnly.

"Interesting priority," Junar laughed.

"It's Malriel's likely order of targets, I would think," he grinned, winking at her.

"Can you stop making fun of me for a moment? You just sprang it on me that you are about to leave me for five days to be on the road with that beast and now you are mocking me? Honestly?" Eryn huffed and stared at him with a piqued expression.

He rose and pulled her into his arms. "Forgive me, dearest. I know this is rather short notice, but there still are a few things I need to discuss with Malriel, and now that she is leaving early there is no more chance for it otherwise."

"What things?"

"Aren business. Trade. How to restore House Arbil to its former glory so they may continue to be a useful ally at the senate," he listed.

"So after a short frenzy of preparation with Vern I will see you again at the Council meeting and then you will have to leave straight off?" she sighed.

He smiled. "I might manage to defer our departure for an extra hour, if you like."

Junar pretended to study the pattern on the curtains while sipping her juice.

Eryn nodded briefly, then returned to her study to put together the notes for the proposal for Vern's impending arrival.

Enric took a seat opposite Junar. "I am afraid you will have to make do with me for now. How is your pregnancy progressing? Is everything the way it should be?"

She smiled. "Yes, everything is fine. I have three healers checking on me regularly. Vern draws these amazing pictures, so I can see everything that has changed from one week to the next. I am sure that is a privilege no other mother in this Kingdom has had for quite a while. Pe'tala stops by casually for a drink every now and then and then finds a reason to examine me. And Eryn, of course." She chuckled. "Also, Orrin jumps every time I cut my finger and heals away every tiny scratch immediately, even if I just poke myself with a needle!"

He grinned. "The big, strong warrior - all soft inside."

"A concept completely unknown to yourself, is it?" she retorted with a quiet smile.

"That is something I would never admit out loud," he replied, good-naturedly.

Junar put aside her empty glass and straightened. "There is something I wanted to ask you. I have put aside a little money. And I would like to do something with it, invest it somewhere. For the baby, you know. When she is old enough, I would like there to be some nest egg for her."

Enric raised his brow in surprise. "You are aware that Orrin is well-off, aren't you? He is in a position to provide for a family without any problem whatsoever."

She swallowed. "I know. But there is Vern, and I wouldn't want him to think that he is being cut out in favour of his little sister. That he has to give up what would have been rightfully his otherwise. I wouldn't want this to be an issue between them, ever."

"I think you are grossly misjudging Vern in that regard,' Enric pointed out. "And that rather surprises me, to be completely honest. He is unusually considerate and has in the past proven more than once that his is willing to accept disadvantages for himself in order to help others. Money has never been a topic for him, as far as I know; he is more than willing to work for his share of it. He is the only boy I know who works in addition to his regular classes and extra training hours."

Junar kneaded her fingers. "I know! It's just that I want to contribute something as well." Her expression became pained. "I wouldn't want my daughter to think that I was just after a rich companion to have a life of idle comfort. I want to show her that I, too, can give her something."

Enric regarded her thoughtfully. Of course she would have had to endure one or other open or covert snide remark or hint in that direction from the noble ladies she was now bound to interact with on such a regular basis. So this was a mission to prove to herself and her family that she was self-sufficient and had chosen them not for wealth, but for much more idealistic reasons. Who was he to deny her that?

"Of course. Why don't you come to my study? I have an idea or two about what we can do here."

He offered her a hand to help her up when she smiled in relief.

"I would appreciate if you didn't tell Orrin about this," she requested.

Enric raised a brow at her. "I won't. It is not my place to do so. And it will not be necessary, anyway."

She frowned. "It won't?"

"No," he smiled thinly, 'because *you* will tell him yourself. I am not a great fan of companions keeping secrets from each other, as you may imagine. I don't have very fond memories in connection with it. And Orrin's learning one day that you have been stashing away money without his knowledge will not be a happy occasion for either of you, I think."

He led her to a chair and motioned for her to sit down. "That is a condition for my help in this matter, in case you were wondering."

Looking concerned, Junar let herself sink onto the chair in front of his large, black desk. "People keep complaining about there not being enough men with principles around. *I* seem to be drowning in them," she said, then looked up with narrowed eyes. "Why do I have the impression that you keep treating me as if you were *my* superior as well?"

"Not a superior, Junar. Just somebody who helps in protecting you from yourself every now and then. But you should be familiar enough with that pattern, it's what Orrin does with that chaotic, foreign healer friend of yours, after all."

"You are returning the favour of Orrin treating your companion as a daughter? That is strange, as we are pretty much the same age," she pointed out.

"It's not a matter of age. Vern has given her protection in the past as well, and he is quite a bit younger than her. It's a matter of family. You were there for Eryn when she was a lonely prisoner; I don't forget something like that," he explained soberly. "Are you going to tell Orrin about your investment plans or do I need to drag you there by your ear and make you?"

She smiled at him in wonder, then nodded. "I will. I promise. Thank you, Lord Enric."

"My pleasure. And it's *Enric* for you."

* * *

Eryn looked Vern up and down as they stood in front of the doors to the Council hall while they were waiting to be admitted.

"What?" he asked with an unnerved expression.

"I wonder if we should have dressed you in healer's robes."

"You can't. The robes are what we get when we have finished our training. The Council would hardly look kindly upon your violating another tradition without so much as asking. And we need them to like you. For now. If that is at all possible since your last appearance," he added, none too lightly.

"I believe at least three of them are reasonably well-disposed towards me," she shrugged.

"Those are not enough, considering the Council has twelve members. Since the most important one to have on your side is Lord Tyront, you might try and manage somehow not to cause him to yell at you this time."

She ruffled his hair affectionately and pulled her hand back when he swatted at it. "That's why I brought you, my friend. You will make it work. I have the utmost confidence in you."

He sniffed. "No pressure, alright? I will try to do most of the talking in there, but they will insist on hearing from you every now and then as well. It is supposed to be *your* proposal, after all. I am a mere underling doing the menial presentation work for you. When they have important questions, they will address you, not me. Having you always deferring to me will not make them happy." He looked at her insistently. "We need a code word or phrase for when you lose control over that spiky tongue of yours. Whenever you hear me say it, you must shut up immediately."

Eryn rolled her eyes at him. "Come on! I am not a child you need to rein in like that. I will behave." She groaned when he just kept staring at her. "Alright! But pick something unobtrusive. I don't want them to notice that I am being kept on a short leash by a sixteen-year-old boy who is supposed to be taking *my* orders," she sighed in defeat.

"How about *sure*?"

"Sure?" She thought about it for a moment. "Why not? Should be easy enough to fit into practically every sentence without standing out."

"Good, then listen for it. If you decide to ignore it, I will resort to stomping on your foot. That is less restrained than you would wish, I imagine. Let's not forget why we are there, shall we? You want something from *them*, so try to be pleasant," he implored her.

At that moment the heavy double doors opened and a guard announced loudly, "Lady Eryn of House Vel'kim. And company."

"*Of House Vel'kim*?" she rolled her eyes. "That is ridiculous. As if such a title made any sense here!"

"*Sure*," Vern hissed at her and followed her in.

That was a good start, she thought resignedly. They had not even started their presentation and he had used the code word already for the first time. She made herself smile politely at the assembled magicians once she came to stand in front of the large oblong table. Her expression became slightly rigid when she beheld the King, who had obviously decided that witnessing this Council meeting was probably worth his while.

She bowed first to the King, then to the Council before she started speaking.

"Gentlemen, I would like to thank you for granting me another chance at speaking before you. Especially as the last time has ended on a rather… unsatisfactory outcome for both sides, I imagine." She noted with satisfaction a few amused expressions. Good. Whatever put them in a good mood. "I have asked my young colleague to assist me today in proposing to you a new structure that will I hope benefit both the Order as a whole and the healers. I believe you all know Vern, Lord Orrin's son."

She then stepped aside and let the boy do the talking for now. He cleared his throat and then spoke.

"Your Majesty, My Lords, it is my honour to address you today in order to present to you an idea that should provide a stable framework for the two very different purposes magic is nowadays put to in the Order. This framework aims to provide both rules and control as well as resources and easier administration for the hitherto rather unregulated area of healing," he propounded eloquently.

Eryn smiled to herself. She had seen some of the expressions when she had told them that Vern would be the one speaking to them. Indulgent, resigned and one or two were even unnerved. But the boy's first few sentences spoken with unusual confidence and in a style that meant business had made them realise quickly enough that they had to take him seriously. A few curious looks darted across to Orrin, who was smiling smugly, undoubtedly proud of his son who had in the past by most people been considered a burden to his father due to his lack of aptitude or enthusiasm for fighting skills.

"We propose establishing a system that allows healers and warriors to coexist within the Order and be subject to its rules. For this purpose we have determined that creating a different set of regulations and guidelines for the healers is sensible, as the warriors currently follow rules that do not either make great sense for the healers nor provide statutes on topics and procedures that are urgently required for carrying out the healing profession in a responsible way that ensures high quality standards and does not endanger the reputation of the Order or the patients' safety."

Eryn was none too happy about the order of his last two arguments, but then it was very likely that most of the men present would prioritise the Order's reputation before the wellbeing of patients.

"We have prepared a list of regulations we would ask the Order to ratify as soon as a structure is agreed on, but this is not of the essence at this point," he went on. "We propose appointing a responsible person for each of the disciplines, one Head of Warriors and one Head of Healers, who will be the first person to be consulted in case any issues arise within one of the two areas." He then turned to Eryn with a slightly pained expression as if he were reluctant to continue.

She lifted her brow at him, then resigned herself. Very well, if he didn't want to say it, she would.

"Lord Tyront would of course be the Head of Warriors, while I myself am surely the logical choice for Head of Healers," she announced, her chin uplifted determinedly.

Lord Tyront folded his arms, his smile restrained. "What a novel idea. So you propose elevating yourself to a rank equal to my own and thus freeing yourself from the need to take orders from me, Lady Eryn?" He looked at her indulgently. "I don't think so."

"Well, I was simply aiming to release you from the burden of having to waste your precious time and making decisions in an area where you clearly have no..."

"I am *sure* there is another way to organise this to our mutual satisfaction," Vern cut in sharply with a scorching look at her.

She fell silent immediately. Oh dear, that had been close. Nodding once, she stepped back and motioned for Vern to go on.

Enric shot her an amused glance, then returned his attention to Vern.

"Another option would of course be that of dividing the Order at the lower hierarchical level, leaving the top ranks in charge of both disciplines, but delegating a greater part of the issues to the previously mentioned Heads to be established. This should ensure that the administrative efforts for the Order's leaders are not increased beyond reasonable amount."

That made both Enric and Lord Tyront smile. After she had clearly been on the verge of insulting her superior once again only a few moments ago, the boy's tact and eagerness to convey the benefits for all parties concerned had salvaged the diplomatic outreach.

"Another concern of ours is the chance to invite healers from our new friends in the Western Territories to work here. As the Order is an institution devoted to the defence of the Kingdom and requires its members to take an oath of loyalty in order to be accepted into its ranks, this is clearly not something we could make guests from other countries undertake. And yet they, too, need to be subject to an organisation that makes sure that they act responsibly in the execution of their duties and are made to justify themselves in case they fail to do so," Vern went on. "For this purpose we suggest forming an institution that is not part of the Order, but still headed by an Order magician, namely the Head of Healers mentioned before."

That earned him several confused expressions.

"An Order magician leading an institution that is not part of the Order?" Lord Woldarn asked with a questioning scowl.

"Indeed, My Lord," Vern nodded. "Consider that the Order cannot as such discipline or even command members of another country due to its purpose of defending the Kingdom. This means an independent institution which would nonetheless be controlled by an Order magician, though not in that capacity, is a viable solution for that. Another benefit is that this will also allow us to include all medical professions that are currently being carried out by non-magicians. Lady Eryn plans to train non-magicians as healers as well, and they, too, would need to be members of a governing institution for the profession. So this solution would enable us not only to enforce our regulations with foreign visitors who wish to work here, but also to include non-magicians who are working in the healing profession and those connected with them."

"You mean the apothecaries as well, I assume? They would hardly be willing to give up their League, would they?" a Council member asked.

Vern smiled confidently at that. "They would eventually. They have signed their services over to the clinic exclusively and would either have to comply with the rules set by us or face an immediate end of our cooperation which would leave them without an income, as patients do not depend on them any longer. But the apothecaries would not be the only profession to be included here. There are also the herb gatherers. And whatever staff will in the future be required in addition to Rolan for the administration of the services." He paused as if to think for a moment, before he continued. "That leaves us with only two more points we wish to address. Firstly, there is the need for an increase in the quota for healers in the near future. The number of patients seeking our services has been rising steadily from month to month. People have started coming here from all parts of the Kingdom since it became common knowledge that there is magical healing available in Anyueel for everyone. We first need to finish training our current trainees so they can dedicate their time both to healing and teaching others. And the second matter is the inclusion of basic healing skills into the schedule of the regular classes for young magicians."

"This sounds like you want to force magicians to learn healing," Lord Aldon pointed out in a less than enthusiastic tone.

"Well, you are forcing them to learn combat skills right now, aren't you?" Eryn cut in. "And healing at least has an immediate and very practical use for everyday life, whereas fighting, if you are really honest with yourself, is little more than..."

"I am *sure* there is space for both disciplines in the teaching schedule," Vern interrupted her urgently. "You are right, Lord Aldon, we propose to make the learning of healing skills compulsory for young magicians as it would enable them to take care of themselves and their families and so reduce the need for them to consult healers at the clinic, who are at the moment busy enough. And it increases young people's independence and self-sufficiency - values which the Order advocates as far as I am aware. Lady Eryn has furthermore proved that the application of healing principles can lead to considerable progress when it comes to fighting techniques. I assume you all remember the double barrier she managed to employ against two much stronger magicians less than a year ago."

Eryn bit her tongue to quell her annoyance at having once more been silenced by him; she had to admit that his arguments were received more favourably than the insult she had been about to deliver would have been. Somehow, standing in front of them and being asked inane questions brought out the worst in her, she realised. It had indeed been a smart move to have Vern do the talking instead of attempting to convince them herself.

"We would of course only propose teaching them basic skills such as repairing skin, bone and muscle tissue damage so they will be able to assist in emergencies. The treatment of diseases and illnesses, as well as more complicated damage, will still be undertaken by trained healers," he added and then bowed. "I thank you for your attention,

Gentlemen, and hope that you cannot fail to see our proposals' benefit for all involved parties and will choose to agree to them."

"Thank you, Vern," Tyront nodded at him, clearly impressed at how he had managed the session. "The Council will now discuss your ideas and decide if and in what form we are able to accept them. We would ask the two of you to leave us for now, but inform the guard outside the door as to where you can be found."

Eryn, too, bowed and followed Vern out the door.

Vern waited until the heavy doors were firmly closed behind them, before he exhaled extensively. "I am glad we agreed on that code word. You would otherwise have spoiled everything! How come you can't manage to keep that mouth of yours shut when it is important to? You are your own enemy with that defiance of yours!"

She rubbed her face. "I really don't know! As soon as I see Lord Tyront before me, my reasoning brain shuts down and I am somehow in fighting mode." Then she smiled at him. "But you did everything beautifully. You are my hero!"

"You bet I am," he snorted. "If you had been the one doing it, who knows what Lord Tyront would have compelled you to do this time by way of punishment for your insolence."

She remembered that Enric had told her about Lord Tyront's threatening to take over her combat training and looked chastened.

"Let's go and eat something, shall we?" she proposed. "We worked through lunch time, after all. I am starving and knowing you, I am sure you must be, too."

He grinned. "Oh, for sure I am! Let's go home - it's the nearest place to get something to eat quickly." He turned to the guard behind them. "Lady Eryn and I will be at Lord Orrin's quarters should the Council send for us," he informed the man before they walked off.

* * *

Tyront exhaled in relief when the two of them had left. "I admit that worked out a lot better than I had feared," he sighed.

Enric saw the King smiling at that remark, though he remained silent.

"Do we really want to grant the healing profession such a large position within the Order?" Lord Seagon frowned. "It is a sizeable step away from our traditions, after all."

"One we will need to take, sooner or later," Lord Poron remarked. "It is also a chance to get back in contact with the people, to be seen to be working with and for them. And whatever you might think, young Vern had a few very convincing arguments, didn't he?"

Another Council member nodded thoughtfully. "That he did, yes. I was surprised at seeing him in that capacity, Lord Orrin. It seems his revelation at the execution that he had secretly learned healing was not to be his last surprise for us."

Lord Aldon chuckled. "Indeed. He himself is the best proof that some of us are clearly not cut out to be warriors, but should be watched closely enough nevertheless. Whoever is going to be Head of Healers, I have little doubt that we have just watched the next in line for the position when he is old enough leaving that hall."

Enric noted how Orrin seemed to radiate pride, while trying in vain to seem modest about it.

"Did anybody else note that unusual interaction between Lady Eryn and the boy?" another Council member questioned.

"You mean that he seemed to shut her up somehow at regular intervals?" Lord Seagon asked bluntly.

"Sure."

All of them turned towards the throne.

"Pardon, Your Majesty?" Tyront enquired.

"A code word. They obviously agreed on it before," the monarch explained.

Enric nodded. "Yes. It was the word *sure*. It was in every sentence he used to silence her, he pronounced it a little more prominently than the rest."

"A technique you yourself employ with your companion, Lord Enric?" Lord Woldarn sneered.

"No, I don't," he replied calmly with a cool look at the older man, "I prefer to listen to her instead of stopping her from speaking her mind, though I appreciate that this might not be everyone's approach to showing respect to one's companion."

"Be that as it may," Tyront cut in before they could continue to throw sniping remarks at each other, "we had better come to a conclusion concerning the ideas that were just presented to us. We are on a tight schedule since Lord Enric is due to leave for Bonhet in only a few hours. I myself found the idea of dividing the Order reasonable enough. The Order's high command and the Magic Council would be responsible for both disciplines, the other magicians would be directly answerable to their respective Head. Are there any objections to this?"

"We all saw how difficult she still finds it to control her temper," Lord Aldon raised his voice. "I am told it is a family trait where she comes from. Somehow the idea of giving her full responsibility over an entire discipline that will probably expand very much in the years to come does not sit too well with me, I have to admit." He gave Enric an apologetic smile. "Not that I wish to disparage your companion's considerable gifts and abilities, Lord Enric, yet I think she still has quite a lot to learn when it comes to leading herself before she can be expected to lead others."

"She is doing a very good job in keeping the services running," Lord Poron pointed out in her defence. "Also the healers enjoy working with her immensely. Even young Rolan eventually started respecting her. I fail to see how she lacks leadership qualities."

"She treats you all as equals," Enric stressed, "not as subordinates. That makes you like her, but there is the question how she will react if she really needs to ask you to do something unpleasant. With her aversion to leadership, she will probably rather take over those unpleasant tasks herself instead of delegating them."

"So you do not wish her to take over the healers - do I understand you correctly?" Orrin enquired with a quizzical look. "Even though she is doing a fine job at it and has been the one to make all that possible, working hard for it over many months? She will not be pleased about that."

"No," Tyront consented and added wryly, "I imagine that Vern will find it quite a challenge to make her behave after *that* revelation."

"So I suppose it is Lord Poron who will be made Head of Healers, then?" Lord Aldon ventured.

"That would be appropriate, yes," Tyront agreed and turned to the old man. "What do you say, Lord Poron? Do you accept the position?"

He looked unsure, a little sombre. "I feel as if I would be tak ng on a position that I am not entitled to."

The Order's leader shook his head. "No, you would not. If we divide the Order into two, we need to maintain at least three people on top who are responsible for the entire institution. She is too powerful to be assigned to only one area. Lady Eryn is third strongest in the Order, so it would be inadvisable to completely remove her from the warriors to have her work in an area where her superior strength is being under-used. And I believe it wiser to make her focus her extraordinary abilities on discovering new things in more than one area, in any case."

Lord Poron nodded reluctantly. "I accept, then. But not happily."

Tyront acknowledged this with a nod and then turned to the King. "Your Majesty, as the healing services as such are still officially in the Crown's hands, I would ask for your approval in appointing Lord Poron as Head of Healers."

King Folrin nodded once. "It is granted. Congratulations, Lord Poron. You will not find me unreasonable to deal with as I have no intention of disrupting services that run well enough without even requiring any financial input from my side."

"Then we will also establish that organisation outside the Order? For the non-magicians and foreign healers?" Lord Seagon asked.

Enric shook his head. "No, *we* won't. Lord Poron as the new Head of Healers will. The Order as such is not responsible for that part."

"Who is to be given the position of Head of Warriors?" Orrin asked with a raised brow.

"Yourself," Lord Tyront replied. "Who else?"

That earned him several amused smirks, and for once not a single Council member objected.

"No token offer for me?" the warrior sighed.

"No. It wouldn't make sense to put any other warrior above you, Lord Orrin. Are you telling me you object to being given this appointment?"

Orrin thought for a moment, then brightened. "No, I don't."

"Good. Another matter taken care of," Tyront nodded with satisfaction.

"How do we stand with her request about teaching all students the practice of magical healing?" Lord Aldon then enquired.

Lord Poron smiled thinly, "I am in favour of it."

"That is hardly a surprise," Lord Aldon sighed, "You are biased."

"As I should be," the older man smiled smugly. "Anything else would suggest a serious lack of commitment to my discipline, wouldn't it?"

"I, too, agree with that idea," Orrin stated.

Several hesitant nods followed. If the new Head of Warriors didn't object to having warriors being taught healing, then there was not much sense in anybody else doing so. Additionally, he had demonstrated quite effectively several months ago that he had learned the skill as well before the clinic had even opened.

"This leaves us with the proposed increase to the quota of healers as our last point," Tyront went on. "But that is something we will need to determine with the new Head of Healers as soon as the current trainees have progressed far enough to be able to train new healers." He rose. "Now I am going to send a messenger to fetch Lady Eryn and Vern."

Enric nodded tensely. What a rotten timing that he would have to leave her alone for several days after she was given such a message.

* * *

Eryn took a deep breath and looked at Vern. "Ready?"

He nodded and she didn't wait for the guard to open the doors, but did so herself.

She let her gaze wander over the faces as they walked inside and towards the table and said under her breath so that only Vern could hear, "Can you read their expressions? A few of them seem rather stiff, don't they? That probably means bad news."

"Wait. Maybe your nerves are making you imagine things," he whispered back. "But whatever they say, the code word remains intact."

They came to a stop in front of the large table, all thirteen pairs of eyes on them.

Eryn turned to Lord Tyront and bowed to him.

"Lady Eryn," he began, "I am happy to inform you that the Council has agreed to your proposal of dividing the Order into two disciplines. This is quite something to have accomplished within a very short time."

Enric watched a broad grin spread across her face.

"We have also agreed to put the new Head of Healers in charge of an organisation outside the Order, in order to govern non-magical healers and other related professions," Tyront went on. "Furthermore, next year's intake of students will find their teaching schedules enriched by an additional subject we have not yet chosen the name for, but which will aim to familiarise them with basic healing skills."

Eryn closed her eyes for a moment. That was more than she had dared dream. With the novices learning healing, it would be no more than a matter of a few years until the ability would become so very normal among magicians, and that those who still refused to learn it would be outsiders. That would strengthen the healers' position in the Order even further after that first significant step of being granted their own discipline.

"The healers' quota?" Vern asked carefully.

"Will be discussed directly with the new Head of Healers when the time and opportunity to train them comes," Tyront replied.

Eryn smiled joyously, her eyes sparkling. "May I be bold enough to request one final thing? As the Head of Healers is no longer subject to the warriors' requirements, I would ask to be released from my combat training obligation."

There was silence. The Lords exchanged tense looks, while the King, too, looked serious. She looked at Orrin, who seemed displeased with something, as did Lord Poron. Enric and Lord Tyront were sporting rather grave expressions as well. She had a sinking feeling and moistened her lips before asking, "Why do I have the suspicion that I am not going to like what you are about to tell me?"

"Lady Eryn," Tyront spoke softly, "the position of Head of Healers will not be yours. Lord Poron will take that responsibility."

She blinked once. And then another time. Her ears had heard something, but the words made no sense. They were completely absurd. Either her ears or her brain had to be playing tricks on her for some reason.

"Vern?" she asked quietly.

"Yes?" he swallowed with an unhappy expression.

"Is it possible that they just...?" She gestured helplessly.

He nodded with a grimace. "Yes. They have appointed Lord Poron Head of Healers."

A cold fist seemed to be squeezing her stomach and she put a hand on it, knowing that healing away the sensation wouldn't be any use, as reactions caused by emotions would just return again moments later.

She saw Enric looking concerned, undoubtedly a reaction to the emptiness, the feeling of betrayal, the disappointment, desperation and impotence that threatened to overwhelm her. She closed her eyes for a moment to put a shield around that small area in her brain that would stop him from feeling the full impact of it, wishing she could shield herself like that as well.

She stared at the floor. After everything she had accomplished, fought and worked for so very hard, now they had taken it away from her just like that. Boiling outrage flared up inside her. Dangerous outrage, she knew. But this felt so much better, so much more liberating than the pain. It would return later sure enough, but right now fury would save her from seeming pathetic and hurt.

"How dare you!" she growled. "This is *my* clinic! Why have you done this to me? Is this some punishment, a chance you were waiting for to pay me back tenfold for whatever disrespect I ever showed you?" she snarled at Tyront. When he just shook his head, she turned to the King. "Or did *you* tell them to deny me this? Because of what I said to you in your study? Because of what I did there?"

"No, Lady Eryn, I assure you this was the Order's decision," he replied calmly.

"Eryn." She felt Vern's hand grab her shoulder. "I am *sure* there is a reasonable explanation for this. Why don't we listen to it?"

She gave him a pained look. A code word would not be enough to restrain her this time, she knew. Not with that ball of rage that kept expanding outwards with every second. Vern seemed to come to the same conclusion a second later.

"Let me help you, please," he said urgently. "Just don't fight, alright?"

She was about to ask what exactly he was talking about when she suddenly felt warmth from his palm at her shoulder and a moment later a familiar sensation of strange happiness spread inside her, a wave of bliss that calmed her down immediately and left no more than a slight tension at the edge of her consciousness.

Enric sat up in surprise at the strange feelings he suddenly received from her. So it seemed the boy had learned a useful thing or two from Pe'tala.

"I didn't know you could do that," she murmured and smiled. "I myself forgot to ask my uncle how this works. How pleasant. Now *you* can show me."

Vern swallowed. "Easily done." He was clearly amazed by the effect it had on her. "Eryn?"

"Yes, Vern?" she beamed.

"Why don't you ask Lord Tyront again about the Council's motivation behind deciding in favour of Lord Poron instead of you?"

She thought for a moment. "What a splendid idea," she then nodded and turned back to the table.

The men looked confused, she noted.

"Lord Tyront?" she asked sweetly. "I would so love to hear your reasons for that decision, if that is not too inconvenient right now."

He stared at her, then ran fingers across his chin, clearly astonished by that unexpected metamorphosis from ire to rapture.

"Certainly," he said carefully. "I am aware that this must seem to you as if we didn't appreciate all your efforts or have not valued your skills, but let me emphasise to you that this was not the case. We consider you to be too precious to be claimed by only one discipline and are convinced that the Order will benefit a lot more from your dividing your efforts between both areas. You are dedicated, smart and have skills in being able to discover new things and find creative solutions. I have no doubt that you will come up with valuable ways of using the essences of either discipline for the benefit of the other, as you demonstrated so impressively with that double barrier of yours. And how you overcame it."

Eryn smiled broadly. "How very nice of you to say that!"

Enric watched her carefully. Was it possible that Vern had overdone things a bit? She had at least been able to still make sarcastic remarks despite her uncontrollable felicity when her uncle had infused her like that the day he had met her.

Tyront seemed to wonder whether she had gone crazy or was just messing with him.

"Ahem... well... yes. We furthermore think that there should be a certain number of magicians in leading positions who are responsible for both disciplines, and as you are the third strongest in the Order, that includes you. In addition to which you will very likely undertake occasional trips to Takhan to see your family, and with Lord Poron in charge of the clinic you would not have to worry about that part at least." He looked carefully at her. "Is everything alright with you?"

"With me?" she exclaimed with wide open eyes. "Of course it is! I feel fabulous!"

Tyront turned to Enric and muttered, "I don't know what is going on here, but I don't have a good feeling about this. Get her home. Now." He then stood to address the other Council members. "I think we have taken care of everything we had planned for today. With that, I close this meeting."

Enric rose immediately and stepped next to his companion, putting an arm around her centre to guide her out the doors into the corridor.

"Vern? I think that was a tiny bit too much," he sighed.

The boy grimaced. "I know! I have only ever tried it once before, and that was with a large man. It seems medium-sized women need a lower exposure..."

"Yes, obviously," he remarked and cursed himself for agreeing to having the meeting so soon before his departure. He wouldn't even be there when she awoke from that tranquil space.

"Wait!" Orrin's voice boomed behind them. "What exactly is going on here?" he hissed when he had caught up with them. "Why is she like that?"

"I treated her with a bit of exhilarative magic," Vern admitted. "To still her tongue."

He stared at his son. "You can do that? That's good to know," he said. "Don't try that on me, ever, my boy! How long will the effect last?"

"Several hours, I fear. I was a bit too generous," the boy said apologetically.

Orrin pinched the bridge of his nose and looked at Enric. "You will be gone by then. Alright, bring her over to my quarters. Junar and I will make sure she is not alone when this all wears off. We will keep her with us over night. Just send a servant with some clothes and whatever else she needs for one overnight stay."

Enric nodded gratefully. That was *not* how he had envisioned the last one or two hours with her before his departure. But at least she would be in good hands.

"Can you have an eye on her as long as I am away? Or two eyes?" he asked the warrior. "After this here I dread what will happen when she is alone here for five days."

Orrin nodded curtly. "I would have, anyway. I will make sure she doesn't attend any social dinners, I'll increase the training interval for that time and ask Junar to invite her and Plia over every evening for dinner. I'll try to keep her busy enough so she doesn't have any time to get into mischief."

Vern sniffed. "Have you met Eryn before? That woman would manage to get into trouble if you shackled and gagged her in a dungeon cell."

Eryn burst into a ringing laughter. "Oh my! Did you ever notice that strange pattern on the walls? It looks like little cat ears!"

The three men exchanged weary glances, then Orrin rolled his eyes.

"Let's just get her safely behind closed doors, shall we?"

CHAPTER 20

Royal Trouble

Eryn slowly opened her eyes and stared at the different but still familiar ceiling. Orrin's guestroom, where she had stayed for several days before her commitment to Enric. There was daylight behind the curtains, so he had let her sleep in, even though there had been a combat lesson scheduled for today, she remembered dimly.

She couldn't exactly recall a lot from the evening before, only that the three of them had brought her back here instead of home for some reason. She slowly sat up and the memory oozed back. The Council meeting... the news that they had granted her proposals as such, but had no intention of letting her lead the healers. And then Vern had done his thing and had once more saved her from getting into hot water. She had been about to insult or oppose every high-ranking person in that room and with that pretty much the two most important people in that Kingdom. That would not have gone down well.

She dimly remembered Lord Tyront and snippets of his explanation why they refused her the position and then Enric's worried expression when he had left, clearly torn between staying with her and making the trip. Orrin had finally pushed him out the door with the promise that he would take good care of her.

She cleared her throat and pushed aside the blanket to get out of bed. She was wearing an unfamiliar blue nightgown which had to be one of Junar's. Pulling aside the curtains she stood there for a moment with closed eyes until the daylight ceased being painful.

It looked like late morning.

Without bothering to change into daytime clothes she walked out into the parlour and looked around. It was empty, which was of course not much of a surprise at this time of day. Vern would be at his classes, Junar was surely working and Orrin was probably in his study as his training session with her had been cancelled.

She strolled over to his door and knocked, entering when he called her in.

He raised his brow when she walked in barefoot and in her sleeping attire.

"What exactly do you think you are doing?" he asked instead of a greeting. "Get yourself dressed for your training. You slept long enough, after all."

She stared at him in dismay. "My training? I had practically assumed that it would not take place today. My shift at the clinic is starting soon!"

The warrior shook his head. "No, it is not. I sent a message to tell them that they will have to make do without you today. Now go and get yourself ready. It's sword fighting today, so put on your leather armour."

"You are aware that I had a rather trying evening yesterday, aren't you? How about exercising some leniency by not compelling me to do this today? I am sure my progress will not be hampered too much by skipping a single lesson."

"No," he said firmly. "Get ready. Now."

Eryn muttered to herself grumpily and went reluctantly back to the guest room.

"Fresh clothes you'll find in the parlour, on the chest of drawers," he called after her.

When she returned from the bathroom, fully dressed and fumbling with the clasps of her armour, he was leaning against a wall with the wooden box that contained her shackles under one arm.

He then opened the door and indicated for her to step out first.

"You are not particularly wordy today," she remarked. "What's *your* problem? *I* was the one to be told that I can't take over the healers. Why the sour face?"

He just motioned her on impatiently down the stairs and along the corridor towards the building's exit.

"Who is to be the Head of Warriors? That doesn't happen to be you, does it?" she enquired when they stepped out into the open.

"It does," he replied and walked on.

"Well, and why wouldn't they appoint you for the position? It's only logical. Not that this seems to be a major consideration in the Order lately, mind you," she sulked and then asked, "Where are we going? You are aware that we just passed the arena, aren't you?"

"That's not where your training is going to take place today," he commented and moved on towards the Palace.

"Why? I don't want to go to the Palace! I don't have very fond memories of that place, in case you forgot. Why can't we do it in the arena as usual?" she complained.

"Stop pestering me, Eryn," he just sighed.

She followed him through the Palace gate and along a set of corridors. What had put him in such a foul mood today?

Wondering whether he wanted to show her something special that was not meant for everybody's eyes, she walked one step behind him. He stopped in front of a thick wooden door and pushed it open. It led into a small square courtyard, very similar to the one Enric had used when he had started training with her. It was just as private, with high stone walls and it had two tall trees sharing a generous area of grass.

"Charming," she commented. "At least it's friendlier than the arena."

Orrin opened the wooden box and held out the shackles for her to put on. She hesitated for only a moment before taking them, still not happy about having to wear them so frequently, even if it was only for one or two hours each time.

When she had closed the clasps, she wearily lifted her wrists for Orrin to seal the seams.

There was an immediate feeling of wrongness.

"Orrin?" she frowned. "What happened with the enchantment? They are blocking my magic entirely instead of just limiting it!"

"That, my dear Lady Eryn, is the idea," she heard the King's voice behind her and whirled around to the door through which he stepped. He was not clad in his usual elaborate garments, but instead in simple trousers and a shirt. And leather breast armour. Her gaze then dropped to his hip and the sheathed sword that hung there.

Oh no, this had to be a cruel joke!

"Orrin?" she said quietly, her eyes still fixed on the King's weapon. "Tell me that this is not what it looks like, will you? You have not brought me here and blocked my powers to deliver me to *him*?"

The warrior gave her a look of warning that clearly conveyed that he didn't consider this way of expressing herself very suitable.

"Lord Orrin was under orders to do so without letting you know anything," King Folrin explained.

She looked at Orrin with annoyance. That was why he had been so uncommunicative! The order did obviously not sit well with him, yet he had had no choice to do anything but obey.

"You may leave us now, Lord Orrin," the monarch told him and the warrior bowed stiffly with a last cautioning glance toward Eryn.

She ground her teeth and watched him leave and close the door behind him. Then she looked back at the King, not bothering to hide her dismay. He looked different in his attire, disconcertingly so. Less... kingly, more lean and trained that she would have thought after only seeing him in his flowing elegant robes. She needed to remember that she was still bound to follow his commands, no matter how casual he appeared right now. Taking any liberties would just make him retaliate.

"Is this a version of the testing in political strategy?" she asked in a worried voice.

He pretended to think for a moment, glancing at his sword, then replied, "No, not quite."

She raised an eyebrow at him, waiting for him to volunteer more information on his motives. He didn't and merely smiled.

A chance to take revenge on her, she considered, for what had happened in his study a few days ago? It was the most likely explanation, given that he had made sure that her powers were blocked. She was completely at his mercy. Not promising.

"Why am I here?" she asked when he didn't say anything.

"Because I am curious as to your progress in this discipline. I do receive reports, of course. But first-hand impressions are always more accurate."

"Why would that be of interest to you?" she asked directly. She felt awkward in his presence, in one way angry at him for his affair with Malriel, as well as wary of his unresolved issues with her that he might be eager to settle. With swords.

Was he even able to properly handle the weapon? She disregarded that concern almost immediately. He would not risk making himself look inadequate by not at least being her equal in a discipline he wanted to challenge her in. The more likely option was that his skills surpassed hers by far. His stance was confident enough.

"I don't think I have to justify my actions to *you* unless I am very much mistaken," he replied, his smile still in place.

She pressed her lips together in annoyance and watched him draw his sword in a smooth, elegant move. So much for her deliberations about his fighting skills. Watching him, she made no move to draw her own weapon.

He raised his brow at her. "If a person facing you draws their weapon, it is generally considered an invitation to do the same."

She folded her arms defiantly. "You are putting me in a difficult situation, Your Majesty. I assume the law provides for unpleasant consequences for people who draw blood from you or injure you otherwise."

"Let me assure you that this does not have to worry you, my dear Lady. But I admire your confidence that you could. Draw your weapon now," he added mildly. "That is an order."

Reluctantly she unfolded her arms and did as he had told her, not even attempting to hide her discontentment.

He slowly advanced and made a rather lazy first thrust as if to check that she was ready to defend herself. She blocked it easily and waited.

"I hope you are not worried too much about Lord Enric and Malriel being on the road together?" he asked conversationally.

"Hardly," her acerbic reply came, "I rest safe in the knowledge that he is too *old* to be a target for her attentions." She shot him a telling look. "She prefers her lovers quite a bit less... mature, from what I know."

He smiled at that. "And you object to that."

"It's not my concern who she chooses for her libidinous frolics," Eryn remarked stiffly and parried another blow.

"That was not the impression I had a few days ago. Your reaction was rather... disapproving, I seem to remember."

"That was because I was surprised... shocked," she amended. "I wouldn't have pegged you for the type to fall for her. As somebody who likes to play games with people himself, I wouldn't have thought that she would find playing *you* so very easy."

He raised his brow at that. "What makes you think that I was being played?" he enquired after she had ducked out from another attack.

"Even though I don't know her very well, the little I do know about her is that she is manipulative and never fails to act in her own interest. If she hasn't made you do something for her already, she is very likely to accomplish this in the future," she answered.

"Interesting," he said quietly before smiling. "This is how many people would describe *me*, too. What makes you think that there was no benefit in it for myself?"

She sneered. "You mean the chance to have physical relations with a female magician? I suppose I have to grant even you to act on... less sophisticated motives at times."

"My being just a man, you mean?"

She decided that it was probably prudent not to answer that and simply shrugged. She quickly lifted her sword and hastily blocked several thrusts in rapid succession. He was fast, she had to admit. And not exactly clumsy with a blade. Maybe he could be persuaded to end this here rather sooner than later if she proved to be not much of a challenge, or rather entertainment, to him. Shutting up and letting him disarm her without much effort should do that trick.

She let the next strike knock the weapon out of her hand and watched it land on the ground with a loud clang.

He sighed. "This is not exactly what I had in mind, Lady Eryn. This passive stance will not make me release you any sooner. Pick up your sword and show me a bit more of what you can do. You have been trained by the two most able sword fighters in this Kingdom for quite a while now, and I refuse to believe that this is all they have managed to teach you."

She bent down to retrieve the weapon and then let herself be driven several steps backwards, determined not to provide the entertainment he clearly wished for.

After several more attempts to engage her in a fight instead of just defensive manoeuvres, he pursed his lips and considered her for a while before sheathing his sword again. "Alright, let's try something else."

She watched him untie his sword belt and put it aside on the ground under one of the trees before he unbuckled the clasps of his breast armour. She frowned when he stepped towards her and took a step back, but he hooked two fingers into her belt and pulled her back towards him before taking it off her as well. He then put it next to his own and returned to her, obviously to unclasp her leather protection.

Pushing away his hands, she narrowed her eyes at him. "*What* else do you want to try, if I may be so bold as to enquire?"

He lifted his hands to her side once again and frowned when she turned away. "Unarmed combat. From what I know this discipline is less objectionable to you. And now hold still. It will be quicker if *I* help you out of your armour than your fumbling around under your arms where you can't see."

Unarmed combat? With him? She stared at him. Surely not! That was not appropriate, not at all! She either had to let him come much closer than she wanted to or try to hurt him to avoid it.

She once more pushed away his hands when he made to free her from her protector and a moment later he had a knife in his hand.

She drew in a sharp breath, but he had already grabbed the leather and cut open the two straps that held the armour together on one side and half turned her briskly to do so at the other one before lifting it over her head and tossing it on top of the swords.

"No. I am not going through this." She shook her head and lifted a finger at him. "And you can't make me." Then she turned on her heel and stomped towards the door. She didn't care if he gave her an order to stay and fight. There would be consequences for not complying, but she would deal with them later. Whatever he thought of to punish her for her disobedience would hardly be worse than being made to fight him like that.

To her surprise he made no move or gave no command to hold her back. And when she pushed down the door handle with determination, she realised why. She was locked in with him. Or out, depending on how one wanted to look at it.

She turned slowly and saw him standing on the patch of grass, his arms folded, his stance broad and his expression smug.

"Come back here," he instructed calmly. "There is no getting out of here before Lord Orrin returns with the key."

Eryn braced herself and walked back hesitantly, stopping a few paces away from him. It wouldn't make much sense to ask him to spare her. Whatever his reasons for tormenting her were, he was clearly not yet satisfied.

Maybe the other way round would be more effective, she considered. Surprising him with a few painful strikes when he wasn't counting on them would probably discourage him. He seemed to consider making her give up her passiveness a challenge, so why not oblige him?

She quickly spun and aimed a kick at his stomach, but he evaded her easily, blocking the blows intended for his side and shoulder. So he was trained well enough in that discipline as well. What a nuisance.

He smiled. "Yes, I can see that this is more to your liking. A nice chance to rid yourself of some of that anger you are keeping for me, isn't it? One I don't normally grant people."

Yes, she thought dryly, because in that case he wouldn't have much time left to do anything else.

She let herself fall back a little and waited for him to attack next. Her surprise had clearly not worked, but instead pleased him.

They circled each other for a while, before the King resumed talking. "I heard about your little plots at the last two dinners you attended. A pity I can't really go to such occasions; it would imply undue favour towards certain individuals unless I attended all of them. But I would love to have been there. I am even considering hosting one of them every now and again myself, just to see with my own eyes what it is you will come up with next."

She smiled weakly. "Let me save you that trouble, Your Majesty, by assuring you that I would show a lot more restraint in *your* presence."

That made him laugh. "Indeed? That is not the impression I had in the past. I explicitly remember you sticking a fork into Ambassador Ram'an's thigh in my presence."

She shrugged. "That was not meant to be noticed by anyone, so I would hardly call that a *plot*. More like surreptitious retribution.'

She yelped in surprise when a swift move aimed at the back of her knees swept her off her feet and made her land on her back on the grass.

That was another possibility, she thought. Evading him had not worked, neither had surprising him. Maybe letting him push her around a bit would do the trick. At least without a weapon she was not in great danger of losing a limb.

She attacked him a few more times, making sure to give him ample opportunity to send her to the ground.

After what had to be the fourth or fifth time, he held out his hand to help her up. She grabbed it and let him pull her back onto her feet. A moment later she found herself with her back against a cold stone wall, one of his hands at her throat, his face too close to hers.

"Don't think I am not aware of your strategy," he growled. "But petting my ego by letting me win is no way to make me happy, let me assure you. Quite the opposite. It makes me think I have to prove something by making you see that it is not necessary. So you either cooperate now," he leaned closer, his lips almost touching hers, and continued in a much lower voice, "or I will have to resort to other measures to make you."

She swallowed hard against his palm and tried to shove him away by pushing hard against his shoulders.

"That's the spirit," he remarked dryly and stepped back again to release her.

She breathed heavily and glared daggers at him, wishing she had her magic at her disposal, even a little bit. If Orrin weren't so damn diligent about carrying out his orders! He might as well have left her with a tiny amount of her powers, just a little edge to help her hold her ground here. But then the King would very likely have worked that out soon enough and made Orrin pay for it. That would not have been so good, either. How much longer until he returned to free her from this yard?

She nodded deliberately and felt warm, welcome anger coursing through her veins. He wanted to fight? Alright, he could have that. No more holding back.

Walking towards him slowly she halted when she was only one step away from him, not taking her eyes off him. In a quick move she let her fist shoot forwards towards his chin. He deflected it easily and then staggered back when she followed the move with her shoulder and hit him with her elbow instead, twirling away from him before he had recovered from the blow enough to retaliate.

He lifted a hand to his jaw and opened and closed it a few times experimentally, nodding appreciatively at her.

"Good. I see we understand each other."

She smiled thinly. "Perfectly."

That had felt good, very much so. Maybe being allowed to hit him was a nice opportunity to pay him back for everything he had done to her in the last year. Taking her prisoner. Letting the Order force her into fighting training. Coercing her to join Enric. Trying to make her heal the apothecaries to be executed. Manipulating her into going to the Western Territories by making her mad at Enric. Yes, she reflected, hitting and kicking him was a chance she should definitely not spurn, but embrace. No matter what she did, there would very likely be consequences either way.

She ducked from a blow and a moment later felt a strong grip on her wrist. He twisted her arm on her back and pushed her against a wall face first none too gently, holding her there for a few seconds before releasing her again.

She lost the next four bouts before she managed to hit him again, this time in the stomach, making him bend over and brace his hands on his knees for a moment until he could breathe again.

His expression was determined when he straightened again. "I think we will end this now," he announced and stepped forwards to grab both her wrists and push her backwards against the wall once again, pressing against her.

She cursed and glared up at him. "What is the point of doing what you tell me to, anyway? This is one of your games again, isn't it? Damn you, why can't you just say what you want and I will accommodate you if it is not completely insane!" She tried to wriggle out of his grip, but he deftly twisted both her arms behind her back, holding on to both her hands with only one of his, using his other to keep her from averting her face.

He chuckled. "But where would be the challenge in that, my dear Lady Eryn?" His blue-grey eyes bore into hers when he slowly lowered his face towards hers. "You know what first induced me to take Malriel as a lover? Her striking resemblance to *you*."

Panic made her heart increase its pace and cause the blood to rush loudly in her ears. Her breathing had become more rapid and she stared at him frozen in dread. He wouldn't really do it, would he? He tightened his grip around her wrists when she tried to pull free and still kept her gaze locked in his.

She breathed in through her nose, shocked as his lips met hers and he kissed her. She was unable to move for several moments before she began to writhe in his grasp. What was he doing? How could he just violate the connection he himself had forced her into like that? In vain she tried to turn away, frantically trying to get her brain to emerge from this sea of panic it threatened to drown in. Was there something she could do to stop him that wouldn't get her locked up in a dungeon? Would biting him fall into that category? How was a woman supposed to free herself from the unwanted attentions of a bloody King? Not at all, probably. She was very likely supposed to consider them a compliment instead.

He pulled back several seconds later without loosening his grip, keeping her in place. His usual aloof façade had given way to a tense expression and he, too, was breathing faster. He stared down at her, his demeanour none too happy, a hint of frustration in his penetrating gaze.

"You are a very compelling woman, my dear. What a pity that you have inherited your parents' magic," he sighed regretfully. "Otherwise I would have made you *mine* instead of Lord Enric's."

Her stomach clenched at his words. "Am I supposed to consider the idea of being made your sexual plaything some kind of honour? It's not, in case you were wondering," she snarled at him.

"Not merely my sexual plaything. My *queen*," he replied calmly. "And spare me your assertions that you wouldn't have agreed to that. I think I have established that I do not require your consent for my actions, whether they include you or not."

Her heart seemed to skip some beats and her mouth dropped open in astonishment. What? His *queen*?

He chuckled. "So surprised, dearest Lady? I didn't think that I was that nuanced in my admiration of you. And you turned out to be the daughter of an influential foreign family, after all. Of *two*, even. You would have been a more than advantageous match for me both politically *and* personally. But, alas, your magic has saved you from a fate that seems so obviously anything but desirable to you."

She closed her eyes. She didn't want to listen to this any longer. "Enric will learn about this," she spat at him, squirming to free herself, but again to no avail.

"I see," he replied, and the ghost of a smile played around his lips. "Then this is probably the only chance I will ever have to indulge myself by getting this close to you. It might be advisable to use it thoroughly."

When he attempted to lower his lips to hers once more, she desperately tried to lift her knee to hit him in the groin, no longer caring what the consequences would be for her, but he trapped it between his thighs before it could to any damage.

"Try to remember that I am your King, will you?" he growled. "Kneeing me *there* would not earn you any points."

"Right now I don't see any king," she hissed back, "I see nothing more than a savage who is forcing himself on me! And neither is winning points with *you* any priority of mine right now! But why don't we get Lord Tyront to settle this matter of my disobedience against my King? I am sure he would have very definite views on this here!"

"Not entirely untrue, I admit. But not at all in accordance with my intentions right now," he murmured and a moment later pressed his mouth onto hers again and opened her lips, applying more force than before, pressing her harder against the wall in her back with his body.

This felt so very wrong, nothing like being kissed by Enric, even when he was more assertive. This was being plundered instead of conquered. There was no affection or attempts at persuasion, just blunt domination.

She fought to hold back the tears of outrage that wanted to escape the corners of her eyes. *He* was not to see them.

Her knees almost gave in with relief when she heard a key being turned in the heavy wooden door. Orrin! Finally! He had come to take her back!

If the King had heard the sound, he had decided to ignore it. He neither freed nor stopped kissing her. She imagined Orrin's reaction to the sight that presented itself to him right now and shivered.

Suddenly the pressure on her wrists, lips and body was gone. She found it surprisingly hard standing on her own and had to lean against the wall for another moment before she managed to push herself away without looking at the King. Clasping a hand over her mouth, she walked as fast as she could on wobbly legs towards safety, towards Orrin, who stared at her open-mouthed.

She let the hand sink from her face and lifted shaking wrists to him. "Remove them. Now."

His gaze sank down to the manacles, then to the King, his expression turning into something bordering on horror. As if in trance, he slowly touched each of them and she immediately felt magic course through her when the seams opened again. She took them off and threw them on the ground.

"Don't you *ever* make me wear them again," she whispered.

The warrior shook his head as if under water, the disbelief in his eyes slowly turning into fury when his glare returned to the King who just stood there and observed them with interest.

"No," he pressed out from between clenched jaws, "I won't."

She saw how Orrin's breathing had become heavier and knew that she had to get him away from this place immediately before he did something foolish.

"Take me away from here now," she urged him. "Please."

He nodded and put an arm around her shoulders to press her against him when he turned and stepped back into the corridor with her.

"I am so sorry," he growled and leaned his head against her temple for a moment. "Forgive me. If you can."

"Of course," she swallowed, grateful for his comforting presence, the smell of him, his strong arm around her. "Just get me out of here."

* * *

He pressed a glass of something clear and potent into her hand and motioned for her to drink.

She tipped back the entire glass, scowling at the bitter aftertaste and immediately felt warmth spreading in her stomach. Her hand was still shaking slightly.

They stared at each other for a few long, silent seconds.

"What exactly happened in there?" he then asked and took a seat opposite her, leaning forward with his elbows on his knees.

"I don't know. I was trying to get out of fighting him again and again, and he was not happy about it. He changed from armed to unarmed combat after a while." She looked at him. "Did you know that he is such an able fighter? I only managed to hit him twice, more out of sheer luck than skill."

He nodded. "Yes. He trains regularly, though not with me. Go on."

"He pressed me against the wall and told me he took Malriel to bed because she resembles me in appearance. Then he kissed me. And when I told him that Enric would learn of this, he said that he might as well make use of the chance as it would very likely be his last, and then kissed me again. You came in at that exact point."

Orrin nodded slowly. "I see."

She leaned back on the settee and closed her eyes, still holding the empty glass in her hand. "I can't tell Enric. Do you have any idea what he might do? When Ram'an tried to dance with me in Takhan, he hit him so hard that he was thrown over an entire seating arrangement. Without even using magic."

"You *have* to tell Enric," Orrin objected. "It's what the King wants."

She opened her eyes again. "What?"

"He wants Enric to hear about this. That's why he kissed you again when you threatened him with it. And that's why he didn't stop before I came in. He wanted *me* to witness it, too. Whatever game he is playing now, provoking Enric is part of it. He wants something Enric would very likely not agree to otherwise. Though I wonder if he is fully aware of what he is letting himself in for. Even I can't really tell how Enric is going to react, only that it won't be pretty. His self-control has been remarkable over these last fifteen years, but when it comes to you..." He gave her a meaningful look.

"Then we should probably not tell him. Why risk his doing something stupid? And if the King wants him to know, then this is probably the very thing we should try to avoid, don't you think?" She lifted the empty glass and looked at him. "Can I have more of this? I like the dulling effect it has."

He took the glass from her hand and put it aside. "No. This was just to stop you from shaking and to relax you. We don't want you to develop any pesky habits."

"I am not in any danger of becoming addicted with a second glass," she sighed.

"Maybe not physically, but dulling your pain may lead to a different kind of addiction. It's good to remember that this is not how we deal with problems. Neither is withholding information from Enric. The King wants him to know that he has crossed this line with you. There is not much we can do here. If we don't tell him, there will be another attempt at provoking us to do it. We don't want that."

She gulped. "So either I tell my companion that his King kissed me and hope that he doesn't go berserk, or I might find myself in a similar situation again? Just fabulous."

"Think about it. What is the better solution? Telling him ourselves and having an eye on him, or risking his hearing it some other way with no one around to stop him from following his first impulse and doing something utterly destructive? If he finds out that there was another incident that was kept from him, he is not likely to appreciate it. I don't want him mad at you or me. Let the King deal with whatever he deliberately got himself into."

"What if the King wants to get rid of him? Or of us? He could be trying to provoke Enric into doing something that is bad enough to get him locked up, banned from the country or even... executed," she pointed out, staring with a wistful look at the empty glass, wishing it was full and within her reach. Would Orrin hold her back if she got up to refill it herself? Probably he would.

"I don't think that this is what he wants. Enric has never even once shown any sign of being disloyal to the King or the Order, so wanting to get rid of him wouldn't follow. It would even be dangerous, as having Enric on our side is better than making him our enemy. He knows too much and is too strong to be easily replaceable. And Lord Tyront wouldn't stand for it. Neither would the other high ranks, including yourself." He spoke with conviction. "No. The King wants him to do something. I am almost certain of that. But I can't tell what."

"You said we need to keep our eye on him so he doesn't do anything foolish after he hears of it. How can we prevent it? Neither of us alone is as strong as he is, and we can't both be tagging at his heels all day long."

"We will involve a higher authority," Orrin said matter-of-factly.

She thought for a moment, then groaned. "Oh no, not Lord Tyront! I don't want *him* getting wind of this!"

"Of course he needs to know it, Eryn. Don't be an idiot - he is the one who is most likely to be successful in keeping Enric under control. He is magically stronger and can order him to stay away from the King. And I think you should not be there when Enric hears about this. Let *me* talk to him."

"*You* want to tell him? Without my even being there?" she asked incredulously.

"Yes. He will be furious enough, without having to see you replaying the scene in your head when I talk about it."

"He will think I wanted to withhold this incident from him if you exclude me!" she protested.

"Which is *exactly* what you wanted to do, despite your threat to the King," he pointed out with a raised brow. "But as we don't want Enric angry at you, I will inform him that I asked you to stay away. The important thing is that you don't talk with him alone after he returns from his journey. He must know that something has happened thanks to that mind bond of yours. So he is likely to ask you what it was as soon as he is back."

"So I am to refuse to talk to him?" She rolled her eyes. "That did not work very well for me in the past."

"You are to be sure not to meet him alone after he returns. We will have the gate guards inform us when he is first sighted. That will leave us with a bit less than one hour to get you to my quarters and leave him a message to meet us and Lord Tyront here. Then you will leave while we talk to him. You really will have to go, even though he is very likely to try and make you stay. Understood?"

She nodded reluctantly. That was absolutely not the kind of welcome she had intended for him after that farewell, which had also been anything but pleasant.

Sighing, she got to her feet. "You know, I wonder if he will one of these days reach the conclusion that I am not worth all the trouble I cause."

"That is not very likely," Orrin smiled thinly. "Enric is good at dealing with trouble, even though he might need a bit more... assistance than usual this time."

She looked at him with a momentary concern. "One more thing. I noticed that you have stopped referring to him as *Lord*. When did that happen?"

He chuckled. "After I learned that Junar is pregnant. A life changing situation and a good bottle of something potent have that effect every now and then."

"A *bottle*? And you begrudge me a second glass? Is it possible that you are applying double standards here?"

"No, my girl. *I* know how to handle my drink. That is not the impression I have of you. I dimly remember your returning my son to me from Ambassador Ram'an's quarters in a drunken state. I bet you were not exactly in a sober condition yourself that time, either. Which shows a certain lack of judgement, if you ask me."

"Having a glass or two too many shows a lack of judgement? That is a bit harsh, don't you think?"

"If you do it with a boy in the quarters of a man who wants to steal you away from your companion, I would definitely say that, yes," he retorted.

"Oh my," she called out. "So late already? I'd better get back home now."

"You do that. Pity Enric has taken the cat with him. I would feel better if you had her with you as long as he is not around. Can I persuade you to move to our quarters with Plia as long as he is away? The bed in the guest room is large enough for the two of you."

"That is very sweet of you, Orrin. But I don't want to start hiding away because a man assaulted me. I would rather demonstrate that this hasn't intimidated me." Most of this was pretence, however, and she knew it. The King was dangerous enough and not being completely aware of that would be unwise.

"As you wish. But you must return here for dinner. Make sure to bring the girl. From what I have heard she has adopted your unhealthy habit of staying on at the clinic too late. Some role model you are," he said.

She managed a smile for the first time since she had arrived in the quarters. "You are in training for raising a girl by practising your father mode with every female you manage to find, eh?"

"Only with those in dire need of some fathering. And neither of you has that."

Noble, kind Orrin, she thought with a rush of affection. "I would value it enormously if you didn't mention anything about this whole incident to Junar, Plia or Vern. I don't want to worry them unnecessarily."

"I won't. Be punctual," he added as she opened the door to leave. "You know our dinner time. And what score I set by punctuality."

"Yes, *father*," she sighed and rolled her eyes before she escaped into the corridor.

* * *

Enric yawned and stretched. That had been very long three days. Departing in the evening instead of morning was unusual, as hardly anybody was keen on riding through the night. But Malriel had promised at the dinner to leave the next day, and there were still a few things she had wanted to take care of before her departure, which meant she had needed the day.

They had opted against a coach, even though they would have been able to sleep fairly comfortably in it. But horses were faster, and Malriel's things would be shipped, so there was no need for her to take along more than a small bundle with the things she required for the four days until she reached Takhan.

The night had passed quickly enough. They had ridden at a brisk trot that had still allowed them to talk comfortably. She had told him about the situation in the Western Territories, how the conflict with their northern neighbour had become slightly more intense over these last few months since his departure from Takhan, and how people were getting rather nervous owing to their lack of defensive knowledge, practice and structures in case there was a war coming. The sticking point was that they were equally unwilling to give up the mineral resources contained in the bordering mountains.

Enric had suggested to her that the triarchy could ask the King for the Order's assistance in this matter, but she'd had to decline. She had tried to convince the senate, but her proposal had not been received well. The connection to the Old Kingdom was still too tentative. They first wanted to see how things developed with their new trading partner, see if it could be trusted before asking a delicate thing such as that of them.

It had not been a great surprise to him when she had then asked him if he could imagine an extended stay of visiting his House in Takhan. Enric simply turned her down with a look of regret. Taking Eryn to Takhan again so soon after what had happened there last time wouldn't be wise. And Eryn had just managed to get the Order to agree to those few very necessary and innovative changes. She wouldn't want to leave here but help make them happen, contribute, shape, implement and criticise everything that was going on. Her clinic was finally running, but there were still things she wanted to achieve, such as training non-magician healers to send them to all corners of the Kingdom to provide medical services over a wider area; specifically in the countryside, where coming to the clinic would mean a journey of several days that not everybody could undertake easily, especially not severely injured or ill people.

Then she had to complete her own training finally and fully to assume her rank as third in command of the Order.

He himself was also not too fond of the idea of leaving Anyueel so soon again, especially for who knew how long. He wanted to settle into a daily routine with his companion that was not interspersed with one catastrophe after the other, come to rest, take care of the plans he had for Bonhet and the trade with the Western Territories as well as get on with his other businesses.

Malriel had listened to his reasoning and expressed her understanding with his reluctance. He had been surprised that she had not tried to persuade him to do it nevertheless, wondering if she had truly given up or if there was more to come at another time. But for the sake of a relaxed journey they had left that topic behind and spoken of things that concerned House Aren, such as trade opportunities with the Kingdom and himself and what to do about House Arbil and their fragile status that made them so vulnerable right now.

He had seen her send off a bird she had been keeping with her in a small woven basket, once she had considered herself unobserved when they had finally halted in the morning at an inn to eat and snatch at least a few hours of sleep. It had not flown towards the sea but back in the direction they had come. So she must have sent a message to the Palace, as this was the only place in the Kingdom, apart from his own house, that kept birds. To the King, most likely. He wondered what could be important enough for her to write about to him only little over a day after their departure from the city.

He had been raised from his sleep only a few hours later by a powerful wave of emotions. Dismay, shock, helplessness, disbelief, fury, worry. It had held on for several minutes with unbroken intensity, until she had either managed to cope with whatever unpleasant situation she had been made to face or had remembered to shield her feelings. He hoped it was the first. He had kept thinking about what might have happened to her, hoping desperately that she had not managed to get herself into trouble yet again. But then there was still Orrin. He had promised to look after her as long as she was alone in the city. Yet he had not been able to let himself stop wondering.

Malriel had kissed him good-bye and boarded the ship that had been left here at her disposal no more than an hour after their arrival in Bonhet. He had to admit that he was glad to see her off. Having her so close to Eryn had not exactly been soothing.

He returned to the here and now and went to inspect the tally house that had been completed only recently. The docks were still under construction in places which made them a little behind schedule, but two out of three were usable and ready to receive ships from Takhan.

The little village looked completely transformed. He had expected it, of course, but seeing it with his own eyes was still something different. A significant number of families had relocated here and built small houses to live in. The local trader had expanded his small shop and offered more goods to the constantly growing number of people. And of course the range of the products he would offer was about to increase as soon as the goods from the Western Territories arrived regularly and in more dependable quantities.

He had another meeting with the head builder in the afternoon to discuss the shipyard, then he would once again mount his horse and return home. He had brought a few of the birds from his own roof and instructed the builder how to accommodate them to make them breed. It would be good to have a quick way to communicate with Bonhet.

He rubbed his face and felt the stubble on his cheeks. He had not bothered shaving this morning and probably looked more like a vagabond than a high lord of the Order, he realised. But thanks to his robes and his impressive height it didn't stop people from treating him with the reverence he was used to.

Only a few more hours, he reminded himself and pushed away the weariness with a little magic.

CHAPTER 21

Taking Measures

Enric let out a sigh of relief when he finally reached the house and was able to dismount. He motioned for the two servants who had stepped outside to take care of his bundle as well as the horse and opened the door for Urban to enter first.

"Eryn?" he called out. It was evening, so he would have expected her to be here as she had to be aware that he was due to return today. He heard steps on the stairs, but they were not Eryn's impatient, rapid ones, but Plia's more deliberate, quieter footfalls.

"Good evening, Lord Enric," she smiled. "Eryn is at Lord Orrin's; she asks you to go over there as well."

"Hello, Plia," he replied. "Thank you for the message." An evening at Orrin's? That was not exactly how he had envisioned the evening. He had been looking forward to a quick meal and an early night with her in his arms. But it looked like he was to wash off the dust and dirt from the road, get changed into something clean and be sociable for a few hours.

He watched Urban yawn and then flop down on the next handy carpet, her eyes closed almost before her head had sunk down entirely. He ruffled Plia's hair playfully and made her smile as he passed her and took two steps at once so he could turn himself back into something remotely human.

When he stood in front of the mirror after climbing out of the tub, he regarded his reflection thoughtfully. Five days without shaving had altered his appearance considerably. He tried to decide if he liked it, turning his face this way and that. If he trimmed it just a little, it might even look presentable. Why not give it a try, he thought. If Eryn didn't like it, he would just go for the clean-shaven look again.

He opted for a dark shirt and trousers, deciding against robes. Since returning from Takhan, wearing them had somehow transformed itself into an annoying duty - something which had never bothered him before.

He waved to Plia, who had made herself comfortable on a settee in the parlour with a book and a hot drink, and walked the distance to the warriors' quarters briskly in the clammy evening air.

Orrin opened the door only a moment after the knock and nodded to his guest while stepping aside to let him enter.

"Welcome back."

"Thank you," Enric replied and walked past him to the settee where Eryn was sitting.

He lifted both brows when he saw Tyront on a chair to her left. What was going on here? He pulled his companion up from her seat and kissed her on the lips more chastely than he would have preferred. She seemed unsettled, even though she was clearly happy to see him. She lifted a hand to touch his bearded cheek.

"Interesting. Is this something permanent or an experiment?" she asked.

"That depends on you, my love. Do you like it?"

"I'm not sure. Ask me again in one or two days."

He nodded and kissed the hand at his cheek, then turned to his superior without letting go of Eryn.

"Tyront. This is an unusual setting. Seeing the two of you in the same room voluntarily is unexpected. I must say I am curious to find out why."

He saw the two men exchanging a glance. There was tension in the room, so whatever they were about to tell him was not going to be easy to hear.

"Alright," he said slowly, "I sense something is clearly amiss here. Out with it."

Orrin nodded to Eryn once and she gulped nervously and stepped out of his embrace.

"I am leaving now, Enric. I'll see you later at home."

He quickly grabbed her hand before she could step away. "What is going on here? Why is she being sent away?"

"To spare her your reaction and to make it easier for you to keep control of yourself," Tyront said calmly.

Enric's eyes narrowed. This sounded serious. Whatever it was that made them think he would lose control of himself had to be connected to Eryn. There was not much else that tended to have that effect on him.

"Is everything alright with you?" he asked tensely and looked her over as if to determine any illnesses or injuries, which was of course foolish as she was a healer.

She nodded. "Yes, I am fine."

"Does it have something to do with what happened four days ago around noon?"

Another nod. He released her hand reluctantly.

"Alright, then I will see you at home," he said slowly.

Eryn looked at Orrin with a pleading expression. "Maybe I could just..."

"No. You'd better leave. We talked about this. Several times," he insisted.

She got up and stood on her tiptoes, suddenly looking quite unhappy, to kiss his bearded cheek before going to the door, where she took her cloak off the hook and left without further comment.

Enric folded his arms and remained standing. "Talk," he just said to no one in particular.

Orrin, too, opted for standing when he started speaking. "You might want to do your shielding thing in your head."

The younger man closed his eyes for a moment, then nodded. "Done."

"The day after your departure when Eryn was still asleep, I received a message from the King in which he ordered me to bring her to the Palace to one of the small courtyards. He instructed me to make sure she was outfitted for sword fighting and to omit informing her that he was the one wanting her there. He also told me to enchant the manacles we use for training so they would block her magic entirely."

Enric's eyes narrowed, but he didn't interrupt.

"She was not too thrilled to find herself without her magic and in front of him, as you may imagine. And in addition to this I was also under orders to leave her there alone with him and lock the door behind me."

Now Enric was grinding his teeth but still didn't say anything.

"I returned an hour later to take her back. When I unlocked the door and entered, I saw the King pressing her against a wall, holding her immobile. And kissing her passionately."

Both men jumped when Enric's fist came down on the small table to his side, making it collapse under the force with a loud crack, wooden splinters large and small shooting off in all directions.

"You!" he thundered with his index finger raised at Orrin. His voice had taken on a different quality, something strong and threatening reverberated in it. "I asked you to look after her! And you delivered her defenceless without her magic into the hands of a man who has once already mentioned taking her to bed? And you locked her in with him?"

Tyront got up when he felt the floor under his feet vibrating. "This is enough, Enric," he warned. "Don't make me shackle you. He was ordered to do all this by the King. And you know as well as I do that he couldn't have known that such a thing would happen."

Orrin hadn't moved, he just remained standing. "No, let him. He is right," he said quietly. "I wouldn't take it well either if he had failed Junar like that."

Enric saw the faint shimmering of the protective barrier Tyront had raised in front of the warrior and stared at Orrin's tense features. He was angry at himself. Whatever anybody else did or said to him would hardly hit him harder than what was going on inside his own head. Enric felt his anger shifting direction and concentrating towards the man on whom it should have focussed from the beginning. He turned on his heel and marched towards the door without another word.

When his hand reached for the door handle and was stopped by a powerful barrier, he turned and snarled at Tyront, "Remove this at once!"

"I cannot," his superior replied calmly. "I can't let you jump into doing something stupid. Sit down and we will talk."

Enric's hand raised up suddenly and released a bolt which shot towards the older man before it hit another shield in front of his target. A moment later Tyront retaliated, and his own bolt struck Enric full in the chest, the force of the blow heaving him against the wall with his back and making him slide down it to the floor. Both men were breathing heavily.

"Lord Orrin, the shackles."

Enric slowly shook his head to get rid of the disorientation and felt cool metal being placed around his wrists. A moment later all his magic was gone. He groaned and looked up at the two men towering over him with folded arms, their expressions resigned.

His gaze wandered back to the gold at his arms, fighting the urge to try and pull it off. He knew it would be to no avail.

A moment later he felt hands grabbing his upper arms from each side and pulling him back onto his feet with a jolt. He had to lean against the wall for a moment longer until the room had stopped spinning.

"I forgot how damn strong you are," he murmured.

Tyront raised his brow. "Obviously. But I am confident that your brain will resume its work as soon as it is no longer awash with fury." He took Enric by the shoulder and guided him towards a settee. "And now sit. We need to talk about this."

"I don't exactly feel like *talking* right now," Enric growled.

"And yet you won't leave here without doing so," his superior retorted and pressed him to sit down.

Orrin took a seat opposite him, careful to stay out of his immediate reach.

"Why can't they just keep their hands of her?" Enric hissed. "Wherever I go, some presumptuous bastard thinks he can take liberties with her, no matter which side of that damned sea we are! Do you have any idea what it was like watching Ram'an pawing her every opportunity he could find? Knowing that he was sleeping in a room next to her for ten days during that bloody trial? I wanted to chop off his hands every time I saw him with his arm around her shoulders, holding her close under the pretence that he needed to have physical contact with her as long as I was nearby to keep us from fleeing together. Nevertheless, whatever Ram'an tried, he never forced her into kissing him like that." His eyes shot daggers. "You can't keep me shackled forever. I can't allow the King's treating her like that to pass without action. And you both know that."

Orrin cleared his throat. "Let us consider a few things first. Then you can still plot revenge. I am sure the King has no intention of stealing her away from you. And he wanted you to hear about this. That's why he made certain that I witnessed it. He wanted to provoke a reaction. So you had better think very carefully about what you will do next."

Enric stared at the warrior for a long minute. The picture of a messenger bird flying back towards Anyueel in the early morning hours returned to him. And only a few hours later the King had been kissing Eryn without restraint while she struggled to free herself.

"I know what he wants," he said suddenly, kicking the broken table at his feet once more for good measure. "He wants me to go away to Takhan again. For longer this time."

Tyront frowned. "Why would he want that?"

"Because Malriel asked him to make sure of it. I can only speculate what he got or is going to get in return. I don't think that he would be content with having just a few whirlwind nights of passion in return, however skilled she may be in pleasing him," he snorted. "She asked me to come to Takhan for an extended stay. They are having trouble with their bordering country and don't want to involve another country. They don't trust us. Yet they are in dire need of some tutoring in the mechanics of fighting a war, it seems. How very practical that Malriel happens to have a son with exactly that kind of expertise. Getting me to stay in Takhan would allow them the make use of my knowledge without needing to be seen officially requesting it from the King. Or risk being refused."

"What did you tell her?" Tyront enquired, not too thrilled about that titbit of news.

"That I have no intention to go to Takhan for anything other than a brief visit. And not long after that she sent a bird to the King, undoubtedly telling him that I was not cooperative and that he needs to step in." He shook his head. "I could happily choke that woman. I wonder if she was aware what methods he would employ to force my hand. Eryn is still her daughter, after all!"

"What are you going to do now?" his superior asked, with a face that expected to hear the worst.

"If I could do as I wanted, I would take Eryn and move somewhere completely different where nobody has ever heard of us or magic and has no political or diplomatic affiliations with any other region or country," he grunted. "But as my choices are rather limited, I consider there is only one thing to do: to go to Takhan and remove her away from his clutches. If I don't, he might feel inclined to try another ruse aimed at persuading me. And I don't even want to think what he might resort to next time if forcing himself on her for a kiss doesn't do the trick." He felt the anguish taking a step back and cool deliberations beginning to take over. "But my going there will not happen only under his terms." He would, he decided, write a message to Vran'el first thing in the morning, telling him to make sure that all revenue created from trading his own goods in Takhan would be kept from being sent to Anyueel, but instead be held in the vaults of House Vel'kim. Malriel would very likely learn about this and thereby realise that he didn't trust her enough to let her hold his trading profits, but he didn't care about that right now.

"Eryn will not like that at all," Orrin pointed out carefully.

"No," Enric agreed. "But does she have much of a choice, after what happened? She knows as well as I do that the bond would keep pulling us together if she stayed put. Not that I would let her, mind you. And if I have to knock her out and lift her bodily into a coach, then so be it."

Tyront sighed heavily. "Can I impress on you that you stomping into the King's study and inflicting bodily harm would be an unwise thing to do? It would destroy not only what you have been working for all these years, but also rebound seriously on your companion. Whatever you plan to do, I implore you to ensure that you will still be welcome here in Anyueel. If the King makes me take disciplinary measures against you, I will be utterly furious with you, my friend. You are therefore from now under orders not to approach the King of your own accord without my express permission. Should he be so unwise as to summon you on your own, I additionally order you to contact me immediately and await my reply, which will very likely consist in my coming along with you."

Enric nodded once.

Tyront rose. "Good. Then I propose you return to your home, put Eryn, who is undoubtedly worried sick about you right now, at ease and get a good night's sleep. You look like you could do with some rest. Good night."

Orrin waited until their superior had closed the door behind him, then smiled weakly.

"You won't obey that order. I can see it in your eyes."

Enric raised an eyebrow at him. "I beg your pardon?"

"He is either fairly tired himself or he is choosing to delude himself into thinking that you will comply with that order."

"And *you* are planning to stop me?" Enric sneered.

"Don't be such a foolish fellow. I am not strong enough to stop you from doing anything. I am asking you to let me accompany you."

"Accompany me? When I go to the King? Why?" he asked suspiciously.

"He involved me in his scheme in a way I do not like at all. So I feel that I, too, deserve a share in your retribution, even if it is only watching your threatening him. You will wear shackles that limit your powers to my own, so we can pretend that I am there for the King's protection. That will at least save us both some trouble with Lord

Tyront." He sighed. "And if we are both kicked out of the Order, at least we will not have to separate Junar and Eryn, as wherever you go, you will be damn sure to take us with you."

Enric looked hard at the warrior and asked wearily, "So you are calling me foolish, Orrin? Risking your rank in the Order for a touch of revenge? I know you are very attached to Eryn, but you still have a family to think of."

"It *is* my family I am thinking of," he replied grimly. "You are aware that I am about to have a daughter. She was conceived after the barrier in our heads was removed. There are good chances that she will be the first female magician to be born in the Kingdom after a gap of more than three hundred years. I want to make it very plain to the King that she is not at his disposal for any plots once she is old enough to be of use to him."

"Very well, then," the younger man said slowly. That was indeed a valid enough reason. "I need to take care of a few things first, but be ready to face him in about four days."

Orrin nodded. "I will."

* * *

Eryn tremored when she heard steps approaching the entrance door. She put aside the book she had been staring at - reading would have required the ability to take in the content of the text, and that had not been accomplished. Her attention refused to stay with the rather dry text of cosmetic bone alterations and kept returning to three men in a parlour. There had been fleeting impressions of unpleasant emotions, but Enric had shielded them well enough to have her receive nothing but hints instead of the full impact.

Enric pushed open the door and stepped inside. She stood up and stared at the manacles around his wrists. Oh dear. That had clearly not gone too well.

He followed her gaze. "Orrin thought it better to let you remove them. He thinks being here with you will reduce the chance of my storming over to bite off the King's head, for now anyway. Taking them off while I was more or less in front of the Palace was too risky for him."

She smiled with tiredness in her eyes and stepped in front of him, touching the restraining tools with her fingertips and making the manacles fall off and land on the floor with a jingling noise. He felt the familiar surge of power returning to him then wrapped his arms around her to press her close, inhaling the scent of her hair, kissing her forehead.

"I am going to take you away from here, my love," he murmured.

He felt the tension in her body when she tried to lean back, but he kept embracing her. "No, not yet."

She leaned against him once more. "Don't tell me you are about to ship me off to Takhan and back to Malriel to get me out of the King's reach? It would be subjecting me to torture in order to escape torment," she said. "What's more, a holiday would hardly change much in the long run, would it? Orrin thinks the King wants to make you do something you would otherwise not agree to."

"I know. He wants me to go to Takhan," he explained.

She stiffened. "What? How can you know that?"

"Malriel has asked me to go. And when I refused she sent a message to the King, very likely to do something that would make me change my mind."

He released her when she took a step back to stare up at him.

"That means that I have to thank *her* for his assaulting me? That woman really knows no bounds! How is it possible that she is even more of a pain, a burden, a nuisance now that she has left?" Eryn raked her fingers through her hair and then balled them into fists. "I could hit her! Honestly, one of these days I will hurt her. Physically smash her. With my fists. Really badly." Then she looked up at him again. "Then we are going to oblige her by doing what she wants? By going there? Really? What's the next option down?"

Enric's expression became heavy. "Staying here and subjecting you probably to even more unpleasant Royal attempts at persuading us to leave."

She grimaced. "And the option after that?"

"There is no third option, I am afraid. Unless you are counting getting rid of the King and replacing him with somebody less susceptible to Malriel's charms," he remarked tartly.

"That would more or less solve our problems, though, wouldn't it?"

"Yes," he admitted. "But let's consider regicide only as a last resort, shall we? Tyront would not at all take well to that. He's ordered me to stay away from the King."

She shrugged. "I think Lord Tyront would be the least of your problems. He is your friend, after all."

"First and foremost he is my superior. Friendship is his second priority. And after the strike I took from him today I wouldn't dare thinking of him as the least of my problems should I disobey his orders."

"What kind of strike?" Her gaze returned to the shackles on the floor. "Not a magical one, surely? We are talking about a heated discussion here, right?"

"Not quite. There was a little... well, let's call it a tense exchange of arguments with slightly explosive qualities, shall we?"

She stared at him. "You were fighting? Really?"

He nodded uneasily. "Yes, you could say that. Though a stronger magician fighting a weaker one is not a circumstance that provides for lengthy battles. I shot one bolt at him, but he was prepared for it. He sent back a stronger one which my shield couldn't hold. And while I was lying dazed on the floor they shackled me."

"You really attacked him?" She swallowed. "Are there going to be consequences for you? Will he discipline you?"

"I don't think so. They both expected a reaction like that, or Orrin wouldn't have asked him to come. He knew that he needed a stronger magician there to keep me from following my first impulse and storming across to the Palace. And Tyront was prepared. He had a shield raised in good time. I'd think he considers knocking me down a peg and shackling me a sufficient reminder of the balance of power between us."

She grinned lopsidedly. "Brilliant. And I wasn't there to see it. That was the last time I let myself be sent away when somebody wants to give you bad news."

"How very supportive and sympathetic of you, dearest," he sighed and pulled her close again. "I would like to greet you properly now that we don't have witnesses, if you don't mind."

Eryn slung her arms around his neck. "Go ahead. This is the first test for your beard. If it pokes or tickles me I will make the whiskers fall out."

He smiled and leaned down to kiss her.

"And?" he asked when he pulled back again.

She shrugged. "I can't really say. Unusual, but I would need to do more testing in order to reach a reliable conclusion."

He nodded seriously. "I am at your disposal for any testing you feel you need to carry out. Any time."

"Indeed? That is very dedicated. I appreciate your cooperation." She took his hand and pulled him towards the stairs.

"Always at your service, my love." He followed her up the stairs, glad that he had managed to avoid the discussion about going to the Western Territories for now.

* * *

"Erbál?" Eryn called out as she saw him in the corridor of the clinic on his way to Pe'tala's study.

He turned and smiled at her. "Lady Eryn! How nice to see you! It has been a while, has it not?"

"Indeed. Which is rather surprising considering how many social events I have been attending lately. Why haven't I seen you there?"

He grimaced. "Sanaf managed to insult Inad gravely once more, so he is not exactly someone people like to invite to their dinners nowadays. There is the dread of being his next victim in connection with not wanting to make Inad angry."

"So he basically caused both of you to become social outcasts? Lucky you," she sighed.

"I am not quite as pleased with that development as you would be in my place," he grimaced, then added with a grin, "I would very much have preferred watching your two most recent performances instead of just being told about them. It was quite a remarkable feat, by the way, to force Malriel to leave a week early."

They both stopped and looked towards Rolan's door when they heard loud voices coming out of his office. Eryn rolled her eyes.

"I swear to you, if those two idiots don't stop feuding before long, I am going to hurt them both. Hard."

Erbál smiled. "I would not worry about those two too much if I were you, Lady Eryn. They are enjoying themselves well enough."

They heard something fragile burst into shards. She lifted an eyebrow at him.

"That's your idea of enjoyment?" she asked.

He shrugged. "Passion. Nothing wrong with that, is it?"

"Passion?" She pointed a thumb over her shoulder at the door behind which they had resumed shouting at each other. "Well, that s certainly one way of referring to it."

"Is it possible that you have not noticed that the two of them are starting to fall in love?"

Eryn shook her head at him pityingly. "You suffer from delusions, I am afraid. Do you want me to have a look at it? You had better not consult Pe'tala in that matter, she might not be very gentle with you if she learns about their nature. Not that she is known to carry gentleness with patients to the extreme in general, mind you."

"What are you willing to bet that I am right?" he grinned.

She pursed her lips. He was pretty sure of himself, but the likelihood of Pe'tala and Rolan becoming romantically involved was practically zero. They either shouted at or ignored each other whenever they were in the same room.

"What do you want?"

A slow, calculating smile spread on his face. "I want you to put in a good word for me with your King. I know that Inad complained about Sanaf, and as soon as the first mentions of replacing him start coming up, I want those who can influence the decision to remember my name fondly."

She grimaced. "I am afraid even if in the very unlikely case of your winning this bet, it wouldn't be much of a favour I'd be doing you. The King and I are currently not exactly on speaking terms," she said.

"Are you not?" he asked in surprise. "How very interesting. Did you have a fight?"

Eryn straightened and gave him an even look. "That is not something I wish to share, I am afraid."

"Neither was my having been involved with Malriel in the past anything to share, and yet I answered you truthfully," he retorted without showing any sign of being insulted. "Tell me, did he overstep some boundary with you?"

She stared at him incredulously. Wherever had that come from? How could he possibly rumble a thing like that? After having spent hardly any time here at all?

"This is no discussion for a place like here," she replied stiffly.

He nodded. "You are absolutely right." He turned her back to where she had come from and pushed her back into her study, following closely before closing the door. "Let us instead talk in here, shall we?"

She fought the impulse of kicking him back out the door, tired of letting herself be bossed around by whichever man was in the mood for it. Erbál at least had no chance against her magic. But then his assumption had been so dangerously close to the mark that she at least was curious to know where it came from.

"What makes you ask a thing like that?" she queried, with arms folded.

He went to her desk and uninvited took a seat. Eryn remained standing, not wanting to give him the impression that he was welcome here after insinuating himself into her study without invitation.

"Malriel told me that the King admitted to being attracted to you."

She clenched her teeth. That meant that Malriel had very likely known what she was unleashing by sending that bird back to the King after Enric had declined her invitation to Takhan. Had she plotted together with him what measures of persuasion he should resort to in that case? That insight was hardly a great surprise, but somehow it still irked her. When would she finally stop expecting consideration from that woman and save herself the continuous little stabs of being let down each time?

"Why would Malriel tell *you* about a thing like that?"

"Because she thought that a little advance information would be advantageous for me. I am pursuing a certain position I would very much like to take over in the not too distant future, after all," he smiled.

Oh my, that was open and honest, she thought and scowled at him. "Then if Malriel is in favour of your becoming Ambassador, I should probably try to prevent just that."

"You do not need to worry about Malriel and me, Lady Eryn. She is not doing this primarily to have an immediate advantage, but to nurture my career. It really does pay to part with Malriel amiably; she has a soft spot for her former lovers."

Eryn snorted. "You confused, misguided fool! How can you be so blind? She is not doing this because she is so soft-hearted, but because having friends in high positions tends to turn out useful."

He shook his head. "I am neither confused nor misguided. Of course, I am going to come in useful to her one day, as she has been and will be to me. I rather wonder at your own perception of the circumstances involved when taking a lover. Have you only ever had liaisons with men to sate a physical need?"

She stared at him, taken aback. "I certainly never considered when and where they could one day be useful to me and whether I am supposed to be of use to them! This is so... cold and calculating! But I suppose you consider me naïve for taking somebody as a lover merely because I am attracted to him without considering birth rights or status."

Erbál considered her with interest. "You know, I would consider this a cultural difference between us, but I know that others here think the same way as I. So this is a personal opinion of yours and does not really reflect how people generally think in the Old Kingdom." He shrugged. "But then even if I became ambassador sometime soon, it would hardly concern you as you are bound for Takhan anyway, are you not?"

Her jaw dropped and she quickly returned to what she had learned to take control of herself again: breathing in and out slowly.

"Malriel might have been a little too forward in imparting that bit of news to you. Nothing whatsoever has been decided, agreed or even discussed yet with regard to that," she retorted coolly. "If I have any say in it, I will definitely not be obliging her by going over there."

"I see why you would not want to, but honestly, she will not abandon her efforts if she has set her mind on having you and your companion over there. But it does not have to be a disadvantage for you to go Takhan for a while, does it? You have family there you discovered only so very recently and who will be delighted to have the chance to spend more than a few weeks with you. Also there is a lot in Takhan to learn for you as our society is more advanced in quite a few areas. No offence meant, my dear Lady, but you are surely as aware of this as I am."

She smiled at him without humour. "Spending time in the same city or even country as Malriel for a longer period of time is a very definite disadvantage, as the only two times we were in the same city, a few weeks turned out to be vastly too long. Both times."

Erbál nodded slowly. "I see. But then this is a consideration you will not really have to worry about."

Looking puzzled, she took a step closer. "What do you mean by that? Why do I have the feeling that you know a little more than you are telling me?"

He got to his feet with an apologetic expression. "I am afraid this is all I am at liberty to tell you right now. And do not forget our wager. And do not worry about your little disagreement with the King - I cannot imagine that he would not listen to you."

"Little disagreement?" she hissed. "I would definitely not cal..." She stopped herself in time.

"Yes?" he enquired curiously.

"Nothing. Just that you seem to underestimate the depth of my displeasure a little. But I don't see that I have to worry about having to see the King on your account anytime soon. Your assumption about Pe'tala and Rolan is still ridiculous."

"Good," he grinned. "Then you have nothing to lose."

"True enough. What do I win in the very likely case of your losing?"

"What would you like?"

"All and any information you have on Malriel. Every little scrap," she replied immediately.

"I agree. I was afraid you would say something tedious," he laughed, "but I see that I was wrong. If they do not end up together before you leave for Takhan, you may consider me the loser of the bet."

"I may never even have to leave! So please be more specific with your time frame," she insisted.

"Oh, you will leave," he nodded confidently. "Would you care for another wager on that account as well?"

"No, thank you," she huffed.

"Let us say two months, then."

"Alright. You win, I shall go to the King and tell him what a superb fellow you are. I win, you have to give me every dicey, juicy, compromising, embarrassing detail you have on her."

He bowed. "Agreed."

"Good. And now go. I need to return to my students."

She watched him leave and began to consider what he had said. He was so very sure that Enric would take her to Takhan. That was disconcerting. She needed to talk to Enric about this, and soon. It was time to find out how serious he had really been that evening about taking her away from here.

* * *

Enric unrolled one of the two paper slips a servant had just collected from a bird that had arrived earlier that day and scanned the message Vran'el had sent. It related to his request of having the gold he earned through the shipping and sales of his produce in Takhan stored wherever House Vel'kim had their wealth locked away. Vran'el had not asked any questions as to the motives behind it or any particulars, but had taken care of the matter expeditiously and in a way that he himself had saw most useful. Enric appreciated such an efficient approach and knew he could trust the lawyer with his money without being cheated or having the arrangement made public knowledge.

He had managed to avoid talking to Eryn about going to Takhan so far, even though she had tried to broach the subject several times. He kept putting her off from day to day, but he was more than aware that her patience was beginning to wear thin. She was clearly not in favour of it and had told him about Erbál's cryptic remark about her not having to worry about being in the same city as Malriel if she went over there. It seemed the ambassador's assistant was rather well-informed. Being in Malriel's good books did seem to pay off.

But with the little matter of keeping funds safely in Takhan being taken care of, he could finally move on to something he was both looking forward to and dreading: confronting the King. He had no doubt that he was about to learn a great deal more of Malriel's plans and what the King really wanted him to do. King Folrin had not summoned Enric since his return, which was more than convenient for

Enric, as he had wanted to communicate with Vran'el first. That meant that the monarch was waiting for him to come on his own accord. Well, he would oblige. That was about to happen.

He put aside the first paper slip, informing him of the details of monetary measures that had been taken, and unrolled the second one. It was noticeably less formal; an interesting way to switch between the two roles Vran'el had taken over in Enric's life: legal consultant and friend.

The second message supplied information on what was going on in Takhan. People were talking about the situation up north, and so was the senate. He wrote about Malriel's attempts at convincing the senate about asking the Old Kingdom to officially advise them in the matter of defensive measures, just as she had intimated when they had been on the road together. Vran'el warned him that Malriel might be planning something to involve him in this in a more unofficial capacity - as her son, as it were. Enric felt himself deflating at that snippet of information. It had come a little late.

He pulled out a sheet of blank paper and wrote a single sentence in which he formally requested an audience with the King. He signed and sealed the note with his emblem, then summoned a servant to have it delivered. The reply would surely not be long in coming, as his request was very likely expected, and would have been since his arrival a few days back.

* * *

Orrin was leaning against the wall when Enric turned into the corridor that led to the throne room. Their determined gazes locked and the younger man came to a halt next to him, speaking quietly to make sure the guards around the corner didn't overhear them.

"There is a realistic chance that I am about to get myself into a lot of trouble. I would advise you to think twice before accompanying me. I won't think less of you for employing common sense and returning home."

The warrior just looked at him and silently pulled a pair of golden manacles from his pocket. Enric studied the objects for a few seconds, then nodded and took the shackles to fasten them around his wrists. Orrin touched them to affix them and then they turned the last corner that would bring them into view of the doors to the throne room.

The guards watched them approaching and opened the double doors for them in time so they didn't have to break their pace and could walk on to meet the King.

King Folrin stood on the topmost step of the dais, both hands tucked behind his back. Marrin was to his right wearing a slightly concerned expression. Enric wondered if he was aware what the reason for this meeting was. Probably, or otherwise the King would very likely not have let him join them. Or was that for reasons of security? Did he think that having a witness on hand would protect him from physical retributions?

Both magicians stopped in front of the dais and bowed briefly.

"Lord Orrin. I had not expected to see you here," the King remarked.

The warrior smiled faintly. "I am here to ensure your protection, Your Majesty."

"Protection. I see," the monarch pondered with narrowed eyes. "Though I fail to see how *you*, however unparalleled your fighting skills may be, would be able to stop a magician that much stronger than yourself from doing whatever he chooses."

Enric wordlessly lifted his arms to make the sleeves of his robe fall back and reveal the gold at his wrists.

"I see," King Folrin mused with a mildly amused expression. "I wonder why this fails to reassure me. Perhaps because it appears to be more of a justification for Lord Orrin to witness whatever is about to happen here, and very likely also a little concession to Lord Tyront, who is, I am sure, unaware of our little meeting here." He lifted his chin. "Go on, then, Lord Enric. I have been waiting for you to come to me for some time now."

Enric regarded the man in a seemingly placid way. "I have come to talk to you about your... efforts to make me go to the Western Territories."

"Then let me first elaborate the exact nature of what we are talking about here, Lord Enric." The King looked down at him. "Malriel wishes to summon you to Takhan to take over her position as Head of House Aren."

Both magicians stared at him.

"Pardon me?" Enric enquired, barely able to hide his surprise at this revelation.

"Only temporarily, that is. You are certainly in the picture when it comes to the current political situation between the Western Territories and their northern neighbour. Our new friends have decided to despatch an exalted delegate there to attempt negotiations in a situation where the fronts are continuing to harden. Malriel of House Aren. There is no saying how long she will be gone from Takhan. Furthermore, their laws state that she requires somebody to take over her House for the duration of her mission."

Enric forced himself to remain calm. That was unexpected. He remembered Erbál's remark about Eryn not having to worry about spending time with Malriel in the same city. So that was obviously what he had meant.

That meant that their stay really was meant for an indeterminate time.

"Malriel travelling into what might soon turn into enemy territory could result in her not being able to return at all," he stated soberly. "That could mean that my position as her substitute would become a permanent one."

"This, Lord Enric, is of course a possibility, though not one I am anticipating. This is, after all, meant as a mission to avoid any war, not to start one."

"Then I wonder why you are sending a high-ranking warrior to a country that is discussing how to prepare for a war, but which lacks the knowledge," Enric replied.

"To show our support and understanding, of course," the King explained slowly. "And your connection to House Aren allows us to do so without forcing them to lose face by having to request such a thing officially."

"So what you want me to do there, apart from taking over the responsibility for a family I don't know and their businesses I have no idea about, is to prepare them for a war that is in your opinion unlikely to happen? Do I understand that correctly?"

"A rather simplified way of looking at it, especially from a man with your political and diplomatic experience, but I do admit that basically, yes, that is what you are meant to be doing there," he agreed.

"What kind of preparation?" Enric enquired. "Training them in fighting? Teaching them military strategy? Erecting defensive structures?"

"The exact nature of the measures to be taken to make them feel more secure and demonstrate both our expertise and eagerness to assist I shall leave to your discretion, Lord Enric."

The magician nodded slowly. "You are aware, Your Majesty, that taking the position of a Head of House includes holding a seat in their senate? This would constitute a conflict of interests as I am already part of a similar organ here."

The King smiled. "That is correct. And this is why for the duration of your stay in the Western Territories you will no longer be a member of the Magic Council. Or the Order, for that matter."

Enric released his breath gradually. He was being expected to leave the Order. After more than two decades, more than half of that time in a leading position very close to the top.

"I see that this might be an unpleasant thought right now, but let me assure...," the King started, but Enric jumped in.

"No, this is quite in order. I will comply. It is a sensible course of action." He saw Orrin beside him slowly turning his head to stare at him, puzzled.

King Folrin raised his brow at him and regarded him closely. "I see. I admire your ability to adapt to unexpected circumstances so quickly. Though I admit that your willingness to leave behind you everything you have worked for so eagerly *does* rather surprise me."

Enric smiled at him coldly. "And yet you have taken such bold measures to ensure that I would."

The King remained silent for a time before he replied, "I did what I thought necessary."

"Also, you managed to connect the pleasant with the necessary I think, didn't you?" Enric responded dangerously calmly and slowly climbed the few steps until he was facing the King on the same level. He stopped directly in front of the younger and yet so very confident man, who showed no fear despite the immediate danger he had to know he faced.

"Or was kissing my companion much of a strain on you, Your Majesty?" Enric's voice was little more than a low grumbling.

"No, Lord Enric, it was not," the King replied equally softly. "Quite the opposite, I assure you. I got a first-hand impression why her recalcitrant nature appeals to you."

Enric's hand shot forward to grasp the King's throat in a movement so deft it took the other two men several moments to realise what had just happened. Marrin's eyes widened in panic, and he went to step forward. And stopped where he was when the King lifted a steady hand to him to keep him in place.

"Lord Orrin!" Marrin called out urgently. "I think that this is a situation that warrants your taking action if indeed your purpose in coming here was to protect His Majesty!"

Orrin frowned and pretended to think, before he shook his head. "No, everything is good so far. I don't see any immediate danger yet."

The advisor looked at Orrin as though he were witnessing a different scene entirely, frantically thinking if there might be anything he could say or do to make the magician release the King's choke-hold without inflicting further damage.

The King's eyes remained focused and still he showed no fear, Enric had to give him that.

"Let me be very clear about one thing: I will not tolerate your touching her in such a way ever again. Should you fail to comply with this very simple and yet very emphatic *request*, then I see myself entitled to take measures that will remove her from your area of influence. Permanently. I would take her and go to Takhan never to return. I would leave the Order and the Kingdom and everything I own here behind if this was what it took to protect her from being used as a bargaining chip against me and for your own gratification." He increased the force of his grip for a moment for emphasis before releasing the King. "However, you have accomplished what you wanted. We will go to Takhan."

Once released, the King subtly tried to swallow, but refrained from placing a hand to his throat - never breaking eye contact with the man who had just committed an offence punishable by death.

"Good," the King replied in a voice that sounded slightly raw-edged. "Consider one thing, though, Lord Enric: Lady Eryn's oath to the Kingdom will *not* be lifted following your departure. She will remain an Order magician, and even rise to your rank during the time of your absence, continuing to be bound to us. This is just a small reminder in case you decide to carry out your threat without provocation. I am not prepared to lose either of you."

"I am positive that there would be ways to work around that," Enric said evenly. "I trust that we would be able to convince somebody in Takhan to remove the binding from her."

"That may be so, but in doing it without my consent, they would considerably degrade our diplomatic relationship and risk losing us as their trading partner. They may look down on us and consider us less developed in some areas, but you know as well as I that they are keen enough on buying our natural resources. So I am convinced that you will be very careful and avoid acting in a way that will lead to insurmountable difficulties between our countries, especially now that they are struggling to get a grip on the situation with their northern neighbour," the King pointed out. He then smiled and raised his voice. "Lord Orrin will accompany you to Takhan, as you have indicated that you will have to take care of duties such as being leader of House Aren and also taking on the political function of senator. Lord Orrin will accordingly be a useful man to have with you for the other matters related to defence they are expecting your assistance with."

Enric looked at the King in dismay. "No. I will not take Lord Orrin away from his family for an indeterminate time."

"Of course not! His family will accompany him," the King replied. "Consider this a token of goodwill on my part to make going to Takhan a little less unpleasant for Lady Eryn."

Enric turned to the warrior, whose surprise was evident from his facial expression and posture.

"Orrin, I will do everything in my powers to fight this order if you require it," he promised. "I will not have you forced to take your pregnant companion to a country that might or might not be on the brink of war."

The older man pursed his lips while thinking, then he said, "No. We will go. This is about helping to prevent a war, after all. You will instead make sure that if indeed the situation should escalate, both our families will be safe. A ship reserved to leave only with them on board. Or not at all."

Enric closed his eyes for a moment, then nodded. That made not returning to Anyueel even less likely. The King really wanted to make sure that they would go. And he was right, of course. Orrin and Junar coming with them would make going to the Western Territories a lot more pleasant, especially with Malriel away from Takhan.

"Excellent," the King smiled. "You have three months to settle everything for your extended period of absence. This should be sufficient, I assume. Lady Eryn might wish to use the time to instruct the new Head of Healers in his duties and make sure the clinic continues to run smoothly without her. I will inform Lord Tyront of this. I expect he will not be too thrilled at losing the three of you at the same time and for so long, but I am confident that he will not be too surprised at this development. He usually isn't." He then nodded to both magicians. "You may leave now."

The two men turned and briskly walked to the doors, but halted when the King's voice once more rang out.

"Lord Enric? One more thing: Do not count on my continued leniency after today. If you ever again talk to me or handle me in such a manner, you will find yourself locked up in a dungeon cell," the monarch said coldly.

Enric nodded slowly. "Yes, Your Majesty. Then should you ever again give me a reason as potent as that to consider hurting you, I doubt you would be in any shape to have me locked up afterwards."

Thus he turned and left the throne room, Orrin close behind him.

"A very dangerous game you were playing, Your Majesty," Marrin remarked somewhat reproachfully. "I was rather concerned for your safety for a moment. Lord Orrin should not have stood watching but acted!"

"That was not why he was here, Marrin. He was here to observe. It was his own little chance to contribute to making sure I was punished for making him deliver Lady Eryn to me after rendering her defenceless. He would have interfered if Lord Enric had gone too far, though not to protect *me*, but him. The consequences for disobeying Lord Tyront's order not to meet me without him will be dire enough without the added gravity of having hurt me."

Marrin sighed. "Then maybe the period until sending them away should not have been that long. Three months is a long time to have the three of them feeling discontent at you here, Your Majesty."

"And yet I need the time. I will have to use it to make amends. I can't afford to send them away with fire in their bellies at me. I need them to act in the interest of the Kingdom while they are gone. And to return to me afterwards."

"An ambitious aim," Marrin remarked with some doubt.

King Folrin smiled. "Indeed. But not impossible. The key to success is to start with the right person. The first target for my efforts will at the same time be the easiest one: Lady Eryn herself. In her case there were no protective instincts violated, simply pride."

"So you wish to cater to her vanity? A concept that does not seem very promising to me, if you don't mind my saying so, Your Majesty."

"No, not to her vanity. I intend to focus on the things she takes pride in, such as her work and the people close to her. As opposed to Lord Enric, she has made herself susceptible to efforts of that kind almost from the day of her arrival in the city by making friends so easily."

CHAPTER 22

Public Punishment

Orrin and Enric stepped out into the bright daylight.

"It doesn't really pay for you to return to your home," the warrior said calmly. "Lord Tyront will summon us in less than an hour, I imagine. Come with me to my quarters and have Eryn summoned. We may as well tell them together."

Enric nodded and lifted his wrists to have the shackles removed. Orrin opened them with a little magic and let them slip back into his pockets.

"That went well enough. I am rather surprised at it, to be honest," the older man stated. "I would have counted on his making us pay for insolence somehow. Or is that to come yet, do you consider?"

"No, I doubt that. He is well aware that my reaction was still a very limited one. Too limited for his taste at the beginning, I would think. He even provoked me to make me demonstrate a reaction. Bravery bordering on light-headedness." Enric shook his head. "That man has a very particular and dangerous taste in entertainment."

Orrin shrugged and lifted an arm to summon one of the gate guards over. "He knew I would step in in case you were too enthusiastic in demonstrating your disapproval. So not too much of a risk for him there."

When the gate guard stopped in front of him and bowed, Orrin instructed him to take a message to Lady Eryn at the clinic to see him and Lord Enric at his quarters at her earliest convenience.

"I think it's a treatment day today," Enric pointed out when the guard had left and they set in motion towards the warriors' quarters. "That means she will either come to us soon because it's a quiet day or not at all because they are swamped with patients."

"Vern should soon be home now. I can send him to the clinic to take over for her. I want this taken care of before we get our hides tanned by Lord Tyront," Orrin said resignedly.

"How will Junar react to that bit of news?"

"I am not sure. She could go either way. I don't have to ask how Eryn will react, do I?"

Enric smiled tiredly. "No, not really. It is merely a question of her bothering to hurl breakable objects around first or going for my throat straight away."

"It can't be that unanticipated for her," Orrin replied and opened the heavy door to let Enric step into the corridor first.

"No, she has been jostling to discuss this with me for several days now, impressing on me that she has no intention whatsoever of going to Takhan again."

"*Jostling to* implies that you have avoided the topic so far, I assume?"

Enric nodded. "Yes. I first wanted to see what the King had to say. And give her a little more time to get used to the thought of going over there again so soon. My revelation that we will indeed do so in a few months should not be too much of a surprise for her then. Which does not mean that she will take it any better, mind you. I have great hopes that the fact of the three of you accompanying us will console her at least a little."

Orrin shook his head. "Perhaps eventually, but surely not when she first hears of it. I am wondering how to break it to Vern. He will not be happy about seeing us go."

Enric stopped. "You are not considering leaving him behind, are you? I would think he is a little too young to be left unsupervised for whoever knows how long."

"You think I am taking him there?"

"Well, that's why I said the *three* of you."

"I thought you meant the baby! I am not taking *Vern*! He needs to continue his studies here, and I can't just take him away like that. He is too young and inexperienced to be moved over somewhere like that. Who knows what kind of trouble he would get himself into!"

The younger man looked at him doubtfully, but didn't contradict him. He had a very clear idea of how the boy would react to being left behind.

They climbed the stairs and followed the dimly lit corridor to the door of Orrin's quarters. The warrior preceded him into the parlour, where Junar was busy with what looked like staring at pieces of fabric. She raised both eyebrows at the unexpected return of her companion and the guest he had brought along.

"Hello. I don't intend to be rude, but what are you doing here?"

"Waiting for doom to befall us," Enric murmured darkly.

"That is not exactly enlightening," she replied. "But it does give me a rather uneasy feeling, as if you are about to give me bad news."

"That would depend on one's point of view," Orrin sighed. "We are waiting for Eryn to join us, so I would ask you for a little indulgence for now. What are *you* doing, anyway?"

"It looked like a staring contest with lifeless objects to me. And as you looked up when we entered, you have lost," Enric commented.

Junar rolled her eyes. "I am examining the quality of the fabric the traders want to sell me, if you must know. Texture, weave, feel, mistakes in the pattern, sloppy storage, durability and things like that. And it's good I have you here, Enric. One of your men tried to sell me a load that was seething with vermin! Not exactly the kind of quality I am used to when it comes to your produce."

Enric frowned. "And not the kind you should have been expected to buy. If you write down the trader's name and the type of fabric he tried to sell you, I will take care of this."

She smiled broadly. "Great. It does pay to know the mighty and powerful."

"Glad to be of use," he bowed.

Orrin stepped to the drinks cabinet and seemed to ponder over a particular bottle before he relented and grabbed a carafe of juice instead.

"Scruples about drinking alcohol during the day, Orrin? Or are you trying to keep a clear head for what we have yet to face?" Enric chuckled.

"There is that, yes," he growled. "And I lectured your companion about handling her alcohol responsibly after... you know. I don't want her to see me drinking before dinner. She has accused me of applying double standards already."

"After what?" Junar frowned. "Are you keeping something from me?"

"Yes, my dear," Orrin nodded to Enric's surprise. "But nothing I can share with you right now."

Her eyes narrowed, but she didn't try to make him talk. He wouldn't budge, there was no use in pestering him.

They turned to the door as Vern entered. The boy bowed to Enric.

"What is this? Some kind of conference? Am I supposed to leave you alone?" he enquired, unsure.

"No. You should hear this as well. We are waiting for Eryn to join us," his father said.

Vern sighed. "That could take a while. Today is a treatment day."

"We know. We are hoping it was a quiet day," Enric remarked.

At that instant the door pushed open once more and Eryn rushed in.

"What is the matter? Has something happened?" she demanded, her breathing still heavy from sprinting along the corridor.

Enric nodded approvingly. "That was fast. I take it you didn't have very many patients today?"

"We have enough patients, but I asked the other healers to take on mine for an hour when I got your message. Being told to meet the two of you at this time of day does make me very wary, and I want to know if I am in any trouble before I return to my work instead of having to fret all afternoon. Out with it, then! I am expected back soon."

Enric cleared his throat. "Eryn, I have agreed to go to Takhan again."

He saw her lips tighten. She folded her arms and her eyes narrowed. "Have you, now. And how long will you be gone?"

"I have, yes. And it is not yet fixed how long *we* will be gone."

"If you say *we*," she said tensely, "you surely don't mean you and *me*, do you? Because I distinctly remember telling you repeatedly that I do not, under any circumstances, want to return there at all soon. That was over the course of the last few days, when you refused to talk about this to me!"

"The term includes you as well, yes," he replied calmly. "But not only you." His gaze darted to Junar. "Orrin and Junar will accompany us."

"What?" Vern exclaimed. Junar dropped the measuring tape she had been holding in her hand. It silently landed on the carpet in a zigzag line.

The boy turned to his father. "You are not leaving me behind while you go to Takhan, surely not? You *have* to take me!"

"You can go in my stead," Eryn said from between clenched teeth.

Enric went on slowly, shielding his brain to dull the wave of anger he received from her. "You will go, Eryn. Your remaining would defeat the purpose of taking you away from here. This is an order."

She unfolded her arm to ball her hands into fists. "I am not taking such an order from *you*!" she hissed.

Enric's gaze became set. "I was not aware that taking orders from a superior magician was something you are at liberty to decide on, depending on your mood or if the command is to your liking. I gave you an order, and you will comply with it. Insubordination is not something we take lightly in the Order, whether you are my companion or not. But should you wish to discuss this with the King instead..."

"Don't you dare throw the threat of *him* in my face!" she snarled and jabbed her index finger at him. "Why don't you *think* for a moment instead of letting your jealousy and unfounded fear of losing me guide your decisions? The last time we went there we were in danger of never being permitted to leave again! And now the very source of that calamity, twisted malicious Malriel of bloody House Aren, feels that it's cosy idea to have us there! This is more than enough for me *not* to go there!"

Enric took a step towards her and caught her finger in his hand. "Just you listen to *me*. I have agreed to go there to protect you, and you know as well as I do that your staying here can't be a choice. There is the little matter of the third level bond, which would begin to make us both feel miserable after a very short time. I already start feeling restless when you work longer! So if you once more suggest that I go there alone, I will not even bother discussing this with you anymore but knock you out and have you shipped over in a crate together with the cat," he snapped.

"To protect me? By dragging me to the place where that villainous, scheming minx is at home? She is in league with the King - what kind of protection would that be, anyway?" she howled in frustration.

"She won't be there," he said calmly.

Eryn narrowed her eyes suspiciously. "What do you mean, she won't be there? Of course she will be there, she has a bloody residence in that bloody city and leads a damned House! Where else would she be?"

"She will travel to Pirinkar to negotiate an agreement that is intended to prevent war. She will be gone for a longer time. Which is why she wants me to take over House Aren for the duration of her absence."

"What?" she exclaimed. "You are to be Head of House Aren? Really?" She looked about in confusion. "But what if she doesn't return? What if they capture and kill her there? That would mean that we are marooned in that place forever!"

"It would also mean that your mother would be dead, but never mind such details..." Vern mumbled with a rather shocked expression.

"You shut up!" Eryn snapped at him. "Your eagerness to go there is not something I look on very well right now!" Then she turned to Junar. "You say something! They are about to push *you* there, too!"

The seamstress nodded slowly. "There is quite some planning to be done, I would say," she spoke calmly. "I need to be able to communicate regularly with the women who work for me. I want the business to go on while I am gone. That means I need somebody to make sure they are paid regularly and to handle the orders in addition to all the organisation."

Eryn closed her eyes for a moment, then pulled her finger from Enric's grip before stepping in front of Junar and grabbing both her shoulders, shaking her slightly. "Have you lost your mind? Your child will end up being born in that country!"

"No shaking the pregnant lady," Vern murmured and ducked when she sent another withering look his way.

"I know," Junar replied stiffly. "But I imagine there are worse places for having a baby than in a place where there are a lot of well-trained healers available for the delivery."

"*I* will deliver your baby, Junar!" Eryn cried out. "You will be taken care of wherever you are! No need to go to Takhan! The journey is long and unpleasant, two days on the road and another two days on a pitching ship that makes you seasick all the voyage!"

"Not much of a difference for me, then," she retorted dryly.

Eryn shook her head, wondering if everyone but herself in the room had lost their mind. She lowered her voice, careful to sound reasonable and collected.

"Enric. I have very valid reasons not to go to Takhan. There are so many things about to happen here in the Order, things that concern me and my area of expertise. This would be an immensely bad time for me to leave the Kingdom for who knows how long. I am the only fully trained healer here, and I cannot ask Vern to handle the clinic for such a long time."

He nodded. "I see your point. And I wish I could spare you returning over there so soon and for such a long time, honestly I do." He took both her hands into his, noting how she tensed at the contact. "But we don't have much of a choice here."

"*You* were the one who made the choice," she accused him. "And I don't like it! You can't keep pressing me into things like this! This is not how a mature relationship works!"

"Eryn," he implored her, "open your eyes! The King wants us to go there, so you may be assured that he will resort to other means of *persuasion* if we don't go along with him now. And if he does resort to other means, I know that my reaction will be a very risky one for us all. However, if you think you have a better solution, I would be very interested in hearing it," he added tensely. "And this solution better not leave you at the mercy of the King."

"Enric, he just did this to manipulate you into going! He won't do anything else when he sees that it doesn't work, I am sure!"

"You are sure?" He looked at her, his expression bordering on incredulous. "How can you be sure of a thing like that? He has some kind of agreement with Malriel, and he will not risk appearing impotent by having to admit that he can't get his own subjects to obey him! He will take other steps if we don't leave, believe you me." He placed a gentle hand at the back of her neck and pulled her close. "I for one won't wait for him to increase the pressure by another intervention with you that is meant to make me react the way he intends."

Junar cleared her throat. "Another intervention with her?" She turned to Orrin. "What is going on here? What *has* he done to her?"

"Nothing that bears repeating here and now," Eryn gulped and took a step back to free herself from Enric's grip. "I will return to the clinic now. I don't think that we can discuss this reasonably right now. I need some distance. I need to think." She turned and rushed out into the corridor, leaving the four of them behind.

Enric rubbed his face. "Well, that went rather more smoothly than expected."

"That was smooth?" Vern exclaimed.

"It was," Orrin nodded. "Nothing was smashed, no magical fighting happened, no screaming or kicking... I would say that it really did go quite well. Though I am sure that this is not the last any of us will hear from her about the plan," he added with a telling look at Enric.

Vern looked at his father with an angry expression. "And you are planning to leave me behind? Just like that? To go to another country full of knowledge that would help me? I could meet healers and artists there! I could use the time to learn so much!" His voice had taken on a slightly pleading quality.

Orrin turned away. "No. I don't have time to keep an eye on you there. And I don't even know what kind of trouble you could get into there. You will stay here and I will have Lord Poron look after you. You need to continue your classes here, I can't just take you with me like that!"

Vern pressed his lips together and turned angrily to storm off to his room. When he had slammed the door behind him, the two men looked at each other.

"Superb," Orrin sighed. "Now they are both going to be difficult until we leave here."

"At least your companion goes along with it all."

Junar smiled thinly and folded her arms. "That might have been a bit too optimistic an assessment, I fear. You both take a seat now and tell me what exactly is going on here between Eryn and the King. I am also on Vern's side, by the way. How can you even consider going without him?"

The warrior rubbed his face with both hands. "Going along with it all indeed."

* * *

Tyront stood in front of the window behind his desk and looked outside with his hands on his hips.

"Close the door, will you?" he said softly without turning when the two magicians he had summoned entered his study. Only after he heard the quiet sound of the door snapping shut did he slowly turn and regard his two tense subordinates with a glacial look. He walked around his desk placidly as if he had all the time in the world, stopping directly in front of them.

Enric could see the effort it took the Order's leader to keep his wrath under control. There was a certain blood vessel at his throat that tended to protrude on the rare occasions when he was truly enraged. Though those occasions had not been so rare in this last year, he remembered. Not since Eryn had been brought to the city. And every single time Tyront had been irate had always been connected with her. So it was this time, though it was hardly her fault for once.

"You two imbeciles!" he all but whispered with eyes narrowed to slits. The low volume did not fail to convey his fury. "What were you thinking?" His stared into Enric's unmoving eyes. "I am crushingly disappointed in you. This is the first time in more than ten years that I have asked myself whether you can be trusted any longer. I could have understood an immediate reaction - your storming up to the King and shaking him because you didn't have your emotions under control is one thing. Not one that speaks for your grip on yourself, mind you, but a reaction I might have granted you in a situation like that. However, waiting for several days, obviously planning what you did and then disobeying my orders with cold determination is a punch to my own face." He swivelled his head to look at Orrin, who was staring ahead almost unseeingly. "And for you, Lord Orrin... Frankly, I am astonished at such stupidity from *you*. What in the world made you think that accompanying Enric to see the King the course of action which was preferable to stopping his doing so?"

"I ordered him to come with me and shackle me," Enric spoke calmly.

Tyront closed his eyes for a moment before he asked the warrior, "Is that true, Lord Orrin? Did Lord Enric truly order you to disobey a direct order of mine?"

"No," Orrin just replied, still staring ahead.

The leader's face came close to Enric's when he hissed, "Should you lie to me once more you will be spending the next month in shackles." Then he turned back to Orrin. "Why did you go with him?"

"To hold him back in case he went too far. To witness the King being told to keep his hands off Eryn in the future."

Tyront stared at him, then nodded slowly. "I see. Protecting Enric and Eryn. And being seen to protect them to make the King think twice about one day using your daughter, who might very well be the first female magician born to the Kingdom in centuries. A lot of daughters around to be protected by you lately. I understand your motives, but cannot endorse your course of action." He rubbed his face. "And letting yourself be sent away like this for *months*! This is something that should have been discussed between the King and myself, not with you! I am losing three out of five leading ranks, and my second-in-command is even being removed from the Order for that time!" He lifted an index finger up to Enric's face and the younger man couldn't help but notice that this was the second time within one hour that he found himself peering at this accusing gesture. "Don't you get any ridiculous ideas about not returning here, my dear boy! Eryn will remain in the Order, and having the binding removed from her will cause severe tensions between the two countries. So I will advise you to think very carefully about your course of action regarding this. If you don't come back after Malriel returns from her mission, I will personally come after you. You can depend on it."

Enric nodded once. He had no doubt that Tyront was deadly serious about it.

"Incredible what havoc a single woman can wreak within what until now I considered a stable institution lead by level-headed people." His stare remained focussed on Enric. "Did you touch the King?"

"Yes."

"Where?"

"His throat."

Tyront closed his eyes and exhaled slowly. "You throttled the King? Did he punish either of you in any way?"

Enric returned the glare evenly. "No."

Tyront returned to his desk and seated himself without offering his guests the same. "That means that it falls upon me to do so," he uttered with a determined look at each. "Thank you so much for that, you idiots. You have brought disgrace to your ranks. It means you have volunteered for a public beating. I need to show the King that despite all contrary evidence I am still in control of the Order. Lord Orrin, you will spread the news that I am going to use the arena tonight. That should attract enough attention."

"Yes, Lord Tyront," Orrin replied resignedly.

"I shall see you both there before dinner. Don't dare be late," he barked. "And now get out of my sight!"

"Fantastic," Orrin murmured quietly when they were out in corridor and walking back towards the Palace gates. "And there I was, thinking the worst part of the day would be over after facing him. It seems I was wrong."

"Obviously," Enric said, none too cheerful. He hoped Eryn would at least be a little more well-disposed towards him after watching him taking a proper beating from Tyront. Then he closed his eyes, feeling his stomach clench when it occurred to him on what this punishment would mean for her. Every blow Tyront dealt him she would feel, too, thanks to the mind bond.

* * *

Eryn looked up as her study door at the clinic flung open and Vern stormed in. She felt the weight of everything crushing her. Having only come here only a few minutes ago after sending the last patient on his way, it didn't seem like she would be able to take care of the patient reports as planned.

"Come with me," the boy demanded impatiently with wild eyes.

"Where? And why?"

"To the arena! Lord Tyront has reserved it for himself tonight."

"So what?"

He rolled his eyes at her. "This is not an everyday occurrence! Something is about to happen there. When did you last see him in the arena?"

"When I knocked him out with my new bolts."

"Exactly!"

She nodded and got to her feet. When he put it like that it probably would pay to have a look at what might be going on. Especially as Vern seemed to term it either important or potentially entertaining enough to temporarily shelve his discontent at being left behind while his family planned to go to Takhan.

She raised her brow at the number of people who had assembled around the circular fighting space.

"It's that unusual to have the big man claim the arena for a bit of exercise, eh?" she commented.

Vern didn't bother with an answer but pushed aside two watchers, who hurriedly stepped out of the way to make room for the two magicians. Eryn frowned when she saw Lord Tyront in what looked like common training attire, but which made him look completely different, as she couldn't recall seeing him in anything other than his robes of office. Like the King, he appeared strangely transformed. Less pompous. More dangerous.

Enric and Orrin both entered the arena from one side, each sporting identical attire with black leather chest armour and forearm protection. Both looked grim and less than thrilled about the audience, but progressed with determined strides towards the centre of the arena, where their leader awaited them with folded arms and a stern expression. Eryn had never seen him fighting, but thanks to his immense magical strength he would very likely be in a position to defeat his two subordinates despite their superior fighting skills.

Vern next to her whistled. "He is fighting them both? But why in public?"

Eryn pursed her lips. "To humiliate them, I would think. For whatever reason." She looked to her side when a familiar figure elbowed her way to the front of the crowd.

Pe'tala stopped next to them. "What is going on here? Savage entertainment for the masses?"

Eryn didn't answer but watched Enric being sent back to the edge of the training area. So it was Orrin who would be dealt with first.

Lord Tyront was the first to draw his weapon, and Orrin followed suit, changing into a fighting stance in an instant.

Their swords met several times with a series of clangs, some of the strokes too fast to appear as more than blurs for the eyes of their audience. Eryn drew in a sharp breath when Lord Tyront's knuckles hit Orrin's nose in a punch that made his head snap to one side and caused him to stumble several steps backwards until he managed to steady himself again. A thin trickle of blood was running from one nostril.

"Dear me," Pe'tala murmured, "Your fighters do have a rather harsh way of dealing with each other."

They watched the warrior take another hit in the stomach. Vern's jaw clenched.

"This is a bit above average," Eryn swallowed and laid one hand on the boy's tense shoulder to squeeze it reassuringly.

Lord Tyront approached the warrior anew and drove him back another few steps with powerful strokes. Orrin blocked them skilfully. Then the stronger magician dealt him a blow to his side with the hilt of his sword and Orrin went down on one knee, supporting himself with his sword to remain as upright as he could manage. His face was a mask of pain.

Eryn watched her companion, who was observing the scene with folded arms and an expression of foreboding. Probably a combination of having to watch the thrashing being dealt to Orrin and being aware that he was next in line.

Orrin struggled back to his feet and lifted his weapon to ready himself for the next attack. The next few strikes were less fervent, as if Lord Tyront intended to let his opponent recover his strength. Orrin was careful to remain outside the immediate reach of both sword and fists.

"He is not attacking," Vern complained. "Not at all! He just blocks all the time!"

Eryn studied the action, then nodded. He was right, she saw - Orrin was no more than defending himself, either not daring or not wanting to do anything else. Would fighting back seem like he was not accepting what was looking a lot like a very physical kind of punishment? Would Enric follow his example and let himself be battered in such a way as well?

Lord Tyront had obviously decided that Orrin had regained enough of his balance and his blows became forceful again.

Eryn considered sending Vern away so he didn't have to watch this any longer, but of course it would not be much use. He wouldn't just leave while his father was being squashed publicly.

She drew in a sharp breath and heard the boy do the same when Lord Tyront aimed a forceful kick at Orrin's knee which sent him once more to the ground. This time Orrin didn't attempt to get up again, but grasped his knee in both hands and pulled it towards his chest with an expression of agony. Not a single sound had issued from his lips.

Lord Tyront stood over him and looked down at the recumbent figure, slowly sheathing his weapon and waiting for Orrin's pain to recede enough for him to get up again.

"He is not going to continue this, is he?" Vern hissed and Eryn held on to his arm to stop him from rushing down there.

"No, look. He has motioned for Enric to help him up. I think Orrin has taken all the beating he seems to have been due," she said in a voice breaking with emotion. That had to mean that now Enric's turn had come. They watched him walking down the steps and across to Orrin, then lifting him back to his feet before escorting him to the edge of the arena. Then Enric returned to face his superior.

Eryn swallowed when both men drew their swords at the same time with a slow, deliberate move, staring at each other. Somehow she doubted that he would accept this rough treatment with as much passivity as Orrin had. She worried about that. Lord Tyront would very probably not take such pluck well and would make him pay for it. But then the thought of Enric just taking a beating without fighting back seemed so unnatural and uncharacteristic that it was even more upsetting to her.

Lord Tyront was noticeably more cautious with his new opponent. He scrutinised Enric's each and every step carefully and after a few moments she could see Lord Tyront's lips moving. She wished she had taken the time to cultivate Enric's trick in redirecting airstreams to listen to distant conversations. Unfortunately both distance and angle made reading their lips impossible.

* * *

"So you are determined to make this difficult," Tyront commented.

"You knew well enough that I would. That's why you took care of Orrin first. And to make me watch him. My punishment is to be the more severe of ours, isn't it?" Enric replied calmly.

Tyront smiled thinly. "True enough. But I was hoping that you would surprise me by showing remorse and accepting willingly what you brought upon yourself. But then you never were very good at dealing with corrective measures. Although as it was such a long time since they were necessary in your case, one is tempted to neglect that after a while."

"You assisted the King by not telling me about the Ambassador's impending visit back then, making it possible for him to manipulate me into making her join me. It was your doing as much as his, even though your role was a more passive one. And now you act surprised at the consequences of my actually protecting her, treating her as *mine* instead of some trophy for the Kingdom and the Order," Enric retorted coldly.

"No, my dear boy," Tyront sighed. "Yours she is, as you have never failed to make clear. Yet I did not expect you to set aside all common sense, nor even openly to disregard a direct order of mine. This is a precedent I cannot let pass, as you are very well aware. This was not about protecting Eryn, but about taking revenge. Retribution is not something you can afford when it comes to the man you are supposed to obey. If I don't punish you, the King might have cause to do so himself."

"Doing his dirty work, old friend?" Enric murmured. "That represents how far we have come. His imposing his attentions on my companion, and your dealing out chastisements because I didn't tolerate it. Really a low point."

Tyront answered with a low growl and a first thrust, which Enric blocked swiftly.

Their swords met several times with tremendous blows that rang loudly through the arena.

"Listen to yourself, you fool!" Tyront snarled at him when their weapons had locked. "You allowed your feelings for her to cloud your judgement. How can I rely on you if I have to fear your doing something mindless as soon as she somehow becomes involved?" He pushed mightily with his weapon, making Enric stumble two steps backwards.

"What do you want me to do, Tyront? Put the Order before her?"

Tyront's reply came as though thunder from the sky. "Yes, that is damn well what I expect you to do! You have been in the Order since you were a boy - you are responsible to it and the Kingdom! Catering to your own personal tastes cannot come before that!"

Enric nodded slowly. "I see where our problem here is, then. Your priorities are not actually in accordance with my own."

"I am not telling you to leave her unprotected! Just to make yourself less susceptible to manipulation of any kind. The King keeps using Eryn to steer you into doing what he wants."

"What is the alternative, then, Tyront?" Enric shot back. "My not letting him force her to become his partner for one sordid fling was as much in the Order's interest as in my own. How else would you have stopped her from leaving at the first opportunity? Would you like me to consult with you from now on about which situations you see my interference acceptable and which not?" He then ducked quickly, barely escaping the blow aimed at his shoulder.

"That would be a good start, yes. And following my orders from now on. Your own agenda cannot come before what I think best for the Order. Not ever."

"I, too, am a part of the Order," Enric pointed out.

"And this is why I am trying to protect you, as well. But I can't do this when you keep acting on your own," Tyront insisted.

"How can I trust you to protect me and also Eryn, if I discover that you are keeping essential information from me, as with the impending arrival of the ambassador back then?"

Tyront sighed. "I see now that things between us have not been as smooth as I thought for quite a while now."

Enric slowly shook his head. "No, not really. And as long as Eryn is being used against me like that, I don't see how this is likely to change soon. Political measures I can tolerate - they are part and parcel of the game. But as long as the rules do not prevent the King from disrespecting the commitment he himself pressured her into, I am not bowing to them. Or to either of you, for that matter."

"Dangerous words, my young friend," Tyront replied with narrowed eyes. "Very dangerous ones, indeed. They do not only declare open insubordination, but push very close to treason."

Enric didn't reply. He could see from his superior's unrelenting expression that there would be no more talking for now.

* * *

Eryn grabbed the divider in front of her to keep her hands still. They had stopped talking and started circling each other. Every blow from either side was preceded by careful consideration. She watched Lord Tyront lashing out with a speed her eyes had difficulty following. Enric blocked the strike, but at the same time whirled away. She realised that he was merely diverting his opponent's blade from its course as a complete block was not very promising in the long run with a stronger adversary. He didn't expend any more strength than necessary, but focussed on something he could better work with in this particular fight: speed.

"That is very impressive," Pe'tala mumbled next to her. "I cannot even see some of their moves clearly without straining my eyes. But this is a more interesting fight. At least Enric has no qualms about fighting back."

Yes, Eryn thought - and it remained to be seen how he would be made to pay for this eventually. They watched Enric lift his blade to stop the other sword from cutting into his thigh and in turn aim a blow at Lord Tyront's seemingly unprotected side.

The subsequent exchange was so fast that it was hard to distinguish between the single crashes of naked metal when the swords met.

Eryn couldn't help but smile ironically when she saw Enric moving with the blows, using their superior energy to make the other fighter stumble forwards and land him a hit on the back with the flat of his weapon that almost sent the older man to the ground. This was something Orrin had taught her for unarmed combat: using another person's strength against him and just adding a little of her own to redirect the attack. Enric had adapted those principles marvellously to fit his own needs in sword fighting.

She only now saw how proficient he truly was with a blade. Fighting with her had never pushed him to his limits. She was neither skilled nor magically strong enough for him to be anything else but a diversion, an amusement. And she never would be, judging from what she was witnessing right now. This was skill honed over two decades, true proficiency that had so far even managed to withstand a battering from superior strength.

Unexpected pride welled up inside her and she quickly shielded her emotions. Distraction of any kind was the last thing he needed now. Could he somehow win this fight and escape the public beating? Would that be advisable? Very probably not. Lord Tyront would not take well to being sullied as a loser. And he would hardly have chosen this setting if he wasn't sure of winning. But right now it seemed as if he had underestimated either Enric's considerable skill or his determination to resist Tyront's chastisement.

She felt the wood under her fingers giving way when they tightened. Enric had just taken his first blow to his right upper arm and she felt the surge of pain through their mind bond before he quickly shielded himself. Vern and Pe'tala both turned to her with a worried expression.

"Did you just feel that?" Vern enquired, clearly disturbed by the idea.

She nodded silently, not taking her eyes off the two men in the arena. Lord Tyront had to be aware that whatever pain he caused Enric she would also feel, even though with less intensity. Was that why Enric refused to take the beating with the same resignation Orrin had shown? To protect her from suffering the mirroring of every hit he took? Had the Order's leader intended for this to be a disciplinary measure for her as well for her uncooperative response to learning that she was not to head the healers?

If yes, then it was not any course of action that would secure him Enric's goodwill, she thought.

She watched Enric take the sword in his left hand and raised both brows in surprise. She had not even been aware that he could fight with his left hand at all. After being made to train with him so often there were obviously still a few surprises to be discovered. But then she had never managed to hit him hard enough to make it necessary for him to resort to such a manoeuvre.

Enric blocked the next few blows using the sword in his left hand, not showing any sign of weakness.

Lord Tyront began to look more and more peeved. He observed his opponent with tightened eyes, his blade at the ready before him. Then both of them attacked at the same time, which was unfortunate for Enric, who quickly had to change direction to avoid being stabbed in the chest. Lord Tyront took advantage of this and pursued him, all the while keeping his opponent busy with hard strikes. Enric was driven backwards step by step, getting closer and closer to the wooden barrier that separated watchers and fighters.

Eryn could see from his sideways glance that he was aware of the disadvantageous situation he was in and that he had to do something soon before he truly had the wall in his back. He tried to duck away sideways several times, but Lord Tyront thwarted his attempts and kept him where he was.

Enric then drew in a deep breath, took a few quick steps back and took a short run-up before jumping up into the air and somersaulting right over Lord Tyront. The watchers around her let loose exclamations of delight. That was not something one witnessed every day in a sword fight.

A moment later Enric landed on his feet, unfortunately with his back to Lord Tyront, who had turned quickly instead of being awe-struck like all others around him. He took immediate advantage of the situation and kicked Enric hard in the small of his back, sending him flying to the hard ground face first. When Enric attempted to rise again, he was kicked hard in his side and collapsed back again.

Eryn bent forward and braced her hands on her knees. Damn! And this was just a dampened echo of the pain *he* was feeling right now!

She felt a hand on her back, rubbing it comfortingly and was surprised to see that it was Pe'tala's when she looked up. So it seemed that pain that almost brought her to her knees seemed to trigger sympathy, even in her cousin.

She straightened again to look what was going on in the arena. Enric was lying on the ground, his sword knocked out of his hand and lying beyond his reach. He was moving slowly, pressing a hand against his painful side and seemingly content to remain down.

Lord Tyront used his foot to flip him forcefully onto his back and then held his glinting blade to Enric's throat. Eryn pressed her lips together. A gesture to make the crowd realise that the fight was over and clarify beyond a doubt who had won it.

She climbed over the wooden barrier and jumped down the other side to quickly walk towards the decumbent figure in the centre of the arena.

Lord Tyront watched her coming closer and sheathed his sword. She bent down to Enric and took his hand to press it reassuringly.

"Where does it hurt most?"

"You will not heal him," the older man growled. "He is to endure the pain until it has healed naturally. Same goes for Lord Orrin."

She looked up at him in disbelief. "I cannot believe I am hearing this! I am definitely not going to watch him suffer for a few weeks, depending on what damage you did to him!" she exclaimed angrily. "There is a Code of conduct for healers, principles we follow! You may as well consult your *new Head of Healers* over that. I have no doubt that he will inform you of this Code in as much detail as you could wish for," she then added with a hiss and returned her attention to Enric, who had managed to make himself sit up.

"Careful," Lord Tyront said in a severe voice as he placed a hand on his sword hilt, warning her. "You will either follow my order or you will be the next one crossing blades with me right here and now. Since both of your colleagues here are more proficient in the art of sword fighting, you can probably imagine how unpleasant this would be for you."

She was about to say that taking a few punches from him was a price she was more than willing to pay to be able to heal her companion and stand true to her principles, but Enric's low moan stopped her. He was still sitting on the ground, but his glacial stare was no less effective because of it.

"If you so much as lay a hand on her, I shall give you an even better reason for making me pay for being disobedient. Here, in front of the assembled people. How will your standing be influenced if your second-in-command publicly defies you just after having been dealt a pasting, I ask you?"

Lord Tyront returned the stare, but with fire instead of ice in it. After a while he nodded slowly while letting his hand sink from the sword hilt. "Very well. I see where we are standing. I am beginning to think that your going away from here for some time is not such a bad idea, after all. Get your head clear again, remember where your loyalties lie."

Enric tightened his lips, holding back the comment that he knew exactly where his loyalties lay and that he had no intention of realigning them to the Order's preferences. But saying this out loud would be to no avail and only serve to heat up the current conflict.

Tyront turned towards Eryn. "You! I will see you in my study in two hours. Alone," he added with a sideways glance at Enric. "That should give you enough time to cool your temper and get into a cooperative and reasonable state of mind. There are things we need to discuss." He smiled coldly. "You are to be the new number two soon enough, after all." With this he turned and walked away towards the Palace.

Eryn stared after him, then her gaze returned to Enric.

"Why do I have the unsettling feeling that things in the Order are not running very smoothly and that we are on the verge of some kind of escalation?" She frowned, then looked down at him pointedly. "And how could I have been promoted to *your* position?"

He looked away. That little detail he had not yet mentioned to her. She would not like it.

"Because the King has decided to release me from the Order for the duration of our stay in Takhan, since serving two different governing councils would constitute a conflict of interest."

"You are to be excluded from the Order?" she cried. Her thoughts raced. Obviously that was not what they intended with her, as Lord Tyront had just announced that she was to be the second-in-command then.

"So I am to remain in the Order while you are freed from it?" The thought was so absurd that her first impulse was to laugh it off. But it was soon overshadowed by dread. She would be caught in the Order alone, without him to protect her. That was not good, not at all.

"Only until we return. As soon as we get back, I will resume my former position. You will only be second as long as we are away," he tried to reassure her.

"What sort of sense does *that* make? How can I take up a position of second-in-command without even being in the country?"

"It's a matter of keeping up appearances," Orrin's voice supplied from behind her. She turned her head, surprised. She hadn't realised that he had joined them.

She rubbed her face. So much to consider. But there was one thing she wanted to know first.

"What did you do to him? Why did this spectacle take place here?"

"First, he ordered me not to see the King alone. I went nevertheless. With Orrin accompanying me," Enric explained tiredly and carefully climbed back on to his feet, clasping Orrin's shoulder for balance.

Eryn folded her arms and glowered at him. "You are not serious, are you? And you had the nerve to threaten *me* with consequences for insubordination only a few hours ago? Honestly, if you weren't bruised and battered already, I would give you a solid beating myself here and now." She turned on her heel, muttering under her breath while walking away with long, angry strides.

Enric exhaled slowly. "What a day. Is there currently anybody who is not irritated at me in this Kingdom?"

Orrin thought for a moment, then said, "No, none that I can think of. You were very thorough. As with everything else you do."

Enric sighed. "She has even stomped off without healing me first, and that after defying Tyront because he forbade it. I suppose I will have to take care of the broken leg myself somehow. How about you?"

"A broken rib and my nose hurts, but nothing major."

They turned and saw Vern and Pe'tala walking towards them. The crowd was beginning to break up and disperse now that the entertainment was over.

Vern wordlessly stretched out his hand for his father to take, his face was still pale, his lips held together. Orrin grabbed his son's fingers and squeezed them, instantly feeling the magic that was released into his body to check the damage. The boy closed his eyes for better concentration.

Pe'tala turned towards Enric.

"How about you, plucky fighter? Do you require some healing as well? It seems you managed to annoy Eryn enough to rush off without even fixing you up first."

Enric shrugged. "If you are offering it, I won't turn you down. I have read about mending bones, but practical application is something different, I think. And in my state..."

She smiled and took his hand. "Do you want a thorough check or just having the broken leg taken care of? I assume it *is* your leg, judging from your stance?"

He nodded. "Yes. The leg will be enough for now. Should there be any other trouble I hope I will manage to have Eryn heal it soon."

"You think my *big sister* will be annoyed if she finds that you were treated by me?"

"No, not exactly. But as she is annoyed at me right now I would employ any remaining injury that doesn't stop me from walking painlessly to make her take pity on me," he smiled.

That made her laugh. "All-powerful Lord Enric has to resort to pity to make his companion forgive him? How unexpected. Not the kind of method I would have suspected as working on an Aren woman. I thought they had to be either begged for mercy or dominated into acquiescence."

He chuckled. "So I seem more the dominating than the begging kind to you?" He watched her close her eyes as warm magic flowed into his hand and followed the outline of his arm up to his shoulder and back down towards the broken leg.

She smiled. "As befits an Aren man, especially one having been granted the privilege to be adopted into the family. They are not usually the adoptive kind. They do believe in bloodlines."

"Yes," he commented dryly and thought about the prearranged commitment between Eryn and Ram'an. "I noticed."

She remained silent while she knitted back together his broken tibia, then opened her eyes again and released his hand.

"Thank you," Enric said and nodded to her.

"It was my pleasure," she shrugged. "Is there any chance that you could tell me why you received this public thrashing?"

He shook his head. "Not at this point, no. But what I can tell you is that we will be joining you in Takhan not long after you have left here."

She raised both eyebrows in surprise. "Will you now. How interesting. Especially as I am currently considering prolonging my stay here."

Enric felt a smile tug at his lips. "Indeed? That would be very fortunate for the clinic."

Pe'tala grinned. "Also for your companion and myself, I would say. We would be rid of each other again."

"You know," he said slowly, "I am rather beginning to think that this is a downside."

She wrinkled her nose in disgust. "You are not implying that we are starting to like each other, are you? That thought is appalling." Turning on her heel, she marched off, leaving the three men looking after her.

"They are more alike than they would care to hear," Orrin commented.

Enric nodded. "Yes. And the nice thing is that Eryn will be less troubled about going to Takhan if she knows that the clinic will be in Pe'tala's hands for the duration of our stay. They may not like each other, but they can't help respecting each other professionally."

"And our stay in Takhan will probably be a lot more relaxed without having both of them and Malriel around us," Orrin said.

Enric exhaled. "Yes, there is that."

CHAPTER 23

Mending Fences

Eryn stood in front of the door to Lord Tyront's quarters and stared at the dark wood. The prospect of meeting him was not exactly a pleasant one after what had gone on in the afternoon. And yet she didn't have any choice but to follow the order. Enric had impressed that on her when she had wanted to stay at home instead. He had also tried to make her wear her robes, but she had refused outright and told him that if he insisted on making her put them on, she would get rid of them as soon as she was out the door. He had finally relented and decided to be content with her going there at all.

She moved her head in circles a few times to loosen her neck muscles and then lifted her fist and knocked at the door. Vyril opened it with a tense smile. So she had obviously been informed of what had happened that afternoon.

"Lady Eryn, how nice to see you. Come in, you are already expected."

Eryn followed her to Lord Tyront's study and entered through the open door without knocking. She saw him perched in his large chair, appearing transformed again from the victorious swordsman of earlier, and walked on until she stood directly in front of his heavy desk.

"Here I am," she announced calmly, deliberately avoiding the customary bow she owed him.

She heard the door being closed behind her and continued to stare at Lord Tyront, who regarded her intently with pursed lips.

"Yes, that I can see. I was curious whether you would come. But then Enric wouldn't let you ignore my direct order, would he? No matter how incensed with me he is right now."

She waited for him to go on and tell her what exactly he wanted to talk about. Or first offer her a seat, for that matter. Or was it to be such a short conversation that sitting down wouldn't be necessary? That would be the most pleasant option, of course, if not the most likely one.

"Why don't you have a seat, Lady Eryn?"

She smiled faintly. "Why don't you tell me what *you* want from me and then I'll decide if sitting is what *I* want?"

She spun around when she heard a low laugh from the direction of the door and sucked in a shocked breath. The King was leaning against the wall next to the door, his calm gaze locked onto hers. So it was not Vyril who had closed the door behind her, as she had assumed. It had been him.

"I admit it amuses me to see that I do not seem to be the only one you delight with your bold manner," he said in that clear and clipped way of talking he had.

Eryn turned back to her superior and gave him a murderous look. "After all that happened you dare to play a trick like that on me?" she hissed and turned without waiting for his reply to stomp back out the door. The King watched her with interest walking in his direction, making no move. She cursed when she saw the faint sparkle of a magical barrier in front of the door and stopped abruptly to avoid bumping into it. She stepped to one side to have both men in her field of vision.

"I am sick of being pushed around, locked in, manipulated, tricked, used, punished and forced by you! I am sick of you *both*!" she snarled. "Why can't you just let me be? What have I ever done to either of you?" She felt the bookshelves in her back and fought to get her composure back. Being hysterical wouldn't help, it just made her seem weak and pitiful.

Lord Tyront got up and rounded his desk slowly, perching on the edge of his desk. She let her suspicious gaze switch back and forth between the two men, reluctant to leave either one out of her sight.

"Eryn," the magician said softly, "there is no need to be afraid. I have asked you to come here so we can talk about the things that have happened. Also about what is to happen in the future."

"Well, *Tyront*," she emphasised the name unadorned by his title, wanting to show him how little she cared for his attempt at being familiar with her, "I would say there would have been better moments to choose for a conversation such as this than after your performance in the arena today. As for surprising me with this particular guest," she nodded at the King, "let's just say it does not exactly serve to strengthen my trust in you."

He regarded her calmly, showing no sign of annoyance at her foregoing his title without his invitation to do so. "I see how neither of these circumstances has exactly helped you to relax, but let me reassure you that you are safe here. His Majesty has accomplished what he needed, and you must be aware that you have nothing to fear from *me*."

"Apart from being disciplined with a sword instead of a shovel, you mean?" she lobbed back, referring to his threat of only two hours ago.

"A threat I did not carry through, if I may remind you," he replied gently. "Despite your intention to ignore a direct order."

Eryn folded her arms and leaned against the bookshelf in her back. "Alright. What do you need from me?"

"Your help."

Her eyes bulged and her brow furrowed. "*What*?"

Now the King pushed himself away from the wall and walked towards the magician's desk, very likely to ease the impression of her being trapped between the two of them. "Recent events, my dear Lady Eryn, have had a rather detrimental effect on the Order's stability," he said carefully.

"Recent events?" she asked, her voice loaded with faux innocence.

King Folrin smiled at her attempt to make him uneasy. "Our kiss."

"Your kiss," she amended tensely. "I don't remember participating in it."

"My kiss, then," he agreed. "In hindsight this provocation turned out to be rather more effective than I had hoped. Lord Enric is not only leaving both the Order and the Kingdom behind with a measure of enthusiasm, we even fear that he might decide not to return if he does not regain the impression that Anyueel is a safe place for you."

She ground her teeth. "And you approach *me* of all people about that? What in the world makes you think that *I* could consider this a safe place after all that has happened to me here? You are keeping me barricaded in here as we speak!"

Lord Tyront let the barrier at the door melt away, and lifted a questioning eyebrow at her. "Better?"

She nodded slowly. It would hardly make much of a difference. If she tried to leave again, the shield would fly up again in no time. And yet the atmosphere in the room seemed different. Breathing suddenly became easier than before.

"So what you want me to do is to convince Enric to return here?" she enquired. "What exactly makes you think that I could be capable of doing that? It's not like he was listening to me when I told him that I did not, under any circumstances, want to go to Takhan. And why would I even want to? I was serious when I told you before that I am not happy about the way you treat me! What makes you think that asking me for my cooperation might be a fruitful course of action?"

The King gave a hint of a smile. "Because I have come to know you somewhat in the short time you have spent with us here in the city. I would not mark you as a person who feels comfortable knowing that you are the reason for considerable tensions and disadvantages for both countries. Yet this would definitely be the consequence if they allowed you to stay against my own and the Order's wishes. As for your first concern, let me tell you that your influence on Lord Enric is greater than you give yourself credit for," the King explained. "If he was to see that you and I agree on a truce and that you and Lord Tyront manage to get along amiably, he would almost certainly consider relocating the less attractive option. You would have to leave close friends behind, after all. Not to mention admirable accomplishments, such as the clinic and the orphanage. Would you be able to accomplish as much in Takhan, Lady Eryn? Would they benefit from your efforts as much as we have? Think of everything you have achieved here. Would you want to leave all this behind?"

She intensified her gaze at him. "Are you trying to manipulate me through flattery?"

The monarch smiled lopsidedly. "Not if it doesn't work, no. Maybe I could offer you something more to your liking. To provide a basis for the motivation you seem to find hard to come up with at the moment."

She sighed. "And now you are trying to bribe me? Seriously?"

"Bribing you? The companion of the man who is about to rise to the top of the list of the richest people in the Kingdom?" the King called out in feigned astonishment. "What good would that do me, my dear Lady Eryn?"

"Pity," she smiled without humour. "I was hoping for you to try and propitiate me with offering me the position of Head of Healers."

Lord Tyront spoke up. "No, this is not something we can do. And the current situation with your forthcoming stay in Takhan should demonstrate why it never was a good idea in the first place. But I remember giving you the Council's reasons for choosing somebody else for this position."

"I was not exactly in a receptive state of mind towards the end of that particular Council meeting," she replied acidly. Not with Vern's little trick at keeping her from lashing out.

"Your unconventional approach to solving problems and making new discoveries does not make assigning you to only one discipline a very wise move. We want you to divide your efforts in accordance with what is needed. And your interests, of course."

Eryn raised her brow at him. "My primary field of interest is healing, as you are surely aware."

"Not according to your testing in Takhan, unless I am very much mistaken," the King tossed in. "You were tested for the rare class of explorer. And with an exceptionally high score, too. From what I was told this usually does provide for a more interdisciplinary range of interests."

She glared at him, dismayed. So he had already managed to establish a halfway decent information network on the other side of the sea. How intensely annoying. That meant that he would have an eye on them while they were staying in Takhan.

"You will be gone for several months," Lord Tyront then continued. "The clinic needs somebody in charge who is available not only intermittently, but permanently. As you will be taking your seat in the Council after your return..."

"My what?" she interrupted him. "I have no intention of taking a seat in the Council! I don't remember agreeing to that!"

"It's what your rank entitles you to," the magician explained patiently. "Moreover, I would not disregard the seat too readily. It is a chance to influence our processes: a vote."

"Is it? Considering the way many of the Council members regard me - namely as a nuisance, a disturbance - I don't see much chance of achieving so much with my participation." She flashed the King a look. "I was once even described as an element disruptive to the Order's values."

"Not the Order's values, Lady Eryn," the King rebuked mildly, "but to how I need people to envision the Order. Though when it comes to issues you wish to be discussed and voted on in the Council," he smiled, "there is always the option of a Royal Recommendation. The Council hardly ever votes against those."

Eryn stared at him. "Are you offering to give backing to my motions?"

The King wagged his head. "Just let us say that there would be some change of perception in order. Being seen to support you too much would not look good for me. However, we might agree to have me put in a Recommendation every now and then before it is known openly that you are in favour of it. Only if I see your ideas as sensible, that is," he added.

She nodded slowly. That did not sound too shabby.

The King regarded her for several moments with raised eyebrows as if waiting for something, then sighed disappointedly.

"Nothing at all you would like to say, then, Lady Eryn?" he enquired.

She looked at him in despair. "What do you want to hear? A heartfelt promise that I will do whatever I can to make Enric return here with me?"

"We just told you how much we depend on you," he said pointedly. "So there is nothing that comes to your mind with regard to this?"

Eryn blinked. What did he want from her? Some kind of commitment? A pledge to come back? She had no intention of putting words to anything of that kind. She saw a small smile on Lord Tyront's lips.

The King shook his head. "This lack of opportunistic attitude in you causes me some frustration. I decree that you are to be given another ten lessons in political strategy before your departure."

She gulped. Oh no.

"You showed such promise in the past, but I can see that applying the principles of the game does not yet come naturally to you. We need to work on that, my dear Lady. There might be challenges to face in the Western Territories that would require a certain awareness of your own interests and how to protect them."

"What?" she protested. "Lack of opportunistic attitude? Are you telling me, that because I didn't try to extort you for what I wanted just now, I am to be trained to be more reckless and demanding in the future?" Was he completely cracked? Why was he trying to make her act to his own disadvantage?

"That would be another way of putting it, yes," he admitted.

She folded her arms and raised an eyebrow at him. "Another stack of books to read for me? I don't remember learning very many useful things that way."

"True," the King nodded. "That is why you are going to be coached by somebody with considerable expertise and experience in that area: myself."

"You," she said, deadpan. "I am not sure if you are aware of Enric's... consternation concerning your little method to make him go to Takhan, but I must tell you that he will not take the news of your spending any time at all with me very well," she explained carefully, sending him a look that clearly conveyed that she herself was not in favour of this new plan, either. "And from what you said before I was of the impression that you wanted to motivate Enric to return here, not provoke him to consider the opposite the more attractive alternative."

"Let me assure you that I am fully aware of your companion's disapproval. A hand clasping one's throat tends to get the message across quite explicitly," he remarked dryly.

Eryn stared at him, not sure if she had understood him correctly just now. Enric had done *what*? And the King had put up with it just like that?

"Thus I will permit an additional person, of his choice, to join us on these occasions," the King continued. "Not that this would be necessary, as I imagine that you would hardly comply with another command not to use magic against me a second time to protect yourself should you feel that I came too close to you. But I am more than willing to make this concession to his urge to protect you."

"Is there any chance for me to turn this down? Or request somebody else to coach me? With all due respect," she added hastily.

"None at all," he said simply.

"I don't like this," she growled.

"This is of no consequence to me. You will comply with my order. We are to meet once a week, starting tomorrow following your work at the clinic. I expect you and whoever your chosen chaperone is to be in the throne room. On no account be late. I have not much tolerance for being kept waiting," he warned her, and then walked towards the study door without waiting for her reply. "She is all yours now, Lord Tyront," he spoke and left.

"Why don't you take a seat, Eryn?"

"No, thank you, *Tyront*, I prefer to stand," she replied in an offhand manner. "Why don't you tell me what you want from me so I can return to my companion who has obviously broken quite a few important rules on my account today."

He nodded slowly. "As you wish."

She noticed that he raised a soundproof barrier around them before going on. "You should make use of the lessons the King wishes you to undertake with him, however little you may appreciate the prospect right now," he said urgently. "You have become a potent weapon to employ against Enric, and we need you to be more aware of this and, we hope, learn how to counteract any attempts at ensnaring you. Enric was for a very long time as good as impossible to control, bribe, coerce or manipulate, so the King is using his chance at doing so to the full, as you must be aware."

She shook her head in confusion. "Why then would he be interested in teaching me how to counteract this? This would work against his advantage!"

"He wouldn't do it if he didn't expect more benefits than drawbacks from instructing you in political strategy. Using you against Enric in the future has become too risky for the King, so he has to make sure nobody else is able to use you either. An advantage Enric will recognise and appreciate at once. Even though he will not be thrilled at King Folrin being the one to be teaching you. But then I expect that he himself will be there as your chaperone for at least the first few lessons." His expression became determined. "What you must do is accept this order without any attempt to gainsay it. It might provoke Enric to act against his own interests just to make you happy. There is no way around your having to endure these ten sessions with the King, however uncomfortable they may turn out to be. You may safely depend on his not overstepping any more boundaries with you, especially with you retaining possession of your full powers and with a witness willing to protect you."

She considered his words, then nodded reluctantly. He was right, of course. There was no other sensible course of action.

"Will you be trying to make up again with Enric before we leave for Takhan?" she asked.

"I have to. He is my second-in-command. I need him on my side."

"Has the King ordered you to do so?"

Lord Tyront smiled thinly. "He has, yes. He is afraid of the Order disintegrating, being divided into those who stand with you, Enric and healing, and the rest. In any case, I would have recognised the necessity to make amends so even without being told to. Enric has been my friend for quite some time now; not managing our friendship properly would lose me more than a reliable right hand."

"So your treating me well would make reconciliation with Enric easier for you," she pointed out. "Which means I am once more being used as a tool to make him do what you desire."

"Not a tool, Eryn. A powerful factor that must be taken into consideration. The King is right on this. You must learn to seize that power that is the consequence of Enric's considerable attachment to you. Or others will do so instead."

"And this powerful factor you are trying to use for your own benefit right now. Is omitting my title when addressing me part of that? Is this meant to make me like you because you know that I am not a great fan of being called *Lady* Eryn?"

He chuckled. "Yes to all of that. Though please do not be indignant as your first reaction, but think about the possible merits for yourself."

"Such as?" she enquired without much enthusiasm.

"Such as being seen to be on familiar terms with a powerful man such as I. There are not many people in this Kingdom who are permitted to forego my title when addressing me. You are one of only a selected few to be accorded that privilege," he explained calmly. "It will make quite a lot of people very eager to avoid having you against them as the consequence might be the risk of annoying *me*."

She sighed wearily. "So we are basically using each other."

"I prefer considering it an alliance for mutual benefit," he corrected her. "And in my case there is also the conviction that the two us finally starting to work *with* instead of *against* each other will also benefit the Order as a whole. And the Kingdom, for that matter, as your efforts are aimed at helping the people."

Eryn closed her eyes for a moment when a slight dizziness befell her. "I need air," she murmured and a moment later felt fresh, cool air around her after the barrier had been removed.

"Go home now," he told her. "Talk to Enric. And listen to him carefully. The King is probably one of the most skilful players in this game, but he is not the only one you might glean something useful from."

She nodded once and turned to leave. Yes, talking to Enric was exactly what she had to do. But there was somebody else she wanted to see first.

* * *

Erbál raised his brow in surprise when he opened the door and found himself facing Eryn. "Lady Eryn! What an unexpected pleasure," he smiled then and stepped aside for her to enter. "Do come in."

She smiled knowingly and entered his quarters. "Unexpected. That is what I use instead of *unwelcome* when I need to be diplomatic."

He took her hand and kissed it in the style of his home country. "A beautiful woman at my doorstep could never be unwelcome to me."

"Smooth," she nodded appreciatively. "But that is not what I require of you right now."

He looked puzzled. "Really? I am not entirely sure which impulse is the stronger right now: the one making me hope that you are about to make me a salacious offer or the one that makes me shiver when I think of the consequences your companion would make me face."

She rolled her eyes and removed her hand from his. "None of that. In his current mood you would probably not survive his revenge." She folded her arms and looked at him thoughtfully. "You are cunning, sly and manipulative."

Erbál chuckled and turned to a wooden chest she instantly recognised as a container for liquor. "I think this kind of conversation needs to be eased with something to drink."

Eryn watched him carefully take out two gold-rimmed glasses and then uncork a bottle. He then nodded towards a sofa and followed her with the glasses in one hand and the bottle in the other.

"I see you don't have the usual sitting arrangement. No reorganising your room to make yourself feel more at home? Or have you come to prefer our local furniture?"

He shrugged and took a seat, putting the glassware on the table. "I do not see much sense in holding on to habits from my home when I intend to stay here for some time. Adapting should turn out more useful than trying to pretend that I am still at home as soon as I close my door behind me." He poured their drinks and handed her a glass. "To my less flattering character traits that have yet brought you to my doorstep."

They clinked their glasses and took a sip.

"How may I be of service to you? I assume that your visit is not a purely social one."

She licked a drop of the sweet, thick, heavy wine from her lower lip and leaned back. "People here like to practise something we like to call *political strategy*."

He nodded. "I know. It is the art of manipulating others into acting in accordance with your wishes without the necessity of bringing force to bear. Well, in most cases no force is used as I understand it. As you should be aware, this way of dealing with others is also common in Takhan, even though we have not yet seen fit to elevate it to an official discipline being taught to our young people."

Yes, she thought, she had experienced at first hand Malriel's and Ram'an's manipulations during her stay in Takhan. "I have since the time that I was brought here found myself both the target of intrigues and their agent. This has at times led to considerable... inconvenience." She played with the stem of her glass, twirling it between her thumb and forefinger. "I was only very recently employed as an agent against Enric. Again. As I still don't understand everything that is going on, I wish to do something about that, but not just in the way the King sees fit. I have become a liability to Enric, a dangerous weapon to be used against him because I don't know how to see through manipulation attempts or to counteract them."

"And you want me to...?" he prompted.

"I want you to help me stand my ground in these last few months until I leave for Takhan. I want you to help me understand and advise me how to act, help me interpret the forces that are influencing events around me."

He regarded her curiously. "You are aware that this would require sharing a lot of personal information with me. Is this a wise course of action for you, Lady Eryn?"

She snorted. "Why not? It simply saves you the trouble of buying such information from spies. I have no doubt whatsoever that many of the things I will tell you would not remain unknown to you for very long, anyway."

"On account of my being cunning, sly and manipulative?"

"Quite," she nodded with conviction. "Though I have to warn you that I will skin you alive if you dare to use anything I tell you against me in any way. This includes passing it on to Malriel or anyone. I can tell you honestly that having me, and therefore my companion, on your side will turn out to be a lot more beneficial than opposing us."

"Duly noted," he smiled unperturbed. "Why have you come to *me* with that particular concern? Why not to Lord Enric, who has ample experience in that field? I am sure he would be more than willing to oblige you."

She raised her brow at him. "Your smug smile informs me that you think you have the answer to that already."

He chortled. "I dare say I do, yes. I want to know if *you* do as well. If coming to me was a matter of intuition or the result of careful thinking."

"What would you prefer?"

"Neither. Whatever your reason was, developing the other aspect will then be important. The most effective way to determine a course of action is having a good feeling and then applying reason to see if it really is the best alternative. Go on, tell me what brought you here."

"Thinking. Even the King thinks I need more coaching, and he is the one using me essentially to make Enric do what he wants. He decided to invite me to see him once a week and improve my skills. However, I can't trust him. Since Enric is emotionally involved whenever it comes down to me, I am not sure if he always thinks clearly these days. He lets himself be provoked. You are used to partaking in gaming yourself. And you are not against me, at least from what I can tell. You hope for my assistance in getting the position as ambassador, after all. My approval does seem to play a pivotal role."

"I see. Valid reasons," he said approvingly. "You are smart, but as you are more often than not a victim to your impulses, your ability to analyse and think does not help you very much when you come under pressure. The trick is to practise assessing situations until such a thing comes so naturally that it seems like another form of perception," he explained.

She looked at him despairingly. "I was pushed into this whole world of intrigues and politics only recently. My life before that was uneventful compared to this here. People left me more or less alone unless they needed my help. And then they made sure to pay and avoid annoying me. I am starting to adapt, but slowly. I am struggling with these people here. I was raised to say what I think and act in accordance with my principles. This has not exactly served me well in recent months."

"Yet you are doing very well from what I can tell," Erbál replied. "You have been the mover of quite a few changes in the Old Kingdom from what I was told. And in the Order - which is probably a most remarkable accomplishment, judging from the dusty, conservative members of the Magic Council that I have met so far. But you are right - you should work on your ability to assert yourself." He took another sip from his glass. "What was it that brought you here at this particular time? Something has happened, has it not? Something in connection with why you are not exactly on friendly terms with the King right now, I would imagine. Was it something he did that you did not approve of?" He thought for a moment. "Something which has some bearing on how you are being made to go to Takhan again," he speculated and raised his brow questioningly.

Eryn nodded slowly. He really was competent at this. She had come to the right place, it seemed.

"He forced a kiss on me to compel Enric to take me away from here, save me from being bothered by him again," she told him hesitantly.

Erbál pursed his lips. He didn't appear overly shocked by that piece of news. "Not entirely unexpected," he commented. "Malriel told me that he is attracted to you. Choosing this course of action is a sure way to make Lord Enric comply with his wishes and at the same time do something about his own frustration with you and the distance he is supposed to keep from you. Though I think he is very much aware that he cannot get that close to you again without risking escalation."

"From what the King and Lord Tyront told me tonight they are afraid that this escalation might happen anyway, that he could decide to stay in Takhan for good. They want me to convince Enric to return here again after Malriel is back from her peacekeeping mission. What I don't understand is why the King wants me to be more aware of the danger of being manipulated. He has done the same himself in the past, so this would also be a drawback for him. Lord Tyront thinks he will stop using me against Enric from now on and wants to make sure nobody else can. I don't really believe that. Not using me against Enric doesn't mean that he can't use me at all for his purposes."

"But not having you used against himself is the more powerful objective here," Erbál pointed out. "I honestly believe that he will not stop manipulating you. He just makes it more interesting for himself. He is a player, and a very able and confident one. Coaching you in the art of seeing through other people's attempts does not necessarily mean that you will be in a position to withstand *his* attempts anytime soon. Maybe not even in a long time. He is making things more interesting for himself, improving your skills to build you up into more of a challenge."

She scowled. "So he wants to transform me into a more amusing plaything than before?"

"With the added benefit of protecting himself from having you and Lord Enric used against him by others," he reminded her. "Do not let this bother you too much. It is for your own good as well, after all. I am sure coming to me is a first step towards making his playing you harder in the future. I can assist you."

"In exchange for what?" she enquired calmly.

"For having a powerful ally in you when I need one. I am relatively vulnerable here, especially as I am neither a magician nor currently anybody of importance as assistant to an ambassador who regularly manages to antagonise the mighty, rich and powerful."

"Alright," she smiled. "I can be that. How do we do this? Weekly meetings as I have with the King?"

He shook his head. "No. I am not a great friend of routine when reacting to circumstances is the more sensible course. You will come to me whenever you learn of something you cannot quite comprehend, something that puzzles or nags you. Be aware of everything that triggers a strong emotion in you. Emotions are the easiest way to steer people. You should take advantage of these lessons with the King. Take liberties you would not normally take by asking him about his motivation for past actions. He will not mind but instead welcome your enthusiasm."

"Do you think he will answer me honestly if I do?"

"Probably not every time, but you might also learn something from the things he does *not* disclose," Erbál explained.

"He has allowed one additional person to be present when we have our little lessons. I'll make sure to bring somebody who is at least a little experienced in the discipline."

He smiled. "I do not think that you will have much of a say in that, my dear. I dare say Lord Enric has very definite views on who he wants to be with you there: himself."

She nodded. "Yes, that is very likely. I would try to persuade him to let you accompany me every now and then, but I suppose it is not too smart to let the King know that we are seeing each other so frequently."

Erbál smiled patiently. "I would not worry about that too much, my dear Lady. I am virtually certain that he will know it anyway. His information network is very thorough."

"I will talk to Enric now. He doesn't know about my forthcoming lessons with the King yet. He will not be overjoyed," she sighed and got up. "Thank you for the wine. And for your help."

"It is my pleasure, Lady Eryn." He bowed his head to her.

"Eryn to you. Make sure to address me like that in public," she smiled. "I am told that this lends a person more importance when they are seen to be on friendly terms with a high-ranking magician."

"Does it?" He thought for a moment, then smiled. "The one telling you this does not happen to be Lord Tyront, who is trying to mend fences with your companion by making you more well-disposed towards himself?"

Eryn smiled despite herself. "You are really good at this, aren't you?"

He shrugged. "That is why you came to me."

"True enough, I just had no idea that you are that good."

"What is a modest man to say to that?" he smiled.

She smirked. "Why would *that* be a concern of yours?"

He laughed when she closed the door to the Palace corridors behind her.

CHAPTER 24

Royal Instructions

Enric waited in Eryn's study at the clinic, leaning back in her chair, wondering how she could find that thing even remotely comfortable. He thought briefly about surprising her with a more luxurious model, but quickly dismissed that idea. If she came here and found that he had exchanged her trusty furniture she would probably see it as unwelcome interference instead of the gesture it was meant as.

They had been together for almost exactly ten months now, and he wondered if it was normal that there still were things about him she didn't understand, intentions she misinterpreted. He wondered about the extent of her trust in him. It was not that he worried about her holding back on purpose. Joining in the third level bond with him was a really good sign that she trusted him as much as she was able to. But there was probably still a certain degree of healing necessary until she could feel completely comfortable with being more or less in his hands. Of course him making her do things she was opposed to did not exactly help that process along.

When she told him about her conversation with Tyront and the King the evening before, he had not been too surprised. He had expected some kind of attempt at reconciliation, and soon, too. It was too risky for them to let him depart for Takhan in his current state of mind. Approaching Eryn was the logical choice. She was easier material to work with than him, and they knew well enough that making her happy would in the end mellow him as well. If they were convincing enough, that is.

What had surprised him was that she had sought Erbál's assistance. He had tried not to be annoyed at that. In vain. She had explained to him that she needed somebody whose interests she could trust to be selfish enough to help her in exchange for her good word on his behalf. That had cut. When he had wanted to know why his own intentions were not to be trusted, she had just folded her arms and given him a pointed look as if the answer was self-evident.

He appreciated her openness, though. Not that he would have tolerated anything else, but it was reassuring to see that she had obviously overcome her reluctance about sharing important details with him. That was a considerable step in the right direction, in his book.

The door opened and in she walked. She stopped for a moment when she beheld him sitting in her chair, then sighed and shut the door again behind her.

"You know, I wonder how you would react if you came into your study and found me sitting in *your* chair. That is a bit territorial, if you know what I mean. Like demonstrating that you are in charge wherever you go. Even in places where you are not."

He smiled. "But I *am* most of the time. Unless I am in Tyront's or the King's presence, of course."

She rolled her eyes. "You disobeyed one and started to throttle the other. My being a touch disrespectful at times does seem harmless by comparison. Yet I don't see *you* shovelling horse manure or teaching children for a change."

"I was punished in a rather more physical way, if I may remind you," he remarked pointedly.

"That was over in a matter of minutes. Cleaning the stables entails getting up really early, doing smelly work and last time it also included being mocked by the dark-haired sisters of doom. Over five days. And I had to teach the boys for two entire months! Do tell me again why you were the one being dealt with more severely?"

"My chastisement was aimed at breaking my pride," he commented.

"So is mine, usually," she shrugged. "Only *my* pride can't be cracked by a minor thing like that. My father told me that nobody else can debase you, only you yourself."

He nodded approvingly. "A lesson well internalised, as I can see. Unfortunately for you, Tyront has by now almost certainly worked out that the only thing that bothers you about it is getting up early. This means I can only repeat my warning about provoking him."

She grinned. "Oh, I wouldn't. Not now that we are to become great chums."

"That is something I will only believe when I see it with my very own eyes. Speaking of teaching the boys, today was your last time with Orrin's class, wasn't it? I was rather surprised there was only one complaint about you with regard to your using the shield that one time."

"What can I say? It was obviously a well-chosen example I set. The rest of them were too afraid to provoke me after that." She grinned. "I bet they are more than glad to be rid of me now. Though I have to admit that it was not as demanding as I had anticipated. And

I even learned a thing or two. Such as how my healers sometimes tend to show the same behaviour no matter what their age. I don't know how often I had to point out to Lord Poron that he is not supposed to talk to his colleagues during class, no matter if his thoughts on the topic at hand seem more relevant to him than what I have to say."

"The trials of teaching. I admit I have never found that profession particularly attractive. And listening to you confirms that assessment." He rose from her chair and rounded her desk. "Which brings me to my reason of turning up here. Are you ready for our appointment with the King? It seems he enjoys teaching you more than I appreciate. He doesn't seem able to get enough of it," he concluded with a sour expression.

Eryn grimaced. "As ready as I am ever going to be, I would say."

He lifted her chin to kiss her mouth. "I will be there with you. No need to worry."

She had a sinking feeling; that he was with her was probably more reason to worry. She had tried to persuade him to let Orrin, Vern or Erbál accompany her today, though she had been aware from the start that his agreeing to such a thing was fairly unlikely. True enough, he was adamant. So she had to rely on the King's not doing or saying anything inappropriate and Enric's keeping his composure to avoid escalating the current tense impasse between them. Superb.

"You will behave, won't you?" she enquired as she let him fasten her cloak around her shoulders.

"I will if he will," he replied matter-of-factly and took her hand to walk out with her.

"You know, you could be the older and wiser one here," she suggested. "Demonstrating your superior command over your impulses. Something you keep telling me I need to learn myself."

"I play the part of the older and wiser one with you already. I don't feel any particular wish to assume that role with the King for now. I doubt he would thank me for it. It might seem that I consider him young and unwise. And I *am* in control of my impulses, my love. Actually, if I do anything to him, it will not be due to lack of control but a well-considered course of action."

Exasperated, she let herself be pulled out onto the wet streets and towards the Palace. "That is not at all reassuring, you know." Especially not when she recalled how his last meeting with the King had gone only the day before.

"Well, it is all I can offer for now."

They turned the corner into Kingsway.

"I want you to tread carefully with him. He has a way of knowing things and getting you to tell him what he doesn't know before you are aware of it. I can't exactly interfere, but I will try to use the mind bond to warn you in case the direction of your conversation warrants particular guardedness."

She looked up at him in surprise. "How? Don't tell me you can conjure up a strong feeling of unease or worry on command?"

"Honestly, I will be uneasy enough with you and him in the same room. The only thing I will need to do is to lower the mind shield to let you feel it."

She nodded. That did sound like a viable plan. In the distance she could already see the Palace gates with the regular two guards on duty.

They walked on in silence, hand in hand, passing the gate and walking along the corridors towards the throne room.

The guards in front of the double doors had obviously been briefed to admit them without any ceremony and to let them enter without even announcing them.

Eryn looked over to the throne, but it was empty. Then her eyes darted across to the other end of the large hall, and there he was. He was standing in front of a medium sized table with twelve chairs around it, watching them enter, his expression placid, waiting until they had walked towards him and bowed.

"Lady Eryn," he smiled. "And Lord Enric. Your presence is not entirely unexpected."

Enric smiled back frostily. "I had not assumed that it would be," he replied.

The King indicated a chair for Eryn to sit in, then cleared his throat. "Lord Enric, I would ask you to sit a little further away. I would like to keep the distraction your presence might at times cause to a minimum. This includes keeping your emotions shielded."

"As you wish, Your Majesty," Enric replied and took a seat at the other end of the table. The King pulled out the chair for Eryn and took a seat at the head end of the table right next to her.

She willed herself to relax. And cooperate. Resisting him would just prolong this unnecessarily. And cause him to take measures that would probably provoke Enric.

"Tell me why you think you are here today, Lady Eryn. Why I insist on coaching you in this discipline myself instead of delegating it to another," the King began.

"Because you took offence at my not coercing you yesterday when you told me you needed my help. And you doubtlessly consider yourself the expert in manipulation and trickery, something which is not entirely unjustified judging from my past experiences with you," she responded pertly and regretted her tone instantly. "You seem to object to my lack of skill," she went on more cool-headedly. "Because you don't want others to find me such easy prey and use me against you."

He nodded. "True. All of it. Though I do not warm to your tone," he chided her in a calm voice.

"I apologise," she replied at once.

"Accepted. Let us start with Malriel's agenda. Why do you think she went to bed with me?" the King asked.

Eryn swallowed. This was something she had no wish of talking to him about. But it seemed that she didn't have much of a choice.

"To enjoy your undoubtedly honed skills as a sexual partner?" she ventured.

He chuckled in a low voice. "I wish I could believe that, my dear Lady, though I doubt that rumours of my accomplishments in that area have managed to find their way to Takhan as yet. Try again without such transparent attempts at flattering me."

So much for that, she thought and tried again. "She was aiming at having a favour granted by you. As well as following her penchant for young lovers. I dare say a foreign King is quite a feather in her cap."

"Much better, yes," he agreed. "So I am confident that you can imagine what that favour might have been."

"Permitting Enric to go to Takhan. Then, after he refused following her asking him, *inducing* him to agree to it."

"Exactly," the King smiled with satisfaction.

Eryn regarded him with narrowed eyes. "Was Malriel aware of the measures you would take to accomplish this?" she asked tensely.

He shook his head slowly. "No, she was not. Though I can't promise you that she didn't have her suspicions. I would be rather surprised if she hadn't. Getting too close to you is such an obvious choice of action to make your companion react, after all. It had worked so well once already, when it came to making him claim you officially. Speaking of Lord Enric's reaction," he went on, "let us have a look at that, shall we?"

She raised a brow in surprise. He really wanted to talk about this with Enric present and listening to them?

"Lord Orrin did a very smart thing when he insisted on telling Lord Enric about the kiss in the presence of Lord Tyront, the only magician in this Kingdom strong enough to restrain your companion. I assume the situation was not exactly a pleasant one for either of the three of them, but if there is one thing that one may rely on with Lord Orrin, it is that he does not shirk from what he thinks needs to be done, however troublesome the task."

Eryn narrowed her eyes at him. "Which is exactly why you made sure that he was the one to witness that kiss. You didn't trust *me* to tell Enric about it."

The King smiled approvingly. "Well done, Lady Eryn. Yes, you have shown a certain propensity for keeping things from your companion in the past, so I thought it advisable to make sure the information would be passed on in any case." He looked at her with a knowing smile. "Would you have told him?"

She looked him straight in the eyes. "Of course I would. I told you as much, didn't I?"

He clicked his tongue, shaking his head disapprovingly. "That was a lie, my dear. A rather brazen one. You would not have told him. Due to some misguided need to protect him from himself, I would imagine. But luckily Lord Orrin is quite a clear thinker. He was aware that keeping this a secret from Lord Enric would prompt me to resort to other measures as a consequence, was he not?"

She forced herself not to move a muscle. He was aware of a lot more than she was comfortable with. And having Enric overhear the King plainly stating that she had intended to keep another important incident from him meant trouble. She could already feel a rising level of annoyance through the mind bond. Curse him and his maddeningly pinpoint insights!

"You are aware, of course, why Lords Enric and Orrin were dealt punishments by your superior yesterday. What do you think the reason was why Lord Enric waited several days before contravening Lord Tyront's order not to see me alone?"

She frowned. "Getting a grip on his violent urges to do you harm, probably," she guessed.

King Folrin smiled. "No. Although he did show admirable restraint when I provoked him. He first wanted to take care of a little matter that required exchanging messages with Takhan. With your cousin Vran'el of House Vel'kim, to be precise."

She saw from the corner of her eye how Enric's posture had changed only slightly. He seemed more alert now than before. The current topic seemed to have awakened his interest. And no more than interest it clearly was, as she didn't receive any sign of unrest.

What reason could he have had for contacting Vran'el? Nothing came to her mind.

"What matter?" she then enquired with a sideways glance at Enric. At least she now had something against *him* if he later held her intention to keep the kiss a secret against her.

"He contacted your cousin in his capacity as lawyer to arrange for the revenue generated from business with the Western Territories to be held in Takhan instead of being sent here. So he made sure that - what will in time doubtlessly become a considerable amount - is stashed in Takhan to enable both of you to have a very comfortable life there in case you should decide not to return here."

She felt a little undermined and tried to look unruffled by this news. "A cautious course of action, I would think," she remarked.

"It was a little more than that, Lady Eryn. Lord Enric made sure that I would learn of his action. He wanted me to know that he was considering leaving his life here behind him. To force me into acting somehow."

"And?" she asked lightly, "Did that work out?"

"It did indeed. Lord Enric is not known for making idle threats. People who deal with him regularly even consider themselves lucky if he warns them before making them pay for whatever they did to upset him. Did you know that one of the traders selling Lord Enric's products tried to sell to your friend Junar several bales of cloth that were infested with vermin?"

She shook her head.

"As the condition of the merchandise suggested that he was aware of the quality of his goods, he was punished by having his license to trade products in the city of Anyueel and several other towns confiscated. He will also never again be permitted to trade in any of Lord Enric's produce," the King explained. "A very good example of how your companion likes to take care of matters: expeditiously, thoroughly and permanently. No room for empty threats or futile warnings. Yet he is known to be dependable when it comes to paying his debts and for granting generous bonuses if things run the way he expects them to. The timely completion of his building projects has caused many a worker to find himself with notably more than the promised pay afterwards. You may count on them to be more than willing to leave whatever other engagement they may in the future have as soon as word gets out of Lord Enric's planning the construction of another structure."

Eryn fought the impulse to turn her head and look directly at Enric. She had never had any insight into how he managed his businesses, but from what she had just been told he was clearly somebody to be wary of. And somebody it paid to keep happy.

"You see why I had no doubt that he was serious about relocating?" the King enquired, waiting for her hesitant nod. "Good. It means that both the Order and I myself need to make sure you are both willing to return here." He regarded her expectantly.

It took her several moments to realise what he was hinting at. "Which is obviously my cue to commence making demands," she stated.

"That is what political strategy would suggest, yes," he confirmed with his thin smile.

"I wish to be made Head of Healers," she said at once.

He shook his head indulgently. "Now you are just being difficult, my dear. You must be very well aware that I can hardly grant you something that pertains to the Order's inner structure and has already been decided differently by the Magic Council."

"I want Sanaf gone and a proper ambassador instated. Somebody better suited and less clumsy," she then offered.

The King let out a low laugh. "Is there somebody particular you have in mind, Lady Eryn?"

She nodded curtly. "Erbál of House Feral. I was given to understand that his House's decision to vote against me at the trial and a possible grudge I might hold against his House due to this, is one of the main reasons he was not considered fit for the position."

"Now we are talking," the monarch nodded. "I cannot *promise* you anything, as you must be aware, but my recommendation - and your being in favour of it - will carry quite some weight, I expect." He leaned back and winked at her. "It is good to see that you are starting to make useful connections. What is more, I hope that Erbál will turn out to be a hugely advantageous one. If you trust him not to be too close to Malriel, that is." He smiled when he saw a look of unsureness in her eyes at the mention of her mother's name. "House Aren will of course support his being made ambassador. House Feral voted with them at your trial, after all. And then Malriel prefers having a friend in charge here instead of Sanaf. Though I wonder if she has taken into consideration the fact that Erbál's own interests might cause a shift in loyalty from herself to you. Although this would be good for House Feral, as they risked their good standing with House Vel'kim by voting against you."

This man was truly well-informed, she thought with an uneasy feeling. He was aware of which House had voted for or against her, of Malriel's past affair with Erbál, and judging from his last remark, he was at least partly in the know when it came to the alliances between the Houses. It seemed that Kilan was very busy sending information over here.

But at least the King had agreed to promoting her request of having Erbál made ambassador. She wondered how much further she could push him. He had told her that he and the Order depended on her making Enric agree to returning here, after all.

She lifted her chin. "I want to be released from the Order for the time of our stay in Takhan. The same as Enric."

"No," the King replied curtly.

She waited for him to provide his reasons, but he didn't. Damn it. That very likely meant that he was not to be shifted when it came to that point. She considered asking him, but hesitated. Then she remembered Erbál's advice to be bold with him during their lessons, that he would see it as enthusiasm and not her questioning his decisions.

"May I ask why?"

"You may," he said graciously. "You are my guarantee that Lord Enric will return here. As long as your status in the Order and with it your magical binding to the Kingdom remain intact, I can rely on such a thing."

"Can you?" she replied mildly. "People in the Western Territories know how to lift a bond like that. What would stop them from doing so?"

The King raised both eyebrows at her. "What indeed, my dear Lady? I invite you to ponder this question yourself. I am sure that one of your family could be persuaded to free you from the oath, but consider the consequences."

"You wouldn't declare war on them, would you?" she asked lightly but with a certain tenseness.

"Not at once, no. Though it might come to that eventually. But there would be more immediate if less bloody consequences. Think," he commanded her.

She let her eyes roam the throne room in search of inspiration. "No further diplomatic relations," she ventured, then went on, when it dawned on her what he wanted to hear. "No more trade or exchange of knowledge. They might even strengthen the barrier again somehow to hold us to our side of the ocean."

"Exactly. Even though it seems at the moment that we would be the ones to suffer most from this, let me tell you that the Western Territories, too, would consider this development not to their advantage. They do have a vested interest in our resources. Wood, for example, has turned out to be a very sought-after commodity. So have the fabrics Lord Enric makes. They are sturdier than fibres they have managed to grow and weave so far. I am told they are currently being tested for their use as sails as they are less likely to fail when subjected to great strain." His expression became serious. "In Lord Enric's case releasing him from the Order makes sense, as he needs to be free to act in accordance with the interests of the House he is about to lead. Especially as this entails a seat in their senate. He can't serve two masters, as it were. But this does not apply in *your* case. You will continue to be an Order magician during your absence. I am adamant about this. And I earnestly hope that you will not endanger the warm relationship between our two countries by serving your personal motives. You are not the type for that; you wouldn't wish to make so many others suffer the consequences of your selfishness."

She didn't reply. There was nothing much to add to that. He was right. She wouldn't.

"What would be the consequence of this attitude of yours for people who might try to manipulate you, if you would hazard a guess? Or even better, think about it properly?" he enquired.

Eryn blinked. An interesting question, she had to admit. Being aware of that answer would probably make resisting such attempts easier in the future. She thought for a minute.

"Making me think that what I do wouldn't harm others, I suppose. It is a major part of the healers' principles, after all. A way of going through life that does not only concern healing."

"You are on the right track, my dear, but not quite there." The King turned his head to look at Enric. "Lord Enric, would you care to elaborate?"

Enric smiled and looked at her. "Not harming others is not enough to make you comply, my love. Helping others or enabling you to do so is the trick. This applies both for the anonymous masses you provide healing services for and the people close to you in matters not at all connected to healing. It is what His Majesty's commitment gift, the building for the clinic, was aimed at. And granting his support to Erbál being made ambassador. He knows that rejecting requests that relate to you alone is no danger at all since you wouldn't hold a grudge for long. This is why you will not become Head of Healers, nor will you be released from the Order. Your chances of having favours granted that you ask for people other than yourself is greater. Your priorities run that way."

She scowled. "Are you saying I am a selfless benefactor to everyone around me but myself - willingly suffering disadvantages for myself in order to make others happy? This does not exactly fit my own picture of myself, I must say."

"No," he shook his head. "That would be a little more self-sacrifice than you currently practice. You do not mind having favours for yourself disregarded, even on those rare occasions you ask for them because you are proud enough to think that you don't depend on anybody else to achieve what you want. But your understanding of society, namely that those who can should help provide for those who can't, is what makes asking for others easy for you."

She narrowed her eyes at him. "Is this why you agreed to funding the orphanage? To manipulate me into accepting that you are filthy rich without my feeling bad about it or having me telling you constantly that I believe there is a limit to how much wealth one single man should possess?"

The King laughed at that before Enric could answer. "I admit that the dynamics of your relationship are somewhat different from what I normally witness. I have never before met a man who had to justify his wealth to his companion. Usually it is the *lack* of it that must be explained. How very bizarre that a women born into two rich families and joined to an immensely prosperous man should have so little consideration for gold."

"I was taught that relying on things that can be taken away from you is not a way that will ensure long-term happiness," she replied curtly.

The King smiled. "Of course. Your father would have known about that, wouldn't he? Leaving his own fortune behind and building a whole new life with his healing skills. He found a life of luxury to be less appealing than staying true to his principles, however objectionable many people may still find them."

Eryn battled the urge to ball her hands into fists. This was not a topic she wanted to talk about with the King. It was too close to the bone. And after only recently learning what had been the reason for Ved'al's flight to the Kingdom, it was also too painful.

"But let us talk of this no more. I imagine this is not the most pleasant of topics for you," he then said with his usual unnerving feeling for what was going on inside her. "Let us move on to the last question I have for you today before you are dismissed. Why do I insist on teaching you political strategy?"

She frowned. Hadn't he asked her something like that at the beginning already?

"Because you don't want others to use me against you," she repeated her answer from before.

"Yes, my dear Lady, I think we have established that," he replied patiently. "What else?"

She thought about what Tyront had said yesterday evening when she was alone with him. But was it prudent to repeat it out loud here and now? Yet if it was the answer he was waiting for he wouldn't stop pestering her in any case. "Because Enric sees the benefit for me as well as himself, which may in time even lead to his seeing you as a proper King again instead of somebody he mistrusts because you crossed a dangerous line with me. It may take a few years yet. but I might in time become proficient enough to be impervious even to *your* strategies. Though I assume this is not something you would consider a likely outcome. You prefer playing your games with skilled opponents, which at the moment I am not. However, not using me is not something you can consider, either, because Enric turned out to be so very resistant to other attempts at steering him in the past. I am a useful tool, though at the moment not someone who challenges or amuses you as much as you wish," she ended.

"Exceedingly well put, Lady Eryn, I have to say. Though it pains me to see how much you underestimate your own skills in that area. You have learned a lot in this past year and will continue to do so, I am absolutely sure of it. Another reason is that I want you to be able to hold your ground in Takhan. As the daughter of two powerful Houses you will very likely find yourself the object or means of other people's plans there, especially given Lord Enric's new position."

She smiled. "So even though we are no longer official representatives of the Kingdom, you still don't want us to look weak and easy to manipulate."

He sighed. "You are both powerful and important. You must be aware that you can be used not only against your companion, but also against the Kingdom. Or against myself. Those Houses not allied to Malriel or your uncle may see in you a welcome chance to cause them trouble. Not all senators are in favour of establishing permanent contact with us, which means your being very careful when it comes to breaking any laws. Fortunately, your cousin is in a position both to advise you before any such transgression takes place and to get you out of trouble should the worst happen," he concluded dryly.

She considered him several moments, before she slowly said, "What do you get in return? You granted Malriel a sizeable favour in making sure that we would go there, even risking our not coming back. What is in it for *you*?"

The King arose. "That is not for you to know presently, Lady Eryn. But I am very confident that it will one day become a topic of conversation between us. You are dismissed. Be back in seven days at the same time."

Both Eryn and Enric got to their feet as well and bowed before walking out of the throne room.

"That was not too bad," she murmured after they were back out on the streets and had left the Palace precincts behind them. "I could have imagined worse."

Enric took her hand and squeezed it. "That was his intention. He wants you to feel unthreatened in his presence as well as placate me. He completely avoided any physical contact with you this time. Though I hope you have realised by now that being in his presence is never without risk."

She snorted. "Judging from how much he knows of the things that are going on in Takhan I would say that not even leaving the Kingdom means being safe from him."

He smiled grimly. "Well spotted. We would both be well advised never to forget that." Then his expression became dark. "And now to the little matter of your planning to keep that damn kiss from me," he hissed and she groaned when his grip around her fingers tightened.

* * *

Enric looked up when the servant knocked at his study door to tell him that Vern would like to see him, if it were possible. He instructed the servant to send his visitor in.

That was unusual, he mused. The boy had never before come to see him about anything, especially not unannounced. If he needed something, it was more straightforward for him to go to Eryn instead. He permitted himself a quick smile. Unless, of course, what Vern wanted was not something Eryn would agree to. Such as being taken to Takhan with them.

Vern entered, his shoulders straightened, his chin lifted defiantly, as though he had just pushed himself enough to approach this very powerful man, a man, who had lost some of his mystique in the past year, but had nevertheless turned out to be more dangerous in other respects than people would previously have credited. Especially when it came to Eryn. But whatever people said about him, the tales never mentioned anything to do with unfairness, despotism or undeserved harshness. So at least it was not likely that he would be yelled at or otherwise humiliated if his request was not received favourably.

"Lord Enric," he said rather breathlessly, then bowed. "Thank you for seeing me without an appointment. I appreciate that very much. I hope I have not come at an inconvenient time?"

Enric smiled at the grown-up way the boy tended to express himself. From what he had seen, he also did it with his peers. Eryn seemed to be the only one where he dared behave like himself, a teenage boy.

"Not at all," he replied in a friendly voice and indicated a sofa to one side of his desk. "Take a seat." He got up from his chair and rounded the desk. "What can I offer you to drink?" Holding on to a glass would surely help Vern deal with any nervousness, he thought.

"Water would be fine, thank you," the boy said and frowned when Enric stepped towards a drinks cabinet. "I can do that...," he stammered, aghast at the thought of being served by this important man.

Enric chuckled. "Relax, Vern. In the Western Territories serving one's guests is not humiliating for the host, however much higher his position in the hierarchy might be." He paused a moment for effect and turned to fill two glasses with water from a carafe before he went on, "This is something you might have to get used to if you are to accompany us to Takhan."

He smiled when he heard the boy behind his back gasp and gave him another few seconds to collect himself before turning back to Vern to hand him the glass.

Vern took it with both hands and held on to it, his eyes wide. "Pardon me, My Lord?"

Enric took a seat on a chair and placed his own glass on the small table before him. "Takhan. I think you should accompany us. In my opinion you have a very interesting career in the Order ahead of you and should accordingly be trained properly in all areas connected with it. There is no better place to train healing than Takhan, I would suggest. It is what Eryn will be doing while we are staying there, after all. As she will clearly not be at liberty after our return to spend as much time at the clinic as she has done in these last months, another well-trained healer here is a necessity."

The boy's stiff posture slowly started to change. He began to let himself breathe more naturally after holding a single breath for what seemed minutes, when Enric had wondered how much air there could still be left inside his lungs.

"How did you know this was why I have come?"

"An educated guess," Enric smirked. "Though you are of course aware that I am not as such in a position to grant or deny anything here. You need the King's and Lord Tyront's permission." And he had a fairly good feeling that they would agree if Enric recommended sending the boy along. They still had quite some reconciliation to get through, after all. "In addition to that you require support and careful planning. My support you can be sure of, but your father and Eryn are not in favour of bringing you along. As you know they both think it is too dangerous for you to go with us. Orrin would even choose to leave Eryn and Junar behind. But as going there puts him in a position to protect them both, he puts up with the Royal command without protest."

"How do I convince them, then?" Vern asked without much hope.

"You don't. You bypass them by applying to higher authorities, namely the King and Lord Tyront. But in order to convince *those two* to release you, you need to give them valid reasons and show them that you have given the matter some thought. Your going to another country for several months will interrupt your classes for a long time. I would recommend that you arrange for tuition in Takhan. I will give you one of the Arbil message birds. Ask Ram'an. I am convinced he will be more than happy to help you with this. Then you need to talk to Lord Poron in his capacity as Head of Healers; you need him on your side. Lord Tyront won't agree to your going if Lord Poron doesn't approve. Prepare convincing arguments when you face the King and Lord Tyront," he advised.

Vern summarised what he had just heard, using his fingers. "Prepare arguments, talk to Lord Poron and Ram'an, address His Majesty and Lord Tyront. Is there anything else?"

"Yes. Let me know as soon as you are ready to meet the last two. I will put in a good word for you."

The boy grinned broadly, then looked downcast. "Eryn won't be pleased about my going behind her back."

"Let her be my concern," Enric said mildly. "She might not be too happy to take you to a place that turned out to be quite disaster prone for herself, but once we are there she will appreciate having you with us. She will also see that you have a lot more opportunities in Takhan than here."

Vern jumped up, clearly excited that what had only a few minutes ago seemed an almost impossible plan had suddenly now become a realistic option.

"Thank you! Thank you so much! I will start working on this right now!"

Enric sighed when the boy rushed out the door.

"Vern?" he called after him.

He returned. "Yes?"

"The bird?"

He grinned sheepishly. "Oh, yes."

CHAPTER 25

Losing a Bet

Eryn was leaning against a table, watching Plia meticulously remove small seedlings from their trays and carefully plant them out into larger pots. She took her time, cautious not to pinch the tiny shoots.

"Will you keep them here or are they to go up on the roof?" Eryn enquired.

"They will stay with me for now. I want to have a close look over them for the next few weeks, see how they develop," the girl replied and wiped her hands on a cloth to remove the earth clinging to them.

"Which would be all but impossible up on the roof in your glass house because it's not as if you are spending at least two hours a day up there," Eryn chuckled.

"I don't know. It just doesn't feel right to put them up there yet."

"Are you afraid that the other, older plants will mock them for being tiny?" she joshed.

"Healers," the girl sighed and went to a bowl with water and a piece of soap next to it to scrub her hands and remove the dirt from under her fingernails. "You truly are a strange bunch."

Eryn shrugged. "Not exclusively. I know a few rather weird people who aren't healers. How are things getting on with the apothecaries? Have they finally managed to work out who is going to deliver which products or are we still getting large deliveries of just about the same items once a week?"

"I talked to Lord Poron about this. He promised to look into it," Plia replied with an apologetic look.

Eryn nodded. Fair enough. She was not the one in charge of things like that anymore. Lord Poron had been busy in these last two weeks.

He had been establishing the organisation for healing professions, introducing himself to the people who would from now on deal with him in his new function and slowly running the transition from colleague to superior when it came to the other healers. It helped that he outranked them in the Order structure and that he was far enough advanced in age to be easily accepted as the one in charge. Apart from her, everybody seemed to find adapting to this new situation rather uncomplicated. Which was a good thing, she hastened to remind herself. She had established the clinic to help people, not to preen her own ego. But still.

She had considered bringing up the topic again during one of her sessions with the King, but she doubted that he would react well to that. The first three meetings with him and Enric had been surprisingly smooth. There had been a certain underlying tension, for sure, but all in all they had been polite to each other.

"Eryn?" Plia enquired, waving a hand in front of her face. "Lost in thought?"

"Hmm?" Eryn blinked. "Er, sorry... yes. What were you saying?"

The girl pressed a box with various differently-shaped glass items into her hands. "I asked you if you would mind taking this to Rolan's study. I need him to exert a little pressure on the glassmakers - their quality has not been up to standard lately. They don't take me seriously, so I think having a magician tread on their toes might do the trick better."

Eryn nodded. "Alright. Can you open the door for me?"

Plia did so and called after her, "Don't break anything! These are the last ones I have left!"

Eryn rolled her eyes. "I am a big girl, Plia. I am sure I will somehow manage to carry a box with breakable things from one end of the building to the other, thank you very much."

"Do you want me to open Rolan's door for you?"

"No, I will manage it. Go back and get on with whatever you do at this time of day."

She walked on towards the door next to her own study and stopped, wondering if there was possible to knock without putting the box on the floor then picking it up again afterwards. Using her elbow would be almost inaudible, using her shoe would be a bit too forward as it would probably seem like she intended to kick in the door.

Then she shrugged. He would somehow manage to deal with it if she went in without knocking for once. Carefully turning to one side, she pressed the door handle down with her elbow and pushed the door open with her shoulder.

She looked up and froze at the sight.

Her proper-mannered, over-bureaucratic Head of Administration was pressing Pe'tala - who was currently not wearing any top - against the opposite wall, his mouth locked onto hers, his hands grasping her buttocks. Pe'tala was holding his head in her hands, kissing him passionately. From the unbroken energy with which they kept clinging to each other, Eryn saw that opening the door hadn't interrupted them.

She barely noted when the box slid out of her limp fingers. When a moment later glass and wood smashed into the stone floor with an ear-shattering burst, the two lovers jumped apart and stared at her, open-mouthed.

"What do you think you are doing here?" Eryn hissed. "Go and cover yourself up, woman!"

Pe'tala woke from her dazed alarm and quickly bent down to retrieve her shirt, shaking it a few times to remove a number of glass splinters before pulling it on over her head. Inside out.

Eryn heard footsteps behind her and a moment later Plia groaned. "Eryn! Really? All of them?"

She turned to the girl and said harshly, "Plia, I need to take care of something here. Rolan will somehow deal with this afterwards, I promise you." Then she shoved Plia out of the room, closed the door and leaned against it.

"You!" she glowered at both of them. "I don't believe what I am seeing! Why, you don't even like each other!"

Pe'tala lifted a sweat dampened eyebrow and replied archly, "We were working on that, as you can see."

Eryn narrowed her eyes. "He paid you to go with him, didn't he? He just can't take losing a bet! Admit it!"

Two pairs of eyes stared at her in astonishment, then Pe'tala's eyes fixed her. "I do not know about the Old Kingdom, but where I come from assuming that a woman takes a man to bed for payment is a profound insult."

"It is not exactly a compliment here, either," Rolan remarked, his expression having become annoyed. "Nor is assuming that a man has no other way of convincing a woman to have sex with him."

"You are not sleeping with each other," Eryn stated calmly. Of course they weren't. What a thought!

"Well, the news is we are!" Pe'tala said defiantly. "We were about to when you barged in. Which I find immensely inconsiderate of you. I know for sure that people here maintain the custom of announcing themselves by way of a knock before entering."

Now two startled pairs of eyes rested on Pe'tala. "What?" She threw her hands up into the air. "Oh yes! I forgot for a moment what a prudish place this is." Her tone became mocking. "We do *not* talk about sex in public. We do *not* have sex outside our bedrooms. We do *not*..."

"... *have* sex in public!" Eryn snapped at her. "Furthermore, from what I know this is also frowned upon where *you* come from! So stop your insults right now! You were about to have intercourse in a public building, at your work place! This is not professional!" She lifted her index finger. "I forbid it! You are not to see each other privately. Or talk to each other publicly. You will keep away from each other from now on!"

Pe'tala folded her arms. "You are joking! You may forbid us to engage in public fornication in your precious building, but you can hardly tell us not to see each other. We are both grown people and do not require any consent from you!"

"You are colleagues! That's not something colleagues are supposed to do!"

Rolan folded his arms in defiance as well. "I think you and Lord Enric might be considered colleagues for that matter."

"*That* is something completely different!" Eryn protested. "When we had our affair I was not even a member of the Order!"

"Neither is Pe'tala," he retorted. "And I recall that you were a prisoner back then, so if you want to talk about professional conduct, let us start with Lord Enric's, shall we?"

Eryn rubbed her face. This was not going as simply as she had wanted. And knowing that they were right and she was wrong didn't make it any easier. She let her hands sink again and straightened.

"You will keep your hands off each other while you are at my clinic. If *I* can surprise you like this, anybody else could have. If I catch you like this again, I will kick you both out of that window."

"Very professional," Pe'tala murmured.

"What was that?" Eryn barked at her.

"Nothing," she sulked.

"Good." Eryn looked back at Rolan and pointed to the mess of glass fragments and wood chips on his floor. "Take care of this. Talk to Plia. She needs..." Her mind kept returning to the picture of the two of them from only a few minutes ago despite her valiant attempts to push it aside. "Well, you just talk to her."

Thus she turned and all but fled, leaving the door wide open. When she reached the top of the stairs, she heard Rolan's voice.

"She took it reasonably well, I would say."

"True. Let us try it in her study next. That would not be something Aren temper is up to." She could recognise the glee in Pe'tala's voice.

"The two of you have that same strange sense of humour," Rolan then sighed wearily.

Eryn ground her teeth and all but ran towards the exit. She stepped out into pouring rain and icy air and quickly raised a small shield over her head to protect herself from the rain. There was nothing she could do about the cold now, but suffering a few minutes of freezing air was preferable to walking back up into her study to retrieve her cloak.

* * *

Enric frowned when he heard the entrance door open, and got up from behind his desk. This was unusually early for her to come home. Urban lifted her head lazily, sniffed the air and then let her head sink back onto the soft carpet when she had identified Eryn.

He walked out into the parlour and raised his brow when he saw her kneeling in front of the fire place, her palms stretched out towards the flames.

"Don't tell me you walked home without a cloak," he admonished her without any greeting.

She didn't look up, but closed her eyes instead. "Don't bother. Just... don't."

So something had obviously happened. Something that had caused her to run around in the city without bothering to dress for the weather. She was still wearing her thin work shirt and trousers, not the robe that would at least have provided some protection from the cold.

"What's the matter?" he asked gently and crouched down beside her, pulling her into a warm embrace, rubbing her back.

She sighed, wishing he would have given her a little more time to get over the recent embarrassment before making her talk about it. If she tried to avoid telling him, he would just go on and urge her. That man was obviously never properly brought up to accept the word *No*.

She pressed her forehead against his shoulder. "I just made a complete and utter fool of myself."

"Did you now. What happened?"

"I barged in on Rolan and Pe'tala. It seems they are having an affair." She felt him stiffen in surprise.

"They are? So when you found them, they were in the middle of...?" His expression was a blend of shock and fascination.

"What? No! But it would probably have been no more than a matter of minutes." She felt warmth slowly return into her fingers on his chest. "The idea! I shouldn't be shocked by that anyway – Erbál has predicted it! I even entered into a bet with him because it seemed so very outlandish!"

Enric smiled and shook his head in wonder. "I hope you didn't lose anything significant?"

"No, I didn't. I have even paid my debt already by asking the King to help him become ambassador. And I was thinking I could do it to make him owe me a favour, play the gracious winner and all. Damn it! I really wanted that information on Malriel I would have got had he been wrong."

He looked down at her, when a thought occurred to him. "May I ask how you reacted when you caught the two of them?" That was very likely the feeling foolish part she had mentioned.

She looked uncomfortable. "Not too well. I dropped a box of glassware and forbade them to see each other ever again."

He looked down at her indulgently. "And how well did that work out?"

She sighed. "Not at all, as you may imagine. So I amended that to prohibiting them to have close contact with each other at the clinic."

"So they are now both mad with you?"

"I can't tell. I heard them making fun of me when I left," she growled.

"Better than cursing you. Now go upstairs and change into something warmer. I will start the cooking. And send out the invitations."

"What? Invitations?" she enquired, feeling surprised.

"Yes. We will invite Pe'tala and Rolan to have dinner with us."

"No! I mean, what... Really?" she asked, perturbed. "I find sitting at the same table with that woman difficult at the best of times! This is not going to be a pleasant evening."

"I am serious about it." He smiled. "You may depend on it being not much more comfortable for them, either. A lot less, if you do it right."

That made her swallow her next complaint. "What?"

"How well will Pe'tala respond to having a family dinner with you?"

"Not too well."

"And Rolan?"

"Not much better, I would think." Then a smile slowly spread across her lips. "Are you giving me a chance for revenge here to cheer me up?"

He smiled. "Anything to make you happy." And to get the two cousins talking to each other before this incident could do any permanent damage. However, that was not a concern he considered wise to share with her right now.

* * *

He brightened when she descended the stairs. She had taken a hot bath, changed into something a little more elegant than usual and looked a lot more relaxed than one and a half hours before. The prospect of annoying Pe'tala and Rolan had clearly improved her mood.

He finished laying out the cutlery on the dinner table and then walked towards her to kiss her forehead.

"You look fabulous. Mm, and you smell even better," he murmured.

"The little tricks we employ to keep you boys interested," she grinned.

"No need to on my account. I am still fascinated by you and don't see that changing anytime soon," he said gallantly and bent down to kiss her lips. At that moment the knock at the door came. "Impeccable timing," he sighed and walked to the entrance door to permit their guests.

"Don't complain," she called after him, "*you* invited them."

Enric welcomed them in and took their cloaks to hang them on hooks in the niche beside the door.

Pe'tala wore a bold red tunic in the local style that went very well with her dark eyes and creamy skin. Rolan next to her in his dark brown shirt and trousers was quite a contrast.

Eryn smiled at them with a twist of malice and stepped towards them with wide open arms to noisily kiss a startled Pe'tala on both cheeks before turning to a slightly panicky looking Rolan to snatch his collar and pull him close before he could retreat and bestowed on him the same welcoming.

"So nice of you to find the time to join us at such short notice," Eryn purred.

"Yes," Pe'tala retorted dryly, "being summoned by the almighty second-in-command makes people jump to attention."

"You are not a member of the Order," her cousin pointed out. "What made you jump?"

"His reputation of dealing swiftly with people who do not comply with his wishes, whether they are in the Order or not," Pe'tala snorted.

Eryn laughed factitiously. "Such nonsense! Nasty rumours - nothing more. They never found that poor man's body, so he might as well be up and about somewhere. Theoretically."

Rolan sighed in defeat. "Very funny."

She smiled broadly and put an arm around Pe'tala's shoulders. "It's our sense of humour. It runs in the family, I have heard. Right, *sister*?"

Pe'tala gave her a brooding look. "I suddenly feel the urge to drink something. A lot of it."

Eryn drew in a breath in mock shock. "Dear me, what have I been thinking? I am neglecting my duties as a hostess! Do come along and take a seat, will you? What can I get you to drink?"

Their guests exchanged awkward looks and perched themselves on a sofa next to each other.

"The strongest stuff you have," Pe'tala murmured.

"Coming right up!" Eryn chanted and stepped towards the drinking cabinet. "And you, Rolan, my dearest?"

"I'll take whatever she's having," he replied nervously.

Enric watched her lifting his bottle of clear, distilled liquor to fill two glasses generously and smiled to himself. It was a pleasure to watch her resonating with dark delight at making the two of them as uncomfortable as possible. He could feel the echo of her amusement in his head. Though if Pe'tala and Rolan truly managed to drain their glasses, they would very likely be relaxed enough not to be bothered by Eryn's behaviour any further. Or by anything else short of an earthquake or a direct lightning strike, for that matter. It really was a potent drink, and Eryn had been exceedingly generous with it.

He stepped next to her and took a third glass for himself, choosing the same potion his guests were having. Eryn had opted for a glass of wine.

They turned back to their guests and handed them their glasses.

"To family," Eryn exclaimed grandly and lifted her glass with an enthusiastic upwards tilt and a wide smile.

Pe'tala shot her a withering look and took a greedy gulp that made her cough. She had obviously slightly underestimated the drink's potency.

"Everything alright, sweetheart?" Eryn enquired with exaggerated worry. "You know, with liquor such as that you need to be more careful. As your big sister I feel I should point this out. Maybe you should switch to wine, my darling. It is more suited to a sensitive nature such as yours."

Pe'tala pressed the glass against her chest possessively. "Don't you dare, Eryn. Anything weaker than this would make enduring *you* tonight unthinkable," she muttered.

Eryn shook her head. "Tala, Tala, this is surely not how *our* father raised you."

"*My* father," Pe'tala growled back. "You were only permitted into our House because he pitied you."

Enric watched the scene contentedly. Eryn was doing well, he had to say. There was no trace of the annoyance and frustration from when she had come home. Pe'tala, however, was clearly thrown off track by every other remark.

"Rolan, my *dear* Rolan," Eryn sighed, squeezing herself into a tiny space next to him on the settee, holding on to his arm to avoid losing balance. "Who would ever have thought that you and I would be sitting together in my parlour like this?" she purred contentedly.

He looked at her with a pained expression. "I distinctly remember your promising me that this would never happen."

Eryn raised both brows. "Did I really?"

"Yes. It was when you forced me to stop using your title. You said that just because I wouldn't be calling you *Lady* any longer didn't mean that we would end up in your parlour sharing private thoughts," he stated.

She thought for a moment, then nodded. "You are absolutely right, I did say something like that, didn't I?" She took a sip of wine, then smiled. "But that was before you decided to have sexual intercourse with my dear little sister here. That does change things somewhat, you see."

Rolan closed his eyes and exhaled, so obviously uncomfortable and yet he didn't dare get up and move out of her reach. Enric wondered if she would stop him with her superior powers if he indeed worked up the courage to make an attempt at escaping. But for now he looked as if he had resigned and resorted to suffering silently.

"I can see how immensely uncomfortable this very open way of talking about sex makes you, Rolan," she said conversationally. "Though I feel I should warn you that with a woman from the Western Territories this is something you need to work at. They are so much more open-minded than us here," she said, then chuckled as if a thought had just occurred to her. "Do you remember that one time when I tried to make you undress in front of me, but you kept refusing?"

Pe'tala's eyes flashed at that. "You did *what*?" she barked and gave Enric an accusing look. "Don't you have any control over that woman? I thought *you* were the man to restrain three fuming Aren women at once! Is subduing the pack easier than handling a single one of them?"

Enric just smiled at her with half-closed eyes, determined not to be pulled into that conversation for now. It was Eryn's time to play, and he would grant her another few minutes before he would liberate their guests from her grasp and serve dinner.

Eryn smiled, her eyes hazy as if enjoying a fond memory. "You were so very shy. I remember the other healers asking you if you never before had undressed before a woman. Well, it seems you have now."

Rolan stared at her in dismay. "You are doing this on purpose, to make me suffer. I do not like that."

She pretended to think for a moment, then nodded. "I suppose there is no denying that. But you are right. I shouldn't be doing this." She put aside her glass and turned to him, still sitting too close to him on a sofa that was meant to provide space for two instead of three people. "Let us talk seriously now. Rolan, what are your intentions with my little sister?"

Pe'tala next to them groaned and let her head sink into her hands. Then she looked over towards Enric, pleading.

"Please?" she mouthed wordlessly with so much desperation in her eyes that he sighed.

"Eryn, why don't we serve dinner now? Our guests must surely be hungry."

"Oh dear - how thoughtless of me!" she cried out and held on to Rolan's arm so that he had no other choice than to lead her to the table and pull out a chair for her.

Enric took Pe'tala's arm to escort her to the dining room. When both their guests and Eryn were seated, Enric started serving the dishes he had prepared in the bowls they had acquired in Takhan. He could see Pe'tala's surprised expression.

"Did you...?" she asked.

"I prepared the food, yes," he smiled. "Your brother's instructions did not go to waste. I cook regularly, and I have taken to hunting my own meat."

She blinked, clearly not sure how to respond to this unexpected display of preference for customs from her home.

Eryn observed her closely, wondering if Enric's words and the manner in which the food was served awoke any homesickness in her. Funny how she had never before wondered about Pe'tala missing her home and family. The thought that she had not exactly been very considerate and supportive in making her cousin feel at home here came unbidden and she quickly pushed it away. She would deal with it later.

"*You* cook?" Rolan stared at his superior incredulously. "With pots and pans and chopping and all that?"

Enric smirked. "That is what cooking generally entails, yes. In the Western Territories being able to provide for oneself is considered natural. They sneer at our dependence on servants for things like that."

Rolan turned to Pe'tala. "I have never seen *you* cooking," he pointed out.

She blushed. "Well, my quarters at the Palace do not provide any cooking space. That means that for the time being I have adapted to the local customs."

"If you do feel the need to cook a meal for yourself, you are welcome here. We do have a rather nice kitchen at the other side of the yard, even if I say so myself," Enric offered.

Pe'tala regarded him suspiciously. "Careful. I might take you up on that."

"Please do. We would be delighted," he replied seriously.

She took her glass and drained the rest in one go, exhaling slowly and shaking her head once as if to clear it. She accepted the bowl Enric placed in front of her and then looked at Eryn with a stony expression.

"Alright, cousin, you have had your fun. No more tormenting us with your false, saccharine society behaviour. It makes me want to gag. Though I admit that you are surprisingly good at it. Which I do not at all mean as a compliment, mind you. It just means that you still are a devious Aren with all the twisted skills this entails, no matter what your official name is now." She took a bite and chewed it, nodding appreciatively at Enric, before turning back to the other woman. "Let us clear this up here and now. I do respect your demand with regard to not breaking your delicate rules of common decency at the clinic, but it is not your place to decide who I take to my bed."

Eryn sighed, letting the affected manners drop. "I have no intention of patronising you, but that was quite a surprise you caused me today. Also, I can't help but wonder if you are both aware that this is a temporary thing with your returning back home in several weeks. I wouldn't want either of you to leave or stay here with a broken heart."

"We are both adults. That is something you need to let us come to terms with without your well-meant interference," Pe'tala retorted.

Eryn nodded stiffly. "Alright, duly noted. No more meddling from my side." She started eating, not taking her eyes off her bowl.

Pe'tala exhaled audibly. "Now you are angry. This is not what I wanted. I appreciate that you care, but I am sure that you would not take it very well if I interfered with *your* love life."

"Such as back in Takhan, when you kissed my companion?" Eryn remarked snidely.

Rolan's head jerked upright. "You did *what*?" His gaze darted between Pe'tala and Enric.

Pe'tala waved him off. "Nothing. Just a rather dramatic way of expressing my anger."

He stared at her. "You expressed your anger by kissing *Lord Enric*?"

She looked grim. "I can see that his standing here would make such a bold move seem absolutely inconceivable to you, but for me he was no more than a slightly intimidating foreigner who was too confident for his own good." She grinned. "The shocked look on his face alone was worth it. As well as on yours, of course, cousin." She popped another bite into her mouth. "Priceless."

"I'm glad you enjoyed it," Eryn grumbled.

"There is one thing I wanted to ask you." Pe'tala looked serious. "When you came into Rolan's room today, you said something about somebody not taking well to losing a bet, if I remember correctly. What did you bet on that concerns *me*?"

Eryn rolled her eyes. "Erbál told me that the two of you having an affair was just a matter of time. I thought this was ridiculous."

Pe'tala laughed. "You bet a wager against Erbál?" She shook her head. "Nobody bets against Erbál! He never says anything he has not thought through or cannot substantiate. The chance of his being wrong with anything is remote."

"Yes, thank you for the reminder," Eryn mumbled. "Where were you a few weeks ago when such advice could actually have been helpful?"

"About to start an affair with Rolan, it seems," the younger woman smiled.

Enric took a sip from his glass to hide his smile. Eryn had obviously underestimated her cousin, who had somehow managed to turn around the situation. Now Pe'tala was the one enjoying herself at Eryn's expense.

CHAPTER 26

Vern's Plan

Enric stared out the window, deep in thought. Urban lay sprawled on the carpet in front of his desk, dead to the world. They had been out in the woods hunting yesterday evening and she was obviously still in need of some rest.

He had just returned from the Palace. Today had been the fourth lesson in political strategy Eryn had taken with the King. So far everything had gone smoothly enough, and he noted that Eryn had indeed started to look less tense in the monarch's presence. He just hoped this would not cause her to let down her guard too much when dealing with the King in the future.

The lesson today had been interesting for her, as well as for him as a mere onlooker. The King had brought up political alliances in Takhan, how the Houses interacted with each other and what schemes they had resorted to in the past to keep each other at bay. Even Enric had been surprised at the thorough historical and political knowledge the King had demonstrated of a country they had only recently established contact with. He had encouraged Eryn to have a closer look at the two Houses she was connected to by birth and the companionship agreements they had forged over these last two-hundred years. They had discussed the consequences of her father taking her away and thereby disrupting the plans between the Houses. Eryn had been fascinated, that was easy to witness. And it was a good thing that she showed interest in the place she was about to spend a good portion time soon.

What had bothered Enric had not been the lesson in itself but the exact time the King had set for the next one. It coincided with a Council meeting, meaning neither he himself, Orrin nor even Tyront would be available to accompany her. The King obviously wanted to see who Enric considered trustworthy enough to act as her protector. That was a sensitive question. It had to be somebody who was sufficiently attached to Eryn to step in in case she needed help, even if it meant facing an angry monarch. But then who could he ask a thing like that of? It had to be a magician, because he could then claim that he had acted under Enric's orders if indeed any kind of action was necessary.

Another option was to send somebody along whom the King wouldn't dare to be witness to any inappropriate behaviour towards Eryn. Such as Erbál. The trouble was that he didn't know Erbál nearly well enough to entrust him with a mission like that, even though Eryn seemed to get along well enough with him.

That left only one option he was remotely comfortable with.

* * *

Eryn yawned loudly without bothering to cover her mouth when she pushed open the door to their house after another long, exhausting treatment day.

Enric looked up from his book concerning the merits of hot spices in hot climates which Vran'el had sent him.

"Good. I would have given you another hour before I came after you," he commented, putting the book aside to rise and greet her.

She looked at him thoughtfully. "I thought we agreed on your treating me like an adult every now and then?"

"Well, I also thought we agreed on your not keeping any more secrets from me; yet you then considered not telling me about the King's kissing you," he retorted coolly.

She narrowed her eyes at him. "Says the man who began secretly stashing his riches in Takhan. Oh, wait - not completely secretly, was it? You just kept it a secret from *me*, but made sure the King learned of it."

He sighed. "That's not exactly the kind of welcome I had in mind for you, my love." He took her hands and pulled her closer. "You look tired."

She leaned against him, enjoying his warmth. "I am. I need to go to bed early tonight, I have a session with Orrin tomorrow morning."

"Are you even learning anything, now that he doesn't shackle you any longer?"

She grinned. "I learned that superior magical strength is a great advantage. But I only use it when I am in a particularly bad mood."

"Isn't that the default status when you have a combat session?" he enquired with a grin.

"It used to be. But it turns into my feeling resigned more and more." She yawned again. "Today, Pe'tala told me to set a date for my exams. It seems she is eager to have me take them with her here instead of in Takhan. Another chance to cause me proper anguish, no doubt," she muttered.

"Probably," he admitted. "So? Will you take them with her or wait until we are in Takhan?"

"I can't really say *no* to her, can I? It would seem as if I were afraid of her. And it would be good to have the exams before we leave. Then I will be able to concentrate on preparing for the one with Sarol in non-magical healing. He is rather... demanding, from what I have experienced so far."

"Did you agree on a date, then?"

"Yes. In three weeks."

"That does seem a little soon," he commented. "Are you sure this is enough time for you to prepare?"

She shrugged. "These last two months I have been reading the books Valrad sent me. I am through with most of them and Pe'tala narrowed down some of the areas for me. So I think I should be able to pass."

"So no worries about her being determined to cause you to fail?"

She ground her teeth. "Of course, I worry about that. Though if she does, she had better make sure to convince me that it was due to my being insufficiently prepared instead of her being wilful."

"She has been professional in everything connected with healing so far, hasn't she?"

Eryn nodded. "Yes, I must admit that's true. Though testing me is, strictly speaking, not connected to pure healing. Even if I failed I would go on healing here, so there would be no disadvantage for the patients. Just for me personally."

"I doubt that she is that vengeful, especially as she handled our dinner together rather well after she downed her first drink," he chuckled. "Rolan looked a bit ill at ease all evening long, though. I wonder if we made him regret his choice of lover. I don't know what disturbed him more, your being a nuisance or my just being around."

She raised an eyebrow at him. "Are you starting to feel sorry because you have been making half the Kingdom snap to attention in reverence for these last, what is it, fifteen years?"

He sighed and pulled her towards the stairs. "Maybe I am. I never before had to worry about my companion's sister's lover not being comfortable in my presence."

"She is my cousin," Eryn pointed out.

"You keep calling her your sister often enough," he commented.

"But only when we have witnesses so I can tease her. She isn't particularly thrilled about our officially being siblings, in case you hadn't noticed."

"And how about yourself? I got the impression that you are getting along pretty well considering your bumpy start."

She snorted. "Ask me that again in three weeks after the exam, will you? By the way, I heard that the next Council meeting is to take place at the exact time of my appointment with the King. Interesting coincidence, wouldn't you say?"

Enric shook his head and ascended the stairs right behind her. "Not a coincidence. He timed it like that on purpose. He wants to see who I will send along with you in my stead."

"I opt for Erbál."

"Pity. I have actually chosen Vern," he replied dryly.

She turned and frowned at him. "Vern? Is that wise? And who says that you are the one to do the choosing, anyway?"

"If I didn't think it wise, I wouldn't have picked him. And as long as I am the one worrying about your being safe, I get to choose who I send to protect you."

"Protect me!" she huffed and pushed open the door to their bedroom. "I am a magician in full possession of my powers. Anyway, the King overstepping any more limits for now is highly unlikely. Sending Vern along just makes talking to the King more difficult as I want to keep those recent developments from him."

"Yes, I can see that this might be a challenge," he agreed. "But it still doesn't change my decision. Just don't forget to be more careful how you talk to the King in Vern's presence. It's one thing to let your companion see how little respect you have for your sovereign, but this is not something he will let pass when others are present."

"I could take Pe'tala," she suggested.

Enric grimaced. "You can't mean that! You would very likely get both of you into more trouble than I might be able to get you out from. No, I need somebody level-headed and reliable there, not a slightly younger yet more disrespectful version of yourself."

"Hey!" she protested indignantly, both arms akimbo. "I am nothing like *her*!"

He looked at her directly. "Sure, you go on believing that, my love. And now get off to bed. Orrin tends to exploit any weaknesses he sees."

"Well, we can't all use superior strength on our fellow magicians, can we?" she said pointedly.

"No," he smiled, "that is very true. Fortunately, *you* can't."

* * *

Eryn walked into the small kitchen on the ground floor of the clinic and found Vern and Pe'tala leaning against a wall companionably and talking in an animated way.

"What's going on with you two?" she asked.

The boy sipped from his cup. "Pe'tala just told me about Takhan and the clinic over there. Did you know that they have divided healing into several areas and have healers that specialise in each?"

"Yes," she sighed. "I was over there, remember? That one visit where they almost didn't allow me to leave, a few months ago?"

"Oh yes," Pe'tala smirked, "but honestly I can tell you that it would very likely have been more of a trial for us than for yourself to have you stuck with us."

"Funny," Eryn shot back, "that didn't stop you from following me here and gracing us with your presence."

The younger woman shrugged. "I told you. I just wanted to repay the favour of making my life a little less peaceful for a while. Though I might suggest that you have profited more from my visit than you have suffered. So far," she added with a malicious glint in her eyes, doubtlessly hinting at the impending examinations.

"You be careful, or those charming dinner invitations will become regular events as long as you are here." Then she turned to Vern. "You should stop showing so much interest in Takhan for now. There is no chance of your coming with us, so you might as well make this whole matter easier on yourself and not get to know more about things that spark your interest. You will not be seeing them for yourself any time soon."

The boy shrugged. "I can still educate myself, can't I? Are you ready for your lesson with the King?"

She nodded with a disgruntled expression.

"What is the matter, dear *sister*?" Pe'tala grinned. "Not being happy about the great ruler of the country bestowing the honour of his attentions on you? Or is the thought of having a sixteen-year-old boy as your chaperone the thing that is troubling you?"

Eryn rolled her eyes without saying anything then grabbed Vern's sleeve to pull him out of the kitchen with her. Enric was probably right. Taking Pe'tala along would *not* have been a bright idea.

* * *

Eryn walked into the throne room ahead of Vern, who followed closely behind her. The King was awaiting them, next to the table at the end opposite to the throne. He waited until both of them had bowed, then pulled out a chair for Eryn.

"Vern," he went on to say, "I was wondering if you would be the one to accompany Lady Eryn today."

The boy didn't reply since it had not really been a question, but took a seat at the foot end of the table just as he had been instructed by Lord Enric.

Eryn watched the King regarding the boy pensively for a few moments, probably wondering how much he knew.

"Tell me, young man," the King then addressed him, "what exactly are your instructions concerning this meeting here?"

Vern blinked a few times, then swallowed. "To keep Lady Eryn out of trouble, essentially. If by whatever means possible I am able to do that without getting myself into it."

"I see. What kind of trouble were you told to expect, pray?" the King enquired calmly.

"Lord Enric was not very specific as to the particulars; he only told me I would recognise it when I saw it," Vern said, clearly not feeling very comfortable.

"Let us for one moment, only in theory, assume that keeping Lady Eryn out of trouble would require going against *me* either verbally or physically. Or magically. How would you handle a situation like that?"

The boy scowled. "Very, very carefully, I would think."

The King stared at him for a moment, then laughed. "Well done, my young friend. We will make sure not to have you face such a dilemma today! But I want to assure you that sending you along with Lady Eryn today is a great proof of Lord Enric's trust in you. One day you will probably learn how great it is." He then turned to Eryn and took a seat next to her at the head end of the table. "Today I would like to talk about a topic that is doubtlessly of considerable interest to you: Lord Enric."

Eryn raised her brow at him, which provoked chuckling. "This particular topic we should go through without his listening to us. You didn't think the fact that our little lesson today takes place at the same time as the Council meeting was a coincidence, did you?"

"No, not really," she shook her head. Well, at least not since Enric had pointed it out to her.

"How exactly would you manipulate a man like Lord Enric, then?"

She swallowed and took a quick look at Vern. She wondered if it was a good idea to allow him to listen to this. But then there was not really anyone else she would have considered less dangerous to Enric, unless one wanted to include Plia.

"I wouldn't," she replied slowly.

"No? And yet it would be the only way for you to get your way every now and then in matters where you are not of the same opinion."

Eryn folded her arms. "There are several things against it from my point of view. Firstly, I don't appreciate being manipulated myself, so why should I do it to others, especially my companion? Secondly, he has a reputation of not being easily moulded in his opinions as he is proficient enough in the discipline to avoid it. And thirdly, it seems that since his rise to power, using *me* has been the only way of making him do things he doesn't want to. So I am a medium for others without having any means at my own disposal to pressure him with."

"Well said," the King nodded. "The first reason is clearly one you need to work on. Though I do remember an occasion or two in the very recent past where you had no qualms about resorting to manipulation."

"I don't want to manipulate people close to me. With those I don't have any respect for such a restriction does not apply."

"Obviously," King Folrin smiled. "Your second reason is very true indeed. He has proven to be extremely resistant to being steered in the past. Though I wouldn't have expected this to stop *you*. Quite the opposite; I didn't peg you for somebody who would shirk a challenge, especially as Lord Enric himself has resorted to manipulating and spying on you when it served his purposes. As for the third, I am rather surprised at your not seeing that *your* power over him is greater than anyone else's."

He did have a point there, she had to admit. Enric had withheld information from her more than once, to make her act the way he wanted or stop her from acting on something. And yet having this man point it out to her made her want to reject the idea on principle.

"I can't help but wonder about your own agenda," she remarked. "Why would you want to persuade me to manipulate Enric? You can't rely on my intentions being in accordance with your personal plans. Rather the opposite, I would say. You intend us to go to Takhan - I want to stay in Anyueel. You don't wish me to be Head of Healers, which is *exactly* what I want to be. You intend for me to remain a member of the Order for the duration of the stay whereas I want to leave it."

The King's head moved, signalling his denial quite definitely. "Lord Enric wouldn't have granted any of those demands, even if he had been in the position to do so. He doesn't even support them - not a single one. And manipulation is not always something that requires the object of the mover's efforts being unaware of it. Consider that for a moment, my dear Lady, will you?"

She did, but the concept seemed absurd. "Are you telling me that he would respond to being openly manipulated by complying with it? That is not the man *I* have come to know."

He looked at her indulgently. "Is it possible, Lady Eryn, that the concept of feminine wiles is one unknown to you?"

She laughed out loudly. "Feminine wiles? Really? Like batting my lashes, swaying my hips and wearing clothes that are overly revealing so I get my wishes? He would see right through that!"

"Too proper and professional are you, my dear, to make use of your natural advantages? And there is a lot more than batting lashes and swaying hips. But I dare say your friend Junar would be willing to assist you on those. Or your cousin Vran'el for that matter."

Oh dear! Was the King truly telling her to use coaxing by flirtation and sex on Enric? That was extremely awkward. "My cousin's interests - as you almost certainly know - run in a completely different direction," she pointed out briskly.

"I am aware of that. But I am also told that this makes him an excellent adviser for his female friends." He looked at Vern and smiled indulgently. "But I can see that this topic is making your young friend here slightly uncomfortable."

"How considerate of you to take note of *his* discomfort," she muttered. "I am not exactly thrilled by this direction, either."

"That, Lady Eryn, is something I would advise you to learn to deal with. The Western Territories are a place where such matters are discussed quite openly. This here would even qualify as polite dinner conversation."

That was true, she knew, but it didn't make talking to the King any more bearable. She folded her arms.

"Still, I don't like it. This is not how a self-confident woman reaches her goals. Neither is it a way to earn respect."

"Self-confidence is what makes it even more effective. Only a woman aware of her own skills and value can do this properly. Respect is not something you should have to worry about with Lord Enric, I would say. I would even go so far as saying that he would enjoy it. The beauty of it is that no matter whether he sees through it or not, it will most likely work due to his attachment to you. Do you remember what I told you several months ago about playing with open cards?"

She nodded glumly. "Yes. You said doing it and still winning was the master class."

"You see, I cannot order you to use seductive powers on your companion, nor can I check that you have. But I would encourage you to. Though you might want to consider that having control of your impulses is essential for this. This also applies to being in command of your emotions as you share them through your mind bond."

Eryn briefly considered covering her ears with her hands and hiding under the table until he was done, but that would not look too good, would it?

"Now let us have a look at how others have manipulated Lord Enric so far through making use of his attachment to you. I myself have found this a very useful approach." He looked at her expectantly.

She exhaled. "The commitment which was a consequence of your..." She took a quick glance at Vern. "...threat. Then making him go to Takhan as ambassador first by making *me* agree to go there. And now he has once again agreed to go there thanks to your... persuasive measures."

"True. How about Malriel? What comes to your mind here?"

"She made him agree to be adopted by her by threatening my new House and, through that, *me* indirectly. Also she got *you* to make sure Enric goes back to Takhan for who knows how long."

"Quite," he confirmed. "But you see that his possessiveness has rendered this last move a risky one. He was willing enough to leave here, the trouble now is to convince him to return when the times comes. And here, dear Lady Eryn, we come back to yourself once more. Showing him that this is a safe place for you and making *you* want to return is the key to success. Where you want to go, he will follow. It is that simple."

That was nothing new for her. Maybe she could make him tell her something useful. "How, then, am I supposed to prevent being used for such schemes in the future?"

"How indeed?" he smiled. "Any suggestions regarding that?"

Why was he giving that question back to her? As if she would have asked had she been able to furnish the answer!

"No."

He sighed. "Now you are being stubborn. What does Lord Enric consider the solution?"

She rolled her eyes. "In his opinion most of the time trouble could be avoided by my just talking to him. I don't think the solution is as easy as that, though."

"You discard the idea because it does not appear sophisticated enough for you, my dear Lady?" he enquired gently. "Let me tell you about the merits of *talking*. We have developed the ability to talk to each other to convey information in a more precise manner than mere body language or sound alone would have permitted us. Information, you see, is a valuable currency. You make use of it in the form of knowledge to better be able to do your work. People in politics - and this is what you are, too, to a certain degree - use information to steer others and avoid being steered themselves in return. So I would advise you not to underestimate the importance of information and what some people are willing to do to obtain it."

"By using spies for example?" she threw in sarcastically.

"Exactly," he agreed. "Though I can hear the disdain for this method in your voice. Even Lord Enric utilises them, though not to the extent most others in the Order do. He has resorted to a very minimal yet effective way of using them; until recently he only used them to spy on Lord Tyront, who maintains a very extensive network which can easily compete with my own. Lord Tyront is aware of this, of course. This is the downside, you see? It implies that Lord Enric will only learn what Lord Tyront permits his spies to find. A practice Lord Tyront and I have established, too. This all is unofficial, of course." He cast a quick look at Vern, who needed a moment or two to unfreeze from his state of fascination to then nod emphatically. The King smiled. "Your escort, Lady Eryn, is a more receptive audience than yourself, it seems. Luckily for you, he will in time very likely become another useful asset for *you*. A very talented young man to have around," he pronounced. "And you were the one to discover him, as it were. You were the first to appreciate him and help him develop. Amazingly enough, stumbling across him was no more than a matter of chance, as you did not act out of self-interest - rather the opposite. It seems that luck does occasionally favour good people."

She chuckled. "You think I am a good person? While you are trying to make me see the merits of political strategy. Doesn't this seem contradictory, something that would make your efforts futile?"

"By no means. Being good is a function of two things, you see. One is the things we do, the other is why we do them. Both need to be considered. Somebody doing what is generally regarded as a good deed may well be basing their action on inferior motives. Such a person would hardly be considered *good*. Neither would the term apply to a person performing a questionable deed for pure motives. It is the combination of doing good things for noble reasons. You, as we established in our very first lesson, are determined not to make others pay for your actions. That shows a need to protect those around you - be they people known to you, but also thinking in terms of entire countries. This is an admirable attitude for somebody in your position. You could in the past and also in the future become an excuse if not a cause for a war, after all. So I rest assured in the knowledge that you will do everything in your power to avoid such an outcome. Which includes returning here after Lord Enric's assignment at House Aren has come to an end."

A nice reminder, she thought. And none too subtle.

"So what you are basically telling me is that talking to Enric should lower the probability that I am being used against him?"

The King chuckled. "Talking is one thing. The second and even more essential thing would be *listening* to him as well. Don't look at me like that. *Hearing* somebody and truly *listening* are different activities entirely. You are quick on the uptake, which makes it easier for you. However, you are also at times a captive to your impulses, and that lets your perception become rather selective and you focus on things you want or expect to hear. But the interesting things, my dear Lady, are most of the time those we are not expecting or wishing to hear."

"For example?" she prompted. She had no doubt that he would have at least one for her.

True enough, he didn't even have to think before answering. "When Lord Enric thwarts another of your plans, do you ever listen to *why* he is doing it or do you just focus on the *what*? Consider when he decided not to allow you to go on another expedition in the near future. It was because he is very protective of you - an honourable and understandable motivation. You, I am sure, prefer to see it as unfair treatment, his exerting the higher rank along with the power it gives him over you."

That was not exactly wrong, she had to admit.

"Why would his motivation behind his deeds be of any consequence to me? The outcome is the same to me, whether he wants to demonstrate his dominance or protect me."

He leaned forward. "That is where we come to the really important part: recognising a person's needs. If you can do that, Lady Eryn, you will be able to make them cooperate by either choosing your arguments in accordance with them or considering a course of action that helps their fulfilment. What course of action would lead to Lord Enric letting you go on another expedition and making allowances for his fear for your safety? These two considerations are not exclusive, you see."

Eryn exhaled. There had been discussions about that, she remembered dimly. "Taking somebody with me he trusts to keep me safe. Lord Orrin, for example."

"Exactly. Though I have the distinct feeling that this is not something you just came up with right now. If I had to guess, I would think that either Lord Enric or Lord Orrin himself proposed this to you before. Or rather presented you with a fait accompli by telling you that they wouldn't grant you another trip soon without your complying with that condition. Though of course now it seems that this is no option anyway for quite some time to come, as you will be gone for a while."

Yet again he was dead right. This was really getting annoying. Did he have to be right *all* the time? Though this was probably down to information he had received. Exactly the concept he wanted to impress on her as useful.

"I have another example for you: your mother." He raised a hand when she opened her mouth to speak. "No, don't interrupt me with a throwaway remark about her not officially being your mother. Focus on what is important here, if you will. She tried to keep you in Takhan. There were a number of needs she tried to satisfy with that plan. Which ones?"

"Taking control over my life again after my father removed it so many years ago. Proving to the world that she could. Strengthening House Aren by trapping its heiress over there. Showing me that she is the stronger of us two," Eryn listed, her expression sour.

The King nodded slowly. "They are all true to varying degrees, I would say. Though thanks to your selective perception you have left out the very reason that would make her appear more human and would thereby make rejecting her seem unjust. She wanted to get to know her only child, spend more time with you."

Eryn didn't comment on that. What was the point? Others did want to see that driver in Malriel's behaviour, even Enric. But Eryn didn't share that impression, even though doing so would have brought less pain. Being considered as no more than a political tool by her own mother was not exactly a cheering thought. She thought it possible that Malriel was proud of her to some extent, of what she had managed to achieve here, of what she had become. Nonetheless, pride and maternal love were not the same. One could be proud of a great many things without loving them.

The King watched her expression becoming grim. "I see there is not much to be gained from pursuing that particular topic any longer. You have an adverse reaction to it and will not accept anything I have to tell you in connection with it. What are *my* needs in making sure to have you return here?"

"Taking control of our life. Proving to the world that you can. Strengthening the Kingdom by reclaiming two of your three most powerful magicians. Demonstrating that you are the strongest of us," she said, recycling her earlier statements about Malriel using varied wording and with a smug smile. She could see from the corner of her eye how Vern was covering his mouth surreptitiously to hide a grin.

"Interesting way of putting it," the King said and steepled his fingers. "There are other areas you have not considered. I told you once that I consider you something close to an ally, and that is a good thing to have in the Magic Council, which you will officially join after your return. Lord Enric, too, is not opposed to me normally, save the recent events. I regularly grant him permission for projects, businesses and other plans he has. I make sure he finds having *me* as his King more beneficial than taking the risk of disposing of me. Then there are your efforts that benefit the Kingdom greatly by bringing healing back to us. I wonder what else you will accomplish in the years to come because I fully intend to take advantage of it. Then there is the simple fact that I have come to enjoy your company and would not like to be deprived of that in the long run."

"Quite a lot of reasons," she mused. "And all of those would have to be taken into consideration when asking something of you, I suppose?"

"They would. And what is even more important is knowing what your own needs are. If you are not aware of them but others are, this is a severe disadvantage and makes you easy prey for those who want to use you." The King then turned to Vern. "I believe there is something you would like to bring up, young man, unless I am mistaken?"

Eryn's eyes snapped to the boy. Oh no - he surely wouldn't try to ask the King to send him to Takhan, would he? Not with his father and her as his immediate superiors set against it. She tried to fashion a warning look for him, but he ignored her and cleared his throat.

"Yes, Your Majesty. There is a matter I would very much like to address. I wish to thank you for the chance to do so without first making an appointment," Vern said formally and got up from his chair. Sitting in front of the King while asking him for something was clearly not something he felt appropriate.

King Folrin acknowledged the thanks and nodded for him to go on.

"I request to be sent to Takhan along with the rest of the party. Allow me to present my reasons." He used his fingers to enumerate his arguments. "I am currently the most advanced local healer, save for Lady Eryn, of course, which means I am in a position to continue my studies on a level which would not really be possible here. I am still in education, so I would not be leaving an unoccupied position needing to be filled in my absence. I am convinced that the knowledge I will bring back would benefit the Kingdom considerably, since even a person as intelligent as Lady Eryn may only acquire so much knowledge in the course of no more than a few months."

Eryn folded her arms and waited for the King to reply, instructing Vern that he was to bow to his father's judgement. To her dismay he looked thoughtful when he should instead have been radiating disapproval.

"Valid reasons. Though you would miss quite a few months of classes here."

Vern pulled a small, rolled up paper slip from his pocket. It was obviously a message delivered by bird.

"I have a confirmation of arrangements from Ram'an of House Arbil. He has been kind enough to help me find a tutor in Takhan, as classes with many students, such as we have here, are not common in the Western Territories. I would be taught in the subjects that are common there and would gain valuable insights into their education system from that. Insights that would no doubt be valuable for our Kingdom," he finished.

Eryn stared at him open-mouthed for several moments, then slowly rose from her chair. "Tell me you are joking! Tell me you did not contact Ram'an behind my back to have him aid you in this ill-fated plan of yours! You are staying here - end of the discussion! I am your superior, and that is an order!"

"Lady Eryn, I have granted the boy permission to speak. To *me*. You may discuss this matter with him afterwards. Not now," he admonished her with a levelling look. "Now sit down again and be still or you will have to leave. When I last checked, I was still the one giving the final orders here. And as far as I am aware, his new direct superior concerning healing is Lord Poron. I don't see how your objections are relevant here at this point."

She swallowed her anger and plunked back down in her chair, her expression irate.

The King turned back to Vern. "I see you have given this rather a lot of thought. How about your work as a healer? As you said yourself, apart from Lady Eryn you are the most advanced healer here. Having both of you away might turn out to be a problem for the clinic."

The boy smiled. "Fortunately that would not be much of a problem, because Pe'tala only recently decided to prolong her stay here for another few months. Only this morning did she receive a message from Takhan that it has been granted. From what I know she has already filed a request with Lord Poron for his approval."

Eryn's head jerked up. "She did *what*? Why didn't I know about this?"

"Lady Eryn, you either keep your mouth shut or I will remove Lord Enric from his Council meeting to take you away from here. I mean that," the King hissed at her.

She swallowed and leaned back again, her lips pressed tight into a thin line, arms folded.

"I see. That would solve that problem, I imagine," the King then went on after returning his attention to Vern. "Judging from your very well-prepared plans I assume you have already talked to Lord Poron about this?"

The boy nodded. "I have. He welcomes the chance to have another well-trained healer at his disposal, as Lady Eryn will not be exclusively available for the discipline."

"Lord Tyront?" the King asked simply.

"Is in favour of the idea. He thinks I have a bright future ahead of me in the Order and welcomes the chance for me to obtain a broader education."

Eryn sighed loudly and closed her eyes. Damn that man! Damn them all! That was a bit too well-rehearsed, even by Vern's standards. That looked suspiciously like Enric's handy-work.

"Well done, my young friend," the King smiled. "You have given this matter a great deal of consideration and provided me with reasons that let me recognise benefits for the Kingdom." He turned to Eryn and smiled. "This, Lady Eryn, is how one makes one's King agree to a request. He did not waste a single word on his own interests or wishes but gave me something I was able to work with, something that made listening to him worth my while. You attempted something similar when you first tried to introduce your plan for a healer's association to the Magic Council, but your tempter got the better of you." He looked back at Vern. "Congratulations, young man I herewith officially decree that you are to accompany your family to Takhan to improve your knowledge of healing, whichever arts you are interested in, local education standards and of course cultural and social features of their society. I will have written confirmations despatched to Lord Tyront, your father and Lord Poron in the evening."

Eryn bit her tongue to hold herself back from cursing. He had gone and granted it. What's more, he had even more or less told the boy to have fun and go to parties.

"You are both dismissed," the King then said with a final, slightly amused, look at Eryn.

Vern bowed, torn between immense joy and dread of facing Eryn as soon as they were out the door.

She jumped up with barely hidden wrath and stamped off towards the exit, at which point she heard the King's calm voice behind her.

"I think you have forgotten a little something, Lady Eryn. There is a certain protocol when it comes to retreating in the presence of a King."

She stopped in her tracks, whirled, gave him a devastating look and bowed with fists balled at her sides before turning back towards the doors and storming outside. Vern increased his pace and called after her when he was out in the Palace corridors and the guards had closed the doors behind them.

"Eryn! Wait!"

She didn't stop, only growled back over her shoulder, "I am not talking to you right now." There was somebody else she had to grind this axe with first.

* * *

Enric controlled his breathing from a chest tightened by floods of emotion. Her anger was like a dull throbbing behind his temples. A quick look at the faintly glowing symbols from their commitment ceremony on his wrist told him that she couldn't be far away. In fact, most probably waiting outside the Council hall for him. That was unfortunate. He had been hoping that she had stormed back to their house to await him there, fuming and ready to jump him the minute he got there. It was not to be. It seemed she had plumped for the option that did not require as much waiting, the one that would allow her to rid herself of her anger more quickly. Probably also in public.

At least she had not stormed in here to abuse him in front of the other Council members. Not yet.

Tyront followed the younger man's gaze to his wrist, a hardly discernible smile curling at the corners of his mouth. Enric pulled his sleeve down. He wasn't comfortable with his superior's amusement at his expense; there were still some remainders of tension between them since that day in the arena. Their meetings had so far been professional and guarded. There had been none of their usual private banter for quite a while now.

Tyront had only recently carefully began enquiring about personal matters. Such as how Eryn was getting along with her exam preparations, how the tutorials with the King were going and how the construction of Enric's ships in Bonhet had progressed so far. Those had been his first struggles with getting back to normal again, Enric knew. But he was not yet willing to respond to that. He needed Tyront truly to understand that this was not a matter to brush away as easily as that. He wanted it understood that anybody who messed with Eryn would be directly answerable to her companion - *him*. It didn't matter if this were the King. Or the Order's leader who was going along with the monarch's whims.

Yet he had to give it to Tyront that he had approved of Enric's recommendation to send Vern to Takhan almost immediately. Another signal that he didn't want these tensions between them to go on.

Tyront looked at him sideways for a moment, then cleared his throat to announce that in his opinion all important matters for today had been taken care of and that the next meeting was arranged for exactly two weeks' time. There were a few puzzled expressions at the abrupt ending, though nobody objected. They slowly stood and most of them kept talking while they were walking towards the double doors.

Enric caught a glimpse of a slim figure, clad in purple robes, outside in the corridor. Her face was grim, and she stood in a broad stance with arms folded defiantly in front of her. He saw Lord Woldarn smile and look back at him with a gleeful expression, suddenly not too keen on retreating from the hall so quickly.

When approximately half of the Council members had filed out, Eryn walked in - her movements controlled, yet clearly disclosing her inner tension. She walked towards him and Tyront, who also seemed in no hurry to leave the hall. Orrin raised his brow at her questionioningly, but she ignored him, continuing towards Enric determinedly. The warrior slowly changed his direction to follow her.

"You!" she snarled quietly when she was close enough for him to hear her. "You have precisely one minute to get rid of whoever you don't want to overhear what I have to say to you."

Tyront raised his voice, addressing the few Council members who were trying to linger surreptitiously to watch the spectacle that was quite obviously about to start soon. "Gentlemen, please kindly excuse us, would you?"

The four men looked up, feigning surprise that there was really any privacy required, as if they had not realised that there was any need for it. They murmured their assent and quickly left, the last one closing the door firmly behind him.

"I just had a very interesting meeting with the King. And Vern," she said in an even tone, her voice a stark contrast to the fire in her eyes.

"Yes?" Enric enquired calmly, knowing fully well what this concerned. He considered asking Tyront and Orrin to leave, but the first simply wouldn't and Eryn would almost certainly tell Orrin to stay as he was no doubt an ally in this anyway.

"Imagine my surprise when the King invited Vern to address him regarding a specific issue we know he has been discontented about for a while now," she said with a withering look. "And you know what? It turned out that Vern was exceedingly well-prepared for putting words to that request. Imagine that!"

"We know Vern to be a thorough and earnest young man," Enric remarked calmly.

"That we do," she agreed with a smile that disclosed rather too many teeth. "And yet I couldn't help thinking that this level of insight was just a scratch above what I might have expected. Even from Vern. Would you care to share your sentiments on that with me? Or rather own up to supporting him right away without pussyfooting? How else would the King have got the idea to address the subject, after all?"

Now Orrin spoke up, his eyes narrowed. "Vern addressed the King about going to Takhan? What did he have to say?" he asked a little tensely.

Eryn didn't take her eyes off Enric while she answered him. "The King granted it. Vern is now officially being sent to Takhan with us. To educate himself in all the areas that he terms beneficial for himself, the Kingdom and the Order. Somehow he even managed to arrange for tutoring in Takhan with the help of a certain former ambassador we are all familiar with. I wonder where that idea sprung up from," she concluded with a pointed look at her companion.

"Enric?" Orrin asked sharply.

"I recommended to both the King and the Order that he should accompany us, yes," he admitted unperturbed.

"So you didn't consider that if not *my* objections, then at least his *father's* should be respected?" Eryn demanded, then looked at Tyront. "From Vern's suspiciously well-phrased arguments I gathered that you, too, were in favour of this. Does none of you have any scruples about sending a teenager to a country that might be on the brink of war currently?" she asked, her arms unfolding and balling into fists at her side. "What were you thinking of?"

"If I thought this to be the case, I would not be taking you or Junar there, either," Enric replied in that steady way of his that drove her insane when she felt about to explode.

"Which means my own concerns are not at all important to you? You are not the only one who has to assess the dangers in this! Or bear the consequences should something go wrong over there!" she cried out angrily.

"Neither are you," Enric said. "I wonder about your untypical selfishness, especially with regard to Vern. You yourself have always lamented the Order's and also society's lack of respect and admiration for his talents. Now he has the chance go to somewhere where he has already made a name for himself and where he is admired thanks to no more than a single book of his they saw. He will meet with artists, healers, followers; he will learn, develop and finally get the appreciation he deserves, even according to you. Of course he wants to go there! And he should."

Eryn blinked twice. Selfish? Was she truly being selfish in wanting to deny his accompanying them?

Orrin flashed his superior an irate look and took Eryn's arm, saying quickly and with urgent emphasis, "Don't let yourself be tricked into feeling guilty for wanting to protect Vern. You are not the one who has to justify herself. He is the one who acted behind our backs. He wants somebody to keep an eye on you in Takhan, preferably somebody he can trust and who will be more than happy spending time with you at the very place you are likely to be for the bulk of your time: the clinic. Enric himself knows that he will be too busy with his new position as Head of House and senator to do so himself."

Enric pursed his lips. Pity. That looked as if it would have worked without Orrin unmasking his strategy.

Eryn gave him another scorching look. "You *are* manipulating me! The King was right!" She lifted a finger up to his face. "I have had enough of your playing me like this! And I don't need a teenage boy to supervise me! Bastard!" she spat and whirled around.

He grabbed her wrist before she could rush off. "Wait."

"For what? Wait for you to come to your senses? What is your problem here? Why do you have to have everything I do under *your* control? I am a grown woman, not your daughter! Stop treating me like a child!" she shouted and pulled herself free from his hold. "I am utterly sick of this!"

She turned and stormed off, not bothering to shut the door behind her. Enric went forward to follow her, but Orrin stepped in his way with his arms folded.

"Now you wait for a moment yourself. This is *my* boy we are talking about here, and I do not take kindly to being bypassed in this way. I am responsible for him, after all. You might not think that there is a war impending in the Western Territories, but you'd better make sure you remove my family to safety in case you are wrong."

Enric nodded. "I am insulted you think you have to point that out. There are arrangements to take care of that."

"I consider Eryn one of my family, I case you were wondering," he growled for emphasis.

"That I am aware of, yes," Enric replied dryly. "But do I need to remind you that she is family to *me* as well."

Orrin nodded. "Of course she is. Though she is right enough; you are obviously a bit mixed up when it comes to your role towards her."

He bowed to Tyront, gave Enric a final angry look, then turned and paced out the door as well.

Enric stared at the doors through which both of them had just disappeared, an uncomfortable knot forming in his stomach. Her parting words about being fed up had left a bitter aftertaste. Fed up with the situation? Fed up with *him*? He had received a faint echo of her feeling enraged, helpless, betrayed. She had shielded her emotions, but there was always a little that got through, not enough to overwhelm him, but to give him a good impression of the turbulence going on inside her.

"She is right, you know, at least to a certain degree," Tyront said quietly. "I know why you are doing it, but I see you treating her the way I used to treat you when I first got my hands on you. It honours me that I seem to be serving as a role model, but the situation is not the same. I am twenty years older than you. Nor did we have a personal attachment back then. You, on the other hand, are in a relationship that is supposed to be on equal terms - at least that one outside the Order. You need to get the roles you play in her life under control. You can't act as her superior when it comes to private matters, and taking Vern with you was nothing more than a private consideration, as we both understand."

Enric raised an eyebrow at him. "And yet you gave the Order's permission without hesitating."

"You are mature enough to bear the consequences of your actions. I am not here to protect you from yourself any longer. See? *I* learned that lesson."

"I had better go after her now."

"Yes, you better had," Tyront agreed with a faint smile.

* * *

Eryn walked on, hearing footsteps behind her she recognised as Orrin's.

"To my place," he said once he had drawn level with her. "You and I should have a little talk with Vern. And your companion deserves a bit of steaming, if you ask me."

She nodded, grateful that he was once more a safe haven for her, someone she could go to whenever the world went loopy on her. Having him in Takhan would be a great comfort, and the prospect of having to go there again so soon was somehow not so scary, knowing that he would be coming with her.

They had reached the door to the warriors' quarters when Eryn spotted Enric emerging from the Palace compound. Their eyes met for a moment, then she turned to disappear into the building. That would surely be a clear enough signal that she had no intention of talking to him right now, one she hoped he respected for a change.

When they reached the stairs that led up to the first floor, she listened for the door at the other end of the corridor and nodded with satisfaction when everything seemed quiet. Good - that meant that he had not followed them.

Orrin opened the door to his quarters for her and let her go ahead of him. Vern jumped up from the sofa he had been settled on and suddenly looked slightly daunted when he saw the two of them coming in. Dealing with both of them at the same time was clearly not something he favoured.

"Father. Eryn," he said with an uncomfortable expression, obviously dreading what was to come.

"Sit," Orrin growled at him and the boy complied instantly, sinking back to the settee he had just got up from.

Eryn pulled the healer's robe over her head to hang it on a hook next to the door, then adjusted her tunic before stepping closer to Vern.

"You have some explaining to do, young man," she said with steady eyes on him. "That was rather a sly trick you played on us today."

"I told you that you were to remain here in Anyueel while we were gone," Orrin joined in. "As long as you are not of legal age you are bound to comply with what I think is best for you!"

Nobody said anything for several moments; the argument that what Orrin had just said did not apply in this case - when both the King and Lord Tyront had decided otherwise - hung heavily in the air, unspoken.

"Or should be bound to it," he amended. "As soon as we are back from Takhan, you will be kept on a tight leash until you are nineteen and then no longer legally subject to my care."

Vern groaned. "Father, I am sorry!"

"I'll bet you are. But you are not sorry for going behind my back, you are sorry you have to suffer for it."

The boy's expression suggested that this was not entirely untrue.

"Come on, father! How could I not have tried it? This is a unique chance for me!"

"A unique chance to get into big trouble out there, you stupid boy," Eryn butted in. "It is dangerous for people who do not know the local customs and are unprotected because they are not members of a House. I have been there and know all about it."

"Just because your mother used all her malice against you doesn't mean that this is how they treat all their visitors," he pleaded. "I will behave, I promise! No insulting of important people, no disregard for their traditions, no..."

She sighed, "Vern, I didn't want you to remain here because I was afraid of your aiming to wreak havoc there, more that you would stumble into it. I almost found myself dancing a seduction dance with Ram'an, quite unknowingly, for example. Had Enric not interfered, that would have been a very awkward situation." Not that Enric's smashing Ram'an with his fist so hard that he was thrown across an entire table plus cushions had been any less disturbing, she recalled, silently. "I am sure that you will do your best to show respect and avoid breaking laws, but this is not always easy. Also you are a target, as you are associated with me and thereby with Enric. Not all of them are pleasant people over there."

"You mean, pretty much like here?" he asked pointedly.

"Yes," she admitted, "though here at least we usually know in which direction to turn when somebody makes our life harder. We don't know very much about the open and covert alliances and enmities between the Houses and whoever else is important over there, though."

"But that is something we can learn! Lord Enric is good at this political assessment thing; he will make sure we are safe."

They boy's confidence in Enric's impressive powers of conflict avoidance was touching, but it wasn't something which should make him underestimate the potential for danger and the need to be careful there.

"You will be a liability once we leave here," she said without pity.

Vern's gaze became angry. "You are just saying this to make me feel bad about being permitted to go!" he wailed.

"No, I am not! It is simply the reason I wanted to leave you behind."

"Lord Enric doesn't seem to think so," he retorted with folded arms. It seemed like he had left the state of anxiety behind and moved on to simple annoyance.

"No, but in all honesty, right now I am not at all interested in what all-seeing Lord Enric thinks of anything," she lobbed back.

He grimaced. "You are mad with him."

"Of course I am mad with him! With both of you for that matter! With you because you are an idiot, and with him because he is a manipulative bastard who doesn't take my opinion into consideration but instead acts behind my back!" she hissed. She exhaled slowly when she felt Orrin's warm hand on her shoulder. There she was, starting to let her irritation with Enric out on Vern. Not good. She rubbed her face and let herself slump down into a chair.

"What sense does it make to tell you what an idiot you are?" she murmured. "It is too late now. All in all, Enric is the one to blame here. He should have known better. I trust that without his help, you wouldn't have found gaining the permission quite so easy."

Vern grimaced. "It was not his fault," he said, his loyalty undiminished by Eryn's condemnation of her companion.

"It was from where I stand," she replied sharply. "Listen, no more discussion about that now! Go to your room and think about what you have got yourself into!"

"*You* can't send me to my room! Superior magicians cannot interfere unbidden in purely domestic matters! That's what the law says," he protested.

Orrin shot him a look. "But *I* can. Off with you. And stay in there until dinner arrives."

The boy rose from his seat with a sulky expression, his lips pressed together and marched towards his door, closing it more than firmly.

The two magicians stared at each other for a while, then Eryn exhaled wearily. "Thank you for assisting me against Enric today, when he wanted to play me again. You know, I think you are the only person in this bloody Order who I can genuinely trust in. You are the only one who has the means to play the game, but decides against it. You really are honest and reliable. The King once told me that you are a good person. Straight. I only now see how very true that is."

The warrior raised his brow and smiled. "He said I was *good*? What an unflattering character assessment for a fighter."

"Would you rather go for *devious, manipulative and untrustworthy,* like my beloved companion?" she sniffed.

Orrin sighed. "You *can* trust him, Eryn. Though obviously not always to keep you informed or respect your wishes. But you can depend on him to protect you. That's actually what all this is about. I can understand that well enough. Though I also need to protect my son, hence I am not very thrilled about his choice of strategy. I do believe, however, that he sincerely believes Vern faces no danger. The trouble is, following your first stay there I am not so optimistic."

Eryn nodded; it was a sentiment she shared.

"Is there a chance for us to do anything against the Royal decision?"

Orrin shook his head. "None. The King can't change his mind about that, it would make him appear indecisive. And Enric wouldn't like it either. Lord Tyront and the King are still working on making him happy. Unfortunately, they are not squeamish about how they treat others, namely you and me, in the process."

"Hypocrites," she grumbled. "First they tell me that they need me to cooperate as making *me* happy is what will ultimately bring Enric around, but when the question is angering him or me, I see what their priorities really are. That's what cooperating with them gets me!"

"Political strategy, my dear girl. It's a dirty game."

She snorted. "As if I didn't know. I have been their pawn ever since I have arrived here. It's just that I was not really prepared for Vern to go behind my back like that. He is in the game already, and against *me*!"

"I know." He looked at the door to Vern's room. "But you should understand why he is doing this. You are pretty much the first real friend he ever had, as he was always just too different from the others. The thought of seeing you, Junar and I go away for several months was undoubtedly not an easy one. We are all bound for some great adventure, and he was to be left behind. That is not something a determined lad like him is going to swallow just like that. I underestimated his determination, though."

"You are proud of him!" she exclaimed in an accusing voice.

"Shut up! We don't want him to know that! It would only encourage him. Yes, of course I am proud; it shows that he can take care of himself and protect his interests, stand his ground. Those are useful strengths in a young lad."

"Then I suppose I should be proud of Enric, too? As standing his ground is even better for a *grown* lad?" she snapped.

"No, you should be mad with Enric because he didn't treat you with the respect you as his companion deserve. It's a good idea to make sure he learns that lesson soon, or it will be something to haunt you for years to come."

"Something to look forward to," she murmured. "You know, I thought that our being willing to enter into that third level bond kind of meant that we had reached the end of a journey, that we would then find our rhythm. I thought that reaching that state of loving each other is a sign that we are safe, in a manner of speaking."

"Says the woman who almost chokes on the words *I love you*? When did that happen? Finally working out that you want him is not the end of the journey, it's the beginning. And you are *never* safe. The bond is no guarantee for being happy together forever. It's work - not a blissful state of peace where you can kick back for the rest of your life. And what you need to work on right now is to make that man stop treating you like his subordinate all the time."

"Any bright ideas how to accomplish that particular feat?" she said, slightly exasperated.

"I can't do all the work for you, can I?" he said, smiling benevolently.

"I knew it," she snorted.

"I have to take care of a few things now. I assume you have no intention of returning home to Enric, so I suggest you find a way to occupy yourself."

She nodded. "I will send a messenger to get me a book or two from the clinic. I still have some preparation work to do for these exams in two weeks."

Orrin got up. "You do that. How long are you going to let him stew? Am I to have the guest room prepared for you?"

"No, that would be taking it too far, I think. I don't want him to come over, throw me over his shoulder like a sack of flour and haul me home. I'll have dinner here and then return. That should be enough time for him to think. He is a quick one, after all. Well, mostly."

* * *

Enric pushed the book aside after re-reading the same paragraph for the second time without remembering a single word of it. He was still waiting for Eryn to return home.

He had been at Orrin's place about three hours ago when she had not turned up for dinner. He wanted to let her know that he was willing to give her some space, but that did not include her sleeping somewhere else.

She had explained to him that she had no intention of doing so, but that returning home with him at this moment was also not what she wanted. A bit more time to calm down and speak ill of him, then she would return. That exchange had been very polite and civilised. He had then left and returned home, waiting for her to come back ever since.

He had used the time to think, of course. He wondered if trying to persuade her to take Vern would have been successful. Or if simply letting her know that he intended to support Vern's plan would have made a difference. She had told him to stop treating her like his daughter. Was that what he had been doing? Protecting his companion was surely not the same as treating her as a child, or was it?

He remembered his father and his views on the role of a woman. Namely that she needed every aspect of her life overseen by the man she was bound to. Or, if there was none, by her father. His sister had not taken well to that line and left home as soon as she was old enough. So it had not been a very serviceable approach.

How much of this was he carrying inside him and applying unconsciously? Being confronted with it during the formative years of his life probably had left its mark.

He pushed aside the thought, feeling mad with himself. Only a coward blamed others for his own mistakes. Perhaps manipulating others had just become second nature to him in these last fifteen years since his rise to power. So much that he didn't even hesitate employing it with the person closest to him. He hadn't had the luxury of being able to trust anybody completely in a long time, he realised. Yet he did now. Only his head did not yet seem to have got around to this new reality. He had to work on that, he thought. Or he would make it impossible for her to trust him in return.

Both Orrin and Tyront had told him that he needed to do something here. He might not appreciate their meddling in his relationship very much, but he still valued their opinion - no matter how tense the situation with each of them was. They were right, he knew.

His thinking stilled when he heard the entrance door opening and he rose from the study sofa.

He leaned against the door frame and watched her taking off her robes and hanging them on a hook. He noted the exact moment when she became aware of his presence by the jerk of tension in her shoulders.

"Hello, my love," he said, sheepishly.

She turned to him and nodded once. "Enric," she said formally.

Funny, he thought, how after all these months he had been using his term of endearment for her, yet she still addressed him by his name. She had once called him *darling* in Takhan, shortly after their arrival when she had been under the influence of her uncle's happiness spell. He had been hoping that it would become more common. In vain, however. The only other name she did use for him was not exactly flattering. *Bastard*.

He strolled towards her, noting the warning showing clearly in her eyes. He thought it wiser not to kiss her for a greeting but instead took her hand and led her to a sofa in the parlour.

"I have been thinking," he said slowly and took a seat next to her, keeping her hand in his. He was glad she didn't try to pull it away. That meant that her level of anger had subsided enough to make a sensible conversation possible.

"Have you now."

"Yes. I can see why you are mad at me. And you are right." He smiled when she blinked in surprise.

"I am?"

"Yes, you are. I have become so used to having to work around people instead of with them that I don't take the trouble to check what is appropriate. Now I see that my asking you to share information and getting irritated when you won't is not exactly fair considering my own recent doings. Tyront and Orrin both told me that my perception of our roles needs some revision."

She raised her brow in surprise. With Orrin such a thing was not unexpected. But Tyront, too, being on her side on this? His input was probably what had induced Enric to do some serious thinking.

"So... what exactly does this mean? Are you about to promise me now that you will improve your behaviour toward me?" she asked, feeling sceptical.

"No. No promises. I am simply going to do it."

That made her smile. With any other man that might have seemed like grandstanding, but with him it was simply a statement of fact.

Which was so much more believable than any promise would have been.

"Very well. You do that."

He lifted her hand to kiss it. "I will."

"Orrin said you did all this to protect me. So I assume you are not sorry about assisting Vern in that way?"

Tricky, Enric thought. But he couldn't lie, not now. "No, I am not. I am just sorry about the manner in which I did it. I should have discussed it with you instead, whether we reached an agreement or not. At least it wouldn't have taken you by surprise when you saw me helping him." He smiled. "Though I know you would still have been mad at me. But not as much."

She breathed easier. Not much sense in denying that, was there?

"Are we in trouble?" she asked quietly. "With each other, I mean? Why do we keep stumbling into these situations? Look at Orrin and Junar, they never go through anything like this."

Enric put his hand tenderly against the back of her neck and pulled her close, resting his forehead against hers. "Their circumstances are not quite as complicated as ours, my love. Junar is no long lost, exotic foreign princess with magical abilities who we more or less drafted into the Order under pressure. Our relationship did not exactly kick off the classic way, so we first had to come to terms with that. Also, it has overshadowed the way we deal with each other for quite some time now. It's high time to get it behind us." He smiled. "Imagine the two of us working together. We could make the whole world tremble in trepidation."

She chuckled. "Then let's start our reign of terror. Though *after* my exams, if you don't mind."

CHAPTER 27

The Exams

Eryn chewed on her third sweet bread bun that morning, careful not to drop any crumbs on the book in front of her. The text considered the impact of dehydration on the human body. She was almost finished with that particular topic, with three more books lying on the desk in her study beside her. These were the last few she needed to get through within the next ten days.

Pe'tala had started teasing her by dropping hints about the exacting nature of the exams, how much they were dreaded back in Takhan – and how very justified that was. Eryn had taken to ignoring those little attempts at unsettling her. Unfortunately they still worked well enough on another level. She had taken quite a few exams since she had joined the Order, basically in all subjects they kept insisting on teaching her. Yet she had had no particular regard for any of those subjects and couldn't have cared less if she had failed. It was just something the Order wanted her to do, nothing she herself felt compelled to accomplish. With healing that was different, very much so. These were the ones she *wanted* to pass, and preferably before she had to leave for Takhan. How much nicer would it be to arrive there as an almost fully certified healer, with just one exam lacking instead of having to take all of them there!

She knew that Pe'tala would not make it easy on her. She couldn't anyway, even if she wanted to. Testing her own sister - legally speaking - might earn her the accusation of making it too easy for Eryn. Or too hard, if she was too demanding and caused her to fail, or made it unnecessarily gruelling for Eryn due to the enmity still between them. The first case would make people in the Western Territories think she had not really earned the certificate and so they would not really look at the qualification seriously. And in the case of her failing she would be considered a helpless victim of her cousin's desire for revenge. Neither of those alternatives was appealing.

The only option for both of them to come out of this without having to justify anything would be sitting fair exams that she would pass and that were duly documented for review by healing experts in Takhan.

No pressure, Eryn thought sarcastically, and returned to her book, swallowing the last bite of her bread bun. Without looking she felt for another one in the small basked to her right and frowned when she just felt the weave under her fingertips. Empty already? But maybe that was better, anyway. She had started snacking on these buns in unusual quantities since she started her preparations for the exams. It seemed her brain needed the extra sugar to deal with all the extra work it was having to do. Unfortunately, her stomach did not seem to go along with her cravings. It kept complaining, like now.

She closed her eyes, healed away the queasiness, knowing fully well that it would be back in just a few minutes, and concentrated once more to get through the last few pages of this book.

Just when she had managed to focus her thoughts on the topic once again, she heard a knock at her door frame and groaned before looking up. It seemed there was no chance for her to get through all this right now.

Enric stood in the doorway, holding up a thin slip of paper. So there was a message from Takhan.

"Malriel asks what we prefer with arrangements for servants while we are there. Do we want them to be available all day long the way we are used to from here or do we want to adapt to the local customs?"

Eryn frowned. "Why would that be any of her business?" Then it dawned on her, when her thoughts had left healing and caught up with the conversation. "Wait a moment! No! You can't mean it!" She rose from her chair. "I am *not* going to stay at the Aren residence!"

He sighed. "Eryn, as new temporary Head of the House I can hardly choose to stay anywhere else. It would look like a lack of commitment to my responsibilities, and rightly so."

She folded her arms. "Very well. I understand that - I admit that it wouldn't look good."

Enric nodded and smiled. "Good, I..."

"But this need not apply to me. I am not a member of her House, and considering our falling-out I doubt that anybody would object if I kept my distance from her and her House."

His eyes narrowed. "Are you telling me that I am to stay there alone while you move in with Valrad and Vran'el? How likely do you think that is? What makes you think I would agree to a thing like that? Where I go, you go."

"Not if you go to the Aren residence," she corrected him, her expression determined. "I am not going to stay under one roof with her. This is not open for discussion. I understand why *you* need to reside there, but I don't. I will not attempt to cause you to neglect your duties. And we can still see each other every day. The residences are not so far apart, after all."

He came closer and gave her a stern look. "That is very noble and generous of you, but I have no intention of letting my duties separate me from you. That is a promise."

Her eyes narrowed. "I hope you are not trying to tell me that you will *make* me stay there."

"No. I am trying to tell you that you are more important to me than House Aren and that I hope to find a compromise that works for both of us."

Her tense shoulders relaxed and normal breathing resumed. They were making progress. Good.

"What do you suggest, then?" she asked.

"How about staying somewhere else while Malriel is still in the city? Although I can't stay at House Vel'kim; I can't be seen to prefer another House to my own. It has to be somewhere neutral."

"Like the ambassadorial residence?"

"Exactly like that," he nodded. "I suppose we could trespass on Kilan's hospitality for a week or two. Though we would of course have to make do with another part of the residence, since he is now entitled to the master bedroom."

She smiled. "I wouldn't want to kick the poor fellow out of his bed."

"Very considerate of you," he smiled back, then became serious again. "Then, after Malriel has left Takhan, you will come to the Aren residence with me. I have no intention of spending a single night without you."

She scowled, thinking of the unpleasant times she had endured there. The notion of having to live for several months there was not exactly one packed with delight. But then Enric had been understanding enough not to try and force her to stay there while Malriel was in the city. That meant that it was now her turn to meet him halfway.

"I agree," she sighed. "As soon as the Queen of Darkness has left Takhan, we will move into her noxious lair."

"Queen of Darkness," he mused and grinned. "I like it."

"Good. I intend to keep on referring to her as such."

"Not in polite company, I hope. It would make people start wondering how stable the newly forged alliance between our Houses really is."

"Fair enough," she shrugged. "What about Orrin, Junar and Vern? Where are they going to stay?"

"With us, of course. Both residences are spacious enough to easily accommodate two families. Unless you prefer to have them settled elsewhere?"

Eryn swallowed. "I was just thinking about their forthcoming new family member. Their baby will be born about two and a half months after we arrive there. Do we really want to have a crying infant around us? They are said to be rather disruptive for people's sleeping habits, you know."

"That is not a very sympathetic thing to say, my love," he shook his head disapprovingly.

"You think? I *am* sympathetic. Just with my own needs first in this case."

"You do remember that her being pregnant is to a certain degree your accomplishment, right?"

She rolled her eyes. "So you think this is how I have to pay for it? Fabulous. Just let me remind you that your nights would also be less restful than you are used to. What's more, once we allow them to stay with us, we can't send them away again after their baby has started robbing us of every minute of sleep. That would look really bad."

Enric just smiled. Getting her in one house with a new-born infant would probably make her reconsider her negative attitude towards having one herself. Most of them were immensely likeable, after all. He hoped that Junar and Orrin's would turn out to be a well-behaved one with high cuteness appeal.

"Don't you worry about living with a subordinate? Two of them, in fact," she tried another approach. "It might seem a bit inappropriate, don't you think?"

"Firstly, that would be *three* subordinates, counting you as well. And secondly, I am about to be released from the Order for the duration of our stay there, so I would be no longer part of that hierarchy."

"Yes, alright," she mumbled, "keep reminding me of it, why don't you?"

"Cheer up, dearest: I am then no longer authorised to issue you with any orders for rather a long time. I would have thought that this counted for something in your book," he chuckled.

She rolled her eyes. "You will hardly be any less powerful over there, as Head of House and senator, than you are here. I am confident that you will find some legitimate reason to push me around somehow."

He grinned. "What can I say? I am a born leader."

She sniffed. "Not according to the stories *I* have been hearing. They suggest that there was quite a lot of pressure necessary to turn you from an obstinate, insubordinate, disrespectful, lazy young man into this *born* leader."

"You know how stories tend to change with telling over time," he shrugged.

She laughed. "Not to such an extent."

His gaze fell on the empty bread basket. "Have you ploughed through another helping of bread buns? I worry about your eating habits while you are boning up on theory. I am no healer, but this does seem a bit one-sided."

"I have it under control. I can stop anytime I want to. It's just that I don't want to right now. A few sweet buns a day won't kill me. You are not worried about my turning to flab, are you?" she snickered. "The love you keep insisting you feel for me will hardly be lessened by a few extra curves, will it?"

"No, it won't. Though I don't really worry about that as long as you have to improve those fighting skills regularly through training. That should keep you fit enough. And as you will continue to be a member of the Order and we happen to be taking your combat trainer with us, there is nothing to stop you from continuing to train in Takhan. Isn't that handy?"

"Just fabulous," she growled. "Go. I need to finish this book or I will have to face Pe'tala's satisfied sneer, with her telling me that she knew all along that an Aren woman can't be a proper healer, if I fail."

"You won't fail. You are too stubborn for that." He kissed her lips gently and then turned to leave. "Ah yes, one more thing: Tyront asked me to remind you that he expects you to pass all your other exams as well before we leave. He wants you to be fit and ready to join the sacred halls of the Magic Council when we return."

"Just terrific. Marvellous," she snapped. "As if I have nothing else to do." Well, at least Pe'tala would be taking care of the healing part while they were gone. That was quite a lot off her shoulders, even if the manner of being informed about it by Vern during her meeting with the King had not been the most agreeable way to learn about it.

"Go!" she said once more and tossed the empty basket at him, watching him catch it expertly with one hand. "And bring me more bread buns."

He nodded. "I will. Just to prove to you that I will continue to love you if you become rounder."

"I might repeat that very statement back to you one day," she chuckled and sat down to launch on another attempt at finishing the book.

* * *

Eryn parried a low blow with her sword and received an appreciative nod from Orrin for it.

"Nicely done. I wouldn't have thought you capable of using that weapon properly today after your hardly being able to keep your eyes open when we started."

"I am supposed to pass a couple of very important exams in only a few days, so you may at least have *some* patience with me. Not that you ever showed me any before when I was in dire need of it, mind you."

"I tell you what I think you are in dire need of - a kick up the backside for whining and whingeing, you miserable weakling," he growled.

"Insensitive brute!" she cried out. "How does Junar manage to live with somebody like you? Especially now that she is in need of sympathy and understanding?"

"That's simple. I satisfy all my need of tormenting others with *you*. So all that is left for her is a loving, considerate companion who fulfils her every hope. Now how hard can that exam really be?" he shrugged. "You have been a healer for what, fifteen years?"

"It's not as easy as that," she corrected and tried to kick his shin while aiming a thrust at his shoulder. He avoided both easily. "The things I need to know for the exams are rather more extensive than what I used in my work in the past. So it's not like I don't have to sit down and prepare, quite the opposite. And Pe'tala will make this as gruelling as possible for me."

"Can't you two finally start acting like adults and leave this ridiculous squabbling behind you? I shudder when I think that you are the two most skilled healers in this Kingdom right now. How is a person to trust either of you when you behave like children as soon as you have left the clinic?"

"I am not forcing anybody to subject themselves to my services if people don't consider me professional enough," she huffed. "And the trainees are getting more and more accomplished, so there is enough choice now. Who needs me anyway? I am not even in charge of my own clinic anyway!"

Orrin groaned and looked upwards. "Not that again! You are aware that you have been given a position *superior* to the one of Head of Healers, aren't you? The Head of Healers is subject to *your* orders!"

"And I am subject to his in my capacity as a healer!" she retorted angrily. "Seriously, how strange is it all? How can I be superior and yet subordinate to the same person? Who thinks up structures like that? Does the Order pay somebody just to make my life as tricky as they can? As if being subordinated to my own companion wasn't tedious enough!"

"Whining again," Orrin sighed and made a few quick jabs to keep her on her toes. "But you know what," he said with a sinister glint in his eyes, "none of it should be too much of a problem in the future, since the Order does not intend to let you have enough time at your disposal to perform so much healing anyway."

"Oh, just shut it," she hissed and ducked under a high blow to then retaliate quickly by hitting him in the small of his back with the flat of her blade. "You are dead," she smiled sweetly and sheathed her sword. "Which sort of ends the lesson, I would say."

"By no means," he smirked. "A true warrior doesn't let himself be detained by a minor detail such as that. You draw that weapon again or this is going to be rather painful for you."

"You wouldn't strike an unarmed lady, would you?"

"I think I have proved to you in the past more often than once that this doesn't stop me. Remember our first training session?"

She ground her teeth. "The one where you hit me with that wooden stick until I picked up the other one? I was black and blue all over!"

"Though it seems it wasn't memorable enough to judge me correctly. Pity."

She quickly jumped back when he aimed a kick at her thigh. Well, at least he had attacked without the blade. That probably counted for something.

"How is that unfaithful, disobedient son of yours doing?" she said, changing the topic.

"Well enough. He is keeping himself busy planning for his long absence. Judging from how you phrased the question I assume you are still mad at him for having accomplished permission to be sent along?"

"It's that obvious, eh?" she said, face grim.

"Yes, rather," he nodded. "Junar is relieved that he is coming with us. She was nagging me about wanting to leave him behind."

"Junar's opinion doesn't count," Eryn snorted. "She is currently not exactly clear in her head with that baby developing inside her. Those hormones do strange things to a woman's ability to think like a proper human being, from what I have witnessed."

Orrin raised his brow at her. "I would very much like to watch you repeat that very statement when my lovely companion is around to hear it."

"Are you crazy? She would tear my head off!"

"She would, yes," he nodded. "You know, I really hope I will be lucky enough one day to see you with a child, despite your determination that it is never going to happen. I wonder how you would react to someone saying something like that."

"Good luck there, then," she sneered. "Anyway, I would probably react like any other pregnant, and so completely irrational, woman - I would tear your head off. I shiver at the thought of taking Junar to Takhan. It is a four-day journey, after all. There are two days of bumpy roads and another two days at sea that will very likely make her already queasy stomach empty itself at even more frequent intervals. I really wonder why you accepted an order like that."

He shrugged. "Curiosity, probably."

"Curiosity? You?" She stared at him. Down-to-earth Orrin? That did seem uncharacteristic for him.

"I find the insinuation in your astonishment insulting," he said calmly and knocked the sword out of her hand in a move that didn't even require any finesse or magically-enhanced speed. "As well as finding your lack of reaction disturbing. What did I tell you about letting yourself become distracted while fighting?"

She sighed and bent down to retrieve her weapon. "Not to let it happen."

"Exactly. Now, why do you think me incapable of curiosity? This is an adventure, a chance to experience something different from this here." His gesture encompassed the city, and probably what lay beyond. "A challenge. Something new. A chance to *do* something." The last words had been spoken with an unusual wistfulness.

Eryn considered him thoughtfully. Why had she ever thought him immune to the lures of an adventure in the great big unknown? Because he had been for her a pillar of this dusty institution called *the Order*? But then he had proven to be among those few open for new developments, hadn't he? Befriending her had been a more than ample proof of that. She was more or less the personification of frequent change around here, one might suggest.

Focus returned to his gaze when he looked at her. "It is something I know you understand, but weren't expecting in my case. You attribute curiosity for new things to intelligence, and this is a concept you find hard to apply to a man holding a sword." It was not a question, but a simple statement.

Not an entirely untrue one, she had to admit. He was right, she did tend to forget how quick on the uptake he was. That was why his reacting level-headedly to the intrigues around them was a surprise for her every time. He kept proving to her that he was an able thinker, but since it didn't fit her picture of his profession her head kept disregarding it.

"I live with a capable fighter who I know to be quick-witted," she remarked, reluctant to admit his appraisal of her attitude.

"You don't have that much to do with him in his capacity as fighter," Orrin replied. "Also, in his case it is a matter of strategy not to let you forget that he is in good shape up here." He tapped his forehead with his index finger. "You wouldn't respect him otherwise."

She blinked. Was it a matter of strategy for Enric to constantly remind her that he was intelligent?

He smiled. "I can see that doesn't sit too well with you. You would rather like to think of you as a person who does not feel regard or disregard for others according to their mental capacities but on their character. The things we learn about ourselves, eh?"

She glowered at him, knowing he was right, but still not happy about it. She did feel a certain disdain for the people she had met that did not waste so much time on thinking before they acted. Or spoke. Such as Inad. Or Sanaf.

"So you are saying that I am a snob with regard to intelligence if not for money or status?"

He considered the question for a moment, then nodded. "You could put it like that, yes. Though it is nothing I would worry too much about in your case. We all have our preferences for the people we surround ourselves with. Myself as a trainer I prefer people with the ability to learn quickly, with determination and a certain rebellious streak."

She lifted an eyebrow at him. "Really? A rebellious streak? Then being made to take my training when I was first brought here must have been a genuine pleasure for you. A dream come true even."

"I am a fighter, Eryn; I do appreciate a challenge. But this doesn't mean that I enjoyed every aspect of that in your case. I do have a conscience as well, even if this, too, is something you would not credit a mere fighter with possessing. I was not happy with the idea of training somebody who was being held prisoner not because she had done anything wrong, but merely because she happened to be born as a magician with the wrong hair colour. With Enric it was a matter of overcoming his idleness and his intention not to do anything too well so he could continue to disappoint and anger his father. In your case you were dead set against fighting for other reasons that came up against your very beliefs. You might have been aware that it was the King and the Order who wanted you to do it, but it was still *me* you were facing in the arena every day."

She nodded slowly. She hadn't been aware that for him, too, this had been quite a burden.

"Yet I somehow managed to start liking you."

That made him grin. "Of course you did. I am likable, after all. What's more, I let you befriend Vern, which surely was a great point in my favour."

She grinned back. "You devious trickster. Using your own flesh and blood like that."

"It's not like I am not paying the price for it," he sighed. "You haven't always been the best influence on him, if I might remind you. And let's not forget that a fighter might have other preferences for his only son's choice of profession than healer."

She waved him off impatiently. "Nonsense. As if you would prefer his turning into a mediocre fighter instead of a brilliant healer. Also, his starting to learn healing must have appealed to that weak spot you claim to harbour for rebels. Brave Lord Orrin's son, who disregarded the Order's and the King's possible wrath by following the path of a pioneer, learning what no other Order magician had been able to do for hundreds of years. Don't pretend you are upset because of his choice of career," she snorted. "It's wasted on me, I am afraid."

Orrin chuckled. "I see there is no deceiving you." His expression became serious again. "How will he do in Takhan? What should I be worrying about?"

She thought for a moment then admitted with a sigh of helplessness, "I don't really know. We spent five weeks there, but we were almost always in the company of some local every time we went out. So most of the time there was somebody around to keep us out of trouble. I dare say there is still a lot I have to learn myself when we go back there. When I am working and undergoing training there, I will be expected to adapt to their customs more than I did before. We all will be. But luckily for you, I happen to be a member of an influential family over there, so we will get all the help we require.

Most of them are healers as well, so that should smooth the way for Vern."

Orrin nodded slowly. "I suppose that is alright for now. Anything we can do to prepare? Learning greetings conventions, cultural blunders to avoid and things like that?"

"There are a few things we will share with you, but there will be enough time once we get on the road, as well as on the boat," she added with an expression of dread. "It's important not to take too many clothes with you. You will need new ones for the local climate. It's really wasted baggage carrying our heavy garments. Anyway, as you happen to have your very own seamstress with you, coming up with new clothes won't be much of a problem. If she is still up to doing any work there with her swollen belly, that is."

"I imagine they have tailors there if she can't," he remarked. "How about our living arrangements in Takhan? Where will we stay?"

"At the beginning we will all stay at the ambassadorial residence because I refuse to spend a single night under the same roof as Malriel. As soon as she has departed we will move in to the Aren residence, as Enric can't be seen to stay anywhere else as the Head of House. Don't worry, though - there is enough space for all of us. The Houses do like their residences to be spacious; it's a matter of prestige. If you can't quarter a small army there, it does not befit one's social class."

Orrin raised his eyebrow at her harsh tone. "An interesting thing for you to say. May I remind you that you inhabit *two* houses here? It's not as if your own style of living is exactly modest."

"This is nothing compared to what *they* seem to feel appropriate, honestly. Oh, yes - you will have to get used to napping after lunch. Which is not as bad as it sounds owing to its being too hot to do anything else around noon anyhow."

His expression was doubtful; the idea of lying down for a snooze in the middle of the day not too enthralling. "Like a small child."

"Basically, it is," Eryn grinned. "But you can stay up longer in the evening."

* * *

Eryn closed her eyes for a moment and breathed out in the way she had learned. It was stupid to be nervous. This was her clinic and the exams would concern the work she had basically been doing all her life. Well, and a few things she had never even heard of apart from finding out about them in books. Why couldn't all her niggling thoughts still themselves in time, now she was trying to calm herself?

She made herself press down the door handle of the room that had been prepared for her exam today. Pe'tala and Lord Poron stood by one of the windows, conversing in a relaxed manner. And why not, Eryn thought - it was not as if *they* had much to be nervous about.

There were three desks arranged at one end of the room, two of them pushed next to each other, one facing those, a little further off. That was where she, as the candidate to be tested, would sit.

"Good, you are here," Pe'tala nodded and then added, "I was starting to worry that you might not turn up."

Eryn decided not to give any response to that. It would hardly be wise to provoke her examiner minutes before the exam.

Lord Poron smiled at her reassuringly and took a seat at on one of the desks, pulling a pen and several sheets of paper towards him for the documentation task he had been given.

"Are you ready or do you need anything before we start? Water? A last trip to the bathroom?" Pe'tala enquired and sat down next to Lord Poron.

"No, I am ready," Eryn replied, a little stiffly.

"Good," her cousin smiled. "Take a seat, then."

She did and watched Pe'tala slowly pulling a few sheets towards her, looking them over thoroughly, as if she didn't know exactly what was on them, despite having written the questions herself. That was surely no more than a little game to make her nervous, Eryn thought with trepidation.

"As you were informed before, this examination will consist of four tests in total, three of which will be carried out by me. Those are Anatomy, Disease and Injuries. The fourth test, Non-magical Healing, Sarol of House Roal will take care of when you are in Takhan," Pe'tala started. "I will ask you three questions about each topic. You will answer them and Lord Poron will note your answers for later review in Takhan. You need to answer two out of three questions completely in order that the topic can be awarded a pass grade. You need to pass each of the tests separately; outstanding results in one area will not counteract poor performance in another. Do you have any questions about the examination procedure I have outlined?"

Eryn shook her head. "No." They would ask her the questions and then she would answer them as best she could. Not so very complicated.

"Then we will begin. You may choose the part we start with."

"Injuries," Eryn said immediately.

Pe'tala nodded and flicked through her papers until the desired sheet was uppermost. "Injuries it is. First question: Why are injuries to the head so dangerous if untreated?"

"External head injuries may result in a considerable loss of blood as the head is very well supplied with blood. This can quickly lead to the body being denied sufficient blood flow," Eryn replied, and watched Lord Poron jotting down her reply with a surprising speed she wouldn't have thought possible. He probably used a little magic to extend himself.

"And internal ones?" Pe'tala further enquired.

"Internal injuries may cause the blood to pool where it is not intended inside the head, to clot there and block the supply of other regions. Or it may even press the brain against the inside of the skull. If brain tissue is damaged through pressure, it will not, unlike most other body tissues, recover without the aid of magic. Important functions may be lost forever through this."

Pe'tala then asked about the long-term effects of these injuries, how assessing and treating them was expected to be done and what external indications an untreated injury might present.

Eryn answered all questions, but had to waffle a little with the last one. Having magic at her disposal often made looking at external indications unnecessary.

"I shall consider this question as a whole answered adequately. Now the second question. What different types of bone injuries are you aware of? Tell me about their nature, how they may typically occur, how they should be treated and what the consequence of their not being treated often is."

That, as well, was not much of a challenge and after around ten minutes of non-stop explanation, Pe'tala interrupted Eryn. "Very well, I can see that you are up to speed with bones. That question has been answered to my satisfaction. Question three, then. Which different kinds of soft tissue damage do you know of and what is the difference in the treatment of them?"

Eryn gave a silent groan. That was a very wide-ranging question, one that could easily have been split into several smaller ones. But there was no sense in complaining, especially as she was able to answer the question, even if it would probably need about half an hour.

* * *

Eryn greedily gulped down an entire glass of water in one go. She had finished the first part of her exam well enough and Pe'tala had allowed her a short break. Vern had been waiting for her in the small kitchen downstairs and watched her refilling the glass.

"So? How is it going?" he asked, eagerly.

"So far, so good. I passed the first part, though she has tried to make it a little tricky for me. Which I admit was not exactly unexpected."

"What was the first part?"

"Injuries. She asked me about head, bone and soft tissue damage. Nothing too challenging. I am a bit worried about the other two parts, though. I kept forgetting the things from my uncle's books. There are so many of them I have never encountered before, so I hope she will stick to the more common ones and leave me alone with the unusual things."

Vern grimaced. "How likely is that?"

She sighed. "Probably not very. Why are you here, anyway? Aren't you supposed to be in your classes at this time of day? Don't tell me you are staying away without authorisation?"

"I am not. I'll tell you later."

"There you are," Pe'tala's voice sounded from the door behind them. "It is time to carry on. We do not intend to sit around all day long."

Eryn nodded, taking her replenished glass with her, and followed her cousin back up the stairs and into the room for round two of the ordeal.

* * *

It was early afternoon when Pe'tala leaned back after listening to the answer to the last question. "Very well, question answered. Which brings us to the end of this exam. Let me summarise the results. Lord Poron, if I may use your notes for a moment?" She pulled the sheets towards her. "The first part about injuries was very well done, you answered almost all of the questions completely. The second part about diseases was a little less impressive, though still sufficient to consider it passed. Part three, on anatomy, was nicely done as well, two and a half out of the three questions were answered to my satisfaction." She then looked up at her cousin and smiled in a guarded way. "Congratulations. You passed! Not with the above average performance we generally pride ourselves on at House Vel'kim, but then I would say it is not such a bad result for an Aren."

Eryn exhaled slowly and shook her head. "Is having to let me pass such a strain that you can't be civil about it but still have to insult me? Is seeing me achieve something so distasteful for you?"

Pe'tala looked at her for a few moments, then pursed her lips. "You are right. It was not an appropriate thing to say. Let me try again. I congratulate you on the passing of your exams. You did well. Especially as my personal standards are known to be a little higher than others'. You may not have been born into House Vel'kim, but it is good to see that you have not shamed us. So far."

Eryn chuckled. "Close enough, dearest *sister*." She got to her feet. "If you would excuse me now, I have some serious relaxing to do." She nodded to Lord Poron and strolled out the door, relieved, happy and hungry for an entire basket of sweet bread buns.

* * *

Enric got up from his chair when he heard the entrance door opening and closing again a moment later. He had been waiting for her for quite a while now.

"Where have you been? I have been wanting to congratulate you for these last two hours," he said and walked towards her while she unbuttoned her cloak.

She smiled. "It seems news travels fast. I was on a walk through the city to clear my head." She lifted a paper bag with bread buns. "And got myself a few more of those."

"Didn't you tell me they were a means to supply your brain with sugar while you had to revise?"

"They were. But it seems I can't do without them from one day to the next just like this. I'll start weaning myself off them tomorrow. Today I feel I shouldn't have to begrudge myself such little pleasures."

He nodded solemnly. "Indeed you shouldn't. You have deserved every single piece of pastry in that bag."

"That I have," she agreed. "How come you know about my exams? No, wait – it was Lord Poron, wasn't it? I somehow can't imagine Pe'tala spreading the happy news. He was probably under orders to inform Tyront of the outcome right away."

Enric nodded. "Exactly." He took her hand. "And now sit with me and tell me if your cousin was particularly cruel."

She chuckled. "Incredibly so. She tried to obliterate me, but I sidestepped every single one of her attempts with my unparalleled brilliance."

"That's my girl."

She let him lead her to a sofa and watched him go to fetch a bottle of sweet wine with two glasses.

"Lord Poron said you exceeded the estimated time for the exam slightly."

She snorted and accepted a glass. "Slightly? She grilled me for three hours instead of the two that seem to be customary. She phrased the questions so generally that my answers had to be very extensive. And at times she asked in such detail that I wonder that we needed only *a single* extra hour."

"But you won through," he smiled and clinked his glass with hers. "I am proud of you. It now means that you have accomplished three quarters of your certification for Takhan."

"That I have! And I am glad this is over for now. Now I can concentrate on the exams Tyront wants me to finish finally to turn me into a useful member of the Order," she grimaced.

"As opposed to your current state of uselessness?"

"Well, obviously. It seems my being a healer is not enough for Tyront, is it?"

He sighed. "Are we back to the discussion of why you were not made Head of Healers?"

She shook her head. "No. It wouldn't make much sense, would it?"

"None at all," he confirmed. "No more of that, you will have to learn to live with it."

She bit back an acid remark and took a sip from her glass. "Vern was at the clinic today during one of my breaks from the exam. Do you know why he was not at his classes?"

"As a matter of fact, I do. But I think Vern should be the one to tell you. He came here twice to look for you within the last two hours. The second time I took pity on him and told him that you had passed your exams. I have asked him, Junar and Orrin over for dinner tonight. I thought it might be a happy opportunity to celebrate your success and re-introduce a few of the foreign eating customs they need to familiarise themselves with."

She grinned. "I hope it does not mean that I have to share my bread buns with our guests, does it? As those are to be my last for the next time, I have become very possessive of them."

"No, my love, they are yours alone," he promised. "Our guests should be here in about two hours, which means that it's time to start cooking. I have asked the servants to remove the dining room furniture so we can use the seating cushions we brought back."

She stretched lazily. "Does this mean I have to come and help with the cooking?"

He shook his head. "No, I can't have you working on your gloriously triumphant day, can I? Why don't you go upstairs and take a bath while I take care of providing for our guests?"

Eryn nodded enthusiastically. "If this is what you want me to do, I suppose I have to comply, although with a heavy heart."

"I appreciate your sacrifice," he smiled and stood.

* * *

Eryn looked up from her book in surprise when there was a knock at the door to the bathroom. Enric normally entered without knocking and everybody else tended to wait for her to come out.

"Yes?" she called out and dropped a little deeper into the water.

The door opened and Junar stuck her head in. "Hello you. Do you mind if I come in?"

Eryn shrugged. "No, not at all. Though I am afraid the seating in here is not so comfortable. All I can offer you is the small stool I use for my book when I am taking a bath."

Junar waved her off and closed the door again behind her. "That's fine. As long as I can rest my feet a little. I have been up and about all day."

"Preparing for our big adventure?" Eryn enquired and let her book slip to the floor as the stool was now occupied.

"Yes, I need to. I would like to have a business to come back to, after all. I suppose having Pe'tala stay here instead of returning soon has made your preparations a lot easier, hasn't it?"

"My preparations? They've mostly consisted of revising stuff for exams so far. The clinic has a Head of Healers who has to worry about keeping the services ticking over. He has Pe'tala to assist him in both healing and administrative matters. Members of House Vel'kim have been in charge of healing in Takhan for generations, I was told. It's more or less the family business, after all."

Junar grimaced. "I would congratulate you on your relatively low-key preparation efforts, but I know that you would have preferred being in charge of the clinic yourself, so I will save my words."

"Oh my, don't get me started," Eryn sighed. "Can you hand me one of those bread buns?"

"So you are still eating them all the time? Even while you are taking a bath? That is rather unusual, if you ask me. Is it possible that you are pregnant?" Junar asked pointedly and handed her a pastry.

"Pregnant, me?" Eryn snorted. "If I know anything, I know this is most unlikely. I have means to avoid that and am very thorough in following the procedure."

"Pity. I like the idea. Can you imagine the two of us, bringing up our children together? We could let them grow up as if they were siblings. Vern is too old to be a brother to our little one. He will be more in the role of an uncle, I expect."

Eryn thought for a moment, then shook her head. "No, I don't see me raising a child. Too loud. Too dependent. Too helpless. Too impressionable. Orrin already claims I have been a bad influence on his sixteen-year old." Her grin became twisted. "Imagine how much your daughter will be able to learn from me."

Junar's face fell. "You will have that child over only under strict supervision. Or I will end up with a three-year old who curses the Order in a very colourful language."

"That is a valid worry, for sure," Eryn admitted unabashedly. "I have always thought having that a certain vocabulary at one's disposal for airing one's rage is good for general wellbeing."

"Not for your company's wellbeing, though," Junar pointed out.

"Well, one has to set priorities. Are you the only one who has come early or are your men downstairs?"

"We are all here." She rolled her eyes. "They try to let me out of their sight as little as possible. As if I were about to drop to the floor unconsciously as soon as I am left alone for a minute. Whenever I take too much time in the bathroom in the morning, Orrin comes looking to make sure I haven't slipped on the wet floor or fallen victim to some other calamity."

"That's rather sweet, actually," Eryn shrugged.

"Is it? Then I wonder why you tend to react rather angrily whenever Enric protects you from something."

"That's completely different. They protect you because you are in a state of increased vulnerability due to your carrying another life inside you. Enric just protects me because he thinks I can't take care of myself."

"Which is complete nonsense, of course," Junar muttered.

"Pardon?" Eryn snapped.

"Nothing."

"You know something? My bath has become a lot less relaxing since you have barged in here and disturbed the peace and quiet."

The seamstress smiled and reached out for a towel. "Good. Than you may as well get up, dry and dress yourself then come downstairs with me."

Eryn watched her friend walking towards the door and called after her, "You didn't even congratulate me on passing my exams!"

"Congratulations!" Junar threw back at her while closing the door.

Right. That had felt very sincere.

* * *

When she came down the stairs, she saw Orrin and Vern standing next to the drinking cabinet, discussing something.

"No, one glass is enough for you," his father said in a rather unnerved tone.

"It's just wine!" Vern protested and lifted his empty glass accusingly as if withholding a refill was an immensely cruel thing to do.

"You can have another one after dinner, but not on an empty stomach. It is still alcohol, after all."

Vern sighed heavily and put the empty glass aside in a resigned way.

"Don't worry, my lad," Eryn said while descending the last few steps, "He keeps telling *me* how much I should be drinking in his opinion - and I am really old enough, one might think."

"Yes, that's what one might think indeed," Orrin remarked, his eyebrow raised.

Enric entered the parlour through the dining room door. "You are here, good. Dinner is ready as well, so if you care to follow me.'

Vern stepped away from the drinks cabinet to take Eryn's arm and lead her to the table. Junar was in the dining room already and dished out the food Enric had prepared.

"So tonight we really will dine Western style," Vern commented and took in the seating cushions on the floor, the low table and the exotic-looking tableware.

"Oh yes," Enric nodded. "This is meant to be educational and give you an insight into what a dinner in Takhan will be like. One important difference is that the food is prepared by the host and not by servants. Another is that if meat is served only if it is game hunted by the host himself. Anything else would be a great shame. Now take a seat, please." He waited until everyone else was seated before letting himself sink down onto a cushion between Junar and Eryn. "You see the bowl of water in front of you? It is meant to clean your hands in." He leaned forward to demonstrate, then dried his hands on a small towel.

Eryn followed suit, then their guests washed their hands, too.

"Now you will take the bowls Junar was kind enough to fill beforehand and begin eating. As the host, I am expected to be the last to start eating so as to make sure all my guests are content."

"Somewhat spicy," Junar commented as she drew in air through her mouth.

Eryn handed her a piece of bread. "Eat this. Don't drink water, that would just spread the spices around more on your tongue."

"I don't find it particularly spicy," Vern frowned. "Just right for me."

"Pregnant women do have a changed perception of impressions both of smell and taste," Eryn explained.

Vern gave Junar a thoughtful look. "That means things tend to taste and smell differently than before? That does explain a lot. Some of the things she has started combining lately..." He shook his head as if putting words to the strange and unnatural events he had been made to witness was too much for him.

"Poor boy," Eryn nodded with mock sympathy. "There Junar goes, spitting out her meals at regular intervals, and nobody acknowledges that you are the one who is suffering most."

Enric sighed. "I don't think this is an appropriate table conversation - neither here nor in the Western Territories. While eating, it is customary to talk of pleasant things to show respect for the host's efforts."

"Sorry," Eryn murmured.

"You should be. It's not as if you weren't aware of this."

"Then I suppose we can as well talk of my success today in the exams. That is something cheery. And I have to say that congratulations have so far not been expressed as abundantly as I feel is warranted."

Orrin sighed theatrically. "It's not as if anyone really doubted that you would pass, Eryn. But congratulations nevertheless."

"She didn't really make it easy for me, you know," Eryn sulked. "It was not a walk along Kingsway, but a real challenge!"

"Try walking along Kingsway in the early evening or on market days. That is quite a challenge as well," Vern shrugged.

She flashed him a withering look. So there was not much chance of her getting the recognition she felt she deserved, she thought grumpily, before leaning back with her bowl. It was nice that they had such a high estimation of her abilities, but a little display of admiration would still have been healthy for her ego.

Vern lifted his empty bowl. "Is it polite to ask for seconds?"

Enric shook his head. "Not particularly. You place your empty bowl on the table and wait for the host to offer you one. Asking for that yourself implies that the host is negligent of their duties."

The boy nodded and placed the empty bowl in front of him, looking at Enric expectantly.

"Vern, would you care for another helping?" Enric asked as if he weren't aware of the answer.

"Why, yes, Lord Enric, I would really like that so much," Vern replied in earnest.

Enric leaned forward to refill the empty bowl and hand it back to him. "I am glad you enjoy it."

"I do. I wonder if learning to cook might be something I should try. I mean, I do like eating very much, after all. And it seems like we will be doing our own cooking in Takhan, doesn't it?"

"I would recommend that, yes," Enric nodded. "It is a skill everybody in the Western Territories is expected to possess. They are amused at our depending on our servants so much. We may as well prove to them that we are not completely helpless in that regard."

"Father said we will be staying with you at Malriel's place?"

"You will, yes. I think staying together is advisable." It also meant that more people could keep an eye on Eryn, he added silently. In his experience there couldn't be too many for that job.

"You did consider that we are about to introduce a crying infant to the happy group in only a few months, didn't you?" Junar smiled.

"That's exactly what I said," Eryn sighed. "Yet he insists on keeping you with us."

Orrin gave her a stern look. "Charming."

She shrugged. "Hey, you made that baby. Why should I have to give up my peaceful nights?"

"I dimly remember that you had your share in the conception of that child," he pointed out.

"True enough," she admitted. "And I will have my share in raising it. Somebody has to teach the child how to read lips and other such helpful little skills."

"I'll repeat my previous statement. You may look after that child only under supervision," Junar threw in.

"I thought *I* was the one supposed to be the bad influence?" Vern frowned.

"You?" Eryn chuckled. "Come on! The child prodigy? What bad influence could *you* possibly be? Make the kid study hard and diligently?"

"I resent that! It's like I never did anything vaguely forbidden! I taught you magical fighting!" he protested.

"Yes, because you wanted me to teach you healing, which goes along the lines of the child prodigy thing. Give me a better example," she chuckled.

"I went behind your back to come to the Western Territories with you. That was sly and devious!"

"Doesn't count. Again, you did it to be able to learn more. Your arguments just prove what a harmless little swot you are. No bad influence-material in my books."

Vern thought for a moment, then laughed. "I have something! I painted naked women on an ancient city map in the library."

Orrin cursed. "That was *you*?"

Enric smiled. There went Tyront's little hidden crumb of information to blackmail the boy with one day.

Vern folded his arms proudly. "Yes, that was me. I did it. It was selfish, destructive and irresponsible. Just what you need to be a bad influence on a child."

"Congratulations," his father growled. "I am sure these are just the character traits your patients will appreciate when they come to you for treatment."

Eryn leaned forward, smiling broadly. "You really did that? On an ancient city map?"

Vern nodded. "Sure. I sneaked in after dark. It took me three nights to finish it and then another week went by until Lord Poron found out. There was quite a lot of anticipation after that," he grinned and put his bowl back on the table again.

"Another serving for you?" Enric asked.

"No, thank you, Lord Enric. I am quite full."

"Good. Then I would say you should share your news with Eryn. She already asked me why you were not in class today," he suggested.

"Because the King has decreed that I am no longer to be taught with the others my age. I will from now on receive private tutoring to enable me to finish my training ahead of time." His grin grew wider. "It seems my little initiative impressed him. He said that forcing the slow pace of shared classes on me is a shame. He thinks I will profit more from a different arrangement that focuses more on my individual needs."

Eryn nodded appreciatively. "I approve very much. So, how will this work? Like my own tutoring where I keep reading books and was tested on them afterwards?"

"Pretty much so, yes. I can go and ask the teachers if something is unclear, but otherwise I am fairly independent. I have to pass a designated minimum of tests every month, but I can pick in what order I choose to do them."

"How much earlier do you think this might enable you to complete your education?" she asked.

"I expect I should be able to shave about two years off, judging from the pace in my classes in the past. And there are a few subjects I think I can skip. Such as advanced botanical studies, for example. I have already learned more about plants in the last year, thanks to you, than the teacher could ever know," he said.

"That means I should have you available as a fully trained healer in about three years," she speculated. It was all good news.

"At the most," he remarked confidently. Then he looked downcast. "The only thing I still have to do the old way is the combat training. It seems there is no way around that."

"No," Orrin confirmed. "But I will be more than happy to assist you there."

Vern's expression didn't show any more gladness. "Thank you so much. Lucky me."

Eryn grinned. "Why should you be any better off than me? If I have to do that bloody training, you should, too. It is only right and fair."

"Yes, whatever you say," he sighed. "I still don't see why healers have to undertake combat training."

"Because the Order is still in the process of working out how to deal with all the recent changes," Enric explained patiently. "I can't promise you that healers will be free to stop training fighting skills in the near future, but I assume that one day there will be different standards concerning their required level. However, we first need to let the Council members get used to the idea of not all Order magicians being fighters any more. This is a process that needs time. They have had to adapt to a number of changes recently, thanks to our newest addition here." He took Eryn's hand and kissed it. Then he got to his feet and stepped towards a wooden box to take out a bulgy, foreign-looking bottle.

"Hey, I recognise that one!" Vern beamed. "That's what we had when Ram'an invited us to his quarters. He said it's bad luck not to finish it once it has been opened!"

Enric looked at him, his expression indulgent. "That, my lad, was not entirely truthful, I am afraid. He just said it to get Eryn drunk."

Eryn stared at him. "He did?"

"Yes, my love. There is no such custom. I checked."

"Brilliant," she murmured. "And I fell for it. Just like that."

"You did. And this is exactly why I am asking you to drink only when you are in my presence."

"Taking your stewardship duties seriously again. How fatherly," she sighed and saw Junar smirk.

Vern watched Enric bringing the wine bottle, another bottle with juice and several gold-rimmed glassed back to them. "The juice is for...?" he asked carefully.

"Junar. I heard your father has granted you another glass after dinner," Enric replied, amused with the boy's smug expression.

"Where is Plia, by the way? Why does she never join us when we have dinner together?" Vern enquired.

"She keeps very long hours," Enric explained with a sideways glance at his companion while he filled the glasses. "Somebody seems to have been a bad role model here. I have instructed Grend to make sure she doesn't return here too late. I am expecting her back any minute now."

"You pay somebody to escort her here when she works late?" Junar asked with a tellingly high-pitched voice. "That is really thoughtful of you!"

"You are not going to cry, are you?" Eryn asked suspiciously.

"No, of course not! That would be silly," she protested then dabbed away a tear from the corner of one eye with her finger.

Orrin smiled and put an arm around her shoulders to press her close.

"Oh my. So it seems you have entered into the emotional phase of your pregnancy," Eryn smiled. "This is going to be entertaining.'

"No mocking the pregnant lady," Vern stated and accepted a glass.

"No shaking, no mocking... That's a fair number of privileges she has been given now."

"Envious, Eryn?" Junar smiled sweetly.

"No, dearest friend, I am not. At least not enough to want to follow in your footsteps," she replied.

"Good thing, too," Vern snorted. "Frankly, I find the thought of your having even less control over your emotions frightening."

"Well, thanks a million. Orrin - I think it is not too late to discipline Vern for that defiling of historic property with his naked ladies."

"Oh, come on! You are so mean!"

She chuckled. "Oh, I am. And you know what? Being so didn't even require losing control over my emotions." She emptied her glass and held it out to Enric. "I'll have another one, please. Even if drinking all of it is not required for avoiding bad luck, there is no use in letting it go stale, is there?"

They all turned towards the parlour door when the sound of the entrance door being opened reached their ears.

"Plia?" Eryn called out. "Come here and eat something."

The girl obeyed and blinked when she beheld the party. "I am sorry, I was not aware that you had guests."

Enric indicated a cushion for her to sit on. "That we have. It would have been nice to have had you with us a bit earlier. We need to talk about your working hours, Plia. But not now; sit and eat!"

The girl swallowed. "Yes, Lord Enric. I am sorry."

"Don't be. Just try and keep more civilised hours in the future. I don't feel good leaving you here alone for months if I have to worry about whether you are even returning here to sleep. That would result in my having to make somebody move in here with you to keep an eye on you." He filled a bowl for her, reheating the food with a little magic, and then handed it to her.

"Thank you," she said and took the bowl with an unhappy expression. "That won't be necessary, I promise. I will make sure I return before dark from now on."

"Good." Enric took a sip of his wine and leaned back.

Eryn rolled her eyes when she saw Junar surreptitiously wiping away another tear. "Come on, Junar! His being bossy again is not touching - it's just annoying!"

"Oh, shut up, you," the seamstress murmured and held on to her juice.

CHAPTER 28

Stomach Troubles

Eryn absentmindedly smoothed her hand over her belly while going through the list of changes which Pe'tala, after watching the clinic work for a few months now, had suggested. Rolan had worked on the list with Pe'tala and even though Lord Poron was officially in charge of healing now he was still reluctant to take away competences from her for now and had asked her to stay in charge until she left for Takhan. She supposed that he didn't want to subject himself to her looking over his shoulder all the time. It was probably a matter of self-preservation to wait with taking control until she had left the country. Not entirely unwarranted, she had to admit.

"Something wrong?" Pe'tala asked with a frown.

"What?" Eryn looked up. "Nothing severe. My stomach keeps acting up because I have developed a rather unhealthy addiction to sweet bread buns. I have been trying to do without them, but somehow I don't manage to summon the strength of will to stop eating them."

"Are you sure your stomach is alright?"

"Of course I am sure. I check it regularly, so everything is fine. It must be a reaction to all the buns. But I suppose as long as the hankering after them is stronger than my aversion to my stomach troubles, I am not going to be sufficiently motivated to do anything to help it."

"How long have you had this craving? And when did the stomach troubles start?" Pe'tala enquired, obviously switched into healer mode.

Eryn rolled her eyes. 'There is no need to walk me through an examination. I happen to be a healer, too, you remember?"

Her cousin stared at her impassively. "I hear words coming out of your mouth, but none that are helpful. Want to try again?"

Sighing, she gave in. "It started with my learning marathon for the exams. That's when I got addicted to bread buns."

"Any other complaints, or just the stomach trouble?"

"Just the stomach."

"Have you been having these complaints often? Could they be connected to your monthly cycle?"

"No. I don't have a monthly cycle. I keep it held in the pre-ovulation phase to avoid getting pregnant."

"How long have you been doing that?"

Eryn did some reckoning in her head for a moment. "For more than ten years now. Though there was a slight disturbance when they blocked my magic with the shackles. But I managed to avoid any unbidden... developments."

Pe'tala then lifted her hand. "Would you mind if I took a look?"

"Really?" Eryn sighed. "So little confidence in my healing abilities? I have checked my stomach over several times, there is nothing wrong."

Her cousin shrugged. "Indulge me, will you? What do you have to lose? If I find something you overlooked, you can do something about it. If I do not, you can be smug about it."

"Suit yourself, then," she sighed and placed her hand in Pe'tala's. A moment later she felt warmth where the magic entered through her skin.

Several minutes went by until Pe'tala opened her eyes again, regarding the other woman with an unreadable expression.

"Well? You look like you found something," Eryn observed worriedly.

"How often do you check your body?" the younger woman asked instead of answering the question.

"I do a quick check once a week, the way my father showed me. Why?"

"How thorough is that check normally?"

"Well, if I have no complaints it is not very extensive. Why do you ask?"

"When your stomach problems started, did you check any other areas of your body to exclude other sources that might cause your complaints?"

"No, I did not. Are you going to tell me if you found something or do I have to turn you upside down and shake the answer out of you?"

Pe'tala nodded slowly. "Yes, I did find something."

"What?" Her voice had become tense. "Out with it!"

"You are expecting a child," her cousin said slowly.

Eryn lifted her eyes and breathed out slowly while she leaned back in her chair. "Very funny. You almost had me there for a moment. That was a bit in bad taste, I have to say. And a bit unimaginative, especially after I told you that I take certain measures as a precaution. The chances of my falling for that clumsy joke were not that great. Better luck next time! Does that mean you didn't find anything? Can I be smug now and tell you that I told you so?"

Pe'tala closed her eyes for a moment, then she leaned forward, looking right into the older woman's eyes. "Eryn. Listen to me carefully. This is not a joke. You are pregnant. Really."

"Pe'tala," Eryn replied patiently, "I am not. Honestly, I know. Can we stop this now? I find your insistence a little tedious. Just accept that your little prank didn't work, will you?"

"You bloody fool," Pe'tala hissed. "You just take a look for yourself instead of arguing with me! I am a healer! For the moment you are my patient, and I pride myself on being a professional, even though you are making that very hard for me at the moment." She folded her arms. "What are you waiting for? Go on!"

Eryn stared at her for several seconds. Her mouth went dry, but she pushed away the uneasy feeling. That woman was just a good actress, nothing more.

"Alright, I will check. What do I get when I find I am not pregnant, that this was just a tasteless joke of yours?"

Pe'tala stared up at the ceiling, shaking her head. "Why me? Why do I end up being the one to tell her? I cannot even knock some sense into that thick skull as it does not look good for a healer to strike a pregnant woman." She returned her attention to her opposite. "What do you want? Pick whatever you like. I can afford to bet anything, as I am not going to lose it."

Not a good answer, Eryn decided. Not at all. "I want you to write a statement with a public apology for treating me badly because Ram'an refused to be joined with you."

"Fine!"

Eryn gaped at her. "Seriously?"

Pe'tala folded her arms. "Yes. Now do it."

She felt tiny beads of sweat forming on her forehead. This was not the reaction she had expected. Or hoped for. For the first time in her life she dreaded looking inside her body, afraid of what she might find there. She slowly closed her eyes and focussed on her stomach. Maybe there was a tiny little something that she had overlooked in the past. Something that explained the recurring queasiness. She noted how her heartbeat had increased.

Her stomach looked fine, just like it had every time she had checked it in these last few weeks. She moved her attention further down, hesitantly focused on her womb. She immediately noted that something was different. The organs there were not in the state they used to be. They were supposed to be dormant, but there was some activity. She felt her breathing becoming heavier and forced herself to look deeper.

And there it was. A tiny lifeform inside layers of protective tissue. She sprung up from her chair, causing it to fall back and hit the floor with a loud thud. Her eyes were wide, her head spinning and her lungs refused to suck in the air she needed.

Pe'tala rose as well, grabbing her shoulders. "Eryn? Listen to me! You need to breathe! Slowly. In and out. Come, we will do it together. In. And... out."

Eryn grabbed her arms. "This is impossible! How could this have happened? I was always so very careful!" She shook her head, feeling how first tears formed and blurred her vision. "I don't want this!" she whispered frantically.

"Sit!" Pe'tala commanded and Eryn obeyed instinctively. "Now you listen to me: This is not a catastrophe. You are in a companionship, so you will not have to raise this child all alone. You are very wealthy, so you do not have to worry about whether you can afford a child. Your companion is good with children - at least with our niece, Obal - so it is not likely that he will be hostile to this news."

"*I* am really hostile to this news!" she wailed. "I can't believe it! How could this happen? I don't understand it at all!" She grabbed Pe'tala's hands. "I am a healer, I am good with preventative measures! Tell me how this could have happened!"

Pe'tala sighed. "I cannot tell you for sure. You might have been negligent in maintaining the dormant status of those particular organs..."

"I was not," Eryn growled, her voice shaking, "You can be sure of that."

"Then there is the chance of... some external influence."

"What do you mean, external influence?" she asked sharply.

"Somebody else with the required medical knowledge and magical powers superior to your own could have overruled the measures you took," Pe'tala explained uncomfortably. "I am not saying this is what happened, I am just giving you the possibilities here, mind you."

Eryn stared at her for several moments, then rose shakily. "Enric. He is the only one who could have done that," she whispered. Suddenly she felt cold.

"How would he know what to do? He is not trained in healing."

Eryn raked her fingers through her hair. "He can do simple repairs, like skin tissue. And he knows, well at least in theory, how to repair bones and muscles."

Pe'tala shook her head. "This is hardly sufficient for the complicated manipulation that this required."

"He keeps reading books on healing! And who knows what he managed to learn while we were staying in Takhan! Or what Malriel showed him when she was here!"

"Eryn," Pe'tala said carefully, "I think you are talking yourself into something here. You have no evidence for any of this."

"Evidence?" Eryn shouted and pointed at her lower abdomen. "This is evidence enough, one should think! This is just something else he made me do, regardless of my own choice! That's what our relationship has largely consisted of so far - my being made to do things I never wanted! Joining him, being bound to the Kingdom, travelling to Takhan again..."

"I will send for Enric right now. You are not exactly in any reasonable state of mind and I do not know what to do with you," Pe'tala sighed.

"You don't have to do anything with me! I am a grown woman, I can take care of myself! But call for him, by all means. Let's see how he reacts, shall we? That should show us well enough if he was involved or not," she hissed. "He is probably on his way here anyway, the damned mind bond doesn't allow for strong feelings to go unnoticed," she added with a shaky voice before letting herself sink down onto the chair again. "I feel quite sick."

"This is very likely a stress reaction. Your body is reacting by getting rid of the things that make dealing with the situation difficult right now. It wants to use the energy your intestinal system otherwise needs for digesting and that means considers getting rid of the food in your stomach," Pe'tala explained.

"Damn you, I know how this works! I am a bloody healer!" Eryn snapped at her. "Remember?"

Their eyes snapped to her wrist, where the dark symbols were flaring up, indicating that Enric was approaching, it seemed quickly.

Only moments later the door to Eryn's study pushed open and he came in without knocking, his gaze immediately locked onto Eryn.

"What happened?" he demanded, a worried frown on his forehead.

"That was fast," Pe'tala murmured.

Eryn forced herself to maintain some calm. Now she would find out.

She rose from her seat. "Enric, I am expecting a child," she announced with as much composure as she could manage.

A rush of wild joy breezed through her, and she braced herself on the surface of her desk. So it was true. He had been wanting a child. And obviously made sure he would have one.

She needed to get out of here and quickly, as long as her legs still worked properly. That was just a matter of time now. She wanted to curl into a ball and hide in some dark, hidden place.

She straightened and stepped towards him, glaring daggers toward him. "You bastard," she all but whispered, "How could you do this to me? This was one step too far, one thing too many to force on me!"

She pushed past him and rushed out the door, leaving him staring after her, dumbstruck.

He slowly turned towards Pe'tala. "What just happened here?" he asked in a stunned voice.

Pe'tala sighed and rubbed her face. "She thinks you forced that child onto her."

He stared at her. "How?"

"By somehow learning how to manipulate a woman's fertility cycle."

"What? I have no idea how to do that!" he exclaimed.

"I pointed out that chance, but she was not exactly open to the argument," she sighed.

"I didn't do anything of the sort! Even if I could, I wouldn't!"

"I know," Pe'tala remarked dryly, "Too proud, too principled."

Enric lifted his palm to his forehead. "Pe'tala, I am aware that deep inside you there must somewhere be the remote, underused ability to connect with people, to show them sympathy. I would be very grateful if you somehow managed to dig it out, because I am in dire need of it. I will not take well to another snide remark right now," he said, remaining calm yet somehow threatening.

Pe'tala gulped and stepped towards him, taking his hand between both hers. "Look, I *am* sorry. This was a rather nasty shock for her. Her attitude towards having children is well known and not exactly positive. The easiest way out for her right now is to blame you. She has no idea how this happened to her, and your having done this intentionally is the easiest explanation for her presently. She has not much capacity for clear thinking at the moment."

"I need to find her," he murmured. "Talk to her."

"You may try, but I do not have any great hope of her being especially open to anything you might say at present. You might want to give her a little time to get used to the new situation, to calm down."

He closed his eyes for a moment. "She wouldn't do anything stupid, would she?"

"I doubt that very much. Let us not forget where she comes from. She was raised by a healer who fled his country because he fought against wilful early terminations of pregnancies. Added to which, she is a healer herself - which entails a certain conviction to not harm but help. And she has taken on the home for orphans here, so I strongly suspect there is a weak spot for them somewhere deep inside her, even if her fear of raising a child herself is very strong."

He exhaled slowly and nodded. Good, valid arguments. Just what he needed right now.

He lifted Pe'tala's hands to his lips to kiss them. "Thank you. If you will excuse me now, I should go home. I want to be there when she returns."

She nodded and watched him leave, his expression a mixture of disbelief in the news he clearly considered delightful and the sadness when it came to the seething, accusatory packaging it came wrapped in.

* * *

Eryn wandered the streets aimlessly. She hadn't brought her cloak, but she didn't feel the cold. Dusk was falling and after more than one and a half hours she felt how her feet were getting more tired by the minute. It had been a long, busy day at the clinic before she had received the news.

The news. She pushed aside all thought of it and tried to get back into the dreamlike state she had been in before. A haze of pleasant dullness that wrapped around her thoughts and stopped them from concentrating on what she had learned not long ago. Only a slight, indistinct feeling of unease had remained, but not intense enough to bother her too much.

But now her brain was back in active mode and refused to return to its former state of carefree bliss. Probably as a reaction to the basic needs her body was starting to remind her of. Such as rest for her tired body, food and protection from the cold, things that could now no longer be ignored.

She wondered where to go. She wasn't ready to face Enric yet, nor did she know what to tell him or what to do. Could she even continue to live with him again after he had smashed her trust in this way? Was that something that could ever be forgiven, even less forgotten? How could she ever again relax in his arms, rely on him, believe anything he said? Yet he had made his choice with regard to that, hadn't he? Or was he naïve enough to believe that things would return to what they had been before after her anger had subsided, the way it usually did? She pushed away these thoughts as well. She couldn't deal with them now. To sit and to warm up - those were her priorities for the moment.

She found that her feet had traced their way to Kingsway. The way that led to Orrin. An automatic reaction to stress of whatever kind. She slowly walked on, running over her options. Orrin's quarters were where Enric would seek her first. As much as she wanted to go there, staying away from Enric was more important for now. She needed time to consider the options first.

Where would he not look for her immediately? The answer came readily enough and made her sigh in resignation. Pe'tala. This was probably the last place anyone would suspect her of going when in trouble. Either there or to the King. She had no intention of following the latter one, however. She increased her pace and walked on with more determination, pushing aside the image of her cousin guffawing and closing the door in her face. Would she?

She straightened. There was only one way to find out.

When she stood in the dimly lit Palace corridor in front of Pe'tala's door, she stared at it while she tried to bring up the courage to knock. How bad would a rejection from her cousin really be? It was not as if they were friends or even disposed towards each other in a friendly way. It was ridiculous to be afraid of being sent away. Only people close to her had the power to hurt her, didn't they? And Pe'tala was not among them. Definitely not. And yet...

If Pe'tala didn't let her stay, she would go to Junar's sister. She and her companion owned a pub that also let rooms. It was not as if she would be forced to spend the night on the street if she didn't want to return home.

She closed her eyes, counted to three and then knocked five times rapidly, not sure if she preferred the door being answered or not.

She heard feet moving towards the door and a moment later blinked against the lamplight, making out the surprised figure of Rolan.

"Eryn? You look terrible!"

She sighed. Ever the diplomat.

"Tala? Eryn is here," he called out, and a moment later her cousin emerged from the bedroom, clad in a dark red night gown of the flowing kind which managed to be alluring without revealing much skin. Her cousin Vran'el had given Eryn one like it when she had been in Takhan.

"Eryn." She frowned. "You have not been roaming the streets in those clothes all this time, have you? Come in and sit," she instructed.

Eryn entered hesitantly. "I was wondering...," she began and stopped again. Coward! "I need a place to stay for tonight," she stated, inadvertently making it sound like a challenge. Not good. "I mean," she tried to amend, "I would very much appreciate..."

Pe'tala rolled her eyes. "Of course you can stay. The guest room is over there, but from what I have seen, quarters here are pretty much all laid out the same, so I am sure you will find your way around. I will bring you one of my nightshirts. Use whatever you need in the bathroom. Rolan, be so good as to order one extra breakfast for tomorrow."

Rolan nodded and went to the door to summon a servant, resigned that he was spending a night in the same quarters as Eryn. As well as having breakfast with her in the morning.

Eryn stared at her. "Just like that? No making me beg? Humiliating me? Mocking me for being wrong?"

"Do not be so silly, Eryn. Why would I kick you when you are on the ground? It is more fun when you are in a position to be able to fight back properly. You know, where I come from hospitality is a virtue, whether it concerns strangers or friends. Whatever else you may think of me, I do not send away people who come to me for help. Or a place to stay. Not even family," she smiled a little stiffly.

Eryn nodded gratefully. "I would be happy if you didn't tell Enric that I am here, not for now. I need some time for myself."

"As you wish," she shrugged. "But do not take too much time. Looking for you here may not be his first or even second choice, but he will find you soon enough."

Eryn nodded tiredly. "I know. I will think about this tomorrow."

Pe'tala stepped towards her drinks cabinet and took out a mug, a few herbs and a bottle of water, mixing a few spoonsful of the powder into the clear liquid and heating it before handing it to her cousin.

"Here - drink this. It will warm you through."

Eryn accepted the mug gratefully and drank it down greedily without even tasting anything, welcoming the warmth that spread immediately in her stomach. She leaned against the backrest of a chair and closed her eyes for a moment. She opened them again when the empty mug was taken from her hand and a soft bundle was pressed into them instead.

"Here. You can wear this for tonight. Now go to bed. You look like you are going to collapse on me any moment," Pe'tala commanded and pulled her along to the guestroom, eased her inside and closed the door behind her.

Eryn stood in the darkened room, bundle in hand, blinking. That had all been... unexpected. She hadn't really counted on such hospitality from Pe'tala that seemed to be offered so freely. There had been no reluctance or hesitation whatsoever, just a natural understanding.

She felt her way towards the spacious bed and removed the day cover, letting it drop to the floor untidily. She would take care of that tomorrow. Then her clothes landed right next to it and she slipped into the nightgown she had been given. It smelled slightly of the perfume Pe'tala tended to use.

Eryn felt a little dazed and wondered if the herbs she had just gulped down had not only a warming but also a sleep-inducing effect. If so, that was fine as well. Sinking into oblivion was a welcome thought and she slipped under the thick blanket, pulling it up to her chin. Moments later she felt the heaviness of sleep, dimly aware of a pulsating worry at the edge of her consciousness that had to originate from the other end of the mind bond.

* * *

The King let the page with the message sink and pursed his lips

"It seems Lady Eryn is not well which is why her companion is asking for my permission to have the lesson scheduled for today at some other time." He looked up at his advisor. "Marrin, why does this seem suspicious?"

"Probably because one would expect a trained healer to be able to take care of common ailments," he replied immediately.

"Exactly. So this is either a lie or the good Lady is facing something that cannot be healed away like that. Either way, we should find out about this. I wonder..." The King's eyes narrowed. "Find out for me if Lady Eryn is currently at her house. Also whether she spent the night there. If the answer is *No* to both, I want to know if somebody has ordered an extra breakfast tray anywhere today."

Marrin raised his brow. "You think she might have run away from Lord Enric?"

"Let us say that Malriel hinted at something that slowly starts taking shape. I need to see Lady Eryn. And soon. Inform me as soon as you have located her whereabouts."

"Yes, Your Majesty." Marrin bowed and left the study to get a hold on one of the servants who tended to Lord Enric's household.

* * *

Eryn woke slowly when heard dim voices through the door that separated the guestroom from the parlour. One of them was Pe'tala's, the other... she sat bolt upright. That was the King's voice! Him of all people!

The memory of the evening before came back like a wave and made her slump back onto the cushions, her hand covering her face as if blocking the world from her sight would make it all go away.

She heard a determined knock at her door and groaned, "Go away!"

The door opened nevertheless and she pulled up the blanket when the King stepped in.

"A very good morning to you, Lady Eryn. I think there is a little matter we need to discuss."

She gave him a pleading look. "I know we do have an appointment today, but I am really not in any shape to keep it. I would not be of much use today." She closed her eyes. "Honestly. It would be a waste of your time."

"Get dressed, Lady Eryn, and meet me in five minutes in Pe'tala's study," he replied unmoved. "Don't make me wait. I am not accustomed to it, neither do I appreciate it."

"Oh, please?" she wailed, her expression desperate. She couldn't deal with *him* right now.

"Would you prefer to talk to me here?" He looked around the room. "In your nightgown? I am fine with this, though I would have expected you to opt for a more... dignified setting."

She let her head sink in surrender. So it seemed there was no wriggling out of this.

"Five minutes," she sighed.

The King smiled. "Excellent." Then he turned and left the guestroom.

Eryn jumped out of the bed, cursing, all but ripped off her nightgown then quickly donned the clothes from yesterday that she had dumped on the floor the evening before so carelessly.

How did the King know where she had spent the night? Enric didn't seem to have worked it out yet, or he would undoubtedly have barged in here already. But then it was the King's Palace. Enric had told her once that walls had ears, as it were.

She dashed into the bathroom for a very quick wash that was anything but thorough, but one didn't want to face a King completely unwashed and unkempt - however much of a nuisance he currently was making himself.

Pe'tala watched her dashing from the bathroom to her study with some alarm.

Eryn stopped in front of the door, breathed a few times to calm down, then entered without knocking.

The King was standing at the window and looking out when she entered. She expected him to take a seat behind the desk, but he instead walked around it to take a seat at one of the corners, motioning for her to sit on a chair in front of him.

She hesitated for a moment, then took a seat. The thought that Enric wouldn't be pleased about her being alone with the King came up briefly, but then what did she care any longer what he was pleased about or not?

"Talk to me, Lady Eryn," he said softly.

She stared at him. "What about?"

"Why you spent the night at a place you had counted on not being found in for a while, instead of at the very comfortable residence Lord Enric and yourself have, for example," he prompted casually.

"That is a private matter. I was not aware that my relationship with Enric was subject to Royal intervention whenever there was a... slight variance of opinion," she replied coolly.

"Slight variance of opinion? That is a rather mild way of putting it, I would say, considering that you seem to be hiding from your companion who, as you surely are aware thanks to the bond between you, is currently not exactly in a relaxed state of mind," the King said unperturbed. "As grave dissent has the potential to unbalance the Order, thanks to both your high ranks, I always take the liberty of intervening when I see fit. However little it may be to your liking. And maybe I can even be of assistance to you."

"Of assistance?" she asked weakly. Him?

"Yes. You would be surprised what talking to somebody who is not involved can accomplish."

"With all due respect, Your Majesty," she remarked testily, "but *you* would hardly be my first choice for that kind of conversation."

And there was his thin smile again. "Duly noted. And yet it seems that I have to remind you that when facing a King *you* are hardly ever the one making the choices."

"You can't order me to talk to you about private things!" she protested.

"Order you?" he asked with both eyebrows raised in surprise. "It is an offer, no more. You are free to refuse it, of course."

"I am?" she asked suspiciously.

"By all means. If you feel that you cannot in any way profit from my insight, who am I to force it on you?" he shrugged.

His insight. Damn him. That probably meant that he knew more than she did. But when had that ever not been the case?

"So you would be willing to share those... insights with me?"

"Let us say I would, to the extent I am able, yes," he agreed.

That was very likely all the commitment she would get from him, she knew. How could she learn as much as possible from him without giving away too much herself?

"Very well. Then why don't we start with your view of the recent events?"

King Folrin smiled and folded his arms. "Nice try, my dear. But no - this is not how it works. You start. Tell me why I received a message from Lord Enric telling me that you do not feel well. You do look well enough, physically speaking. At least at the moment."

She thought quickly. "A digestive problem, one where the cause has turned out to be rather elusive." This was not a lie, technically speaking.

He grinned. "Has it really? It doesn't happen to be related to your recent avid consumption of bread buns, does it?"

Eryn glared at him. "I find your interest in my diet very disturbing, if I may be so bold as to remark on such a thing."

"Lady Eryn, I make it my business to be as well-informed as I can. And you would be surprised what interesting insights apparently random fragments and snippets of information provide at times."

"Such as?" she asked warily.

"Well, let me see," he said thoughtfully. "There is your craving for sweet bread, something that seems to be a digestive problem that you have been seen to suffer from for a while now, plus the fact that you apparently are furious with your companion right now. This does lend itself to certain inferences."

She raised an eyebrow at him, waiting for him to go on.

"If I had to guess, my dear, my suggestion would be that you are expecting a child and are not particularly thrilled about it."

She exhaled and sank back in her chair. He was quite the guesser.

He smiled. "I take your reaction as confirmation. And I will even be bold enough to congratulate you on the forthcoming family addition. I am confident that you will in time come to see it as a blessing, instead of a curse. I take it that you somehow hold Lord Enric responsible in the conception of that child? Apart from fathering it, obviously."

Eryn closed her eyes and let her head loll back. How did he do it? Was he a mind reader? Even with his extensive sources of information he still had demonstrated amazing powers of deduction here.

"Lady Eryn? I feel I have done quite some talking already. May I invite you to contribute a little something more than reluctantly confirming my suspicions by your resigned gestures?"

She exhaled and straightened again. It seemed that she could probably learn more from him than he would from her.

"He forced that child on me by counteracting the preventative measures I had established in my body," she murmured without looking at him.

The King looked down on her thoughtfully. "Did he really, now? Is that a fact, Lady Eryn?"

She lifted her gaze to his face, feeling angry. "It is a very valid assumption, if you must know! From what I know there are not too many other means by which a healer with magical abilities may be impregnated when she does not wish for it."

"From what you know...," the King repeated slowly. "How confident are you that you are in possession of *all* the facts?"

She narrowed her eyes. "You seem confident that I am not. Can we stop pussy-footing around? Just tell me what you know!"

He sighed and shook his head. "Knowledge, my dear Lady, is always a matter of subjective perception. What I might term knowledge would by somebody else be considered insinuation. And that can in my position be a dangerous distinction."

"Are you telling me that you can't tell me anything because you might get yourself in trouble?" she said, trying to simplify his statement.

"You might put it like that, yes," he admitted hesitantly.

"What about those insights you wanted to share with me, then? It seems there is not much chance for me to profit from them," she sighed.

"I may not be in a position to share my knowledge, suspicions or assumptions with you directly, but what I can do is point you in a direction that may lead you to the satisfactory explanation."

"What makes you think the one I have does not satisfy me?" she asked coldly. "It seems logical enough for Enric to do that, doesn't it? A powerful man landed with a companion who was chosen for him by his King and who turns out to be unwilling to grant him his wish for children. What would hold him back from doing what he has been known to be so good at - taking what he needs."

"You do not appear satisfied to me," he pointed out. "Moreover, I think it is time for you to start using your brain again, even if you still are in that emotional state that makes accessing common sense rather challenging." He watched her press her lips together and smiled. "No contradiction. Good. Now consider what you already know about Lord Enric. What you have learned about him in this past year."

"Dominant, possessive," she started listing. "Proud, intelligent, resentful, dangerous, devious, headstrong."

The King nodded. "True enough, though some of these characteristics tend to come up only in connection with *yourself*. Your current state of mind does not exactly let you focus on his more constructive character traits, apart from intelligence. Try to think of a few positive things about your companion, even if that is a challenge for you right now."

She sighed and pressed her thumb and forefinger to the bridge of her nose. "Very well. Positive traits. Protective. Generous. Supportive, when it suits his needs. Annoyingly skilled in whatever he decides to undertake."

"Trustworthy? Honourable?" the King supplied.

She raised her brow at him. "Not from where I am standing right now."

"I am trying to establish that your current stance is a rather shaky one, so I would ask you to consider his actions prior to what you suspect he did to you regarding your current situation."

"If you insist... Honourable, maybe. Trustworthy? No - he tends to withhold things from me. Which brings me to another trait of his. Secretive."

The King smiled. "Yet *honourable* is definitely something we should concentrate on. How does what you allege he did tally with that very quality? Or with pride?"

"It goes well enough with *devious*," she snapped.

The King scowled at her impatiently and lifted his index finger to tap her forehead several times none too gently. "I told you to *think*! Let us leave aside that he finally committed to the weakness of loving a woman. It is not an argument you would acknowledge at this point. But how does tricking you into conceiving his child go with the honour he as one of the two highest-ranking warriors in the Kingdom has displayed in every aspect of his life so far?"

"Desperation?" she suggested.

"Really, Lady Eryn? Does he strike you as so desperate for fatherhood that he would do a thing like that after less than one year? What was his approach in the past in making you comply with what he decided was the right course of action?"

"He simply ordered me."

The King nodded. "Yes, the direct approach. What else?"

"Persuaded or convinced me."

"The logical approach with arguments. Go on."

"Cajoled me," she admitted reluctantly.

That made him smile. "The funding of the orphanage, I imagine."

"And he tricked me," she added angrily.

"Into doing something you didn't want to? Or rather into not refraining from doing what you had planned? As in Takhan when he decided not to inform you of his adoption to make sure you followed your plan of renouncing House Aren?"

Eryn fought hard to swallow her rising irritation. There was no discussing with that man. He knew too much, which was so incredibly annoying!

He chuckled when she didn't answer. "I will take this as confirmation. I would think that he also may even have begged you at times."

That, too, she didn't deign to comment on, however close to home it was.

The King observed her closely. "Would you agree with me, then, if I argue that your companion was in the past either very direct in his authority, used arguments to change your mind, bribed you to give you an incentive or tricked you into following your own plans?"

She thought for a moment, then nodded slowly. "That is probably one way of putting it, yes."

"So he has never tricked you into doing something you didn't want to do anyway? If it came to things you were averse to he always chose the open, direct, mostly authoritative way to make you comply?" the King clarified.

"Yes! Yes!" she exclaimed and threw up her hands. "I see what you are getting at! Tricking me into having a child when I am dead set against it is just not his style! Are you satisfied? But I have not heard you give me a better explanation about how it happened yet!"

"No. Because you would probably not accept whatever I told you. You don't trust me, especially after my last... manoeuvre to induce you to go to Takhan." He leaned forward. "I will offer you something better - a path to follow. Talk to your cousin, or sister or however you currently refer to her. Ask her if the unlikely scenario of your companion stealthily acquiring advanced healing knowledge in a very short time and using it on you like that is the only possibility of making a powerful magician conceive against her will. After that you will talk to Lord Enric." With that, he rose. "I shall expect you tomorrow morning for the lesson I am so graciously permitting you to postpone. I am looking forward to hearing about the conclusions you have reached by then." He bent down to lift her hand and pressed his lips against her knuckles, rolling his eyes impatiently when she flinched.

"That is something you should work on, Lady Eryn," he sighed. "It is the traditional formal greeting of your own home country, and if you can endure it with strangers, you should definitely bring yourself to accept it from me. Good day to you."

Eryn watched him leave and remained seated, pondering what she had heard. Her head was spinning. He had made sense, of course, as always. The King had manipulated her in the past, more often than once, but he had never actually lied to her. At least not as far as she knew. He had at times even been surprisingly open about engaging in his games with her. He undoubtedly had his reasons for talking to her about her current issues with Enric, but it didn't feel like one of his usual games this time.

"Eryn?" she heard Pe'tala asking carefully from the door to the parlour. "Is everything alright?"

"I don't know," she sighed. "Would you come in here for a moment? There is something I was told I need to ask you."

* * *

Eryn looked up and swallowed when a sharp knock resounded in Pe'tala's parlour. So the King had obviously told Enric where to find her.

Pe'tala rose slowly and shoved her breakfast tray aside. "I suppose I do not have to ask who *that* is," she said with a meaningful look and went to answer the door.

Eryn looked down at the symbols on her wrist that had darkened at their counterpart's proximity. "No, not really."

Enric pushed open the door after Pe'tala had opened it a crack and all but knocked her down when he stormed into the parlour. Even without the mind bond his anger would have been obvious.

He walked towards Eryn, grabbed her upper arms to pull her up from the chair and growled, "*There will be no hiding, no running from me*," he said, quoting the line from his commitment oath between clenched teeth. "I meant that, damn you! What did you think by just running off into the night without returning home, without letting me know where you are? I have been searching half the city for you, dreading every moment that some sensation through the mind bond would indicate that you are in peril, helpless, the victim of a mugging..." His words trailed off and he forced himself to calm down. Then he turned his head to Pe'tala without releasing Eryn. "And *you*. You and I will need a little conversation regarding the proper course of action if my distressed, pregnant companion shows up at your doorstep! It's not hiding her from me, in case you were wondering!" he snarled.

Both women stared at him, neither daring to move. A tall, enraged magician of above average strength had that effect on people. He released Eryn from his grip, closed his eyes for a moment and then let himself sink on a chair, suddenly looking forlorn and exhausted instead of intimidating.

"Eryn," he sighed tiredly. "That was the last time I shall go through something like this. You will from now on have somebody shadowing you wherever you go. We talked about running, I threatened you with an agent, and yet that doesn't seem to have helped at all. From tomorrow onwards every step you take will be monitored and reported to me. If you ever again think you can run away, always consider that I will know where to find you."

She stared at him. "I do not think this is a sensible way to tackle our issues."

"It is a very effective way of tackling *my* issues, namely keeping you safe and close to me," he retorted. She could see the muscles in his jaw working when he went on, "What in the world induced you to believe that I forced a child on you? What is it about me that makes you think that this could be an acceptable method for me? Apart from your seeming to overestimate my healing skills grossly, I find that idea insulting and wonder what your picture of me truly is. But," he raised a hand to stop her from talking as she opened her mouth to reply, "I will grant you that you were under shock and not entirely yourself yesterday."

"You were happy!" she exclaimed. "I could feel it!" She tapped her forehead.

He stared at her in disbelief. "That's your reason? The fact that I was happy when learning that I am about to become a father equals having tricked you into a pregnancy?" He exhaled slowly, remembering his own words about her not entirely having been herself last night. "Is that still what you think?"

Eryn swallowed and slowly shook her head. "No. I have come to hear of something that in the past also resulted in unplanned offspring despite thorough magical protection."

Enric's eyes widened and his head snapped to Pe'tala. "How far along is she?"

"Pretty much the end of her second month," the healer supplied.

He nodded slowly and turned back to his companion. "When you had that glass of wine with Malriel the evening before she left here, did you ever, even if it was for only one moment, turn your back on her?"

"Yes," she replied calmly. "I avoided looking at her and stared out of the window while she was pouring the wine. What a very interesting question to ask me," she added with narrowed eyes.

Enric became agitated, raking his fingers through his hair, making it stand on end. "There is a potion. It is very powerful and can overrule virtually any kind of protective measure which is in place! That's what must have happened!" He closed his eyes. "That woman. I simply can't believe what she does."

Eryn and Pe'tala exchanged a look.

"I myself learned about the existence of such a concoction only this morning. How would *you* of all people know about that potion, if I may ask?" Eryn asked, her voice soft yet threatening.

Enric instantly realised the trouble he was about to get himself into. "Not because I used it or knew that *she* intended to use it," he said slowly, looking her straight into the eyes. "And this insinuation is hardly any less flattering than your first one," he finished with a warning undertone.

"Then how do you know?" Pe'tala asked, arms akimbo.

"Because Malriel offered me a vial when we were in Takhan."

Eryn stared at him. "She did *what*? How did you react?"

"I refused it, of course! What do you think I did?" he shot back angrily.

"How would I know?" she cried out. "I only know what you *failed* to do, namely tell *me* about it!"

"That was when I still had hopes of you and Malriel somehow managing to get along with each other. I didn't want to let one ill-judged action on her side get in the way of the two of you finally forming some kind of mother-daughter bond," he said, justifying himself.

"Well, that worked out fabulously," Eryn said sourly. "Not only do I now detest her more than ever, but I have also been landed with having a baby soon! If you had told me about all that beforehand, I would have been more careful! Had I known about the existence of such a potion, I would never have agreed to drinking anything as long as she was even in the same building as me!"

"We," he said softly.

"What?"

"*We* have been landed with having a baby soon. Not *you*."

"Oh yes," she said dryly, "I forgot that you are happy enough with the situation."

She saw the anger flaring up again in his eyes. He sprung up from his chair and pulled her close by grabbing her arms once again.

"Listen to me, and listen very carefully," he said slowly as if to make sure that not a single word was wasted on her, "I do not require trickery and intrigue to manage my relationship with you. I may not have been too happy about your resolution not to have children, but I would have accepted it. I would not have put the need to have a child before having *you* with me. I would have tried to change your mind in the years to come, worked on making you see that there are worse things than creating a new life with me and raising the child together. I strongly disdain Malriel's course of action, and the trouble it unleashed upon us. This might very well have led to my losing you, and that is a price I would never have paid for having a child with you. Are we clear on that?"

Eryn stared up at him, feeling the echo of his wrath and desperation in her own head through the bond. Yes, he truly meant it. She felt relieved. This honest anger at Malriel's plot was better proof than any of his words that she could indeed trust him.

She nodded. "We are."

"Good. Then I never again want to hear you accusing me of either having assisted Malriel in this or applauded her actions."

"I won't," she promised. "Can I take revenge on her? I don't know what I will do or when, but I will not rest until she has paid for taking this liberty."

Enric smiled grimly. "I think you should. I want her to think twice next time she considers messing with our lives. So whatever you do, you'd better be thorough."

Pe'tala sighed. "How delightful," she deadpanned, "Reunited through plotting terrible retribution on the grandmother of their child, whoever wants to claim her as a parent now."

Enric slowly turned towards Pe'tala, making her consider her harsh words.

"Tala, my dear, why don't we have a little talk about how you can improve your own way of dealing with a situation like this, should you ever again be caught in the middle of one?" he purred, with a glint of looming fury in his blue eyes.

Eryn had to admit that her cousin did stand her ground well enough, even though her expression seemed a little apprehensive. But then that was a fairly normal reaction for whoever had to face Enric when he was aggrieved.

"I do not see any need to improve my actions, thank you so much, mighty Lord," she said with her chin lifted defiantly and arms folded. "I granted my sister a safe haven when she was in trouble, as is expected of me. I invite you to verify this by contacting my father and having him educate you on the value of hospitality in my country."

"Thank you, I am quite aware of the merits your culture places on hospitality. And I am not telling you to close your door in her face next time. What I am asking you is to send a message next time." His smile showed rather too many teeth. "We wouldn't want this to turn into an occasion that may one day lead to tension between our Houses, would we?"

Pe'tala narrowed her eyes at him. "You would not intentionally harm your own companion's House when you took the trouble of letting yourself be turned into an Aren to protect it in the first place."

"No, you are absolutely right, I wouldn't. The tensions would rather result from your father being angry at me for causing trouble to *you personally*. You are planning to stay here in this country for a while longer, and I am only stating facts when I tell you that my influence here is considerable. I can make your life very difficult indeed should I set my mind to it," he promised and put an arm around her shoulders, squeezing her close to his side. "Don't get on the wrong side of me, my dear girl. It doesn't pay."

"Alright, alright," she grumbled. "No more hiding her from you. I got it."

"Good." He removed his arm from around her shoulders. "I am so glad we understand each other."

Now Eryn folded her arms. "That leaves only one little matter to be discussed. You told me that I will from now on be tailed by a spy. I do not feel that this is warranted after we just established that this is basically all *your* fault, since you didn't tell me about Malriel offering you that damned potion."

"As long as you do not give up that unfortunate habit of running from me, I do not think my measures are disproportionate," he replied mildly.

"But you have obviously not overcome your own tendency to keep things from me! I thought it was what we agreed to work on. I don't flee, you don't keep secrets, remember?"

He nodded. "True enough. But there is one little detail you seem to forget - my not telling you about Malriel happened *before* we agreed that, your running happened *afterwards*. It means you were the one to break it while I did not."

"But your actions caused me to run!" she protested. "I insist that you give up the idea with the spy!"

"I will make you an offer, my love," he smiled good-naturedly. His mood had improved considerably since he first had come here. "I will have an agent on your heels for the duration of your pregnancy. I think we can both agree that your judgement is questionable at the best of times; being in this state of increased vulnerability now does not seem to have improved it."

"I do *not* agree with a thing like that! That *you* do not agree with many of my decisions doesn't mean that my judgement isn't correct!" she huffed.

"Then let us at least agree that your decisions do not always keep you out of trouble. This is unpleasant enough when it concerns you alone, but is now even more of an issue since you are carrying my child under your heart."

"Alright," she grumbled.

"Fine. Then let us consider the agent as an additional means for keeping you both safe from harm. Should you prove to me in these remaining seven months that you have finally overcome your inclination to run from me when there is trouble, I will no longer have you watched. I consider this a very reasonable offer."

She pursed her lips. "When you say *offer*, does this mean I am in some position to reject it?"

"No, my love, this was just diplomatic wording. It is in truth a final decision that you cannot discuss, negotiate or otherwise change."

"Brilliant," Eryn sighed. "It seems I don't receive anything like Junar's pregnancy privileges."

"You will get your own set of privileges, I promise you," he smiled and kissed the top of her head. "Now, please come home with me. In addition to our other preparations we now need to have the second guest room turned into a nursery."

She groaned. "I'll ask Junar to do that. She will be so happy with the two of us raising our children together that she will be eager to help me out with it."

Enric looked up sharply. "Orrin. I need to tell him that I have found you and that you are well. He was quite upset when I stormed into his quarters yesterday night and demanded that he send you home." He took her hand and pulled her towards the door. "Come. I think we should take care of this little matter before we go back home. You can break the good news to them."

"Actually, I don't consider it *good* news - not at all," she scowled.

"Very well," he conceded, "just the news, then." He nodded to Pe'tala. "Have a good day, Tala. Dinner in three days at our place. Bring Rolan. I decided that we should turn this into a regular thing." He grinned broadly at her expression of dismay.

Eryn stopped in front of her cousin, feeling awkward. "Thank you. For everything. Really."

"Do not mention it," Pe'tala waved her off. "If you want to reciprocate, get Enric to give up the dinner-idea."

She grimaced. "Not much chance of that, I am afraid. It's the penalty you have to pay, in a way. Just defy his expectations by enjoying yourselves."

"Oh yes, that's a great idea. Simply fabulous," they heard her muttering as Enric closed the door behind them.

CHAPTER 29

Spreading the News

Enric held on to her hand when she tried to change direction and walk along Kingsway instead of across the Palace square towards the warriors' quarters.

"You know, I don't really want to tell them right now." Or at all. She could imagine their smug, satisfied reactions only too well after her repeatedly insisting that having a child was never somewhere she wanted to go.

He smiled and tugged her along. "No shirking! We have to tell them sooner or later. Especially as a few people know already. Let's make sure they hear it from us."

"It's just the King and Pe'tala," she protested.

"For now. It's only a matter of days until Tyront hears of it. You may depend on the fact that he knows that you spent last night somewhere else."

"Bloody spies," she mumbled.

"Can't be helped," he shrugged. "We are persons of interest, after all."

He stopped when she pulled on her hand and looked down at her questioningly. "What's the matter, my love? So reluctant to share this news?"

She grimaced. "I don't even know how to deal with all of it myself! I haven't even had a chance to get used to the thought of... of..."

"Having a child," he supplied.

"Yes, that," she sighed. "You see? I can't even say it out loud!" Her expression became panicky. "What if I turn out like Mariel? A nightmare of motherhood – bossy, wicked and insufferable?"

"You won't. I'll be there to avoid that happening," he promised and pulled her close, kissing her cool lips. He smiled. "This is the first time I have kissed a pregnant woman."

She gave him a tired look. "No, you haven't. I have been pregnant for two months. You just weren't aware of it before. And there can hardly be much difference. I don't feel any different, so how can kissing me have changed in any way?"

"I don't know. Must be me, then. Come on." He walked onward with his arm around her shoulders.

"You are awfully eager to spread the news," she commented sullenly. "Didn't you use to be that hermit who avoided making friends? What happened to that person?"

"You happened to me," he chuckled and opened the door to guide her inside. "I discovered my social side thanks to you."

"How lovely for you," she murmured.

"If you slow down any more, I will lift you up and carry you the rest of the way," he warned her. "I wouldn't mind, but you haven't taken very well to being carried in the past, so I assume you prefer walking. Which means you should hurry up."

She did so reluctantly and found herself in front of Orrin's door not much later.

Orrin answered their knock quickly and gasped in relief when he spotted her. "Good. You found her. What is going on?" He stood aside to let them enter.

Junar came out of the bedroom, both hands on her rounded belly. "There you are! We were so worried! Where have you been? Why did you run *this* time? When will you start behaving like an adult and take care of matters instead of rushing off, you reckless fool?" she scolded.

Eryn rolled her eyes and gave Enric a pleading look. Nonetheless, he just smiled and led her to a chair, pushing her down gently with a hand on her shoulder.

Vern's room door opened and he stepped out. "Hey, what happened? Good to see you turned up."

Eryn was about to ask him why he wasn't at his classes, but remembered in time that he was being tutored now.

"We are waiting," Orrin growled and stared down at her.

"We have news," Enric stated, stepping behind her to lay both hands on her shoulders. He looked down on her. "Would you?"

"No," she murmured, "you do it. It's you who is the one who can't wait to tell everybody."

"Very well, then." He lifted his gaze to the three faces looking at him expectantly and grinned broadly. "We are expecting a baby."

Their faces showed assorted expressions of disbelief. Vern's mouth dropped open, his eyes widened. Junar's left hand went up to cover her mouth while her right rested on her belly, while Orrin blinked and shook his head.

"What?" Vern whispered after a while. "How? I mean, I thought you did your precaution thing?"

She nodded. "I did. But it seems like Malriel had other plans. We think she gave me a potion that overruled my means of protection and kicked my fertility cycle into action."

"She did *what*?" Vern exclaimed in utter astonishment. "How could she? Which person does a thing like that?"

"A truly evil one," Eryn said darkly.

Junar awoke from her shock and shook her head, taking a seat on the chair next to Eryn and squeezing her hand. "I am so sorry she did this to you." Then a smile slowly spread on her face. "Thinking back, it seems that I diagnosed you correctly that day. You know, when you were trying to give up the bread buns."

"Really?" Eryn shot her an angry look. "Gleeful? In a situation like that? I got pregnant through no fault of my own!"

"Oh really," Junar snorted, giving her a penetrating gaze. "And what would *I* know about that?"

"Come on!" Eryn hissed, "Don't tell me you consider this some kind of cosmic revenge or I will smack you, pregnant or not!"

"I recall your telling me that a child developing inside me was nothing bad, but a gift from nature. It seems you have received that very same gift. Congratulations!" she smiled, the delight clear in her eyes. "What was it you told me about how *you* would react in my place?"

Eryn lifted a finger to silence her, "Honestly, if you don't shut up right this moment I will disable your vocal chords! I mean it!"

"Ah, yes," Junar went on with a smirk, ignoring the threat. "Humbled and grateful. I con't see much of that right now."

"That's it," Eryn growled and let magic flow through her fingers, doing to Junar's vocal chords what her uncle had done to her own several months ago. "I warned you."

Junar's mouth opened, but no sound came out and both her hands flew up to her throat. She shot Eryn an accusing look and turned to her companion with a pitiful expression.

Orrin sighed and shook his head. "I am sorry to say this, but you had that one coming. Teasing her when she is upset is a risky thing to do."

"Eryn!" Vern sighed. "That is not a responsible use of healing magic, no matter how upset you are right now." He stepped next to Junar and put a hand on her shoulder, closing his eyes.

Eryn watched him drawing his brows together.

"I can't fix this," he murmured and looked at her. "What have you done here?"

Junar's expression became slightly panicky.

"A little something my uncle showed me," she explained coolly. "Don't bother. You won't be able to fix it. I will do it when we leave here again."

Orrin crouched in front of her and regarded her thoughtfully. He took both her hands in his.

"How are you doing, my girl? I can see that Enric is dealing with this well enough, but you never wanted children. I am sorry this has befallen you. That mother of yours really should be publicly flogged."

She exhaled slowly and smiled tiredly. Sympathy. That felt good for a change. "I am not sure how I am doing. It's still a bit unreal. I don't *feel* pregnant. If I hadn't seen it with my own... well, magic, I still wouldn't believe it. I am worried. Mad. And I feel guilty about not being happy or feeling some kind of mystical mother-child bond with this tiny life inside me. And I feel guilty about not wanting to be happy about it. I just want to hide somewhere and make it all disappear."

"You are not thinking about...?" Vern whispered, wide-eyed.

Eryn shot him a withering look. "I can't believe you would really ask me that question. Of course I am not thinking about that! Enric would murder me."

She looked up and saw him nodding. "Maybe not murder you, but I would not take well to it myself. Not at all."

She returned her attention to Orrin, who smiled at her. "Don't feel bad, Eryn. You will be fine; I know it. And you are not alone. Vern and I will be here for you. And there is Junar, too, even though she might need a little while to get over her indignation at just having been stuck dumb like that."

She nodded and leaned her forehead against his. "Thank you, Orrin. I love you."

"Sure," she heard Enric murmur above her testily, "tell *him*. It's not as though *I* would appreciate hearing it now and again."

"You, my friend, caused this whole thing. I don't see me complying with any of your wishes right now," she growled.

"Well, of course he caused it," Vern pointed out. "At least he should have done, if you have been faithful."

"That's not what I meant! Malriel offered *him* that same potion she must have slipped me, and he failed to tell me of it. Otherwise I would have been more careful around her and been able to avoid this whole predicament!"

Orrin grimaced. "Oh my. You two really should work on a thing or two." He pointed a finger at her. "You, stop running all the time when things get difficult. You are not a stubborn teenage girl any longer but a pillar of society!" Then he rose and scowled at Enric. "And as for you, it wouldn't hurt you to talk to your companion every now and again instead of trying to do all the thinking for her and then wondering why she keeps getting furious at you!"

Enric just raised his brow at him.

"Don't give me that indignant look, I know well enough that you still outrank me. That doesn't make what I just said any less true."

They both turned when they heard Vern clapping his hands together enthusiastically.

"You know what just came to my mind? I can now draw another set of pictures to compare your baby's development to ours! That is brilliant!"

Four pairs of eyes stared at him, nonplussed.

"What?" He looked at them with big, innocent eyes. "I am just making use of an outstanding opportunity here! I mean, how often would I get the chance to document two pregnancies so closely while being commissioned to do just that? That must be some sort of fate!"

"I don't think that my being pregnant is connected with your being destined to illustrate a *book*, but rather with a certain person who we shall meet again in about one month," she grunted and looked at Enric. "You said I could take revenge on the Queen of Darkness. Didn't you tell me that you had fantasies of somewhat violent means of dealing with Ram'an back in Takhan? Can we use any of them on Malriel? We could feed her remains to our mountain cat, if need be," she hissed with eyes squeezed tightly closed in vicarious thrill.

"Bloodthirsty," her companion commented dryly.

"Yes, let's get the huge predator with the pointy teeth and sharp claws used to the taste of human flesh, why don't we?" Vern murmured and looked up at the ceiling.

"I think it's time for us to leave now," Enric said, taking Eryn's hand and pulling her up from her chair. "There are a few things I need to take care of, such as procuring books on the dietary needs of pregnant women, and contacting her uncle."

"You are surely not going to monitor what I eat!" she protested.

"I will if you keep on devouring huge quantities of sweet bread buns," he stated determinedly. "That can't be healthy."

"I am a bloody healer! I know exactly what I am supposed to eat and what not!"

"I am aware that you *know*. I just want to make sure that your cravings don't stop you from employing that knowledge the way you should."

"Patronising me again? Really?" she snarled, her arms akimbo. "Maybe it really is time for you to have a child to look after so you can stop ordering *me* around!"

"Charming," he commented and put an arm around her waist to guide her towards the door. "I can see we are going to have a lot of fun in the next few months."

Orrin closed the door behind them and looked at his son, his expression resigned. "Oh my. And we are going to spend many, many months together with them in Takhan." Then his gaze fell on a wildly and silently gesticulating Junar. Her expression was furious and she kept pointing at her throat.

Vern started laughing loudly while his father cursed and opened the door again to call their visitors back.

* * *

Eryn blinked languidly against the daylight after Enric had pulled aside the curtains in the bedroom.

"Good morning, my love," he smiled and lifted a breakfast tray from the chest of drawers to put it next to her on the bed before taking a seat at her other side.

She sat up, raising her eyebrow at the unexpected luxury and yawned. "Good morning. What is that?"

"Pregnancy privileges. I am experimenting," he explained.

She winced at being reminded of that little detail so early in the morning, then sighed in resignation and even managed a weak grin when she located two bread buns on the tray and snatched one. "Keep doing that, you are off to a good start."

"Glad to hear it." He watched her examine the other components of her breakfast. Her reaction had not been lost on him, she was still anything but comfortable with their new situation. As opposed to him. He found himself wondering about what arrangements to take care of first, whether starting to transform the second guestroom was a bit premature without knowing the gender of the baby. Or whether such a thing really mattered. Why stick to the traditional colour patterns and toys, anyway? He himself remembered entertaining himself with his sister's playthings just as often as with his own, so why impose any limitations on that child of his before he or she was even born?

"A touch more fruit-heavy than what we normally have here," she commented, interrupting his train of thought. "You are not by any chance starting to sneakily alter my eating habits already, are you?"

"I wouldn't say sneakily. Let's call it doing so gently, shall we? I brought you your bread buns, after all."

"That you did," she admitted generously.

"You are aware that bread buns will be difficult to come by in Takhan, I assume?" he asked carefully.

She stilled for a moment, then frowned. "I suppose so, yes. I bet I can learn how to make them, though," she mused. "But then it might be just as much of a challenge to get the ingredients there."

"Pity. But we can always switch you to fruit," he suggested with mock resignation.

She smiled. "No need to go to such extremes. I will just have to try the local pastries there and see if something strikes my fancy."

He tucked a strand of hair behind her ear. "That sounds like a plan. And I am sure that you will have a more than willing accomplice in Junar when it comes to getting through that demanding task."

"I don't think Junar will be very concerned about food when we are in Takhan. She will be well into her seventh month by then."

"Four months ahead of us...," Enric mused. "That is looking rather practical, you know. We can use most of the things their daughter outgrows for the first year or two, I would imagine."

She blinked. "That is unusually pragmatic of you, considering that you insist on ordering new clothes of me all the time."

He laughed. "I can't have you running around in somebody else's castoff clothes, my love."

"No, maybe not," she conceded. "But you could let *me* wear them long enough for them to become worn instead of having anything with even the tiniest hole in it exchanged for something new. Clothes can be mended, you know?"

He let out a long sigh. "Not the clothes discussion again! And a small child hardly manages to wear out a piece of clothing since it doesn't fit them long enough for that. I wouldn't have our firstborn clad in rags, you know."

She stared at him open-mouthed for a few moments. "Our *what*?"

He realised too late what he had said. "I didn't mean to imply that I intend to have another one," he assured her quickly.

"No?" she growled. "What did you mean to suggest with *firstborn*, then?"

"Nothing. Just an unfortunate choice of words."

"You learned about this child less than two days ago, how can you be planning another one already just like that? Are you insane? Do you have any idea what raising *a single* child will involve? Sleepless nights, a helpless creature that depends on you for everything from feeding to cleaning, no more time for yourself..."

"Well, that does sound like our life as we know it is about to end anyway," he joked. "How bad could a second one be, then?"

She glowered at him and put her half-eaten bread bun back on the tray to get up. "Not funny."

"Come back," he called after her when she got up without finishing her breakfast. "I am sorry. We won't have another one if you don't want it."

She whirled around to him. "Damn right you are! We won't! What makes you think I would be open to having a *second* child while I am still in shock after learning about the first one?" She raked her hair, then pointed at her abdomen. "I will be more thorough next time. I will do something permanent. Should there ever be another potion, it will find me less... susceptible to external manipulations," she promised.

He frowned. "Permanent? How permanent?"

"What do you mean, how permanent? That is a rather unambiguous term, I think."

"Permanent as in *never again reversible*?" he enquired in disbelief.

She lifted a finger at him. "I am really not going to discuss this with you right now. You will have one child, which is one more than I ever planned! If you want another one, find somebody else to have it with you! What is going on with you? Why was having no children easier to accept than having *one*?"

The question made him think. It was not exactly an unwarranted one, he had to admit.

"I am not sure," he said slowly. "Maybe because I grew up with siblings. The thought of being an only child is rather sad."

She shook her head at him. "You don't have close contact to any of them! To one of them none at all!" And he was not exactly raised by an affectionate father himself, so how could he be that eager to breed? She needed some distance to him, to all of this.

He got up from the bed as well to follow her into the bathroom and hugged her from behind. He held her close when she tried to disentangle herself from his arms.

"I am sorry," he murmured. "I would very much like to enjoy this with you, experience it together as something positive. Making you angry is not what I had in mind." He linked his fingers with hers and kissed her temple when she closed her eyes and exhaled.

"I need time, Enric," she said tiredly. "I am not ready to see it as something positive. Right now I am still trying not to consider it a curse."

"I will do my best to help you with that."

She felt his cheek against her hair. "Just don't be too enthusiastic about it for the time being when I am with you. It makes me fume. And it causes me to feel guilty because I don't share your sentiments. Not to mention your plan for more children – plain scary!"

"I know, that might have been a little too much," he sighed.

"Yes, you could say that," she nodded and made to turn to the basin to wash her face.

He held on to her. "Wait. Can I... see it?"

She hesitated, then nodded. "Alright. Do you know what to do?"

"I am not sure. I know how to explore injuries, but this... I don't want to do anything wrong."

He sounded a fraction nervous, she realised. "Then follow my lead."

She felt his hands on her abdomen and a moment later warmth travelled from his fingertips into her body. Closing her own eyes, she guided him to her reproductive organs and the small embryo growing there.

"Its size is about the width of your finger," she said softly. "There you can see the head and where the arms and legs are starting to grow. If you look further and deeper, you can see its tiny heart. It is beating slowly right now, but that rate will increase later," she explained soberly. Strange, even though she had direct contact with it, it didn't feel any more real. It was like looking into a stranger's body. Maybe that was because she hadn't really felt any changes yet in herself that would make it more real.

"When can we see whether it is a boy or a girl?" he whispered, clearly awed.

"I can see it already. I assume you would like to know?"

"I would, yes," he nodded and opened his eyes again while turning her around to face him.

She saw the wonder in his eyes after this first contact with his child and couldn't help but think that this minute blob of life was indeed lucky to have him as a father. Right now it didn't look as if she was going to be a very dedicated mother.

"Which would you prefer?"

He blinked, surprised by the question. "I don't know. Which probably means that I don't really have a preference." He let his fingers glide over her cheek softly. "Maybe a girl with your brown eyes and your fierce temper. Or a boy with your quick wit and your complete lack of respect." He smiled at her indignant expression.

"No charming traits you intend to pass on, then?" she asked, her brow raised.

"My devastatingly good looks, I assumed," he joked, then became serious again. "And? Which is it to be?"

"A boy," she stated calmly.

"Quick witted, disrespectful, but immensely good looking," he grinned broadly and kissed her lips. "Maybe with a bit of Aren temper. Or is that only passed on to girls?"

She moved away from him and got on with washing herself. "I have no idea. I don't think I met any Aren men yet - not counting you, since you can't have inherited anything from them. But having seen you in a few of your less controlled moments, I dare say vitriolic temper in this child is not necessarily passed on through *me*."

He leaned against a wall and watched her cleaning routine, which started with fixing her hair together into a tail to avoid getting it wet.

"Do I need to meet Tyront to tell him that I will no longer be undergoing combat training or is that self-evident?" she asked while scrubbing her face.

Enric furrowed his brow. That was a very good question.

"I am not sure. I suppose that means that we should see him. And soon. We should pay him a visit today after we are done with the King."

She turned to him, her face wet and slightly sudsy at the sides. "Are you expecting difficulties here?"

He pursed his lips. "Nothing we won't be able to handle. I have no intention of letting anyone attack you."

He watched a slow smile curve her lips upwards. "Good to hear. We are finally moving along with the really interesting pregnancy privileges."

* * *

The King smiled when he saw them entering the throne room, hand in hand, and waited until they had stopped in front of him and bowed.

"Good morning. I am pleased to see that the two of you have reconciled with each other. Do take a seat."

Eryn noted with amusement that he refrained from kissing her hand in Enric's presence.

Enric pulled out a chair near the head end for her and then moved to the other side to sit as well.

"I am very interested in what conclusions you have reached regarding your present situation," King Folrin said and leaned back in his chair, his eyes on her.

She felt annoyance bubbling up almost immediately at the thought of Malriel, but fought to maintain control. This was neither the time nor place for hysterical, flailing emotional display. They were so much more satisfying when there were handy breakable objects around to hurl against walls.

"Evidence has led us to understand that a certain person might have decided to present us with the unexpected gift of a child," she said stiffly.

The King raised his brows. "That was phrased very carefully, I must say. I do appreciate that you seem to take to diplomacy, yet you really do not need to worry about that in here, behind closed doors."

"You seemed to worry about precisely that when we were in Pe'tala's study," she reminded him.

"There is quite a lot of difference. I have little control who might be listening in to me in certain places as I do not have the very convenient ability to create magical shields that stop sound from travelling where it should not. I am confident, however, that in here we can talk as privately as possible."

"So what you want to hear me say is that we strongly suspect my pregnancy stems from a potion Malriel managed to administer to me without my realising it at the time."

He nodded. "Yes. Well done."

She narrowed her eyes at him. "Looking back to our little conversation of yesterday I can't help thinking that you were somehow aware of this before. In turn that makes me wonder if you lowered yourself to assist the plan."

"Be very mindful, Lady Eryn, of what you are accusing me," the King warned her calmly. "I was not involved in any of this - at least not in the planning or execution of it. In hindsight, however, I see that Malriel did indeed want me to play a certain role by providing me with just enough information to work out her intention after the plan had already been executed."

"What role?" she asked, not entirely convinced of his innocence.

"I was to ensure that it would not cause a permanent breach between you and your companion through alerting you to other possibilities than Lord Enric having forced this child upon you."

"Of course," she pressed out between clenched teeth, "Having us separate would not be to her advantage, would it?"

"No, not at all," he agreed. "Quite the opposite. With the two of you continuing to be attached to each other, she has a chance of seeing her grandchild every now and again while if you were the only one to determine who was to see it she would be excluded."

"Why did she do it?" Eryn blurted out. "The child will be a member of House Vel'kim, so she has no hold over it."

The King raised both eyebrows. "Why would you assume that I am fully aware of her motives, Lady Eryn?"

"Don't tell me you don't harbour a theory or two on that," she said.

That made him smile. "I certainly do. But let us see if you can figure out possible reasons yourself. You are aware that the Houses in the Western Territories are keen on preserving and enhancing magical bloodlines and keeping alliances between the Houses in place by strengthening them with strategic companionships."

"So you are saying that my being joined to a strong magician, who happens to be a member of her own House, is too good a chance for bearing empowered offspring to let it pass?"

"Isn't that obvious? The bloodlines have been mixed so often in the past that any fresh addition will be a blessing."

"They could introduce fresh blood anytime by not limiting their breeding programme to members of the Houses," she growled.

"But that would be a political disadvantage, especially for a House as powerful, and thereby in need of strong alliances, as House Aren. And now you have provided a very good solution for both problems: fresh blood with a magical background as strong as she could wish for and a reaffirmation of the bond with House Vel'kim, which was strained by your father's actions."

"The bloodline is now no longer officially Aren since I joined another House," she pointed out. "So how can she profit from it?"

"That is a question I would expect you to be able to answer yourself," he said and looked at her expectantly. He sighed when she just frowned at him. "Think of your companion."

"You are not suggesting that she will try to adopt our son into House Aren as well?" she snorted. "As if I would ever agree to an outrageous thing like that!'

"Ah," the King smiled, "so you have already determined that it is to be a boy? Congratulations! And yes - in your place I would in the future expect an attempt of that sort. Not as long as your son is the only descendant of House Vel'kim and so is the sole heir of that generation, of course."

Oh no, she thought and closed her eyes for a moment. He was right. So far she hadn't even thought about the fact that her child would be the only available heir of House Vel'kim. Vran'el's daughter and whatever other children he might have yet would belong to their mother's House, and Pe'tala didn't have any children so far. And who knew if she ever would? Marvellous. So, no matter to which of his parents' Houses her son belonged, he was bound to become a Head of House one day. So much for determining his own path in life.

And if Pe'tala really should be persuaded of the joys awaiting her and enter motherhood one day, thereby providing for another available heir for House Vel'kim, then that would be Malriel's signal to try and start getting her fingers on her and Enric's son to secure the succession for House Aren.

Or, if Pe'tala showed no inclination to have a child, Malriel might even try to ensure that she would have another grandchild either by trying to slip Eryn another potion or using whatever other tricks she knew. Two children meant two heirs; one for each House.

"So keeping my son here in the Kingdom would only work if Pe'tala procreates as well. Just splendid. I suppose I am now the one who is supposed to slip her a vial or two of that noxious brew that has worked so well on me?" she sighed. "What do *you* want? Which is the more attractive option for you, having my son in the Order, because you hope for him to inherit our considerable magical strength, or having a good connection to one of the Houses by promoting his rise to Head of whichever damned House manages to dig its claws into him? Where do I stand with you?"

"I assure you, Lady Eryn, that at this time either option is equally attractive to me, meaning I have currently no plans to help along either outcome."

"*At this time*. That means that there might be a preference for one outcome depending on how things with the Western Territories develop. Which means that I had better take care of keeping not only Malriel's and Valrad's hands off him, but also yours." She cursed under her breath.

How could one growing embryo the size of her thumb nail start all this? These were considerations that would only be realised in twenty years at the earliest, depending on when the current Heads planned to pass on the responsibility of their Houses. Vran'el would very likely be the one to take over House Vel'kim, but it was not even sure who was to be Malriel's successor. She could hardly count on Enric genuinely intending to take over her position, could she? But then it was hardly possible to guess what that woman's plans were. If there was no other heir available, she would surely try to make him do it. And having her own grandson, blood of her own blood, take over the House after his father would be the ultimate victory. Her direct bloodline would continue to be in charge of the House after skipping one generation, due to the adoption.

"I detest that woman," she murmured. "I really do. I thought I had hit rock bottom with her already, but she keeps extending the limit of my loathing."

"Do try to see things from her point of view for a moment," the King suggested.

Eryn scowled at him. "That I can't do, I am afraid. I have too much conscience and too little ruthlessness in me for that."

"Tell me of a Head's responsibilities towards his or her House. This is an interesting question also with regard to the role your own companion will soon be taking on."

"Don't try to make me understand or condone her actions," she snapped. "That will not work with me. I have no comprehension of the measures she sees fit to employ against me, and I admit that I have no wish to develop one!"

The King gave an exasperated sigh and looked up at the ceiling. "Before you came along, I was not really used to having to repeat my instructions. Since being acquainted with you, dear Lady, I have come to realise what a luxury that was. I intend to return to that very convenient state of affairs," he ended sharply. "One should think that you have managed to get used to the concept of obeying one's King by now, despite having been raised in the countryside."

She felt Enric's unease through the mind bond and the warning it was to behave appropriately. Very well, she could do that. But she didn't have to pretend to like it.

She smiled without humour. "In this case it will of course be my pleasure to follow that very appealing line of thought, if it so pleases you, Your Majesty."

"Well done," he remarked dryly. "That only leaves the sarcasm open to improvement."

She swallowed and nodded. "A Head's responsibility includes providing for the family's wellbeing, forging alliances and protecting its reputation."

"Good. What else? I know you are aware of it. Say it!"

"Ensuring succession," she mumbled.

"Well done. Ensuring succession. I am sure you agree that this particular task had to be quite a challenge for Malriel considering the way she kept losing you. Twice. First through your father's actions, then through your own."

"*She* was the one who made me renounce her House," she hissed. "That was no one's fault but hers!"

"Be that as it may, it is not part of our current discussion. Whose fault it was is of no consequence to the House, only what is done to rectify it. Let us return to the situation House Aren faced: Their only heiress taken away to another country and remaining elusive for twenty-two years. When she is found again after hardly anybody had counted on it any longer, she is bound to another Kingdom by a magical oath. Removing that oath would of course have been a path to consider, but one that would have angered the sovereign of that Kingdom, namely myself, considerably. The Triarchy would not have agreed with that in order to satisfy a single House, especially as we have turned out to be stewards of resources they wish to engage in trade for. Yet that alone would not have made it impossible for you to follow in your mother's footsteps."

"No," she supplied. "But my renouncing her House has."

"Exactly. So there is a woman who had her daughter returned to her, only to lose her again. And with it the heir to her House she needs if she doesn't want to leave it without any successor. Adopting Lord Enric was an ingenious move on her part. A man who is not only a high-ranking politician with valuable connections and almost unparalleled magical strength, but has also proven to be an able business man. And he happens to be joined with the daughter who rejected her. How could she not have taken advantage of that opportunity, I ask you?"

"Yes, a brilliant move by a brilliant woman. I am glad you pointed this out to me. Now I can leave my resentment behind and admire her the way I should," Eryn muttered angrily.

"Lady Eryn!"

She flinched when the King's fist came down on the table and his booming voice echoed through the vaulted ceiling.

King Folrin closed his eyes for a moment and breathed in and out a few times before returning his attention to her. He slowly moved his head from side to side and she wondered if it was at her or himself.

"I am beginning to understand how Lord Tyront and Lord Enric are driven to lose patience with you," he spoke in his usual calm manner. "You could probably provoke a dead man into outrage."

She felt Enric's amusement and fought hard against letting it show on her face. Unfortunately, her body did not always distinguish where the emotions came from and displayed them automatically. Which was somewhat inconvenient at times. Such as now.

And true enough, the King seemed to have noticed something and shot Enric a disgruntled look. "I am glad you seem to find this amusing, Lord Enric. Do try to remember that your companion tends to display the feelings you yourself are managing to hide so well. This does make her a rather handy indicator of your moods, should one know what to look for."

Enric nodded once, but remained silent.

Eryn wondered how much longer this would go on. Apart from her feeling rather uneasy in the King's presence, the lessons had so far been informative and even helpful, but this one was an ordeal. If there was one topic she did not want to elaborate on, it was Malriel of House Aren. The only thing that would have been helpful was how to dispose of that woman instead of trying to understand her motives.

She frowned. But maybe she could give this conversation a twist in exactly that direction... If there was one man who might have an idea how to handle her, it was one who had at times turned out to be as devious as herself.

"How would you have handled all this in my place, may I ask?" she asked with a challenging look.

He smiled. "It seems you are finally realising that you may profit from this topic. Excellent. I was beginning to worry about your emotions shutting down your brain entirely." He waited, watching as she opened her mouth to reply, but closed it again, having thought better of airing her thoughts and smirked at her restraint. "Yes, I can see we are definitely making progress here." Then he returned to her question. "In your place, Lady Eryn, I would not have renounced House Aren. Your status was one in some dispute, since it was unclear to which country you truly had citizenship of at that time. By joining House Vel'kim and thereby causing Lord Enric to become a member of House Aren you have given Malriel greater power over the two of you than she had before."

Eryn ground her teeth. She knew he was right though that didn't make hearing it any more bearable.

"I see. Then I suppose the question of how you would progress from where I stand now becomes superfluous. You would very likely do what I mentioned before but meant as no more than a tasteless joke."

"If you are referring to making sure that your cousin will have a child, I agree. But I am aware that this would hardly be a palatable course of action for you after suffering from having this very trick done on yourself. This is a great difference between the two of us, you see. I would not hesitate in doing to others what had been done to me if it aided my own objectives. If I had to bear it, why should somebody else be spared?"

She swallowed her words about loyalty and how one could ask to be treated fairly when not willing to show others the same courtesy. That would only make him grin indulgently at her again.

"But saving your son from having to take over House Vel'kim is only the first step, mind you. The consequence of this is the real challenge: stopping Malriel from ultimately appointing him as her heir. She has a lot of time to attempt different approaches in the years to come. You will have to thwart every single one of them, because if she gets lucky once, she has won."

She looked at him in dismay. Those were sinister prospects indeed.

"And yet you are sending us there."

"I must. She might have managed to summon Lord Enric in any case, even without my consent. This would not make me look good - as not being able to avoid it would imply a certain weakness. And it would not improve the relationship between ourselves and the Western Territories. The logical course of action was to harness this state of affairs in a way that will enable me to profit from it as well." He lifted a hand when she attempted to speak. "No, do not ask me again what I get in return. I am willing to answer this question no more now than I did when you asked me the first time."

She exhaled and looked at him discontentedly.

"How are your studies for the exams required by the Order before your departure progressing?" he enquired, switching tack.

She frowned at the abrupt change of topic. "As well as I might wish, I would say."

He raised a brow at her. "Really? And would you also say that this correlates with what Lord Tyront wishes? You will forgive me for applying *his* standards here. Your own priorities here are well known," he concluded dryly.

"I will be able to take one exam per week before we leave. That will cover all the remaining subjects," she explained, not rising to his remark implying a certain lack of commitment on her part. He had a point there, nevertheless.

"Good, I am glad to hear it. I do look forward to having you in the Council after your return, Lady Eryn. The meetings will doubtlessly be more... animated."

She grimaced at the thought of having to attend them regularly. That did not make the prospect of returning here exactly a joyful one.

"Let us conclude our lesson for today. I am sure you are eager to meet Lord Tyront. I imagine there is an issue or two you might want to address with him regarding your new status," he smiled knowingly.

Eryn pressed her lips together in annoyance. Talking to him always gave her the impression that all her actions and intentions were completely and utterly predictable.

Enric rose first and stepped next to her to help her up from her chair. They both bowed and turned to leave the throne room.

"I don't like it when he does that," she muttered in a low voice once they were out of earshot. "I bet he does it on purpose. To make me feel easy to see through and insignificant next to him."

Enric nodded. "That you may safely rely on. And being the King, basically everybody *is* insignificant in comparison."

"That doesn't make it any easier to bear," she sighed.

He nodded. "Yes, I know. Unfortunately for our self-esteem, we are about to go to the only other person in the Kingdom who has any claim to being higher ranking than the two of us," he smiled. "But following this train of thought leads to the conclusion that there are quite a number of people who are less important than either of us."

"How lovely," she snorted. "What a bad thing then that I don't believe in assessing people in accordance with their magical strength."

He nodded. "Yes, I admit that is a setback. But then the thought that Lords Seagon and Woldarn are among those who have to follow your orders should cheer you up at least a little."

She sniggered. "Yes, that it does. That will be my remedy when I am in a bad mood; I will find a reason to give them an order and watch them comply with it grudgingly."

He squeezed her shoulders. "That's my girl. Learning how to abuse your position of power for your own satisfaction. The King would be so proud."

She grimaced. "Thank you for dowsing my dark fantasies like that. You could have allowed me that little pleasure a few minutes longer."

"Too dangerous, my love. We wouldn't want you to deviate from the path of virtuousness."

"We wouldn't?" she sighed. "Pity. Being nasty does hold certain appeal, you know."

"I suppose. That's why Malriel enjoys it so much, I'd bet," he chuckled.

"And this was the most convincing argument against it you could have given me," she growled. "Come on, let's see that important superior of ours and impress on him why not making me train my combat skills is a splendid idea."

CHAPTER 30

Combat Training

Eryn stared at the high ceiling and forced herself to keep her hands from fidgeting nervously. She was once again in front of the double doors to the Council hall, waiting to be called and to present another request. This time it would be a personal one.

Tyront had listened to her yesterday when she had told him about being pregnant. He was surprised at first, then was pleased and had gone on to congratulate them warmly by hugging her gently and slapping Enric on the back heartily several times. He had also expressed understanding for her request to have her combat training suspended for the months ahead, but had told them that it was too risky for him to make a decision like that on his own. The combat training was a requirement for being a member of the Order, and making an exception for her needed to be agreed upon by the entire Council, or his standing in the Order and even her own might be compromised in the long run. Some of the Council members might try to use it to make it seem as if he was showing undue partiality towards her and Enric. He promised that he would support her request, but the final decision needed to be the Council's, not his alone.

At least it never took long to convene a meeting. The Council members were used to being summoned at short notice. She wondered what to do if they decided that she needed to continue her training.

She hadn't had any chance to discuss this with Orrin, who would undoubtedly not be too thrilled at having to train with an expectant woman.

The doors were opened for her and she straightened herself and walked in. This would, she hoped, be no more than a formality.

She came to stand before the great oval desk around which the Council members were seated and bowed once.

"Good afternoon, Gentlemen," she greeted them and received several nods in return. She saw Enric rise from his chair and waited until he had stepped next to her. They had agreed on addressing the Council together over their request.

"I have asked you to receive me today as I wish to inform you that Lord Enric and I are expecting a child." That fragment of news triggered different reactions. Lord Poron smiled broadly and winked at her, the rest of them looked at Enric as if for confirmation and only seemed to believe it when they saw the small smile on his face. Her feelings about having children had been widely known, after all.

"Well done, Lord Enric," one of them called out. "We were wondering if you would manage to convince her." That earned him a few chuckles.

"What can I say?" Enric replied good-naturedly, "I am hard to resist."

Eryn looked at him intently and cleared her throat. "There is an important matter in connection with this that I need you to consider and hopefully grant. I request to be released from any and all combat training with immediate effect, for the duration of my pregnancy until such time as I am physically able to resume it." She counted several frowning faces and continued, "I am aware, of course, that honing one's fighting skills is an important condition for being in the Order, but I would ask you to consider the risk to my unborn child as well."

"What risk?"

Eryn didn't even have to look who had said that, she recognised Lord Seagon's voice instantly. She turned to him.

"Blows, hits, strikes or basically any kind of impact could endanger the child's life," she explained calmly.

"Is that the case, Lady Eryn?" he smiled in obvious mistrust. "I wonder if this is the genuine assessment from a healing point of view. Your unwillingness to train in fighting is commonly known, after all. This might just as well be another ruse for shirking this duty you find so very bothersome."

"I can assure you, Lord Seagon, that it is not," she replied coldly. "I am aware that the issue of how to treat a childbearing magician has not been an issue for the Order for a significant time. Let me tell you as a healer that avoiding the strains I spoke of is definitely advisable, whether the mother be a magician or not."

"Be that as it may, but your healing skills are not exactly up to the standard that is common in the Western Territories, are they? You might not even be able to assess the situation correctly," the Council member said with a smirk.

She gulped and glared at him, fighting hard to maintain her countenance. This was one occasion where she could not afford to give in to temper, however appealing the idea of grabbing his hair and crashing his face against the large table's stone surface might be at the moment. She could feel an echo of Enric's feelings that went in practically the same direction.

"Are you telling me, Lord Seagon, that you consider my healing skills insufficient for determining what any clear-headed person should be able to grasp instinctively?" she said slowly, staring into his eyes. "My skills may well not as yet be able to compete with those of a fully trained healer in Takhan, but they are advanced enough to pronounce on a risk to a pregnant woman. You may safely rely on that."

She felt Enric's arm around her shoulders and gladly let him take over. If she had to go on discussing risks with that bloody fool, she would sooner or later lose her rag. Actually, rather sooner.

"I understand your consideration, My Lord. This leaves only one sensible course of action, does it not?" Enric's voice reverberated through the spacious hall.

"I agree, Lord Enric," Lord Seagon nodded with obvious satisfaction. "And I am glad you are not making this unnecessarily difficult. Of course proceeding in accordance with our traditions is the only..."

Enric opened his mouth for an acid remark, but Orrin got ahead of him by stating loudly and clearly, "I object, Lord Seagon. I demand that Pe'tala of House Vel'kim be summoned here before us to provide the expert opinion *you* seem to consider necessary for informed decision."

"Lord Orrin," Lord Seagon sighed, "I can see why this is a particularly sensitive topic for yourself right now with your own companion bearing your child, but for all we know magicians could be a lot more resilient to external physical disturbance. Even in the unlikely case of Lady Eryn's unborn baby suffering injury, she would no doubt be able to heal it away in the blink of an eye."

"You will surely be able to relate to my own priorities of avoiding my companion or my child suffering any injury at all," Enric said with such deadly insistence that several of the Council members exchanged telling looks, and those seated next to Lord Seagon surreptitiously moved away from him a little.

"I did not intend to imply...," he then amended quickly, but was interrupted by Enric, whose smile was not exactly a friendly one.

"Excellent. Then I am sure you have no objection to consulting a fully trained healer at this point. How very fortunate that we happen to have one so conveniently available."

"Of course not," Lord Seagon agreed hurriedly.

A guard was instructed to fetch Pe'tala and bring her to the Council hall immediately, and Eryn had to smile when she looked in Orrin's direction and saw him rolling his eyes and shrugging at her. If they made him work as a trainer with her despite the fact that it might be dangerous, he would not respond well to it.

Only a few minutes later the double doors swung open and an irritable-looking Pe'tala marched in, quickly taking in her surroundings and stopping next to Eryn. She didn't bother addressing or even acknowledging the high-ranking magicians, but spoke to her cousin.

"I sincerely hope this is important. I was interrupted in the middle of a patient's treatment," she complained.

"It is important for me," Eryn nodded. "I would be extremely happy if you could inform the Council whether there are any risks connected to a pregnant woman becoming involved in physical combat training."

Pe'tala stared at her for a few moments, then blinked. "This is a joke, surely?" She slowly turned when Lord Seagon addressed her.

"No, it is not a *joke*. We need a valid opinion in this regard."

"A valid opinion?" Pe'tala snapped, her voice incredulous, and stared at him. She lifted the index fingers of both hands to her temples and started massaging them. "Please do not tell me that you dragged me here for a question that not only is completely stupid, but could just as easily have been answered by my cousin here. It can hardly have escaped your notice that she, too, is a healer? I could instead have continued to treat my patient's liver disease! Do you have any idea how serious such an illness is?"

"You would consider this question stupid because...?" Orrin prompted with an amused sideways glance at his colleague.

"Because every person with at least half a brain should be able to see that combining a woman carrying a child in her womb with fists or a sharp-edged weapon is utterly reckless," she explained in a voice as if talking to a group of four-year-olds. She shook her head, appalled. "You short-sighted primitives are surely not going to force her to continue her training, are you? I would personally make sure that this had very severe consequences for all of you!" She glowered at the assembled men. Several of them stared at her, taken aback.

"You are surely not *threatening* us, are you?" Lord Seagon called out.

"What?" Pe'tala exclaimed. "How could you have mistaken that for a *non*-threatening statement? Of course it was a threat! My father, who happens to be not only Lady Eryn's legal parent, but also a very high-ranking and influential healer in Takhan, would not just sit by idly if you went ahead, you can be certain of that!"

Tyront cleared his throat and shot her a warning look. "Thank you very much for your valuable opinion, Pe'tala. Are there any further questions concerning the healing aspect in this?" he asked the men around him. When all of them had shaken their heads or otherwise indicated that they felt no desire to address that woman again, he looked back at her. "I appreciate your help here; you may now return to your work. Though I would counsel you to be a little less blunt in phrasing your less than flattering opinion when facing the Magic Council."

"Then you may want to attempt to display your lack of common sense a little less bluntly in the future," Pe'tala snorted and turned on her heel to storm out.

Eryn worked hard at keeping a straight face.

"That was... enlightening," Lord Woldarn commented when the doors had closed behind the healer.

"What a disrespectful creature!" Lord Seagon huffed. "Somebody should teach her manners!"

"I think we can attribute her behaviour to her wish to protect her cousin. Or sister. Quite understandable, I would think if the danger truly is as dire as she was saying," another Council member said soothingly.

"Gentlemen, this brings us to our vote," Tyront announced. "I ask those of you in favour of suspending Lady Eryn's combat training for the time being to raise their hands."

Eryn exhaled slowly when ten hands around the table were lifted plus Enric's right next to her.

"This is a clear majority and the matter is thereby decided." Tyront turned towards Eryn and Enric. "We will discuss the appropriate time for resuming your training after your child is born."

"Thank you," Eryn smiled and bowed to him. Enric winked at her when she turned to leave the Council hall. When she had entered the Palace corridors and closed the massive double doors behind her, Pe'tala's voice came from her left side. She was leaning against the wall, still looking put out.

"So? What has that bunch of fools decided?"

Eryn grinned. "I am officially freed from training for now. Your maverick statement impressed them, it seems."

Now her cousin couldn't help but smile in return. "I admit I enjoyed it a tiny bit. I could not really get away with things like that back in Takhan, so I might have taken advantage of not being answerable to them."

"I envy you," Eryn sighed. "Ah, the days when I was a prisoner and more or less entitled to behave like that! Nowadays one wrong word from my side tends to have unpleasant consequences."

"Such as having to clean the stables," Pe'tala smirked.

"Yes, exactly that. If they ever offer you a place in this bloody Order, don't accept it!"

"I will remember that. You are not worried that my joining them would make *you* less unique, are you, though?"

Eryn snorted. "Hardly. You would be a welcome distraction. With you among them they would soon start appreciating how uncomplicated and harmless *I* am by comparison."

"Says the woman with the Aren temper."

"I don't see that your own temper is far behind. But then after centuries of inbreeding there is bound to be some Aren-blood in your veins as well, isn't there?"

Pe'tala grimaced. "A surprisingly painful and yet accurate statement." They walked on silently for a few steps. "I received a message from father today. He asked me to do a thorough examination on you and the child. We tend to keep an eye out for inherited illnesses due to any inbreeding as you mentioned before. In most cases we can counteract any unwanted developments without problem. And we like to keep track of what is being passed on." She shrugged. "Professional curiosity, you see."

"So you told him about my baby."

Pe'tala looked at her in surprise. "Of course I did. Your child will be the first-born Vel'kim in that generation. The Head of House needs to be informed that a new heir is on the way. Though I could see from his message that he would have preferred learning this from you instead of me."

Eryn grimaced. "My child is *not* going to be his heir, Pe'tala. You are his real daughter and your children will take over your House one day. Additionally, we live at the other side of a sea. How great are the chances that our child will relocate to Takhan one day?"

"Bad luck for you, *sister*. I do not plan to lay claim to the position of Head for my children, should I ever have any. It is nothing but trouble," she sneered. "But why think about this now? Let our children sort this out amongst themselves in a few decades' time."

Yes, that was a sensible idea. "So you will need to examine me to determine whether my child has too many ears or fingers as a consequence of our ancestors having kept the same alliances alive too long? What an appealing thought. When do you want to do it?"

"I will be rather busy over these next few days. It is sowing time in the fields which means injuries are frequent. Let us say in four days?"

Eryn nodded.

"Good. And bring something to write. You may as well use the opportunity to learn how to do a proper Vel'kim check. We tend to be a little more thorough than the others. It is a family thing." She regarded her cousin thoughtfully. "How are you dealing with the pregnancy? You look a lot better than you did two days ago."

"There is not much I can do about it now, is there?"

"There is. But I am pleased to see that you have no intention of going that way."

Eryn looked at her sharply. "It never was somewhere I intended to go!"

"I know," Pe'tala said softly. "Too much Vel'kim in you for that."

* * *

Tyront poured his second-in-command a hot drink then leaned back in his chair again. The atmosphere was more relaxed than it had been since the incident with the King three months ago, but they were not yet adjusted to normal. Tyront wondered if they might be anytime soon. In less than a month Enric would leave the Kingdom for quite some time, and after that there would be little chance for remedy before his return. But letting him go away like that was unimaginable as each of them depended on the other to stay informed. Enric needed to be kept updated regarding everything that happened in the Order, despite the fact that he would cease being a member for the time of his stay in Takhan. On his side, Tyront needed a reliable source of information posted in Takhan.

"I see you are taking to your new situation well," the older man commented with a smile. "It is normally the women who are said to radiate composure and happiness, but in your case it seems the other way round."

Enric nodded. "True enough. But Eryn is getting used to it - especially as now she no longer has to attend combat training. Getting her to resume the training at a later date will be somewhat of a challenge, though. She will try to find reasons and excuses to postpone starting."

Tyront smiled. "We will see how well she behaves up to then. If I am pleased with how she takes care of her duties in the Order - and especially in the Council - I might even indulge her a little longer."

The younger man raised his brows in surprise. Leniency in something that was essential to the Order?

"Don't look at me like that. I could use another ally in the Council. Lord Seagon has turned into quite the adversary since Eryn joined the Order. He is not happy about her. A woman, a healer - and what's more, she is the one in his opinion who is to blame for your breaking his nephew's nose. Unfortunately, he has managed to recruit several of the other Council members onto his side."

Enric nodded. He knew about this of course, being in the Council himself. So making sure Eryn was on Tyront's side when she too got a seat was the sensible course of action. It was all a little contradictory. While the matter with the King had opened quite a gap between himself and his superior, Eryn seemed to be getting along better with him since that occasion. They had even stopped using their titles with each other, though not yet publicly.

"You will doubtlessly have to deal with things like that when you join the senate in Takhan," Tyront said into his thoughts. "But then you already have a pretty good picture of the Houses' alliances. They do not really keep them a secret, after all."

Enric snorted. "That would be hard as they tend to seal them with companionship agreements. But I am lucky already to have good connections with House Vel'kim. They are not after glory and power, but like to advise and keep an eye on things. Just the kind of ally I need, especially in the beginning."

"True. Though another official ally of House Aren is less reliable."

"House Arbil. I know. In any event, I have been working on them by establishing trade agreements between themselves and me. As Ram'an is currently fighting hard to save his House from bankruptcy, I expect he can't afford to have House Aren pitched against him.

Unfortunately, that makes him more susceptible to bribery in the event somebody wanted to make him side against me."

Tyront nodded. He was pleased that Enric was well enough aware of the hurdles he had to take and knew what to keep an eye on. He had learned rather a lot since his rise to power in the Kingdom, and yet there was no telling what exactly was awaiting him in Takhan. He was the legal heir to a powerful House and yet he still was, and would always be, a foreigner, a stranger. His rank would not help him much there, even though it was a lofty one at home. But then with twelve Houses there were eleven others on the same level as himself plus the three triarchs who outranked him.

Observing him dealing with this from afar would be interesting.

"I had the impression that Eryn and Pe'tala are getting along better since your companion's pregnancy came to light. Or am I wrong there?" Tyront then asked.

"I would say they are, yes. They have started respecting - and even liking - each other, but each of them would rather bite off her own tongue than admit the same." Enric sighed. "A pity. Owing to Pe'tala's continued stay in Anyueel it seems there will not be much chance for them to work on their relationship for the time being."

Tyront smiled when he saw his chance. He could assist here, and Enric would have no other choice but to be grateful for it.

"What you need, my dear boy, is a common enemy to get them to connect."

Enric sighed when he saw in what direction his superior's thoughts were leading. "And you are offering, aren't you? I thought you wanted to make Eryn work with you."

"That is the beauty of it. It will leave her with the impression that she has won against me. Judging from her character, she is the generous type in victory - someone who will want to show me that there are no bad feelings between us, which aids my purposes just fine."

He took out a sheet of paper, a pen and his sealing wax, writing a short message before he closed it with his embossed seal. Then he got to his feet to have a servant take care of delivering it.

"Have you summoned her here? She doesn't take well to being called at short notice. Prepare for her to be not too compliant when she arrives."

"Thank you, but there have been a few occasions up to now which prepared me for her foul mood after being summoned."

And true enough, when Eryn stormed in several minutes later, she did not look at all happy.

"Why is it so difficult to plan in advance? Why is it not possible for once to send me a message asking me to see you in the evening? Or the next day? Why do I always have to drop everything to come running here at your beck and call? How am I supposed to carry on with my work like this? You are aware that I am not simply sitting around in an office, pushing paper about? I work with patients!

Treatment should not be interrupted in this way! This only causes confusion and increases waiting times for the other patients!"

"Take a seat," Tyront instructed without responding to her t rade.

She rolled her eyes impatiently and let herself drop into the chair next to Enric's. "Out with it, then. What is so damn important that it requires my immediate attention?"

"It is about your... sister."

"Pe'tala?"

"Yes. Or do you have any other sisters I should be aware of?" Tyront remarked tartly.

"What about her, then?"

"Her behaviour at the Council meeting two days ago was questionable, to put it mildly."

Eryn frowned. "I can understand why you see it that way. But what do you want me to do about it? Confine her to her quarters or the clinic? Take away her desserts for a week? Make her stand in a corner and consider how to address the venerable Council members properly the next time?"

"Quite amusing, Eryn. But you are on the right track. I want you to punish her for her insolence. It doesn't look good if we let her get away with behaviour like that. We have a reputation to maintain, after all," he replied calmly. "I can't punish her myself, as she is not a member of the Order and so not subject to my authority. You, on the other hand, are currently the highest authority when it comes to healing, as Lord Poron has not yet officially and fully taken over the position of Head of Healers."

She blinked at him. "You are not being serious, are you?" Her tone was incredulous. "You want me to deal out punishment to her for being disrespectful when she acted to help me and the growing child inside me? I won't! How could you even ask a thing like that of me?"

"This is one of your responsibilities as a leader: disciplining those under your care who do not comply with the rules."

"Being nice to some of your slow-witted Council colleagues was never one of *my* rules! So from where I stand there is no reason for chastising her!"

"Not even if I tell you that not punishing her will result in unpleasant results for yourself?"

Eryn raised her chin defiantly. "No. And I can see that we have very different approaches to leadership. My own includes standing up for people if I feel that they are to be subjected to wilful censure in preference to saving my own hide!"

Tyront nodded slowly. "I see. An admirable sentiment. Yet it has just earned you another three days of stable duty. I trust that your and your child's wellbeing will not be endangered by this, on account of your magical powers."

She shot him a furious look. "Really? Again? Is this a little something to help you over the months you will have to manage without punishing me?"

"You can easily avoid this if you wish. Discipline Pe'tala instead, and you won't have to clean the stables. Your choice."

She rose from her chair and leaned forward, bracing her hands on his desk. "I won't do this to her. I will clean your damn stables! And you'd better remember this for the next time when you want to get me to do your dirty work for you!"

"As you wish. You will start tomorrow morning."

"Fine!" she hissed and turned to storm out of his study and subsequently his quarters.

Enric sighed. "I don't see the two of you working together peacefully in the Council in the near future."

He waved his hand unconcernedly. "She will have got over it by the time you return here. And she will figure out soon enough that working *with* me is more rewarding than against me. The only thing that now remains is for Pe'tala to learn of the sacrifice her beloved sister has just made for her. And this is where *you* come in, dear boy. I would suggest you do it soon to give them a little time for bonding before you leave."

The younger magician nodded and got up from his chair. "Nice trick, old fellow. It has worked well enough so far. For both Eryn *and* myself. Thank you."

Tyront watched him walk out, and smiled to himself. A smart lad. He would sorely miss him and that temperamental spouse of his.

* * *

Enric watched the entrance door to the clinic, had been for about one hour now. On a treatment day it was always hard to tell when the healers would be able to leave as it always depended on the number of patients. He watched Lebern and Lord Poron come out, both looking tired. This meant that the healing work was pretty much done for today and it would only be a matter of minutes until Pe'tala, too, would leave.

And true enough, only little later the door opened again and Pe'tala stepped out and turned towards Kingsway. She sighed when he approached her and fell into step next to her.

"Waylaying me in front of the clinic seems to be turning into a habit," she sighed. "Does Eryn know of this small disturbing detail?"

"Don't worry, this time I have not come to warn you about slandering my companion. I want to ask you something. A question pertaining to healing, as it were."

"You do?" She raised both brows and stopped. "It must be a very sophisticated question if you think Eryn is not able to answer it. Or it is a question that concerns her or the baby?"

"The latter. I want to know if shovelling horse manure is dangerous for her in her current condition."

Pe'tala rolled her eyes, and sighed loudly. "Ha! Not again! How does that woman manage to keep getting herself disciplined so often?

I mean, I am not exactly known for *my* genial nature, but she is even worse! And you gave that woman such a high rank? It makes me question the Order's approach to hierarchy. Do you not worry what kind of role model she sets for the less exalted members of your institution?"

"Not exactly an answer to my question," Enric commented dryly.

She sniffed. "No, if she uses her magic to enhance her strength I do not see how this will be harmful for her. And now that I have been so cooperative, you tell me as a reward why she has been punished this way. It will keep me happy for the rest of the day."

Enric seriously doubted that, but nodded. "If you insist. She refused an order Lord Tyront gave her today. It had something to do with the Council meeting two days ago."

"The one where I was called to state that pregnant women should not be made to swing edged weapons or be kicked in the guts?"

"The very same," he nodded.

"What of it?"

"Lord Tyront was not exactly pleased with the way you addressed the Council members. For whatever reason he seems to think that this was a lot more disrespectful than warranted by the situation."

She frowned. "Do not tell me that he disciplined *her* for it? That would be immensely daft!"

"No, he didn't." He noted the relief in her expression and went on, "He disciplined her because she refused to punish *you* for it."

Pe'tala drew in a sharp breath. "*What*?"

"Without being in the Order, Lord Tyront cannot discipline you. He is not your superior in any capacity. Eryn in her capacity as the highest healer in the city would be so able. But she did not agree and, well, that was seen as an act of disobedience which is not accepted at all in the Order."

She stared at him. "She took on *my* punishment? And you just stood by and watched it happen? Why did you not intervene or object or whatever means of disagreeing you have at your disposal?"

He shrugged. "I couldn't have done much. And it was her decision to accept the sentence as a consequence of defying her superior. She would not have thanked me for patronising her by treating her like a little girl who needs my protection."

"Is this not how you have usually treated her?" Pe'tala growled. "What made you change your approach now?"

"I have learned from my mistakes," he retorted. Then he turned and waved. "Thank you for easing my mind about the stable duty. I shall wish you good day."

"Wait!" he heard her call after him and smiled briefly before schooling his expression into one of polite interest and turning back to her.

"Yes?"

She raked the fingers of both hands through her hair and turned the neat ponytail into a minor ruffle.

"Would it help if I, you know, apologised? To those stupid blockheads, I mean? Will that make Lord Tyront take back the discipline he handed out?"

He shook his head. "No. The discipline is not for you, but for her unwillingness to act the way he wanted her to. Your apologising would not change that. And from the way you have phrased the question I can imagine that your apology would hardly sound very convincing, if you don't mind my pointing that out."

She scowled. "And what am I supposed to do now? I can hardly stand by and watch her do this!"

"I dare say she would appreciate if you *didn't* watch her undertake it this time," he remarked. "From what I remember, she didn't find having watchers very pleasant the last time."

"Back then I went there to tease her! This is something completely different!" She scowled at him. "You are trying to make this as difficult as possible for me, are you not? Is this your way of getting back at me for causing her to be disciplined?"

"Don't be ridiculous, Pe'tala. This is not the first time she has been made to clean the horse stables. It is the third so far, so she knew exactly what awaited her when she accepted the punishment. And it is not as if she will overexert herself, as you confirmed to me just now. The only unpleasant things about this for her are having to get up a few hours earlier, plus the smell. Well, and the occasional sneer - but people learned from their mistakes and resort to jibing only when she is out of earshot."

"This does not make it any better!" she exclaimed and wrung her hands. "Tell me how to make this right again!"

He pretended puzzlement. "Make it right? This is not your fault. I don't see what there is to be made right."

"Enric," she hissed, "you are doing this on purpose! Stop being such a bloody obstruction and help me!"

"Pe'tala," he sighed. "I don't see what you could do. Taking on the punishment yourself would not sit well with her. It would also mean that Lord Tyront got his will, and that would just make her furious. Doing this and having the feeling that she has prevailed over him will make her much happier, believe me. And I would prefer if you could avoid mentioning that you learned about this, especially from *me*. And now you'll really need to excuse me, there is an appointment I need to keep. Good day to you."

He took a last look at her miserable expression and grinned widely when he walked back the way they had come from. Healers. Sometimes they made things almost too easy.

CHAPTER 31

The Rules of Inheritance

"Take a seat," Pe'tala instructed. They had waited until all patients had been taken care of for the day so they could have this examination without being disturbed.

Eryn sat on one of the two chairs in front of Pe'tala's desk and took a look at the sheet of paper her cousin pushed into her hands.

"Here. This is a list of the things we are going to check. Most of them are completely harmless and only of interest because we want to keep track of how things are being passed on. Some are a bit more intensive, while others are dangerous and need to be dealt with immediately should they be discovered."

"That's quite a list," Eryn murmured. There had to be at least twenty diseases and other inheritable disorders on the sheet.

"Well, things have been passed on between the same Houses for a while, so we need to be thorough to avoid any unwanted consequences for our offspring. But your child is lucky as its father is from outside the usual pool of candidates. This makes certain things being passed on less likely. Always provided that Enric does not have any nasty diseases himself, that is."

"Red-green colour blindness," Eryn read out. "Eye mutations with uncontrolled growth, lack of hearing or ability to speak, lack of capability for blood clotting, degenerative muscle diseases ..." She looked up, wide-eyed. "All of those and the rest on that sheet are hereditary? I had no idea that having a child held such great risk! I admit I am getting rather nervous now."

Pe'tala plucked the sheet from her cousin's weak grip and put it aside. "Then maybe we will not let you have a look at that any longer for the time being. There is no need to be nervous. If I find anything,

I can take care of it. The lethal diseases would have caused you to lose the child already, so I am confident that if we do find something, it will not be a great problem." She sat down on the chair facing Eryn and held out her hand. "Relax and follow my lead. This will not take long."

Eryn nodded, took the offered hand and closed her eyes. She followed Pe'tala's weak stream of magic down into her womb and the small embryo in its comfortable nest.

"A boy," Pe'tala whispered.

"I know," Eryn replied, equally quietly.

"Eyes... fine. Blood... fine," Pe'tala listed. "Muscles... fine. Heart... fine. Lung... fine. Brain... fine so far. Needs to be checked regularly. Bones..."

Eryn swallowed when the pause became longer. "Fine?"

Both opened their eyes again.

Pe'tala frowned and shook her head in confusion. "This should not be there."

"What?" Eryn demanded, feeling the blood drain from her face. "What shouldn't be there? Is something wrong with his bones? Can you repair it? Damn you, talk to me!"

"There is an inherited disease, but not one your child should have." She noted Eryn's panicked look. "Do not worry - I can deal with it in a matter of minutes. There are several variations of this disease, and the one your child has is the weakest form we observe. Even if left untreated, he would have hardly any deleterious effects from it, and none that could not be taken care of later."

Eryn closed her eyes for a moment. "I see. So you can and will do something about it now?"

"I will, yes," Pe'tala nodded and took her cousin's hand again. Both of them closed their eyes again and Eryn watched how the tiny bone structure was strengthened with minuscule portions of magic.

"That is taken care of," Pe'tala announced a few minutes later and then rose from her chair, clearly agitated.

"Well, what is the matter, then?" Eryn enquired worriedly. "You don't look like everything is fine!"

"This is... I..." She exhaled. "Eryn, this disease... it is a recessive bone disease. It is passed on by both parents, yet only men suffer from it. It has not been found in House Aren over these last few generations. Ved'al did *not* have it, either."

Eryn frowned. "What is that supposed to mean? You know, isn't it a good thing if my father didn't have it? It might have skipped a generation. Isn't this something that happens every now and again?"

Pe'tala stared at her. "The laws of inheritance! Think!"

"I have never really managed to figure out that particular discipline, to be honest," Eryn admitted. "My father had one or two books about it, but they were not exactly digestible for beginners and I didn't understand a lot. Much too obscure. And as I have never really had the impression over the last years that I needed it for my work, I stopped trying to grasp it."

Pe'tala closed her eyes for a moment. "You really are a fool. I could easily have asked you something about it during your exams. It is well within the remit of topics you were supposed to know about."

"Alright, I neglected one area and I solemnly promise to catch up. Will you tell me what the problem with my unborn child is now or not?"

Her cousin opened her mouth to speak, but changed her mind and closed it again, shaking her head. "No, I will not. And I do not see why *I* should be the one to do it. Eryn, your son is alright now. Everything is fine with him, there is no need to worry about that." She looked pale and troubled, her eyes roaming the floor as if desperately looking for an answer that wasn't there.

Eryn swallowed. "You scare me. Tell me what is going on here!"

"I promise you, your child is healthy."

"Why do you keep emphasising that? Something is wrong here, and you are avoiding telling me about it! It obviously has nothing to do with the child, so why can't you tell me what it is?"

"Please, I need to..." Pe'tala shook her head and stormed out the door, leaving behind her alarmed and distraught cousin.

Eryn stared after her, distractedly picked up the sheet with the list and slowly paced out into the clinic's corridors. It was time to give those books on the laws on inheritance another try. They had to be in her study at home, somewhere on the bookshelves. From what Pe'tala had implied, this was where she would find whatever had unsettled her cousin so much.

* * *

Enric smiled when he walked into her study and saw her bent over a book, her head propped on both hands, a frown of uneasiness on her face.

"Good evening, my love. This is the kind of mood I normally find you in when you have to read something in connection with political strategy or history. What is it today?"

She looked up at him with an agonised expression. "None of those. It's healing."

He raised both brows in surprise. "Really? *That* gives you such trouble?"

"This particular area does, yes," she sighed, marked the page she had for the last half hour been rereading with little comprehension, then closed the book before pushing it aside.

He stepped closer and read the title upside down. "*Inheritance and the rules it follows*. Not your favourite topic, then?"

"I just don't manage to understand the principles. The book is too advanced, and I have nothing that explains the basics. I could ask Valrad to send me one, but this would take a few days."

"And you are in a hurry for what particular reason?" he enquired.

"Pe'tala found something when she examined me today." She saw his alarmed expression and quickly reassured him. "No, don't worry - everything is fine with the child. What she came across does not seem to be bad in itself, but completely threw her off track. She all but fled her own study when I asked her to tell me what the matter is. From what she said I think that understanding the rules of inheritance should actually be the key to working out what she avoided telling me. But I am stuck with this damned text."

Enric picked up the book and leafed through it. She took a sip from the water glass on her table.

"If you tell me that you can understand it after looking through it for a few seconds, I am going to hit you," she promised.

"You know," he said slowly, "this looks a lot like the principles that apply to breeding horses."

She stared at him. "What? Horses?"

"Yes. Same principles, just different characteristics. With horses, you try to breed for things like the right colour, strength, speed and similar. This book states that certain diseases follow the same principles. Some are passed on through the maternal line, some through the paternal one while a few depend on being passed on by both parents. In some cases you can pass on the disease without suffering from it yourself..." He stopped when her eyes had widened.

"You really *do* understand this?"

"The basics, yes. I used to be interested in horse breeding for a while, but gave it up when there was no more time for it. I still own a horse stud farm up north. Why?"

That was so incredibly convenient that she could hardly believe her luck. She had been sitting here for at least three hours, trying to slosh through the things she had given up learning more than ten years ago, only to discover that her very own companion possessed enough knowledge that would be the key in uncovering the secret Pe'tala was keeping from her!

"Sit," she commanded. "And explain this all to me." She took the book back and opened a page. "Tell me about the eye colour thing. They write as if everybody should be aware how it works, but I am completely lost. This was clearly not written with beginners in mind."

He smiled and took a seat. His being in a position to teach her something in connection with healing was a rare event. The first time had been when he helped her refine her shielding skills so she could use them for medical purposes and the second time was when they had discussed the mind shield. This time, however, it was about pure knowledge, about understanding principles.

He quickly read the chapter she had opened for him, then nodded.

"Alright. Do you have a sheet of paper and a pen for me?"

She took the items from her top desk drawer and pushed them towards him in silence.

"Imagine your eye colour as something that was given to you by your parents. By both. It comprises two halves, and each parent has passed on one to you. The colour they pass on to you is not necessarily always the one they have - that would depend on what had been passed on to them by your grandparents."

"Stop right there. You are starting to confuse me already."

He nodded once and started drawing. "This here is your mother. Her eyes are brown. What was Ved'al's colour?"

"Dark brown."

"So your brown eyes stem from one of your parents, though we can't say which one, as each could have passed it on to you. Let's look at my side of the family. My father's eyes are blue; my mother's are green. Mine are blue as well."

"Which means that you have inherited your father's colour," she stated.

"Not necessarily, no. According to this book, there is an order of dominance of eye colours. Brown is the strongest. So, if a child gets the brown part from one parent and the blue part from another, the child's eyes would be brown."

"Brown is stronger than blue. Alright," she murmured.

"The dominance according to strength is brown, green, blue and grey," he explained after consulting the book once more.

She frowned. "But if your mother had green eyes and your father had blue ones, then *her* colour should have been the stronger one. Why aren't your eyes green, then?"

"Because she has obviously had a blue-eyed parent herself and passed on that half to me, instead of the green one. Remember? I told you before that what our parents pass on is not necessarily what you can see in them. So I ended up with one blue part from my father's side and another blue part from my maternal grandparent's side. The result is that I have blue eyes. My sister has green eyes, so she got one green and one blue part. And green dominated, as it is stronger."

Eryn nodded slowly and looked at the drawing he had made for her. "So if we carry this on to the next generation, namely the one we currently have in the making, our son will very likely have brown eyes, because brown is stronger than whichever blue parts come from your side, isn't it?"

He nodded. "That is basically right, yes."

She leaned back. That was a bit involved, but when it was explained in a diagram, then understanding became possible.

"And inherited diseases follow the same rules," she mused.

"It is a bit more complicated than that, I am afraid," Enric contradicted her while skimming over another page in the book. "The basic rules are the same, but there are additional ones Some diseases depend on the maternal or paternal parent to be passed on, others can be passed on by either parent, but only show themselves when the child is a boy. Then there are some that require being passed on by both parents at the same time, otherwise they do not come into expression." He looked up from the book again. "What exactly did Pe'tala find?"

"I don't know. It had something to do with bones." She jumped up. "Wait! She gave me a list of things she wanted to check on." She dug in her pockets and pulled out a crumpled looking piece of paper. "Here. It should be the one fairly much in the middle here. The others all relate to other body parts."

Enric opened the last few pages of the book to check for a reference list and then leafed back to the page that dealt with the disease he was looking for. He quickly read the chapter, then frowned.

"Could she heal it away?" he then asked.

"Yes, she assured me that everything is fine. And it would have been the weakest variation there is, anyway. She said it was also easily treatable after he was born. But then, why wait?"

He looked down at the page again, thoughtful. "I don't understand the problem, though. According to this, the disease can be passed on by both sides and only expresses with male offspring. So either of your parents could have passed it on."

Eryn remembered her cousin's words. "She said something about House Aren not having passed it on for several generations, which means it must be on Ved'al's side. Although he didn't have it himself, he must simply have passed it on."

Enric's head snapped up and he stared at her. "What? Are you sure? He *didn't* have it?"

"Yes, that's what Pe'tala said. Why?"

She saw him regard her carefully and bite his lower lip. Then he got up.

"I will be back. There is something I need to check," he said slowly.

She jumped up as well and glared at him. "You stay where you are! If you also run away now without telling me what is wrong, I will hit you! And as I am pregnant, you can't hit me back or knock me out!"

He looked pained, but sat down again.

"Out with it!"

"I am not entirely sure, it is just... well, I could be wrong. Let me ask you something first: How does Pe'tala know that Ved'al didn't have this bone disease? She was what - two years old when he left the country?"

"She told me that House Vel'kim keeps exacting records to keep track of the damage which politically-motivated inbreeding between the Houses causes. So every Vel'kim child is checked for all the disorders you see on that list, and the results are always documented."

He nodded gravely. "I see."

"Enric!" she groaned. "Please?"

"Eryn," he said slowly and pushed the book towards her with the page on the disease still open. "It says here that male offspring cannot pass it on without suffering from it themselves. Malriel has not passed this on to you as it does not run in House Aren. And Ved'al..."

She swallowed hard. A cold shiver ran down her spine and she felt the hairs on her arms prickling.

"Which means Ved'al can't have passed in on to me, either." She looked up at him, her eyes wide. "This is impossible. Either this book is wrong, or..."

Enric rose and took her hand to pull her up as well. "Let's not jump to premature conclusions. Come. We should have a little talk with Pe'tala."

* * *

Pe'tala opened the door and glowered when she saw who had come to talk to her.

"Go away! I am not going to tell you anything about it now. And bringing your big, strong companion along will not change my mind! I am not afraid of him."

Enric raised his brow at her.

"Well, not much. And only if you are really angry," she amended quickly.

Eryn just flashed her a warning look and pushed past her into the parlour, where Rolan quickly got up from a settee. On the small table in front of him she saw a game she recognised. It was one she had played with her cousin Vran'el several months before. He had given up playing with her when she had tried to explain to him that the rule about needing three magicians to sink one ship didn't make any sense, as she could certainly accomplish that feat entirely alone.

After Enric had entered as well and closed the door behind him, she said, showing more calm than she felt, "I know what you didn't want to tell me. My companion used to breed horses and gained very helpful knowledge of how the rules of inheritance work through it. Imagine that!"

Pe'tala threw a desperate glance in his direction. "Really? Bloody scholarly types! Why are you not the kind of warrior who uses a book to *slap* others with instead of reading the thing?"

"Is it true?" Eryn barked.

"Is what true?" Pe'tala asked evasively, clearly hoping that whatever conclusion her cousin had reached was not the one she herself had arrived at several hours ago.

"I checked the symptoms of that bone disease in one of my books. Enric shows none of them, so he cannot have passed it on. As the disease currently doesn't seem to run in the Aren family, my paternal side must be the source. So Ved'al of House Vel'kim cannot have been my father, or he would have inherited this disease himself."

Pe'tala closed her eyes for a moment, then nodded. "I am sorry. This is what the evidence suggests."

Rolan stared at both of them, shaking his head, but decided against speaking. This was not a discussion he wanted to be involved in.

Eryn gulped hard and shivered. "So that woman managed something I wouldn't have believed was possible. She has now even taken my father from me." She covered her face with both hands. "She betrayed him! She is a hideous mother now and was obviously a terrible companion back then. The only thing she has been good at is making money and gripping tightly on to her power. I can't tell you how much I detest her!"

She looked up when she felt a warm hand on her shoulder. To her surprise, it was not Enric's but Pe'tala's.

"I wish I had not told you about this. I wish Enric was not so damned fast at conclusions. I wish...," she sighed. "I wish your mother had not betrayed your fa... betrayed *Ved'al*. And I wish I could do *something*. This is not a good moment for you to learn about this."

Eryn shook her head and wiped away a tear. "When was there ever a good moment for learning of something like that? Learning that the family I finally found is actually not even mine? I have to face Valrad and tell him that he has not adopted his own niece, but Malriel's bastard child from a sordid affair! But I suppose for you that is something you can live with. For you, being my cousin was never much to be joyful about!" The thought of Vran'el not being her cousin, her not even being entitled to all the kindness that House Vel'kim had shown her in the past made her drop to her knees, sobbing softly.

Pe'tala quickly sat down on the floor in front of her, grabbing her shoulders and shaking her slightly.

"Stop this!" she hissed. "Stop talking such idiotic nonsense! You were raised by one Vel'kim and adopted by another. That makes you Vel'kim enough in my book. Now get a grip on yourself and stop worrying your companion."

Eryn swallowed and looked at Pe'tala through teary eyes. "I thought you would be glad to get rid of me!"

"I do not see how this helps me get rid of you," Pe'tala sighed. "Or do you expect my father to kick you out of the House for being fathered by somebody other than Ved'al?"

Eryn blinked and the younger woman grimaced in disgust. "Really? That is what you thought? I am trying to comfort you here, but you are making it very hard for me to show you any sympathy right now! You have another man's blood coursing through your veins. So what? Nothing will change for you. You will continue to be Eryn, or rather *Maltheá* of House Vel'kim in Takhan. The only person who might have had a good reason to be upset about this is Ved'al, and he is gone. So stop pitying yourself for no reason at all and stop projecting all those destructive feelings onto my nephew. This is not good for him, you know."

Her nephew, Eryn thought and fought against new tears, this time affectionate ones. Pe'tala - who had rejected her from the minute they had met - was suddenly proving to be loyal beyond expectation; beyond reason, even. She regarded this child as a member of her family, though instead she should have been relieved at not having to treat Eryn as her cousin any more.

Enric slowly let his tense breathing relax when he saw Eryn fling both arms around Pe'tala's neck and pull her close in a clumsy hug.

"Splendid," Pe'tala murmured, "A teary embrace. This might ruin my shirt, you know. It was expensive." But her arms, too, encircled Eryn and held on to her.

When they released each other again after about a minute, Eryn used her sleeve to wipe her eyes.

"Funny, you know. It took nothing more than learning that I am not really your cousin for you to finally start seeing me as one. I think you just enjoy being difficult."

The younger woman shrugged. "As you said, there might still be a drop or two of Aren blood in me from a few generations ago. I will from now on blame that for each single one of my less amiable character traits."

"Fair enough," Eryn nodded slowly and her eyes narrowed when she thought of Malriel. "I will never again blame you for any cutting remark about House Aren. Every single one is deserved. Richly so."

Pe'tala smiled and nodded her chin at Enric. "I would not go quite that far. House Aren does not only consist of Malriel, after all. There are other, less sinister members in that House, remember."

"I take offence at hearing that you had to be reminded of that," Enric smirked.

Rolan finally seemed to have found a voice again. "Sorry, but I am a little confused here. Did I understand this correctly? You aren't cousins any longer?"

Pe'tala nodded. "You did." Her gaze returned to Eryn. "No more cousins. But still sisters, it seems." She screwed her face in disbelief as tears welled up in Eryn's eyes once more. "Enric, get her out of here. I hope this tendency to weeping is a side effect of her pregnancy and not a sign that she is going soft in the head."

"Just dust in my eye," Eryn sobbed.

"Sure it is. Then go home and rinse it out. Really. I mean it; I am not good with tears."

Enric saw a hint of moisture in Pe'tala's own eyes and pulled her close to press a firm kiss on her forehead.

"Then I will free you of our disturbing presence, Tala." He nodded to Rolan and put an arm around Eryn's shoulders to guide her outside.

He stopped before closing the door behind them. "I will write to Valrad when we are back home."

Pe'tala shook her head. "Do not bother. I have let him know already. We will hear from him soon."

He nodded gratefully. That was not a task he had been looking forward to.

* * *

"Hey, what are you doing here?" Eryn called out in surprise when she went into the small kitchen at the clinic to refill her mug and saw Enric leaning against a wall, deep in conversation with Lord Poron.

He smiled and leaned towards her to kiss her cheek. "A little something from Takhan was delivered today. I thought you might want to look at it right away."

She swallowed hard when she beheld the small tube the messenger birds carried. It had been two days since Pe'tala sent the message relating recent developments to Valrad. Exactly the time one bird needed to fly to Takhan and for another to return.

"I have a short break now. Let's go up into my study, shall we?"

Enric pushed himself away from the wall and nodded to Lord Poron before following her up the stairs.

She closed the door behind him. "Have you read it?"

"No." He handed her the small container. "*You* are the one it is about."

She unscrewed the tiny metal cap clumsily and shook the paper slip from the tube. It landed on her desk. Enric nodded encouragingly when she just stared at it for several moments.

"Come on, my love. It is not going to bite you."

"That's what you might think," she murmured and finally picked it up to unroll it with shaky fingers. She recognised her uncle's handwriting immediately and started reading. Enric stepped behind her and looked over her shoulder.

Dear Eryn, Pe'tala has written to me about what she found when she examined you. I am sure that this came as an unpleasant revelation to you. I know this is a lot to ask of you, but please do not worry. We will talk about all of this when you come to Takhan in a few weeks' time. Everything will turn out for the best. I promise you that. Do take good care of our youngest Vel'kim until then. I love you. Valrad.

She let out the breath she had been holding while reading the message.

"You know," Enric smiled and leaned his chin against her shoulder from behind, "I think Pe'tala was right. It does not look exactly as if they are about to expel you from House Vel'kim."

"No, I suppose it doesn't. I expect my offering to revoke the adoption would not be received very well by them."

He shook his head. "Don't. It would seem ungrateful."

Eryn nodded and unrolled the paper slip to read over the warm and affectionate lines once again.

"You know, this is an immense relief. I am glad he doesn't bear me any grudge due to this. Though I wonder how this might affect the alliance between the Houses. Malriel basically already broke the companionship agreement by being unfaithful to my father and with that to House Vel'kim."

"Why would he be angry at *you* of all people?" Enric frowned. "You were hardly the one to cause Malriel's infidelity, rather the result of it."

"Yes, but neither was I to blame for Ram'an's stepping back from the agreement with Pe'tala, though she took it out on me."

Enric sighed. "Anyway, your uncle is not the kind for harsh, unfair judgements. And Malriel's actions so many years ago hardly caused him as much hurt as Ram'an hurting Pe'tala by pursuing you." He smiled bleakly. "And no matter who your father might turn out to be, Valrad still has a good connection to House Aren, thanks to our companionship. As well as that, we are about to give him an heir for his House. So it's not as if he is at a disadvantage, politically speaking."

Eryn was about to pull a face at that remark, but paused for a moment's thought. Political considerations were not normally her first choice when it came to assessing a situation, but in this case the fact that House Vel'kim truly did not suffer any unpleasant consequences, would even profit from adopting her, did make her feel better.

"How great are the chances that this is not going to become common knowledge anytime soon?" she asked.

"For now only the four of us know. And Rolan. Probably Vran'el as well. That makes six. With Malriel I can't tell, but if she is aware of it, she has not been eager to make it public so far, so I don't see much danger on that front."

She snorted. "Really? How could she *not* be aware of it?"

"I would think that having sex with two men within a short time span would make it hard to say which of the acts resulted in her becoming pregnant," Enric reasoned.

"Are you defending her?" Eryn narrowed her eyes at him.

"Me?" He looked at her with true astonishment. "Are you really asking me that while you are carrying my child beneath your heart? I would *not* take well to learning that I was not the father. Not at all. One could say that this might cause me to forego any restraint on my violent urges to inflict real harm on whoever got that close to you."

"Which would not be at all justified, as long as I permitted somebody to get that close to me," she pointed out. "As Malriel did."

"True enough. Though I don't think that even after doing a thing like this to me I could ever raise a hand against you."

"That is kind of charming. In a twisted, disturbing way."

"Yes, but when have we ever been the traditional kind of couple?" he shrugged. "What is the plan when we get to Takhan? Will you confront Malriel? Ask her who she had that fling with back then?"

She sighed. "I don't know. I really don't. Do I even *want* to know? But then I will probably end up wondering whether each man I meet above a certain age is the one who fathered me. I am not sure which is worse - knowing or not knowing."

"Then let's see what is to come. Maybe Malriel isn't even willing or able to share that knowledge. Or she might do so despite your not wanting to hear it. Or Valrad might have good advice for you."

"Alright then - no planning," she nodded. "I should get back to work now. I'll see you in the evening." She stood on her tiptoes to kiss his cheek. He swiftly turned his head so that they kissed on the lips instead.

"Don't work too long. You don't seem as tired today, so I would like to enjoy your company for a bit."

"Today was the first morning I didn't have to get up to muck out the horse stables, so it's no wonder I look fitter. If you cook something nice for me today, I might make it worth your while," she winked and left, leaving him standing in her study with a broad grin.

CHAPTER 32

Ambassador Erbál

Erbál stepped aside to let Eryn enter his quarters. She inhaled the aroma of freshly prepared food appreciatively.

"Good. I am starving," she said.

"And a good day to you, too, Eryn," he smiled.

"I'm sorry, Erbál", she apologised. "Hello and thank you very much for your invitation to have lunch with you. I am afraid that I will be completely useless until you have fed me, though. My attention does focus on eating a lot these days."

"Understandable. You have two to feed, after all," he said gallantly.

"That's what pregnant women like to hear, but unfortunately it is not really a valid excuse for bingeing on everything that looks or smells good. Nourishing a developing child when it is such a small thing hardly requires eating twice as much," she said, rather technically.

"Eryn," Erbál shook his head. "You need to indulge yourself a little. If there is one time in a woman's life where she can let herself go without being talked about behind her back, it is during pregnancy."

"Oh, I am not exactly restraining myself. My consumption of sweet bread buns has gone through the roof, I think. I am already nervous about going to Takhan in a few weeks as there won't be any over there. Yet from a healing point of view stuffing myself is not healthy, especially as I am no longer being forced to exercise. I have been exempted from fighting for now."

"I think the little matter with sweet pastries should be solved easily in Takhan," he mused. "We do have quite a variation at home. Maybe a little sweeter than what you have been used to, but as you seem to be craving sugar at the moment, this will probably not be much of a problem."

"No, it won't", she grimaced. "I will simply turn into something vast and spherical."

He laughed and took her arm to escort her to the table and the lunch tablet which was laid upon it. "Do not worry, Eryn, they will make you engage in combat training again after your child is born, so you will get back in shape in no time. I am sure of that."

"If that was some attempt at comforting me, let me tell you that you failed miserably. This does not cheer me up at all," she said sourly and took a seat. She noticed with relief that he had ordered something without meat for her. She had not exactly kept her dietary habits a secret, but every now and again it happened that a host simply forgot about them, and she had to either wait for something else to be sent up from the kitchen or make do with a piece of fruit from a bowl that served for decorative purposes.

When Erbál had taken his seat as well, they both started eating, Eryn forcing herself to eat slowly and with good manners, chewing the food thoroughly instead of just gulping it down to fill her empty stomach.

When she had finished, she put aside her cutlery and leaned back.

"Very well, talk to me. You didn't ask me to have lunch with you because you had been missing me. What news do you have?"

Erbál pushed aside his empty tray and smiled. "You make me seem unsociable, my dear Eryn."

She raised both eyebrows. "So there is nothing new you want to share with me?"

"That is not what I said. As it happens, I do have something I wish to tell you. And there is another matter where I wish to satisfy my curiosity. But let me start with my news." He got up and fetched two glasses and a bottle of red juice. When he had poured them each a glass, he handed her one. He cleared his throat, obviously about to deliver significant news. "Eryn, you see before you the new ambassador to Anyueel."

She stared at him for a moment, then a slow smile spread across her face. "Really? Congratulations! That was fast!"

"It was indeed. The King informed me only today in the morning. He also told me that you are the one I have to thank for it all. Let me do this straightaway: Thank you so very much. I am greatly indebted to you."

Eryn waved him away. "Don't. It was part of our wager, wasn't it? Pe'tala and Rolan did end up together, after all."

"But you talked to the King before you knew about that. Which means that you would have helped me either way."

She shrugged. "Talking to the King did not exactly require great effort on my side."

"That maybe not, but asking a favour of him when there was such tension between you was without doubt not overly pleasant, either."

She raised her glass. "I drink to the new ambassador! May you do your country proud and put that training of yours to good use here."

Erbál clinked his glass with hers and took a sip of the sweet juice.

"What about Sanaf?" Eryn then enquired. "Will he stay on here as your assistant or return to Takhan under a cloud?"

"His staying here would not be too pleasant for either of us. The official reason for his return is that he has been recalled to take care of important matters at his House."

She snorted. "A lot less embarrassing than having to tell people that he kept making enemies due to being an insensitive oaf who exposed too many important people."

"True. Though most people who know him at least a little will be able to guess the true reason easily enough."

"A pity that he has been exchanged now that I am about to leave here. It means I will have to try and avoid him in Takhan. How inconvenient," she sighed. "I assume he will not be too eager to meet me, though. I expect he will learn sooner or later on whose prompt his untimely dismissal was initiated by."

"Yes, that is a reasonable assumption," Erbál nodded. "But then Takhan is a sizeable place and I do not think that the two of you will move within the same circles very much. You are quite a bit younger than he, so you will probably not encounter him when you go out in the evenings. And he is not of such importance as to be invited to the same dinners and social gatherings as you."

That was a relief, she had to admit.

"But tell me now why you were made to clean out the stables. What did you do to upset Lord Tyront this time? Did the famous Aren temper get the better of you again?" he asked.

She shook her head. "No, this time I think I was actually the innocent party."

He smirked. "An assessment that does not say a lot, coming from you."

"He wanted me to discipline Pe'tala for being... a *touch* disrespectful when she told the Magic Council that letting me continue my combat training was not a sensible idea."

Erbál pursed his lips. "Knowing Pe'tala quite well I assume that *a touch* is a gross understatement. He wanted *you* to punish her in some way?"

Nodding, she put her empty glass back on the table. "Yes. He told me that he had no authority over her since she is not a member of the Order. The only one she is responsible to is the Head of Healing, which is strictly speaking Lord Poron's position, but he asked to be spared taking it on as long as I remain here."

"You refused to punish her, I assume?"

"Of course I refused! The audacity of trying to make *me* discipline her for helping me out! I mean, she was not exactly polite about it, but then a few of the Council members didn't really deserve much better, if you ask me."

"He then gave you the punishment for refusing his request or - more likely - his order?"

"Exactly. Another three days of shovelling horse manure. The stable hands started carving the dates when I have to work at the stables into the wooden beams! I heard them discussing how long it would likely be before they saw me there again."

He narrowed his eyes for a few moments, then looked at her thoughtfully. "This does not feel right."

"It shouldn't! It's unfair!"

"No, this is not what I mean. It is not exactly Lord Tyront's style. Was somebody else present when he talked to you about this?"

"Yes, Enric was there."

His brow shot up. "Was he indeed? How very interesting."

She frowned. "Why? They meet on most days, even if there is a certain tension between them still. Has been since that day in the arena."

"How has Pe'tala behaved towards you since you were made to clean out the stables?"

Eryn thought for a moment. "Rather civil. Why?"

"Eryn, you have been played," he informed her mildly.

"How?" she exclaimed, clearly disgruntled. "And why this time?"

"Lord Tyront was well aware that you would refuse his order. I would bet that he had your companion present so he could inform Pe'tala of the sacrifice you made in order to spare her. He did this simply to improve the relationship between the two of you."

She stared at him, then slowly shook her head. "But why would it be of any consequence to him how well I get along with my cousin?"

"Because Lord Enric cares about it. Accomplishing the two of you starting to befriend each other is something your companion will surely appreciate as well as making him better disposed towards Lord Tyront."

"But Enric would surely have been aware of that. Why did he play along and inform Pe'tala? That doesn't make sense."

"Of course it makes sense. Lord Enric is aware of why his superior did it. It was a peace offering, a sign that Lord Tyront wishes things to return to how they were. By contributing to making it work, Lord Enric accepted it."

She sighed and looked grim. "So I was used once again. How perfect. Well, at least the only harm done was my having to get up much too early on three mornings."

"It was but a little scheme, one that might have cost you a few hours of sleep, but which improved things between you and Pe'tala."

"I know. Yet being played still leaves a nasty taste in my mouth." She got to her feet. "I need to get back to the clinic now. Thank you for the meal. When will your new position be announced officially?"

"At the next official occasion. That should give Sanaf enough time to regain his composure and manage to smile while still boiling inside," he told her.

"Then I would think you want me to keep it to myself until then?"

"You may tell Lord Enric, if you wish. I assume he will have earned about it anyway by the time you return home in the evening. Lord Tyront tends to be rather well-informed, from what I have seen."

"True enough," she confirmed. She wondered if informing Erbál about her recent revelation concerning Ved'al would be a smart idea. He might pass on that fragment of knowledge to Malriel, though. But then again he might have an idea how to deal with this situation properly when Eryn went to Takhan. Would he tell her something if it meant creating a disadvantage for Malriel, his former lover?

"You look like you are pondering something," he said into her thoughts.

"I am," she said honestly. "But I am not yet sure if telling you about it would be a wise move."

"That wounds me deeply," he sighed.

She rolled her eyes. "No, it does not. You are just annoyed that there is some piece of information you don't know yet."

He chuckled. "Quite true. I will wait patiently for you to come to your senses and share what bothers you with me. You really should, you know."

She couldn't help but smile. "We will see about that. I couldn't take up an ambassador's time with minor things."

"Oh, but you should," he nodded solemnly. "You are one of a few people important enough around here who is entitled to waste however much of my precious time you see fit to."

"I would have expected some flattery along the lines of *whatever concern of mine leads me to you, will never be a waste of your time*."

Erbál shrugged. "Ah, but how tedious would it be for you always hearing what you expect?"

"At times I would appreciate a little predictability," she sighed.

"No, explorers always seek the unknown. Surprising you is my best shot at keeping you interested in me," he grinned. "And now I will let you return to those patients of yours and no longer keep you to myself when you could be healing their ailments. I trust I will see you again soon, owing to whatever is occupying your mind right now."

She thought over the exchange once she had stepped out into the corridor. He was confident, she had to give him that. She just wondered if that would turn out to be justified on this occasion.

* * *

"You look preoccupied," Vern commented when he had put aside his pen after completing his drawing of her unborn child.

Eryn looked up at him and smiled. "Well, that is surely warranted, considering that I am still getting used to having another human being growing inside me. And I am supposed to be preparing for an extended stay in a foreign country." And there was the fact that she had only recently learned that the man who had raised her was not the one to father her. But that was not something she wanted to share with him presently. She wondered whether keeping it a secret would be possible. One could only hope. Malriel would not want to let the world know. As for Valrad, it would definitely not look too good for his House should it become public knowledge that his brother was not the father of his companion's child. He would effectively have abducted another man's daughter, after all.

"How are your own preparations coming along?" she asked, determined not to spend any more time thinking about Ved'al for now. "And how about that cat of yours? I doubt if the servants will be too keen to take care of it for such a long time."

"Ram'an will come to Takhan, of course!" Vern huffed. "If the two of you can take a fully-grown mountain cat along, I can hardly be refused permission to bring my own pet. He is only about one tenth of Urban's size, after all!"

Yes, he had a point there, she had to admit. Though having that vicious beast live with them was not a cheerful prospect.

"That might be a bit dangerous, you know," she tried. "We don't really know how Urban will react to another feline that is so much smaller than herself. She might consider your cat as a snack."

"Not if you keep her fed properly," Vern retorted with a raised eyebrow.

"Do we know how Ram'an reacts to infants? I mean, there are about to be two of them soon," she pointed out.

"Really?" He indicated his cat's size with his hands, then Urban's. "Are we truly discussing which one of our animals is the more dangerous when it comes to babies? I do have the impression that you are trying to make me leave Ram'an behind. Give it up. I won't! You bring your cat, I'll bring mine. If yours looks funnily at mine, she will bear the consequences."

Eryn lifted her hands in a placatory manner. "Alright, alright - you bring that little monster with you. Though I wonder how people there will react to your choice of name for that beast."

He shrugged. "It's a tribute. I'll explain that to whoever wants to know."

Maybe that was the problem, she considered. A compliment to the man who was currently treating her in such a cold manner was not something that sat too well with her. The cat was hardly to blame for it, though.

Vern sent her an offended look. "And I resent how you refer to him. *Monster* and *beast* are hardly very flattering terms."

"He keeps hissing at me," she pointed out.

"You stunned him with magic and brought him here as a test object for me to practise my healing skills on! How would you react to anything like that?"

"Since this improved his health status considerably, I do not see why treating me the way he does is justified," she grumbled.

"Do you want me to talk about this to him?" the boy said, sneering.

"To the cat? Very funny."

"How are things going with you and Pe'tala? I have the impression that there is less bickering, but she also keeps out of your way."

She nodded. "Yes, it seems we have found a halfway civilised way of coexistence."

"Did something happen between the two of you?" Vern enquired in a suspicious voice.

Apart from the fact that they had discovered that they were not really cousins, but that she was an unknown man's bastard? And Tyront's little game that made Pe'tala feel guilty about Eryn's having to clean out the stables on account of her misdeeds?

"No, not that I recall," she replied casually. "Maybe she became tired of opposing me, now that she is about to get rid of me. By the way, my uncle told me that he has asked Pe'tala to accompany us to Takhan. He writes that he will feel better if there is another fully trained healer with us when there are two expectant women on the trip. He asked me to tell you that he didn't mean to disparage your abilities. I also suspect that he wants to see her again, now that she decided to prolong her stay here in Anyueel. Maybe make her change her mind about it."

"That's alright, I don't mind. I dare say if something goes wrong, I will be grateful enough to have her with us," Vern offered generously. "How long will she stay in Takhan? She is supposed to be keeping the clinic here running, after all."

"About one week. She will accompany us to Takhan, spend a few days with her family and then return here. I am sure the clinic will not sink into total disorder over the two weeks she is gone."

"Will Rolan be coming as well? I suppose she will want to show him off at home after being rejected by Ram'an like that?" he asked.

"No, not as far as I know. I don't think they are far enough advanced in their relationship, or whatever it is they have, to introduce each other to their respective parents," she remarked.

"I am looking forward to meeting your uncle, the healer," he grinned. "Or father, officially speaking. I wonder if he would help me to be permitted work as a healer trainee or something."

Eryn smiled. "Don't worry about that. From what he has written, there will be no lack of opportunity for you to improve whatever skills you wish to work on. Thanks to that book you gave Ram'an you are a local celebrity there already." She watched him sit up a little straighter and grin broadly, and added, "Just don't get conceited. Or I won't bring you back home again."

He laughed. "If I am famous there, why would I even want to return home?"

"Fair point, my lad. Though you might expect to find explaining this to your father a challenge. You have another three years until you come of age, meaning you are not the one to decide this on your own. But let's not get ahead of ourselves here. For all you know you may find Takhan terrible and may be eager to return home sooner than planned."

"Possible," he admitted, "but not very likely. I survived camping out in the woods, I will surely be able to adapt to a civilised city easily enough."

"That was an expedition of 10 days!" she exclaimed. "You can hardly compare this to going to a foreign country where you are immediately discernible as a stranger and don't know the rules and customs."

"I will have my family along with me," he pointed out. "And you. And I already know one local - Ram'an. I don't think adapting to it all will be such a big thing."

She nodded reluctantly. It was good that his attitude was optimistic, though if his expectations were too high, they would be dashed more easily. A certain degree of scepticism and caution was surely no mistake when venturing into the unknown like this. But just like before the expedition, he was not open to any impulses of that kind. Well, he was a growing lad, he had a right to choose his own experiences.

She looked down at the paper that showed a detailed drawing of the current stage of development of her foetus.

"I assume you are done for today? The picture looks finished."

"It is, yes. Do you need to leave?"

"I should, yes. Enric has invited Pe'tala and Rolan for dinner today and has taken Urban on a hunting trip. He wants me to help with cooking."

"He is trying to make you bond. How charming," Vern sneered.

"Yes, isn't it just," she snorted. "Poor Rolan is the one who is suffering. Pe'tala has started to like Enric and actually tolerates me, but Rolan is at a loss about how to behave properly. Enric ranks so far above him that under normal circumstances they would not be moving within the same circles. And now he is forced to interact with him in a private capacity and is so afraid of transgressing any rule of politeness that he doesn't even dare talk to him all evening."

The boy smiled. "Sounds cosy."

"It really does." She got to her feet and took her cloak from the hook next to the door. "Though you might want to get used to facing that scenario yourself. You are to spend many, many evenings with Enric once we are in Takhan. So if you are still feeling awkward in his presence, you will have to start working on overcoming that before long."

Vern gave an uncomfortable gulp. It seemed he had not yet thought through that particular aspect of their stay.

When she opened the door, she stared right into the startled face of a Palace messenger who had just lifted his fist to knock at the door. She looked down at the envelopes he held in his other hand. The uppermost one showed the Royal seal.

"Vern? It seems there is some important mail."

"Lady Eryn." The messenger bowed hurriedly before her, then quickly flipped through his messages to pluck out one that was addressed to her and Enric and held it out to her.

She grimaced and sighed. "Wait, don't tell me: This is an invitation to a ball?"

The messenger nodded. "Yes, my Lady."

She heard Vern cackling behind her, but decided to ignore him. Maybe this was another chance to see if her pregnancy would serve as a reason to be exempted from that unwished duty as well.

* * *

Enric leaned over her shoulder as she broke the Royal seal and unfolded the message. He started laughing when he saw the single word that was written in the centre of the paper in neat capital letters: NO.

Eryn turned to him and gave him a piercing look. "Oh, just shut up!"

"Come on, my love, what did you really expect? Being pregnant does not work as an excuse to get out of everything you are not fond of. You may be the first *magician* to have a child here after a long interval, but not the first *woman*. Other expectant mothers before you have attended balls without suffering any bad effects at all."

She crumpled the message and threw it against the wall. It bounced back and hit her right on the forehead.

"Damn it all!" she exclaimed and rubbed the spot where the paper ball had made contact with her skin. She watched Enric's fight to keep a straight face and her expression darkened even further.

She moved to give him a good shove, but he caught her wrists and pulled her into his arms.

"No fighting, dearest," he chuckled, "otherwise we might just as well resume your training sessions."

"I don't want to go to that ball!" she moaned. "Why does he think that this is an appropriate way to bid us farewell? Why not just wish us all the best and warn us to be careful? Why do we have to go through another tedious evening, talking to and dancing with tiresome people?"

"There are not just tiresome people. Orrin, Junar and Vern will be there. As will Lord Poror, Aurna, Tyront and Vyril. Plus Pe'tala and Rolan."

"And Lord Seagon, Lord Woldarn and Inad," she added. "And the King."

"Yes," he said dryly, 'there is no avoiding the King, I dare say. Especially as he is the one hosting the ball. Though I wouldn't consider him tedious."

"Well, not tedious," she admitted, "but he is a trial. Disconcerting. Disquieting. Malign."

"Yet meeting him at a ball is surely preferable to any other location. It is public and he can't focus all his attention on you. He is supposed to dance and converse with a lot of other important people there, when all is said and done," Enric pointed out.

"True," she sighed. "But I have to talk to these allegedly important people, too, so not having him around doesn't mean that I can relax."

"I can always break another nose, if that makes you happy," he proposed.

That made her chuckle. "It would certainly provide for entertainment. And people would be a lot more eager to see us leave the city, I'd imagine."

"Probably would, yes. So, as your attempt at squirming free of attending the ball has failed, can I rely on your seeing Junar for a ball gown?"

"You can, yes."

"Because Junar will turn up here anyway, no matter whether you send for her or not?"

She flashed him an irritated look. "You should know, shouldn't you? You keep paying her to make sure I have whatever clothes you two consider sufficient even without my bothering to order them."

"I wouldn't if you took care of that yourself. This time I would ask you to show her a bit more consideration, though. She is not so able to withstand stress at the moment, so don't put up a fight this time," he warned her.

"Would I ever?" she murmured.

"Yes, you would. And I have to warn you, from what I have heard she tends to weep easily these days."

Eryn grimaced. "I know already. When I visited her the other day, she started snivelling because she had run out of fruit juice. Orrin and Vern were both running off to fetch her some, and only then did she calm down again." She shook her head. "Plain worrying." Then she grinned. "It's funny to see them like this, though. Orrin has never lived with a pregnant woman before, so he is completely overwhelmed whenever she is in a bad mood. Vern comes running every time she is upset to check if everything is alright with her. Hilarious domestic theatre. And of course they both scold me every time I say something harsh and implore me not to make her cry. She has never started crying with me, probably because it doesn't work on me."

"Or her annoyance exceeds her desperation when she is with you," he suggested.

"What a lovely thing to say," she sighed.

He shrugged. "I aim to please. Speaking of pleasing people, I received the report on your latest test. Not exactly impressive, but you scraped through. Tyront considered making you take it all again, but I managed to convince him that in light of your current state this is an acceptable result."

She exhaled slowly. "Thank you. I swear to you, if I have to read another book on battle strategy, I will adopt Junar's method and cry until somebody takes pity on me."

"If you keep passing your exams, that will not be needed," he assured her hurriedly.

"Nervous?" she grinned.

"Slightly, yes. The thought of you in tears is a frightening one. There are only two more exams left, then you are done with them. Forever."

"Well, with the ones the Order defines as necessary, not with all exams *per se*. There is still one left in Takhan," she corrected.

"But that's one you are taking voluntarily, so it doesn't really count."

"I would say it counts even more. Your exams here just serve to entitle me to a take a seat in that bloody Council of yours while the one with Sarol makes real sense."

"Oh dear," he rolled his eyes. "That discussion again."

"No discussion," she shrugged. "Just sharing a sentiment. By the way, you are aware that I will be the highest-ranking Order magician in Takhan, aren't you? That means *I* can give orders to Orrin and Vern while you can't."

"A very reassuring prospect." He narrowed his eyes. "I can rely on your common sense not to take advantage of that, can't I? Don't forget that this will only be temporary. As soon as we are back here, your and my status will be back to normal. Which also means that I will be in a position to...," He paused for a moment as if to think for suitable words, "take whatever measures I determine as appropriate."

She pursed her lips. "You are not by any chance telling me that you intend to use your position to take revenge should you not like the orders I give, are you? That would be unprofessional."

He smiled. "Whatever you say, my love."

"Why do I have the feeling that the two of us being in the Council is going to be a standoff sometimes?"

"Because you are a pessimist by nature?" he suggested.

"Oh, of course. That must be it," she sighed and stepped out of his embrace. "Now you'll need to excuse me. I have to prepare myself for a further two exams."

He nodded appreciatively. "That you should. Did you have a look at the date of the ball? It coincides with the day of your last exam. Isn't this great? A chance to celebrate properly afterwards."

"I see that our notions of what *celebrating* means diverge quite a lot," she muttered and turned to walk into her study.

* * *

Eryn turned to one side and examined herself critically in the full-length mirror in her bedroom.

"You know, I don't really look pregnant, do I? This is the end of the third month, and I don't see anything. Nothing. Not the smallest hint that something is supposed to be growing inside me."

Junar smiled and stroked her own very round belly. "You wait for it. It's just a matter of weeks now. While you may not yet see anything, I definitely had to add a little to your girth or that dress would have been rather uncomfortable tonight. And from what Vern told me you are tiring more easily at the clinic. That is a side effect of being pregnant. You should go easier on yourself now."

"Gossips," she sighed. "And I know about how to do all that, thank you; I am a healer. The human body starts to get used to the strain of providing for two which results in less energy for taking care of everyday tasks."

"Good girl, nicely quoted from one of your smart books. Now let me have a look at that cleavage." The seamstress pursed her lips. "Your breasts also seem to have swollen just a little. But this doesn't matter. It just makes your neckline more... interesting."

"The way you tailor my dresses, *more interesting* verges on indecent exposure," Eryn scowled.

"You may as well give people a pleasant image to remember you by," Junar shrugged.

"I don't see *your* breasts about to jump out," the magician commented.

"That is because I am the one making the dresses. It allows me to cater to my personal whims. And unfortunately for you, making you comfortable is not one of them," she smiled innocently.

"Don't make me hire somebody else to make my clothes."

"You wouldn't. Enric wouldn't let you. And who else would put up with you in the long run, anyway? Now let's get going, shall we?" She shook her head when Eryn tried to grab a wrap, and pulled her along. "No, none of that. The winter is over, you don't need such a thing."

Orrin and Enric stood, already dressed, next to the drinks cabinet. The latter was about to open a bottle and raised his brow when the two women descended.

"That was unusually quick," he commented and put the bottle back in its place. "So eager to get to the Palace?"

"Of course I am," Eryn said in a high chirp while batting her lashes. "There is simply no other way to spend the evening that would give me as much pleasure!"

Orrin stepped forward. "Congratulations on passing that last exam today. Enric just told me about it. So you are finally a fully-fledged member of the Order, our official third-in-command."

She rolled her eyes. "Yes, thank you for pointing that out so elaborately."

"My pleasure. I need to make sure my new, fully initiated superior is favourably disposed towards me, after all," he smiled.

"Oh, quite," she nodded solemnly, "so let me assure you that you are well on the way to accomplishing that very thing. Let me give you a small token of my appreciation."

She stepped next to him and deliberately trod on his foot. He drew in a sharp breath and manfully kept the expression of pain within.

"Well done, Orrin," she grinned. "I respect such restraint in a man. You shall become my favourite minion."

"Minion," he growled. "I will to show you what..."

"Children!" Enric interrupted them with mild disapproval. "Can we leave now? Let's put this last official evening here behind us with some dignity, shall we?"

Then he opened the doors and ushered them out to where the coach was waiting, catching Orrin's disapproving look at the term *children*.

Enric helped both women into the carriage and then got in before Orrin.

"How are you going to spend your last day here tomorrow?" Junar enquired.

"Firstly, I am going to sleep in after all this tonight," Eryn sighed. "Then I will probably take a walk through the city one last time and drop by at the clinic. In the evening the King wants to see us to say his goodbyes. And the three of you?"

"Go through our packing lists one final time, have last minute hysterics... the usual," Junar shrugged.

"You plan your hysterics? That's what I call organised," Enric commented.

"Oh, it is," Eryn nodded, "mine are too spontaneous for your taste."

"Not true," Enric contradicted, "I do appreciate the element of surprise. It's never dull with you."

"A declaration of love that makes me want to weep from the emotion," she chortled.

Her companion leaned forward, the hint of a smile on his lips, his gaze intent. "Would you like me to declare my love to you properly? Here and now?"

Eryn gulped and quickly shook her head. Surely not with an audience. "No, thank you. That will not be needed right now."

Junar sighed. "You still haven't got over your reluctance to tell him that you love him, or even of hearing it? Really now! You have been joined for more than a year, isn't it about time to come to grips with that?"

"None of your business," her friend growled and watched Junar's eyes become teary. "Stop it! I have no intention of going easy on you just because you feel you can start sobbing anytime you want now! You just keep that nose of yours out of my affairs!"

A first glistening tear ran down Junar's cheek and Orrin took both her hands in his and kissed them fervently. "Don't listen to her," he growled with a reproachful look at Eryn, "you know what she is like."

"Great, being pregnant seems to be a splendid excuse for getting away with a lot of things," Eryn muttered. "Though it seems some of us are entitled to more leniency than others. Not fair."

Enric looked up in relief when the coach stopped in front of the Palace gates and a guard opened the door for them to get out.

Junar dabbed at her eyes with a handkerchief Orrin had given her, careful not to smear her makeup.

They walked in and followed the dark carpet right to the magicians who had formed the usual line in front of the throne room doors. They moved aside to let Enric and Orrin take their companions close to the front as was in accordance with their ranks.

Vyril and Aurna turned to greet them, but when they beheld Junar, both of them hurried towards her, taking her between them and murmuring platitudes that were meant to comfort her.

Eryn rolled her eyes at each sentence such as 'Everything will be alright, dear' and 'Don't you worry yourself, darling'.

"What did you do now?" she heard Vern's unnerved voice behind her.

"That's it," she turned and hissed at him, "just assume it must be my fault, why don't you?"

"Is it?"

"Yes," Enric offered.

"Thank you so much," she said and looked up in relief when the doors to the ball room opened and the magicians and their companions hurriedly returned to their places in the line.

"I appreciate your support just now," she whispered to Enric and plastered a smile across her face when Tyront and Vyril were announced to the crowd. When they had walked in and reached the throne, they bowed to the King and moved to one side when their attendance was acknowledged.

"Lord Enric of House Aren and Lady Eryn of House Vel'kim," the words echoed through the high room and made Eryn groan.

"Really? That much detail?"

"These little details are the reason why we are about to leave the country," he murmured and began to walk towards King Folrin, who patiently watched them approach.

"Thank you, I was in no danger of forgetting that," she replied almost without moving her lips.

They bowed before the King, who nodded at them.

"How very fortunate that you have managed to attend despite the onerous circumstances you presently find yourself in, Lady Eryn," he smiled.

She forced herself to refrain from sniffing. That was the wording she had used in her message to him to try and make him excuse her for tonight.

"Of course, Your Majesty. Nothing whatever would keep me from one of your balls," she beamed. "Only today I was saying to Lord

Enric about how very vexing the prospect of not being able to attend such an event in the months to come is..."

"Try not to get carried away with your rapture," the King replied dryly and added, "Though seeing how enthusiastic you are about being here warms my heart. I will see you on the dance floor. Do not wander too far away."

Enric gently pulled her to one side of the throne next to Tyront and Vyril when Lord Poron and Aurna were announced.

"Is it too much to ask of you to stop provoking him?" he murmured close to her ear.

"He started it," she retorted sullenly.

"That is not a very mature justification," he pointed out.

Vyril smiled. "Don't worry, Lord Enric, I think even the King enjoys a bit of backchat every now and then. Hardly anyone else dares taking any liberties with him."

Yes, Enric thought grimly, and there was good reason for that. The trouble in Eryn's case was rather to avoid his taking any more liberties with *her*.

They watched the stream of magicians entering and stepping off to one side of the throne to make room for the next in line.

"Pe'tala of House Vel'kim and Rolan," they heard the words echoing through the hall.

"They named her before him?" Eryn chuckled. "Not very flattering."

"She is the stronger magician," Tyront stressed.

"But he has risen to some importance with his position of administrative Head of the clinic, hasn't he?"

"That's true. But the Order has not changed its approach to hierarchy yet," her superior pointed out. "So far we are still putting magical strength above function." There was a warning in his tone not to start a discussion here and now. "However we may decide to handle this differently in the future."

Eryn watched the pair proceeding towards the throne. Pe'tala looked pretty in her dark red dress and an elaborate hair style that accentuated her long, slender neck. She had gone for the exotic touch tonight. One tended to forget about her origins when seeing her in her plain everyday clothes or healer's attire that were both in the local style.

"What a nice-looking couple," Vyril sighed. "How fortunate they have found each other. I assume young Rolan is the reason she has decided to stay for a while longer, which is very lucky for us. Who knows? Maybe they will join into a companionship with each other and she will relocate here for good. You could invite her into the Order in that case, couldn't you?"

Tyront raised an eyebrow at Eryn's expression. "I assume that should this ever become a realistic choice Pe'tala will very likely be warned against joining us."

Vyril furrowed her brow at Eryn. "Surely not? You have done so well in the Order yourself, my dear, that I cannot believe that you would advise your sister against becoming a member?"

"She keeps trying to resign from her position in the Order," Tyront informed his companion. "That does imply a certain lack of enthusiasm."

"You do?" the older woman asked her, the surprise evident on her face.

"Well, it was just because of leaving the country and everything, you know...," Eryn replied lamely.

"I am afraid there is not much chance of their allowing you to leave the Order," Vyril remarked sympathetically. "It took them quite some effort to secure your admission to it, after all."

"There is no need for your commiseration, Vyril," Tyront sighed. "We don't exactly keep her locked up in gold."

"Not any longer," Eryn murmured.

"Yes, the good old times...," the older man smiled thinly.

Eryn ground her teeth and continued to watch the magicians entering. Vern was the last one to be announced as he was the youngest magician present and had not yet been assessed for taking his place in the hierarchy.

Once Vern had stepped to stand along with the crowd as well, the King rose to welcome his guests and remark upon how delighted he was about their plentiful attendance. Then he stepped down from the dais to select a partner for the opening dance.

They watched him stroll along the passage that divided the guests and then stop before Pe'tala, smiling at her and reaching out for her hand. She bowed and accepted the honour graciously.

Eryn frowned. Why had it never before occurred to her that Pe'tala could be a possible target for the King's attentions? He had pointed out to her that she herself would have been a suitable queen for him due to her family connections. Pe'tala, too, was part of a powerful foreign family. Would King Folrin care that she was in a relationship of some kind with another man? But then making Pe'tala join him would not be as easy. She was a free citizen of another country, after all. Would she leave Rolan to become queen? Would the King offer the title to her despite her magical abilities? That was a contradiction somehow.

She looked up when Enric took her hand to lead her to the dance floor as well.

"Do I have to?"

"Yes," he said simply. "And I would thank you for not making me feel as though dancing with me is such a strain. I happen to know for a fact that it is not."

"Then my reaction should not be able to make you feel otherwise," she retorted.

"It shouldn't, no," he agreed and smiled at her when he started moving to the music with her. "Yet even my considerable self-confidence suffers in the face of your disregard for my dancing skill."

"Does it?" she smirked. "I wasn't aware I had such power over you."

"Oh, but you *do*. My self-esteem rises and falls in concert with your opinion of me."

"I doubt that very much," she sniffed. "As long as people still become frozen in awe whenever you enter a room, your self-esteem is hardly in danger of being neglected too much."

He pondered that for a moment, then shrugged. "You know, the freezing has become a lot less since we were joined. People have started perceiving me as somewhat remotely human."

"How very inconvenient for you. There is nothing like fear and terror to make people jump out of your path wherever you may walk."

"True, very true," he nodded solemnly, "but, alas, there is the time in a man's life when he has to face up the fact that he is not as intimidating as he used to be in his younger days."

"You will be able to intimidate your own son in a few months," she offered.

"Spoken like the compassionate mother I know you are," he grinned. "Let's intimidate him together, shall we? Couples should have common interest, after all. And as you haven't taken to hunting, this is the next best thing."

She laughed. "I wonder what Valrad and Vran'el, those dedicated Vel'kim fathers, would say if they heard us talking like that."

Enric sighed when he watched her face fall. "Don't think of that now, my love. I am sure they would not approve if they knew that thinking of them makes you feel bad because you are not of their blood."

She squeezed his hand. "You have come to know me quite well, haven't you?"

"I like to think so, yes. This mind bond has been very helpful in that regard," he confirmed. "Tyront has just given me a signal that he wants the next dance with you. Will you oblige him or should I pretend that I didn't see it?"

She looked up at him in surprise. "Defying your superior, Lord Enric? You remain a member of the Order until we board that ship, if I may remind you."

"Pregnancy privilege, my love. You get to decide who to dance with, especially as you were not able to wangle your way out of coming to the ball."

"Grand words, Lordling. Though you would hardly be able to stop the King from dancing with me."

"Back to that honorific term, I see," he sighed. "And if you really want me to, I will find a way."

She shook her head and smiled. "I do appreciate your determination, but I will save us both the trouble and rather spend a few minutes on the dance floor with him."

"Is your mood generous enough to extend the same courtesy to Tyront?" he asked once more.

"Sure, why not? I'll be free of them for a long time after tomorrow, so I may as well indulge them tonight," she nodded.

"That is very magnanimous of you, my love."

"I know," she sighed. "But then being the companion of such an important man as you requires a certain awareness of one's status, does it not?"

"Definitely," he grinned.

Eryn let her gaze wander over to the other dancing couples and the people standing together in small groups. "People keep looking at me," she commented.

"I know. At your abdominal area, to be precise. It is common knowledge by now that we are expecting a child. I suppose they are looking for outward signs."

"Pity for them. I have none yet."

"You have for the trained eye," he contradicted her and pointedly looked at her neckline.

"I shouldn't really be surprised that you noticed *that*," she chuckled.

"No, you shouldn't," he agreed.

The last notes of the music died away and he held on to her hand to guide her across to Tyront, who accepted her hand with a nod.

"Will you make do with me, Vyril?" she heard Enric ask.

"I will, yes," Tyront's companion replied with a smile, "but only because I feel charitable, mind you - not because you are a formidable dancer or any other such selfish consideration."

"You are too kind," Enric replied.

Tyront nodded at Vern, who led Junar onto the dance floor. "Very considerate lad, Orrin's boy."

Eryn followed his gaze and smiled. "That he is, yes. When I see him right now it is hard to believe that he has a sly side to him."

The music started anew and Tyront gently eased her into the dance.

"You are talking about his managing to be permitted to join his family going along to Takhan, I assume?"

She nodded. "Exactly that, yes. I would have missed him terribly, yet I don't really feel that Takhan is the safest place for him. Well, not for any of us, for that matter."

"This time you are going there much better prepared," Tyront pointed out. "And Enric's status as Head of House in combination with your uncle's position should provide a large measure of protection, I would think."

"Probably," she agreed tentatively.

"I expect you to put your time there to good use," he continued. "One thing is to keep in contact with me. Regularly. I am well aware of your aversion to written reports - or *any* reports, for that matter - but I need you to cooperate with me here."

"I don't really think you will need *me* to keep you informed. Even though Enric is not officially in the Order while we are away, you will hardly be breaking off your communication with him. And Kilan is still a member of the Order as well, as is Orrin. So you have three other people in Takhan to write to you."

"And yet I am ordering you to do so, in addition to them."

She gulped and then nodded reluctantly. His objective was clearly not so much getting valuable information from her while they were gone, but rather to make sure she didn't forget who she was answerable to.

Tyront looked down at her with a thoughtful expression. "When you come back from the Western Territories, there will have been a few significant changes. You will probably have given birth to your son by then. I regret missing the chance to watch things unfolding. I would have liked to see if you will be as prone to mood changes as Junar as your pregnancy progresses."

She blinked at him in surprise. That had been unexpectedly affectionate.

"Don't look at me like that," he said mildly. "We may have had our differences, and even though you tend to strain my patience more than I would have thought possible, I still have a soft spot for you."

Eryn smirked. "Is that why you took the trouble of helping along my bonding with Pe'tala?"

"So you have worked that one out? Well done. In your position a certain awareness of being manipulated can be a survival tool."

She didn't tell him that Erbál had been the one to point it out to her. Why take away his illusion, when they were getting along so buoyantly right now?

"In this case I decided to let you go through with it," she smiled. "I did profit from it, after all. Also, I am currently really good with stable duties. Should I for whatever reason not be able to work as a healer anymore one day, I have acquired a handy new skill to make a living."

Tyront raised his brow. "I dare say we would find another task for you that is more suited to your talents than cleaning out the horse stables."

"I suppose. But it is always nice to have something to fall back on."

He chuckled and shook his head. "I wouldn't think that this is a major concern for somebody possessing your considerable resources."

"You mean Enric's money?" she grimaced.

"In addition to the allowance the Order is going to pay you for serving in the Magic Council upon your return," he nodded.

"Oh dear," she rolled her eyes. "You are going to pay me for sitting through a tedious meeting every two or three weeks? The Order really is a drain on public funds, you know."

He closed his eyes for a moment. "This is the kind of remark you might want to work on rephrasing or keeping to yourself when in foreign parts," he advised. "Diplomacy, you know?"

She nodded slowly, amused. "I dimly remember the concept, yes."

"Excellent. Then you may as well put it to good use right now, because the King has just indicated for me to take you over to him after our dance. Which is about... now," he concluded, once the music ended.

"No asking the expectant lady if she is fine with that?" she grumbled when he held on to her hand and turned to where the King awaited in front of the dais.

"I wasn't aware that your status entitled you to choose whether or not to follow Royal instructions," he retorted and walked on.

"It should," she murmured. "I am working on expanding my pregnancy privileges."

"Good luck there, then," he muttered and took her the last few paces towards the King before placing her hand in his.

"Lady Eryn," King Folrin smiled when Tyront had retreated. "Tonight is the last occasion for me to dance with you for the next few months."

Yes, she thought wryly, what a great pity. She frowned when he made no move to take her dancing.

"I must ask you for a little patience, though, there is an announcement I wish to make first."

She noticed Erbál and a rather sour-faced Sanaf edging closer. Ah yes, that little matter was still not official yet.

King Folrin climbed the few steps of the dais and turned to face his guests. It took no more than a few seconds until every last person had fallen silent.

"Ladies and Gentlemen," the King's voice rang out, "I have an announcement to make. Ambassador Sanaf has decided to return home to Takhan for personal reasons. It is my pleasure to announce that Ambassador Erbál will succeed him in the office and remain with us in Anyueel. I trust that you will welcome him warmly in his new function. The transition will no doubt be a smooth one as most of you are acquainted with him already. Ambassador Erbál will from this evening onward officially assume the position."

Eryn cast a sideways glance at Sanaf. His face was a stony mask, only the upwards curve of his lips suggested that he was trying to appear halfway cheerful. If he aimed at avoiding the impression that he was being encouraged to leave against his will, he was not very convincing.

She saw the people in front of her nodding and murmuring; many of them flashed Sanaf gleeful looks, clearly relieved at being rid of him.

Erbál did a much better job at hiding his sense of triumph than Sanaf did with his resentment. He winked at Eryn when she looked in his direction. She smiled and took both his hands when he lifted them towards her.

"My dear Ambassador," she cooed, "let me congratulate you on this unexpected development. How very fortunate for us to have you here, willing and able to take over the burden of filling the gap Ambassador Sanaf would undoubtedly have left."

He shook his head at her slightly and murmured, "You are a mischievous creature. A pity His Majesty is determined to claim this dance with you, or I would have done so myself."

The King cleared his throat next to them.

"Then let me welcome you to your new position, Ambassador, by granting you this very dance. Be sure to return her to me when you are finished, if you will."

The freshly instated ambassador smiled gratefully and bowed. "I esteem your generous gesture highly and accept it gladly. Only, of course, assuming Lady Eryn wishes to dance with me at this point?"

She smirked. "As if you left me much of a choice. Rejecting you here and now in front of all these people wouldn't make either of us look very cultured, would it?"

"Very diplomatic of you," Erbál grinned back and let go of one of her hands to lead her to the dance floor.

Once the music had started, Eryn sighed. "Don't tell me Sanaf is returning to Takhan with us. The thought of being stuck with him for four entire days makes my flesh creep."

"Hardly, my dear. He is not too eager to spend more time with you. You have not exactly made it a secret how you regard him since he shared your little secret with Anyueel society concerning your bedroom fainting spells."

She rolled her eyes. "Thank you so much for reminding me of that tiny detail. I had almost forgotten about it."

"You should not. I intend to remind you of it every time you doubt that aiding me in my efforts to be considered for his position was a good idea," he promised.

"Really? That means I had better start looking for a more compliant replacement for you when I am in Takhan," she jested.

He laughed quietly. "I would very much prefer it if you did not. I could become a valuable source of information for you, after all."

She raised both eyebrows at him. "Could you now? Are you offering to share the intelligence your spies collect for you with me?"

"Let me put it like this: I would be open to an arrangement that includes the mutually beneficial sharing of information."

"Oh my. You really do work fast, don't you? You have been Ambassador for hardly more than a few minutes and are already attempting to have me share secrets with you. I am supposed to join the Magic Council after my return. That means I am not exactly at liberty to share any juicy bits of information with you."

"Of course not," he shrugged. "That you would pretty much be the only person in the Council *not* doing it should not make any difference to you," he said briskly.

She narrowed her eyes at him. "Are you trying to trick me?"

"Trick the third most powerful magician in this Kingdom?" he looked shocked, but there was a glint in his eyes. "That would be a bit audacious, would it not? But then it should be fairly easy for you to determine whether it is a trick or not. You are acquainted with a few Council members, after all. Though Lord Tyront would hardly admit to it, and I wonder if Lords Orrin and Poron would. You are their superior, after all. That is one of the things one does try to keep hidden from the upper ranks. But there is always Lord Enric to ask. I am sure he would be pleased at your efforts at securing your own sources of information."

She snorted. "I wonder how pleased he would be if I considered passing on information about confidential Order business. And I seriously doubt that he himself participates in such exchange of information you imagine to be so very common within the Council."

"Suit yourself," he smiled. "Just let me know in case you change your mind. Takhan is a long way from here. I wonder how long you will be content with receiving only filtered information by those who are supposed to be reporting to you."

"Will you shut up if I promise to consider it?" she sighed.

"I will, yes," he promised.

"Will you now get your own assistant?" she asked, changing the topic.

"I should do, yes. Though I have been thinking about asking for a local person instead of having somebody sent here from home."

"You have?" she enquired. "That is unusual. Why?"

"It would enable me to access local knowledge better. There are still quite a few things about your country I have to learn. A person born and raised here would without a doubt be better able to help me in this."

"And you are not worried about confidentiality? I mean, somebody from here might be vulnerable to selling information about you to whomever pays enough," she pointed out.

"Eryn, my dear, do you seriously think that a person from my home would be any less susceptible to the temptation of gold? Do not paint us foreigners better than we are, or you are in for quite a disappointment as you spend more time in Takhan."

"Thank you for the warning, but I think after Malriel there cannot be very much that will surprise me over there," she sighed. She chuckled at his sceptical expression. "Don't tell me you don't like my speaking ill of your former lover?"

"She is your mother, Eryn; I would say you are free to speak of her as you choose," he replied in a neutral voice.

"Don't say that," she grimaced. "I went to great lengths to make people stop saying that."

"Renouncing her House does not stop people from considering you mother and daughter," Erbál pointed out. "Especially not since you bear such an uncanny resemblance to each other."

She aimed a dark look at him. "You know, I am rather glad the music is about to end. It saves me from striking you publicly on your very first official evening in the new role."

"You would not do that," he grinned and took her hand to lead her back to the King. "You are glad that I have replaced Sanaf, even if you are a touch annoyed at me right now."

"Yes," she admitted and winked at him. "You are the lesser nuisance. For now."

King Folrin raised his hand to receive hers when they had arrived at the foot of the dais.

"This is going to be a very busy evening for you, Lady Eryn," he stated once Erbál had retreated.

She let herself be led back to the dance floor and suppressed a breath heavy with weariness. "I expect it will, yes," she agreed.

"I can see that the thought of this being the last ball for you for quite a while lets you weather the trial in a rather calm manner," he commented.

"What can I say? I knew what awaited me after you so eloquently refused my request to be excused tonight."

The music started and he raised his brow at her when they started dancing. "You could hardly expect me to agree to an exemption on the evening of your own farewell ball, could you?"

"Well, if this truly is *my* farewell ball...," she started but fell silent at his glare.

"Stop sulking and use this last opportunity to talk to me," he said, a hint of annoyance in his voice.

"Do you have any particular preferences as to the topic of our conversation or does the current state of the weather suffice?" She smiled coolly.

"If the weather is what you would like to converse about, then I should warn you that you may have to prepare yourself for a rather chill breeze blowing your way from Sanaf's direction."

She shrugged. "We were not exactly close while he was ambassador, so I don't see what changes there are likely to be."

"The fact that he is aware of your giving assistance to Ambassador Erbál in being appointed to his current position might cause him to harbour some resentment against you, I would imagine."

She cast a quick look at the man in question. "I suppose I will manage to endure the evil eye on the few occasions where I might meet him in Takhan, if there are any."

The King shook his head at her. "So careless, so very careless...," he murmured.

She spotted Pe'tala dancing with Lord Poron not far away from them and frowned. "What is your interest in my sister?"

He blinked at her. "I beg your pardon?"

"You opened the ball with her tonight," she pointed out impatiently. "Why?"

"I opened a ball with *you* once as well, if I may remind you," he remarked pointedly.

"Yes, and you cornered me to tell me that you would have liked to make me your queen. Do you have a similar intention with Pe'tala?"

The King slowly shook his head. "Whatever brings you to a notion such as this, I wonder? You are aware of the ban on magically-gifted heirs to the throne, of course."

"And yet you planned to have offspring with me shortly after my arrival here," she growled. She remembered the day well. It was in this very room when his advisor had ordered Enric to check for the protective barrier she had claimed was inside her to prevent unwanted intrusion.

"Did I now?" he asked softly.

She frowned in confusion. "But Loft said..."

"Loft, my dear Lady, said what I led him to believe was a good idea. Angering the Order by making you bear my children was never something I considered. It was no more than a little pressure I applied to induce to Order to make you an offer to join them. Unfortunately, your barrier made that unnecessary and they could afford to take a lot more time over it."

She stared at him. Another political strategy. And for once one that had foundered.

He chuckled. "Don't tell me you are upset because I had no intention of having children with you? I assure you that it was not your lack of appeal that stopped me from going down that path, but political considerations. One of them was retaining my place on the throne for a while longer," he concluded wryly.

She shook her head and looked deflated. "Is there ever anything you say or do that is not part of a game you play?"

He smiled wistfully. "I only wish I had that luxury sometimes, My Lady."

She searched his face for a sign of sarcasm, but found none. That had sounded joyless and for the first time she couldn't help but ask herself whether he was lonely. No companion at his side that he could entrust with his private thoughts, just his circle of advisors. She frowned. Advisor, that had become. There seemed to be only Marrin at the moment, and had been for a while.

"I haven't seen Loft with you for quite some time now. Months."

"It has taken you a long time to notice that," he smiled. "I have transferred him to an administrative position that does not require such close contact with, hmm... foreign influences. He has not taken well to the recent changes that have occurred over this last year. A traditionalist, Loft. Yet a useful sort of man if one knows where to place him."

"Like in a windowless cell with plenty of *other* vermin," she muttered.

"Now, now, that was not a very sensitive remark, was it?" he chastised her gently. "I sincerely hope you show more restraint in Takhan."

"Why should I? People are so delighted whenever they catch a glimpse of the famous Aren temper," she shrugged. "Who am I to deny them their entertainment?"

"Somebody who does not lower herself to being little more than a source of amusement to others, I would have thought."

Well, that put her in her place, she thought, disheartened.

"Have you given any thought yet as to what the name of your son will be?" he then asked after some long moments of silence.

Eryn slowly shook her head. "No, we haven't. There is still time left before he is born."

"But in your case picking a name will not be such an easy matter, will it? Being the heir to a House in Takhan requires taking the Vel'kim naming traditions into consideration. And then it is not supposed to sound too foreign, as he will be spending a good part of his childhood here in Anyueel as well. Lord Enric might also be inclined to pay heed to the Aren traditions in this regard."

Naming traditions? How in the world did he know about the naming traditions? The only thing she had worked out so far was that Aren women all seemed to have names that started with the same syllable. That did not apply to the men as well, did it? And even if this were the case, she didn't care about it one jot.

What were the Vel'kim traditions when it came to picking names? The first letter being a V, at least for males? Was she even expected to comply with them now it had turned out that she wasn't really one of them?

"We will probably start thinking about this soon," she said, curtly.

"Splendid. I am curious what you will come up with."

She spotted Enric leaning against a column, watching with a controlled calm the King and herself.

"How long am I required to remain here tonight?" she ventured.

"I expect you to be not among the first guests to leave," he informed her. "I advise you to take frequent breaks and sit down between dances to avoid tiring quickly in your current condition."

"Too kind," she murmured. "I suppose Junar is not subject to the same stipulation?"

"But of course not. Her pregnancy is a lot more advanced than your own. What is more, she is not a magician with the capability to keep exhaustion at bay with the aid of a little magic, is she?"

"Of course she isn't," Eryn sighed and braced herself for a long, strenuous evening.

CHAPTER 33

Farewell

Eryn strolled along the familiar streets, as she had been doing so for more than one hour. The thought of leaving here for a longer period was unappealing. She had spent only about one and a half years here, and yet it had become a home to her. The town she had spent about twenty years of her life in was still present enough in her mind, yet she realised that she never actually missed it as such.

Home, she wondered. What made people think of a place as home? Familiar surroundings? Surely one part. Friends? Definitely. Family? She had family in Takhan, technically, yet it did not occur to her to consider it home. Love? That was definitely a helpful aspect if available. A purpose in life, she mused. That she had found here, too.

What of these things would also be available in Takhan? Familiar surroundings, to a certain degree. Family had turned out to be a tricky term, as Malriel's infidelity had changed the meaning of it, to what extent she wasn't really sure yet. Friends would definitely be there, as they were more or less part of her baggage. Love, of course, as Enric was the reason she had to go there.

A purpose. She would be little more than one healer among a multitude, nothing defining her as special the way it did here, since she was not particularly talented, experienced or well-trained compared to others in Takhan. She could hope to pass as average, at best. She wondered if what disturbed her was the prospect of not being considered distinguished and advanced in skills, being one of many.

Taking charge of rambling thoughts, she forced herself to look at things from a more cheerful perspective. If she wanted her stay in Takhan to serve a purpose, she would simply have to give it one.

What did it matter if she was perceived as backwards and barbaric over there? Learning as much as she was able would in the end benefit the Kingdom after her return.

She thought of the people she had come to like and that she would have to get along without for who knew how long exactly. Elia. She was the one person she would miss most. Her healer colleagues. And even Pe'tala, to a certain degree. Rolan, especially teasing him and watching him gather the courage to repay her in kind. Tyront, who she had yet to figure out whether she liked or not. Vyril, who had performed miracles with the orphanage. Erbál and his strangely twisted way of candidness.

She realised that going without Orrin, Junar and Vern would have made leaving tomorrow bear a lot more heavily, and felt a surge of warmth and relief knowing she could just take them with her. That was something to be grateful for. Not that she intended to let the King know that. But then he was very likely aware of it anyway.

The King. She wouldn't miss him as such, she knew. Not after his getting too intimate with her in the past. But he was an intellectual challenge, somebody she had learned from and surely would continue to do so in the future. Nonetheless, a break from him and his manipulative games was definitely welcome.

The bakery she usually bought her bread buns from came into view and she decided to indulge herself one last time before their departure. This would be the last batch of them before they left, and she was determined to enjoy them to the full.

The baker smiled when he spotted her. She had become a good customer over the last months, after all. A minute later she walked out with a paper bag under her arm and strolled towards the river. It had become warm enough already to sit outside for a while, the sun bathing the city in a pleasant light as if to present it to her as favourably as possible, making her want to return. It worked.

She sat down on a stone bench, watching the birds that came closer cautiously at the prospect of some bread crumbs dropped or even pieces bestowed on them willingly.

There was some construction work going on to her left. The city's port was being extended. She dimly remembered that Enric had said something about negotiating the terms of funding such a project with the King. It seemed they had reached an agreement. She really needed to keep herself more up to date on things like this.

Her eyes followed the course of the street on the other side of the river. It led to the city gate through which she had tried to flee, more than a year ago, when she had shocked the magicians by using her double barrier to keep them at bay. The repair works on the inner city wall into which Enric and Tyront had blasted a hole with united forces was finished many months ago, but where the newer stones had been inserted was visible. It would take a while until they were weathered enough to blend in completely.

Her gaze fell on the bracelet on her wrist, the one Ram'an had given her on the day of her commitment. A token of friendship, he had said. She let her fingers glide over the links and wondered whether to take it off or not. There was no more friendship, if there ever even had been a connection like that between them. He had been frosty and distant in the scant few messages she had received from him before they had ceased communication completely. The right thing to do would be to return the bracelet to him once she was back in Takhan. Yet the thought of doing so made her sad somehow. She wondered why he had given it to her in the first place. Had he even wanted to be friends with her at that time or had it been no more than a token gesture? Had he talked about friendship in order to induce her to wear it so people would see that Houses Vel'kim and Arbil were on amiable terms? Unfortunately, that possibility now became the most likely explanation for his gift.

She decided to keep the bracelet on for now and give him another chance when they met again in the Western Territories. If she arrived there without wearing it, that would be a clear signal of her severance, something that putting it back on again later could hardly make up for.

She looked up in surprise when she felt a warm body rubbing against her legs. Urban.

"Are you through with roaming the streets or are you just taking a break?" Enric's voice came from behind her.

She smiled without turning. "I think I am pretty much through; I am getting tired. It was a long evening yesterday, after all."

He stepped next to her to take a seat on the bench and linked his fingers with hers.

"How did you find me?" She shook her head at herself. "No, don't answer that - you have somebody following me around who informed you."

He nodded. "Yes. Just like I told you I would."

She considered telling him that this was demeaning to a certain degree, that she was a grown woman entitled to her freedom and no longer a prisoner. But then they would just end up discussing her tendency to flee from him again. After spending that one night at Pe'tala's place when she had thought that he had manipulated her into becoming pregnant, there was not much chance for her to make him call off his spy. At least he had agreed to stopping this practise after their son was born if she managed to convince him that it was no longer necessary and she had outgrown her fondness for flight.

"You have agreed with the King on the construction of the port, I see," she said instead.

"I have, yes. I have taken over the funding and construction and he will in turn grant me tax relief over the next seven years following completion. That is usually the way it goes when a private person offers to fund a public structure," he explained. "It is useful for the Crown as there is no outlay at first in connection with the project.

Since my taxes are likely to increase anyway due to my enhanced trade volume, this is a favourable enough deal for the Kingdom."

"And for yourself, I dare say," she amended calmly. "You are not doing this out of pure benevolence, but to be able to increase that trade volume and earn even more income from it, after all."

"True enough," he confirmed and smiled at the reproach. "This was not meant as a complaint. I am pleased enough about the arrangement." It was probably time for a little reminder that the riches she still despised so much were not only being used for their own comfort. "I have topped up the money box for the orphanage's expenses with ten thousand gold pieces," he mentioned casually. "Vyril is authorised to withdraw whatever she needs. This should cover expenses for about one year judging from what has been spent on food, clothes and education over the last few months."

Eryn swallowed. "*Ten thousand* gold pieces? That is... a lot." Then she frowned. "How do you know about the expenses? I wasn't aware that you had access to this information. I thought she only reported to *me*."

"No, my love, she doesn't. She has to inform the King as well. The orphanage is still a public utility, you were just granted the *privilege* of managing it."

"Yes," she murmured angrily, "one he had neglected shamefully."

"Society did not exactly pressure him to improve things there," he pointed out.

She snorted. "As if he usually gave a damn about what others want! And don't talk to me about society - the rich just caring about themselves and the poor suffering what they have to without the power to change anything."

"The rich have been raised to protect their own interests from each other, in the main."

"So they are not to blame for their lack of care and compassion? I wonder who is, then. I think the rich have a certain responsibility towards the rest. Especially as most of them have not earned their wealth through their own hard work but inherited it from their forebears."

He took her hand, regretting already that he had got onto the topic. This was their last day here and he wanted things to be amiable between the two of them.

"I am not saying they are not to blame, my love. Just that they need to get used to the new idea that helping others is actually something worthwhile. Which is exactly what you have been doing since your arrival here. Your commitment has put quite a few of them to shame. This is why some of the evening invitations lately have become occasions to raise money for the orphanage. If this keeps up, Vyril will not have to use much of the money we have put at her disposal."

"Yes, I suppose so," she sighed and scratched Urban's furry cheek when she offered it. She had to smile when she remembered their first hunting trip in the Western Territories. "I just had to think of Vran'el and his wariness about Urban. She is fully grown now, so I suppose he will be even more careful around her, if such a thing could be conceivable."

Enric chuckled. "I would say her size will be an unpleasant surprise to him, yes. But watching her flee from his daughter back then restored some of his faith in the world."

They watched several passers-by giving them curious looks.

"We are not usually to be seen sitting out in public doing nothing," he smiled. "It confuses people."

"We? They are looking at *you*, my friend," she corrected him. "*I* am a regular sighting on the streets."

He sighed deeply. "I know. You are one of the *people* while I usually just glare down at them from my marbled tower."

"Well put," she grinned. "As long as you are aware of it..."

He watched her take another bread bun from her bag and bite into it. "Can I have one or is that question too cheeky?"

She shook her head and took out another one to press it into his hand. "No, it isn't. I am feeling generous."

"I shall consider it as a sign of your devotion to me," he commented. "You are known to be very possessive of them lately." He took a bite and then broke off some tiny pieces to throw to the birds that were brave enough to venture closer despite the feline predator. One just had to reward bravery like that.

Eryn blinked. The sight of mighty Lord Enric sitting on a bench and feeding the birds was so uncharacteristic that it seemed almost unreal. Judging from the fingers being pointed and curious glances people were giving them she was not the only one thinking that. It was touching somehow. The wealthy man, who could afford the finest rooms and goods to deck them, being content with sitting at her side by the river and throwing bread crumbs to birds.

She reached out for his hand and pulled it towards her, squeezing it. "You know that I have come to like you very much, don't you? I value your efforts at keeping me safe and healthy. Well, and reasonably happy. Even though I don't always agree with how you go about it," she said without looking at him but instead staring at the murky water in the river. It was a little higher this time of year due to the melting snow in higher regions.

He squeezed her hand and looked at her in profile - serious, intent, reflective. It didn't seem like she had finished and he liked where this seemed to be going.

"Junar is right; I need to get over my dread of telling you this. I am going to be working on it." She kept her gaze on the water. "I love you," she said simply, feeling embarrassed.

She felt his arm move around her shoulders, pressing her closer and his other hand squeezed her fingers.

"I love you, too." He kissed her on the temple. "And I appreciate your efforts, I really do. You will see - this is something you will get used to. It will be less awkward with each time you say it." He grinned. "That means the fastest and most effective way of fighting your dread is telling me as often as possible."

He felt her relaxing under his arm and returning to a less solemn mood.

"Don't think you can establish a different kind of training programme with me," she smirked. "I am not going to say it whenever the mood to hear it strikes you."

"Then I might have to resort to tricks to make you say it. Such as *not* buying you clothes."

That made her laugh. "You are a devious man. I will from now on be extra careful whenever you fail to insist on buying me something."

"Do that, dearest. If our son takes after you, I will be saving a lot of money in the years to come. But then children are not always known to follow the way their parents think, are they?"

His words reminded her of something the King said the evening before when he had been dancing with her.

"Have you given any thought to what name we will give the child?" she asked. "I was given to understand that this might be a bit more involved than just picking whatever name sounds nice to us."

He nodded slowly. "I know. The naming traditions of the Houses. House Vel'kim has very uncomplicated ones; they abandoned a number of such rules last century. The only one that remains is that the male descendants' names have to start with a V."

She smiled faintly. "I shouldn't really be surprised about you knowing about this, should I? You probably found a book on this somewhere in Takhan."

He shrugged. "I had a lot of time to kill while waiting for that trial to take its course. And Golir granted me access to his very extensive private library. Probably to keep me occupied and out of his way."

As would she have, she mused. Irritated, nervous Enric was not a pleasant influence to have around. Keeping him busy somehow was the best course of action.

"As for House Aren..."

She gave him a stern look. "I don't really see how *their* traditions have to be taken into consideration. The boy will not be of her House, so it will not be necessary to apply their rules."

"May I remind you once again why we are putting up with all of this? We want to avoid the two Houses doing any harm to each other - or rather of Malriel harming House Vel'kim. So adhering to the Aren naming rules will be a powerful signal of goodwill that will force her to show her appreciation. If she fails to do so, her reputation would suffer."

"Alright, alright," she mumbled. "Out with it, then. What are the Aren rules? Apart from putting the syllable *Mal* at the beginning of every girl's name, obviously."

"The boys' names usually contain a syllable of their father's name."

"So the name needs to start with a V, contain either En or Ric and is not supposed to sound too foreign neither here nor in the Western Territories. This is all it should take to please both Houses and also avoid making our son an outsider wherever he goes. Simple enough, isn't it?" She rolled her eyes. "Lucky for us we still have about six months to find a name that meets all those requirements. Maybe we should just call him Ven. Or Vric."

Enric grimaced. "Not exactly what I had in mind."

"Don't tell me that in addition to all of this a name also needs to appeal to *us*?" she chortled.

"I would appreciate that, yes," he remarked dryly. "I don't want to give myself a nasty shock for the rest of my life every time I say or hear my son's name."

The rest of their lives, she thought and saw the perspective it meant. That was how long they would both be connected to that child, worrying about it, supporting it and probably scolding it.

"Is everything alright, my love?" he enquired.

She nodded slowly. "This is quite a commitment, isn't it?"

"It is, yes," he agreed softly.

"Nothing that scares you at all?"

"No. I have committed to you, after all. How much harder can dealing with a child be?" He laughed when she jabbed him with her elbow, then became serious again. "Actually, I wouldn't have minded having you to myself for another year or two, but I am still looking forward to raising a child with you. I will do beautifully as a father, of course, but I am curious to see how you turn out as a mother."

She rolled her eyes and got up. "Oh dear."

Enric quickly crumbled the rest of his bread bun to throw it to the birds, then whistled for the cat to rise and follow him when he walked after Eryn.

"Judging from the direction I assume you are off to the clinic?" he asked when he had caught up with her.

"I am, yes. I will sit down with the healers and Rolan for an hour, officially pass on my responsibilities to Lord Poron and say my farewells to them. Any last things you need to take care of before we leave?"

He shook his head. "No, not apart from our appointment with the King in the evening where he will tell us to play along nicely with the other politicians, write to him regularly and return home safely."

She grinned. "I doubt that he will put it quite like that, but in essence that is probably what he wants."

He took her hand while they walked along the street. "Do you have any particular preferences as regards our last evening here in Anyueel?

She thought for a moment, then nodded. "Yes, a quiet evening at home and a nice, relaxed dinner with Plia."

"I can arrange that. Just make sure to tell her to come home at a reasonable hour today for a change when you see her, or I will send Grend to drag her home."

Eryn sighed. "You do have a way with women, you know."

"Yet they still find me irresistible," he smirked, bending down to kiss her once they had reached the crossroads where their ways parted.

"That's just because your face is a lot prettier than your manners," she pointed out.

"One has to work with what one was given," he grinned and winked at her before he turned left into the street that would lead him back to their house, the cat trotting at his heels.

Eryn smiled at the picture they made. Confident, tall Enric with the fearsome predator that had accepted him as her master. A pair that wouldn't fail to impress anyone, wherever they went. She imagined him with a child on his shoulders and oddly enough it was a picture easy enough to conjure up, especially as she had seen him with Vran'el's daughter. They had taken an instant liking to each other and he had picked her up and talked to her as if it was the most natural thing in the world for him to do.

She sighed and turned to continue her way to the clinic. He was right, even though he had meant it as a joke: he would do beautifully as a father. Good - that meant that at least one of them would know what they were doing.

www.ingramcontent.com/pod-product-compliance
Lightning Source LLC
Chambersburg PA
CBHW070539030726
47505CB00001B/93
9783904142076